The Disappearance of Henry Hanson

Also by J.L. Larson:

The Raid at Lake Minnewaska

The Accident at Sanborn Corners...and
other Minnesota Short Stories

The Disappearance of Henry Hanson

BOOK II OF THE MINNESOTA LAKE SERIES

J. L. Larson

iUniverse

THE DISAPPEARANCE OF HENRY HANSON
BOOK II OF THE MINNESOTA LAKE SERIES

iUniverse books may be ordered through booksellers or by contacting:

iUniverse
1663 Liberty Drive
Bloomington, IN 47403
www.iuniverse.com
1-800-Authors (1-800-288-4677)

Because of the dynamic nature of the Internet, any web addresses or links contained in this book may have changed since publication and may no longer be valid. The views expressed in this work are solely those of the author and do not necessarily reflect the views of the publisher, and the publisher hereby disclaims any responsibility for them.

Any people depicted in stock imagery provided by Thinkstock are models, and such images are being used for illustrative purposes only. Certain stock imagery © Thinkstock.

ISBN: 978-1-4917-5772-7 (sc)
ISBN: 978-1-4917-5771-0 (hc)
ISBN: 978-1-4917-5770-3 (e)

Library of Congress Control Number: 2015900230

Printed in the United States of America.

iUniverse rev. date: 01/21/2015

Preface

It was a fluke when those five people met in the small lakeside community of Glenwood, Minnesota on that June weekend back in 1931. The ten-day town festival was coming to a close. There were hordes of locals and visitors enjoying the final days of the celebration of the coming summer lake season on Lake Minnewaska. In many ways that setting could easily have been a logical venue for various people to meet. However, for those five individuals the popular event had little to do with their paths crossing.

As told in the first of the Minnesota Lake Series novels, 'The Raid at Lake Minnewaska', the coincidence of their chance encounter on Saturday, June 6 would later be described by each one as not so much a fluke, but fate. In just hours after being together casually at a Saturday afternoon charity golf tournament, they committed to taking on something very risky...that is, if you define 'risky' as deceiving a lake resort full of known criminals, convicted felons, bail breakers, and members of a high level Chicago crime family.

The story originated when one of them, an undercover investigator from the Minneapolis branch of the U.S. Attorney's office, was desperately seeking a way of putting away one of the slipperiest Chicago conmen the authorities had ever pursued. There was a small window of opportunity for some kind of action against this well-known mobster who happened to be hosting a charity golf tournament that weekend at a local area lake resort. But, that opening would close abruptly on Sunday afternoon with the completion of the event.

Lindy MacPherson, an undercover investigator from the Minneapolis branch of the U.S. Attorney's office, had been working the previous three weeks in Glenwood claiming to be a travel magazine writer. Her actual assignment was to check out rumors of a possible gambling ring somewhere in the Lake Minnewaska area. It was supposed to be a relatively danger-free job lasting but a couple days... the primary purpose to give her some worthwhile field experience. However, she kept on discovering additional factors pointing to a much bigger crime scene at that same secluded lake resort five miles from town. There was enough proof of wrongdoing at Chippewa Lodge lake resort for her to schedule a police raid Sunday morning, June 7. The bust could have been arranged earlier, but unfortunately she had yet to find the uncontested evidence that would put the infamous gangster, Loni D'Annelli behind bars once and for all. While the police raid on Sunday would be highly fruitful with the number of expected arrests, without the undeniable proof in pinpointing D'Annelli as the true ringleader of the grand mob operation at the Lodge, the incursion would not fully succeed.

Fate came calling that Saturday when the paths of the other four individuals crossed the previous night and that morning. Two of them were law school buddies who never intended to be in Glenwood, Minnesota that weekend. James Lawton, a lawyer from Minneapolis, was piloting his dilapidated, reconstructed former World War I biplane up to Lake Ida near Alexandria to see Charlie Davis. The two thirty-year olds were supposed to enjoy two days of golf with other friends including a lot of eating, drinking, and playing cards. Sleep was low on the list of priorities.

Unfortunately, Lawton's flying machine was forced down Friday evening by a major thunderstorm. He made an emergency landing on Hwy. #28, just two miles east of Glenwood atop the bluff overlooking Lake Minnewaska. Seeking safety, he literally drove his plane right up the driveway to a farm owned by, John Bailey. In that evening's conversation with Bailey's son, Adam, Lawton would learn of a rather unique charity golf tournament complete with large sums of under-the-table prize money scheduled the very next morning at the Chippewa Lodge nine-hole golf course...and there was still one invitation available.

With Adam Bailey being the caddy for the tournament host, Loni D'Annelli, that led to the next twist of fate. With young Bailey's assistance, Lawton, a top amateur golfer in the state, would gain entry. He then called his friend, Davis, to drive the thirty miles down to Glenwood and bring money to cover Lawton's exorbitant entry fee. At that point Lawton had no idea the field was composed of wanted criminals and notorious mobsters. At the breakfast before the group teed off, he would make that discovery. By then it was too late to back out.

That Saturday morning the series of coincidences that brought the two Baileys together with Lawton and Davis would set the stage for MacPherson to encounter them at the big golf event. As a nondescript spectator she was trooping around the golf course area completing her final list of recognizable hoodlums and gangsters to be arrested during the following day's raid.

Observing John and Adam Bailey who were carrying the golf bags of two of the golfers, she made a special note that the authorities were to leave those two locals alone. They were not part of the unholy assemblage of wanted criminals and members of the mafia. Along the way she also came to notice Lawton and Davis. One was golfing in the tournament; the other was following the action very closely. Both seemed nervous and preoccupied. Their behavior was distant, as if they wished they were anywhere but at that golf course. She ended up walking with the four men that afternoon as John Bailey was caddying for Lawton. In the same foursome coincidentally was Adam carrying the bag for none other than the notorious gangster himself, Loni D'Annelli.

Following that group would become the final quirk that would eventually bring the five together. MacPherson couldn't help but take delight in being around Jamie Lawton and Charlie Davis on that Saturday afternoon. She got a kick out their kibitzing with each other as well as their privately said disparaging comments about the other golfers in the tournament. They showed little if any regard for their opponents... and maintained a cordial but reserved manner with D'Annelli and the other two players in the foursome. She would add Lawton and Davis to her short list, along with the two Baileys, of individuals who should not be picked up by the authorities during Sunday's raid.

With limited time remaining and blinded by her frantic desire to corral the Chicago mobster, she made her way to the Bailey farm where Lawton and Davis were staying the night. She'd decided to ask Lawton, Davis, and the two Baileys for help. In taking the other four into her confidence, she explained her urgency. They were not so surprised at the number of gangsters and racketeers at the Lodge that weekend as they were about her evidence of the on-going illegal businesses operating at the lake resort. They were also not astonished that Loni D'Annelli was involved in the unlawful businesses, but troubled that MacPherson's lengthy undercover investigation had not unlocked the absolute, irrefutable proof that the cunning D'Annelli was indeed the leader of this major mob operation at Chippewa Lodge.

When she then described the circumstances that would exist for only one more day at the lake resort to possibly entrap the Chicago racketeer, there was a collective sigh around the farmhouse. What followed were MacPherson, Lawton, Davis, and the two Baileys brainstorming that Saturday night on how to find that crucial evidence or to at least not let the high-powered, slippery Chicago mobster escape arrest and prosecution once again.

In an impulsive decision they committed to make one secret attempt at lassoing D'Annelli. They figured a clandestine sting directed at this key racketeer on Sunday morning before the raid just might have a chance of succeeding. At that point they didn't consider their own safety or the danger they might face. All they could see was the advantage they had...for the moment.

Maybe if they had more than a few hours to think about it, they might have come to their senses. Their scam was full of risks. Anyone of sound mind that night might have convinced them their actions were not only reckless but suicidal. If they had known the long term impact on their lives, they might have reached that conclusion by themselves.

Caught up in the deep belief that the cards were in their favor, they felt strongly their scheme could be pulled off without them being seen or even considered to be part of the scam against Loni D'Annelli. Besides, they also figured they had nothing to lose if the sting failed. The raid would still go on as planned. Numerous arrests would take place. The mob operations would be immediately closed for good even if D'Annelli was able to dodge the real blame.

Their chance meeting and unwary decision to take action that weekend would result in a highly successful con. In fact, their rash and whimsical plan would go far beyond what the five of them had envisioned. Their scam directly caused fifty-four arrests, the closing of a very profitable mob operation, a very visible embarrassment to the Chicago syndicate....and D'Annelli being arrested on five felony counts. He fell victim to the sting as if he was led by hand.

*   *   *

If the story had concluded with Lawton, Davis, the two Baileys and MacPherson savoring their incredibly successful secretive plot against the crime syndicate and a key crime boss, it would have been a logical and comfortable conclusion. As long as those five collaborators lived on in silence and relative obscurity telling no one of their hijinks that weekend, it would be assumed their lives would continue unthreatened by any potential retribution from the mob.

Unfortunately the story would not end so conveniently. It took only hours after the police raid for all five individuals to realize the unseen consequences of their success. They especially hadn't considered the response from the Chicago mob. That brotherhood in crime didn't take lightly to having their isolated golfing sanctuary invaded by throngs of law enforcement. In addition they were enraged on having been completely surprised by the influx of cops. In the chaos not one shot was fired; the only scene was hoodlum after hoodlum in their fancy golfing attire being led away in handcuffs... including D'Annelli and some other prominent mafia members.

The complexion of the story would change within a day of that raid at the Lake Minnewaska lake resort. If the five collaborators were ever found to have been involved in the overall sting that Sunday morning at the Lodge, reprisals would be swift and quite final. It was evident that confidentiality among the five conspirators from that weekend on would be crucial.

In this sequel to the original story entitled 'The Disappearance of Henry Hanson', it would be told how the five collaborators would be haunted repeatedly in the months and years following their spur-of-the-moment exploits in Glenwood back on that June weekend.

MacPherson had to remain firm in her explanation of her involvement and how she worked alone. She never wavered from her story that her efforts had been relatively simple after accidentally stumbling upon the obvious indiscretions at Chippewa Lodge. It made her actual participation in the huge raid sound inconsequential thereby averting any reprisals aimed at her by the mob. Of course that avowal could not have been any further from the truth, yet critical to the lives of her fellow accomplices, Lawton, Davis, and the two Baileys.

It helped that her statement was generally accepted by the state patrol and the Bureau of Investigation, especially since both law enforcement bodies wanted to be credited for the results of their raid. Doubts to her claims did prevail, however, especially from a few skeptical reporters as well as many mob members who were present at Chippewa Lodge that weekend. They all sensed a scheme had occurred, in particular because of the easy way Loni D'Annelli had fallen. But, none could prove a sting had actually happened.

Those reservations amongst nosy reporters and embittered mobsters at times created some complications in the lives of MacPherson and her four stealthy associates. It would require them to come to each other's aid quite often, especially in the coming months and years of that decade of the1930's. In doing so, each episode secured an even closer relationship. They actually became more like family.

Not brought to light until this sequel was the importance of another person in the original story. His name was Henry Hanson. He was depicted as a minor character, a quiet, supposedly unassuming general manager of the local feed and grain mill in Glenwood. This next volume will illuminate some startling details how he actually had a direct impact on the demise of the D'Annelli era. Without the five collaborators knowing it, he was as integrally involved in the success of their scam as they were.

Hanson had been working virtually alone for over a year to undermine the mob operation at the lake resort. Among the many things he did, it was he who dropped some last minute hints helping the five conspirators prove D'Annelli's actual guilt. And, he did so just hours before he disappeared from town forever.

Without this local man's efforts there would not have been any investigation at all. Lindy MacPherson would never have had any reason to be assigned to Glenwood, Minnesota. It was he who sent an anonymous note to the U.S. Attorney branch office in Minneapolis about a gambling ring in the Lake Minnewaska area. Without his hint to the authorities, the noteworthy numbers of crooks and racketeers that weekend would have finished the golf tournament and calmly returned to their home cities. And, Loni D'Annelli would have dodged arrest yet again.

Henry Hanson was actually a trustworthy and unassuming town leader. He shunned any limelight and showed little ego. His retiring character but competent business nature resulted in many people including the mayor and town council members often seeking out his advice. Even his church pastor recognized Hanson's financial abilities and had asked this grain mill manager to be the church accountant despite there being several public accountants in town quite capable of performing the task.

When the town began a series of annual ten-day June festivals welcoming in the summer boating and fishing seasons, Hanson was asked to be the overall chairman. It would be in this capacity he would get to know another de facto leader of the town...someone who wasn't even a resident of the community...none other than Loni D'Annelli himself.

Loni D'Annelli had become a very popular fellow in Glenwood since his arrival in 1926. No one knew much about him other than he was some kind of union head from Chicago who preferred the relaxing Minnesota vacation spot with his colleagues and friends from around the Midwest. He often repeated how Chippewa Lodge was the perfect place for him to get away from the pressures of the city. The town in turn was fond of the man for his great generosity to the churches and his bringing more commerce to the town. Chippewa Lodge depended upon the local businesses to supply the goods and services required by the 'guests' staying at the isolated lake resort.

Throughout those five years up to June, 1931, the mutually beneficial relationship worked as well as one could hope. While the town did notice the rather strange collection of guests renting cabins at the Lodge, they were not about to be too curious. Locals didn't want to say or do anything to rock the boat. The town was prospering quite nicely thanks to the free spending lodgers.

As head of the huge June celebration, Hanson gradually got to know Loni D'Annelli. As part of the events during the festival, the Chicago man had been hosting a charity golf tournament at the nine-hole Chippewa Lodge golf course. As the event grew in spectator popularity each June, D'Annelli sought out Hanson to solicit civic and church organizations to support the tournament as well as to be the financial man to manage the high stakes Calcutta. From parking to transportation to food and ticket sales to golf course maintenance during the event, it would turn out those organizations made a lot of money for their involvement. It was another example of why people wanted this symbiotic relationship to endure as long as possible between the group at Chippewa Lodge and the townsfolk.

Both men carried a respect for each other as much as anything for the good their relationship did for the town and the lake resort. But, in time that deference, at least from Hanson's perspective, would begin to wear thin. By 1929 the local businessman had become quite mindful of the year-round shenanigans being played out at the lake resort. Hanson's inclination was always to inform the state patrol and end the sordid affair. However, by the time he fully understood the magnitude of each of D'Annelli's illicit ventures, Hanson was inclined to hold his tongue. In the years he'd been festival chairperson, he'd also become the de facto middle man between Loni D'Annelli and the local townsfolk. As long as Hanson and D'Annelli worked together and maintained the balance between the ignorance of the town and any snags caused by the large mixture of reprobates, wanted criminals, and mobsters who stayed at the lake resort during the rest of the year, then the precarious relationship between the town and those 'guests' at the Lodge could continue unabated. Furthermore, he could not ignore the positive impact D'Annelli's operation was having on the town. Most farm towns all across the U.S. were simply trying to survive; Glenwood was thriving.

Despite all the good being derived from D'Annelli's needs from the town's businesses, by 1931 Hanson had had enough. He was experiencing increased personal guilt as he witnessed more and more his counterpart's complete disdain for the law. Holding back what he knew for the good of the town no longer controlled his thoughts. Realizing it was just a question of time before D'Annelli's entire operation would be discovered in one way or another, he had to face the only alternative he felt he had. He had to move on. His being wanted by the law as an accomplice to the mob or his being sought by the Chicago syndicate as a stool pigeon when D'Annelli's operation would finally fall had become as predictable as day and night. The stress was sucking the very energy from his mind and body. He was in a no-win situation. He knew he had to take more control if he was to have any future at all.

And, taking control was what he did. It included his creating a vast plan to lay the groundwork for the Loni D'Annelli era to end while creating an alias and finding a new place to set up his own business after disappearing from town.

The sequence of events following the police raid happened much as he expected. After he vanished, he would hear that law enforcement had some interest in talking with him but that importance would wane given the windfall of arrests that occurred at the Lodge. More serious was the key matter of his disappearance making him the primary suspect as the stool pigeon in the eyes of Loni D'Annelli and his mob associates. He knew whether he'd stayed in town or not, that accusation would be difficult to overcome...especially since it was true.

Knowing that threat of mob retribution would be his biggest future challenge, by the time he drove out of Glenwood, he had that new identity and an itinerary to a faraway destination. Very soon thereafter, he also would scrap his recognizable old Plymouth and alter his appearance.

By all measures those plans to stay hidden would succeed over the next three decades. Having set up a new life and basing his new business out of Charleston, South Carolina, Henry 'Granville' would become a very prominent but reclusive businessman. His privately held holding company, Triple H Development, Inc., owned over twenty-five hotels along the east coast and Florida gulf coast as well as the silent ownership of two lake resort properties in Minnesota....and of all things, a publishing company in Minneapolis.

But, this concealment would too often face challenges. Keeping the confidentiality of his past was never easy. Although those challenges were reduced as the years passed, he always had to remain vigilant. By 1960 it was more the threats of nosy business magazine writers and curious newspaper reporters wanting to know his past who remained. Underworld interruptions had mostly dried up by that time. And, in the thirty years since leaving Minnesota, his concern had become more about preserving the image of his very profitable, well-established privately held corporation as well as the reputations of those key people who'd been so loyal and had protected him from being found out over those many years.

With the advent of that new decade, Granville was also facing imminent retirement. He knew his job was not only to find a competent successor, but a man willing to take on the possible challenges the corporation might face if Granville's background was ever made public. He'd also been contemplating more and more a completely radical idea, that is, might it be better for the future health of his organization and the reputations of those people close to him if he'd just come clean with the details of his past life? At least he would be assured his side of the story would be better represented, especially if he, at times, had to twist some of the details to his favor.

Granville had been mulling this idea over for the previous year. He wanted to find a scribe...someone who knew nothing about him or his early personal history...someone who could listen and paraphrase his story without past prejudice for or against him.

Discussing this matter with his few close associates, most were opposed to it. They thought it wiser for him to stay quiet about his past. His board of directors for Triple H Development, Inc. thought Henry's concern after thirty years wasn't necessary. They argued that most if not all of the mobsters who might want revenge from that time back in the late 1920's and early 1930's were likely not even alive, especially given their occupations. They further argued that if he admitted being the long missing Henry Hanson, why face any penalties that might follow from the law or the mob, even after three decades? Finally they contended that Granville's reputation as a highly respected hotel magnate would likely minimize any possible negative impact on himself or Triple H Development, Inc. anyway...but why chance it?

While appreciating their points, he had a more complete perspective than his close advisors. Most of them didn't know how checkered his last years in Glenwood, Minnesota actually were. He truly wanted the chance to explain his motives and actions in context to everything else that he'd done before leaving his home state. Also, if legal questions ever arose or rumors ever developed even after his passing, Granville wanted his key people on his board as well as his replacement to understand his full story. Only then would he feel confident they could effectively protect the corporation's image and the reputations of those individuals who helped him build Triple H Development, Inc.

It was for those reasons he moved ahead with his plans. It was in the spring of 1960 that he finally resolved to confidentially tell his story in a series of interviews in Charleston, South Carolina at the headquarter hotel of his conglomerate.

He hired a young writer who met the qualifications he was seeking...a person with no past knowledge of anyone named Henry Hanson or even Henry Granville. Because of the hotel mogul's busy schedule, it would take the interviewer months to complete the interview sessions and then collate the notes before drafting a final manuscript.

Then Granville could decide for himself if the exposé on his life might be made public or whether it should just remain as a private legal document only to be used when and if needed.

In addition, Henry Granville hoped the drawn-out time requirement for his chosen scribe to complete the project would also fulfill another notion he'd been carrying in his mind. Time would only tell, but he looked forward to the possibility.

Chapter 1

It was after midnight on that Saturday night in June, 1931, when the rusty 1926 Plymouth quietly made its way through some familiar back streets in the driver's hometown of Glenwood, Minnesota. His hope at that late hour was to reach the east edge of town below the bluffs and then quietly ascend the E. Hwy. 28 hill without anyone seeing him or recognizing his automobile.

Finally approaching the main highway, his biggest concern was the other vehicles crossing in front of him. A few dawdlers were on the road after leaving the downtown street dance even though the band had quit playing almost two hours before. He was hoping those occasional vehicles were being driven by young folks from out of town who wouldn't know him if they saw him. His real wish was that his old, plain car would simply blend into the night.

He stopped at the side street corner. Just a left turn and he'd be on his main escape route out of town. Only the familiar rumble of the Plymouth's engine interrupted the otherwise calm of the late evening. His dream was now in front of him. All he needed was a clear road before he took his turn, accelerated forward, and gathered speed so his trusty Plymouth could challenge the long hill out of town. If his worn sedan was made to work too hard on the incline, the engine would moan and cough until the straight away at the crest was reached. The sound would echo for blocks into the town below and he'd feel as if he was naked…the noise easily recognizable by too many people. Townsfolk kidded him about the sound of that old engine; it was as identifying as if he shouted his name across the valley. He'd lived in the town for over ten years and owned the vehicle for the previous four years. The car was as part of him as a preferred piece of clothing.

Yet, it was so late. Those people who knew him would be asleep. It would have to be extreme bad luck that some friend or neighbor might be awake, might identify the hilarious whine of his old Plymouth and then wonder why he was departing town at such an hour. Normally he could take their jesting, however, on that particular night he didn't want any townsfolk to recall his distinctive engine noise once it was determined that he'd left town so surreptitiously. He could not let that happen; he didn't want anyone, not even that late night light sleeper to have any idea when, how, why, or in what direction he'd left town.

Sitting in his jalopy on that street corner under an overhanging oak tree where even the moonlight couldn't find him, he scoffed at his own paranoia. He was being too worrisome. He'd planned this secret departure for months for just the right time…and that time had occurred earlier that day. Now it was the hour to leave…just as planned. He wanted nothing to foul up his exodus.

With his headlights off, he gazed past some trees to his right down four long blocks toward the main intersection of town. He prayed no one would see him. At that late hour, what were the chances? It wasn't that much of a prayer to get answered.

His minor plea, unfortunately, went unrequited. A slightly familiar decrepit Model A Ford with headlights pointed his way had slowed down just past the main intersection and a man with a startlingly vivid colored shirt suddenly came running out from the side of Big Bud Bunsen's General Store. He jumped into the open-door passenger side of the old Ford as it then lurched forward. The driver seemed equally desperate to get out of the town.

The driver in the Plymouth had to make a decision. He'd seen that old Ford around town. There were others of the same model, but even so it looked too familiar. Some sweat appeared on his brow. Whose car was it? He couldn't think. If that old Ford coming in his direction drove by him as he waited at the corner, the driver might stop just to chew the fat. He couldn't take that chance.

He'd barely got started with his escape and he was facing a problem he hadn't expected. He thought he was ready for anything. Apparently that was not true.

He momentarily considered dropping down in the front seat hoping the old Ford would simply drive by and not see his vehicle. Yet, what if they actually slowed wondering what his car was doing at that corner in the middle of the night. They might think his car had been stolen. They'd get out of their car and check things out…and they'd see him sprawled across the front seat. Then he'd have some explaining to do.

He shook his head again. There he was being paranoid again. Yet, the possibility was real. Clenching his teeth, he breathed out some unaccustomed profanity. It was just circumstances and plain bad luck that the old Ford was heading his way at the exact same time he wanted to leave town undetected.

Suddenly the old Plymouth shot forward peeling out of the stationary position at that residential corner. It was as if the driver's foot made the decision before his brain voted. As he shot onto E. Hwy. 28 toward the bluff, he was four blocks ahead of the approaching Model A Ford. Turning on his headlights, he had his accelerator on the floor in order to have any chance of ascending the hill and not having that Ford catch up to him. If he could just maintain the four block distance to the apex of the bluff, he could race off on flatter terrain into the dark night hopefully leaving that Ford back in the foggy mist of the humid night.

Frantically he crouched behind the wheel sweating and willing his vehicle to go faster. Pushing his worn down car to its fullest, he knew he was testing the ultimate power of his overextended Plymouth engine. The whine from the engine began echoing over the valley below as if shouting his name…just like he feared. His old beater was not used to such maltreatment. The normal moans of the engine sounded differently…more of high-pitched gasping. The varying sound made the driver smile. Even he'd never heard his car emit such a distressing cry.

Finally succeeding to the top of the bluff with the Ford well behind him, the driver now anxiously begged for the car following him to slow or turn off the highway as soon as possible.

With his heart synchronizing with the his vehicle's overworked engine, the driver saw the old Ford finally make it to the crest of the hill and maintain the distance from him as they both sped eastward along the state highway. Pressing harder on the accelerator he would not let himself believe the old Ford had his same urgency.

He gritted his teeth and wiped the sweat from his forehead as his vehicle gathered more speed on the straight away and the engine settled down to its normal drone. Another unfamiliar expletive reverberated from his lips. He just did not need the added anxiety of being followed.

With every blink of his eyes he glanced from the road ahead to the headlights tailing him...back and forth...back and forth. Then, despite his anxiety, he felt a painful nostalgic twinge in his chest as he stared into his rear view mirror beyond the headlights behind him. There was nothing but a broad dark nighttime sky that seemed to drop lower than the ground. He knew what it was. The huge gulf of blackness was Lake Minnewaska...a sight he didn't expect to see for a long time if ever again.

Slowing only slightly for some train tracks, he then floored the pedal to pick up his pace once again. Now his eyes were glued more to his rear view mirror than out the front windshield. As he sped along, he waved at the John Bailey farmhouse giving what he thought would be another final farewell to a good friend most likely asleep at that hour.

Wiping his brow to keep the sweat from clouding his vision, the old Ford continued to trail him as the headlights reflected out onto the rolling Minnesota landscape. He spat out a couple more loud swear words in frustration, something he normally did only under his breath. Leaving so late at night was not supposed to be this traumatic.

Then, as if the Almighty was jolted by the driver's uncustomary profanity, the car then a half mile behind him suddenly slowed. The Model A Ford veered onto the same John Bailey farmhouse road the driver of the Plymouth had just passed.

The lead car sped on as if bolstered by the driver's sudden relief. He'd done it...not easily...but he'd done it. He'd made it out of town without being recognized. He patted the old satchel beside him containing enough money to ensure some comfort during his long flight to safety. And, that was just some of the money he had with him. There were other packets of money hidden within the lining of his car's interior, some packed tightly under the very seat he was sitting on, and some stuffed behind the back seats. He had enough money with him to start a bank. All he had to do was remain attentive, not do anything stupid, keep himself from being recognized, and just keep driving... and driving...to his final destination.

The driver...one very highly respected businessman from the very rural lake town he'd just left was now free to travel wherever he wanted...and conceivably do anything within reason he wanted to experience. Despite that freedom, he was not going to do anything unlawful or immoral. On the contrary he was going to continue the honest and honorable life he'd tried to live in Glenwood for the past ten years…or at least eight of those ten years. However, he'd be undertaking that new life with a new name and a new location some fifteen hundred miles away.

He had the chance for a new beginning…not that he really had a choice. He'd been planning to leave the town for over a year, but it had taken him until that very June night before he truly felt ready to make his journey. From that weekend on, he expected to be a marked man. For a time…and he didn't know for how long…he'd have to look over his shoulder until he became more established with his alias and likely a new look. He also had to concoct a background story that would be believable, not create curiosity, and not be easily checked out. Though he wished he could have left his community under better circumstances, it just hadn't worked out that way.

Easing off the gas pedal ever so slightly, the engine sounded more relaxed. The pace of his heart calmed as well. He smiled knowing only God had any idea what direction he was traveling. He still had to be very careful. There could be no accidents, no tickets for speeding, and no stopping until he was out of his home state.

He had to stick to his strategy, stay awake and keep a cool head. He would be moving south and east to his destination. It would require days even a week if necessary to reach his endpoint. Along the way he would rid himself of his old Plymouth and buy a new car to further thwart anyone trying to locate him.

The driver was exhilarated as his old Plymouth purred along the roadway. The next town would be Westport, then Sauk Centre. He knew each time he entered a town, he would feel some trepidation. But, as he got further from Glenwood that feeling would gradually dissipate. Once he passed through the Twin Cities, the fear of being recognized would be greatly reduced…not completely…not ever completely…but enough that he could breathe easier.

The moon shined brightly as he raced along the dark rolling farm land. He was excited. The escape was moving along so smoothly until he passed through Sauk Centre. Then it was as if the previous weeks with little sleep was telling his eyes it was time to close. The sleepless nights had snuck upon him. The thrill with being underway had set him at peace rather than making him more attentive. Falling asleep at the wheel was a problem he'd not considered in all his planning.

As his brain unwound from the months of stress, the adrenalin that had been his primary fuel was melting away with each mile.

For the next few hours his eyes would close…then abruptly open only to be drawn closed again seconds later. At times he snapped awake swearing that he'd been asleep. He knew he should rest, but he felt it more crucial to keep moving. He had to keep that old Plymouth on the road and get out of the state. Once in Wisconsin, maybe then he could allow himself some shut-eye. Even then, a truly restful sleep wasn't possible until he was well into central Illinois moving southward toward Kentucky.

As he mushed on, he appreciated that there was still some adrenalin dripping through his brain as his car sped onward down that dark two lane road. His attention was spurred by the constant reminder he was ending one life that night and beginning another. Henry Hanson was not about to let the impulse to sleep overtake him. He had a much stronger urge to remain alive and witness what his second life had in store under his new name, Henry Granville.

*   *   *

When the raid at the Lake Minnewaska resort ensued on that Sunday morning, June 7, 1931, Hanson had been gone from Glenwood, Minnesota and on the road for about eight hours. Judging that a police bust on Chippewa Lodge was_looming, he had only hours to finalize some last minute details before departing. What he knew above everything was once D'Annelli and his associates were arrested, he would become a target of the Chicago syndicate.

Weighing on his mind as well was that the law would be looking for him, at least for a while. It would be logical for investigators to be inquiring how entangled he might have been in the whole mess out at Chippewa Lodge. After all, there was no getting around his middle man activities between the miscreants at the lake resort and the detached townspeople who preferred to look the other way.

Above all, it was D'Annelli's people he had to be most concerned. His innocence could be proven to the state patrol and the Bureau of Investigation once they found out it was he who wrote the incriminating letters to the Minneapolis U.S. Attorney's office. Whether he'd written those confidential notes or not, though, the perception by D'Annelli and his boys could only be that Hanson knew what was going on at Chippewa Lodge. He'd seen everything. He'd known D'Annelli was thumbing his nose at the law. He'd stayed quiet for the sake of the town right up to the moment he disappeared. Who else could be the stool pigeon?

With his timely departure from Glenwood, he no longer had the vision of himself in a barrel at the bottom of Lake Minnewaska. He already had an out-of-state license plate he'd acquired and placed on his old Plymouth. With his new identity and a large amount of cash, he hoped within two days to be south of the Mason-Dixon line with the name Henry Hanson literally fading into thin air forever.

Of course he hadn't been able to counter every concern. His friends and townsfolk would be worried about his health. There would be constant chatter of where he went. His quick departure would also spur the probability that he indeed ratted on D'Annelli and his boys at the Lodge. He also failed to consider how public the news would become on where D'Annelli had stored his illegal business profits. Hanson had given the racketeer the little known feed & grain mill office basement rent free as a place for storage. To D'Annelli's people it was too obvious that Henry Hanson could easily have stockpiled some of the conman's fortune to finance his escape and set up a new life. Over time there would be plenty of others who would surmise the same thing.

That conjecture above everything kept anyone connected to D'Annelli very dubious about the mysterious and timely disappearance of Henry Hanson. There would be a number of gangsters who sought information to the whereabouts of Hanson for a number of months... some for as long as a year. While retribution was their claim, the supposed money Hanson had taken was their primary incentive.

These selfish efforts would dwindle with the passage of time; many hucksters gave up when most of them believed they were chasing a ghost. A few got close to him, but they didn't know it. Also, what helped Hanson in these instances was that there was rarely any shared information as to Hanson's whereabouts. Their own selfishness kept them silent. No one was the wiser when anyone happened upon his actual location.

The threat of being found under the alias of Henry Granville lessened as the months turned into years. He had added to his new name a fabricated story that he was in the long line of South Carolina

Granvilles whose descendants had mostly died off. Preferring to keep his first name, he felt 'Henry' was common enough and therefore not a threat to his secrecy.

After six months of living in the Charleston area, he'd developed an even better camouflage with a longer hair style, a graying beard and moustache, and his constant effort to speak with a surprisingly acceptable southern accent. Nonetheless, he would always be on guard. Henry Granville, as CEO of a large hotel and lake resort development corporation, was always mindful that someone could be looking for him…or worst of all…that something he did or said could be a tip off as to who he really was.

*   *   *

Despite his efforts some threats did materialize as the Henry Granville name became better known around Charleston and in business circles along the east coast. His new guesthouse, the East Bay Street Hotel, was gaining more notoriety with each passing year. It was natural during the 1930's that people would become curious about this successful businessman. Nosy reporters wanted to get the real story behind the successful hotel owner. It was those meddlesome reporters and business magazine writers who created more of the discomfort. His staff was even trained to respond. The message was that Mr. Granville preferred not to be in the limelight and therefore was not interested in being interviewed. That desired response would echo throughout his business career.

Unfortunately the name 'Henry Hanson' would not die easily amongst the underworld. Someone had ratted on Loni D'Annelli and the name 'Hanson' stayed fresh in the minds of the Chicago syndicate for a number of years. At the least, many gangsters wanted to hear if Henry Hanson's denial was plausible. There would be times during the 1930's that attempts from the wrong side of the law almost disrupted Henry's cover. Luckily each of those extortion efforts was derailed quietly and promptly.

It was usually a small time gangster working alone who'd somehow tracked Hanson to Charleston, South Carolina. Granville developed a close group of colleagues. They made the possible blackmail venture more trouble than it was worth. The small time hood would suddenly have to contend with an unexpected wave of bad luck in dealing with the law. Two different would-be blackmailers found themselves back in Italy facing charges still on that country's books. A couple other potential extortionists were arrested by the Charleston police force for crimes they may or may not have committed back in Chicago. They found themselves being given a choice of incarceration or freedom. The latter always was the more popular decision.

From the war years to 1950, there were fewer problems of Henry Granville's background being revealed. By then his East Bay Street Hotel had become the headquarters for Triple H Development, Inc., a holding company with a growing number of sea side hotels up and down the Atlantic coast. While all his facilities remained opened and solvent during the war, there were some tight times. He did choose to have a few of his hotels become rest and convalescent centers for returning injured military men and women. It turned out to be a worthwhile bit of beneficence with one hotel in St. Petersburg, Florida operating as a hospital until 1946 thereby enhancing the reputation of his organization.

From that year through 1960, his privately held corporation doubled in numbers of hotels with more acquisitions on the east and west coasts of Florida. Triple H Development, Inc. had become a quiet giant as a holding company with over twenty hotels along the Atlantic Ocean and the Gulf of Mexico. The rumors that he also owned some lake resorts back somewhere in the Midwest were never verified.

The increased size of the corporation during the decade of the 1950's fostered more interest in Henry Granville. Prying newspaper and magazine writers became even more challenging. Granville handled these subtle but potentially dangerous requests for interviews with the same time tested strategy he'd used back in the 1930's. Reporters and business magazines writers were passed off to low level managers who knew little about the history of the corporation and even less about their boss. It was always repeated that he was from that long line of South Carolina 'Granvilles'. He allowed the admission that some family money got him started, but it was understood his own business acumen and the abilities of his staff were the key ingredients in building the hotel empire. And, the understanding by most employees and local Charleston friends was that Henry was raised in Europe.

On a happier note through the 1950's, there were virtually no gangster problems. No one from the D'Annelli era had been prowling around trying to link Henry Granville to the Henry Hanson who disappeared from Minnesota two decades before. Age and attrition as much as anything depreciated the number of gangsters interested in finding the man rumored to have singularly brought down the incomparable and legendary mobster, Loni D'Annelli. The buzz, however, had grown into a fantasy that Hanson had absconded with 'all' of the conman's illegal business profits. Despite that compelling hearsay there were very few days by the end of that decade when Henry Granville even thought about his background being discovered.

It was in Granville's sixtieth year in early 1960. Then he got two wake-up calls.

First was his health. His doctor had become more emphatic at Granville's annual physical about slowing down. There was a blood pressure issue. The doctor scolded him for smoking too many Cuban cigars, not eating correctly, and enjoying too much wine. He also didn't like that Granville had a constant and tiring travel schedule. The personal physician hinted strongly that Henry needed to abruptly change his life style.

The words of warning weren't voiced as if the grim reaper was having a drink down in the hotel bar, but the cautionary tone was enough to make Granville ponder more thoughtfully what lay ahead for those in charge of his corporation when he did retire. While he expected to be Chairman of the Board to his last breath, he also knew he had to groom a successor as head of Triple H Development, Inc. This presented some challenges. Though he had many capable people working for him, too many of them were later in their own careers. As for his younger staff members, they just weren't ready to take on the complete job as CEO. Some of them could protect the profit line, but none of them could be expected to stand up against future prying and intrusive questions about how Triple H Development, Inc. got started. To Granville, a successor determinedly protecting the reputation of the organization was an absolute priority.

As the months had gone by in 1959, no answer as to his possible replacement was materializing. Though retirement was not imminent, he had to face the reality that if his health broke down, there might be no option to his stepping away from his business life.

He was unmarried...or at least he had no offspring...and he had no close relatives. Therefore, there were no heirs to which his estate would automatically be transferred. In his will the corporation would become part of a foundation. For a while that foundation could be led by some very competent people on his board of directors...at least until they retired. But, who was capable enough to eventually take charge and continue to grow and protect the corporation. It was a quandary festering more in Granville's mind than he cared to admit.

The second wake-up call was the first threat in years from someone determined to expose Granville's actual background. In February, 1960, an unrecognizable voice from a caller claiming to be from Henry Hanson's past made contact. The call was so unexpected, so disconcerting...like the reoccurrence of an old illness. The man sounded even more sinister because of the accuracy of the statements regarding Granville's past. While the caller didn't make any demands for money, his aim seemed initially to cause apprehension and stress.

Granville normally would have handled the bothersome contact as he had many years before by simply laughing off the claims, informing the potential blackmailer he was on the wrong track, and then hanging up the phone. This call was different. This man wasn't guessing; he knew dates and times...and the people.

In the coming weeks Granville would receive more unnerving telephone calls describing details how Henry Hanson had worked with Loni D'Annelli at Chippewa Lodge...how he'd offered the Glenwood Feed & Grain Mill office basement as a storage area for the Chicago mobster's illegal profits... how he'd taken huge sums of that money before disappearing to South Carolina...and how he'd been the turncoat who'd called in the state patrol to close down D'Annelli's operation. While the caller's points were not entirely accurate, it didn't matter. Made public, the perception would be strong enough to make Granville appear guilty of aiding and abetting a known criminal for many years during his years as Henry Hanson.

And, that insight was bad enough just from the law side. Worse still was the reaction by the mob even after so many years. How would Granville publicly refute the accusations even though some of the allegations were exaggerated? The adverse publicity would be bad regarding the apparent mob money as the means by which he made his initial hotel property investments. That would catch the attention of the

Chicago syndicate even if it was thirty years later. He could see Triple H Development, Inc. following a similar pattern of domination by the mob in the same way Chippewa Lodge on a much smaller scale had been dominated by D'Annelli's group back in the late 1920's through 1931.

By the middle of March when the caller made yet another of his threatening phone contacts, Granville continued to remain calm, but finally insisted the caller name his price for silence. Only then could a reasonable counterattack be planned. But, the would-be extortionist seemed more interested in continuing to make Granville twist in discomfort. The caller began naming some of the members of the Triple H Development Board of Directors who helped bring down the huge mob operation at Chippewa Lodge.

That was too much. The hotel mogul's temper finally flared. There was now no doubt this nefarious caller was out to ruin not only the hotel conglomerate and its owner, but to cast dangerous and often incorrect aspersions on those people closest to Granville as well.

When Granville's impatient rage echoed over the phone line, he noticed a slight change in the caller's confidence. The man's voice became hesitant...as if he wasn't ready to name a price. Creating more angst seemed to be his real aim for the present. No longer in complete control, the man seemed flustered until he suddenly just hung up the phone.

The reaction gave Granville some hope of defending himself. The would-be blackmailer wasn't able to counter when hearing an outburst he didn't expect. It appeared the caller wasn't particularly smart; he was only good at giving rehearsed lines over the phone. While that could mean the caller could become more unpredictable and even dangerous, to Granville it also cast doubt whether the man had the intestinal fortitude to carry out any extortion plan.

Granville didn't hear from the strange man again until Monday, March 28 just days before his quarterly board meeting. Again, no money was mentioned...nor did Granville ask right away. There were only continued implied threats with the caller this time naming the five people who supposedly collaborated with Henry Hanson against the mob. That would be the first time the man revealed some inaccuracies. Rather than incriminating the two Baileys, he named the two key law officers in town at the time, County Sheriff Clarence Petracek and

Glenwood's Chief of Police, Rich Brey as among the accomplices who closed down Chippewa Lodge.

Relieved that John and Adam Bailey were out of the extortionist's loop, Granville remained cool. Through gritted teeth he more cautiously demanded, "O.K., you obviously want something from me. It's time you name your price...or are you just going to continue these idiotic accusations against me?"

This time he heard the caller literally gurgle with delight. "Hanson, we might as well face the real question. You have to wonder once you pay me off, what's the assurance I'd stay mum?"

Henry responded sharply, "Finally we're on the same page. That's exactly what I'm thinking."

The voice chuckled again. "That's why I'm going to suggest a payout completely out of the ordinary. It will guarantee my word not to breathe anything about your questionable history to anyone. My proposal is that you make me a silent partner in your organization. I want a monthly stipend from the ongoing revenues of your businesses... as if I was an employee earning a salary. I would want the payment routed to my foreign account every month. With this arrangement why would I ever want your hotel enterprise to suffer with bad or damaging publicity? On the contrary, if I required you to pay me a lump sum, there would be no guarantee of my silence, would there be?"

Without waiting for a response, the extortionist continued, "Of course not agreeing to my terms would be perilous for your company and your friends. It would be a shame if the careers of some of your longtime associates dating back to the D'Annelli era would suddenly come to a disheartening and disrespectful conclusion. Most of all, though, the newspapers will converge on you when they hear that your entire hotel domain was started with mob profits from your friend, Loni D'Annelli...funds you likely stole the night you disappeared from Glenwood."

The man paused to let his points settle. Granville said nothing... only listening carefully in case the caller slipped up and gave any hint as to his identity.

But, no tip-off was forthcoming. The only positive result of the call was that Granville finally had the blackmailer's cards on the table. Now the real game could begin.

As in the past when faced with possible threats, Henry's voice displayed no particular angst. He simply cleared his throat and replied, "O.K., I understand why you want to be some kind of silent partner in Triple H Development, Inc. You understand I'll have to bring my company financial officer into this matter. We'd have to somehow make these payments...whatever amount you might be requesting...legal. Also, documents will need to be signed so monthly installments could be transferred to your foreign account smoothly."

Granville was now into delay mode. He wanted to leave some questions on the table so as to create some consternation within the caller's mind. It worked immediately as the extortionist seemed puzzled not knowing what to say or do next. It was evident the blackmailer was a novice crook...and everything indicated he was working alone. All these factors could be made to work in Granville's eventual favor.

Granville maintained control. "O.K. ...I have an appointment waiting for me. We'll have to talk later. I'll need more specifics from you...your foreign account number, whatever name you are putting on that account, and of course the amount of each monthly installment you are demanding. I'll be gone on business for the next ten days, but next time you call, I'll need that information."

Then the hotel mogul simply hung up giving the caller no chance to respond. He smiled at his forceful theatrics. Granville had no meeting to attend. He had no immediate travel plans. Abruptly hanging up the phone was all an act. He found it interesting how he'd so easily wrestled the control of the conversation away from the extortionist. The fellow had not been given a chance to set a time next for the two of them to further discuss the demands.

Granville had left the impression the blackmail scheme was just another business matter. Most importantly he'd further curtailed any reason for the caller to make public any background details that could damage Triple H Development, Inc. and himself.

Chuckling, Henry sat at his desk evaluating the telephone call. The man had to be in his same age range to have known so much about those years back in Minnesota. Age could be a factor. The man needed to maintain his energy and determination to carry out this blackmail scheme. The question remained whether this man had the smarts and the courage, attributes also needed if he was to succeed. Further, if this huckster was short of money...which he likely was...he might get desperate. That could lead to him making a mistake. Granville took a deep breath sensing he'd gained an improved chance of winning against this intimidating adversary.

Pouring himself one of his favorite local ice tea drinks, he sat back thinking how this latest blackmail attempt had brought to light his desire to possibly come clean with his background in some kind of signed and notarized document. He wouldn't have to tell everything, but he'd become more convinced the manuscript could be a valuable defense in standing up to any counterpoints or slander aimed at him or his organization in a court of law...even after his demise. His current mêlée with the extortionist made the idea seem even wiser. He'd worked too long and hard not to take whatever necessary precautions to sustain the positive reputation Triple H Development, Inc. Furthermore, he owed it to the people who worked for him...and his friends and colleagues who had so faithfully backed him up over the years. Telling his story in his words and beliefs would reflect his efforts to have done the right thing considering the circumstances at the time.

For a moment he wiggled uncomfortably in his chair knowing that he hadn't always done the proper or even lawful thing throughout his life. Nonetheless, the more he thought about it, the more the document seemed like an obligation.

It was that very morning Granville took time to further ponder the qualities of a scribe. He wanted a writer with no knowledge of his previous life. It would be a series of interviews conducted by the scribe who would have no preconceived notions about guilt or innocence in his dealings. Then, as if lightning struck, he had the most serendipitous brain wave ripple through his head. In those seconds he had the writer in mind. It would take some manipulating, but what in his business life hadn't required some of that kind of action.

He got up and walked out of his office with a brisker step. The caller was still on his mind, but now there was a silver lining to the blackmail attempt. It was causing Granville to realize it was time to move forward on some other overdue plans.

Chapter 2

James Lawton and Charlie Davis had been friends of Henry Granville's since the aftermath of the D'Annelli episode back in Glenwood, Minnesota. In fact two years after Henry arrived in Charleston, South Carolina and after he'd launched his new hotel, the East Bay Street Hotel, the bond among the three had become close... for a number of reasons. By 1933 Charlie Davis had been working as the general counsel of Triple H Development, Inc. since 1929 before Henry Hanson had even become Henry Granville.

Now twenty seven years later as the three of them sat in Henry's office after a late March board meeting, Lawton and Davis detected their old friend was more edgy than usual. As they talked, Granville was wiggling around in his leather desk chair like he was sitting in poison ivy. They knew he had something on his mind. Anticipating he'd eventually spout out what was bothering him, they helped themselves to another drink from Henry's cabinet and waited.

Finally, Henry began lamenting his problem of succession... something he'd discussed with them often in the past year. His concern had not changed. "Gentlemen, we've just got too many fine people in this organization too advanced in age to take over for the many years ahead. And, the younger folks in the company just don't yet have the background knowledge or long term concern to take over the operation. I need someone who will defend the confidentiality of the people who've helped me build this vast corporation. You two hucksters are perfect examples. We've had quite a history together. Your backgrounds with me have to be protected for the sake of your legal reputations back in Minnesota to say nothing of your personal lives."

Henry meant no harm with his joking reference to them and they knew it, however they had already discussed their disagreement with him. They were not concerned about their reputations.

Lawton was first to shake his head. "Henry, for God's sake, the D'Annelli days are gone. The Bailey's, Lindy, Charlie and I...and even you...we're not going to have any more trouble with the mob discovering our story. It's just been too many years."

Henry poured another brandy for his two friends. He nodded, "Jamie, you're probably right, but I still want to seek out someone more appreciative of the enterprise we've created and respect the special circumstances of the secrecy we've been able to maintain for over a quarter of a century. I'm not going to retire until I find that individual, even if it takes me a couple years of training the person to be the businessman he has to become. But, above everything I must have that understanding and compassion from any person I name as my successor.

Lawton and Davis listened with some amusement. They'd heard Henry rattle on about this successor issue for a long time. They sensed it was not the only reason he'd poured them another drink.

It was Davis who knew him best who got to the heart of the matter. "O.K., Henry, what's really bothering you. We'll figure out this successor thing all in good time. You could retire now and the hotel chain would be in good hands with the group of managers you've got. So, let's get off that topic. What's up?"

With that Granville leaned back in his desk chair and simply said, "I've had another caller."

A half hour later with Lawton and Davis listening closely, Lawton picked up Henry's phone and dialed three numbers while saying, "Henry, it's about time we call Lou. He'll need to be involved."

Lou White had been the hotel's maintenance manager since he'd joined the East Bay Street Hotel staff shortly after World War II. His war record gave the man special qualities that made him quite valuable in dealing with problems of any type including nosy reporters and a few possible blackmail attempts early in the 1950's. Though he had lost his left arm in the war, the handicap was anything but debilitating to this resourceful character. He'd also taken on the role as a kind of body guard for Henry. That responsibility was only recognized by a few including Lawton and Davis.

Known mainly as just 'Lou' around the hotel and to locals, he handled the day to day maintenance issues as if that was his only job. However, over the previous fourteen years whenever a problem transpired that could potentially disrupt Henry Granville's life or the reputation of the hotel chain, Lou had taken charge. He also knew he was protecting a number of other people's backgrounds and careers connected to the hotel conglomerate. His value was without measure.

Within five minutes he was strolling into Henry's office and cordially greeted by Lawton, Davis, and Henry. This taller, more serious man acted towards them as if they were brothers. He'd conspired with them on a number of occasions to protect the company's image as well as to seek out any sordid details before any hotel acquisition was finalized.

Pouring his own ice tea, Lou sat down on a couch opposite the three of them knowing he was being called in because there was a problem. He didn't have to say anything.

Henry carried the ball. "Lou, we've dealt with reporters, mobsters, and opportunists over so many years to keep my true identity under wraps. We've managed to outwit them by any means and usually within the confines of the law."

There was a momentary silence as Lawton, Davis, and Lou White stifled their grins.

Henry tried to ignore their noticeable responses. "Of course in those few instances where that wasn't possible, we moved ahead anyway all for the common purpose of keeping the secrets of our pasts out of the public eye."

There was an understanding nod from all three men.

Henry continued, "Lou, I've already told Jamie and Charlie about a threat that really didn't become serious until recently. I didn't think it was severe enough to bother you fellows. Unfortunately, each conversation I've had with this periodic caller has reached the point where it is now a blackmail scheme. I've been a bit surprised how much this man seems to know about all of us going back to those Glenwood days. He spoke of Charlie, Lindy, and Jamie by name. He knows about Clarence Petracek and Rich Brey being employed by Loni as quasi-security guards. And, he has deduced enough about me that is frighteningly correct."

Lawton and Davis looked at each other and smiled. It always tickled them the way Henry still referred to D'Annelli often on a first name basis. The gangster and the feed and grain mill manager had maintained if not a friendship then certainly a respect for the four years they knew each other. Their chemistry and trust had maintained that profitable relationship between the resort and the townsfolk thereby postponing Glenwood from falling into the hard times of the Depression.

Henry then added, "This blackmailer is asking for not a lump sum payment for his silence, but rather to be placed on the payroll of Triple H Development, Inc. He wants to receive a lifelong monthly check delivered to what I would guess is his Swiss bank account. He represents his idea as a guarantee he'll never divulge our secrets to anyone…or in his words, "Why would I destroy my gift horse?" He emphasized that with a lump sum payment, what would keep him from going to the authorities, the mob, or the press the day after he cashed my check. He claims his way would assure me of his trustworthiness. Frankly, I have to give him points for logic and creativity in the art of extortion."

Gulping his last swallow of brandy, Charlie Davis mashed his cigar into an ashtray and stood up tall. Over the years he'd remained the small town attorney in Alexandria, Minnesota. Now, both he and Lawton were respected attorneys of law back in their home state. Few knew their life as it related to their connection with Triple H Development, Inc. They were quite aware of the importance of ending any threats to Henry or to the conglomerate because eventually they could face the same type of extortion to preserve their own reputations. In dealing with hoods and gangsters, they had no sympathy. They had learned to be as ruthless as their competitors.

Davis growled, "Henry, first of all, I want to find this guy as much as anyone. But, let's keep this latest attempt in perspective. As patient and knowledgeable as this blackmailer appears to be, there's been a lot of water over the dam since those days back in Minnesota. The chance of reprisal from the mob has been greatly reduced just through time. Most of those birds who were part of the D'Annelli organization are gone just because of the nature of their work. I can't imagine who this fellow is, but just the fact that he knows so much about us…well, I believe it's advisable to let this man play out more of his hand. I can't believe he has the contacts on the wrong side of the law who even care any more about the D'Annelli legacy. I don't think the mob will come after us. I believe he's in this only for himself, like others we've dealt with over the years. And, if he went to the authorities or to the newspapers, he'd be destroying his whole purpose of relieving you of some of your money. I get the feeling this guy has a grudge against you that will never be satisfied. Besides, if he does open his mouth to the press, it's the word of this joker against individuals like us who have generally been law-abiding, contributing members to society. Whose words do you think would carry more significance in the public's eye?"

Lawton nodded, "Still, it's the inferences by this man that could be damaging. What he has to say could be corroborated. But, I agree with Chas that we have to let this rascal show a few more cards. The more rope he gives us, the better the opportunity we have of hanging him. Like the other threats we've had to handle, these lowlifes eventually show their vulnerabilities. We can find ways to intimidate this guy once we find out who he is. And, be assured this guy has a past. I'm certain he doesn't want his name given to the authorities."

Nodding his head, Lou finally replied. "Henry, I know it puts some heat on you to listen to this rat make more threats, but let's play with this guy. We'll have a better chance of setting up our most effective offense. Now that we know what he wants, we already have some possible ways of bringing him out of the shadows. He wants money transferred to some overseas account from the corporation on a monthly basis; that's great. The bank documents will have to be signed. He'll use a different name, but there are other ways to pick up his scent. The game we play with him is to assure that ultimately he's going to get what he wants...but that it will take time to put the process into place legally. He's been abnormally patient so far, but the smell of money will test his endurance. That's when he's apt to make some blunders and we start making his life miserable."

Hearing everyone's input, Henry showed relief. He'd been sitting on this situation for too long alone. Now he had the key people who were always there to assist him. Breathing easier, he nodded in agreement with the consensus of the group. "You're all right. This guy will make some error along the way and we'll nail him. No reason to get too worked up. I'll handle his next call telling him of the paperwork we'll need for money transfer to his account...and then add that he's catching me in one of my busier travel schedules of the year. He'll have to deal with postponement after postponement until he might snap. It's then he'll be most prone to make a mistake."

With nods of the head from everyone in Henry's office, Lou left the office obviously deep in thought as to what else should be done. Lawton and Davis remained as Henry indicated he still had something else he wanted to discuss.

He then said to the two of them, "Before we dispense, I want to talk a bit more about putting something in writing…something that can be notarized and included in my will. It seems even more pertinent in light of this latest extortion attempt. The goal of this document is to have a recorded explanation of my background and what and why I did what I did back during those Loni D'Annelli years in Glenwood. I want this legal document to stand up in court against any future attacks against this enterprise or the people involved in it…even after I'm gone. I don't want anyone's reputation involved in this organization maligned…even accidentally…after my death. When the manuscript is completed, I'll want each board member to read it thoroughly and make certain it would substantiate my purpose."

Davis, as the general counsel, shrugged and then nodded. "Henry, you should probably go ahead with this journal idea if only to relax your mind that Triple H Development, Inc. will live on despite some of your actions in the past. Jamie and I…and the others… appreciate your concern about our own reputations and safety. Just to repeat, we're not as concerned as you are."

Lawton nodded. "All of our reputations will withstand what we've done in the past. It might make for some juicy copy for a while, but nothing of any longstanding damage. Most importantly, I'll guarantee most of our friends and clients won't believe the accusations or what horrible things we've supposedly done in our past lives anyway. We'll survive…so will Lindy…and John and Adam…and Clarence and Rich. Individual attacks against you, the company, and us just won't stand up. The blackmailer's claims lack credibility."

Not hearing the full backing for his journal idea, Henry finished his ice tea with a large gulp and then added, "Thank you for your half-assed support. I was going to go forward with my idea anyway."

The three of them laughed as Henry picked up the phone on his desk saying more energetically, "O.K.…I know you two want to go play some golf. I'll have you driven over to the country club. Bring a change of clothes. We'll have dinner out there. I've got a property in Phoenix, Arizona I'd like to discuss with the two of you. Also, I already have an idea who I want to employ as my scribe for this background manuscript, but I may need your support in getting him to remain here in Charleston as he puts the document together. I'll have him stay here at the hotel where we can more conveniently have some interview sessions. Then he can edit his notes and drafts while completing my story. I'll treat him first class just to make certain he's leaning my way as he frames his paragraphs."

Again there was laughter. Lawton and Davis knew it wouldn't be Henry to leave anything to chance.

Lawton and Davis sprang to their feet ready for the golf course. As they were about to exit Granville's spacious office, Davis asked, "So Henry, do we know this chap you're thinking of hiring?"

Henry looked confident. "Yeh, you know him quite well. It just won't be an easy task to convince him to spend a few months in this city. I hope to talk to another business associate this afternoon for some assistance in helping me convince this fellow to take on the writing project. I hope to tell you his name over dinner tonight."

Lawton and Davis showed no distress in having to wait. Their minds were more on stealing as much sunlight for golf as possible. The office door closed and Henry was already picking up the phone.

*   *   *

In truth Henry had known who he'd wanted as his scribe since the very idea of his background manuscript first percolated in his mind. The candidate was a young man who wasn't local and hadn't even been to South Carolina. Therefore, he would have no preconceived prejudices and knowledge of Henry Hanson or Henry Granville. The applicant had no idea his parents and Henry had been dear friends since a couple years after Henry had disappeared from Minnesota. The young man also had no idea his father and uncle had been members of the Triple H Development board of directors longer than the chosen journalist had been alive.

His name would be very familiar to Jamie Lawton and Charlie Davis since the scribe-elect was none other than Matt Lawton. Henry had known of Lindy and Jamie's son throughout the young man's formative years. Though Henry had been up in Minnesota numerous times since the end of World War II, he'd never met the younger Lawton...for reasons relating directly to confidentiality.

That didn't keep Henry from always asking about the Lawton's three offspring. As proud parents they couldn't help but boast of their children. Henry was particularly fond of hearing about the eldest son, Matt, and his accomplishments.

As Matt Lawton finished up college and sought employment, Henry made certain the journalism and business major had a job offer from University Publishing, Inc. in downtown Minneapolis. The company was owned by Triple H Development, Inc. and was managed by the younger brother of Rich Brey, the longtime friend and manager of one of Granville's original lake resorts in White Bear Lake, Minnesota.

Matt began working for Bud Brey at the publishing house just months after his graduation from the University of Minnesota in 1956. In four years the young man's career at the publishing house had been steady but underwhelming.

Henry periodically checked in with Bud Brey about Jamie and Lindy Lawton's son. Brey was satisfied but never overly enthusiastic about the young man's progress. Those kinds of evaluations eventually got Henry's attention. Henry's assertion was that University Press was a rather stodgy company, probably not that exciting for any young person looking to get ahead. Brey casually mentioned one day in early 1960 that young Lawton seemed bored enough in his job to more likely already be seeking a new direction in his career. That warning coincided conveniently with Henry Granville's need for a scribe.

Sensing he could steer Matt toward a more fulfilling future, he realized the biggest challenge would be pulling the Lawton son from Minnesota where he'd been born and raised. Logically, the young man would be more inclined to use his network of friends and business associates to advance his career in his home state. Taking on a journal assignment on the southeast coast in an old southern city might not be the kind of path...even if it was for the short term...that young Lawton might favor.

Granville had a habit of winning, however, and formulated a scheme to make the temporary assignment as lucrative as was required to gain Matt Lawton's attention. While he could have used the influence of Lawton's parents, he wanted the decision to be Matt's. Henry just wanted the chance to have some continued influence on the young man's future.

It was the last week in March, 1960, when Henry discussed the idea with Jamie and Lindy Lawton of offering the writer job to their son, Matt. The two parents thought it a grand idea agreeing the decision should be their son's alone. And, with the Lawtons and Charlie Davis embarking for Europe just days away, the timing would force Matt to truly make his own judgment.

Chapter 3

When Matthew J. Lawton first met Henry Granville in April 1960 he had the strange sensation he'd known the man for many years. Despite their age difference, there was something familiar about him. Maybe it was because he'd heard the hotel magnate and recluse was apparently born and raised in Minnesota. Maybe it was the frenetic days leading up to their first handshake. Whatever the case, Lawton's coming to Charleston, South Carolina would be a turning point in his young life.

It was Wednesday, April 6 when his boss, Bud Brey, the president of University Publishing, Inc. in Minneapolis, Minnesota asked him to come into his office. The young man had been trying to forge some kind of career out of his experiences with the conservative publishing house, but sensed he was going nowhere. After four years he'd decided it was time to move on. At twenty-six, he'd gained some worthwhile business experience and some accomplishments. More importantly, he had built a small group of potentially helpful business contacts in the Twin Cities. As spring hung in the air, he figured to begin the process of calling those connections and get the ball rolling in search of another career path.

That morning as he made his way to Brey's office, he wondered if his more recent unenergetic efforts were too obvious and his boss might be ahead of him. There was no threat of being fired. He wondered if Brey might hint that Lawton was wasting his time at University Publishing and he should contemplate seeking a career change.

Instead, the meeting started right out with a surprise ring of a new opportunity. Brey wanted Lawton to consider a new assignment. It was peculiar the way it was communicated. Brey didn't order him to take on the task...rather he used the word 'consider' several times. Their conversation centered on a short-term job requiring a host of interview sessions followed up with writing a journal or manuscript from those interviews on a particular person's life. The subject of the task was a former Minnesotan now living in Charleston, South Carolina. Most intriguing was how Brey's tones became very hushed as he relayed further information. He kept reiterating that the assignment would be extremely confidential, even obliging young Lawton to swear to secrecy about what they were discussing at that very moment.

Shrugging, Lawton agreed to the confidentiality request and Brey then continued to fill in in more details. "Matt, the assignment will also require you to live in Charleston for possibly as long as three months since it will take you that long to conduct the interviews. You have to understand this man is quite busy in his work. Upon completing the interviews you would write and edit the memoir or the journal, whatever format the gentleman wants. You'll stay right there in Charleston until the project is completed."

The mission seemed less enticing to Lawton, especially the part about living in Charleston, but he continued to listen respectfully to his boss. Brey went on to explain that the man's name was Henry Hanson when he lived in Minnesota, and then due to some things that happened in his life, he changed his name upon moving in the 1930's to South Carolina.

Then he looked straight in the eye of Lawton as if trying to observe even a hint of untruthfulness as he stated, "Matt, you may have heard of or read this man's name in some business journals. Henry Granville is known for having built in the last thirty years a large conglomerate of major hotel and lake resort properties.

Lawton felt almost embarrassed having to admit the man's name was unfamiliar. Even the name Henry Hanson was no one he'd ever known. For a moment Brey looked disappointed and Lawton found himself not really caring.

As Brey brushed briefly over the many hotels owned by a company named Triple H Development, Inc., Lawton found it strange how Brey would switch back and forth between calling the man Mr. Hanson or Mr. Granville.

Brey was then interrupted by his secretary. It gave Lawton time to think back from his childhood. He tried to remember if he'd ever heard of some guy named Henry Hanson. In Minnesota that last name was as common as snow...Granville not so much. No one came to mind. Focusing on his life since college, there was still no memory of that name. In his work he'd just met so many more people in the four years since he'd graduated from the University of Minnesota.

He then pondered men who may have been clients of his father, James Lawton or his uncle, Charlie Davis, both lawyers and friends going back to when they'd attended law school together in the 1920's. Matt often met their clients but always it was understood whatever got discussed in front of him...at the golf course, at a restaurant, or even in the Lawton or Davis household, the talk was not for his ears. Frankly, that precept had been easy to follow. In his formative years he rarely paid much heed to their business discussions anyway.

As his boss finished his conversation with his secretary, Lawton sat there trying to understand whether the offer to take on the task was a kind of promotion or just a way of sending him down the road. In the past few years at University Publishing, Inc., he'd received some accolades from Brey...not many, but a few. Taking on this temporary job, might lead to something better, like an increase in pay or more and better assignments. The more he thought about it, Lawton felt even grimmer. His work at a staid publishing house wasn't offering him the excitement or advancement he wanted in his life's work. It fit with his degree in Journalism, but that was about all. He knew he should be taking a more determined look for other opportunities, but it had been easier to stay put...especially with the warm spring and enjoyable days of summer approaching. He had been thinking the following fall would be the best time to look around.

Now his timetable was getting screwed up with this very unappealing writing assignment. It was just another sign that he was overdue in seeking out other job opportunities. A college degree, his work experience and his relative youth...those factors had to be good for something better than what he was doing.

When the secretary left, Brey talked on only after she'd closed his door. Lawton found himself sneaking looks at his watch and wondering where he wanted to get lunch. The conversation then became more uncomfortable. It was as if Brey could feel Lawton's disinterest. His boss began selling the obscure job. He must have said three times how the assignment would give Lawton the chance to truly use his Journalism degree. He also repeated how the new surroundings where Lawton had never traveled would give the young man a real shot in the arm.

Not feeling like he needed a shot in the arm, Lawton politely nodded and maintained a patient smile. He'd never been to Nome, Alaska either, but that didn't mean he wanted to invest three months at that location either. Besides, Brey was talking about leaving Minnesota when the weather was the most inviting. Lawton couldn't imagine missing the warm months up at the lake or the time spent with his golfing buddies at various golf courses around the Twin Cities area. It was the best time to be in Minnesota.

Sensing Lawton's lack of enthusiasm, Brey showed that he had more arrows in his wick. His voice then got more urgent. "Matt, I want you to know that you have been specifically requested to carry out these interviews and author the complete biography of this man. Given his prominence, if you do a decent job, I promise you, this book would sell. Wouldn't it be nice to be a heralded author?

Lawton's response then took on a different path...one of confusion. He was confused. His only thought was that this Mr. Granville...or Hanson...must have made a huge mistake. There were certainly many more capable and experienced writers in and out of University Publishing, Inc. Why would such a reputable business executive want some inexperienced journalism major to do something as important as authoring the man's memoirs.

Brey seeing some curiosity in the eyes of his young employee then hit Lawton with some more appealing food for thought. "Of course, Matt, we want you to be comfortable while you're gone. You'd be receiving a small raise in pay, company paid housing including a per diem, and finally an allowance for some wardrobe needs since you'd be living for a while in a much warmer, humid climate."

Lawton brightened when some more tangible personal benefits were mentioned, but Brey knew he wasn't close to getting a commitment. He was hoping not to have to surrender too much more information about Henry Granville, but he was getting more desperate. Moreover, he was not blind to the probability that the young man might already be interviewing with some other companies.

The president then then pulled out all the stops. He leaned toward Lawton who sat in a slightly lower chair across from Brey's desk and said, "Matt, I want you to listen to me very carefully because what

I'm about to say to you must stay only between you and me. In no way will I force you to accept this opportunity. It's your decision and whichever direction you choose, I'll respect your choice. With that said, you'd be very wise to take on this task. You can't admit to knowing this, but you actually have a close tie to this man. I won't say what it is, but he has abundant confidence you can do this writing job fairly and competently. He truly did request you…and only you.

Brey's openness jarred Lawton. Brey could see he'd hit a nerve and was not going to let this emotion die. His voice regained a more steady tone. "Matt, not only would I prefer you not talk about this portion of our conversation to your father or to Charlie Davis, but obviously not to Mr. Granville if you should eventually meet him. Now, I said your expenses and your salary will be covered. Do understand you will be paid directly from Mr. Granville each week until you complete the interviewing, note-taking, writing, editing and the manuscript itself. I sincerely believe taking on this undertaking will catapult you to some new and unseen directions in your career."

Seeing Lawton's growing indecision, Brey tried to set the hook more firmly. "As for your present work here, we'll cover for you. You'll not have to feel responsible for anything you are doing here at University Publishing. You're current job will of course be waiting for you upon your return."

Lawton could sense his eyes had gotten quite big. He'd actually been requested by someone he'd never met. How could that be? Who was this mystery man whatever name he used?

For a moment Brey felt more saddened than disappointed with the lack of zeal from the young man he'd hired four years before. He hated to think the bright, enthusiastic attitude young Lawton had brought to the publishing house fresh out of college had been summarily expunged due to the repetition or monotony of his work at University Press, Inc. If that was the case, Brey knew his young charge should be looking for other employment even if he didn't take the South Carolina offer.

Brey sensed he'd gone as far as he could in their discussion that morning. His young employee apparently needed time to deliberate. Brey glanced at his watch as he always did when he felt a meeting should be over. As he stood up extending his hand to Lawton, he added, "You'll have the night to sleep on whether you want the assignment or not. Mr.

Granville wants to know your response as soon as possible. I suggest you take the afternoon off and ponder this opportunity. While it might not be exactly what you might be looking for as future work, I frankly think it's an experience you'll not want to miss."

Lawton left his boss' office following one of the weakest handshakes he'd ever shared with another person. In the previous ten minutes he'd gone from having no interest in Brey's offer to ambivalence. In itself, that was quite an upsurge.

Lawton indeed took the afternoon off. He would always recall how he traveled around the remainder of that day in a kind of daze. He had a couple beers later in the afternoon at a bar named Pudge's in St. Paul...something he never did on any other work day. Pudge's was a college hang-out in Highland Park he still frequented. He didn't stop there often anymore but that afternoon he needed a place he felt comfortable just to think.

The timing of this offer was unbelievably inconvenient. With his father and mother and even his Uncle Charlie on a transatlantic trip, he didn't have the key people he always depended upon for advice. However, given this assignment had some adventure and intrigue to it, Lawton already had a hint which way the advice would swing.

But there were other considerations. Just having the meeting with Mr. Brey had convinced Lawton that he shouldn't wait any longer opening some new doors for other job opportunities. Unfortunately, whether he got rolling right then or in the fall, he still had the problem of being undecided what other kind of work he should seek. Why look for something when you don't know what you want? He could procrastinate...again...and entertain the idea of law school. Genetically that seemed a logical choice. He just didn't savor having to live like a pauper again or depending on his folks for financial support while he finished more schooling.

Still, at University Publishing he was nothing more than a fledgling young sales and marketing representative trying to carve out a path to promotion. Maybe this new assignment could lead to some kind of advancement in the privately held publishing company. Lawton didn't know much about the real owners but he did know his father was the outside legal counsel. That inroad was how he got his job. He hadn't figured to be with the publisher for any length of time. But, here it had been four years. He was learning the business from the ground up, making a decent salary and gaining apparent valuable business experience. He'd gained something in his four year ride.

Finishing his second beer he contemplated what kept him at University Publishing, Inc. The part of his job he liked least but invested more time was the advertising sales. Upon starting, he was given some large Minneapolis based business clients. Mostly he had to find his own customers. He'd been fortunate. His clients seemed to tolerate his many ideas and feeble attempts at being aggressive. In time he relaxed and served his clients creatively and with some success. The result had been that he raised his advertising revenue each quarter. Unfortunately, the accomplishment gave him no sense of delight.

As a sidelight he also wrote a column that occasionally made it into one of the publications. Just in the last year, his articles became a permanent addition to a couple of the company's state-wide magazines. His articles had to do with golf courses and resorts around Minnesota. His mother always showed particular loyalty to his writings. At least he knew he had her and three of his buddies who were regular readers.

Lately his commentaries had become more focused on the popularity of the second home…the lake home…for those Minnesotan's well-heeled enough to afford such an added luxury. He wrote about new lake housing developments and lake resorts as well as the better lake properties among the 10,000 lakes Minnesota took pride in claiming. By the letters he was receiving from folks around the state, he had to admit he was developing a degree of readership. That did give him some sense of satisfaction, but he wanted more than writing promotional columns.

Minnesota lake resorts were a very natural subject for him to cover having gotten a taste at a very early age. Though growing up on Lake Johanna in suburban St. Paul, he'd spent his formative years during the summers on his family's lake or traveling with his father to Lake Ida where Charlie Davis lived outside Alexandria. He also worked during high school and college at two lake resorts…one on White Bear Lake and the other at Lake Mille Lacs. The two general managers, Clarence Petracek and Rich Brey were close friends of his father and Charlie Davis…and had become friends of Matt's as well.

As for Charlie Davis, the 'uncle' reference was actually a misnomer. There was no blood ties between the Davis and the Lawton names, but Charlie was so close to his family…and Matt's 'godfather' that he always thought of his Uncle Charlie as kin. In fact, he often wondered why his 'uncle' didn't have his office closer to Minneapolis. His father and Davis were constantly doing something together whether traveling, golfing, or dealing with shared clients.

But, Charlie had a very active law practice up in Alexandria. Young Lawton had spent a lot of time during his summer breaks at Charlie's lake home. Charlie always seemed to have a need for Lawton to clean up a property he bought…mostly clearing trees and brush and mowing grass. Of course there had been plenty of time to play the municipal golf course in Alexandria. The younger Lawton made some good money from Davis both from his employment as well as on the golf course. Davis complained often that between his losses on the golf course to both older and younger Lawtons, he was the real breadwinner of the Lawton family.

The front entry door slammed at Pudge's bringing Lawton out of his dreamy state. His mind returned to his current job and the peculiar task he was being offered in South Carolina. There was little doubt his interest level at the publishing company had declined. For the first time, whether it was the effects of two beers or not, he wondered if the experience in Charleston, South Carolina might spur him onto a more focused career plan.

Then his mind retracted back to his youth once again. Still there was a part of him that didn't want to grow up. He enjoyed his free time with his buddies from college. They were a fun bunch. Then again they were stumbling around in their jobs trying to figure out where life was taking them as well. It seemed as if all of them… including Lawton …were just putting in the time with the blind hope that whatever they were doing would certainly move them on to a better job…whatever that might be. The present ride they were all on seemed mostly for the purpose of financing their free time. Parties, golfing, other sports and chasing women seemed to highlight their thoughts and not just their non-work hours.

Lawton left Pudge's about 5:00 and drove back to his apartment near the University. He was a bit foggier after those beers. He normally would eat and he hadn't done so all day. He was able to make it down the River Road without having to make any important driving decisions. He stopped by another college hangout in Dinkytown and had a large hamburger. Arriving later at his apartment, he crashed without so much as changing clothes.

At 3:00 AM he bolted upright with an abnormal headache. Sleep was no longer of interest. He got up disgusted that someone of his age had a headache from either the three beers or the stress of how to politely turn down the Charleston, South Carolina offer.

He got some aspirin feeling better that he had reached a decision, though by no means was it firm. Sometime between leaving Pudge's and waking in the middle of the night, he'd rationalized that he was busy enough at his present job and he should begin seeking immediately other job opportunities in a city where he preferred to live. He'd made some accomplishments...as low brow as they might be...but enough to dress up his resume and provide some fuel for future interviews.

Five minutes later Lawton went to his book case and pulled out an encyclopedia...a gift from his folks before he went to college. He began to read about Charleston, South Carolina. In some ways it looked like a pretty city...and it was located along the Atlantic Ocean. But, his image of the southern city was anything but positive. To him it was still an old Confederate stronghold with the residents still fighting the Civil War. Lawton liked history, but he didn't want to go back and fight in the battles.

A half hour later he tried to lay back down and sleep. The headache had eased but not ceased. He tossed and turned for the next few hours and then got up as the clocked ticked to 6:00, a good hour before he usually awoke. He walked along University Avenue to Dinkytown where he'd lived as a student. He had some breakfast...something he rarely did. Then he strolled the mile back to his apartment. It occurred to him that in four years since earning his college degree, he had progressed only twelve blocks from his alma mater.

He scoffed at himself. That was an unfair thought. His life was on an upward trend. He had to be patient.

When he made it to his office barely on time that morning, he'd decided for certain he wasn't going to leave his home state...not for something so ill-defined and frankly unexciting as having to live for a couple months in a dilapidated old southern city. He didn't feel like listening to an old guy talk about his life...not for two or three months. 'Hell,' he thought, 'In those two or three months here in Minneapolis, I could already be working at another job...something that fit better in whatever unclear direction I might want to go. It was nice to be considered for a rather unique assignment, but it just didn't fit.'

Those were Matt Lawton's thoughts as he calmly and slowly walked up two flights of stairs to Bud Brey's office that morning. Once there, he shook his boss' hand in greeting…and promptly told him he'd accept the assignment in South Carolina. He sat down without being offered a chair feeling a bit light-headed. He couldn't believe he'd just said the words that had flowed from his mouth.

*   *   *

Bud Brey seemed inordinately pleased that Lawton was accepting the South Carolina project. In fact, it was the most pleased the young man had ever seen Brey. Yet, his boss seemed more relieved than ebullient.

Lawton wasn't prepared for some of the things he would learn next from his boss. He wondered if he'd spoken too soon as Brey began unraveling some other details connected with the assignment. The man actually had a list to cover as if he expected Matt's positive response.

Focusing on his notes, he proclaimed, "Matt, you'll be leaving in two days this coming Saturday morning. From this point forward, you are on this job. Take what time you need to pack, store your belongings, and we'll handle your apartment rent until you return. Also please give me a list of your present tasks here at the office. I'll see that someone takes charge of your work."

There was something unsettling in Brey's words. He made the separation with his present responsibilities sound so easy to find a replacement. Additionally, he still felt apprehension over not discussing his decision with his folks or even Charlie Davis. Their travel couldn't have come at a worse time.

Committing to a task that would see him gone from Minnesota for a couple months now seemed impulsive. Still he knew his family wouldn't be disappointed. They'd certainly see it as something good. Besides, he'd likely be back by the Fourth of July in time to take the ritual vacation to Charlie Davis' lake home on Lake Ida for five days. At least it would be something he could look forward to when the days got long in South Carolina.

That thought bothered him too. What would he do in his free time in Charleston, South Carolina? His impression of an old beaten down southern city would not leave his mind. He figured he'd have to rent a car on the weekends just to find some entertainment in some other nearby cities like Atlanta or Savannah or at some Atlantic beaches.

Lawton was still daydreaming as Brey completed his directions by phone with his secretary to arrange a flight through Atlanta that upcoming Saturday morning. When he hung up, Brey continued his show of enthusiasm. "You know, Matt, this could be quite an experience for you. From the description I heard about South Carolina at this time of year, it'll be mighty hot and humid even this early in the spring. Pack whatever light clothing you have. Like I said yesterday, Mr….ah… Granville will provide a clothing allowance for you so you can buy more comfortable attire once you arrive in the city."

Lawton blankly nodded. He wasn't paying much attention to Brey since his mind was stuck on what a colossal error he'd probably just made. With all his friends, family, and anyone who cared about him back in the north country, he visualized himself in some small one window, one room bungalow rapping away on his typewriter after interviewing some mysterious character he'd never met or heard of before.

About the time he was mulling over how to withdraw his acceptance, Brey nudged a thick envelope over to Lawton "You might be interested in browsing through the contents of this envelope. It has some information about the city…and don't lose the $200 stipend intended for you to enjoy your first couple days in Charleston. The man you're going to see doesn't want you sitting around feeling low upon your arrival. He would prefer that you get to know the city…and maybe do what I suggested…buy some appropriate clothing.

Lawton couldn't hide his surprise. That small little thought by the man named either Granville or Hanson showed someone who cared about his comfort and could imagine his probable loneliness. At least the older man had some empathy.

Brey interrupted Lawton's befuddled thoughts adding, "Matt, your accommodations are already set. You'll be staying at the East Bay Street Hotel in the historic section of Charleston. From what I hear, you'll like your lodgings. It's right on Charleston Bay."

Lawton again nodded silently. These additional factors were very helpful, but his doubts about his rash decision remained. The hotel's name meant nothing to him. Not knowing much about Charleston, he also was inclined to take the word "historic" for "old and decrepit". With his more current image of a non-progressive and dilapidated city ensconced in racial matters, he pondered if he'd even be safe walking the streets.

Upon leaving Brey's office, nothing on his desk carried any significance other than his typewriter. He handed a couple files he'd been working on to two cohorts who seemed generally displeased with the additional work. As for his magazine article, Brey mentioned there would be a notation in the following magazine additions that 'Matt Lawton was on assignment'…indicating that his contributions would continue when he returned. That comment was reassuring. His old job would be waiting for him.

With not much else holding him back, he was out the front door of the publishing company before 10:30 that Thursday morning and already thinking about what he should be packing. He wondered if he had enough time.

By noon he was done. He actually played golf that afternoon at the University golf course. Just opened after a long winter, the fairways were soaked and the greens bumpy, but he had a smile on his face the entire nine holes. He wasn't certain if his cheerfulness was finally being able to play golf again…or if he found himself actually looking forward to a new escapade.

As he drove from the golf course, it occurred to him that he was just happy to be away from his hum-drum job at the publishing company. He hated to admit it, but taking a break from his office duties was quite energizing. He found that emotion somewhat discomfiting.

On Friday he had lunch with his sister and dinner with his brother…and played another round of golf despite some blustery winds. The meals with his siblings were upbeat. Nick was a senior and Mary Jo a freshman at the University of Minnesota. He was pleased to see how envious both were of his new assignment. Of course, he figured he could be going to Butte, Montana and they'd be enthused. Any kind of departure from their study grind would be inviting.

When he mentioned Charleston, South Carolina, as his destination, both siblings did pause for a moment. Yet, they recovered and their zest returned although somewhat contrived.

When he expressed disappointment in not talking to the folks before taking the assignment, Nick scoffed. "Matt, for Christ's sake, given the business and friendly relationship between Dad, Uncle Charlie, Bud Brey, and Rich Brey, our folks probably knew of your offer before you did. They likely wanted you to make your own decision… and then commit to it one hundred per cent. As they've said to us many times, "keep building experiences.""

While that statement would turn out to be true, Lawton voiced his concern to his brother he was doing something that took him too far away from the career path he was developing. Nick's reaction was a quick response that only a brother could offer. "Don't be a dumb ass. It's not as if you're committing your life to this assignment. It's for two or three months. Enjoy it."

As for his sister, Mary Jo, her comment was even more direct over his hesitancy. She bluntly stated, "What are you waiting around here for, big brother…for Brey to keel over so University Publishing can declare you president….you, the lowest ranking employee on the roster?"

While he wasn't the lowest employee, she'd made her point. Lawton walked away from both his brother and sister shaking his head thinking how siblings have a funny way of showing support.

Lawton took off on his opening leg to Atlanta the day before Palm Sunday on April 9, 1960. It was a windy and rainy Minnesota day. The weather made him feel as if he was making the right decision after all. He only hoped the hearsay was authentic about the milder ocean climate in Charleston. He wondered if his golfing buddies were playing their regular Saturday morning round of golf…even if there was a steady rain. It had to be a monsoon for them not to play on the weekends. Once April arrived, they squeezed every ounce of free time onto the golf course. Often they played until dark on Saturdays.

As his plane took off to the west and circled over the downtown area of Minneapolis, Lawton focused on the miniscule roof of University Publishing, Inc. The smallness of the building relative to the remainder of the downtown area was a nice simile, as if his opportunities at his present job were likely as comparable. As the plane made a half turn and straightened out, he gazed down upon the fairways of Midland Hills Country Club where his friends would be golfing that morning. Not being there with them was painful. He rationalized that in packing his golf clubs, he would look for a golf course within hours of arriving in Charleston. There had to be some kind of golf course in that city. He'd rent a car and find it. His impression was that most Charlestonians spent their time fighting integration or lamenting over the loss of the war ninety-five years before. Golf was likely a very unimportant pastime.

In addition, if his new job was to shadow some old gentleman as he related his past life and then collate the notes each evening, free time didn't seem probable. Starting Monday he expected to have little time of his own. He was not looking forward to the tedium.

Connecting through Atlanta Lawton barely made his regional commuter flight to Charleston. It was a sixteen-passenger aircraft with most of the seats empty. It appeared others were reluctant to make the journey to the former Confederate stronghold as well.

Approaching what was described in his encyclopedia as the low country of South Carolina, he pressed his nose against the airplane window seeing mostly flat, swamp-like back country. He couldn't even make out a highway. It occurred to him the folks he was about to meet might have the same negative outlook of flying over his flat, lake-filled and marshy home state. They would likely think he wore a parka most of the year, spend a good part of his time shoveling snow, and huddle around a fire most of the day trying to survive the perpetual frigid weather.

Descending into the airport at Charleston, he remembered a story his father shared with him about flying an old mail plane into Charleston back in the early 1930's with Charlie Davis. The two of them had always said that particular flight was a 'pleasure' trip to Charleston. Yet, when the younger Lawton saw how the two smiled slyly at each other, he sensed the adventure had been a bit more hair-raising. His guess was further confirmed when he'd ask his Dad for more details and his father would just laugh and change the subject. Even the question about how he'd happened to be flying an old 'mail' plane went unanswered.

He thought about his folks and Uncle Charlie currently in France…apparently. That wasn't even a sure thing. Even his mother had been closed mouth about their actual destinations. He'd learned.

The three of them were always quieter about their travels when it was more than just sight-seeing.

As the flaps noisily protruded from the wings and the plane jolted as it descended and adapted to the wind conditions outside, Lawton still couldn't make out the coast line given the faint cloud cover. He wondered if it was just swamp and trees right up to the ocean's edge. As the plane got lower to the ground he finally observed some thin two lane roads. Now the terrain showed more greenery, pine trees, rough unplowed ground, ponds, and a few farmhouses. The farm homes looked more like shanties. He hated to think people actually lived inside. Everywhere he gazed, it looked like a forgotten land.

His mind returned again to that long ago story about his father flying the 'mail' plane to Charleston. The geography had to have been even more remote back then. Chuckling, he thought how Charlie was such a jumpy flyer…and how his father liked to play on that nervousness by appearing to be even more nonchalant than normal. Charlie must have gone crazy not seeing any place to land.

His Dad always had a passion for flying. He'd grown up loving airplanes. He'd even owned a biplane during college and only got rid of it as part of a deal if his mother was going to marry him. Anyway, that was the tale. He recalled Charlie describing the biplane as perpetually on its last flight and looked like a casket with wings. His dislike for the air machine was legend. He claimed that Matt should not have even been born since his father had used up all his nine lives years before he actually got married.

His father countered calling the contraption a grade 'A' World War I biplane. Charlie in turn refuted that statement claiming Jamie's definition of grade 'A' and his definition were so far apart it wasn't worth debating. Matt had seen a few pictures of his father's biplane. He agreed with his Uncle Charlie.

Approaching the Charleston Regional Airport landing strip, he hoped it was paved. Recalling what Brey had told him, upon landing he was supposed to seek out a lady named Lill Hamilton who would transport him to the hotel. There was no description of her. He was told she would recognize him. Lawton had no idea how that was possible. He wondered if South Carolinians thought Minnesotans had a certain look…like Eskimos in Alaska.

When the commuter plane edged up to the small terminal baggage area, he saw no woman waiting for him or anyone anywhere. As the airplane's exit door opened he finally noticed a nice looking very dark-skinned gentleman dressed like a limousine driver and standing next to a very shiny large Cadillac. He was standing beside a scruffy looking lighter-skinned baggage worker who looked as if he wasn't thrilled with how life was treating him. Lawton wondered if the poor man had unloaded one too many bags in his life and suddenly realized he'd likely hit the pinnacle of his career. It flashed in his own mind how similar he felt with his University Publishing job back in Minneapolis.

There were only six other passengers on the flight. As Lawton emerged from the fuselage and carefully stepped down the precarious staircase to the tarmac, a wave of humidity and heat hit him like a blast from a furnace. It was similar to the temperature he felt during a hot Minnesota summer day. The difference, though, was how this blanket of moist, stifling air seemed heavier and thicker. There was also a noticeable odor of decaying vegetation, yet with some redolent smells of spring mixed in. The scent wasn't exactly bothersome…just different.

While he waited for his suitcase and his golf clubs to be unloaded from the airplane, Lawton gazed toward the fence separating vehicles from broaching the landing strip. He hoped in one of those cars was the Hamilton woman.

Seeing no one looking for him, he began to give up on the ride he'd been promised. He looked hopefully at some taxis. There was a chance he might be able to share the cost of a cab into town with one or two of the airplane passengers. Why not save some of the $200 advance he had carefully split up between his wallet, his shaving kit, and inside one of his socks. Once downtown, he'd depend on the cabbie to know where the hotel was he'd be staying. He hoped the hotel was well-known enough for the cabbie to recognize the name.

The inconvenience didn't bother him. He figured he wasn't the most important person arriving in Charleston, South Carolina that day. He just wanted a room and a cold drink before the day ended. Anything else would be frosting.

The airport was on the far edge of the city. Thick forests of tall, thin pine trees and low brush surrounded the airport. Leaving the air field in any direction, he felt like he'd need a rifle to ward off the local wildlife… and a machete to carve his way through the foliage into town.

Suddenly there was a tap on his shoulder. The tall distinguished looking Negro gentleman was holding his suitcase and had Lawton's golf clubs slung over his shoulder. He politely put down the suitcase, removed his hat and gave Lawton a refreshingly bright smile while offering his hand. His soft deep accented voice said, "Mr. Matthew Lawton." It was said as a statement, not a question.

Surprised, Lawton grabbed the man's hand and stuttered, "Yes sir. I'm Matt Lawton."

He then became immediately concerned with his response. The man was only a decade or two older and very articulate and professional. Matt didn't want the polite gentleman to think Lawton was being condescending. He was brought up to say 'sir' to his elders. This man was definitely his elder. Why shouldn't he refer to the man as 'sir'? He wondered if local society might frown on him, a young white man, referring to an older black man in that manner.

Then Lawton shrugged and thought, 'The hell with the local society.'

He was relieved when the man's gaze didn't waver. Pointing to his vehicle, he said, "Miss Hamilton is waiting over in the limousine for you. She's anxious to say 'hello'. Have no concerns. I'll drive you directly to the East Bay Street Hotel."

With the suitcase and golf clubs already in his hands, he also took the Remington Rand typewriter case from Lawton's hands and escorted him to the limousine. Lawton thought he could have helped, but the guy seemed very determined to do his job right. Setting down Lawton's things, the driver opened the door to the back of the large vehicle making Lawton feel a bit conspicuous. His fellow airplane passengers looked at him as if wondering what kind of VIP had been on their same flight.

Entering the vehicle, he was pleasantly surprised to see an older, very attractive lighter-skinned Negro woman sitting comfortably with a very pleased and sincere smile directed his way. Her hair was a mixture of gray and black and finally styled. But, it was her eyes that were the most striking. They were warm with a depth leaving no doubt her self-assurance and classy style. Lawton would find out very quickly her genuineness as well.

Her smile got even wider as she greeted Lawton with a hug. He accepted the gesture somewhat startled but certainly with appreciation. It was nice to be welcomed in such a kindly way.

She was immediately enthusiastic. "Matt, it's so good to finally meet you in person. You look just like your dad, but you have your mother's eyes. What a great combination. You've had a long trip today. Please sit back and relax. We're so excited to have you come down here and help us with Henry's project."

His wonder must have been apparent because she started to laugh. Holding his hand as the limo pulled away from the small terminal, her touch was so gentle and caring. He found himself not feeling uncomfortable in the least. In many ways she gave him the feeling of being a long lost relative...as impossible as that likely was. When she spoke, her voice was confident and smooth... like maple syrup dripping from a northern Minnesota tree...yet with the loveliest southern accent.

For the first few minutes of the drive into the city, her eyes couldn't seem to focus on anything but Lawton as she kept up a line of chatter about Charleston in the spring. His head swung back and forth between her and the green-filled outdoors. As the limo crossed a large body of inland water, he could finally see what there was of the skyline of the small city. The things most noticeable were a number of church steeples and one office building of roughly fifteen stories and a high bridge. Finally what had seemed like a tourist guide monologue, she suddenly switched over to what likely were his obvious questions. She said, "Matt, no doubt you've got to be wondering why we sent for you in such a secretive way. You can be at ease in that your father, mother, and even Charlie Davis know exactly where you are right now, where you will be staying, and everything about the task you've been assigned."

Lawton hadn't said a word yet and began sensing it was about time he reciprocated something...anything...so she didn't think he was a complete verbal incompetent. Awkwardly he replied, "Miss Hamilton, thank you for meeting me at the airport. I could easily have taken a cab."

Her eyes showed momentary shock as if the very thought of him being shuttled into the city in a taxi was somehow beneath him. Feigning astonishment, she whispered, "Now Matt, don't you worry. We're going to take very good care of you. We promised your folks."

He couldn't think of anything else to say but a lame 'thank you' and then turned his attention to the outside as they entered the city. The window was slightly ajar. He couldn't get over the smell of the warm air. There was definitely a difference compared to the warm summer air where he lived. He detected a faint smell of a paper mill, like the stronger odors up in the Cloquet and Duluth areas of northern Minnesota. Mostly he felt the humidity.

He had definitely flown into a very different climate…and so early in the springtime. With it already so hot, he speculated what summer must be like in South Carolina. It occurred to him the clothing allowance should promptly be put to use. Half the clothing he'd brought along was so dark and heavy looking.

Moving through the downtown, there were additional smells. The odor of fish and a whiff of garbage were strong enough for Lawton to covertly rub his nose. Driving further, the foliage was blooming and a sweeter smelling aroma took over. He would always remember the change of smells being so distinctive.

As they drove down an avenue called 'Meeting Street', the limo passed an old marketplace. Lawton visualized slaves being sold on that location in the 1700's and early 1800's. That was one question he didn't feel like asking Miss Hamilton given her heritage. The inquiry might make her uncomfortable.

He would learn later she was open to any question. In addition, he would learn the 'market' was not the location for those many horrible human transactions. The actual slave market was conducted closer to where the hotel was located at a shoreline location known as the 'wharf'.

Lawton's limited knowledge of eighteenth and nineteenth century history was being tested as he visualized this old city being the stalwart of the South. He recalled the state having been the first to secede from the Union after Abraham Lincoln was elected to the presidency in 1860. Matt's impression had always been that the state must have been controlled by a lot of hot-headed Southerners. He wondered if some of those personalities would show in their modern era descendants.

Miss Hamilton then interrupted his rapt attention to the sights in the city. With some urgency, she hurriedly expounded, "Matt, I need to tell you a few things before we arrive at the hotel. First, I want you to call me Lill. I am a very old friend of your parents and your Uncle

Charlie. You'll learn that we have worked together for years and serve on a board of directors for a privately held corporation primarily owned by Henry. Don't feel embarrassed that you didn't know this fact, but for reasons you'll find out, we've had to keep this relationship confidential. There is nothing illegal or anything you should be concerned; it was just the way the cards were dealt many years ago.

Our association with your parents and Charlie go back to before you were born. You and your brother and sister among everyone else back in Minnesota were never aware how often your folks and Charlie traveled down to Charleston for what we'll describe right now as periodic board meetings. As you think of your past, you might have wondered why your mother and father...and Charlie Davis...often made trips to Florida. They must have seemed numerous to you. Actually they were most often coming here to South Carolina.

Lawton found her familiarity with his parents and Charlie Davis fascinating. And, she was exactly right. He'd always wondered why his parents took off so often to 'Florida'. They still did. All that was said about their frequent trips south was that it was mostly business.

Nonetheless, he was surprised he'd never heard the city of Charleston slip from their mouths or for that matter, the name 'Henry' or even 'Lill Hamilton'. He couldn't comprehend why there had to be so much secrecy.

Her voice was fast, yet flowed smoothly. "We'll speak in more detail of your assignment later, but first I should mention more about the person you'll be interviewing. I believe your Mr. Brey only mentioned the name Henry Granville to you...and that at one time he lived in Minnesota. Back then he was known as Henry Hanson. Since arriving in Charleston back in 1931 he has used the alias Henry Granville. Also, because of his background, you'll hear another of his aliases...this one more endearing from some really close local friends. Don't let that bother you. He's basically known as Henry, but sometimes some more elderly local folks will refer to him as Reverend Hank. It's a pet name he earned from some church folk he got to know when he first arrived in this city. To outsiders including clients and business associates, you'll hear him referred to as Mr. Granville or more often, just 'Henry'. You'll find that true even down to the most recent person we've hired or our newest client. So....you should not hesitate calling him by his first name right away.

You should also understand back in Minnesota he lived in a beautiful little lake community called Glenwood, apparently quite near Charlie Davis' town of Alexandria. I've never been to Glenwood, but with Henry's descriptions, I feel I know the town as well as most local folk might...at least as it looked back in the Depression era. I have it pictured as a pretty little town with bluffs overlooking a lake the size of Charleston Harbor. I even like the name of that lake. Lake Minnewaska must be lovely."

Lawton found himself smiling. He knew that lake very well and had played the municipal golf course often while his father and Charlie attended to some business in the town with a local guy named John Bailey.

Returning his attention to Lill, she was again talking about Charlie Davis. She laughed, "What a contagiously funny man. While you already know that, what you might not know is that Charlie has been Henry's general counsel since before you were born. The company's name is Triple H Development, Inc. I shan't think you've ever heard of that company."

Lawton shook his head. She was right. He truly hadn't heard the name, but out of deference to his father and Charlie, he would disclaim any knowledge anyway. It was something he'd learned being a son of an attorney. He knew the importance of confidentiality in his father's world. If he hadn't shown this type of respect, he certainly would not have accompanied his father or Charlie Davis on the many client trips they made together.

Lill wasn't done. "Matt, I can see you still look a bit bewildered, but that should clear up real soon. What you should understand is that our dear Henry would like to tell his story. Over the years his background has created quite a tale including many rumors...some things true...many things not. He has a need to clear up a lot of these falsehoods that have followed him over many, many years. He feels some of the wild accusations and hearsay could cause some damage to the future of our business. Stories about Henry have ranged from him being part of the Chicago mob to being an undercover person for the FBI to being a coward and fleeing your state to being an accomplice in murder and even being touted as a burglar of preposterous success. We'll get all that cleared up. He is nearing the end of his career and wants to be certain the positive image of his vast network of hotels and resorts will be sustained. He does not want incorrect publicity to cast aspersions on Triple H Development, Inc., especially when he wouldn't be around to defend his company's reputation.

Naturally none of us who work with him want that to happen either…not for the sake of the enterprise, but especially not for the sake of Henry's own character. Therefore, my dear Matt, you will be asked to listen to his story and document the truths about his background. He's led a very interesting life and certainly not always righteously. But, then again, not many people have?

Our aim is to have you write a biographical manuscript. Whether the text will ever be actually published, this is something Henry and a few of his close friends and associates will determine. But legally we want this document to establish Henry's clarification of his past life. In the meantime we just want you to take on this assignment with an open mind and complete the manuscript without prejudice."

Lill suddenly stopped talking as if to let Lawton digest the depth of what she'd just said. After a slight pause, a lighter tone returned to her voice. "You should also know that Henry has been aware of your work, Matt, even before you started your job at University Publishing. He's followed your growth, as well as your sister's and brother's development through talking with your folks. I think you'll come to understand that your family kind of extends right down here to Charleston. When Henry discussed with your folks the idea of stealing you away for this extended writing assignment, the whole thing kind of fell into place. You'll be a sort of ghostwriter and one we know we can all trust to write the truth. Our only concern was whether you'd be willing to invest the time here in Charleston. We're truly happy you decided in favor of our little undertaking."

Lawton gave her another vapid nod. It appeared if he ever wanted to reconsider his decision to come south, that time had passed.

Lill Hamilton then gave him a very serious look. "Now Matt, don't think we expect you to be sequestered in some dingy room poking on your typewriter for the next couple months. We are in no particular rush to get this account of Henry's life completed. There is no deadline. That is all right with Mr. Brey and certainly with Henry. We think it's just as important for you to get to know our business and organization. I believe you'll then better appreciate what Henry's done with his life and how he's put his heart and soul not only into this enterprise, but into this city as well. We think you'll write a more comprehensive manuscript if you understand the man as much as possible.

As for the timing, please be patient and understand this assignment might take longer than you might expect. Henry, myself, and the staff still have a business to run. His schedule keeps us all quite busy. We have the agreement with your publishing company that we have what time we need…within reason…to complete the manuscript as long as you're willing. You're salary will be maintained back in your Minneapolis bank. Here in Charleston you will have a bank account with per diem and living expenses that should keep you very comfortable. You'll find this allowance will be credited into your local account every Friday. You need only to walk down the street to our bank if you need any cash. Beyond that, we plan on providing you any other support you might need."

She paused with her lively eyes shining brightly. "How does that all sound so far?"

Lawton couldn't help but be impressed. She made the assignment sound down right pleasant. He did detect there might be a delay in returning to Minnesota in July. He figured to cross that bridge later. He had landed in a very friendly place. Any feeling of homesickness was dissolving by the minute.

His growing interest now produced endless questions. He didn't know where to begin. He could only think to ask, "So, is…Mr. Hanson…ah…Mr. Granville in today? I'd certainly like to meet him."

Lill looked at her watch. "Well, it's Saturday. Henry normally takes his sailboat out onto the bay for a couple hours. He'll be back soon. He's looking forward to meeting us for dinner at the hotel promptly at 6:00."

She began to laugh. "Oh yes, there is something else you may as well understand. Henry's definition of 'prompt' might be different than yours. 6:00 means sometime around 6:15… or after. He tries to be timely, but he ends up stopping to talk with people. He can't help it. It's his nature."

When the limousine reached the corner of Meeting and Broad Streets, a left turn onto Broad caused the limousine to slow for some pedestrians. Lawton noticed numerous Negro ladies making baskets out of a sort of long stemmed grass. They were sitting on the sidewalk alongside a very old, distinguished church named St. Michaels.

Seeing his interest in the street life, Lill explained, "The baskets those ladies are creating are being made out of a grass vine indigenous to the area. It's simply called sweet grass. The skill at making the baskets was handed down through many generations of black folks. Tourists buy these baskets certainly for their usefulness, but for their historical charm as well.

Lawton nodded while pondering if there were enough interested tourists to make the basket business profitable. The ladies looked like they hadn't improved their lot in life since their ancestors were brought over as slaves. Cultural enrichment or not, the ladies looked bored and very poor.

Continuing down Broad Street, the limo made a right turn on East Bay Street and a block later a left into a circular driveway along Charleston Harbor. That was the entrance to a grand looking hotel. In the distance he could make out the relative narrow opening to the Atlantic Ocean. After his mellowed feeling about the Negro ladies, the sudden classic look of the East Bay Street Hotel left him astonished.

The elongated hotel had eight stories within sight of the Cooper River and the Ashley River flowing into the picturesque harbor. He would hear often from the local populace how the two rivers converged to create the ocean. The spurious statement was said with both pride and arrogance.

Arriving, Lill introduced him to some staff people as his bags were taken from the limousine trunk. She explained that many of them had been with the hotel for years…and were actual small stockholders of the property. One stately Negro gentleman came forward and introduced himself as Thomas Rutledge Brown with a name tag that simply said, 'Thomas'. He was the head of the valets and bell boys. When Lill mentioned Lawton's name, Brown burst into a large smile and immediately asked Matt how his father and mother were….and if Charlie was still slicing the golf ball.

While accepting the vigorous handshake, Lawton couldn't help but be overwhelmed with the kindliness of the people he was meeting and their apparent intimate knowledge of his family.

He responded with similar enthusiasm to Thomas. "Charlie's swing hasn't changed at all. As you apparently know he couldn't hit the ball left if his life depended on it."

The head valet closed his eyes and laughed heartily as if visualizing the flaws of Charlie's golf swing.

At the check-in desk, no registration was required. A key was simply given to the porter who headed for the elevator without delay. Lawton anticipated staying in some basement room of the hotel. That belief was quickly withdrawn as Lill ushered him up a staff elevator to the eighth floor where the larger suites were located. When she opened the door to one of the rooms, Lawton's suitcase and golf clubs were already there. He hadn't even had a chance to tip the porter.

As she opened a sizeable floor to ceiling drapery, a splendid view of the convergence of the two rivers and the harbor was displayed. The wall was more glass than wall board. The vista was spectacular.

Lill pointed out Fort Sumter in the middle of the bay. Lawton was almost ashamed how the fort was one of his few memories about his limited Civil War studies. She pointed in the direction of Ft. Johnson and Ft. Moultrie whose names meant little.

Pointing across the Cooper River, Lill said, "Matt, that's where I live, in the town on the other side of the harbor. It's called Mt. Pleasant. As you can see, the 'mount' doesn't refer to any particular high ground in the area. In fact, the highest geography you'll probably see in this area is a sand castle on the beach."

Grinning at her comment while ambling around the spacious suite, his excitement took over. "Miss Hamil…rather…Lill…I may not leave this room for a couple days. I don't want to walk away from this view."

Seeing his giddiness, she reacted, "Matt, I hope you didn't think you were going to be staying in some windowless little closet. We want you to be with us for a while. We're not going to let you get bored or be the least bit uncomfortable."

Pleased with his response, she wasted no more time. "Matt, I'll let you get settled. You may want to walk around town this afternoon, get your bearings, and do some clothes shopping. Henry and I will meet you here at the hotel around 6:00."

She winked about the time and gave him another hug. He couldn't help it. He returned the hug.

* * *

When she left his suite, Lill Hamilton was pleased. Time would tell, but she was generally encouraged about the young man. He was obviously well-mannered and respectful, not surprising considering who his folks were. She could only hope he had the depth to eventually understand Henry's past and current plight as well as the maturity and good business sense to appreciate the thirty-year history of Triple H Development, Inc.

She knew Henry would be relieved with her initial optimism. He had plenty of expectations regarding Matt Lawton.

Chapter 4

Less than thirty minutes later after entering his hotel suite, Matt Lawton had changed into the lightest clothing he owned. Rolling up the sleeves of one of his white dress shirts to better blend into the warm spring day, he strolled along what was called the 'battery' on an elevated sidewalk above the waters of Charleston Bay. With Fort Sumter off in the distance, the Civil War cannons in a park by the harbor, and the vision of grand old homes nearby had him surrounded by history. He'd never sensed anything like he was feeling back in his home state. The Minnesota lakes were beautiful, but the spectacle of the harbor, the ocean in the distance, and the ante-bellum homes made him aware there was so much more to this southern city.

He strolled along Meeting Street his attention attracted with the historic descriptions attached to a number of the antiquated homes. Some were splendid but too many were in deplorable condition. Modern builders in the 1950's in so many cities were inclined to tear down old buildings and start fresh. He wondered if many of these rundown properties might be destined for the same.

Further up Meeting Street, he strolled through the St. Michael's Episcopalian Church graveyard appreciating some of the headstones dating back to the early 1700's. Continuing on toward Market Street, the buildings were even more in a state of decline. He chose to go no further as he was about to enter what looked like an especially rough part of town. Along that street was an open market with people trying to sell everything from food and clothing to art as well as those sweet grass baskets. Heading back to the hotel on East Bay Street, he sauntered by more shops and restaurants noting a couple bars he'd likely frequent during his time in the city.

Just blocks from the hotel and feeling parched, he decided to stop at one of those taverns. The beer tasted the same as it did in the Twin Cities, even more appealing in such hot weather. With still some time remaining before his 6:00 dinner with Lill Hamilton and Henry Granville, he browsed around some shops intent on buying more suitable clothing.

At one of the shops just a block from the East Bay Street Hotel while perusing some cotton shirts, he had the oddest feeling someone was looking at him. He eventually accepted that his pale, white skin after a long northern winter made him stand out. Adding to that feeling was the more prevalent Negro population walking by him. More interesting was the nod he often received no matter the color of the person...something that simply didn't happen or was it expected to happen in downtown Minneapolis.

It was just past 6:00 when he was ushered to his seat at a reserved table in the hotel restaurant. Two fans had been set up next to a bay window overlooking the harbor. A shy waitress asked his drink preference. What he wanted was a cold beer, but he dutifully asked for an ice water instead.

He sat there for the next ten minutes looking out at a large cargo ship coming into port as he contemplated what his first impression of Henry Granville might be. With what he'd been told so far, the man was older and apparently had adapted well to South Carolina. For that reason Lawton expected to see a tanned figure with the stockiness of a high country Swede. There might even be a trace of a Minnesota accent remaining in the man's speech pattern. He recalled Lill Hamilton mentioning her boss was sailing that afternoon. That meant the guy liked the outdoors.

Towards 6:20 Lawton detected some animated movement amongst the restaurant staff as well as some noise coming from the hotel lobby. Standing up by his table, he saw the energetic Lill Hamilton walking across the lobby talking with some of the staff as she moved along. At first he thought she was walking alone until a taller gentleman caught up to her. He was talking with Thomas Rutledge Brown who Lawton had met earlier that afternoon.

Waving farewell to Brown, the taller man then stopped by the front desk to chat with the check-in staff. There was much laughter before he finally pulled himself from that conversation. Lill joined him after signing some papers handed her by a staff member. The two of them seemed to know everyone.

Lawton kept focusing on the taller figure. He was lanky and even athletic looking for his age. He moved swiftly. He was a couple inches over six feet tall and wore a light suit and a white open-collared shirt. His hair was full and longer than the current style as it fell about two inches below his back collar. The hair even covered his ears! There was some black hair on the top of his head, but his flowing mane was mostly gray. He reminded Lawton of a nineteenth century southern senator in the ilk of a John C. Calhoun, only with a much friendlier countenance. He also had a full but manicured grayish beard and mustache.

Lawton estimated the man's age to be close to sixty years, even though his gait was that of a much younger man. The most noticeable attribute was the warmth on the older man's face when he smiled and greeted people. He wasn't as ebullient as Lill, but you could tell he was energetic and genuine. Being well-tanned, he was much darker than Lill's skin color.

Together they were a very handsome older couple. It occurred to Lawton that they might be more than business partners, but figured that would be impossible...especially in the south. Down south he was certain a more personable relationship would be unimaginable. They would be ostracized and their business would likely be ruined. Nonetheless, it was a great bond to observe.

Lill seemed to want to keep moving. It was Henry who was lagging, although he kept looking in the direction of the restaurant as he spoke to members of his staff. Lawton sensed the man was as interested in acknowledging his chosen young writer from Minnesota as Lawton was in meeting him.

When the older man entered the eating establishment, his gaze went directly to the corner table where Lawton was standing. When both their eyes met, Henry just stared for a moment as if seeing something from his past. Then he marched purposely toward the table smiling brightly. In a voice with but a slight Minnesota lilt said, "Matt, my boy...you look like your father when I first met him so many years ago...although you don't wear the knickers he always favored. And you've got your mother's eyes. They are very dear friends of mine. I'm just so delighted you've chosen to come down to Charleston and help me out."

Lawton felt overwhelmed by the robust and sincere welcome. His own retort seemed so inadequate. "Sir, it's a real pleasure to meet you. I'm just surprised how some of the people here at the hotel know my parents as well as Charlie Davis."

He was going to add another statement saying, "...especially since they have never mentioned your name". He wisely let that aside go unsaid.

For the second time that day Lawton felt like he'd arrived in a kind of second homeland. Without hesitation Lill came up and hugged him. This time it felt very natural.

As the three of them sat down by the bay window overlooking Charleston harbor, three attentive waiters suddenly were ready to serve them. One waiter moved some potted plants as a temporary screen for more privacy and adjusted the fans for better comfort. There was no one sitting within twenty feet of them...and there wouldn't be throughout their dinner.

Henry continued his excited cadence with periodic Minnesota pronunciations on some words. Mostly though, after so many years in the South, his voice and speech pattern displayed plenty of southern influence.

His smile never wavered as he mostly stared at Lawton until the servers went to get the drinks. When the three of them were alone, he calmly stated, "First, Matt, I want you to call me Henry. As far as Lill and I are concerned, you are family. As you've come to understand since you arrived this afternoon, your folks and Charlie and even some other people we know in common who you will learn about later...well, we've all known each other for quite a spell. For now, I'll just leave it at that. The main thing is that we're thrilled to have you with us. I'm hoping this experience will be very worthwhile for you and spur you to bigger interests maybe even beyond your job at University Publishing in Minneapolis."

Lawton was taken aback as if Henry was a mind reader. He noticed Henry winked at Lill after that last sentence.

Henry continued, "It might surprise you how much I know about you. I've been aware of your existence since the day you were born. I realize I haven't been a household name back in your family's home in

Minnesota. The reasons for that will also come out in our interviews and discussions. Just understand that your folks and Charlie and those other people in your home state I know....it has been necessary their relationship with me be more private. Thanks to their conscientious efforts...and certainly my cautiousness as well...we've been mostly able to keep our lives very orderly and safe."

Lawton tried not to blink with that comment, but he wondered if his skin paled slightly. He detected the confidentiality factor he'd been asked to observe by Mr. Brey was more than just for the good of Henry Granville.

Henry kept right on talking not recognizing that Lawton had missed a breath. "Matt, when this idea of documenting a journal on my life came about, I have to admit I had you in my mind given your experience at University Publishing and your family connections. I have to have someone I know and can trust who could make good judgments as to what details should be transcribed in the journal you and I will be creating...and therefore, also what information might not be advisable to include. While I can't expect you to understand totally what I mean right now, I believe the picture will become much more distinct as we get to know one another."

Lawton was getting more of an idea why he was sitting at that table. Interviewing and collating his notes into a manuscript...that was just part of the picture. In the upcoming unforeseen number of personal interviews with Henry Granville, he would have to consider the impact of his writing on various other people.

Lawton finally forced himself to speak just so his hosts didn't think their young scribe was incapable of speech. Awkwardly he responded, "Mr. Granville...er...Henry...I'm really looking forward to working with you on this memoir. I also look forward to getting to know this city. Just in my short walk this afternoon, I can see there's a lot to learn."

It was a bland retort, but the best he could do considering all that had just been laid out to him. Henry, on the other hand, seemed delighted with his reply...maybe more enthusiastic than he should have been. Then again he seemed so naturally cheerful and positive. It made Lawton ponder why such a pleasant character could have a past requiring such secrecy.

The older man continued hurriedly as if to get the preliminary necessities out of the way. "Matt, I can imagine you've got more questions with each passing minute. Don't be concerned. They'll get answered. In fact, before this evening ends I want to give you some of my story just so you have some sense of the work you'll be doing.

As Lill has apparently mentioned to you, I have been a source of many exaggerated stories and accusations in my life. I've had a mind to clear up as many of these falsehoods as possible…everything from how I accumulated my capital in building my hotel enterprise to what I had to do with a group of conmen running a lake resort near Glenwood way back when."

Lawton perked up thinking of the few times he'd traveled to Glenwood, Minnesota. The local flavor of Henry's comment brought out a spontaneous response that Lawton wished he'd kept quiet. "Are you saying there were some gangsters in Glenwood…and somehow you got involved with them?"

Henry pulled out a slim cigar, lit it, and then let the air from the fan blow the smoke away from the table. "Matt, don't jump to any conclusions just yet. You've got a lot of information to digest in order to give you a better perspective on that particular question. But, just by your reaction, you can understand why I want my side of various stories told. It's not just for my sake. Falsehoods could seriously injure the image of Triple H Development, Inc."

Lawton nodded as if he understood. Of course he didn't.

Without missing a beat Henry kept talking. "We'll proceed with a series of interviews or meetings. I have a business to run, so we can't be rigid with our interview schedule. Also, I may not cover the details of my story in exact chronological order, but I'll leave the organization up to you. You'll not be rushed. You'll have plenty of time to complete this task. You'll also have time to meet and talk with many of our hotel staff from which you'll gain further perceptions about the corporation. I'll depend on you to be candid with your questions and to understand when further explanation might be required."

Henry then leaned toward Lill to pour her a special drink from a pitcher kept in ice. Lawton would learn it was called Charleston ice tea. He didn't ask but fully expected there had to be a measure of alcohol in the mix.

Lawton maintained his quiet posture but truly felt he was on a roller coaster...one minute understanding his assignment and the next bamboozled by Henry's inferences regarding his mysterious and puzzling past. In addition, he was baffled by Henry's lack of urgency to finish the manuscript. If anything, there seemed to be no inclination to set a completion date whatsoever.

Whether he was reading the situation correctly or not, Lawton suddenly pulled out his ever present notepad from the breast pocket of his navy blue blazer. He also decided there was no more reason to be shy. He politely asked the waiter standing a distance away, "Excuse me, could I try one of those ice tea drinks? They look quite refreshing."

If the older man was already going to start into his background story, Lawton figured he'd better rely on some caffeine to remain attentive.

He then looked directly at Granville and said, "Henry, whatever you want to share with me tonight, I'm ready. I agree. I'd like to get a better idea of this project. So, if I have one question before you start, it has to be why it's taken you so many years to go forward with this journal on your life. If your background is full of innuendoes and apparent lies, wouldn't it have been wiser to clear up these matters a long time ago."

Pausing, Lawton pressed his luck by asking yet a follow up question before Henry had answered the first inquiry. "And, why have I never heard of you even though you seem to know so many people in my life back in Minnesota? I feel like I've just woken up into a second existence that has been running parallel to the one you've lived in here in Charleston.

Henry grinned enjoying the candidness of his young protégé. He put his cigarette holder down as he looked at his business associate. "Lill, it appears we have another Lawton among us....just a younger version. I say he's more like his mother; she's sweet, but can be very forceful, sometimes more than Jamie."

Lill shook her head. "You may be right, but as we well know, his father never backs down either; it's just that you think he has...and then he hasn't."

They both enjoyed their joking remarks while Matt sat with a slight smile not knowing what to say. Their short descriptions of his parents were spot on.

Henry quieted noticing the young man's sudden discomfort. Then he said, "Matt, excuse our fun. Lill and I really do appreciate your willingness to get on with this task. With what you just said gives me even more reason for my confidence in you. We'll talk some tonight. Your questions may or may not get answered to your satisfaction. I just ask that you give me some leeway and let me attempt more clarity over time. Combining my statements with conversations with the many people you've yet to meet should give you the understanding you're seeking. That's also why we want you to live at our hotel during this project. You'll better be able to get to know the many staff members.

Beyond the hotel, this is also a wonderful city with fine people. If you are willing and want to spend the time with us, we have the elements to make your experience here very pleasant, even educational."

Lawton nodded thinking how interesting it was that only a day before he was playing nine holes of golf in some really lousy spring weather in Minnesota and not motivated about having to invest the next two months in Charleston, South Carolina. And now, there were indications his stay may be extended...and he was no longer concerned if that turned out to be the case.

Another waiter entered the private area and re-filled the Charleston ice tea glasses. Lawton would learn that it was a specialty of the house. With some mint leaves, a sweetener, and a minor touch of vodka, he would develop a fondness for the drink beginning that very evening.

Sipping the tea, Henry now eyed Lawton as if deciding how far he should delve into his background story that evening. Matt in turn realized that his first two questions didn't get a response. He would learn that was Henry Granville's mode. The man would respond when and how he chose.

With that thought in mind, Lawton changed his mode and decided to nudge his host with a comforting statement and then an open-ended question...just like he'd learned in journalism school. "So, Glenwood, Minnesota...I know the town. It's a pretty little lake community on a big, beautiful lake. My dad, Uncle Charlie and I have played the golf course up on the bluff a few times. It's very picturesque. They have a friend in the area named John Bailey. He seems to travel as much or more than my folks and Charlie Davis. I've only met him a few times.

The mention of the town and the name of John Bailey caused Henry's face to relax. His eyes went skyward as if already reminiscing. Lawton couldn't tell if the man was happy or sad as he sorted out his thoughts.

In a very melancholy tone, he apologized. "As I said, Matt, I'll be telling you stories and background of events and people as I feel like talking about them. Some of those folks have been gone a long time... others are still living and breathing...some even are still citizens of Glenwood."

He pulled out a handkerchief and wiped his nose. Lawton was surprised by the sudden emotion.

His voice low, Henry began nodding. "Yes, there were some terrific people I knew back then, besides of course my good fortune in meeting your father, mother, and Charlie Davis. I actually look forward to telling you about them. However, as for tonight, I'll be sharing with you some general background leading up to my time in Glenwood. My intentions are not to make this first meeting too long.

Lawton nodded showing his readiness to take notes. Granville sat back and began his story in his slow, acquired southern drawl.

"First, Matt, let me give you a short explanation of my formative years in Minnesota. Working in my father's general store in Willmar during high school and then after graduation was pure drudgery. He assumed I'd be taking over the store. He'd never been more mistaken. I so desperately needed a change and the 'Big War' provided the impetus. I was still eighteen years old when I went down to the Kandiyohi County recruiting offices and signed up for military duty.

Within a week I was sent to North Carolina for infantry training...my first real time away from Minnesota...and I loved it. I would have liked a bit more free time, but my personal interests weren't the national priority. I was able to drive around the Fayetteville area during some very limited leave time with another local recruit from a town ten miles away. He had a family car and we made it down to Wilmington one weekend so I could say I'd seen the Atlantic Ocean.

On that short trip I recall being so disillusioned. For one of our original colonies, North Carolina in 1917-18 seemed not to have progressed much. The soil didn't look rich like the black loam in the Midwest. It was as if the farmers had worn out the fertile land.

Economically the eastern part of the state looked destitute. The rutty roads made travel difficult. We were forever repairing one of the tires. Not to say Minnesota was that sophisticated, but it seemed I'd traveled into the past...as if the post-Civil War days were only a few years before. Poor black people were walking along the side of the road like they'd just been set free by the plantation owner. It was modern day 1917... but yesterday was 1865!

Whether black-skinned or white-skinned, nobody looked particularly cheerful or successful in rural North Carolina. I'd gathered by what I was seeing those Negroes who'd been slaves likely had to return to those same tobacco and cotton fields after the Civil War. Now here it was years later and sons and grandsons of those same slaves didn't seem as if life had changed much for them.

However, there was one memorable highlight on that sojourn to Wilmington. For a young military trainee, seeing some females at the beach was inspiring. Some of them wore the latest and most revealing swimwear. You could see some leg slightly above the knee. Also, you didn't have to imagine their shape in those swimming suits. It was fabulous.

When training ended I was on a transport boat with my unit to France. We arrived in time to greet the cease-fire. We spent the next three months in Paris and the Rhineland helping those citizens recover and return to some type of normal life. It was important to help maintain order. I certainly learned about postwar abject poverty and illness...and desperation. I appreciated how precious life really was. When people were so highly distressed, they would do anything to eat or live. My military buddies and I commented again and again how fortunate that particular theatre of war had never entered our country.

Later when I returned to the states and eventually acquired my job in Glenwood in the early 1920's I was too often reminded of those images of postwar Europe. The suffering of overburdened farmers and their families in rural Minnesota would constantly dig at my mind.

When I did get an early leave while over in France, I didn't return stateside for almost four months. A friend and I traveled around Western Europe. We had little money but we were long on wanting adventure. We somehow lasted far beyond what our combined money should have allowed. There were times we had to use the food and shelter of postwar charities to survive. Other times we did odd jobs for food and a place to sleep. Having our uniforms helped.

Eventually returning to the U.S., I said good-by to my war buddy and traveled back to Willmar. After journeying through France, Spain, and Italy that return was one of the lower points in my life. I lasted in Willmar about two weeks before I let my father know I be attending the Minnesota School of Business in Minneapolis. He still assumed I'd be returning home following my schooling. Upon leaving for the Twin Cities, I suggested he groom a cousin as my replacement. It just took him a while to understand I'd never be back.

The business school curriculum was easy given my experience at the family store. I had a head for numbers. Once I got that degree I found an audit and accounting position in the Twin Cities. Those kinds of jobs weren't hard for me to find. They were just mind-numbing.

I spent a bulk of my extra money on speakeasy fun most nights. During the day, besides working, I was constantly seeking other types of employment that would get me away from the four walls of an office.

I don't remember how it happened, but out of the blue, I got a call from a friend of my father's telling me of a job in Glenwood, Minnesota. In that town was a cooperative of farmers who owned a feed & grain mill. They needed a manager...someone with a rural background who knew how to store grain, be aware of selling the grain at the right time, and maintain accurate books. That kind of responsibility was right down my alley and I likely wouldn't be fenced up in an office all day.

I called a man named Ernest Johnson up there in Glenwood and told him I was stopping by to interview for the job. He didn't know what to say since normally it was he or his board who decided whether they wanted to talk to a candidate or not. Nonetheless, he agreed to a meeting. I took the train to Glenwood on a Friday night and was sitting in the office of the feed & grain mill when old man Johnson showed up Saturday morning.

He seemed to like my initiative right off the bat...and my background...but didn't like my youth. But, he laid the cards on the table. He was tired of talking with a bunch of unqualified job seekers. He told me the starting salary was $2200 a year for the right man, but he thought the board would only go $2000 a year because of my young age. He quickly added that a small house a couple blocks away owned by the cooperative was part of the deal. He said there might even be a small stipend offered to the right man to fix the place up and make it a home.

That little real estate perk cemented the deal along with my insistence that I'd take one of the other jobs I was being offered down in the Twin Cities if the coop couldn't see fit to pay me the $2200. It was the first time I'd ever been so deceptive in any dealings. I no more had other job offers than Minnesota had palm trees. To my relief he backed down and hired me on the spot for the $2200 a year plus that free rent on the house. Just like that in the fall of 1920 barely into my twenties, I began carving out the kind of independent life I'd been seeking. As a bonus it just happened to be in a beautiful little community along picturesque Lake Minnewaska. Even then I never believed I'd be in that town more than three years. Ten years later I was still there, but I wouldn't be for long.

Matt, you should know that rural life was especially difficult in any farming area around the country at that time. You have heard of the 'Roaring Twenties', but things weren't that way for a farmer during the 1920's. It seemed each day was filled with hopelessness. Crop productivity per acre was low from tired land and no soil conservation. There seemed to be a perpetual and perennial drought in the growing season during those years. Then the rains came during harvest season making whatever crops had grown, difficult to get out of the ground. Farms were being taken over by the banks faster than the banks could open their doors for business. It was in that environment that I had to manage the Glenwood Feed & Grain Mill. The group of farmers I worked for definitely reflected the general feelings of the times. I remember them as being negative, desperate, complaining and always tired. Those kinds of people were my bosses.

The negativity of the farmer's plight caused me to seek solace away from the mill. I'd take the train down to see some friends in the Twin Cities every other weekend. I even started going to a local church. I'd never been a great churchgoer, but it seemed the First Presbyterian Church had about the right balance of religion and social interaction. That Presbyterian minister, Pastor Sven Olson, didn't seem so preoccupied to define sin or make parishioners feel guilty about how they lived. It fit my mentality so I showed up for Sunday church services if I was in town.

Remembering back, I'm always so glad I found comfort in that church rather with some local oppressed woman. Marriage had never been that crucial for me. I was not against the institution, mind you, I just didn't see anyone happy participating in the tradition. I had dated a couple of women in Minneapolis and had some interesting times with some French women while in Europe, but generally while in Glenwood I just stayed busy with my job and got involved in community interests rather than the local women.

Before long because of my financial acumen, I was asked to be the treasurer for the town council as well as for the church. Those responsibilities plus my frequent trips to Minneapolis kept my life busier and apparently more exciting compared to most everyone else's drab life in Glenwood. I guess my single life style made me look like some kind of great adventurer.

By 1926 I had negotiated with the mill owners for more money and more time off for travel. I also had a growing fund as a result of my interest and investments in the commodity markets. My profitable investments provided the means to finance my many trips. I'd be gone as much as two weeks three times a year in my final years managing the mill.

But, frankly as much as the cooperative appreciated my efforts and the townsfolk valued my involvement in civic matters, I was getting itchy to do something else. But, I remained in town...more out of either fear in making a job change or not believing I could find a better gig considering the free house and the extra travel time off my work. I'd been observing in Glenwood, in Minneapolis, and during my national travels a glut of unemployed people. I only wanted to change my life if I had a good chance of making it better. During the 1920's that was hard for me to visualize given the anxiety I was witnessing on people's faces most everywhere I went.

Still, I kept my eyes open for other opportunities. It was in early 1927 that something happened right there in that little lake town. Nothing would have hinted that my future was about to be altered. In fact, I'd paid little attention to the local story about a Chicago businessman bringing some of his friends from the Windy City to the secluded lake resort south of town. It appeared the new owner of the resort, Darrell O'Donnell, had tripped over some luck and was actually getting his cabins rented out...at least for the previous summer and surprisingly during the fall and winter months of 1926 as well.

O'Donnell was a nervous kind of guy who was new to the area. He had shifty eyes and a manner that didn't instill trust. He wasn't past thirty, but he looked much older with his flabby body, stooped shoulders and a constant glum look on his face. I didn't have much reason to talk to the man. He didn't seem to carry much respect in town either.

The story being told that spring was Chippewa Lodge and its small nine-hole golf course had been struggling until the Chicago group showed up. There was an enormous man named Loni D'Annelli who sported a constant cigar in his mouth and a voice that could be heard in the next county. This character apparently liked what he saw. He claimed he was looking for a quiet place for many of his friends to relax. The golf course and the lake answered that need. The seclusion I would come to find out was an even more important ingredient.

As far as O'Donnell was concerned, he'd been facing bankruptcy in the spring of 1926. He would have sold his own mother to make his investment profitable. It didn't take very long at all for D'Annelli and O'Donnell to reach agreement on ten cabins that would be rented out until the fall. For Loni D'Annelli, O'Donnell was the perfect type of puppet. D'Annelli knew he could control the greedy manager of the resort.

O'Donnell didn't know it then, nor did the townsfolk for quite a few years, but D'Annelli was a first rate Chicago mobster. I would learn it much sooner than the townsfolk, but by 1927 I was already being pulled into the ground swell of good fortune that D'Annelli seemed to have betrothed onto Glenwood, Minnesota. By the end of that year I had become the primary go-between with this man from Chicago and the town. What made the entire relationship work even better was the willingness of the community businesses to provide the goods and services for the ever increasing number of 'guests' who were flowing into Chippewa Lodge. The extra business kept the community hopping and cash flows continuing. During a time of economic downturn in the rural areas, Glenwood was like an oasis otherwise surrounded by poverty and discontent.

D'Annelli had a fairly good idea how to manage his questionable boarders at the Lodge, but the townspeople required extra effort. His generosity seemed to hold no bounds, but his altruism did come at a price. He helped the town because it was in his best interest to do so.

As for the townsfolk the many benefits gained from the unique group of men staying at the Lodge made it easier for them to cast a blind eye on anything peculiar they might see. With the increase in local commerce created by all those lake resort dwellers, everyone believed Glenwood was under some kind of lucky star."

Henry stopped for a moment and looked at Lawton to see his reaction. "Matt, you probably find it interesting how I admit to having a cordial relationship with a gangster from Chicago. It was a true dichotomy. Mr. D'Annelli was a model citizen and generally so were the guests who stayed out at the resort. He was still a crook. Once I learned of that fact, that thought rarely left my mind. However, for the good of the town I didn't want to see the town and the Lodge liaison end either."

Absorbed in the story, Lawton's urgent nod indicated to Henry that no judgments were being made about the older man's choices back then.

"Over time the locals naturally became enthralled with Loni D'Annelli. His 'guests' as he called them soon dominated the resort... much to Darrell O'Donnell's liking. Occasionally when those visitors at the Lodge misbehaved, D'Annelli handled the problem immediately. If any damage was done to anyone's property in town, the owner was immediately paid off. As a result the minor inconveniences of some drunks from the resort causing complications were generally overlooked and forgiven.

With the town blindly following him, D'Annelli gradually established his business base at the Lodge. As it turned out, he had several operating out of that lake resort...and not one tracked on the right side of the law. He rented a bulk of the cabins to serve as a safe house for anxious gangsters and wanted criminals who needed a secure place to disappear. The rules were simple. No violence crossed the boundaries of the lake resort...and if any mayhem did occur, it was understood the 'safe house' concept would vanish. The model was amazingly respected by all those 'guests'.

The Lodge also became a center for running illegal booze around the Midwest. Close by in the resort's barn, there was a storage area for stolen goods…even an area set aside for stolen cars. The biggest infraction and the most profitable illegal activity, though, was a gambling operation complete with private phone lines running into one of the larger cabins on the property. Coupled with plenty of 'nieces' being invited to the Lodge from Minneapolis and Chicago, the whole place was as immoral as it was unlawful.

D'Annelli had been conducting these businesses for almost five years by June, 1931. While running smoothly for five years, I'd been detecting more and more signs of stress within the entire franchise. In fact, I wondered if D'Annelli's operation might implode before the summer had ended. Those guests coming and going out of the safe haven were not as discreet. Locals were also becoming more aware of certain lodger's reputations. The *Chicago Tribune* and the *Minneapolis Star* would show periodic photographs of some very renowned gangsters. Often times these same men could be seen having breakfast or lunch at the local Glenwood Café.

But, with D'Annelli's reputation for dodging prosecution, it finally occurred to me how a number of local business people… including me…might be perceived as being guilty of racketeering in the way support was offered and given to those guests at the Lodge. That became as much of a concern as deciding when to make my exodus from Glenwood."

Granville suddenly stopped talking while a waiter filled each of their ice tea glasses. He pulled out a cigarette holder waiting for the server to complete his work. When Lill, he, and Lawton were alone again, he lit his thin cigar and began again as if there'd been no interruption.

"There was another important element to those days in Glenwood. A weekend town celebration on Memorial Day weekend had grown into a ten-day festival welcoming fishermen and visitors to the summer lake season at Lake Minnewaska. It had been a suggestion by Loni D'Annelli. It was another coy idea. He wanted his two-day charity golf tournament at Chippewa Lodge's nine-hole resort golf course to run simultaneously to the town celebration. The golf event was earmarked for his underworld friends. His initial hope was that the festival would keep curious citizens away from the Lodge golf course.

It didn't turn out that way. That golf event grew to be one of the more popular spectator occasions of the entire week. Rumors of the high stakes in the weekend golf affair brought many onlookers. Whether they knew anything about golf or not, it didn't matter. Most just wanted to experience the atmosphere where so much money was trading hands.

As early as the 1928 golf tournament, D'Annelli had to ask local civic and church organizations in town to support the event by handling the needs for spectator transportation, parking, food, and crowd control. That festival was truly a magnificent spectacle. Committees in Glenwood were formed to handle every aspect of the celebration. Planning had to be done starting from the opening events in the town's park on Memorial Day weekend. From that Saturday on, there were nightly dances and band concerts at the park gazebo, softball games at the athletic field, and food tents set up at the park by the local churches. The clanking of horseshoe pitching competitions could be heard late into each evening. Horns were constantly honking as young people sped through town keeping the local police always on alert. Fishing and boating competitions started mid-week and lasted through the final weekend. That last weekend ribbons were handed out to all winners in food preparation, the various sports competitions, as well as the music and sewing contests.

Visitors came from as far away as Fargo, North Dakota and the Twin Cities to enjoy this festival. Most of the attendees, though, were just regular folks from every farm community within a hundred miles of Glenwood. During a time when people all over the country were suffering with the worst farm depression in the history of the United States, that one week represented a slight respite from daily economic, social, and personal woes. The church and civic organizations made more money that week than what a hundred years of bake sales could bring in.

However, where the money was really made by these organizations were their efforts in supporting the charity golf tournament during the final two days of the festival. That event caused the most intrigue. From 1928 onward this collaboration between the festival and the charity golf tournament grew and grew. However, I would learn how the tournament was no more a 'charity' event than Teddy Roosevelt was a socialist. Instead, it developed into the biggest mob run golf tournament in the Midwest with enough money being wagered to make the Pope sweat.

As for my budding relationship with Loni D'Annelli, it's important to know how I was drawn into his web similar to how so many others in that community. The result was that this Chicago conman would have as much impact on my life as anyone else I could name. Strangely, he was never a friend. Yet, he was definitely someone I respected as a businessman. Even now I have to admire how he orchestrated that relationship with the town leaders, civic and religious groups. He had the oddest assortment of thugs and goons you'd ever meet in one place at that lake resort. He managed that entire process as if he was born to do it. It was unfortunate his personal and management skills were applied to business efforts on the wrong side of the law.

Like I mentioned, I'd paid little heed to the developments out at Chippewa Lodge into the winter of 1926-27. By then Darrell O'Donnell was strutting around town like he'd just found gold on his land. I did notice happier faces among my local business friends in town. It was a nice boon to have some out-of-state money circulating around our small lake community. What did get my attention was how many of those lodgers remained at the resort when the summer season was over.

And, what a group they were. They were not normal vacationers. Initially, many of them wore suits despite the heat and humidity. Soon the suit pants with shirt and tie disappeared or at least they'd lose the tie while rolling up their shirt sleeves. Eventually they'd drop down at Big Bud Bunsen's General Store in downtown Glenwood and buy some more appropriate lake clothing.

Another quite noticeable thing was the fancy cars these fellows at the Lodge drove. Most locals hadn't seen these late model automobiles other than in ads in magazines. Along with these sporty cars, often there were some very good looking women in the passenger seats. It was downright humorous to see the local men gaping at these females with all the make-up and wearing the latest styles of clothing. You can imagine the wives of these men in Glenwood were most disapproving.

As for Darrell O'Donnell, he continued to be an odd duck. He was always restless and fretful...not the kind of man a woman found attractive. He lived only for the solvency of his lake resort. Rarely was he seen having a meal or even coffee down at the Glenwood Café. It was as if he didn't want to get real close to the local folks for fear they might find something about him that wasn't socially or morally acceptable. I'll just stop there with any further description of Mr. O'Donnell."

Henry then turned to Lill and rolled his eyes before continuing the story. Lawton didn't pick up on the subtly of the comment.

"It was in the early spring of 1927 when more of my attention was stirred. Charlie B. Good, the mayor of the town, came through the door of the Glenwood Café one morning with eyes ablazed looking for me. He and I had breakfast often together and invariably talked about the problems of the town and ways to improve the community. He'd been repeating often how the nice boost to the town's well-being seemed to coincide with the arrival of those out-of-towners staying at Chippewa Lodge. He was the one who informed me how the cabins out at the resort had remained rented over the previous fall, winter and now into the spring. It was as if some of these visitors were making the Lodge their permanent home.

He expressed mild concern that some of those fellows were on the wild side, but assured me that nothing untoward was happening at the resort. By that time townsfolk were already becoming blinded to the goings on at the Lodge. The churches in town had noticed more money in the plate each week even though attendance was about the same. Big Bud Bunsen's General Store was a big beneficiary of the activity at Chippewa Lodge. That place was the main local conduit for all-purpose supplies. Generally known but conveniently unreported was that Big Bud's place was also the main local dispenser for illegal booze during those years of Prohibition.

Anyway, over breakfast that morning was the first time I'd heard the name Loni D'Annelli. The mayor mentioned that this out-of-towner was apparently responsible for keeping those lake resort cabins rented over the winter. Furthermore, this man had recently attended a town council meeting and suggested some kind of town festival for the upcoming June. It was obvious Mayor Good was completely won over by this D'Annelli.

In describing this fellow to me, he gushed how this man was a bit rough around the edges, but full of enthusiasm for helping the town. I left the café that morning feeling very favorable towards D'Annelli given the benefits he was bringing to the town? And, I saw nothing but good things regarding the festival. What a wonderful opportunity for the community to enjoy a flow of money into the local coffers.

The mayor was very pleased with my positive reactions to both the visitor and his idea of the town celebration. He knew my voice did carry some weight. Though I determinedly stayed away from being on the town council, I'd been drafted to be the town's treasurer. Being trusted to hold the purse strings of the community, my favorable support made that weekend festival in Glenwood a done deal.

The charity event was scheduled and it came off without a hitch on the first weekend of June, 1927. The churches put up tents and sold pies, cookies, and cakes all day Saturday and Sunday in a recreational area of the town called City Park. I could see the preparation every day from my mill office just across the state highway from that park. There was also a street dance on Saturday night that attracted one of the largest crowds ever in the small lakeside community. For the first attempt, most people in town found the whole endeavor both profitable and exciting...words not often heard during those difficult years in any farm community in America.

Concurrently to that festival, Loni D'Annelli did hold his first charity golf tournament. With the festival going on in town, there were very few people gathering out at the lake resort golf course to view that event...at least on the first day. When rumors began to spread that some prominent people were playing for a lot of money in the two-day tournament, the second day on Sunday saw hoards of people making their way out to the resort by any means possible. When the spectators arrived, they didn't really recognize any of the players. The competitors were mostly loud, brusque individuals playing a game of golf that was not in the same specter as how the game was generally described in newspapers and magazines. There was a void of sportsmanship with golfers yelling at one another. Money was often thrown on the grass before a player made a shot as if they were chips at a roulette table. Some people swore they saw one hundred dollar greenbacks being bet on just one particular shot.

Spectators found the entire affair quite entertaining. What none of the crowd realized was that they were seeing one of the biggest social gatherings of racketeers and mobsters ever in Minnesota. Whether playing in the tournament or not, there was copious drinking, gambling, and wagering going on all over the golf course.

I took no notice of anything that weekend. I wasn't even in town. Instead, I had a few social obligations myself in the Twin Cities."

He looked over at Lill and winked. This time even Lawton caught the clever remark, chuckled, and stopped writing until Henry continued.

"Anyway, when I returned to Glenwood, I was swept away by the comments from the local business owners about the profitable weekend they'd enjoyed. Folks from those distant places like the Twin Cities, Duluth and even Fargo, North Dakota were spreading money around various Glenwood businesses during the town festival. The take by the civic and church organizations selling their baked goods was eye popping. There was not a crumb remaining by Sunday afternoon. That first two-day event massaged the treasuries of these local groups in dramatic ways. It truly had been a grand gala for a small lakeside town.

I also heard some muffled comments about an extraordinary number of fancy cars and questionable characters that had pulled into town as early as Thursday before the festival. And, these men weren't in Glenwood for the festival; it was the golf they sought. From my limited perspective, I just figured if a town was going to welcome so many visitors, there certainly would be an assortment of debatable fellows in the entourage. I gave no heed to those initial concerns.

Interestingly, following that tournament those fancy cars continued to pass through Glenwood on their way to and from Chippewa Lodge. For the next couple months of the summer, that resort became one of the more popular places in the area. Heavier set men in suits came into town to eat at the café, get their hair cut, pick up some medical supplies, get their cars repaired, and most of all to spend money at Big Bud's General Store for clothing, food and drink. The town's business people carried smiles unnatural for the times.

Over the next year I couldn't help but notice these high roller people as they came into town. I'd traveled enough places and seen newspapers in New York, Chicago, Milwaukee, Philadelphia and Minneapolis to sense some recognition of a few of those men. I kept my apprehensions to myself, but I swore a few of those guests staying at the Lodge had some previous history of ongoing problems with the

71

law. Not wanting to suspect anything dire, I allowed myself to think they had been exonerated from whatever charges they'd been facing.

In the fall of 1927 I didn't expect Darrell O'Donnell's good fortune to continue. I never thought his cabins would be fully occupied in the fall and winter like the previous year. By then I'd seen Loni D'Annelli occasionally in downtown. He was always laughing and talking with some local businessman or minister. I still hadn't taken the time to introduce myself, but it didn't really matter. He and I had nothing in common. What could a general manager of the local feed & grain mill have that would be of any interest to a man of his ostensible importance.

It was when Mayor Good and I sat down again on a cold December morning toward the end of that year that I got more curious about the Chicago man. Mayor Good said that Mr. D'Annelli wanted to have the second annual charity tournament the next June, but he had some ideas to make the event even bigger. I sat there wondering why and how Glenwood had the lucky star above its water tower when there were so many lake communities around Minnesota and even Wisconsin, a state much closer to this do-gooder's home city.

It was that afternoon that I placed a call to a friend of mine from the war years who I visited often in my travels through Chicago. When I asked him whether he'd heard of Mr. Loni D'Annelli...a steward for some union...he didn't even have to think twice.

He responded, "Henry, where in the devil did you ever run into this fellow? You're right...he's a union guy...like part of one of the largest unions in Chicago. And you might say he's a steward, but in fact he's the 'head' steward...like the president of that entire union. Nothing has been built in this city recently without his stamp of approval.

I was impressed until my friend hinted at another factor. He said, "You should also know, Henry, Mr. D'Annelli is rumored to have some mob connections. Of late he hasn't been in the Chicago news much. His image about two years ago began taking a beating with some shenanigans relating to some building projects in the loop. I heard his advisors had suggested strongly he leave town for a while to get the newspaper guys and the cops off his back. It was good advice. I haven't heard his name or seen a story in the newspaper about him or his whereabouts for a long time."

My friend's comments caused me to gulp. Still, for the good this man was doing for the town of Glenwood, I was inclined to give the guy a break. There were no building projects going on in my town. Hell, we would have welcomed even one. No, everything D'Annelli was doing was to the advantage of the community.

Also, with no convictions, that was another reason I tended to ignore the potential magnitude of what my friend had voiced. Nothing had been proven. Besides, he and his group of guests out at the Lodge had behaved adequately and certainly hadn't created any problems in Glenwood. D'Annelli might have been a bad boy in Chicago, but as far as I could see, he was everything good for my town.

In 1928, I was not yet thirty years old and beginning to get quite itchy about eventually leaving town. The problem I had was finding other opportunities that exceeded the one I had in Glenwood. I was paid reasonably well for the times. I was doing a more than adequate job at the mill paying attention to grain prices and selling the cooperative's grain at the most opportune times. The farmers had no complaints with me or my negotiated free time.

By then I had habitually been taking ten-day to two week excursions periodically. I was really into this new air travel. I arranged flights on mail carriers and even the new Ford Trimotor twelve-passenger plane that was promoting passenger travel. That year I was able to arrange flights from Wold Chamberlain airfield outside Minneapolis to places like New York and Washington D.C. via Chicago. Even after that year there were regional carriers that could take me to places like Miami and Boston. Those trips truly opened my world and enlarged my dreams.

It was my trip to Washington D.C. in the spring of 1928 that made coming back to Glenwood almost intolerable. Seeing the monuments, the history, visiting Mt. Vernon, the nation's capital, and touring the White House motivated me to consider other interests in life. President Calvin Coolidge had not been part of that stimulation. Witnessing a speech he gave one evening, I could not believe he was the elected leader of our country. He would have fit better in my lazy community by Lake Minnewaska. Seeing him speak raised my hope that anyone could succeed if properly motivated.

As you'll learn in our upcoming interviews, my travel was one of many factors that propelled me to think about leaving Glenwood.

However, it would take until 1931 before I no longer would just think about it, but actually do it."

Dinner suddenly appeared and it became silent around the table. Lawton kept noting how Granville quieted if there were any other people within earshot. He was always friendly greeting the servers by name. He had the habit of inhaling whatever he was smoking deeply and blew the smoke high into the air letting the fan disperse the cloud. It was as if some of the untold part of the story was being scattered by the fan as well.

The dinner concluded with a dessert Lawton had never tasted. Key lime pie would become another favorite food item. He was being introduced to so many new things in only his first day in Charleston. It was enough for him to question his own level of education and sophistication. He'd never thought the old southern city with the radical reputation could show him anything new.

With the dessert completed, Henry seemed willing to continue. Requesting more Charleston ice tea, he then asked for privacy from the servers once again. Once they were gone, his well lubricated voice from the ice tea picked up on the story.

"My frustration upon returning to Glenwood that spring of 1928 was interrupted by a note sent over to me at my office by Pastor Sven Olson of our church. As the church's financial officer, he wanted me at a church meeting the following Monday evening to discuss our church men's club possibly taking on a more active role in the charity golf tournament the upcoming June. His note said Mr. Loni D'Annelli wanted to meet with our group to discuss the idea as well as to make a donation to repair the church steeple.

I had of course heard of the previous June's first charity golf event. What I'd remembered was the stories of excessive gambling on the golf course. It seemed peculiar. Running a charity event of any kind with the kind of economic climate that hung over rural America was like a Catholic opening a café next to a Lutheran Church. It was doomed to failure. Though my interest in attending the meeting was low, as the key financial officer of the church, I felt compelled.

My lack of enthusiasm was obvious as I arrived Monday evening at the church just in time to shake hands around the table and be welcomed back home from my recent travels. I appeared to be a quite popular fellow and D'Annelli, remaining seated out of my sight, was looking me over curiously. When the meeting got underway, it was the first time I'd been that close to the guy. I recall being impressed by his girth and how his outgoing personality seemed to explode as he got more involved in the meeting. He was quite a dynamic fellow.

Pastor Olson told us we were there to hear a proposal from the Chicago man. I couldn't help but notice there were many appreciative glances from men sitting around that church table as they gazed at the visitor. D'Annelli cleared his throat a couple times and then proceeded to suggest expanding June's charity golf tournament to include something called a Calcutta. He termed it as a small betting game where people could wager on the golfers participating in the golf event and on teams of players who would be competing. He specified that he needed a trustworthy community organization to assist in managing the tournament as well as the money being staked in the Calcutta. He was especially interested in having a church organization handle the money as it would add credibility to the proceedings.

I recall there were mostly blank looks around the table including a lot of disinterest from me....that is, until he proceeded to say that for our efforts, the Presbyterian Men's Club would get a full 10 percent of the total proceeds of the Calcutta.

When I heard him say 10 percent of the gross amount being bet in the Calcutta, my eyebrows were raised. Most of my friends around the table were used to seeing their wives selling pies and bread at a church bake sale for ten cents apiece, maybe twenty-five cents at best. A great day for charity sales might be clearing fifty dollars.

My fellow men's club members just sat there looking bored. They had no idea what Mr. D'Annelli had just offered our club and church. In my travels I was aware of this type of competition and side-betting. There typically was a lot of money bandied about with this type of gaming device. I realized our small church could make some real money.

When he mentioned the number of out of town visitors he was going to be inviting to the next event, my interest increased even more. It wouldn't be the local people making bets; it would be these guests from the big cities. I figured if only these people made the wagers, I was certain 10 percent of that total amount could well be in excess of hundreds of bake sales.

I sat up straight, coughed, and tried not to show too much interest. While a Calcutta was illegal if done purely for profit, since the golf tournament was for charity and was a singular event, D'Annelli discerned correctly that local law enforcement officials would look the other way. Besides, it could be argued bingo being played in the church basement every Thursday evening could be construed as gambling as well.

Though I still had my concerns about this fellow's reputation back in Chicago, that night I was pleased he graced the carpet of our church and offered such a deal. To ease my doubts, I asked him a couple questions trying to appear casual. Every probe from why he was in Glenwood to why he'd chosen our particular church was answered smoothly…maybe even a bit too glibly.

He mentioned that his wife was a devout Presbyterian. D'Annelli looked at Pastor Olson and articulated how he appreciated a religion not entrenched in the past, but one that cared for the needs of the common man. You'd have thought he was the head deacon in the sky the way the smitten pastor warmed to his words.

Years later I would always wonder why I didn't react to that word 'devout' when D'Annelli described his wife. First of all, Presbyterians I knew were rarely devout. They were spiritually interested, generous with their time if not their money, committed to the support and care they can bring to certain people's lives, and thankful that it was all right to miss Sunday services if you had something else planned. But, devout….. that was a bit zealous to describe that sect of Protestantism. Secondly, the man wore no wedding ring.

But, that evening the 10 percent cut of the gambling proceeds made me deaf, dumb, and blind to any doubts. Playing my role as financial officer of the church, I looked furtively at Pastor Olson and gave him a nod. He smiled back. Our two votes were the two that mattered in going forward in partnership with Loni D'Annelli. I even volunteered to personally manage the Calcutta wagers, so he could trust it would be done accurately.

I detected a suspicious look in his eyes as he evaluated my offer. I had apparently stepped over the line of what he'd intended, but as he thought further, he seemed to like my additional offer more and more.

It would show that the First Presbyterian Church was totally in charge of the Calcutta and there would be no question from the gamblers to say nothing of the law.

When Pastor Olson adjourned the meeting, our big city visitor clapped his large hands together as if saying, 'the business is done, let's eat'. The noise created such a stunning explosion it was as if a gun had gone off. I recall Big Bud Bunsen, the local general store proprietor, who normally slept through our meetings and then recovered miraculously when food and drink were served at meeting's end actually wet his pants hearing the startling sound. As if that was not discreditable enough, his chair also slipped out from underneath him. He kind of splashed when he landed on the hardwood floor of the church meeting room. It was not one of Big Bud's finer moments, but he was not easily humiliated. Wet pants and all, Big Bud was first in line for food that night.

That decision for the church to support and even manage what sounded like an innocent charity golf tournament and fun-filled Calcutta was to be the changing point of my life. My schedule at the feed & grain mill changed noticeably as I was later asked to be the overall chairman of the town festival as well. By then D'Annelli had talked the town council into running the town festival for ten days. His rationale was that if the town and the churches made so much money over a weekend, then they'd make even more over the week prior to his charity golf tournament.

What no one realized, including me, was that the festival was still intended by D'Annelli to be a cover for when all his underworld friends drove into Glenwood. Some arrived as much as a week before the weekend charity golf tournament. What it also meant was that my church men's club volunteers would be busy at two Calcutta tents set up to take bets for an entire week before the actual contest. One tent would be off the property across the road from Chippewa Lodge. The other would be among the food tents down at City Park.

That second charity event and the Calcutta on that first weekend in June 1928 was a real eye opener. It was nothing like the previous year's golf event. This was much bigger. As I'd guessed, mostly it was the out-of-town players and their guests who had the money to make the bets. They were in a different league than my local friends and neighbors in the Glenwood area. You can imagine the shock heard round the county when the total money in the Calcutta was rumored.

As far as I was concerned, the higher the figure being waged the better for our church and church men's club. Before the tournament started, there was well over $100,000 that was bet at our two gambling centers. That 10 percent was an incredible amount of money for a small church organization at that time gained from volunteer work. The First Presbyterian Church was not the only organization to profit. Though lesser in return, other churches showed initiative by offering round trip rides out to Chippewa Lodge for the golf tournament. Still other churches set up food tents outside the gates of the resort.

The earnings from that ten-day festival and concluding golf tournament on the last weekend became a bonanza for the town's businesses, churches and civic organizations. When I tallied up the total dollars wagered, I did have to wonder if D'Annelli had made a miscalculation in paying my church men's club so much money just to manage the Calcutta.

When Sunday evening came and payouts to winning gamblers were divvied out, I brought the total cash ledger to D'Annelli with a complete list of who bet how much and for which individual or team. He was feeling no pain having cleaned up on his own individual bets out on the golf course. Slobbering over a few beers and never expecting such an accurate accounting, he was the one who reminded me about the money owed the church men's club. He said, "Henry, did you remember to take out your 10 percent off the top like we agreed?"

You could have blown me over. The man was true to his word. He was paying our church men's club its first dividend for managing this first charity event at Chippewa Lodge. My calculations showed that our church club would gain $11,500 given as a donation for our club's services. It was a veritable fortune considering the most the club had in its treasury up to that point was $432.

Before Mr. D'Annelli left town two days later, he met with the men's club at our regular Monday night meeting. He was most complimentary about the club's fine work. He told us that his group wanted to continue this wonderful event next June if the Presbyterian group would be so inclined to manage the project once again. With stars in our eyes and nods of the head, Pastor Olson and I agreed to handle the 1929 event.

Loni D'Annelli left that meeting at the church with his stogy latched to one side of his mouth and what I thought was a devious grin on the other side. I would find out later how thrilled he was about pulling off this entire affair. The town seemed happy, the churches certainly were satisfied with their share of the profits, and most of all he was able to continue pulling the wool over the eyes of everyone in Glenwood.

In operating a major year-round gambling operation at the Lodge, he knew there could be hearsay and rumors flying with so many people attending the charity golf tournament. Having the First Presbyterian Church involved in managing the tournament Calcutta gave him a perfect shield. He was able to continue his regular unlawful businesses without a hitch starting the day after the close of the charity golf tournament. What he'd also learned that weekend was another tremendous advantage he had with the church men's club managing the Calcutta. He had me...the most trustworthy non-employee he'd ever duped into working for him. From my perspective I was just bowled over how the community was benefitting from having Loni D'Annelli so interested in our town.

Following the 1928 festival and tournament, the First Presbyterian Church initiated immediate projects of building onto the church, completing the repair of the unsteady steeple, and buying new furniture for the men's club meeting room. Beyond the church needs, the men's club donated time and money to up-grade City Park, the beach area along the lake as well as the local library.

Six months after that tournament, the congregation of the First Presbyterian Church had grown 30% in membership. The accompanying increase in the Sunday offering plate made the now happy go lucky Pastor Olson absolutely dizzy with success at the conclusion of every church financial meeting.

That winter every church and charitable organization had individual meetings to figure out how to skim as much revenue as possible off the upcoming June charity golf event for 1929. I recall when a town council member, Otto Schitzman, the local English teacher, objected because the town was taking on too much responsibility, he was summarily fired from the council. The town was enjoying a streak of good fortune and the town council and business owners in Glenwood had no patience for conservative thinking.

During those next couple years through 1931, this occasion was billed as 'celebrating the coming of summer'. Even more people from the Dakotas, Minnesota and Wisconsin streamed in for a closer look at the fun-filled ten-day event.

For once the mayor's election slogan of 'B good to your town…. vote for Charlie B. Good' finally merited some truth. Getting the entire town wrapped up in a multiday June community celebration was a huge boost to morale and pride for the locals.

There were still naysayers around the town that warned about greed coupled with unholy actions surely would breed depravity. What those blasphemous actions were never got defined, but most citizens thought God was definitely smiling down upon their community. The Almighty was given much credit for the town's good fortune while it lasted; it would be the devil who would make even greater strides when the dream finally ended.

After that 1928 tournament I couldn't help but take more interest in the activities and guests out at Chippewa Lodge. D'Annelli would see me in town and always make conversation. He'd invite me out to the Lodge for lunch periodically just to discuss how to make the festival and golf tournament work better. It was during those luncheons I couldn't help but notice some of the behind the scenes activity. I didn't want to be close enough to see evidence of any malfeasance, but it didn't take a genius to see the trucks arriving and departing with Canadian booze. As for the lodgers I often swore I'd seen pictures of some of them in various city newspapers during my travels. I had the same feeling when some of those fellows were in town having a meal at the Glenwood Café. My fellow neighbors and townsfolk took no notice…or, if they did, their unease was never discussed. I always wondered what they thought observing so many unmarked trucks filing in and out of the resort and passing through town. I certainly didn't blame them for staying mum. I wasn't saying much either.

By the 1929 event I could see Loni D'Annelli was playing our community like a fine pianist. I continued to periodically witness the extraordinary operation at the Lodge, even seeing through an open door the inside of a few of the cabins where call-in bets were being monitored. I'd not seen anything like it and never thought an endeavor like that could work in such a rural area. But it did. Monies were bet on various sporting events all around the country. The bets were made over the phone lines and the wagers were paid at key regional cities. I don't remember how I found out, but I did learn the gambling operation profits were banked somewhere at Chippewa Lodge.

Following that 1929 event I realized I'd become a very significant person in the eyes of Loni D'Annelli. He had learned how absolutely trustworthy I was given my dedication to the town. That year I'd calculated the men's club netted almost $15,000 for our work with the Calcutta and charity golf event. A testament to the success of the ten-day town celebration was that every civic and church group showed an increase in their revenues, even if they were only peripherally involved in the charity golf tournament. Of course they didn't come close to making the confidential sum earned by the Presbyterian men's club.

The Methodists, with their food booths located out at the resort as well as in the park had their buns, breads, cakes, and cookies gone by 1:00 each day. They couldn't bake enough food. The evening hay rides between the Lodge and the city park along the lake was a huge hit even at twenty-five cents a head. The German Lutherans could finally smile with this new revenue stream for their church. They no longer had to depend solely on the meager offerings of the chintzy malcontents who were members of their church.

The Northern Baptists were not as fervent as the enthusiastic Southern Baptists I've gotten to know here in South Carolina. The Southern Baptist would have made a financial killing. Not the Northern Baptists......they tried to sell religious books and bibles in the park... each day of the celebration. God! Talk about uncreative!! They'd have done better selling lemonade. No wonder my feed & grain mill looked in better condition than their church.

The only other church that didn't do so well was the Church of the Nazarene. They were normally against everything and that included what their minister considered a heretical town festival. Parson B.M. Greenslit tried but never did convince people they were going to hell if they participated in the town celebration. There just wasn't a bible passage that supported his claim. I guess every town has to have a Parson Greenslit.

When the June 1929 tournament and the community celebration were completed, I continued my habit of taking time off. Typical of the previous couple years I was gone for two weeks. When I returned everyone was still talking about the success we all shared in hosting that year's festival. The rest of that summer mirrored the previous summers with late model cars driving in and out of town each weekend, more cabins being built and rented for some shady looking guests, and more and more unidentified storage trucks passing through town to and from Chippewa Lodge. It continued that way through the fall and slowed only slightly during the winter.

Then, something happened in October 1929...something besides the crash of Wall Street. I was on one of my trips and visiting that friend in Chicago. The nightlife was fabulous along Michigan Avenue. The second morning I was having breakfast at the Palmer House and reading the *Chicago Tribune*. On page three, ample coverage was given to some recent illegal activities involving senior level officials in a major labor union. It had caused a dispute with various construction firms.

The article pointed out how the union officials were known to have mob connections. At least five of the people mentioned in the articles were Chippewa Lodge guests whose names I recognized from the previous June charity golf tournament. The next day there were follow-up articles covering these five men and their past arrests for burglary, larceny, racketeering, and even suspected murder. I was stunned.

The clincher was the morning of the Stock Market Crash on the last day of my stay in Chicago. I saw a picture of Loni D'Annelli on the front page of the morning paper. The news article disclosed he was being arrested for the eighth time on racketeering charges. The clipping showed him laughing as he was brought into the Dearborn Street police station. The *Chicago Tribune* made it sound as if D'Annelli had his own suite at police headquarters. The disrespect and disdain for the law was etched on his face. It occurred to me how it might be worth having the Chicago police just pay him to leave town for a couple weeks. It would give Chicago law enforcement a rest.

The next few days after returning to Glenwood, I was disgusted. I pondered again whether I had unwittingly committed any crimes while doing the volunteer work for this renegade. While I decided I likely wouldn't be prosecuted, I did feel I deserved jail time for stupidity.

As the weeks passed, I often thought about picking up my belongings and just leaving town. I frankly can't recall exactly what kept me in Glenwood the rest of that autumn through the winter of 1929-30. I still had that sense of responsibility for the town. It was inevitable that D'Annelli would eventually fall on his face and no longer carry out his illegal businesses at the Lodge. For that matter he could pack up the whole operation and retool them at some other remote, secretive location whenever he wished. When that happened, Glenwood would overnight turn into a typical Depression Era town.

But, I dutifully stayed in Glenwood if for no other reason than to appreciate how well the town was faring. I got up each weekday and prepared for another routine day as general manager of the mill...but I had a growing sick feeling in the pit of my stomach.

Admittedly I enjoyed the general respect I had in the community. Two fellows in charge of law enforcement in the town often stopped by the mill to share some coffee and talk about the world's problems. It was after that trip back from Chicago that one of them commented how I seemed more subdued than normal. Usually coming back from my travels I entertained them with various stories. One of the guys, the county sheriff, was concerned I may have been hurt financially from the recent Wall Street implosion. To some degree I had been, but not much. I didn't go in for buying securities. I stayed with small time commodity investing...something I studied.

I recall sitting with them having coffee a bit disappointed that as two officers of the law they had never mentioned any kind of awareness regarding the activities out at the Lodge. I doubted they even knew Loni D'Annelli was mixed up with the rackets in Chicago.

I continued working like an automaton...got up in the morning, went to work, ate lunch and dinner and went to bed. My motivation was at the lowest point I'd ever experienced. I wasn't prepared financially to just quit my job. I had some extra investment income but it wasn't enough for me to just up and leave town. It looked like as long as I was in Glenwood I'd have to work with D'Annelli and his cronies until rumors caused the police to raid the lake resort or his legal problems back in Chicago might prevent him from operating out of Chippewa Lodge.

I remember leaving the mill early that Friday after my return from Chicago. I just walked down along the shore of Lake Minnewaska. It was strange how a lake so beautifully bluish-green in the summer could look so cold and brownish-blue in the fall. It was a cold afternoon. I could hear the high school band playing prior to the late afternoon football game against Starbuck. Despite the stock market crash that month, farming communities were used to surviving in relative impoverished conditions. Bad news was normal. Life moved on. Something like a high school football game could help a lot of people escape for a while from the stresses of everyday life. I was not one of those people. I mostly just heard the howling wind whistling and the crashing of cold waves against the lake shore.

It is often said when you feel absolute despair that was when an individual can witness his true character. You either pull yourself out of the trap of negativity and frustration or you let life's unfairness or cruelty take over your spirit. I guess that evening was a turning point for me. As rotten as I was feeling about life, there were so many people in much worse shape. Even understanding that truism, it wasn't enough to pull me out of my doldrums.

I got in my Plymouth coupe and left town that evening. I had no plans to travel down to Minneapolis that weekend. Alexandria had a movie theatre. I figured to try something new just to jolt me out of my melancholy. Barreling up State Hwy. 29, I made it to town well ahead of the picture show. I stopped by a café for some food. I knew there was some booze available if I said the right thing.

Outside the restaurant there was a 1922 top grade Wills St. Claire A-68 Roadster along with some other newer model automobiles. I stood there gazing at this car wondering what type of character would be driving a classic automobile like that roadster in the middle of rural Minnesota. The driver had a lot of gall showing off such sporty car when only a week before the stock market took so much money away from so many people. It seemed most everyone who invested in the stock market was looking for the best way to die. I figured the fellow who owned the Wills St. Claire had to be snubbing his nose at the world.

Entering the café I wondered if I could pick out the owner of that vehicle. Surprisingly, that became a challenge. Inside there were twelve guys who had just finished a round of golf before the sun had set. There were a few bags of golf clubs leaning against the wall. Given the blustery weather, I figured it had to be one of the last days of golf for our part of the state. Those fellows appeared to be feeling no pain. They were drinking some tasty hot toddies. Obviously one of those fellows knew the magic word in order for the booze to come out of the back room.

The owner eyed me to make certain I wasn't somebody in law enforcement. Prohibition was still the law of the land...if there was a cop around. The proprietor was taking a chance being so open serving booze. I must have passed the test, because he continued pouring more drinks to the group.

As for the golfers, they appeared to be great friends. There was much kidding and laughter. They looked well off enough, but didn't behave as if they gave a damn about the stock market collapse. I figured maybe they were too young to have a lot of money in the market. I was roughly in their age group. I hadn't accumulated that much money to lose in the Crash either.

I sat in the corner and ordered a sandwich and coffee. The group of golfers were the only others in the café. It was actually pleasing seeing a bunch of guys taking pleasure in each other's company. There were a couple guys that stood out. One guy looked like Bobby Jones, the nationally famous golfer with the knee pants and cardigan fitting loosely on his frame. Bobby Jones had been quite a figure in sports the previous years. This blondish, wavy-haired fellow had not only the similar clothing choice, but he looked quite secure and confident. There was another bigger fellow standing next to him. He was more boisterous and was telling the most jokes. When he talked there was such laughter. When he wasn't talking, he listened very intently. He looked to be a very popular man within the group.

I lamented why so many of my true friends mostly lived far away. I saw them only during my travels. Back in Glenwood, I had plenty of acquaintances, but no people I really talked to very closely... except for a guy named John Bailey who owned a farm on the east bluff. He'd been a friend from the moment I arrived in Glenwood. I had my two law enforcement comrades as well, but I didn't talk much about my cavorting in the Twin Cities with them. And, the farmers who owned the Glenwood Feed & Grain Mill were barely acquaintances. They were always sullen. I had not heard them say a nice or positive thing in my lifetime. Finally, the guys at the First Presbyterian Church men's club were reasonably nice fellows, but I didn't spend much time with them either. They were shallow on most subjects. I despised listening to their opinions on matters they had no perspective and even less information. I tended to leave whenever they started ranting about politics or business.

Finishing my food, I smiled at the continuing banter from those golfing companions. They seemed not to have a care in the world. I heard one of the men kiddingly refer to the bigger fellow as 'Counselor Davis'. I'd heard the name. I wondered if it could be the local attorney named Charlie Davis. He was known in the area as being a capable attorney, but even better known in recent years as an astute investor in land and lake cabin properties. Folks said he had recently made a bid on Chippewa Lodge. That thought made me laugh. I thought how lucky that Charlie Davis fellow was in not having his bid accepted. Darrell O'Donnell, the current owner, was enjoying some extraordinarily good fortune as long as Loni D'Annelli was renting the cabins and guests were filling the resort restaurant. The day was fast approaching that D'Annelli's operation was going to go belly up and end O'Donnell's smugness. His solvent little resort would close up faster than an oil town with a dried up well.

I was about to leave and go to the movie house when the proprietor brought over a beer. He said it was on the house from those twelve guys shouting and laughing at the other side of the restaurant. It was meant as an apology for making so much noise. I sat back and lifted my glass to them. The big guy, who I thought might be Charlie Davis, acknowledged my raised glass indicating he was probably the one who'd bought the beer. He didn't even know me, but he was still aware enough to make a kind gesture. His thoughtfulness did have a positive effect. It was the best I'd felt since returning to Glenwood the previous weekend.

Though I felt better walking out the door of the café, my glumness quickly returned when the cold night hit my face. There were so many omissions in my life and so many more things I wanted to accomplish. What had I really done...and time was marching on.

Leaving the parking lot I didn't feel like sitting alone in some movie house. I drove down the block to another café feeling like having another beer in more quiet surroundings, that is, if the owner was willing to sell me one. Since summer had ended, Friday nights had become much slower. People no longer came to the lakes. Lake resort communities tended to become as dormant as the upcoming winter.

Entering that second small restaurant, I didn't even think about prohibition or any particular signal to the café owner. I just put my money on the table and told him I wanted a beer. He took the money and went back to the kitchen. In a couple of minutes he brought out a cold beer in an outwardly colored glass to camouflage the contents. He gave me a wink and walked back to his kitchen.

It was not two minutes later two members of that same party of twelve men walked into that café. Charlie Davis and his nattily garbed friend with the knickers were apparently on their way home and had only made it to the next café...like I had. They were slightly tipsy and didn't even see me sitting alone at a side table. Taking a seat at the opposite side of the establishment, Davis called the proprietor by name and gave him a nod. Soon two more camouflaged glasses came out of the back kitchen and were placed in front of the two gentlemen. Typical of two slightly inebriated fellows, they talked a bit too loudly. I could hear most of what they said.

They were debating whether Davis should buy some property or not. His suave friend kept telling him that this was not the time to do any foolish investing. The friend thought it better to wait until the property could be picked up even less expensively. His main question seemed to be how long before the land would actually increase in value.

Davis then let go with a very sage quip that echoed across the empty café. It was something I've never forgotten. Even in his semi-inebriated condition, he explained very clearly why he was more interested in taking a worthwhile risk than sitting back and letting the world pass him by. He said to his friend, "Jamie boy, every property that I have purchased so far has not been done at the right time. I look what happened last week in Wall Street as opportunity knocking just for me. Now, there are people who want to liquidate anything they've got for cents on the dollar. Even if I make some mistakes, I should have some very potentially profitable land investment opportunities."

His friend had a difficult time disagreeing. He finally said, "O. K...you're right. Do it. You can use our special fund. It's just lying under the mattress gathering dust anyway. I'd say if you feel strongly about the investment, we move on it. You take more chances on land than I do as a pilot in the sky. You've always had a feel for a good buy. Count me in. We tend to enjoy life more when we take a few chances."

Then they chuckled, tipped glasses, and downed that beer... and one more before leaving."

Henry then stopped talking. He motioned for his ice tea glass to be re-filled. He glanced at Lill Hamilton to see if she was tiring. It wasn't that late yet, and the older man seemed to be enjoying reminiscing about those years back in Glenwood.

As for Lawton, he didn't want to interrupt his host with insignificant questions, especially as Henry began talking about Charlie Davis and making reference to Lawton's own father. This was background information the young man had never heard before. He was being transported back in time to scenes when Charlie and his father were only slightly older than he....and just a week after the stock market crash in October, 1929.

Henry picked up on his young guest's increased interest.

"Matt, it was that last statement said by Charlie that hit home with me. I translated it as risks have to be part of life if a fellow wants to have the chance to get ahead. I knew he was right. I just hadn't been around enough forward looking people to hear something so refreshingly positive.

When I departed the second café, that cold northwest wind didn't feel as bitter. Driving back to Glenwood, I was pushing my old Plymouth to go much faster than normal. I was thinking how I took more chances when I was on the road away from Minnesota than when I was home. I never thought of many downsides when I was traveling. Why then was I such a conservative person back in Glenwood? It was as if my regular hometown life dulled my senses. Yet, why was I blaming my community. I'd created my own routine and my own comfort level. I was the one who was allowing the dullness of my rural life preventing me from taking on more meaningful risks.

Chapter 5

That weekend I continued to be in a very contemplative mood. Saturday I caught up on some office work while it rained outside. A few fellows dropped by to warm themselves by my wood burning stove. My chief of police friend was one of them. He seemed to want to talk about something quite important to him, but we were interrupted by Mayor Good who wanted to converse about some town improvement ideas.

I ended up Saturday night sitting by that log burning stove paging through the many magazines I kept on hand. I repeatedly thought back to the two men I saw the previous evening. I recalled another statement I'd heard one of them say, something about "using the money instead of letting it remain under the mattress gathering dust."

I was very reflective that night. Loni D'Annelli and the life he'd created for himself even came into my thoughts. Here was a man who took risks every day. He'd gambled and won in his quest to obligate an entire town to him. But, he'd done it with some balance. He'd given financial support and he offered suggestions to help the community, including the proposal of the popular ten-day June festival. Only time would tell how long the dividends would roll in for both the town and the Chicago gangster. But, until his illegal businesses were closed down he was making a small mint out at Chippewa Lodge...and the town was prospering along the way.

Then again I considered what truly was his risk? If the law ever closed in on him, I had the feeling he'd already covered himself very effectively. How else had he avoided conviction back in Chicago? He had practically the entire town involved with him in his latest venture. Didn't he have the largest church in town as the cover for his gambling business? And, when and if he did get closed down, I guessed he'd only re-start the same action at some other location as soon as possible.

Somewhere through all my thinking that night I came upon a question that would haunt me for the next week. With the types of miscreants at the Lodge, when he did have to travel back to Chicago, wasn't he concerned about the safety of his illegal profits and working capital. That money had to be stored or hidden somewhere and the place was likely at Chippewa Lodge. For a number of reasons he certainly wouldn't use a bank. For one he wouldn't want anyone but himself to know his net profits. Secondly and even more importantly, banks were closing down faster than the shades could be pulled on their windows. And, he likely wouldn't load up his large 1928 Cabriolet with huge amounts of cash for his long drive back to Chicago. Yet, if he didn't, what were the guarantees his profits would still be where he'd left them upon his next trip to Lake Minnewaska?

I recall to this day how an idea hit me so abruptly...that Loni D'Annelli's money was vulnerable. I was thinking so intensely while sitting by that warm stove that my stockings actually started smoking. I'd gotten my feet too close to the burning wood. Jumping out of my chair, my empty coffee cup fell to the floor. It bounced causing a slight echo from the empty private storage chamber below my office.

It was like a lightning bolt. There I was managing a business where grain was stored...at least until the grain was sold...and I had a vacant storage area under the floor of my mill office. I hadn't been in the musty basement below my office in years. The trap door was right below the dusty rug where my desk was located.

I had no clue the amount of capital D'Annelli had, but I figured there had to be a substantial amount of cash to sustain a year round gambling operation. Visualizing the dank, dark interior of the basement storage area, I knew it had size and certainly it had privacy. Most importantly, no one but me even knew there was a basement below my office.

It seemed to me I had an answer to a problem D'Annelli might not realize he had. A plan began to bloom in my newly inspired mind that went far, far beyond just offering D'Annelli the most confidential storage area in the entire town. There would be no risk on my part; it was just a nice gesture.

Another notion, however, was brewing that was not yet clear. It was a risk of unconscionable consequences, but one that could have an upside depending on how far I might want to take my idea. It was exhilarating. In fact, I was kind of flabbergasted how my mind even allowed me to consider such an outlandish thought.

I sat there late into the night throwing more wood into that stove twice more before going home. The entire plan seemed to unfold so neatly, as if I was carefully unwrapping a present.

I had earned the trust and the respect of Loni D'Annelli since taking over the Calcutta and managing the entire ten-day festival. If I could leverage that trust and somehow drop a hint to Loni that I had a very secretive storage area underneath the floor of my office at the mill, the statement might just strike a chord with him. Whatever cash and goods he was trying to keep safe at Chippewa Lodge, the mill basement could offer the safest place yet for storage. He might accept my offer as well since I knew he believed I was generally naïve about his general business practices out at the resort. He would have to think my suggestion would be offered in the most innocent way.

If that long shot could happen and he chose to use the mill basement to safeguard his profits, the second part of my preposterous idea could take place depending on my willingness to take an even more outrageous gamble. Funny how I thought this next part of the idea was more an opportunity than a risk.

From my vantage point, I saw no one including D'Annelli capable of maintaining an accurate accounting of his revenues. I surmised there was no recorded balance of what had to be an impressive amount of cash. After all, he needed cash to support a very lucrative and solvent gambling operation. Another crucial factor...Mr. D'Annelli had some rather reckless spending habits.

If I was right, D'Annelli had no concept of the total worth of whatever cash he had from his businesses. He had the mind of a promoter and a salesman, not that of an accountant.

If he used the space like I was thinking, I wanted to believe there would be a vault full of cash right under my mill desk. Then, if that was the case, I could decide if I wanted to move forward with something truly unconscionable.

In my favor I dealt in a business where commodity profits or losses were made in short periods of time. As part of my mill business responsibilities, I had gained both contacts and worthwhile knowledge in how to invest in the commodity futures market. It was highly unregulated and with my contacts in Minneapolis and even Chicago, I had certain accesses to what today might be called 'insider' information. Also with the market way down since the stock market crash, there were some possible buys of securities if I had the capital and willingness to do that kind of investing as well.

Up to that point my commodity investing in the previous years had been limited to only $10 or $20 investments at a time; no one could ever make money of any consequence with that level of investing. I just had the problem that my knowledge exceeded my meager personal 'fortune'. The possibilities with more money to invest were intoxicating

In the next few days there were hundreds of thoughts rushing through my brain. What if I actually got him to use the mill basement as his own money vault? I kept picturing a lot of unused, unrecorded money waiting to be used for my potential gain. Would I chicken out?

As it turned out the real problem I faced was a moral issue. Stealing was stealing…whether I was pilfering illegally gained money or not. Gradually a phrase came into mind that took the sting out of the word 'steal'. I rationalized that I was only taking out a 'loan' from the money Loni might store in the mill basement. I would be 'borrowing' in order to make some short-term investments. I'd keep my profits and return the borrowed sums. By that procedure I was not stealing. Oddly, throughout these thought processes, I never truly considered I'd be putting my life in jeopardy.

Coincidentally, that next week Loni D'Annelli was to be back in town to meet with the First Presbyterian Church men's club committee and hash out the details for managing the next summer's charity golf tournament and Calcutta for June 1930. D'Annelli continued to amaze me how he could play the legitimate businessman role to keep local businessmen and church leaders in Glenwood on his bandwagon. Even more astounding was how this one man could keep these same people mostly clueless about his activities at the resort. Certainly some of my fellow churchmen had to know something about D'Annelli's mob connections just from newspaper reports and even local knowledge about how Big Bud Bunsen was also dallying in illegal booze from Winnipeg, Manitoba.

Yet, no one seemed to care about the Chicago man's history. They were more concerned about keeping the rig afloat that D'Annelli had brought to their town. Of course, by the time of that early November meeting, even if I had been, I no longer felt predisposed to blow the whistle on D'Annelli's operation. It was in my best interest given this bizarre scheme I was concocting to do everything to keep his illegal businesses flourishing.

When the meeting at the church began, I noticed Loni was not his normal socially active self. He was more fidgety, even intense. My inclination he had some bad news to share with our Presbyterian men's club turned out to be accurate. While we were expecting Loni to perfunctorily contract with the men's club to manage the event once again for the 10 percent stipend off the total dollars bet in the Calcutta, that bonanza would be coming to an end.

Pastor Olson was running the meeting and gave the floor to Loni. The Chicago man stood up tall looking as imperious as ever and began talking about some changes that had to take place in the following June event. He used the crash of Wall Street as a method of gaining some sympathy. The guy was a magician.

He lamented that the 'crash' was affecting all of his charity events...even the ones in Chicago. The boys in my club were commiserating with Loni before he had even dropped the bomb on us. Loni explained he no longer could afford to pay the 10 percent of gross weekend gambling bets that he had paid previously for our handling of the charity golf tournament and the Calcutta. In fact, he stated that he was going to have to put the management fee for our group at 3 percent. If we didn't want to work for that stipend then he'd have to put the management of the Calcutta out for bid among other church or civic groups.

I had to admit it. It was a brilliant move on Loni's part to save the exorbitant fee he had been paying my church group. But now he was established. There was no reason to pay such a high fee. He must have also felt he no longer needed our church affiliation to hide his illegal doings. He could do that under the auspices of any church group in town...and for far less money.

There was silence in the room as Loni asked me how much the men's club cleared last year with the 10 percent bonus he paid us. I told him that we netted over $15,000 adding that the money was earmarked not just for the church, but for further improvements in City Park as well as paying for a new addition onto the local school.

While appearing pleased how we put the proceeds to good causes, he was masterful the way he kept easing into his obvious desire to lower his payment to the club without creating ill will. He again inquired, "Henry, if the Calcutta didn't exist, what money would your men's club probably have made these last couple years?"

Knowing the financial history of the men's club, I went along with his game. I replied, "In the year before the first Calcutta, we had left over revenue of just over $179 after donating $300 to our steeple repair fund…that's not counting the free left-over food we all consumed after the bake sales we held." The entire group couldn't help but chuckle over that ludicrous comment.

He responded simply that he was pleased he was able to contribute so much to our church projects. Then he theatrically shook his head and shrugged his shoulders as if giving in to the fact that he had no choice. The economic downturn and the crash on Wall Street had tragically subdued him.

I almost laughed out loud. He was making more money than the Denver Mint with his year round gambling operation and booze running. I just sat there marveling at this gangster's moxie. If his comments had been a year before or even a month before, I would have been troubled. But, at that evening church meeting, my aims had completely changed. As far as I was concerned, the D'Annelli era in Glenwood was on its inevitable downward cycle. It was just a question of time before his group would be pulling out of Glenwood. I only hoped the dream would last for a while longer for my own purposes.

I believe he was expecting Pastor Olson and me to react very angrily in asking our group to work for far less money. This was where I began my own maneuver against our friend from Chicago.

Pastor Olson was nervously looking at me as to how we should respond. Without looking at Olson and not changing the expression on my face, I stood up and looked at D'Annelli saying, "Loni, I understand your need to cut expenses in these difficult times. To help you out our men's club would be willing to continue the management of the tournament and the Calcutta by reducing our fee to a 5% override." I added that he would of course maintain my services as the accountant for the Calcutta.

I then sat down saying no more. I had offered what appeared to be a major concession, but I had not come down as far as D'Annelli had hoped to reach. He sat there and stared at me quizzically. The men's club members and Pastor Olson glanced back and forth between Loni and me. They knew some kind of match was taking place and didn't want to interrupt the competition.

Finally Loni blinked. He knew he'd been outfoxed on that particular night. He looked around the room and then at me more intently. He'd still done a fair night's work saving 50% of that exorbitant fee he'd been paying us. He'd neither won nor lost. The important thing was that he had the cover of a highly reputable church continuing for another year…and the men's club still had a huge fee for handling the tournament and Calcutta.

He then smiled and reached that meat hook of a right hand over the table to shake my hand. I could see a new look of respect in his eyes. For the first time I sensed there might be a possibility to even propose my storage idea with the man privately…maybe even that very night. I felt my heart beating faster in anticipation…a feeling I hadn't experienced very often in my lifetime. I was more than ready to take a risk.

Big Bud Bunsen, who had wet his pants during our first meeting with Loni two years before, began to wake up with the movement of people and the smell of food tantalizing his nostrils. He looked down and checked the condition of his pants before standing up. They were dry. He was ready to eat. With Pastor Olson adjourning the meeting, food was already prepared by some wives back in the kitchen. Men's club members got out of the way of Big Bud for fear of being trampled.

Loni D'Annelli wandered over to me with an amused look. He had seen a side of me that hadn't existed in previous meetings or conversations with him. I could see he was impressed. That new regard was the impact I was hoping to gain. There was now a chance to extend my little game. If there ever was an opportunity to reel Mr. Loni D'Annelli into my own little trap, it was that moment.

As my fellow church men's club members surrounded the buffet table, I figured he was going to make some quip about how the church would still be making some very good money. That no longer was even in my thoughts. I had my own selfish plan to introduce to him.

I said to him, "Loni, we don't have to talk here, but I was going to make a couple suggestions about the Calcutta. You interested?"

What could the guy do but nod his head. He knew I had to have some hint that things were not all they appeared with his group out at Chippewa Lodge. I had to be very careful how I phased what I was about to say, but my confidence was up. I was highly motivated to continue to outfox the fox.

Still eyeing me favorably, he replied, "Sure, Henry, what's up?"

My chance had arrived. I could sense the next few minutes could radically impact my life. I was surprised how calm I was. I leaned toward the large man and in a very low tone started my pitch. "Loni, I'm glad we could reach agreement. I've been meaning to talk to you about lowering our management fee in fairness to you anyway for all you're doing for this community. However, I'm also concerned about Chippewa Lodge being the primary place housing the flow of Calcutta wagers our group takes in during that week before the charity tournament. These are difficult days; there are some desperate people who could seek out those gambling proceeds. You ever think of how vulnerable that money is?"

D'Annelli just stared at me intently as I continued. "Maybe you feel confident when I give you the money being bet each day, but I have wondered if the Lodge is the best place to store it."

I didn't say anything about the type of people who were guests at the Lodge. I just let his mind digest what I was inferring. He remained quiet but was listening intently. That was when I introduced my offer. I couldn't believe I had gotten that far that fast with my hair-brained scheme to a well-known underworld figure. He could make me into fish bait if he thought I might be pulling something.

I nonetheless trudged ahead and whispered, "I make this offer as another gesture of friendship....let's say, between the town and you. You might want to take advantage of a very confidential storage area under the main floor of the mill's offices. It is used for nothing and no one knows about it except me. I'm thinking you need a place to keep things like the cash being bet. The Glenwood Feed & Grain Mill is set up for storage and safekeeping. The only entrance to that private storage area is a door on the floor covered by a rug under my desk. As far as I'm concerned, the space is yours if you'd like it. I know it would greatly relieve me personally when I see the amount of money being wagered...and I don't want anything to interrupt our association with you and the charity golf tournament."

There was silence for only a moment before he incredibly asked, "How do I know the place is really safe?"

My mind shouted at me, "My God...I've got the man on the hook!

I had rehearsed many of my responses. This was one question I was prepared. I replied, "Well, Loni, not many people are inclined to break into a mill to steal stored grain. How would anyone know if a mill was storing anything else?"

I saw his head moving up and down. Then I added the real clincher. "It's an unused, unknown sub-ground room. I have no use for it. If you want it, I'll give you a key to my office so you have access to that basement at any time."

Then to lighten the moment I kidded, "I'd just ask you not to pocket any of my grain."

It was a joke but I was immediately sorry I'd said it. I thought I'd blown my supposed innocence about his world out at the Lodge.

As it turned out, it didn't matter that he hardly chuckled. His silence made me realize I might have struck more of a cord than I thought possible. He knew what kinds of people were enjoying sanctuary out at the Lodge. Their minds worked in more devious ways. Some would have to take notice D'Annelli was operating some very profitable businesses at the resort. They could easily take interest in the whereabouts of his cash reserves as well.

Before that church meeting ended, things all came together very rapidly. D'Annelli said he'd like to come over to the mill and see this basement area the next morning.

He was there before I'd even brewed the coffee and started up the wood burning stove. We wasted no time. Pushing my desk aside and rolling up the rung, we both raised the floor door to the stairs that led down to a musty smelling room. It was windowless with a dirt floor and cement walls. I could see the satisfaction on his face. An intrusion would be difficult.

Loni didn't hesitate. He said to me, "Henry, it's a good space....of course for just the reason you gave....that is, maintaining the safety of the Calcutta gambling funds. But, maybe I'd like to rent this space year round for some other things...you know...for safe keeping."

At that point I had him. I told him, "Loni, they'll be no rent. It's as much for the church's good that I want you to have this secretive space. You'll have absolutely safety for whatever you put in this basement."

He grinned. I almost felt badly for making such an unequivocal and grievous lie.

He headed back up the stairs not yet affirming that he wanted the space. Then he helped himself to some of my brewing coffee, turned towards me and asked for a key to my office as I'd promised him.

He added, "I'm going to have some of my 'boys'... rather business associates... from the Lodge come down late tonight to place some other things I'd like stored in that basement. I believe if they do it late at night, their actions will draw little attention."

With that he gave me a nod and shook my hand. I gave him a key and the deal was done. When he walked out of the door of the office, I just sat back in my chair not believing what had just happened. I had done it. What particularly thrilled me was that he had no qualms about trusting me. At that moment I realized I was about to take on a risk that few people would ever have the guts, know-how, and foolhardiness to be involved. I knew in a couple days I'd be privy to more of the complete picture of Loni D'Annelli's profits and worth than any one might deem possible.

The funny thing was that I still felt no pressure or fear. I hadn't done anything reckless or problematic as yet. If I went further along with my ultimate idea...undoubtedly I'd feel the gravity of my actions.

For the next couple days, I paid no heed to the basement storage area. I knew some of Loni's boys had been in my office the previous nights. It was fairly obvious. Things had fallen on my desk. The rug and desk were not placed down as I'd left them.

Loni stopped a few days later and thanked me for the space before making his return to Chicago. Winter was approaching and I knew he'd not be in the area that often until February or March. In the meantime he had some of his boys remaining at the Lodge to monitor the businesses and certainly to check on the mill basement.

By the smile on his face he looked relieved and very pleased. He had an ideal, confidential storage area controlled by a local citizen who had a history of being honorable and dependable.

Those following days I was yearning to investigate that basement. I recall choosing the upcoming Sunday morning...very early...about

5:00 AM….to make my first exploration into that basement. I wanted no interruptions. I decided to walk the six blocks to the mill. I wanted no one to recognize my car in the mill parking lot.

It was miserably cold when I arrived that November morning at the mill. I opened the back door and kept the lights off. Knowing my office area, the dark was no concern. Pushing the desk and rug aside, I opened the floor door to the same musty smell. I carefully descended the stairs pulling the floor door shut behind me.

Then I turned on my flashlight. At first my eyes didn't focus. When they finally did, I just sat back down on the steps and stared. I was dumbfounded. I'll bet I didn't move for five minutes. Taking in the vast inventory was spellbinding. To my right on the dirt floor was the oddest assortment of art, statues and old furniture. They obviously had some kind of worth, but I had little interest. It was the currency I hoped he was storing that held my curiosity.

I panned my eyes toward the back of the storage room and focused on what looked like the supply room of a shoe store. Buster Brown shoe boxes were on shelves from floor to ceiling. There had to be a couple hundred of them. I had an idea the shoeboxes contained something besides shoes.

Grabbing one and opening the top, I was so very correct. I actually gulped. Within the box were stacks of twenty dollar bills either bound by rubber band or by a paper strips. I was immediately mesmerized. I couldn't help but count the approximate number of bills in one of five stacks in the shoebox. I determined there were about fifty 'twenty dollar' bills in each stack. It didn't take a genius to realize I was holding a shoebox that contained $5000!

My eyes then gazed again respectfully at the astonishing number of shoeboxes heaped against the wall. My jaw slackened as I counted the shoeboxes on each shelf. I had to sit back down on the steps to calm down as I continued my calculations based on each shoebox containing $5000.

I then shined my flashlight on the opposite wall where more Buster Brown shoeboxes were located. These boxes were much more neatly stacked. I went over and took one of those boxes and opened it. Again, there were piles of currency even more perfectly stacked. The stacks were of absolutely brand new bills. There were primarily ten and twenty dollar bills, but there were some fifty dollar stacks as well.

Even in my astonishment, I was conscious enough to realize something was strange with these bills. They were so new...as if they were straight off the presses. I had taken a tour of the U.S Treasury building in one of my trips out east and had seen uncut sheets of bills. Whether it was the feel of the paper or just the realization that the contents in that box were too pure, the thought did occur to me that the neatly stacked bills might not be authentic. I snickered to myself that I'd just uncovered yet another on the list of illicit dealings by the town friend, Mr. Loni D'Annelli. The sight of the probable counterfeit money didn't faze me other than to make damn certain I knew which shoeboxes contained the genuine money.

It could have been fifty degrees in that basement, but I found myself sweating profusely...and my mind swimming in that perspiration. There now was the possibility of taking on the next phase of my plan which up to that minute had seemed rather preposterous. Suddenly the next step...the most unbelievable and riskiest one...now seemed quite possible. Actually 'borrowing' some of Loni's capital was now more than just a passing fancy, especially given the haphazard way the shoeboxes full of money were literally thrown on the many temporary shelves. The reality of what I could do with this money was abruptly staring me right in the face. I understood the tendencies for seasonal inventory and variances on pricing of corn, oats, barley, soybeans, etc. I had witnessed the dramatic effects of weather catastrophes on pricing in the national and international markets. All I had ever needed was enough money to take advantage of my knowledge and my insider trading contacts and information. And now my dream of having access to a vault of cash was being presented to me on practically a silver platter....or at least within a bunch of Buster Brown shoeboxes.

My heart was racing as I climbed up the ladder stairs and re-opened the floor door. I rolled the rug back over the floor door and pulled the desk back over the rug. It was at that moment I went to the floor as if I'd been shot. There was movement and a flash of light by the front door. In the early morning darkness there was someone moving outside along the windows to my office. The panic that hit me almost froze my heart. I crawled over to some empty grain bags by my wood burning stove. I wrapped myself in a couple of them trying not to sneeze with the grain and floor dust imbedded in the twine. The outside flashlight was now shining all over the inside of the office.

Another panicky thought crossed my mind. Did I remember to lock the back door after I had entered? When the flashlight stopped shining on the office interior, I crawled toward the back door without pausing for a breath. I turned the lock on the back door and fell back among the feed grain bags just as a hand tried to open the back door while shining the light again into the office. I had locked it in the nick of time.

I lay back against the wall rolling my eyes as the person holding the flashlight finally moved on. I then inched toward the front windows hoping to see the person walking out to the front parking lot. And there he was....Glenwood's Chief of Police...my friend...simply doing his duty and making the early morning rounds. I was proud of him for doing his job, but didn't appreciate him taking a few years off my life with the strain he'd just caused my heart. I would have had quite the explanation to fabricate if he'd spotted me lying among those feedbags at such a ridiculous early morning hour on a Sunday.

Waiting ten minutes in that cold office, I finally snuck out the back door carefully locking it behind me. The frigid morning air hit my perspiring face like a cold shower. Steam was rolling off my skin. My shirt inside my coat was drenched. It was also getting a bit lighter with impending dawn as I trotted down some back streets before finally arriving back at my home. I had not run like that in years. My heart felt like it was in my mouth.

When I slipped through the back door of my house, my adrenalin was pumping so hard, I had difficulty catching my breath. I jumped in my small shower with the tepid water. Now chilled, I wrapped myself in my bed covers until the aching cold finally subsided. It probably helped that my mind was so warm from not settling down. I finally did fall into a deep sleep and didn't wake up until late morning. I even missed the First Presbyterian worship service. Of course I'd missed it most of the time for lesser reasons than sleep. Rolling over I went back to sleep awaking after lunch more determined than ever to use some of that D'Annelli money.

It was November, 1929, just weeks after the Wall Street crash that Loni D'Annelli had taken advantage of my offer. He had the confidence in that basement or in me to confidentially store his cash reserve and various other personal items in the mill basement. I took the next step as if I had no choice. I was jumping nose first into the riskiest decision I likely would ever make again. I guess it helped that each step in the process had moved along so smoothly and logically. There had been no obstacles. Even what appeared to be the complete disorganization of D'Annelli's assets in the basement storage area spurred me to take action.

In the beginning I was only contemplating loans of $5000. I had very undefined aims of what I wished to make in my scheme. My primary goal was just to test out my theory. My plan was to deal in some quick short-term investments on the commodity market…and then eventually re-invest my profits into more substantial long-term investments, preferably in land and resort properties.

I finally set my target to make something in excess of $10,000 by the spring of 1930. With my commodity broker friends in Minneapolis plus my own judgment and experience, I felt real anticipation. I didn't intend on losing money, but if it happened, I doubted D'Annelli or his boys would even realize the loss…within reason that is.

During those last five weeks of 1929 I took out my first interest free loan from the cash reserves in that basement. I made one $5000 investment in corn and later that week another in wheat. It was more speculative than I preferred, but it was a good test. Maybe it was dumb luck, but I made money immediately. When I sold those futures a week later for a nice profit, I forced myself to return what I had 'borrowed' back into Loni's shoeboxes. In less than two weeks I had made more than my yearly salary at the mill.

With my initial success, I was conscious of not letting myself get out of control. I talked to those broker friends in the commodity exchange in Minneapolis multiple times a day. This was not like rolling dice as it would be for most investors. I was playing the game with their information and my own experience. My profits made me think bigger. The next week I increased my 'borrowed' amounts to $10,000 and later that week another $20,000 just to test my guile. I wasn't drunk with success but I was on a high.

It was an incredible feeling of unbridled freedom. Still, I knew that if I'd lost any large sums of money from those D'Annelli's cash reserves, then my wild investing would finally be curtailed. As it worked out, I never had to face that question. I just continued making leveraged investments that paid off.

With my own investment profits, I also leveraged more bets in the stock market. The crash had dropped some stocks so low as to be veritable giveaways when you considered the true value of companies like General Electric and Westinghouse. I was making money with those investments as well...to the point that I was afraid I might get careless.

It was during the middle of 1930 when I was borrowing money well in access of $50,000 that I finally slowed down until I saw more return on my longer term investments. I continued to study and take advantage of my sources about farm and commodity prices. I also took into account weather conditions in various parts of the country and needs with European countries pertaining to food, oil, and steel production.

There were still times I felt like I was rolling the dice, but I was in a frame of mind that I didn't care. I had the brashness to believe I could make up for any losses. So, in effect, the portion of Loni D'Annelli's gambling profits that I borrowed were being 're-gambled' by me.

Though parlaying tens of thousands of dollars of loans from D'Annelli funds into impressive profits, I still maintained my determination to pay back the principle I'd borrowed as soon as possible. It helped me maintain some kind of moral code and kept me from getting too insensitive and greedy. It also got to be comical. Each time I paid back Loni's 'bank', I'd take out another loan, usually larger, within a couple days.

I eventually deposited some but not all my profits into a couple large Twin Cities banks under a corporate name called Triple H Development, Inc. At the time I thought the name more humorous, even shrewdly confidential. As time went on it did worry me that someone might figure the initials for 'Honest Henry Hanson', but that label was so indigenous and local to my years in Glenwood, that I didn't think the name would ever raise eyebrows. To this day, it really hasn't.

It was in the late spring of 1930, I had built up a cash reserve enough to make serious bids on some land and resort properties. It was then I began realizing there simply was not enough time in the day or night for me to maintain my schedule. I was trying to run the feed & grain mill, keep up my personal commodity investment interests, develop my land and development business and do this all while being involved in the community. I was gone so much it was important that I maintain that latter activity if for no other reason that to not raise any local eyebrows as to why I was out of town most weekends.

Just after the 1930 June festival I had made an important decision. I needed an attorney regarding my real estate purchases. I'd been checking out the background and business acumen of that attorney from Alexandria, Charlie Davis. I'd seen Davis drinking with his buddies at that speakeasy in Alexandria. I saw him having coffee a few times at the Glenwood Café. Everything I heard about him was positive.

In representing me it was important that I find someone who would be willing to work within some strict guidelines. It was as much for the lawyer's well-being as well as my own. I liked Charlie for a number of reasons and it was a bonus that he knew land and property values. When I finally made contact by telephone with him, it wasn't easy for him to accept me as a client on my terms. I told him I was choosing not to share my name until I felt comfortable in doing so. He in turn kept reminding me that our discussions would be privileged. However I held fast to the way I wanted our business relationship to be. If my plans in using Loni D'Annelli's cash reserves went haywire, I didn't want his name to be connected to mine.

He eventually very hesitantly agreed. Allowing him power of attorney on all business dealings connected to Triple H Development, Inc. and with a generous retainer fee, he finally acquiesced saying he would give my secrecy in our dealings a trial run of three months.

Charlie Davis became my lawyer with my first land purchases in the late June of that year. He was the one who set up my corporation as Triple H Development, Inc....and in a short time came to know me as Henry Granville...the name I'd chosen to be my alias once I left Glenwood.

Initially all of my contact with Charlie was by telephone or letter. He complained often about my being incognito to him. Actually, I seriously feared once he learned my actual name, background, and how I had been accumulating my personal worth, I doubted he would have continued representing me and my new company. That was the real reason for the sizeable retainer. When the day came where he learned my true identity I hoped we'd have a long enough relationship that he'd be comfortable continuing as my corporate counsel.

For more convenience Davis did set up a corporate bank account with one of his trusted friends, Glen Rutherford, the president of a local bank in Sauk Centre. Mr. Rutherford had to accept me as his new client on the same basis as Charlie did. He would not meet me or come to know me. The Triple H Development, Inc. account would be accessible only by Charlie and me.

With my profits, I bought a prime lakeside resort in the Brainerd area. The owners were struggling financially. I took over the property before it went into foreclosure. I considered its location on Lake Mille Lac, a well-known Minnesota vacation area, as very favorable. Though economic conditions were bad, there were still some people looking for places close enough to the Twin Cities where they could relax and escape from the bustle of the city for a weekend. With me as the silent owner, Charlie Davis hired a business friend who was out of work to temporarily manage the property.

In the remaining months of 1930, I was very aggressive with my investing. The basement storage area was like a bottomless pit with my access to D'Annelli's funds. Having not run into one problem siphoning the cash, my loan amount exceeded $80,000. It was not to say that my entire investment year was stress free. It did take quite a toll on my blood pressure and stomach lining. There were too many nights I'd lie in bed not believing what I was doing. Borrowing money from a Chicago mobster without his knowing it…it was beyond just taking a risk. It was suicidal. But, I didn't stop.

A further worry was my belief that D'Annelli's operation was going to be found out at any time. Whether he was arrested or he simply pulled out his team at Chippewa Lodge, I was certain he'd transfer his money and stolen goods he was storing in the mill basement within a short period of time. I might not get the chance to pay back the loan amounts because I had the funds fully invested. It would be then I would find out if he truly had any idea how much cash he had stored in that mill basement. I kept betting he didn't.

I became intoxicated with my success. I had gained a capital and investment reserve that made it possible for another resort purchase on White Bear Lake near St. Paul at the close of the summer in 1930. My commodity investments had some losses that autumn, but my overall returns were still highly impressive.

Admittedly, those days my feed & grain mill job was about the last thing on my mind. But, I had help. That local man, my good friend, John Bailey, would step in when I was gone. He just always seemed to be there for me...as if he was part of my little financial conspiracy. I still don't know why he didn't ask me where I was going or what I was doing on those many, many weekends when I left early on Friday for the weekend. He knew I wasn't long for Glenwood. My guess was that he thought I was looking for other job opportunities in the Twin Cities.... and maybe sewing some wild oats as well.

By that October I was virtually gone every weekend. After my lake resort purchases, I was often staying a night or two just watching how my property was being run. To the staff I was just a traveling salesman. Most weekends I was also socializing with my commodity exchange business friends in Minneapolis. It was still imperative I remained close to them. After a few drinks I was always amazed what I gained from their loose talk about various impacts on commodity trading. With a post office box set up for Triple H Development, Inc. in Minneapolis, I had private firms sending me information about available commercial properties. The state of Minnesota sent me bankruptcy property notices. I also received estate sale announcements. I thought often how opportunities were there as long as a person had the money.

By the end of that year, it became obvious I would have to give up my job at the mill. It was costing me time and money maintaining that job. Conversely, though, working at the mill gave me access to D'Annelli's interest free cash. It was quite a unique problem to have.

Through that year I also maintained my obligation as financial officer of the First Presbyterian Church and the church's men's club. I even kept my chairmanship of Glenwood's ten-day festival, although that didn't take time until after the first of the year. I wish I could say I was being totally civic-minded. I stayed in those volunteer jobs in order to stay as close to the goings on of D'Annelli's operation as I could.

At the start of 1931 it became more obvious than ever how I could be seen as guilty for collaborating with Loni D'Annelli by the law. As much as I hated to think about it, my only true hope of exonerating myself was not to wait but actually cause the downfall of the D'Annelli operation. And, whenever the time was for the state police or Federal authorities to raid Chippewa Lodge, I wanted to be far away from Glenwood."

Granville leaned back in his chair and took another deep puff from his thin cigar. He glanced at both Lill and Lawton wondering their thoughts. Still after so many years he wondered if Lill ever found his behavior or his character questionable during those final years in Glenwood. She'd heard much of his background story, but not all.

He gazed at his young scribe hoping he had not already reached some disappointing conclusions after only one interview session. He was banking on the expectation that Lawton was interested in details about his family and that would be enough to sustain the young man's attention.

Having gone further in his story than he'd intended that first night, he suddenly sat up and smiled. "Let's stop here for the evening. We have plenty of time to get into more detail. Since I have to travel in the upcoming week, how would it be that we schedule an hour or two together tomorrow evening. Following these two interviews, Matt, you'll have more than enough notes to collate and edit before I return.

Once the older man decided to rest his voice, the three of them engaged in conversation regarding the old city and some history of South Carolina. Lawton was a bit embarrassed with his lack of historical familiarity with the city. When Granville related some information about the 'siege at Charleston' during the War Between the States, Lawton raised his hands in surrender saying, "Honestly, I've got a lot to learn. I'm a product of a Midwestern education. The north won the Civil War and South Carolina started it. I hate to be that blunt, but that was how I was educated. Frankly I learned only this afternoon how rich this city's history was going back to almost two hundred years before our Civil War."

Looking at Lill, Granville's eyes shined. "Well, in that light, I believe you'll be delighted to meet a dear friend of ours...someone who I'd like to be part of these interview sessions and a person I want you to get to know. His name is Ashley Cooper. Yes, that's right...Ashley Cooper. He'll claim the two rivers flowing into Charleston Bay were named after him. I've always kidded him that given his age and health, he was probably right. Actually he's a bit younger than those two rivers, but I'll let him explain his convenient name when he meets you.

He's also an important member of our staff at the hotel and a tremendous source for local connections. So, until we meet tomorrow night, I hope you can spend more time Sunday afternoon exploring this fine city."

With that the evening ended. Lawton now had some idea the quagmire Henry Hanson had gotten himself into so many years ago. That it might still be a dilemma after all the years meant there was much more to the story.

Before departing the hotel, Henry and Lill informed Lawton about the East Bay Street Hotel Sunday noon buffet the next day. They suggested he be in attendance describing it as a convenient venue to meet some of the more prominent locals.

Henry began mentioning a few names expected to make an appearance. He missed Lawton's blank expression. Lill leaned over and whispered to him, "Matt, just show up around 11:00 tomorrow morning. You'll have a place reserved at our table. Don't wear a tie, but you might want to wear a sport coat."

Lawton gave her an appreciative smile. He had a feeling he'd never make any serious mistakes while at the East Bay Street Hotel as long as he stayed close to Lill and followed her words of advice.

He would find out later that the Sunday buffet had been part of the hotel schedule since the hotel opened back in the 1930's. It was as much a ritual as were the many church services that preceded the luncheon. It was an expedient gathering where locals interested in talking with politicians or top business heads in Charleston could talk face to face.

In the cooler months, the brunch was changed to a Saturday evening 'tea' either in the lobby or out on the spacious patio overlooking Charleston Harbor depending on the temperature. Both occasions were very popular.

With the evening still relatively young, especially for someone of Lawton's age, he decided to take a stroll down East Bay Street to visit one of the bars he'd wandered by earlier that afternoon. Bellying up to the bar, he ordered a beer. As much as he liked the Charleston ice tea, he needed something that tasted like back home. He was thankful he could get a Pabst Blue Ribbon in South Carolina.

As he sipped the brew, he again had that same feeling as he had during his afternoon walk. He felt uncomfortable…as if being watched. He didn't care, but he couldn't remember ever having that kind of feeling in his life. It was uncomfortable enough that he abruptly turned around from his bar stool and made a quick snapshot of everyone in the bar area who might be looking his way. He focused on one man who looked at him strangely. That man within the next few seconds threw some money on the table and left the bar. As he did, he stared awkwardly at Lawton as if wondering why this sneering person at the bar was looking at him.

Lawton scoffed realizing he'd probably scared the poor man away. Another patron looked his way and stared back. Lawton momentarily sized the man up as if deciding whether he could win a fight with the man. The fellow was twice his age and sweating profusely from the heat as well as carrying way too much weight. Lawton decided if there was a confrontation, he could certainly run faster than the beer-bellied slob.

His discomfort subsiding, he turned around and set his eyes on the attractive waitress serving him. He liked her sexy southern accent. Unfortunately, in their short spurts of conversation as she served drinks, he could tell she distrusted him. He was sure his northern accent discomfited her. It grew tiring to hear her joke about the funny way he talked. He sensed it would take a couple more trips to the bar to break down her defenses and talk about something besides his being from the north.

After two beers and not interested in the fights on the lone television on the shelf behind the bar, he decided to end his first day in Charleston. With one final look at the waitress's legs, he threw some money on the bar for the beer and another couple dollars on her tray as he said farewell to the young lady. She smiled but still didn't show any interest.

Arriving back at his hotel suite that Saturday night, Lawton was tired. It had been a big day since leaving Minneapolis that morning. He'd met Henry Hanson…or Granville…as was the now more preferred last name. Not ready to go to sleep, he sat out on his 8th floor deck taking in the activity on the harbor. Even at that late hour, small motorboats were whizzing by out on the water. He also watched a large merchant ship entering the harbor. It looked like a multi-storied hotel built out on the water. Ten minutes later it still looked like it hadn't moved in the direction of the docking station.

In less than twelve hours since arriving in Charleston, Lawton had become entwined in something unexplainable yet very intriguing. He had every desire to continue the ride.

He sat there on the deck for another hour relaxing and not really wanting to sleep. Drowsiness finally took over as he jerked awake a couple times barely able to keep upright on his chair. Taking one last breath of the now cooler Charleston evening, he slipped back into his suite. Flopping on the bed without removing his clothing, he wouldn't move until the next morning.

Chapter 6

The man Lawton didn't see staring at him that Saturday night was off in the corner of the bar watching the reflection of the young man in a mirror. He memorized every move of the new guest staying at the East Bay Street Hotel. He sought anything to decipher who this new player in the game might be from the way he swigged his beer to the way he smiled and made small talk to one of the pretty waitresses.

The older man in that corner booth was dumbstruck. He'd seen that face...or something resembling it...sometime in his past. He couldn't imagine where, but he'd seen it just as sure as the sun rose in the morning. It might have been years before, but his memory wasn't sharp enough to remember.

The young man looked like he was barely out of college. In the older man's daily surveillance of the hotel, he'd seen this young kid arrive earlier that afternoon. He'd followed the visitor when he went out for a walk. He wondered what was so special about this individual considering he'd had dinner with Henry Hanson Granville and Lill Hamilton that evening. Darrell O'Donnell shook his head exasperated that someone new might have been brought in to find out who was blackmailing the hotel magnate and CEO of Triple H Development, Inc. Any time over the years that O'Donnell had thought about Henry Hanson his blood pressure escalated. It was Hanson who had ruined his life. O'Donnell had been an owner of a moderately successful lake resort back near Glenwood, Minnesota so many years before. But, that success story had ended...and all because of the actions of man who now called himself Henry Granville.

Now in 1960, O'Donnell was more embittered, more conniving, and more cynical as someone of his sixty years might become after years of bad luck and low grade jobs. His fortunes had looked so good when he owned Chippewa Lodge along the east shore of beautiful Lake Minnewaska. But, he'd lost everything, literally in just an hour when the authorities raided his resort on that Sunday morning, June 7, 1931.

The credit for the raid and all the arrests that day had been given to some young investigator from Minneapolis named Lindy MacPherson…a name as clear in his mind as if he'd seen her yesterday. Back then, he'd heard she was a writer for a travel magazine and she was interviewing area resort owners. He'd invited her out to his establishment thinking he'd get some free publicity. She'd seemed legitimate as he showed her around his property. Her questions were appropriate for a journalist. But, it turned out she was undercover. She was only there to spy on his property. She found what evidence she needed and called in a police raid. The result for him was ruin…and bankruptcy…and a couple years in prison.

However, O'Donnell knew the real person who had ruined his life. He was the de facto leader of the community and the one person who had to have been aware of Loni D'Annelli's operation at Chippewa Lodge. How Henry Hanson had escaped arrest and imprisonment was beyond O'Donnell's comprehension. It could only have been if Hanson had made some kind of deal with the authorities after steering MacPherson's investigation in the right direction. There had never been any doubt in O'Donnell's mind that Hanson had set up Loni D'Annelli. After all as further investigation had shown later, most of D'Annelli's illegal profits were being stored in the local feed & grain mill basement…the very business Hanson had been general manager of for ten years.

Finally, even though a host of businessmen in Glenwood had supported the guests at Chippewa Lodge with food, materials, and services, O'Donnell was the one who'd been incarcerated. While there were holes in O'Donnell's thinking, he was unwavering in his animosity towards Henry Hanson. He'd often dreamed of having the chance to destroy Hanson's life in the same way the man had done to him.

While incarcerated, he learned that Henry Hanson had disappeared without a trace. By the time O'Donnell was released from Stillwater State Prison two years after being convicted of aiding and abetting criminal activity at his resort property, he was financially ruined. He was also convinced the former Glenwood community leader was hiding out some place with enough money to be enjoying a very good life.

He'd always promised himself that if he ever got wind of where Henry Hanson was located, he would quit whatever he was doing immediately and take on his lifelong promise of ending Henry Hanson's life and career. Over the years he'd accepted his wild dream as improbable. Nonetheless, he put aside money each pay check for when that day might come. If it never did, he would at least have a small retirement fund. But, his real aim was to invest that money in a devastating blackmail scheme against his hated enemy. He was convinced Hanson would pay a large amount of money to keep O'Donnell's mouth closed.

Over the years that intention disintegrated into a dream. O'Donnell kept moving east working as a waiter until the restaurant was closed or he was let go. He knew his chances of ever finding the man he reviled were as empty as a jobless man waiting for a movie star to marry him. But, he still dreamed.

And then almost three decades later, the impossible happened. The movie star asked for his hand. It was in the summer of 1959. O'Donnell was working at his tenth restaurant in twenty-four years never having moved up from waiting on tables. He was at that time a luncheon server at the main restaurant at the Waldorf-Astoria Hotel in New York. The luncheon tips were lower than in the evening, but consistent. He went through each day with a pasted smile on his face and an obsequious tone to his voice.

His factitious facial expression and fawning voice were on automatic one day as he served a very prosperous looking gentleman wearing a white suit who talked with a slight southern drawl. The accent seemed acquired rather than natural as the man was talking with his clients at the table. To the cynical O'Donnell, he simply didn't like the wealthy looking patron. However, as O'Donnell performed his job with alacrity and routine professionalism, he found himself staring at the southern gentleman. It got so that he couldn't take his eyes off the man hosting the luncheon. There was something about the face...or the eyes...and even the mannerisms that made the waiter sense he'd seen this man before. It became so bothersome that he ambled over and studied the reservation ledger. The table was reserved under the name H. Granville. The name meant nothing to O'Donnell.

As he poured refills of coffee for the group at the table, his eyes and ears were especially sensitive to anything that might hint as to who this man in the white suit might be. Then one of the clients at the table said something that made O'Donnell almost spill the coffee pot he was holding. It was one sentence that was the giveaway and it sparked a flame of hatred that even surprised O'Donnell for its intensity. The man said simply to the host of the luncheon, "So, Henry, when do you expect to return to Charleston?"

He recognized the southern gentleman immediately. The man with the light suit and fancy cigarette holder was no more from the south than O'Donnell was. As if lightning had struck, he'd found his archenemy in the autumn of both their lives. But, time no longer mattered. From that day on, Darrell O'Donnell was possessed. He had found Henry Hanson.

It would take him until the end of that year before he was prepared to carry out his attack against his mortal enemy. O'Donnell quit his waiter job in New York and journeyed down to Charleston, South Carolina in January, 1960. He had enough savings to live comfortably for six to nine months. He expected he wouldn't need near that much time to complete his planned blackmail scheme against the man now known as Henry Granville.

Once there, O'Donnell learned everything he could about the hotel owner. His hatred was fueled with the knowledge that Granville was worth a fortune as owner and CEO of a large hotel and resort conglomerate.

O'Donnell's life had been destroyed while Hanson had been able to take a completely different path filled with good fortune and success. O'Donnell fought his first impulse to simply shoot the man. After a few days of reconnaissance following the hotel mogul, he gradually gathered his wits and focused on extortion over murder...something potentially far more profitable. What he envisioned was the chance for a lifetime income from Triple H Development, Inc. In what had become a form of madness, O'Donnell saw Hanson as being very willing to frame a partnership in exchange for silence.

Moving forward with great caution, O'Donnell assumed Hanson would likely have had to defend himself over the years from others trying to prove his true identity. Also, the man couldn't have built his corporation or maintained his masquerade without a lot of support.

Everything had moved along as O'Donnell had hoped. After getting settled at a cheap rooming house in North Charleston, he'd followed his strategy of gradually building up unease in Henry Granville before making his demands. In a series of short, menacing telephone calls and cold, ominous notes to the hotel magnate from February through March, O'Donnell had taken great satisfaction...even pleasure... in making life miserable for his hated foe. Over time he wanted to make it abundantly clear to Granville that his entire background as Henry Hanson would be made public. He wanted the hotel owner's frustration level to reach an explosive point where Granville would demand the price of silence.

When O'Donnell had finally relented in late March and declared his preference for monthly allotments paid to a Swiss account, he'd expected loud denunciations. Instead he got a jaded kind of response from the hotel owner as if the attempted extortion was just another of many business matters. Granville admitted nothing but spoke of all the paperwork and legal documents that would have to be handled if payments were to be made. The calmness had rattled O'Donnell. He didn't know if Granville was agreeing to the arrangement or not.

Then the man had hung up. O'Donnell had not had the chance to dictate the next steps or badger the businessman with more threats. He'd left it to his enemy's prerogative when their next conversation might happen.

Swearing at himself for his stupidity, O'Donnell noticed for the first time his heart beat was fluttering and his hands were shaking. He wondered if most law-breakers felt the way he did at that moment. There was no turning around. He had committed to his blackmail scheme and shared it with his victim. That made him guilty.

From the phone booth that day, O'Donnell had walked briskly into a King Street bar ordering a beer in hopes the drink would calm him down. While in prison years before, he'd listened to so many criminals describing various crimes they'd committed and where they'd eluded the law. But, why were they in prison telling their stories? Obviously they'd failed in dodging the cops at least once.

They'd made it sound so simple. In fact, O'Donnell now wondered if he could handle the pressure of being a felon. One mistake and he'd be back in the slammer probably for good. He had no other partner, only himself to depend upon.

Before finishing his second beer he'd made the decision to slow down and be even more cautious. O'Donnell had gotten the wealthy owner's attention and the man was now highly agitated. No more threatening letters were required...only a follow-up phone call to solidify the extortion payment and where the money was to be sent.

The slightly tipsy extortionist ordered his third beer and silently nodded his head as if his plan was still going smoothly. He'd maintain his periodic surveillance on the hotel so he knew when Granville would return from his business travels. Then he'd make that final telephone call and demand payment. There would be no further delays.

'Yeh,' he thought, 'that sounded like the best way to proceed.' Yet, as he left that bar he found that his hands would not stop shaking and his heartbeat never seemed to stabilize.

He would not catch Henry Granville again by telephone until the first week of April. Granville was much cooler but indicated that he understood the blackmail demands and that more time would be required to work out a procedure to route a monthly check overseas. Accepting the private bank account number from the blackmailer, the seemingly agreeable Granville claimed his travel would cause some interruptions, but he hoped his corporate financial officer would have the administrative procedures completed upon his return to Charleston. Then Granville simply hung up the phone again not giving O'Donnell a chance to show anger over the delay or voice any further threats if the check wasn't sent within the month.

While things seemed to be going in the right direction, the overweight and slow thinking O'Donnell didn't feel entirely comfortable. His confidence was gradually seeping away. He assumed he'd be strong and determined when dealing with his adversary, but the plain fact was that he knew he was in over his head. Now he was playing in the big leagues of crime...and he felt himself drowning. He never thought blackmail would be such a nerve-racking offense to conduct.

He maintained surveillance on the circled entrance to the hotel hoping to spot Granville arriving at the hotel and then timing that next phone call accordingly. He'd even found a vacant second story office in a dilapidated building across the street from the hotel to more secretly spy on Granville. Each morning and afternoon he'd sit impatiently watching the movements of staff members and guests as they strode in and out of the hotel. There was no sign of the hotel owner. That only gnawed at him more. Granville was not showing him the respect other hoodlums seemed to have had from the target of their crimes.

It was Saturday, April 9 as O'Donnell was sitting on an old orange crate in a dormer of that dilapidated office building across from the East Bay Street hotel when he observed something quite unusual. As far as he knew Granville had to be out of town. The sloppy, sweaty man was about to leave his post when he noticed someone of some apparent importance was being welcomed by the hotel staff. The individual was even being accompanied by the lady O'Donnell had come to understand as the real head of the hotel. He couldn't figure it out but the lady had obvious colored blood and that bothered him. What was Hanson doing leaving a female in charge...and she was a Negro to boot?

Springing from the side door of the hotel limousine was an individual who was oddly very young for getting such special treatment. What O'Donnell kept focusing on through his binoculars was the face of the young man. It was peculiarly familiar even though it seemed a long time since O'Donnell had seen the face. The head of the valets greeted the young man as if he'd known him for many years.

O'Donnell just sat there in his small perch biting his lip in his attempt to recall where he'd last seen this person. He began to worry. Could Hanson have sent for a private detective? Could his archenemy finally have decided to fight against the extortion attempt with a hired investigator? That could be, but why was it someone who looked as if they weren't old enough to have any worthwhile experience.

Perspiring and puzzled, O'Donnell made his way out of the back of the vacant office building concerned that his extortion attempt was seeing a new challenge. He didn't even make a call that afternoon to find out when Granville would next be in his office. O'Donnell's paranoid mind was now working overtime. He'd already been to prison once and the experience was still very clear even thirty years later. That episode could not be repeated. He knew it was essential he find out who this new player was at the East Bay Street Hotel before he felt ready to continue his quest against Hanson.

That evening as O'Donnell sat in a bar exhausted watching the 'damned kid', as he now referred to the young man. He'd followed the energetic visitor on a fast-paced stroll through much of the historic district and over to Market Street that afternoon. O'Donnell wasn't used to expending such energy. Then earlier that evening from his secret vantage point across the street from the hotel, the blackmailer observed the kid having a long dinner with Henry Hanson and that Negro woman. The three of them seemed very compatible…very close.

At the completion of the dinner O'Donnell trailed the kid to the bar thankfully just a few blocks from the hotel. He observed the young man as lonely the way he sat at the bar trying to make time with an attractive waitress. Sipping another beer in his corner booth, O'Donnell caustically snorted how the fellow was getting nowhere with the good-looking female. Somehow that pleased O'Donnell.

Finally the visitor finished his beer, looked around as if trying to find someone he knew, and then lazily exited the bar. O'Donnell didn't have the motivation to follow the kid any longer that day.

The slovenly, overstuffed novice hoodlum was getting frustrated. There had been no progress in continuing his extortion attempt with Henry Hanson since the previous week. Now someone had just arrived only that afternoon causing him to drag his feet even more. Here was a kid who wasn't even born yet when Hanson had brought down Loni D'Annelli and simultaneously ruined O'Donnell's life.

O'Donnell felt discouraged and miserable as he downed another beer at that bar. He was ready to send what information he had about Henry Hanson Granville to every major newspaper in the country on Monday just to gain some satisfaction. He wanted to feel the pleasure of inflicting pain on Granville and his organization. In the next instance, he reminded himself to stay patient. There was a lot of money at stake.

After yet another beer he limped out of the bar and shuffled over to his five year old Ford Fairlane. Big time crime was not as glamorous as he had expected it to be.

Chapter 7

Whether it was the Eastern Time Zone or he was simply exhausted from his first day in Charleston, Matt Lawton arrived at the hotel's first Sunday noon brunch that spring fifteen minutes late. He wore his navy blue sportcoat with an open necked shirt and dark tan trousers. Compared to the light colored clothing of the assembling crowd, he felt like an undertaker. He promised himself he'd spend that two hundred dollar clothing allowance the very next day.

Within minutes of his entering the throng, Lill was introducing him to some locally prominent people. The first introduction was to William Morrison, the mayor of Charleston. Just twenty minutes before, Lawton was still in bed getting the cobwebs out of his brain. Lill introduced him as part of the hotel family. The mayor seemed to understand what that meant and brightened his smile.

Morrison asked how Lawton liked what he'd seen so far of the city. All Lawton could do was nod his head and acknowledge his positive impressions of the historic district and the many antebellum homes. He didn't comment how many of the houses looked weather-beaten and in need of repair but that was what he was thinking. He also stayed mum about striking out in a conversation with a pretty bar maid at one of the local watering holes.

Lill continued making the rounds with him. Lawton met the editor of one of the local newspapers, the president of a local publishing house, the director of the Art Festival, and an owner of a sub-contracting business specializing in renovations. He doubted they'd remember him five minutes later; he knew he'd have the same problem. Nonetheless, her thoughtfulness in making him feel comfortable seemingly had no bounds.

The final introduction of that Sunday social was the close friend Henry had mentioned the night before. Although a generation older than Lawton, Ashley Cooper greeted Matt with a vigorous smile and handshake and an accent that dripped of a quality southern drawl. Though having barely met, Cooper immediately offered Lawton a personal tour of the city that very afternoon.

Lawton laughed, "Given I've been in this city less than twenty-four hours, I certainly have no conflicts. Yes, I accept your offer."

Ashley Cooper enjoyed the wit but then was pulled away by two local middle-aged belles. Ashley shrugged and whispered loudly, "I'll meet you in the lobby at 2:00."

Lill leaned toward Lawton and whispered, "Matt honey, you may as well get used to it. Ashley could be elected mayor tomorrow if he wanted the position. He thinks politics soils the brain. He's a relative to Henry, of sorts. Just having him connected to our hotel is a great benefit for us. He's been a long, long trusted ally and friend practically since the day Henry arrived in Charleston. Just like you, he maintains a suite at our hotel. When Charlie Davis is in town, the two of them play gin for hours. They also like the gin in liquid form as well."

She winked and moved on greeting another guest.

Lawton gazed at Ashley as the man drifted into the sea of people on the outside terrace overlooking Charleston Bay. He estimated Ashley might be a few years younger than Henry. Ashley's hairstyle, like Henry's, was quite contrary to the shorter hair that had become more popular among the male population in the late 1950's. His brown hair flowed over the collar with some natural gray highlights around his temples. He was a shorter man who dressed as a dapper Charlestonian. Like Henry, he also looked like a nineteenth century state senator, but far less serious.

That afternoon Ashley indeed took Lawton on that horse and buggy tour. It lasted a couple hours and was interrupted by numerous stops at local taverns. Though it was the Sabbath, libations were served to Ashley and his guest for the asking.

Lawton would come to learn that Ashley almost exclusively wore light-colored suits and ties. Everyone seemed to acknowledge the man's presence. He was not an athletic man, but he carried himself very confidently. He smoked an omnipresent cigar. He was bright, always smiling, irreverent and funny beyond belief. He knew stories about

Charleston and its history that were always humorous and usually bawdy.

When he dropped Lawton off at the hotel later that afternoon, the younger man was feeling little pain following an assortment of unusual Charleston beverages. Those drinks seemed not to affect Ashley in the slightest.

Walking through the hotel Lawton took extreme care not to giveaway his level of intoxication. He negotiated the entry steps flawlessly and even pressed the correct elevator button on his second try. What surprised him again was how three staff people he'd never seen before greeted him by name. He tried to look bright-eyed as he responded to them in return. He asked their names knowing he'd not remember. However, just trying to reciprocate made him feel better.

After a cold shower, some bicarbonate, and a short nap, he also promised himself he'd have to pace himself better when socializing with Ashley Cooper.

That night Ashley arrived with Henry and Lill fifteen minutes late for the scheduled Sunday dinner reservation. Ashley and Henry were obviously friends as they were bantering with each other while Lill laughed openly. In no time Lawton was involved in their animated conversation. Henry and Lill delighted in his rendition of the afternoon Ashley and he had shared. Lawton, more relaxed than the previous night, referred to their horse and buggy tour as 'bar-hopping'…a term Ashley was not familiar but offered no disagreement over its use.

Lawton suddenly realized he had three people laughing who he'd only known for the past day. While he was likely still showing the after-effects of the many cocktails he'd shared with Ashley only hours earlier, he realized he was finding himself at ease with individuals who already seemed like family.

There was no discussion about Henry's life during dinner. Instead Ashley filled the time with more stories as well as questions to Lawton about his folks and Charlie Davis. It was obvious the Charleston gentleman knew his parents and Charlie as well as Henry and Lill did.

When the dinner dishes were cleared, some desserts with Charleston ice tea were brought to the table. Henry lit a thin cigar, sat back, and said to Ashley, "Well, my good friend, last evening I had a chance to bring Matt up-to-date on part of my life back in Minnesota.

He was rather surprised that I've known both his folks and Charlie longer than he's been alive."

Ashley just shook his head more about the passage of time. Then, with his eyes twinkling, Ashley turned toward Lawton. "Matt, it's good to have you aboard on this project, but I'll need to warn you about this horrible man. You'll have to keep his attention. This bedeviled transplanted Northerner is going to make your life a living hell with his schedule, his propensity to procrastinate, and his flitting about from story to story. Half your battle will be taking your interview notes and putting what you have into some kind of order. You're going to have a holy mess of paper scattered about your suite. It'll take you months just to get the final manuscript organized. In fact, that's why I wanted to give you a tour of the taverns in Charleston earlier this afternoon… so you knew where to drown your frustrations as you complete this memoir. I would advise you to consider escaping now while you still have your sanity."

All four laughed…Henry the loudest…and Lawton nervously. Recovering, Henry's voiced mellowed. He then said, "Well, if we're all willing, I thought, Matt, I might add some more to your notes from last night's interview session."

Lawton pulled out his ever present notebook and simply nodded.

Scratching his chin, the older man showed a temporary blank saying, "Gosh…this all was so many years ago, yet at times it seems as if it was only last week. Matt, maybe to get me started, I'll need a little help from your notes where I left off.

As Lill poured more iced tea, Ashley rolled his eyes at Lawton as if verifying how challenging it was going to be as a scribe for Henry's life.

Paging through his notebook, Lawton found the last notation. "Henry, I believe you were about to talk more about those days leading up to your departure from Glenwood in 1931."

Henry nodded as he blew a ring of smoke toward the fan about their table. He seemed to have another tract in mind as he organized his thoughts. When he was ready, the words flowed easily.

"Matt, I believe I'll start this session sharing information about some other people we both happen to be acquainted. You now know that Charlie Davis and I go back to late 1929. I'd like to introduce two other Minnesotans who I've known since my first years in Glenwood. They were crucial to my life when I was leaving the state; since then they've been instrumental as close friends and business associates right up to this day.

You've known them since you were in short pants, Matt, as general managers at a couple very established lake resorts in Minnesota located along the shores of Lake Mille Lacs and White Bear Lake. Of course I'm referring to Clarence Petracek and Rich Brey. You've stayed at their lake resorts; you've played golf and fished with both of them; you've worked summers during college at the White Bear Lake resort; they've been at your home countless times over the years."

Lawton jerked his head upright. Of course he knew the two men. Charlie Davis and his father handled legal matters for the two men's lake resorts. As a youth, he'd often travel with his father and Charlie to either one of those resorts during the summers. He was now surprised that Henry knew he'd worked two summers at the lake resort at White Bear Lake for Rich Brey. In fact it was Rich Brey who helped Lawton get his job after graduating from college with Brey's brother, Bud, the president of University Publishing, Inc. in Minneapolis. What he didn't know was that those two lake resorts were owned by Triple H Development, Inc.

Enjoying Lawton's captivating stare, Henry talked on.

"My boy, what you also don't know is that not only have they been part of Triple H Development, Inc. since 1930, the two men were officers of the law in Glenwood, Minnesota going back to the early 1920's. They were so very young then. Clarence was the county sheriff for Pope County and his good friend, Rich Brey, was the town's chief of police. We'd always been friends. They'd stop by for some coffee at my office almost every weekday. However, we became much closer by the time I left the town.

Those two had known each other since before the Great War. Both were World War I veterans. The older Clarence had been a deputy at Sauk Centre, Minnesota, prior to the war. When he returned from overseas, he settled in Glenwood as a police officer. He was elected the county sheriff for Pope County in 1922. His younger friend, Rich Brey, worked for him in Glenwood. When the Glenwood police chief resigned in 1923, Clarence recommended to the town council they hire his deputy as the Glenwood police chief. It was done that very day. Those gentlemen worked so effectively together that they even maintained offices out of the same building next to the county courthouse.

The one bit of information we never shared until 1931 was our own relationships, such as they were, with the locally beloved Loni D'Annelli. My interaction with D'Annelli would begin in 1927. As I said, we dealt with each other totally on a business basis. Unfortunately Petracek and Brey, the two primary law enforcement officers in Glenwood and Pope County, had been introduced to the Chicago conman in late 1926 and would soon be caught in the web of this gangster as well.

They were perfect fodder for D'Annelli. There weren't a lot of murders in Pope County, just routine drunkenness, petty fights, family squabbles and general peace keeping. Car accident scenes had become a daily ritual as there were more cars being driven where horses pulling wagons still existed. It was a time when rules of the road were still being formulated. There was also the occasional robbery. Big Bud Bunsen, owner and manager of the General Store, called them up often about food items and clothing items having been stolen from his back loading dock. Given the hard times of rural Minnesota in the late twenties, it wasn't surprising. Desperate people did desperate things when it came to survival. Anyway, my two law enforcement friends tended to help people in any way they could. They were very much respected in the community.

The downside of their life was that they'd accepted the routine of their jobs. Days moved into weeks, weeks into months, months into years and nothing changed much. They were well on their way to accepting what life had dealt them. Having gotten to know them, I'd always felt both men wanted more. The problem was, like with most people, they had no avenue or real motivation to explore other directions. It was this sense of ennui that made them susceptible to ideas they might not have considered earlier in their careers.

It was in late 1926 the charismatic and boisterous gangster from Chicago began making friendly overtures to the two officers whenever he was in town. He'd drop by their combined offices next to the courthouse for some coffee. For someone from out-of-state, they found him personally very entertaining and quite knowledgeable about the pressure of their law enforcement jobs. Of course his perspective was Chicago, but they still appreciated his comparisons. He made their jobs seem quite important. At the time of course, they had no idea of his run-ins with the law or his dubious reputation back in Chicago. To them he was some kind of union steward who therefore had seen plenty of trouble. That he preferred spending more time at the lake in Minnesota made perfect sense to them.

It was while having lunch with them one day that he proposed an idea. He explained it very innocently and compactly. He said, "Gentlemen, I have a need. My associates and I have been coming up to Glenwood during these last few months. Lake Minnewaska and Chippewa Lodge gives all of us the peace and seclusion we enjoy. As we've mentioned this location to many of our friends around the Midwest, I would expect more guests to be arriving as the weather improves."

Clarence and Rich were naturally pleased to hear the compliments. D'Annelli then went on to talk about another endeavor he was involved in…managing some charities in the five-state area. This also warmed the hearts of the two officers despite it being a complete lie.

As the conman explained further, "My charities handle a lot of cash. You can imagine in this world with so many robberies and burglaries this money could be at high risk. With more and more bank closures, I don't necessarily trust those places either. I've chosen to conceal the charitable donations in a secure hiding place at Chippewa Lodge, but there are no guarantees the cash is safe there either.

So, what I'd like to propose to you two officers of the law is to consider becoming a part-time private security unit keeping a general watch out at Chippewa Lodge. I'm not asking you to give up your present jobs. I believe you can do what I'm proposing in your spare time. It would not be necessary to come into the resort property…just your presence as you periodically drive by the resort is all I ask. Obviously, if you see any strangers observing my charity employees at the Lodge, I'd like to know about it. Furthermore, I would expect to pay you for your periodic after-hours service…say in the amount of $100 a month."

Clarence and Rich were taken in like two young boys at a county fair numbers booth. They couldn't believe the offer. Not only was there no conflict, but they'd have some extra money to do some of the things they'd always wanted to do.

D'Annelli put no pressure on them. He told them to think over the proposal and let him know in the next day or two. He told them he'd have the $100 for each of them waiting in advance in the hope they would accept his offer.

Clarence and Rich discussed the proposal and found nothing wrong with taking on the added work. It made sense to Clarence since the resort was on the east side of Lake Minnewaska under his county jurisdiction. Rich rationalized that the Lodge was close enough that he could make some runs out to the resort in his spare time. In fact, what they didn't admit to each other was how much spare time they actually had. Even more ideal, D'Annelli didn't want them driving into the resort; their job was only to make certain the perimeter was safe. Furthermore, dialogue with D'Annelli was needless unless they spotted a problem. The two men saw it as the easiest hundred dollars a month they could ever hope to make

They met their new employer the next morning over breakfast at Chippewa Lodge. The fall day was unusually bright with a temperate breeze off Lake Minnewaska further seducing Rich and Clarence into feeling they'd arrived at a lucky juncture in their lives. They literally bounced up the steps into the restaurant to meet the man involved in charity work.

The two of them did ask a few more perfunctory questions about his charitable organizations and D'Annelli responded briefly and routinely. My two law enforcement friends didn't want to probe too deeply lest they find a problem. They wanted that part-time security job badly. By accepting D'Annelli's offer, they would immediately add about 35% to their respective annual incomes.

Upon leaving the resort that morning, they had become ensnarled in a trap. They would not realize the true consequences for well over a year. By then it was too late. They were indirectly connected to the mob. If found out, it might soil their reputations conceivably forever. Moreover, if D'Annelli and his group were ever found to be doing anything illegal out at Chippewa Lodge, both men could summarily be dismissed from their respective county and municipal positions…or depending on the charges face jail time for negligence of their duties.

That morning Sheriff Petracek and Police Chief Brey drove back to Glenwood each with an envelope containing ten $10 bills. Before they made it into town, they already were talking about pooling their monthly extra pay and jointly buying a small fishing cabin they'd been eyeing over at nearby Lake Osakis.

It was the start of a five-year relationship with D'Annelli. Envelopes containing $100 in cash were waiting for them the first day of each month in their respective mailboxes at their Glenwood residences. Dutifully both of them drove by the resort once or twice a day or night never driving into the resort complex as D'Annelli had requested. Their only job was to be seen on the roadway outside the Chippewa Lodge property as if their periodic presence would thwart any untoward acts against D'Annelli's group. At times they questioned the true value of their part-time security work. However, they reasoned that as long as the man from Chicago was satisfied, then they were earning the money.

As for Loni D'Annelli, he'd just pulled off another coup. He had summarily eliminated the two top law officers in the area from getting in his way. He had bought law enforcement people more times than he could remember and normally it required far more money. This endeavor was almost too easy. He saw Petracek and Brey as dedicated, underpaid civil servants who never thought they'd have enough money to retire. Now they were being paid very well privately to protect his organization from apparent curious eyes and inquiries. If anybody was taking an unhealthy interest in his illegal operations at Chippewa Lodge, these two law enforcement officers would likely notice or hear about it and report it to him. Their part-time security job was similar to working extra hours as a bouncer at a speakeasy.....only better. The pay was higher and they weren't as visible.

Yes, Mr. Loni D'Annelli was a hood of the first order. He was proud of his strong, tough demeanor. He was forty-two years old. He was smart and he knew it. He was in the prime of his life and at the top of his game. During the 'Big War' he'd acquired his talents and tastes for operating on the wrong side of the law. It was far more profitable. And, working with the electrical workers union in Chicago gave him a cover to continue his more lucrative opportunities.

By hiring the two local cops, it didn't really matter to him if they ever drove by Chippewa Lodge. The important thing was that he had them in his pocket. It was just another important step of his grand scheme on how to use Chippewa Lodge as well as the town itself to support his businesses.

As for my two law enforcement friends, over time they would notice the many fancy cars driving in and out of the Lodge. They even thought they recognized some of the guests at the resort as possible racketeers from posters they received from the state police. By then it was too late. Their involvement with D'Annelli was long enough that their own reputations and law enforcement jobs were vulnerable. The months turned into a year…then two years…then more…and the $100 arrived on the first of the month like clockwork.

Yet, there was another factor that kept Petracek and Brey silent. D'Annelli and the many 'guests' he had at Chippewa Lodge were having a very beneficial impact on the town. Not only did these guests need the services and supplies from local businesses, but D'Annelli himself supported both civic and church organizations with cold hard cash. Why would the two law officers want this synergetic relationship for the community come to an end? It was like a dream. The town was prospering when practically all other towns in the state were suffering from the bad farm economy. It seemed inevitable such a good thing would reach a conclusion and the townsfolk would have to wake up, but between the $100 a month and their appreciation for what D'Annelli's group was doing for the town, they gave a blind eye to things that normally would have been questioned.

It was in late 1930 that they could sense D'Annelli's operation was slipping. There was too much talk and too many rumors floating. They knew their security jobs would come to an end and the town would no longer have the financial backing of the Chicago gangster. As bad as that was, they knew their situations would be in jeopardy. If the federal or state authorities ever raided Chippewa Lodge, the two law officers would be questioned about their slackness. More devastating, the authorities might easily find out about their part-time work for the Chicago mobster.

Feeling desperate, they finally decided to approach me for help in their quandary. They reasoned my closer association with D'Annelli might mean that I just might be in the same boat as they. They hoped I might be looking for a way of breaking my affiliation with the Chicago huckster since I was the understood middle man between the town and him.

What of course they didn't know was my plan to resign my job and leave Glenwood. I just hadn't determined the time. For the present my interest was in keeping D'Annelli's businesses in tact until I was good and ready to go. Holding me back was my investment record with the borrowed funds. I was making some incredible returns. By the start of 1931 I'd been taking loans from D'Annelli's funds for over a year. Like any gambler with some inside information, I didn't necessarily want to cash in my good luck too soon.

I had something else gnawing at my mind. When the D'Annelli operation eventually went down, not only did I believe he'd get away scot free, but he'd likely already figured a way to pin the blame for all the illegalities at the Lodge on such people as the mayor, the town council, certainly Darrel O'Donnell....and me. I stayed in Glenwood the first half of 1931 as much as anything to keep his predictable plan from happening.

Henry then stopped and cleared his throat. He appeared uncomfortable with the smoke from his thin cigar surrounding his head making him appear as if his brain was on fire. Glancing at Lawton to give the young scribe time to catch up on his notations, he slowly mumbled, "Matt, there will be times when I'm relaying my story that you'll have to remember I had to make decisions in the heat of the moment. Like anyone, many years later I might have wished I'd said something differently or taken another course of action. But, I dealt with the circumstances at the time in the best way I knew how.

As I tell you this next part regarding Clarence Petracek and Rich Brey, you'll certainly question my motives…they being friends and all. However, with the situation they'd got themselves into while law officers in Glenwood, I admit I took advantage of the circumstances. But, it worked out. I was very lucky. I don't know how I would have continued my business or my life had I not been able to bring them into my business organization.

So, Matt, make your judgments because here is what came about."

"It was a few days after New Year's Day, 1931, just five months before that fateful weekend of D'Annelli's downfall. I had already been strategizing my exodus from Glenwood and figuring out a way that D'Annelli…and no one else… would be taking the heat for the five years of his breaking the law. Charlie Davis was doing his best at handling the changes I wanted in my two lake shore properties. His two friends were only assisting because of their loyalty to Charlie. I needed that kind of allegiance from people who wanted to work with me.

I had often thought about Petracek and Brey. I knew I could trust them implicitly. I even considered ways they could assist me while maintaining their present law enforcement jobs. But, their employment in Glenwood was always a stumbling block. I needed them full-time. Realistically I didn't think their mindset would allow them to leave their guaranteed law enforcement salaries. By working with me, they would have a pay increase, but that factor was not assured. Both lake resort businesses would have to prosper. I questioned if they would be willing to take any risks, especially in those days of a depressed economy. Who would give up a secure job for another with more risk, even if it did potentially pay more?

It was brutally cold that January morning when the two of them made their routine stop by the mill office for some hot coffee. There was virtually no movement in the town with everything seemly frozen solid and the wind blowing snow across the roadway in front of the mill. I'd been gone the previous two weeks, so I expected some friendly smiles and interest about my travels. Instead, I'd never seen them more preoccupied. It was bothersome to the point that I finally had to ask what was wrong. That question was the starting point of one of the more serendipitous conversations that I have ever experienced.

At first they talked as if their lives were over. They related to me the illegal activities they'd seen at Chippewa Lodge and why they hadn't done anything about it. First it was just a convenient part-time security job for D'Annelli. By the time they realized they'd been taken in, they decided to remain quiet for the good of the town. I knew exactly what they were saying.

From their perspective the entire scene at Chippewa Lodge had become a real dilemma for them since the previous summer. Rumors were opening the floodgates of curiosity. The house of cards at the resort was not going to slowly crumble when it fell…and they saw themselves going down just as abruptly.

After four years County Sheriff Petracek and Police Chief Brey were coming to me to discuss if I might have any idea how they might extricate themselves from the mess. Their concern was not just the loss of their respective law enforcement jobs, but they had a real dread about being prosecuted for perceived negligence in performing their duties.

I remember having the opposite feeling of empathy you might think I should have had. I was thrilled over their predicament. What made the conversation almost comic was that when D'Annelli's illegal empire fell...and it was just a question of time that it would...I could more easily be accused of complicity with Loni D'Annelli than my two friends.

Looking skyward to thank the Almighty for my friends' quandary, I recognized my opportunity. Without hesitation, I took advantage of their muddled situation. I had an answer for them, but I hardly knew where to start. The chance to persuade them to join me had just fallen in my lap.

For certain I was not going to start with revealing my own actions in the last year. If Clarence or Rich had any idea I'd been taking loans from D'Annelli's vast sums of illegal money stored right below us in the mill office basement, they'd have tripped over each other running out of that office.

In the silence after their admissions of wrong doing, I remained quiet both to add to their anxiety and organize my own thoughts. It was awful what I was doing. Here I was with two of my best friends and I was plotting how I was going to influence their thinking in favor of my own selfish needs. But, I did feel the opportunity was a good one for them as well.

I had to be cautious. They were conservative men. I intended first to exaggerate their own anxieties they'd just voiced. I had to scare them into submission.

Melodramatically I shook my head, got up from my chair by the wood stove, and exhibited the most exasperated concern I could muster. My theatrics made them restless. Strolling slowly around my office with an anxious look while rubbing the stubble on my chin, I finally sat down, poured them more coffee, and prepared to give them my best performance. They had to recognize my eventual proposal was an opportunity, not just an escape.

I gave them my overstated view of the gravity of the situation. Though embellished, I struck a chord. It was far more than what they wanted to hear. Forfeiture of job, declining income possibilities, damage to reputation, and even possible jail time only repeated what they already feared. Said out loud by someone else, it sounded even worse.

I kept adding more salt to their wounds saying, "...and, the harboring of known gangsters out at the Lodge has likely been going on since D'Annelli first rented multiple cabins almost five years ago. That'll be something else you'll have to explain as pillars of the public trust!"

Clarence looked as if he wanted to jump into the stove. Rich Brey would have joined him if there was room. I got up again and walked over to my front window facing away from them. As I gazed down the frozen main street of Glenwood, I couldn't help but smile. The misery factor had been established and now it was time to change the temperature in that mill office. I turned around continuing to carry that smile. They looked at me slightly confused.

I said to them, "Rich, Clarence, I've painted you a realistic picture of what you're facing, but I have an idea how to possibly save your future. You need to understand, however, what I'm about to suggest will require you to open your mind more than you've ever been required. If you aren't able to do so, then I won't be of much help."

Their faces perked up only slightly.

"First, let me admit something to both of you. I've been aware of D'Annelli's gambling operation plus many of his other unlawful businesses at the Lodge for a long time. I too recognized the good the town was getting out of supplying the goods and services to those fellows out at the Lodge. Hell, I even offered Loni the use of the mill basement storage area as a repository for his business profits or any other valuables. He knew more than I did about those bandits staying at the Lodge. When he was back in Chicago, his working capital he had hidden at the lake resort was vulnerable.

Well, gentlemen, D'Annelli took me up on my offer. It's been almost fifteen months and he continues to use the musty room below us for his personal storage area. I will tell you he has more valuables, money, and stolen goods below this floor than some royalty. I would venture to guess, most of this loot was not acquired legally. And, speaking of laws being broken, he also has a fortune in counterfeit money. I know because I've been periodically looking at his inventory."

That bit of information got a further rise from them. The two men looked at each other and then Rich asked me, "Why haven't you turned D'Annelli and his gang in?"

I had all my answers ready. "My good friend," I muttered, "if you were a mild-mannered general manager of a simple feed & grain mill, would you heroically walk into the sheriff's office and turn D'Annelli in. I wouldn't live to see supper that same evening."

Brey nodded. He couldn't argue the point.

I continued, "That doesn't mean I haven't given it a lot of thought how to end his rein out at the Lodge. But, every idea ends up as me being the stool pigeon with Loni and his boys coming after me. Now that I know your plight with this man, it occurs to me we might be more effective working together against this man. Either way, you both should know that I'm planning on leaving Glenwood, but I'd like to bring down D'Annelli before I do in order to make certain he is the key man brought to justice...and no one in town is inculpated.

Both men looked up at me with some flicker of hope and nodded for me to go on. "Gentlemen, you'll be a bit shocked with what I'm about to tell you but stay patient. I believe we have an ace in the hole. So, please listen carefully. As I mentioned, I've been down in the mill basement a number of times and I have a pretty good idea the worth of his valuables and cash. The result of my intermittent audits has caused me to contemplate how some of that money might be used for better purposes than just sitting in some shoe boxes.

There were only blank stares from both Petracek and Brey. I knew I had to get to the point faster. I then said, "What I decided to do was to take out what you might call 'periodic short term loans' from the D'Annelli 'funds'. With those cash loans I then invested that money for the most part in the commodities markets because that's the type of investments I've followed over my career. I've been very careful to return the borrowed principal after taking my profits. I can report to you today as of the start of the new year of 1931, my investments have turned out quite fruitful."

I thought what I'd said was fairly impressive, but my two friends were not reacting. I realized they had no idea of the magnitude of the amount of money I was borrowing and then investing. I recall thinking on that particular morning I actually owed my downstairs 'bank' more money than at any time in the past. Two weeks before I had pulled out $70,000 from the D'Annelli's funds to make short-term investments on some cattle, hog, wheat, and oil futures. Funny thing, in a year's time I wasn't nervous about that kind of debt. After a year I was certain those funds in the basement were not recorded. No one was the wiser if some of that cash in those shoe boxes was missing. I'd only continued balancing the loans because I still had to look at myself in the mirror. Finally, Clarence mumbled, "Well Henry, we all choose our poison.

If anyone could borrow some money and make a go of it with some investing, it's you. That's all fine and good. But, I'd be careful. You could be putting yourself in a tough spot if D'Annelli ever decides to move his assets to another location. Maybe you should mark a goal as making a thousand dollars or so…some amount that would make you happy. Then stop what you're doing. You're on dangerous ground using his money. You've become a gambler. It could get intoxicating.

I could only laugh inside. He and Rich just didn't get it. I'd moved large amounts of money in and out of that basement as if it was mine for fourteen months. And, as for his comment about the $1000 profit goal, I'd made more than that the very first week I'd used some of D'Annelli's funds.

I had a major challenge just to elevate these fellows' minds. Their low echelon thoughts didn't make them bad people…just wont of imagination. And, so far they could see nothing I'd been saying as having any impact on them.

Getting to the point quicker, I went back to my discomfiting questions. "Clarence…Rich, do you see any chance where you both could keep your jobs once everything at the Lodge is finally found out? The state patrol will be curious how you guys could have allowed a mobster to work under your noses for so long. So, I ask a simple question, 'if forced to resign, what are your future plans?"

They returned to staring at the fire. I then continued but with more urgency. "Gentlemen, to keep from being embarrassed or questioned by your superiors, I'm going to suggest you accept that you should resign your positions in law enforcement…not now, but in the near future. It should be done probably about the time we can affect the closing down of D'Annelli's control at the Lodge. At that time you should admit to being so embarrassed by not being aware of a major gambling operation in the town's backyard that your only recourse was to resign. I think the town's reaction will be momentary irritation, but then they'll come to realize why you stayed quiet. The plain fact is that you'll always have the respect of the townsfolk.

My guess they'll do everything to persuade you to remain in your law enforcement jobs. I will strongly then suggest you thank the mayor and town council for their voice of loyalty towards you, but then stick by your resignations. You should state that your principles will not allow you to continue for having been inattentive in your duties…even though the resort was but six miles from town. That story will sit well with the state patrol."

The two men's momentary brightening faces returned to dejection. Rich lamented, "I don't understand. Why shouldn't we keep our jobs?"

My response was terse. "...because you won't want to stay in Glenwood."

They were clearly puzzled.

I nodded again. "You heard me. I believe you won't want to remain in law enforcement. This D'Annelli episode will follow you for the rest of your days as a cop. Besides, with my idea you'll be convinced that your new line of work will be very much more preferable."

Clarence was paying closer attention. He didn't hesitate. "What do you mean, Henry...another line of work?"

I had piqued their interest. I could sense it. "What I mean is that I'm about to make both of you an offer. I've given this a lot of thought. I want the two of you with me in a business venture I've already established. It'll require that I leave this mill job and Glenwood in the foreseeable future. This alternative might sound unsettling at first, but please stay with me. I want the two of you to join me in taking over two Minnesota resort investments I already own. Your pay will be a lot more than your present incomes. It's just a different sort of work."

Clarence and Rich smiled patiently. They were trying to be respectful. They of course had no knowledge how far I'd come in my development business.

Rich was doubtful. "Henry, these lake resorts would have to be big enough to afford the salaries you are estimating. Clarence and I bought a cabin over at Lake Osakis recently with the private security pay we got from D'Annelli. It cost us almost $1900. What could you possibly own with the small amount of investment money you borrowed and invested from D'Annelli's funds?"

I'd gone too fast. I backtracked and smiled patiently. "What do you suppose the size of the resort would have to be for me to afford good salaries for both of you?"

Clarence and Rich looked at each other not knowing how to respond. Clarence finally guessed. "You'd have to own some of the top resorts in the state with as many as 150-250 units to rent out and have a decent occupancy rate."

It was pleasing to hear they had some basic knowledge of the lake resort business. I calmly responded, "Do you mean like the Lakeside Resort at Lake Mille Lacs that a while back almost went into receivership?"

Rich nodded his head. "Yes, that's the type of place that could substantiate the salaries you're suggesting...as long as it stayed in business."

I chuckled because I had picked up the rights to that lake resort a few months before and already with Charlie and his friend's help, had made some upgrades and marketing changes. I then added, "I guess another property that could pay a decent salary for one of you is another lake resort like the one near White Bear Lake down in the Twin Cities area that also was destined for bankruptcy. It is a 200-unit facility with enough meeting space to attract business groups. Too bad the facility didn't get promoted properly."

Rich and Clarence could only shrug in agreement. They still wondered where I was going with my examples.

Then my voice got unusually light. "Well then, I guess we don't have a problem with your eventual resignations. Is that correct? And I'll need the two of you to allow me to train you so you can take over as managers. In addition, you'll want to invest some of your weekends to get to know the properties as well."

They acted like I wasn't making sense. Then Rich choked out, "Henry, are you telling us that you actually own these properties? Is that what I'm hearing?"

I didn't blink. "That's exactly what I mean and what I am offering you. However, for all our sakes, we're going to have to devote a lot of time in the weeks and months ahead to this plan. I want both of you to be prepared to handle all facets of running those resorts. The longer we can help keep the rumors down about D'Annelli's operation, the more time we have for your preparations, my ultimate departure from Glenwood, and your eventual resignations from your law enforcement jobs."

I don't believe I've ever seen two men more stunned.

I continued without missing a beat. "There are a couple other stipulations. You'll be working for my corporation. My company is called Triple H Development, Inc. If you check the state legal records, you'll find my company owns the properties we just discussed under my lawyer's name. Through my attorney, I have some temporary help from some of his business colleagues. But, I need my own people involved as soon as possible.

As for that attorney, you'll meet him when the time is right. You should know I've gone to great extremes to avoid meeting him personally. It's for his own safety and reputation. We communicate often, but only by telephone, telegram, or through a private answering service I maintain in Minneapolis. I didn't want him tainted if my risks over the past year suddenly back fired. Besides, if he learned who I was and what I'd done to accumulate the capital for my investments, he might walk the other way. I can't afford to let that happen. He's been too valuable to the growth and management of my company.

Finally, when I leave Glenwood, I likely will have to disappear for a while. I'll be the first person D'Annelli will seek out when his entire operation explodes. He'll figure I knew too much and finally blabbed to the cops. He'll want retribution.

So, I don't necessarily see a smooth landing for me once D'Annelli goes down. By vanishing at least I'll have some chance to let the whole thing blow over. I believe there will be enough evidence to lock D'Annelli up without my testimony. Until then, that's why I could use your help in running my lake resort properties together with my attorney."

At that point, I finally stopped talking. They were either going to recognize the opportunity or they were going to continue fretting. Seconds went by. Clarence gave a supportive nod to Rich and said, "Funny thing where life can lead you. Our interest is to move on with you."

With that statement from the county sheriff, the three of us no longer heard the howling blizzard outside the mill office. We talked for another two hours about everything from managing a lake resort to ideas when and how it would best to end D'Annelli's operation.

From that day on, those cold months of 1931 and the early morning coffees at the mill office would take on more purpose and urgency. By the beginning of March, 1931, I was feeling even more confident on both men's abilities to take over as managers for my lake properties. We also agreed on targeting when we wanted D'Annelli's dealings at Chippewa Lodge to be finalized. With the highest number of gangsters staying at the resort during the week before the June charity golf tournament, it made sense that would be the best timing for a raid. Our biggest apprehension was whether the rumors and hearsay would bring in the state patrol and the Bureau of Investigation much sooner. For that reason we had to be ready to carry out our personal plans at a moment's notice."

Granville had been talking intensely for quite a spell. He suddenly stood tall just to stretch. Surprisingly, he didn't seem ready to conclude the second interview session. He began talking again before sitting back down.

"By that April Clarence Petracek and Rich Brey begun taking weekend jaunts to my two lake resort properties. I assigned Clarence to the Lake Mille Lacs resort and Rich's attention concentrated on the lake resort at White Bear Lake. Their purpose was to observe the staffs and take notice of what needed improvement. When both men were away from Glenwood on the same weekend, it was assumed they were fishing at their small cabin in nearby Lake Osakis. In truth they hardly saw the place.

With less than two months before the upcoming annual ten-day Lake Minnewaska festival, I decided to send an anonymous letter to the U.S. Attorneys branch office in Minneapolis suggesting a major gambling ring existed and should be investigated in central Minnesota. I thought the one letter might cause the Glenwood area to be investigated. Once any investigator visited Glenwood and Chippewa Lodge, I presumed the various other illicit endeavors would be discovered as well. Petracek and Brey heard nothing; there seemed to be no interest from the Feds.

By the middle of May I was more direct with a second anonymous note. I addressed it specifically to Ernest Lundquist, the director of the branch investigative unit of the U.S. Attorney's office in the Twin Cities. My note insisted there was some serious infringement on the state gambling laws going on in the Lake Minnewaska area. I was practically leading him by the hand.

By May 15 Clarence had heard nothing from the state authorities or even an inquiring call from Mr. Lundquist. My letters were apparently being ignored. I was then feeling more and more vexed that D'Annelli might just pack up his operation at the Lodge and move his unlawful businesses to some other more convenient spot, like in Wisconsin closer to Chicago. If that didn't happen, then odds were that a raid would happen just because of all the hearsay. I wanted him caught and prosecuted. I didn't want my nightmare to come to pass where prominent local businessmen and leaders would be blamed for the lawlessness as well.

I was getting more and more distressed thinking of a way where D'Annelli wouldn't escape the law. Concerns for my friends in town left me sleepless and eating irregularly.

Then, in that moment of high stress, Clarence Petracek came by my office on Monday morning, May 18, as if he was escaping a stampede. I'd been in Minneapolis over the weekend and gotten back very late the night before. I'd been socializing with some of my commodity broker contacts while completing some heavy investments.

He had a slight hop to his step as he said, "Henry, we've got some good news. I just received a confidential call from that fellow Lundquist in the Twin Cities. He told me about some letters he'd received about a gambling operation in the area. He said he was sending an undercover person from his office to snoop around Lake Minnewaska to verify if the claim was true. He asked that I be alert if this person's cover somehow got exposed and to get that individual out of town immediately if any danger ensued. He wouldn't tell me the guy's name, but suggested I'd likely pick up who the clandestine investigator was very shortly."

When our relieved laughter subsided, Clarence then added another surprise. He gazed over at me and his eyes were literally dancing in his sockets. He grinned, "The investigator has already arrived in town...and he's a she."

That left me momentarily speechless...but not my friend. He chortled, "Henry, she's introducing herself as an independent writer for some statewide travel magazine called *Travel & Resort*. Talk about a great way to talk with anyone in town without creating too much curiosity. When you see this woman, you're not going to believe it. She's a looker. She's going to get more attention in this town...and from those hucksters out at the Lodge...than some royalty might get driving by their subjects. If she's as good of an investigator as she is good looking, you'd better pack your bags now. She's been here for two days and has already been out at the Lodge interviewing that grease ball Darrell O'Donnell.

I've already instructed our deputies there should be a twenty-four hour protection on this gal. My boys don't know her true purpose, but they don't mind following my orders. She's taken a cabin on the other side of City Park by the lake indicating she's going to be in town for a while."

In the days that followed, I never saw her. Our paths just didn't cross. With what I considered an imminent possibility of a raid at Chippewa Lodge, I had too many things to finalize before I left. If anything, I was getting even less sleep; I barely stopped for meals. My chairmanship duties also kept me moving from meeting to meeting. As well, having the two betting booths set up by the First Presbyterian Church men's club volunteers took more time with one of the locations outside the entry gates at Chippewa Lodge and the other near the band gazebo in the park.

I also wanted to liquidate my investment accounts in the Twin Cities so there would be no trail if someone every wanted to find me after I left town. It meant I'd be carrying a frightening amount of cash to my destination upon leaving Glenwood. Furthermore, I had obligated myself to balance my 'loans'. As of the middle of May, a $50,000 debt remained to pay back the D'Annelli funds. That next Friday I took the train to Minneapolis to pick up the cash from the three brokerage houses I worked through. The train ride was as much to let get some badly needed sleep.

As for that attractive investigator, Petracek and Brey kept me posted. She was working alone and keeping her cards close to her chest. In just a few short days she'd become quite popular among the volunteers setting up for the ten-day festival. Folks in town seemed pleased Glenwood was going to get some free promotion in a regional magazine. Naturally I could care less about the publicity for the town. I wanted to get some feel that she was finding some fruit in her secret investigative work.

In the days ahead I found myself stopping by the local café a few more times than normal just on the chance I might meet her. I'd heard she ate most of her meals at the Glenwood Café and had already become a favorite of the staff.

I recall it was just a week before the start of the festival when I took a long lunch at the local café determined to casually bump into her. Rich Brey saw me eating and sat down to share some coffee. He said wryly, "Henry, for God's sake, quit drooling on the window sill. She's in town. She's had breakfast with John Bailey the past couple mornings. It's good to see John smiling again. They seem to have forged a nice friendship."

Brey wasn't so innocent himself. He admitted stopping by her cabin the previous evening just to introduce himself to her and offer any help if she needed it...that is, regarding her magazine article. He gave a subtle wave to one of his deputies as he left her cabin area by the lake. It was that deputy's shift to secretly keep a protective eye on her.

I chuckled, "Yeh, Rich, I suppose you stop by and greet all visitors to our fine community."

Brey caught my humor, but showed no guilt. He said to me, "Henry, she's damned attractive and doesn't seem to know it...just a real nice gal."

Then he added, "She obviously has no idea her boss in Minneapolis contacted Clarence to request we keep an eye on her. Well, after that little incident that took place with her out at the Lodge last Saturday night, we'd be hovering around her cabin anyway. She went out there to interview that twit O'Donnell. She told one of my deputies two days ago she felt like a sheep at a wolf convention. Apparently she didn't react very well to the whistles and innuendoes being thrown at her as she and O'Donnell toured the property.

My deputy said O'Donnell offered her a complimentary cabin for Saturday night. She'd been in the cabin five minutes and some of those wolves started closing in on her bungalow. Well she was no shrinking violent. Let's just say she knows how to use her revolver. She didn't kill anyone, but from what I heard it was only by her choice. Anyway, she drove straight into town and returned to her lake side cabin. That's a relief for the deputies and me. We'll better be able to ensure her safety.

Since that night she seems to be really enjoying herself living right next door to where the main part of the festival is going to be held. She's been talking to our townsfolk and everyone accepts that she's just a magazine writer. The locals of course want her to write nice things about our town."

Abruptly, Henry paused. He looked at Lill and Ashley. Their eyes sparkled. The two of them nodded for him not to stop. Lawton finally glanced up wondering what was causing the delay.

Understanding the astonishment that was about to appear on the face of his young scribe, Henry's voice changed to a softer, more soothing tone. "Matt, I've been referring to that very striking female investigator and it's reached the point where I must share her name with you. Back then, she was Lindy MacPherson...later to become Lindy Lawton and your mother. While I know you were aware of her being head of the U.S. Attorney's branch office in Minneapolis before becoming a law school professor at the University of Minnesota, you might not be as informed about her short career as an investigator."

Indeed Lawton was speechless. Henry only smiled saying, "So... by Miss Lindy MacPherson being in Glenwood in late May, 1931, that meant not only me but Clarence Petracek and Rich Brey were introduced to your mother before she ever met your father. However, don't get preoccupied with what you don't know. They'll be meeting very shortly as I continue this part of the story."

It was then Henry stopped talking. He'd been pattering on without stopping for over an hour and was noticeably tired. As Henry sat back and puffed on what remained of a thin cigar in his holder, Lawton stared at his notes in disbelief. He'd just learned about the involvement of Charlie Davis with his host...and now he was learning that his own mother had been in Glenwood shortly before Henry exited the town for good.

Lawton had heard some references in years gone by about his mother having an investigative legal career, but nothing substantial was ever related to him or to his siblings. Now hearing that she was also instrumental in bringing an end to the Loni D'Annelli era, he was flabbergasted.

With little interest to continue Henry shook his head when the waiter appeared with more ice tea. The atmosphere toned down with the waiter present. Henry leaned toward Lawton and whispered, "Matt, it'll all get explained in good time...all in good time."

Lill gave a slight yawn cuing Henry to end the Sunday evening session. Though transfixed, Lawton understood he'd have to wait. The answers would be forthcoming, just not all in the two evenings since he'd arrived in Charleston. His pages of notes would keep him busy transcribing and editing easily for the next week.

Despite Lill and Henry wanting him to take his time, he had to keep the project moving along. He shared his boss's urgency on all assignments. Bud Brey back in Minneapolis was always pushing his staff to complete any tasks 'yesterday' if possible. Lawton could already hear his boss back in Minneapolis saying, "Well, Lawton, finish up. We've got deadlines!" That kind of insistence, though, was directly at odds with his host's wishes. He wondered why?

Before ending the interview, Henry did make a helpful suggestion for the next day. "Matt, my schedule has changed. I actually have some time Monday afternoon before I take off for the remainder of the week. It might be interesting to take the sail boat out on Charleston Bay. We can continue our discussion on the water. I'll show you some of the sites on the ocean side of Sullivan's Island and the Isle of Palm."

Without being asked, Ashley nodded enthusiastically. "Let's plan on it. The view of the city is spectacular from the bay."

Lawton, anxious to hear more from Henry, readily agreed. He couldn't imagine the choppy water and ocean wind being the best place to gather notes, but he had to work within the confines of Granville's schedule and preferences.

"Well, then it's done," replied Henry. "We'll take off from the city harbor about 1:00 tomorrow afternoon and enjoy the ocean air."

The four of them then parted with Lawton taking the elevator up to his suite while Ashley admitted to yet another engagement that night. That would not be the last time Lawton would notice how Ashley didn't like the night to end.

As for Henry and Lill, they had one of the bellmen drive Henry's Cadillac up to the hotel entrance. When the two of them bid Lawton a good night, he sensed Henry was not just driving Lill back to her home on the other side of the Cooper River. The two of them had a long, long relationship. They didn't talk about it, but they both lived on the same side of the river in Mt. Pleasant.

* * *

Matt Lawton had been in Charleston less than two days and he already felt like he'd been there a month. From his eighth floor suite he stood out on the small balcony feeling the heavy, humid breeze off the Cooper River and Charleston Harbor. He noticed the lonely light at Fort Sumter in the middle of the harbor. Much closer was another lone light he would soon learn was Castle Pinckney, best known as a prison encampment during the Civil War. Looking down to his left was East Bay Street with a collection of bars, restaurants, and shops now all closed on that Sunday evening. The air was mid-summer warm for April 10. He contemplated how long this assignment was really going to last. Despite what would be three interview sessions in three days after the Monday meeting on the sailboat, Henry appeared to be in no rush… only wanting to get the project started and percolate Lawton's interest.

As Lawton leaned against the rail of his patio to take in the harbor breeze, he couldn't help but appreciate his temporary job. Monetarily it was fabulous. His only expenses seemed to be whenever he left the hotel…and those costs were trifling. His salary from University Publishing would simply be deposited in his Minneapolis bank account with no reason to be touched while he also had a local bank account with a generous weekly stipend he was receiving from Henry for supposed miscellaneous expenses.

As for being lonely, that emotion was strangely absent. He was already feeling part of an extended family right there at the hotel. It was not lost on him that he shouldn't be in any haste to complete this unique assignment.

As he looked down onto East Bay Street, he watched as the vehicle Henry and Lill were riding in picked up speed down the avenue toward the Cooper River Bridge…a usual ending to another work day at the East Bay Street Hotel.

It was typical until something rather bizarre happened and only Lawton saw it. As the car crossed the intersection of Broad Street and East Bay Street, there was a man on the corner who stepped out of a darkened door entrance and stared at the late model car as it passed. The man made the most peculiar gesture. He held up his arm and pointed his hand at the withdrawing vehicle as if he was holding a pistol.

Lawton stared hard at the odd spectacle not believing what he was seeing. Did he have a pistol or not? Unconsciously he grabbed a small clay vase with a single flower off a table on the balcony and without hesitation threw it at the vacant street below. In seconds the vase exploded on the street like gun fire less than twenty yards from the strange man. The reaction from the individual was immediate. He pulled his arm down looking frazzled knowing someone had seen him. The street light was not bright enough to identify the fellow except that he appeared to be heavy set and wore a distinctive off-white fedora with an unmatching tan-colored suit. He didn't carry the image of a fast-moving, fast-thinking gunman.

Then quickly the man disappeared into the shadows walking hurriedly the opposite way up Broad Street. Lawton tried to make sense of the incident, but it all seemed so preposterous. Did the fellow really have a gun? Maybe he was envious of the fancy vehicle Henry was driving and made that motion in a silent rage. Or, could it have been a racially prejudiced reaction to Henry and Lill alone together in the vehicle? Above everything else, why was this man standing in a darkened overhang of one of those vacant buildings across the street on a Sunday night so late?

Lawton finally retreated back inside his cooler room and closed the balcony door hoping no one saw his spasmodic throw from eight stories up. What he could have seen was maybe something he only imagined given the intriguing story Henry had been telling about his past. He suddenly became embarrassed about his impulsive action.

He began paging through his notes, but he couldn't concentrate. It was 11:00 when he tossed his notebook on the other side of the double bed and lay down. Resting his head on the pillow, he hardly moved until he woke very early the next morning. For the second night in a row he'd fallen asleep in his street clothes.

Chapter 8

Showered and shaved by 7:00 Monday morning, Lawton marveled again at the vast beauty of Charleston Bay from his top floor suite. He wondered if he could ever take a view like that for granted. With the next few hours free before meeting his three hosts in the lobby to go sailing, he found this type of difficult schedule to his liking.

Deciding a morning stroll would be a good habit, he marched purposefully out the hotel entrance nodding at every friendly face acknowledging him. It was nice while it might last. He couldn't believe that kind of warm welcome by the staff couldn't last too much longer.

At the entry gate there was an older man in a hotel uniform inspecting the front gate and repairing a latch. He unfortunately had only one arm yet showed he was used to the inconvenience. He was a taller fellow who looked like he could have been quite an athlete in his day. The many creases on his face hinted that he'd lived a tougher life. His salt and pepper hair, though, was as thick as in his younger days. He also sported a full beard and mustache that seemed inconsistent to the fitted uniform he was wearing. But, it was the man's eyes that stood out. They were dark and penetrating showing a depth gained from whatever life had thrown at him.

When he saw Lawton, a smile brightened the man's entire face. He stopped working, put down his tool, and held out his one good right hand.

"You're Matt Lawton, aren't you? I heard you'd arrived, but our paths just haven't crossed until now. I know your mom and dad. You're easy to recognize."

Lawton grabbed the man's hand immediately not wanting to appear unfriendly or discomfited by the man's disability.

The man didn't wait for Lawton to talk. He just kept right on chattering. "Henry has mentioned how he hoped you'd take on this writing project he's so determined to complete."

Lawton gave him an appreciative smile not really knowing how to respond. He didn't know how public Henry wanted this assignment to be.

"Matt, my name is Lou White, the security and maintenance manager at the hotel. I've gotten to know your father, your mother, and Charlie Davis over the years during their business travels to Charleston. I've been working here at the hotel for Henry since the end of the war. It's been a great time in my life to meet people like your folks and Charlie. Be sure to give them my best when they return from Europe."

Lawton nodded. Again he was flabbergasted by those who knew his folks and Charlie; this fellow even knew about their being overseas.

He finally spoke. "Lou, I'll definitely do that. I have to tell you I'm still amazed how many people seem to know my father, mother, and Charlie Davis. I never knew they had this connection to Charleston, South Carolina."

Lou only smiled as if knowing that would be Lawton's response. "Yeh, I guess there will be a lot you'll be learning while you're here. Henry is determined to set the record straight regarding his past. He doesn't want any falsehoods damaging this hotel's reputation. I keep saying to him all of us probably have some things in our past we wished we hadn't done or we hoped no one will ever find out. But people forgive and forget. He just seems to forget how very highly he's thought of around this city and within this service industry. I'm a great example of those feelings. It was a very fortunate day when I reestablished my contact with the man."

Lawton reacted immediately. "Oh, so you knew Henry before the war...so you go back even further than when you started working here? Did you know my folks back then as well?"

Lou paused slightly as if looking for a way to end that part of their conversation. He handled the awkwardness, however, like a man who'd dealt with many far more serious dilemmas. His smile returned and the tone of his voice was relaxed and genuine. "Yes, I met your father once, but only saw your mother...never talked with her. Henry, on the other hand, I certainly knew. It wasn't until the post-war that we really became friends. I'll let him fill in the details as he sees fit. It's his story."

The silence was sudden. Lawton realized he should tame his prying for the moment. He changed the direction of their dialogue. "Yes, I've already heard some of Henry's background in two dinner interviews so far... enough to know that Charlie Davis and Henry have worked together for thirty some years. I was shocked to hear he'd known my mother before my father even came into the picture. My folks have never mentioned this part of their lives...ever."

Lou just nodded and put away his tools having completed the repair. About to walk away, he turned and said, "Matt, my office is in the basement of the hotel. Stop by if you need anything. Also, I usually eat lunch around 12:30 if you want to have a sandwich with someone who knows a little about Minnesota."

It was another act of kindness offered by a staff member. Lawton couldn't get over the thoughtfulness displayed by so many of the hotel employees. "Thanks Lou. I'll take you up on that tomorrow. In a few hours I've got to go on some kind of boat trip at noon and continue my interviews with Henry."

He detected a cloudy look in Lou's eyes when the word interview was used. But, the man maintained his upbeat nature and joked, "Well, don't be in too much of a hurry to complete your project with Henry. We want you to enjoy your stay down here for as long as possible."

They shook hands and Lawton headed down East Bay Street towards Broad Street. While walking he had a number of people who nodded or waved to him. It was as if he'd been in the city before.

Approaching the corner of Meeting and Broad Streets, he stopped again as he'd done the previous day at the cemetery on the grounds of St. Michael's Episcopalian Church. He was so impressed with the history reading those gravestones dating back a hundred years before Minnesota had even become a territory. It made the history of his home state seem rather recent.

As he strolled along Meeting Street, there were some Negro ladies already sitting in the shade along the sidewalk. As they conversed with each other, they seemed to be mindless of the skill they were displaying in weaving those baskets from that indigenous grass of South Carolina. The finished baskets were placed out in front of them ready for bartering with the tourists that day.

He stopped in at the Mills House Hotel and read some of the history of the old guesthouse including a framed note from Robert E. Lee hanging on the wall lobby. As a Union officer prior to the War Between the States, the man had an assignment in Charleston and was thanking the hotel's management for their hospitality.

The reflection on the frame's glass gave Lawton a sudden jolt. There was a heavy set man standing at the lobby entrance. He wore a panama-styled hat...like the man the previous night in the shadows. Turning quickly, the man had slipped away. Striding purposefully towards the outside door, Lawton's heart was beating much faster. Was he being followed? If the vision mirrored in the glass was wearing a tan suit then Lawton might have to be concerned. Slowing, he rationalized that there might be many overweight men in Charleston wearing a light-colored panama styled hat.

Another glance across the street and he saw the person again. There were three other men striding down the street wearing the same style hat. Chuckling at his childish paranoia, that same man turned to look back at the hotel entrance where Lawton was standing. The man's face was puffy with no color. What made a shiver go up and down Lawton's backbone was the cold stare the overweight man gave him. It lasted for only seconds, but it was too long.

Undaunted, he crossed the street after noticing the heavy set man had entered a lady's apparel shop. Lawton wondered what any man was doing shopping for lady's clothing on a Monday morning. Passing the store window another chill ran through him as he saw the man staring at him and then move swiftly to the back of the store where he then vanished out the back exit.

With no interest to follow the fellow any further, Lawton picked up his pace and proceeded back to the East Bay Street Hotel. He reminded himself that he was in a new city. He had to raise his familiarity with the idiosyncrasies of Charleston. Walking too far along Hennepin Avenue in Minneapolis was not wise either.

Before he reached the hotel, Lawton stopped by a clothing store and purchased some summery sports shirts and a couple pair of lighter pants. He even wore some of his new clothing on his return trek back to the hotel if for no other reason than to feel more preppy for that afternoon's sailing venture with his three hosts.

Later at the Ashley River marina, Henry's boat turned out to be more than just the small sailboat Lawton had envisioned. Henry would not be at the helm. He had a crew of three men. In the center of the deck was a shaded area with a table and four chairs...obviously rigged for the third interview session.

Once all were aboard, the seven members of the party sailed out onto Charleston Bay. The four of them took their seats and one of the crewmen presented them with some ice teas. Lawton wasn't used to such special treatment. The breeze and the smell of the seawater made him want to lay back and just enjoy the view.

As the sailboat ventured toward Ft. Sumter, it turned slightly offering a panoramic view of the Battery and the water side sighting of the East Bay Street Hotel. Henry placed a thin cigar in his holder and seemed ready to begin. His first statement would become an often repeated one. Looking at Lawton, he said, "Now, Matt, where were we when we cut off our last interview? I know my recollections are somewhat rambled. I'll leave the responsibility to you of putting my babble and your notes in some kind of order."

Rifling through his notebook was not fast enough for Ashley. He'd heard Henry's story or parts of it too often. With a comical impatience, he blurted, "Henry, for Christ's sake, have some mercy on the boy and tell him more what he wants to hear...about his mother working undercover as an investigator...and then meeting his father right there in your former home town."

Through the laughter Granville only nodded seeming to be more inclined to tell his story how he intended. At that moment, he seemed more distracted by the view. He kept pointing out historical places along the coast as Lawton struggled to find the endpoint of his notes. As the boat hit some waves spraying them with a light fog of sea water, it became more fun just to enjoy the ride as the sailboat moved swiftly toward the ocean and the coastline off Sullivan's Island.

It was becoming more and more obvious the pace of his assignment would be entirely at the whim of Granville. The boat slowed as it passed Fort Moultrie. Ashley explained some history in reference to the very old fortress. Half-listening, Lawton marveled how Henry or Lill had so far expressed no interest in discussing a completion date for the manuscript. At times subtly and at other times almost insistent, they repeated how Lawton should learn as much as he could about Henry's current life, how the flagship East Bay Street Hotel had become such a successful hotel property, and how Triple H Development, Inc. had grown and thrived over the many years. The inference was that this information would provide Lawton an even better perspective on the subject of Henry Granville.

They had been out on the calmer waters by the Isle of Palm almost an hour as Granville seemed more interested in listening to Ashley cover some incident of South Carolina coastal history. Lawton wondered if the old man had intended to talk of his past life at all that day.

He watched his three hosts now standing at the stern of the boat enjoying each other's company. One of the crewmen edged up to Granville and pointed at a faraway broad cloud system across the western skies. Both men nodded and the sailboat was put on a return coarse back in the direction of Charleston harbor. There was a possibility of inclement weather, but it was still a long way off.

Lawton wandered along the deck and then returned to one of the four deck chairs letting the wind blow through his hair. Being alone with his thoughts spirited more questions. Why was it now that Henry had decided to document his story? Why in the year 1960 did Henry have this urge? Then there were some more personal reflections. Why really had Henry chosen him? What if Lawton had declined the offer? Who would have been the scribe? For that matter, the choice was his whenever he might want to end the assignment.

As Henry, Lill, and Ashley sat back down on the deck chairs beside him, he wondered if things were more serious than what he was yet being told. If so, could Henry's life be in jeopardy? How about his mother and father, Charlie Davis, even Clarence Petracek and Rich Brey back in his home state? The thought seemed so extreme.

Granville finally interrupted Lawton's deep thoughts. "It looks like our sailing venture this afternoon could be shortened by that far off cloud system moving this way. I guess I'd better take what time we might have to continue where I left off last night at our dinner. I'll see how far I can get before we return to the marina."

There were nods around the table and Henry wasted no more time. He knew exactly where he wanted to begin.

"Matt, I know you're curious about your mother's involvement as an undercover investigator back in Glenwood, so let's continue from that point. I will tell you honestly, I had my doubts how effective she might be. How would a stunningly beautiful city gal get her hands dirty pulling together evidence against those trolls out at the Lodge? Frankly, her presence told me her boss probably thought the investigation was a lark with no sense of any potential danger. How wrong he was about her assignment…and how wrong I was about her.

Under her cover as a writer for that travel magazine, her initial actions of talking with the mayor, various townspeople and even stopping by the county sheriff's office indicated she wasn't wasting time. Then meeting with Darrell O'Donnell at the resort that first weekend showed she had a lot of spunk. What impressed me was her resolve. Most young women would have packed their bags after seeing that motley group of low-grade hooligans at the Lodge and the threat they could be to her. But, not Lindy MacPherson.

Additionally, she got involved with the local organizations as they set up for the ten-day festival. Her friendliness was contagious. Folks in town were not used to having someone of her personality and looks show such interest in their community. You might say she took the town by storm. People were inviting her for boat rides on Lake Minnewaska. She went fishing with some young folks. And, in the quiet of the evening, she could be seen just relaxing and often reading on a rocking chair on her cabin porch. She seemed to be unwinding from the fast paced city life as much as doing her investigation.

The first time I actually saw her, she was walking through City Park on her way to the Glenwood Café just days before the big festival was to begin. I had no doubt it was her and not because of her looks. As she strode along she'd stop and talk with people as if she'd known them for years. Her manner was so sociable…so personable.

I'm not certain what I expected when I finally met the young lady. It was at the Glenwood Café. As Rich Brey had mentioned, she'd already met my friend, John Bailey, and the two of them had been seen having coffee most mornings at the café. John had been my friend since my first days in Glenwood and helped me out at the mill whenever I was taking my trips or gone for the weekend. He never knew the life I led those last two years in Glenwood….at least until a few years later.

I strolled over to their booth at the café to introduce myself. I detected an immediate uneasiness from her when Bailey said my name. She'd obviously heard I was the go-between for the town and whoever the leaders were out at Chippewa Lodge. It wasn't hard to understand she thought I might be one of those lunatics and therefore guilty as hell.

I sat there wishing I could change her understandable presumption, but it wasn't to be. I knew it was better for me if she located the evidence against Loni D'Annelli and his group without my help.

There was not much to our conversation that morning. Whether she realized it or not, she had the future of my town in the palm of her hands. Whenever she felt she had enough proof, she could schedule a police raid at the Lodge any time she wanted. I would never have a forewarning unless she confided to County Sheriff Petracek. That was unlikely or she would have already informed him of her secret investigation. She was perfectly comfortable working alone. I simply had to be ready to leave town at a moment's notice or as the perceived stool pigeon, D'Annelli's men would be on me like hungry lions.

Unfortunately for me, her investigation would turn glacial. I didn't know why at the time. Only later I was informed she had recognized many mob members and even wanted criminals, but she was struggling finding the irrefutable evidence against Loni D'Annelli that he was the ring leader.

Not knowing her reasons for the delay, my frustration was at an extreme as the festival began those last couple days of May. Unperturbed, she could be seen volunteering in City Park at some of the food tents. She seemed not to have a care in the world or certainly no urgency in ending the corruption at the Lodge. Brey even confirmed she was playing cards late into the evenings with the local fellows in the back room at Big Bud Bunsen's General Store...the local speakeasy in town. It was as if she was on vacation and she'd pull the plug at the Lodge when she damned well pleased.

As the ten-day festival progressed, her patience made a little more sense. More fancy cars began rolling into Glenwood indicating an even larger number of gangsters would be involved in the June 6-7 charity golf tournament.

Nonetheless, I was aggravated. It was even more possible she might call in the state patrol at any moment. I was on my last belt loop on my trousers from not eating. Sleep was intermittent at best. I didn't want to fall into a deep sleep and wake up to a gangster's gun barrel following a late night raid at the Lodge. And, if I fled too soon that could be a tip off to D'Annelli that something wasn't right. After all, I was the chairman of the festival. The net effect was that I looked and felt miserable. Even friends expressed concern how frail and haggard I appeared.

As for Miss MacPherson, as Clarence, Rich and I respectfully referred to her, she continued her fun right up through that last weekend of the town celebration. She'd arrive back at her lakeside cabin each evening around midnight. Whether she knew it or not, she had nothing to fear as Rich Brey and his deputies continued to follow her and maintain surveillance at her cabin. She would be observed earlier those evenings often sitting alone on the cabin porch with her feet up on an old wood rail. She'd either be reading or just enjoying the peaceful evening and the view of the vast lake. Later she'd walk the few blocks to the back room of Big Bud's general store and play cards with the boys. She'd somehow proven she could keep her mouth shut about the petty gambling and drinking that went on at Big Bud's place. The cops of course knew that back storage room's reputation. Most every town had a behind the scenes tavern during Prohibition. Generally, the local patrons liked to believe their speakeasy was a secret place away from the law...and their wives. For the most part the spouses didn't know about the back room, but the local law enforcement understood the watering hole would keep the drunks and the cavorters all in one place...and therefore, easier to manage.

Those deputies assigned to secretly follow Miss MacPherson all commented that her life was also a bit sad. Here was a good looking lady being alone each evening. They sensed she had a background with some sorrow tied to it...a story of which no one in Glenwood would ever hear.

That Friday June 5 I was secretly doing some last minute packing before heading over to the two Calcutta tents in City Park and out at Chippewa Lodge. I had to balance the wagers and the money received. Then I'd place the money in the Lodge's office safe.

I recall the talk of a major thunderstorm that threatened our area that evening. Finishing my Calcutta responsibilities, I began driving back toward Glenwood alongside Lake Minnewaska as the mother of all storms hit the Glenwood area. I would learn later that evening from some locals that a crazy fly boy was forced down in his biplane on the highway alongside John Bailey's farm on top of the east bluff above the town. Matt, your father would be able to tell you who that fly boy was."

Lawton looked up to see Lill and Ashley shaking their heads. They'd obviously heard the story a few times before and still found it difficult to believe. Lawton stopped his note taking and looked at his three hosts.

He finally blubbered, "Why would he know?"

Ashley replied mirthfully, "Young Matt, let's just say you wouldn't be sitting here if that crazy pilot hadn't landed safely."

Lawton's eyes clouded over suddenly realizing the meaning. His father was not only the crazy pilot forced down by a storm, but it was becoming abundantly clear that weekend would be the actual time his mother and father would cross paths. Through all the years he was growing up, they claimed they'd met at a party at Charlie's Lake Ida home later that same summer. Lawton and his siblings had always accepted that story as true? Why would his folks not tell the truth to their very own offspring about something as important as that occasion? Now it appeared there was a reason why they hadn't told the whole truth.

Lawton leaned forward toward Henry even more attentively as the older man continued.

"I was watching the torrential rains as I was cleaning out my office desk that Friday evening. There was a small bottle of brandy I found in the back of one of the drawers. I actually had a good luck drink and almost passed out when the booze hit my empty stomach. My intestines made some strange gurgling sounds, but the drink actually relaxed my head. My stomach, on the other hand, simply wouldn't stop turning over.

I sat over by my wood stove with my feet up lazily watching that nonstop storm out the office windows when I succumbed to the relaxing noises of the falling rain and the rumbling in the sky. I fell asleep in my chair for a couple hours before the post-storm silence caused me to regain consciousness. I recall leaving the office quite late that night and returning home to my own bed....one that likely I wouldn't be using again after that weekend.

I woke early Saturday morning remembering that Clarence and Rich had left town for the weekend. This had been their mission since the Calcutta part of golf tournament had first originated a few years before. The town council had first asked them in 1928 to take a two-day vacation while the golf tournament was underway...the thought being that if they didn't see any illegal activities relating to the golf event and the Calcutta, then they wouldn't be obligated to make any arrests. Of course, it was not only the Calcutta, but the town council didn't want the two top local law enforcement officers to witness the open sale of illegal hooch sold off wagons at the golf tournament and behind Big Bud Bunsen's General Store. Chippewa Lodge did not have a monopoly on being a den of sin that weekend. The town participated as well.

Petracek had said he'd leave a message on the door of my house if he'd got wind of any ensuing police raid weekend. There had been no note as I left my home that Saturday morning. I was highly perplexed. I figured Lindy MacPherson had plenty of evidence to prove unlawful activity at the resort. I couldn't imagine what was keeping her from pulling the trigger and bringing in the state troopers and agents of the Bureau of Investigation.

I drove slowly through the town surveying the damage from the previous night's storm. Though there was wind damage in City Park with many uprooted trees and damaged tents, volunteers had already begun the repairs. Word was that the festival would continue that afternoon into the evening. I even heard that town volunteers had been out at the golf course picking up leaves and branches early that morning so the golf tournament would not be delayed.

It was a strange day for me. I no longer cared about the festival or any impending police raid. I just believed it was inevitable, so my focus was when would be the best time to leave town. I still had to fulfill my duties including collecting that day's wagers at the Presbyterian men's club betting booths.

With little food, a restless sleep, and a slight degree of nostalgia knowing I'd be leaving the town I'd lived in for ten years forever, my mind was only halfway functioning. I drove to the charity golf tournament later in the morning after the event was already underway. The First Presbyterian Church men's club betting tent across the road from the Lodge had been my second office that week. While a couple men's club workers manned the front tables for any bets, I sat back in the corner of the tent tallying up that day's wagers. As far as I was concerned, Miss MacPherson should have had a flock of law enforcement officers surrounding the resort a week before. But, there was not a police vehicle to be seen out at the Lodge.

Physically I was miserable. Mentally I wasn't much better. The pangs of never seeing Glenwood for a long, long time were eating away at me. My exodus would be low key. I envisioned simply driving out of town the next morning or at the latest by Sunday afternoon while the party was going on at the Lodge restaurant following the completion of the second and final day of the tournament. There would still be throngs of visitors watching the finals of the various water sport events on the lake.

I had left town the previous two summers similarly following the last day of the festival. I was doing nothing different. The townsfolk would expect me back in two weeks. The difference this time was that a letter of resignation would be found at my house, as I'd planned, by Sheriff Petracek sometime Monday or Tuesday.

It was later that Saturday morning when I decided to return home. I still had yet repaid the last $50,000 loan from D'Annelli's funds. I had to get to the mill and complete that task.

Then I got the surprise of my life. Sitting in the back of the church betting tent I saw one of my fellow men's club volunteers direct a man with the most God awful looking chartreuse golf shirt over toward me. I was lost in adding up the totals of that morning's wagers and wasn't seeing clearly who he was. Then a familiar voice greeted me in a most unfamiliar way.

The man said, "Good morning, Deacon Hanson. I heard you're in charge of this Calcutta booth for your church organization. I guess there's a lot of betting going on and not just related to that charity golf tournament across the road."

Rubbing my eyes I lifted my head only to focus on Charlie Davis, a man I'd not seen for over a year but I communicated with regularly...sometimes a couple times a week. He of course didn't know me at all by sight, but I became immediately afraid he'd recognize my voice.

Choking on some mucous, I probably coughed for a good thirty seconds before catching my breath. He just sat down and patiently waited for me to recover. Apparently he had every confidence I would.

Typical of Charlie, he was casual. He put his legs up on another chair, leaned back, and didn't seem in any sort of hurry. But, I could tell he was confused as he watched some lowlife from the Lodge and his 'niece' stroll up to the booth and place a bet on a National League baseball game to be played the next day. As agreed with D'Annelli over the previous years, he asked if our church booths during the week of the festival could take all bets that people might want to wager since they were away from their home cities where they normally made their bets. Given the percentage the church was getting, it was like frosting on the cake for our men's club. As it turned out, D'Annelli was simply closing down his own gambling operation within those resort cabins at the Lodge for most of that pre-tournament week so no locals or other spectators at the golf tournament might accidentally stumble across any incriminating evidence of a gambling operation.

I was stunned by Charlie Davis' presence. Immediately figuring he was a spectator at the golf event, I also reckoned if he happened upon any irregularities at the Lodge or at the Presbyterian Church Calcutta booths, he was not the type to remain silent. Something was bothering him and he'd come to the man in charge.

As that fellow and his 'niece' completed that bet on the baseball game, Charlie watched the man saunter away. He was even more puzzled. Then in that jovial voice of his, he said, "God dammit, Deacon, your friends over at the table taking bets told me you were in charge of this shebang. You guys must be making a haul with the other bets besides the golf tournament wagers."

He was trying to get me to agree, but I decided to remain quiet. I was aware if I said the right things, Charlie would not delay calling in the police. I no longer would have to wait for Lindy MacPherson to do the same. I responded in a dispirited, despondent tone, quite the opposite of my behavior when he and I spoke on the telephone.

As I purposely slurred my words to camouflage my voice, I slowly began feeding him some minor factors that definitely gave indication the church was taking bets beyond just the charity golf tournament. I said to him, "It's all done in agreement with some fellas over at the Lodge. My church gets a cut of all the bets being made at our two booths all week."

And then as if absentminded, I added, "After this week, the folks over at the resort will take over again."

I could see he was startled at what I'd just admitted. Remaining calm, he asked, "Seems to me there are some shady guys playing in that tournament across the road. If I were a betting man, Deacon, I think I've seen some of those fellows in the national newspapers...and it wasn't for their good deeds. Are you or your fellow townsfolk conscious of the type of people involved in this golf event you're taking wagers on?

I didn't want to be too obvious about giving him so much information so quickly. Instead, I played the role of a potentially scared informant. Getting up from the table, I exclaimed, "My friend, we're just a small town church group helping out. We get some money for our work and we don't want to cause any trouble. Now, I've got to take a break and get something to eat. I hope you enjoy the day."

Then I wobbled away toward the Methodist Church's food tent next door ending our conversation. Moments later I saw him shuffle across the road toward the golf course. His legal mind had to be swirling with the surprising truth as to what was going on at the resort...and not just that weekend. And, he was only aware of the illegal gambling. If he could somehow become aware that there were other illegal businesses, he'd be calling the state patrol the very next minute.

With Charlie Davis now alerted, I felt an albatross gradually being removed from by shoulders. I knew the man. He was a jokester, but a damned good lawyer. Above all, he respected the law. He could never allow blatant lawlessness to continue with impunity.

With that one short conversation I automatically moved up my time table to leave Glenwood. I would not wait until Sunday. Once I completed tallying up the bets that day and dropping the money into the safe at the Lodge office, I saw no reason to remain. I had every confidence Charlie would be calling in the state patrol possibly yet that evening.

I actually ate some food at the Methodist's tent, but my empty stomach couldn't handle the greasy food. Whether my insides were shouting for joy or complaining about the heavier food, I had an acid stomach, heartburn, and gastritis that left my legs weak. I barely made it back to the church wagering tent. I wasn't going to hold the betting booth open too much longer.

I was extremely tired and was resting on a chair in the back of the betting tent when I was bumped. I found myself staring into the face of Charlie Davis once again. In returning I could tell by the look on his face he was after more information from me.

That was fine with me. If I could get him to call in the state patrol sooner, that would be fine. I was ready to leave town.

Maintaining my dour attitude but silently cheering him on, I was ready to give him whatever responses he might need. His approach to me this second time was quite different. The good humor was gone from his voice. He began outlining all the legal problems I might be facing by running a gambling tent that was clearly against the law. It was everything I could muster to keep a straight face. He was actually trying to scare me into divulging more incriminating evidence against the gangsters staying at the Lodge.

That was when he mentioned the name Loni D'Annelli. Charlie apparently knew this man was no good and was taking for granted the Chicago conman was the kingpin. I neither confirmed nor denied Charlie's claim.

Without saying D'Annelli's name I muttered, "Yeh, there's a lot of money being wagered. And, the man in charge needs a lot of cash on hand to run a gambling operation. Thank goodness he's got a secret place he can hide all this money...and all the other profits he's making from his other businesses."

I got another stunned reaction from Charlie Davis but I ignored it and just kept on mumbling, "Yep.....keeping all this cash out here was too dangerous given the kind of clientele staying at the Lodge. I'd like to see how much that man truly has where he stores all his loot in town."

That last loose statement unquestionably got Charlie's attention. I'd given him a major clue, but I sensed he needed another hint. I had to be careful not to be too obvious.

I then got up and told my two men's club members that it was time to shut down the betting booth. I gave that day's totals and the money in the strong box to one of the church volunteers for him to bring it over to the resort office safe. With that done, I nodded to Charlie in farewell saying, "Well, I've got to get over to my real job at the Glenwood Feed & Grain. I've been so busy with this festival and golf tournament, I've got more work on my desk than grain stored in my bins.

Then I chuckled and slurred, "Yep...grain at a grain mill...safer than money in a bank."

I said no more. I had just practically led him by the hand to D'Annelli's funds at the mill. If he hadn't grasped that tipoff, then there was nothing more I could do. What I truly believed from that moment on was that Charlie Davis was not about to ignore the throng of cons and gangsters. There'd be a raid. The only question was whether the proof against D'Annelli would be discovered. As I stumbled toward my old Plymouth, my departure from Glenwood became more urgent. Anything else I felt responsible for regarding the festival or the Calcutta was superfluous. I returned home, completed my letter of resignation and placed it on my kitchen table where it would be found in the days ahead as per my discussion with Petracek and Brey.

I had but one more item to mend before I left town…to pay back that $50,000 I still owed to the D'Annelli funds in the mill basement. To this day I still wonder why that factor had been so important to me. He wouldn't even know the money was missing. Still, I guess I didn't want to leave town thinking myself as just another common thief. I wanted my debt squared.

In carrying out that final accountability, a calamity resulted that almost ruined my secret departure. I delayed bringing that $50,000 to the mill basement until after dark. With a lively street dance scheduled in the park that night, I thought the chaos would provide me some camouflage. I figured to be in and out very quickly. From there, I would unceremoniously leave town trusting that Charlie Davis or even Lindy MacPherson would be bringing in the state police no later than the next day. The D'Annelli era would end abruptly and I'd not get caught up in the dragnet of the ensuing raid. Most importantly I would vanish without a trace. Henry Hanson would no longer exist. It would be Henry Granville driving across the country to points further southeast where I would not be found. It all seemed so simple."

Exhausted, I returned home to take a short nap while waiting for the right time to return the money. Then, whether it was the food I'd consumed or the stress catching up to me, I let myself fall asleep. It turned out to be a deep sleep.

When I finally awoke the daylight was gone. I hardly knew what day it was. Hearing the rumble of noise from City Park where the band was playing and the street dance was likely underway, I jolted from the bed to find the time. I was shocked to realize my short nap had lasted almost five hours. It was 8:30 PM.

Swearing to myself I realized there could already have been a raid at the resort. Charlie Davis could easily have contacted the authorities. If so, I could be vulnerable to either the authorities finding me or some of Loni's associates paying me a visit at my home. The irony of sleeping through the very raid I was trying to generate didn't get past me. It would have been an unforgettable blunder.

Now I moved with purpose. I had no pangs of sorrow or nostalgia saying farewell to Glenwood; I just wanted to get that money to the mill basement with no one seeing me and be off into my new life.

Grabbing the parcel with the exact amount of money ready to be placed back in those shoes boxes, I walked the few blocks to the mill along a back alley. By the clamor and the throngs of people dancing in City Park, there was no indication anything out of the ordinary was happening out at Chippewa Lodge. Certainly if there had been a raid at the resort, attention might have been swayed away from the large street dance.

When I was within a block of the mill, my heart rumbled as I looked ahead to the bustle of people overflowing onto the roadway between the mill and the park. The mill parking lot was filled with parked cars and people. There were young people standing in front of the mill office windows talking, smoking, and drinking. There would be little chance I could sneak into the office and gain access to the basement without a crowd seeing my actions through those front office windows. I had no choice but to retreat back to my house and stay in relative solitude until the events and festivities of the day had tamed later that evening.

With my car packed I remained in what no longer seemed my house. I was antsy. I paced around the house hating my moral stand, but still satisfied I was doing the right thing.

It was past 11:00 when I left the house again on foot aiming at taking an even less visible route across the county fairgrounds to the back of the mill. Meandering through more back alleys to the fairgrounds, I was constantly agonizing over why this effort was really necessary. Eventually D'Annelli's funds would be found after the impending raid. Whether the $50,000 I had in the satchel was part of the vast evidence in the mill basement or not, it didn't really matter. There was plenty of proof in that storage basement to convict the Chicago conman.

I came so close to turning around. Regrettably, I didn't.

Sneaking to the back of the mill, I entered silently through the backdoor. There just outside the office windows the problem still existed. The gathering of young people were laughing and drinking. Some were just standing on the platform right outside the windows of my office.

All I had to do was move quietly in the dark, push the desk aside, roll the carpet back, open the floor door and descend the steps. In the storage basement I could close the floor door, turn on a light and begin filling the empty shoeboxes on the shelves. I expected the effort to not take more than ten minutes.

As I was about to push the desk aside in the unlit office, I began to hear some peculiar noises from the same back door I'd just entered. It was the low excited voices of two young people. I stood motionless praying the two whispers would move on. Unfortunately, God was not listening at that moment.

Hearing the back door latch come unhinged and the door slowly open, I scrambled soundlessly over to a filing cabinet where I could hide. The giggling and whispering young couple was apparently looking for a place to fool around. The amorous evening at the dance apparently had sparked the motivation.

I was now angry at myself. I'd left the back door to the office opened for only seconds and the young couple sauntered in as if they had no doubt the door would be unlocked.

As they found some feedbags to sit on, I was scrunched down in that corner in a hot office, with my shirt becoming drenched with perspiration. Their voices were barely audible. I couldn't believe a feed & grain mill was the most ardent place to stimulate passion. Gritting my teeth I remained calm but swearing constantly under my breath. Five minutes went by...then ten minutes...I was but thirty feet across the office floor from this passionate couple. Constantly looking at my watch and sweating profusely, that painful nervousness in my stomach had returned. If anything I was afraid the loud gurgling might give away my presence.

In those few minutes, I made another decision. I was going to make an exception to my high standards of paying off my final 'loan' from Loni D'Annelli's funds. The very next moment I could escape that office without being heard or seen, the parcel with the money was coming with me. I'd do something altruistic with the money later on. Right then, I just wanted to get on the road.

Still, that decision didn't change the quandary I was in. As I tried not to watch, these two local young folks were locked in an embrace as if Romeo and Juliet. I sardonically wondered if either of them had even read the play.

I was desperately thinking of anything to get these two kids out of my office when the situation got worse. I heard her murmuring something about "not here!"

Peering around the filing cabinet, the two of them were lying on the itchy feed bags. The sweat was now pouring off my head. I was ready to give them the $50,000 in my parcel just for them to be on their way.

It was then that divine providence finally smiled on me. Some flashlights appeared in the window. Other young couples were looking for their friends. They were yelling out the names of Johnny and Becky. With the flashing light, Johnny and the young lady rapidly repaired themselves, snuck out the backdoor and were gone.

As relieved as I was, there was no mercy for me. The other couples continued standing outside the office window shouting the young couple's names. The flashlights kept lighting up the interior of the mill office. I had to remain huddled by the filing cabinet until the young people left.

When that finally happened, I stood up painfully and drenched to the skin. I'd not moved a muscle for easily a half hour. My legs were so stiff. I wasn't able to simply run out of the office.

Unfortunately, that small delay provided time for a second problem to suddenly develop. Another couple was making their way to the back door of the mill office. It was now well past midnight. I wondered how long the mill had enjoyed this reputation of late night ill-repute.

Rushing back to my hiding place behind the filing cabinet, another set of male and female voices could be heard as the back door cracked open once again. Though whispering, their voices were lower and more mature sounding. I was kind of disgusted. An older couple should have more class than having a private moment in a feed & grain mill office.

My irritation was at a high pitch. I felt like a night manager at a house of pleasure.

Meandering into the mill office, they seemed to have something else on their minds besides lust. While I remained scrunched in the corner, they poked around in the dark. I was back to feeling miserable. Not only was I sweating like a leaky pipe, but I was likely about to be rousted from my hiding place.

And then as if the night wasn't rousing enough, a car approached and drove around to the rear of the mill. As the headlights momentarily lit up the office, the couple dove to the floor.

'Good God Almighty,' I thought. 'I've walked down Michigan Avenue in Chicago and experienced less traffic than was coming into the mill that night.'

Two men got out of the car. They were talking loudly with no real reason to be quiet. Their voices brought them right up to the back door of the mill. As they were about to open the door, I saw the male and female scamper up the ladder in my office leading to a small loft. They were desperately trying not to be spotted. Now there were three people in that office trying to conceal ourselves.

The backdoor opened and very confidently two guys with flashlights entered moving the beams around the room. They wasted no time as they marched directly to my desk, moved it aside, rolled the carpet back, and opened the floor door. They went down the storage basement and turned on the light. The subdued lighting caused kind of a lighter haze in the office. I was tempted to peel on out of the office, but now I'd likely be seen by the couple hiding up in the hay loft. I had to stay put.

The two men were down in the basement storage area for only a few minutes before climbing back up to the main level. The light from the flashlight hit the face of one of the men. I recognized him immediately. He was Whitey Malooley, one of the guys who worked for Loni D'Annelli. They were obviously there on a mission to pick up some cash. The gambling at the Lodge hadn't stopped with the golf event that day. Their presence further verified that no raid had yet occurred.

The two men closed the floor door as fast as they'd opened it, unrolled the carpet, and set the desk back where it had been. They were out the back door, in their automobile, and driving back down the road less than ten minutes since arriving. That was more like it. My only hope was the couple up in the hay loft would follow suit.

When the car took off, there was momentarily only the muffled conversation and laughter coming from the loft. In the next instance, they were down the ladder dusting the straw off each other. One of them flicked on a flashlight and pointed it at my desk. Then they repeated the actions of the previous two men moving the desk aside, rolling up the rug, and opening the floor door.

As the female turned on the basement storage light after descending a few steps, I saw her face and almost lost my breath. There looking attractive as ever was Miss Lindy MacPherson. I had no idea how she'd guessed D'Annelli's illegal loot was stored somewhere at the mill. At that point I no longer cared. The important thing was that she had found the funds. In the next few moments she'd be seeing some startling possessions…stolen goods, counterfeit money, as well as the shoeboxes full of legitimate currency.

I could not recognize the male. I had not seen him before. He had followed her down the basement stairway. He had wavy blond hair and was wearing knickers. By his dress, he looked like he'd just gotten off the golf course. I also reasoned that this fellow could be that friend of Charlie's I'd seen in a speakeasy two years before up in Alexandria. Wearing that style of pant wasn't common in a small town like Glenwood. It did occur to me that this fellow was with Charlie out at the charity golf tournament…and somehow they'd made contact with the undercover investigator.

When the couple was downstairs exploring the loot, it was finally my chance to sneak out of that office. I certainly didn't want to be discovered hiding in that office by the two of them with my parcel full of $50,000.

There was no time to delay. I moved away from the filing cabinet hearing Lindy MacPherson and her male friend absorbed in muffled but intense conversation in the basement. I slithered by the open floor door being careful not to cast a shadow over the opening in the floor. Silently slipping out the back door, I snuck carefully away from the Glenwood Feed & Grain Mill. I hadn't imagined slinking away in the dead of night from the place I'd invested ten years of my life would be my swan song, but that was the way it worked out.

Creeping back through one back alley to another, I arrived at my house. Whatever nostalgia I'd had two hours before was gone. My Plymouth was packed. Glancing one last time at the dwelling I'd called home, I remained in the dark shadows as I strode over to the open garage. With a silent prayer for my old sedan not to fail me, the engine rolled over as if it was new. With headlights off, I drove down the grass driveway, turned left and high-tailed it to the intersection of Hwy. 28. Except for a scare of being seen by some folks in an old Ford who were following me out of town, I finally made it to the top of the bluff and sped on down the highway away from Glenwood. It was 1:45 AM Sunday morning.

The life behind me was in my rear view mirror. I firmly believed Loni D'Annelli and his colleagues were going to be closed for business by the end of the next day and I'd be blamed for the raid. Though I'd be sought after, I was well prepared for that challenge."

Henry sat back and sighed as if once again releasing all the stress, exhaustion and even the melancholy he'd felt that particular night in his life. Leaving Lill, Ashley, and Lawton, he got up to check with the crew about the growing cloud system moving towards Charleston Bay.

While the crew was assuring him, Lawton stared out onto the bay in relative bewilderment. There was no doubt the gentleman accompanying his mother late that Saturday night at the mill had to be his father. Somehow his father and Charlie Davis not only were involved in that weekend charity golf tournament...with a bunch of gangsters and thugs...but they'd met up with the undercover investigator...his own mother...and were inexplicably helping her out. He was discovering undisclosed details of his parent's early life seemingly with each Henry Granville interview.

Lawton thought back. He recalled various tales told by his father and Charlie. As he remembered, too many of those stories always seemed to end sooner than they should have. Neither man ever went into detail.

Lawton kept staring at Henry wanting him to go on. There were so many questions brewing. His father had been forced to land his biplane by a farm near Glenwood. He'd called Charlie Davis to come get him. Charlie arrived but they didn't leave the town right away. They didn't attend community festivals. If anything, they'd drive the opposite way to avoid one. So, why did they stay in that town that weekend?

Like a flash the reason suddenly became quite clear...the golf tournament. It was a charity tournament...supposedly. Charlie and his father did participate in those types of events. In fact, with his father being one of the better amateur golfers in the state at that time, there was even more reason he wanted to compete.

Lawton then contemplated, 'Why did his father and Charlie have anything to do with a golf tournament filled with a bunch of gangsters?' It didn't make any sense.

But, the main question was still the mystery. Why had the three closest people to him in his life never divulged...never even hinted... that the weekend his father and mother met happened to be one of the more dangerous periods of their lives. They had not only taken action against the mob, but they'd apparently succeeded!

Then again...had they? All the secrecy surrounding Henry's life meant that they may have been as integrally involved in the Chicago mobster's downfall as Henry Granville. If Henry still felt vulnerable to mob reprisals or damning hearsay against his corporation, was it possible his parents and Charlie Davis felt the threat possibly looming against them all these years as well?

The hypothesis died abruptly as the wind picked up. The huge black cloud system was moving in faster than expected by the sailboat crew and the tacking process would not get them up the Ashley River to the marina in time. The decision was made to head for the East Bay Street Hotel dock on the Cooper River side of the bay.

There were light rain drops falling as the sailboat docked at the hotel. There would be no continuation of Henry's story. There had not even been a suggestion for the next interview session as hotel staffers came running out to the dock with umbrellas for the passengers and crew. All then scurried to the dry comfort of the hotel.

Before the four of them went to their respective offices or suites to find dry clothing, Henry leaned over and whispered to Lawton, "Matt...so...how do you feel about your assignment in Charleston now?

Lawton only nodded his head with his eyes showing absolute interest.

The older man patted him on the shoulder. "We'll talk soon. I'll be gone the rest of this week, so we'll schedule a time hopefully this next weekend after I return. Next Sunday might be best...maybe dinner here at the hotel."

Chapter 9

Henry's statement that he still had a business to run was made very clear that upcoming week. Lill Hamilton was also busy with her many responsibilities. The few times she did see Lawton her greeting was always warm. Invariably she'd ask if he'd been exploring the city, not whether he was drafting his interview notes. The writing assignment never seemed the most important topic on her mind.

She also took time to acquaint him with more hotel staff. He thought it interesting how she kept introducing him as 'a long-term and special guest' at the hotel. What she meant by 'long-term' was never defined but it seemed more and more accurate as each day passed.

The hotel ran like a well-oiled machine with Lill Hamilton in charge. The division of work responsibilities between Henry and she was indistinct. She simply took over when he was traveling.

Through that first week Lawton began establishing a morning routine. Rising early he'd stop in the hotel basement at the staff lounge to have some morning coffee with the Bell Captain, Thomas Rutledge Brown, before the older man went on duty. Brown seemed to know his father, mother, and Charlie Davis particularly well. Again and again he told stories of their many visits to Charleston.

When asked, Brown couldn't really give an answer how the friendship started among Henry, Lawton's folks and Charlie Davis. He just took for granted they all knew each other before Henry arrived in Charleston. Through Brown and those morning coffees, Lawton also learned that Granville pulled a stint as an assistant minister at the local First Presbyterian Church on James's Island when he'd first arrived in the area. There was no explanation why or how an assistant minister could become a hotel owner in such a short span of time back in the early 1930's.

Brown also spoke with pride about being a shareholder of the East Bay Street Hotel having been employed there for twenty-eight years. And he mentioned there were others on the staff Henry had awarded shares of stock for their loyalty and dedicated service to Triple H Development, Inc. Brown also confided that his own son, Jefferson, had earned a college degree in Atlanta thanks to a scholarship provided by Henry. Jefferson now was employed at the hotel as well and had risen to the position of Hospitality Manager.

Through that first week Lawton gave his Remington Rand typewriter a real work out in the mornings and then each afternoon he took a break. The first couple days he routinely repeated his morning walk leaving the hotel about 3:00 to stroll up Broad Street to King Street and stopping by a couple bars. He realized he'd better not make having a few afternoon beers a ritual so by Thursday he got the inclination to find a golf course instead.

Stopping by Lill Hamilton's office that morning, he inquired where he might rent a car. Her reaction surprised him.

With furrowed brow she said, "Matt, naturally you'll need some transportation. We have a couple hotel vehicles available. You need only to get the keys at the front desk or from Thomas Brown. Whenever you need to go anywhere, one of these vehicles will be available to you. We want you to get familiar with the city and the area."

Lawton left her office appreciating yet another perk. It was as if he couldn't ask for too much. His biggest challenge might be to keep his head straight with all the privileges he was receiving.

That very afternoon after driving out to the Sullivan's Island beaches, he found the waves intoxicating. Despite the chilly water, he was happily jumping in the April surf reveling in the knowledge that all his friends and family were at best dealing with moderate temperatures back in his home state.

Several shades redder, Lawton returned to the hotel toward the supper hour. He'd gotten more burned than he'd realized and felt a bit conspicuous. He also had a trace of guilt knowing that staff members had been working that afternoon while he'd been playing. Parking the hotel vehicle in the back lot, he snuck through the hotel's rear entrance and ran up the eight flights of stairs hoping not to be seen. He thought he'd pulled off his small dalliance until he dressed up for dinner and took the elevator down to the lobby. The ladies behind the registration desk muffled laughter when they saw him. He checked his zipper to make certain he was ready to be seen in public.

When he got to the restaurant, Jefferson Brown, the Hospitality Manager, saw him. The two had become friendly over the morning coffee with Brown's father. He wandered over to Lawton and whispered kiddingly, "Matt, you boys from the North don't tan up very easily. Hope you had a nice stroll on the beach today."

Then he laughed and ambled away. Matt looked in the lobby mirror. His choice of wearing a white shirt only emphasized the glare from his obvious sunburn.

Eloise, the restaurant greeter, looked at Lawton with more concern. "My God, Matt, if you need some lotion for that burn, stop downstairs and see Lou. He'll have a remedy that might help you sleep better tonight."

Again he was impressed how everyone was so kind. He wondered when they'd get tired of catering to him.

That evening after dining alone, he made his customary walk down East Bay Street to one of his favorite bars…the one with the pretty waitress. There was a light mist so there were limited locals or tourists sharing the sidewalk.

Strolling solo brought back that previous sensation of being followed. He grinned to himself as he turned abruptly just to satisfy his dark side. He of course didn't expect to see anyone. The problem was that he did. It was only a momentary glimpse, but some fellow seemed to be looking at him and then ducked into a convenient thin walkway between two buildings. Lawton was jolted for a moment. What would be the reason for anyone to be shadowing him? He couldn't imagine he was being singled out as some ignorant northerner who might be easy pickings for a robber. He was certainly not the only tourist in the city and likely more of them were better prospects than some young person in his middle twenties. He scoffed at his paranoia and walked on.

Entering the bar, his favorite barmaid was not working that evening. He felt a twang of disappointment. He had three beers over the next hour while talking with some North Carolina students in town on a college break. They seemed especially overjoyed they were 'down south' and away from the rigors of school. Lawton thought they were already 'south' considering they went to school in North Carolina.

He made another barmaid acquaintance before deciding to walk the four blocks back to the hotel. Her name was Janine. She was a student at the College of Charleston…a school with which he was unfamiliar. She was a sophomore and except for her figure she seemed even younger. She didn't seem to know anything. He was disappointed their age difference accentuated her lack of depth. She had no idea where Minnesota was relative to the other Midwestern states. She only brightened up when Elvis Presley's voice could be heard on the jukebox. Lawton wondered if he was destined to only meet females of this ilk during his stay in Charleston.

Losing interest with the dull-witted waitress, he downed his last swig. A slightly inebriated character seated a couple bar stools away suddenly started to talk to him. His voice was slurred. "My friend, you just came to town from someplace up north and spent the day in the sun, didn't you? You can bet that sunburn will be a bit sore for a day or two."

Lawton gave the gentleman a patient smile. "Yeh, I guess I stand out as a typical tourist. Thanks for your concern."

It was meant to be a final statement on the matter, but the man continued. "So, buddy, where you from? We don't hear accents like yours in these parts very often. You've got to be from the Midwest."

Lawton hadn't considered his speech inflection that pronounced. How did this character pick out his accent in just two short sentences? It only made him feel a bit lonelier. And, he hated to be called 'buddy'.

Sullenly he mumbled, "You've got a keen ear. Yeh, I'm from Minnesota. Ever been up in that part of the country?"

Expecting a negative response, the man surprised Lawton with his reply. "Oh yeh, I've been up there. I was close…in Milwaukee…but that was quite a few years ago. So, are you down here with the other college kids?"

Lawton was tired, but it was kind of refreshing to hear that he still looked young enough to be mistaken for a college student. He responded, "No, I'm done with my college years. I'm down here on personal business."

Then, wanting to end the conversation with the total stranger, he added, "Nice talking to you…have a pleasant evening."

When the man didn't take Lawton's cue and asked what kind of work he did, Lawton realized something wasn't right and he became more cautious.

Immediately standing up, he threw some money on the bar for a tip. He didn't want anything more to do with the drunken local. Before heading for the door, he replied as politely as he could, "Like I said... some just private business. I won't be in town long."

Once out the door, he turned slightly and peered through the huge picture window back at the semi-stoned local sitting at the bar. The man finished his drink and moved over toward a booth as if to strike up a conversation with yet another patron. There seemed to be more familiarity between the two. Within seconds there were some bills being passed to the well-oiled local.

Lawton hesitated. He tried to see the man passing the money, but he was hunched over with his back to the window. Taking the money the intoxicated fellow he'd spoken with at the bar then moved back to the bar and ordered another drink. He sat there alone with his muddled thoughts. Obviously, both men were not close friends.

Lawton would often think how he should have marched right back into the bar and gotten a good look at the unseen face. But, he didn't. There really was no reason for anyone to want to follow him. He'd been in Charleston for only a few days. With that prevailing thought, he marched back down East Bay Street to the hotel.

He looked back twice. There was nobody looking his way.

*   *   *

As for the unseen man sitting in the booth, he already knew where the young man was destined...right back to the East Bay Street Hotel as had been the kid's habit the previous nights after a couple beers. The man shifted his buttocks in the uncomfortable booth wishing he knew more about this latest addition to the people surrounding Henry Hanson Granville. He'd just paid ten dollars for some semi-drunk local to attempt conversation with the young man. The drunk hadn't had much luck; he'd said the kid was guarded and only admitted being in town on 'personal business'.

Darrell O'Donnell shoved a single bill over to the drunk anyway and told him to get lost. He didn't want there to be a scene by not paying the money. No reason to call attention to himself. He'd already had a close call the previous Monday morning when the young man caught O'Donnell following him near the Mills House Hotel. Then upon seeing the kid go sailing with three of the top people at the East Bay Street Hotel that Monday afternoon, it confirmed the visitor was not just a normal guest.

O'Donnell had followed a number of hotel employees to bars in previous weeks trying to get them to talk about their place of employment and Henry Granville. Here was yet another person completely new to the hotel staff and had already learned to be as closed-mouthed as all the others.

Moping over his beer O'Donnell was aggravated about Granville seemingly not taking the blackmail bid with any urgency. There was a delay being caused by Granville's busy travel schedule. O'Donnell frankly wasn't certain if Granville was out of town or not.

Now there was another fly in the ointment...possibly someone brought in by Granville's loyal key associates to find the extortionist. It was causing O'Donnell to be even more cautious.

Every time O'Donnell looked at this young man he scoffed. This kid didn't look old enough to have any credentials as an investigator. Of course, O'Donnell had long ago admitted that most people looked young compared to himself. He'd gaze into the mirror in his rooming house bathroom and wonder how life had treated him so unkindly. He'd aged so badly. Now stocky and slow-moving, he at times contemplated whether he had the staying power to carry out this extortion against the former Henry Hanson. He just wanted to make up for lost times and lost wealth from those times so many years ago when he owned and managed the Chippewa Lodge back at Lake Minnewaska in Minnesota.

He knew he had to remain adamant. To get one last huge payload he had to commit to his blackmail plans. Otherwise, he'd only continue being the loser he'd gotten used to seeing in that same mirror for so many years.

Rubbing his face and taking a strained breath, he ordered another beer and let his mind drift back to his younger, more fulfilling years. That only made the cloud over him become darker and he'd hiss 'Damn that Hanson'. It was all Henry Hanson's fault that caused his life to spiral so quickly downhill never to ascend to any real success ever again. The hotel magnate would always be 'Hanson' to O'Donnell even though he'd been Henry Granville for years. The name no longer mattered. The semi-drunk O'Donnell just wanted to make Henry Hanson Granville pay.

*   *   *

It was Saturday, April 16, the day before Easter, when Henry returned from his business trip to Washington D.C. and New York City. To Lawton it seemed as if Henry had been gone much longer. By then, he'd gotten quite comfortable with the city having access to a hotel vehicle whenever he desired. While he'd caught up organizing his notes from the first three interview sessions, he hadn't begun a manuscript draft. In all past assignments he would have been further along. It had become so easy to procrastinate.

He was toting his golf clubs out a side door of the hotel that afternoon for another round of golf when he got a wave from Lill Hamilton. He was in no rush. He had no foursome to meet; he'd be playing alone again. He found himself truly missing his friends back in the Twin Cities when it came to golf. The only acquaintances he'd talked with more than just a general greeting were Thomas Brown and his son, Jefferson...and of course Lou White. If it weren't for their company, he figured he'd be bored out of his mind.

Approaching him, Lill's voice was upbeat. "Oh Matt, I have an invitation for you this evening. It might sound like something you might not want to do on a Saturday night, but it'd be a good place to meet some people who've known Henry for many years...some since he first arrived. It's a kind of homecoming service at the First Presbyterian Church on James Island. A retired old and dear friend of ours, Reverend John Middleton, is going to be at the church for a dinner in his honor. Depending on your schedule, you're certainly invited to attend. Henry and I can pick you up around 7:00 here at the hotel if you're interested."

Going to church on a Saturday evening was not exactly on his list of preferences, but hearing that Henry had once been an assistant pastor at that church as part of his secret past life gave the invitation a higher priority. The event would likely cast some more light on his subject's early life in Charleston. As for Lawton fitting the invitation into his agenda, that was no problem.

He smiled patiently saying, "Yes Lill, I believe my busy social calendar has an opening tonight. Thanks for the invitation. I'll be out in front of the hotel waiting for the two of you at 7:15."

Then he winked. They both laughed. Lawton had become used to Henry's habitual late schedule.

The church was impressive. The congregation was large for a Saturday night service. Lawton stayed off to the side as Henry and Lill walked into the church. It was as if the two of them hadn't been to church for years. They were greeted by everyone.

Lawton heard many people addressing Henry affectionately as "Reverend Hank". The few people who seemed not to know him just stared and whispered to each other about the unique couple. Most reactions were very positive. A few people appeared a bit troubled when they saw he was escorting a female of a different race. What made that minor reaction somewhat humorous was that Henry actually looked darker than Lill Hamilton with his sun-beaten skin from his penchant for sailing and fishing.

Lawton shook his head over those few people who looked askance. Though she was obviously classy and a well bred, intelligent woman, the times forced ignorant people to abide by their short-sighted prejudices.

Mostly, though, the crowd was overjoyed to see both of them. When the venerable guest pastor, John Middleton saw Henry and Lill come down the aisle toward the front pew, he came off the pulpit to greet them personally. All three had tears in their eyes as they hugged. There was a story there…yet another one. Lawton shrugged hoping he'd hear it before autumn.

The service was short followed by a dinner in the church parlor. Lawton's sunburn had faded to a more acceptable tanned look. Even Henry commented how Lawton appeared healthier looking. While Lill and Henry were involved talking with so many old friends, Lawton drifted away partaking of some of the finger food being served. He not only felt out of place, but he doubted he'd ever have such a congregation of friends.

He spotted Thomas and Jefferson Brown talking in the back of the dinner hall. Thomas was enjoying himself talking with people who were obvious long term friends, but his son, Jefferson, seemed to be of the same mind as Lawton. Tedium at this function seemed to be contagious for anyone in their age bracket.

Spotting each other, the two moved closer to one another since they were about the only two of their generation in the entire church. Above the din of the noisy dinner, Lawton leaned toward Jefferson and exclaimed, "So, tell me what the story is about this old pastor. How far back does he go with Henry? I heard Henry was some kind of assistant minister when he first got to Charleston."

Jefferson was of no help. "Matt, I've asked the same damn question to my father countless times. He evades it like the plague. There're some things to which the older group in Triple H Development simply won't discuss. Whatever you're doing with Henry in those interview sessions, I'd say you have a better chance of getting that information than I ever will. We both know there's always been a deeply held secret about Henry's past. Many of the hotel staff members figure you might eventually supply some answers. I should also tell you, a lot of us wonder why he's telling his story now. Some are even concerned that Henry plans to retire...or worse, that he's sick."

That was the first time Lawton realized his purpose for being down in Charleston was being noticed. It was good of Jefferson to be so upfront. Lawton had learned during the week that the younger Brown at thirty-one was the youngest manager at the hotel. He'd even intimated to Lawton during one of their morning coffees how refreshing it was to have another person of their generation at the hotel.

As both young men leaned on one heal and then the other, Jefferson looked at his watch and then leaned towards Lawton's ear whispering, "Hey, have you fulfilled your obligation for attending this function? If so, are you interested in changing scenes?"

Lawton gave a pronounced nod murmuring back, "I don't necessarily go to church on very many Sundays, so being here on a Saturday night is totally out of my norm. What do you say we go get a beer....like one of those bars on East Bay Street?"

Jefferson eyed him and then patiently shook his head. "Matt, you might want to wake up and remember what city you're in. There are not very many bars that'll serve the two of us unless you get a better tan or I claim to be Cuban. But, I was about to exit all the fun I'm having here and go play some cards with some friends. I believe these guys might be willing to take some of your money if you want to come along."

Lawton was already moving toward the church exit. "You're on."

Jefferson called over to him. "Hey, wait just a minute, Matt. Let me do some quick damage control in case we're missed. I'll be right back."

Then he strolled over to his father standing next to Henry and whispered something in the man's ear. The father listened. A playful grin gradually shone on both their faces.

Jefferson returned and said, "Let's roll."

In Jefferson's car, they drove back toward Charleston crossing the Ashley River Bridge ending up at an apartment complex near the Citadel. When they entered what turned out to be Jefferson's living quarters, there was a poker game already in action. The players were locals all right, and Lawton recognized each one. They were hotel staff members...people he knew mostly only by their first names. There was James, one of the valets. Calvin was an assistant to Lill Hamilton. Ron Taylor was head of Marketing. Coming out of the kitchen with a couple beers under his one good arm was Lou White. In unison they yelled at Jefferson as to what took him so long. When they saw Lawton, they held out their hands in greeting, not so much in the polite manner at the hotel, but the more sincere mode of having another player's money at the table.

Taylor, a white guy with a New York accent, seemed especially pleased to see two new players. He yelled out, "All right...Jefferson has recruited some new money. Welcome young Mr. Lawton. Do you play games of chance?

Lawton grabbed a beer under Lou's arm and then a chair. An innocent look appeared on his face. "Why, if you gentlemen are referring to games of chance...like poker...I guess I can learn."

The entire room lit up with a roar. Calvin shouted, "Watch out boys, we've got a live one. Grab your money while you've still got some. We may get fleeced tonight. This chap from the North may just be buying us lunch this next week with our own money just so we don't starve."

It was an evening that lasted well past midnight. Lou was the one who drove Lawton back to the hotel. Lawton wasn't certain if he'd won or lost, but it didn't matter. He finally had some friends with whom he could be relaxed. His relatively wild night had started out by going to church. He wobbled down the hallway to his room thinking, 'Who would have guessed?'

Sunday arrived quicker than he wished. The matter of going to Sunday church services never materialized even with his first visit to a church the previous evening. Rising about 9:00, he dragged himself down the eight flights of stairs to the back exit of the hotel. Facing anyone that morning was not his plan. The small café down the street was his only goal. He desperately needed a transfusion of coffee.

Upon returning to the hotel, the staff was already setting up for the 11:00 Sunday brunch on the hotel harbor side patio. The staff seemed to be moving at a slower pace consistent with Jefferson Brown who was in charge of the set-up.

It was obvious Jefferson had not had the advantage of two cups of coffee. To add some energy, Lawton jumped in to help out. He assisted spreading table clothes and bringing chairs outside to the patio. He even helped some women staff members set the tables. They seemed to enjoy his kidding around and his added effort. He knew nothing about the set up or even how to place the silverware, but he could follow directions. When the job was completed with minutes to spare of the doors opening, Jefferson gave Lawton a nod of thanks.

Lawton then disappeared up to his room to get dressed properly for the luncheon. By noon it was a packed patio with guests and locals mixing socially. The sun was shining brightly on another successful event at the East Bay Street Hotel.

Jefferson dressed in a tux stood watch over the entire gathering with a satisfied look. Lawton with an open-necked shirt, light-colored pants and light blue sport coat looked more comfortable. He ambled up to Jefferson and whispered, "Does your head feel as badly as mine does?"

Jefferson, ever the professional, put a sparkling smile on his face and replied with a comical strain to his voice, "Lawton, you're a bad influence on me. I've got a headache that would kill most people. We should have stayed at church last night. I would have saved the ten dollars I lost at the card table and I know I wouldn't have consumed near the alcohol. I'll probably live, but an hour ago there was great doubt."

As Lawton stifled a laugh and moved away, Jefferson called out, "Hey Matt… appreciate the help this morning." The nod between the two of them was of two new friends building confidence in their newly found bond.

Waving back at Jefferson, he turned and abruptly came face to face with Ashley Cooper who had been surprisingly invisible the entire week. Lawton was comfortable enough with the older man to kid with him. "So, Mr. Cooper, I have not seen you once since Henry left town. Do you just curl up in your suite until he returns?"

Cooper gave him a quizzical look. "My dear young man, I was earning my keep. Henry and I worked magic up in Washington D.C.... he being the businessman and me being the token southern gentleman enticing our northern friends to bring their meeting business to one of our hotels."

Lawton was a bit embarrassed. He hadn't realized the role Ashley played within the Triple H Development marketing efforts.

Ashley saw the discomfort and patted Lawton's shoulder. "Don't be concerned, Matt. You'll probably be drawn into some business plans while you're here at the hotel. It's quite difficult not to help out where you can. I guess you got a taste of that feeling this morning helping Jefferson's crew out."

Lawton gave him an amused look. Nothing much got past Ashley Cooper. For the next hour Ashley carted Lawton around introducing him to other locals attending the brunch. By the end of the event, Lawton wished it wouldn't end. He hoped he might even remember some of their names.

Ashley sidled back up to Lawton and confirmed that night's dinner. "Henry wanted to remind you that we're on for this evening. He suggested 6:00 unless that's too early.

Lawton gave Ashley a wry look. "Ashley, these last minute confirmations to my busy social calendar are so inconvenient"

Ashley smiled back appreciating the young man's wit. He sauntered away saying, "See you at 6:15."

Lawton found it interesting that he could kid with Ashley Cooper in the same way he joked with Charlie Davis. Both men were like favorite uncles, except he'd only met Ashley the previous weekend.

As the event began to slow down, Lawton headed for his room to relax. He noticed Ashley leading some folks out to a horse drawn carriage in the front of the hotel. He admired the energy of the man knowing that Ashley was not only going to take them on a tour of the historic city, but they would be stopping at a few of Ashley's favorite watering holes along the way.

Arriving 'early' at 6:05 for the 6:00 dinner at the hotel restaurant, he was seated at table overlooking the harbor. Ashley came strolling in shortly thereafter. He looked only slightly worn from his afternoon escapades. He'd showered and changed clothes.

He inquired about Lawton's afternoon. Lawton was not going to let himself be outdone by someone twice his age. He immediately went into a fable about his busy afternoon on the beach jumping the waves and meeting a bunch of co-eds taking their Easter break from college.

Knowing Lawton by now, Ashley yawned and replied, "Oh, so you spent the afternoon taking a nap, did you?"

The gibberish would have continued, but Lawton and Cooper both heard the flutter of noise coming from the lobby. It was the now familiar voices of Lill and Henry talking to staff members and guests as they moved through the hotel lobby. It was a repeat of the previous weekend. The difference was that Lawton was far more comfortable and knew what to expect. This entrance appeared to be a ritual with Lill and Henry. It was ten minutes before they finally made their way to the table in the restaurant.

Being late, Ashley acted irritated at Henry. It was just ceremonial. Henry and Ashley seemed to get a kick out of making jabs at each other. However, neither of them ever made any such comments toward Lill. She was always treated with the utmost of regard.

Lawton marveled at the scene. The three of them had a tie that went far beyond just working together. There was a comfort and a trust only gained by time. He saw the same with the friendship of his father and Charlie Davis.

It was repeatedly being made clear the lack of urgency Henry had in completing his story. Lawton could see it would take a dinner engagement or a sailboat cruise to get Henry truly interested in expounding on his past. If his writing job lasted through Labor Day, it would be of no surprise. Somehow that no longer bothered him.

Henry asked Lawton how the previous week had gone and this time Lawton was able to give a more interesting rejoinder. "Well Henry, I organized my interview notes of course, but I did take time to explore. I found a couple golf courses. I know the history of some of those anti-bellum homes on Meeting Street. I even have some of your staff's money thanks to a Friday night poker game. You of course will have to torture me to get me to name those hotel employees. I picked up a little more suntan on the beach at Sullivan's Island. I also took an excursion boat to Ft. Sumter and drove out to Ft. Johnson."

Thinking he'd passed the test of keeping himself busy while Granville was gone, instead the older man showed some mild concern. Looking at Lill and then at Ashley he murmured, "It looks like we've got to get our youthful correspondent out more into society. He's seen some of the sites. He needs to meet more local folks. Ashley, how about getting Matt a bit more out into the city? He's not getting the proper hospitality!"

Lawton thought his host was joking. In fact he was but only slightly. Lawton was completely void of seeing any problem. Granville obviously thought there was a lot more to experience.

Ashley picked up on the cue. "My young friend, in the days ahead, you will be meeting more of the people of this fair city. I promise."

Matt could only shrug and look forward to the coming days… and evenings. He already knew that wherever Ashley traveled, there'd be entertainment.

With that worry seemingly settled, Henry's brow began to furl. As the ice tea was poured, he was trying to recall where the previous weekend's interviews had ended. Rubbing his forehead, he groaned, "Now, where was I?"

Ashley guffawed into his glass. Lawton, now more organized, took control. "Henry," he said, "You've left Glenwood. You did it. You departed the town without being seen, but it was well past midnight as you were heading for the Twin Cities."

Henry nodded. The recollection brought a smile to his face. He seemed to suddenly know exactly where he wanted to begin that evening's interview session. He was chuckling as he settled in to continue his story.

"Matt, after I'd failed to repay that money I still owed Loni D'Annelli's funds, any guilt I had would vanish with each mile I got further from Glenwood. Yes, it was very late that night of June 6 as I drove toward Minneapolis. In fact, I don't recall much of that journey until I got past St. Paul and crossed the state border into Wisconsin.

I could barely keep my eyes opened as the adrenalin rush that had propelled me had dissipated like water from a leaky glass. I should have stopped to rest, but my instincts kept prodding me to move on. My real fear was that if a raid had occurred on Saturday night there might be a number of 'guests' at Chippewa Lodge from places like Chicago and Milwaukee who might have been able to dodge the police incursion. They would already be speeding along the same road I was taking. I had this constant angst about my car being identified by one of those fellows as I lay sleeping in the driver's seat on the side of the highway. It was paranoia at its worst, but it provided the motivation to stay awake long enough to make it into Wisconsin. At that point I literally couldn't go on. I had to sleep. For that matter I needed fuel and no gasoline stations were yet opened that Sunday morning.

With daybreak on the horizon I made it across the St. Croix River Bridge into Wisconsin into the small community of Hudson. I was bleary-eyed. With nothing opened I still had enough gas to make Eau Claire another hour away providing I stayed awake. Then I'd be forced to stop until a filling station opened and turned on its fuel pumps.

I felt very alone during those very early hours. But, that feeling would change that very day thanks to two gentlemen I would soon meet. Despite my disheveled, haggard appearance, they were willing to help me. When you're beginning a new life and driving blankly down the road, it is hard to forget those special people and events that made a difference.

Eau Claire became impossible. My mind and body wouldn't allow me to make it that far. Fourteen miles into Wisconsin I was approaching an even smaller village named Hammond. There was sudden sharp curve on Hwy. 14 as I entered the town. I had to swerve abruptly to barely miss a corner café built dangerously close to the road. It didn't seem like I was going that fast, but my tires screeched and I came to a dead stop just inches from the corner café's front sign post. Smoke literally came off my tires as my car screeched to a halt. I had turned one hundred eighty degrees facing the opposite way. I was thankful the café was not yet opened that morning. I few customers might have found their coffee in their laps.

The first of those gentlemen I met owned a general store just a block from where I'd stopped. Badly shaken I was thinking how close

I'd come to having an accident and being unable to continue my flight to safety.

With a mounting headache and a low blood sugar level, I was going no further without food and rest. Looking down the dark street I saw a singular light at the side of one of the town's businesses. Shifting into gear I drove slowly toward that light. After having my engine revved up the previous couple hours, the quiet in that town was like driving into heaven.

There was a man unpacking a shipment of goods at the side of the store. It was just past 5:30. I remember thinking here was a man who truly worked for his living. Parking across the street, he watched me approach him and then stopped what he was doing as if to evaluate his situation. I knew what he was thinking and gave him a friendly wave in order to reduce any fear he might have of my intentions.

"Mornin," he said cautiously.

I returned the greeting in the most innocent, non-threatening way I could muster. My voice was very low from my fatigue. I said, "Sir, please don't let me cause you any alarm. I've been driving all night and I'm exhausted. I was wondering if there was a place in town that will be opening soon where I could get some breakfast and a cup of coffee. I'm willing to pay whatever is needed."

He looked me over and decided I looked more vulnerable than vicious. Without further pause, he pointed to the opened back door of his store. "If you'd like, go rest in my storage room. I just put on some hot coffee. You're welcome to have some. In a few minutes I'll come in and see if I can rustle you up some food. How would that be?"

I was so overwhelmed by his kindness that the very thought still warms my heart to this day. It was the tonic my new life needed at that moment. He was willing to take a chance on someone who didn't look in the best of form.

I stumbled into that back room. There was the small pot of coffee on a small wood stove. Next to the stove was a small cot. I couldn't help myself. I chose the cot over the coffee. I was out cold.

It was a few hours later that I awoke with a jump. I had no idea where I was. Seeing the stove, the thought occurred to me I'd fallen asleep in my office and hadn't even left Glenwood yet.

The smell of hot rolls and bacon told me that indeed I was into my new life. I opened my eyes fully to the owner of that general store brewing some fresh coffee and reading some passages from the Bible. The bacon was crackling in the pan and those rolls made my dry throat wet with saliva.

He looked at me and reached over with a fresh cup of coffee. He still had that kind look on his face. "If you want some cream, I've got some in the icebox."

I shook my head. "Thank you. I'll just take it black. I guess your cot looked more inviting than your offer of coffee. I hope I haven't been a nuisance."

He gave me the most patient smile while holding his hand out to shake. He said with a noticeable Swedish accent, "I'm Edwin Nordstrom. I own this store. You looked even more tired than I was a couple hours ago. Rather than have you laid out in some ditch from a car wreck, when I saw you on my cot, I decided just to let you sleep. You never moved while I unloaded the truck and filled my store shelves. Then I went over my bible lesson. In a bit I'll have to leave. Church will be starting."

His thoughtful words caught me off guard. The prematurely balding man then placed a marker in his Bible and served me up some bacon and rolls on a plate. There was no question I had lucked into meeting a very decent man. Having given me his name, I realized I should respond in same. I wasn't yet comfortable saying my new alias, so I grabbed his outstretched hand and mumbled, "My name is… ah…Daniel Johnson." Johnson was another friend of mine back in Glenwood. I figured he wouldn't mind if I borrowed his name for a short time.

Whether Nordstrom believed my fictional name or not, he put more bacon on my plate proving his compassion was stronger than his distrust. Sitting up, my head was still cloudy. I knew I could have slept all day if I'd felt safe in doing so. I hadn't had a good night's sleep for what seemed like months.

Then he just started talking…as if to make me more comfortable. In his mellow accent he drawled, "I'm not used to doing these early morning shipments, especially on a Sunday morning. Usually I'm done reading the bible lesson by now. I teach a Sunday school class before attending church services."

I wasn't certain if he was telling me these things in case I actually was a burglar ready to rob him, but he kept talking and I kept listening.

"My oldest son usually unloads this Sunday morning shipment. He takes his time so he can show up late for church."

Edwin's humor made his face open up into a wide grin. "He's up at St. Croix Falls camping out and canoeing for the weekend. That's even a better way for him to miss church altogether."

We both laughed at that one. His humor was so genuine. The two of us ended up talking until he had to leave for the Sunday school class he monitored. It was surprising the different subjects we discussed. He seemed equally in the mood more to talk than to study that Bible. Our conversation kept us laughing. I was amazed we could talk that long while he never asked where I was from or where I was going. He just seemed to have a sixth sense that I preferred not to talk about my personal situation.

It did occur to me that he was probably thinking I was a poor lost soul running from something. Well, 'running' I was, but 'poor' I was not with a fair amount of cash stuffed in my Plymouth parked across the street.

I asked about his family. He brightened as he told me all the good things about his wife and three kids. He said his oldest son hoped to go to college, but the cost was probably going to be too prohibitive. It was the only time he looked disappointed...as if he couldn't provide the future he wanted for his children. Of course, in those times that was a prevalent feeling among most folks about their kids.

Nordstrom was the first man I'd met and talked with since leaving Glenwood. It already felt like I'd been gone for a much longer period of time. My new beginning had gotten off to a very positive start thanks to the serendipitous stop I made at that man's store.

I recall offering to pay for the coffee and the breakfast, but he acted surprised I'd even made the offer. He'd found pleasure in our conversation as much as I had. Money would have only cheapened that wonderful morning. The sincere thanks I finally gave him seemed to please him more than I could have imagined.

When I finally left Hammond, I was behind schedule and I was traveling on the main highway between Minneapolis and Chicago. I shouldn't have been so paranoid, but I kept looking in my rear view mirror all the way to Madison. I was convinced some of those lodgers at Chippewa Lodge could easily be on my tail.

That obsession, though, did keep me alert. Fueling up in Eau Claire I drove on towards Wisconsin Dells. I still had a dull ache in my stomach but it was not for lack of food. Getting rid of that old Plymouth coupe had become my new fascination. That car and I had been a very distinctive pair for the last couple years in Glenwood. The sooner that automobile and I were separated, the better off I would feel. Unfortunately Sunday was not such an opportune day to be selling or trading an automobile.

In the meantime if anything happened on the highway whether a speeding ticket or an accident, my car could be easily traced. Anyone looking for me...like some of D'Annelli's boys... would try the highway departments in the five-state area to see if my vehicle and license plate could be located. Claiming my old Plymouth had been stolen, they'd even have the cops helping them find me.

I kept on driving south on Federal Hwy. 14. Hunger returned but I couldn't make myself stop for a complete meal. Every café I saw, I could visualize some of D'Annelli's gang stopping in for the same reason. I finally decided that Madison would be my stopping point for that Sunday. I would drive into the city and get a room at a rooming house far off the beaten track.

Yet, even that idea came with another consideration. It would be a bonanza if some robber broke into my vehicle while I slept.

When I finally made it to the outskirts of Madison later that afternoon, my impulse was to get a good meal, and then look for an automobile sales business. I figured I'd sleep in the car lot where there would be safety in numbers. The following morning I'd trade off my car to that car dealer. Paying for a new car would be no problem. Handling my trade-in my way would be the bigger challenge."

Henry paused for a moment, lit a cigar and asked Lawton if the continuation of his story was making sense.

Lawton nodded. Ashley nodded as well. He knew much of Henry's background, but maintained an unwearied ear. Lill had her own interest piqued. She appeared to be hearing some new details he'd not shared with her before.

Henry then winked at Lill and Ashley. The three of them began to chuckle. Lawton sensed they knew the next part of the tale.

"Well, Matt, this next man I met in Wisconsin became a friend of mine just by a fluke. His name was T.W. Thompson. He sold cars. That was his calling and he performed the task with a zeal I've never witnessed in any other car salesman. He was then and continued to be one of the more unique characters I've met in my lifetime. Many of the cars I've purchased over the years came from this man. As I tell you this part of the story, you'll come to realize how important he was to the continuation of my journey.

To begin with, he referred to himself as 'Old T.W.'...always in the third person. He said the 'T.W.' stood for "trustworthy". It was in all his advertisements. Later when we got to know each other, he intimated that at least it was always his intention to be honest in his business. However, with the economy being what it was, he admitted honesty sometimes had to take a back seat to making a sale. All I can say that in my dealings with this man, he was as 'trustworthy' as his nickname described.

He called every man or boy 'Son' even if they were older than him. To best describe him, let me refer to the time years later when I was visiting my old friend T.W. with an associate of mine.

Over lunch I recall T.W. in his wonderful vernacular jump right into telling my business associate about the first time he'd met me. He put his hand on my shoulder and looked at the two of us like he still couldn't believe his own story. His distinct manner of speaking went something like this:

"Tarnation, Son, I recall that first car I sold Henry back in 31. Hell, he wouldn't even give me his name... as closed-mouthed as if his jaw'd been broke. I believe it was a Sunday just a couple hours after most of the church services ended in town. You have to understand, Son, old T.W. doesn't really like going to church, especially to my wife Edna's Dutch Reformed Church. That church was sixteen blocks from my Ford automobile sales business... and sweet Jesus, I felt one hell of a lot closer to heaven in my shop than when I was at that danged church. I placed my

business location north of downtown Madison on Federal Hwy. 14 so I wouldn't miss any potential customers coming in from that side of town. I didn't give a damn about anyone coming up from Illinois from the south. They're just a bunch of penny-pinchin' out-of-staters down there.

Son, I'm a tellin' you that in 1931 customers buyin' any kind of car were thin…and people interested in buyin' new cars were even thinner. Still I had a knack for keepin' food on the table and some illegal beer in the back icebox in my office. I was one of the few men in the car business makin' any money at all.

Sundays were always relaxed days. I liked going over to my car lot whenever I could sneak out of the back pew of that God forsaken Dutch Reformed Church service. Usually the best time was during a prayer. My wife, Edna, always preferred to stay around the church for some gossip, food and maybe meetin' somebody who might claim they had a sure fire idea about havin' a short cut to heaven. But, I think mostly it was the food and gossip. I don't think heaven was in the cards for her given her poor choice in a husband!

Anyway, old T.W. just liked to get in one of his special cars and drive over to my business after sneakin' out of church. I never officially opened my doors for business on Sunday, mind you, but those afternoons if someone came along that was interested in a car, well, by God, Son, old T.W. didn't want them goin' home disappointed. In all them warmer days of the summer, old T.W. likes to just sit out on the porch in front of my office in my favorite easy chair and watch the world go by on Federal Hwy. 14. But, mind you, old T.W. was ready to sell a car on a moment's notice…you can bet your long johns on that fact. But, you know, Son, mostly old T.W. just sat back, unwound, and dreamed of the bygone days like three years before when I was actually sellin' some new cars. Still it was nice just bein' by myself after a long grueling week tryin' to squeeze a dime out of some cheap bastard tryin' to screw me out of gainin' that same dime. I didn't actually see a lot of folks on those Sunday afternoons. Sometimes I'd just grab some of my "IOU's" or look at my inventory sheets and appreciate how I still had some cars in the lot and some cash comin' into my business!

Anyway Son, old T.W. was sitting in my rockin' chair being shaded by an awning out in front of my office. I was watchin' an afternoon rainstorm movin' toward Madison. There'd been a lot of rain the previous days, as the weather systems kept movin' down from Minnesota. Every time it rained I always had a warm thought towards those Scandinavians up there...for sharin' some of the rainwater with their neighbors in Wisconsin. God knows they didn't share much else. I say, Son, those damned Swedes and Norwegians up north of Madison in both Minnesota and Wisconsin were normally so tight I guessed they walked out of a church service early so they wouldn't have to contribute to the offering plate. Of course, those Dutch folks were the worst. I swear to Christ they took change from the offering plate. Those people were the type of customers old T.W. had to deal with every day. Why it was a damned miracle my wife and I weren't liven' some place in a tent and eatin' tree bark! And, Son, when the 'Crash' hit, things got even worse. Of course, no one had to worry about old T.W. By Jesus, I did all right during those days.

Well, Son, old T.W. was almost asleep that Sunday afternoon despite the rumbling of that approachin' storm to the west of Madison. And by God in Heaven without warning, the next thing I know I got this voice talkin' to me not two feet from my ear. I thought the Almighty was comin' down to give me hell about skippin' out on church.

Shitfire, Son, I didn't even hear this tall, skinny fella approach me. The first thing I looked at was the man's eyes...like Old T.W. always did. You gotta read people to see if you have a chance of doin' some business with them...and you gotta read them fast! Well, this man's eyes looked tired, but there was a friendliness that couldn't be hidden. He wasn't there to rob me or burglarize my business. He just looked like he needed a place to rest more than anything else.

But, old T.W. knew that if a man stopped by to look at cars on a Sunday afternoon, he could also be a serious buyer. And, the more desperate they were, the more chance the car was goin' to be priced a bit higher. I just had to figure how desperate this fella was for a set of wheels.

Well, old T.W. was havin' a bit of a task readin' this tired fellow. He was peculiar. He was not reckless or careless lookin', but he was kind of antsy. The guy looked to be on the forty side of his thirties and in need of a shave and a shower. One thing I liked right off about this fella, though, was that he sat right down on a chair beside me. I could tell he was the type who could put his feet up, sit back and relax just like old T.W. liked to do. But, he still seemed a bit anxious…like he needed some kind of help, but not from just anyone.

Well, Son, old T.W. can smell a potential transaction through a den of skunks. I got my business hat on and decided it was time to play out this particular hand of cards. After all, it was a Sunday. There was nothin' to lose.

I tell you old T.W. gave him my friendliest smile and my warmest handshake and said to him, 'Son, this is your lucky God damned day. You're talkin' with T.W. Thompson, the owner of the best gosh-danged car business in all of Madison. If you got your mind on an automobile this afternoon, well, Son, you can consider yourself one fortunate son of a bitch. My wife hates me for it, but my business is open on the Sabbath the same as if it's Tuesday. I say, Son, sit down and take a load off. I've got coffee… or a nice cold beer in the back room… and I've got time. What can old T.W. do for you?"

Well, by golly, that tall, thin stranger suddenly looked like he'd just had his first successful bowel movement in a week. Never saw a fella lookin' so relieved. He accepted my offer of some coffee and sat back on that lawn chair.

The man looked like he could fall asleep any second. Mostly the guy just wanted to rest. That was fine with old T.W.

Well, Son, we jabbered about the weather like most Midwesterners do. That thunderstorm looked like it was going to bear down on us within the hour. That didn't seem to bother him. I could tell this fella was kind of feeling me out as if wondering how much he could trust me. He never offered his name, but I could tell he liked old T.W. And by God, Son, what's not to like about the best danged car salesman the Almighty ever put on earth!

And that was how I met the man who's sittin' next to you...and whose name I only learned years later. We did some business that day and we're doin more today... and I'm a hopin' we'll do a hell of lot more in the future. No matter where the man's livin', when he needs a car, Old T.W. will be there...and if need be, no one will be the wiser."

Lill, Ashley, and Matt were laughing and enjoying Henry's rendition of T.W. Thompson. With the slight break Ashley motioned for a waiter to bring more ice tea. The waiter had barely left and Henry had already continued the story.

".......and I was almost too tired to formulate an opinion about old T.W. that Sunday afternoon. It was absolute coincidence that I happened to even stop at the man's car business. I was just entering the outskirts of the north edge of town when I spotted the large man under an umbrella sitting on a comfortable chair outside amongst all his cars. Though the sun was still shining brightly in the sky, there were some looming storm clouds moving in from the west. It seemed a certainty that a major thunderstorm was going to pass through the north side of Madison. Given my declining condition, I was not about to wrestle a major storm in my old Plymouth.

Call it fate, but I slowed down and ventured into that small automobile business figuring that fellow was the owner. I hoped he'd be in the mood to do some business, even if it was Sunday afternoon.

I parked my vehicle at the end of his automobile lot. I didn't want him to get a great look at the condition of my battered Plymouth coupe. He might have told me to get lost.

T.W. seemed to be sleeping in his chair under that umbrella as I approached him. Not wanting to startle him I made some noise before I got too close to him. He didn't budge. He was sleeping so peacefully, I doubted the oncoming storm would wake him. I had the feeling if I yelled out a greeting I'd scare him so badly he'd drop dead of a heart attack. But, he wasn't moving. I had to say something.

Finally I stood next to him and in a firm voice said, "Good afternoon!" I didn't mean for it to come out so loud. With that quiet Sunday afternoon environment, my voice carried as if aided by a megaphone. Old T.W. almost fell over backwards. He sat up straight while coughing, scratching his enormous belly, and letting go with a hearty belch. He looked me over in seconds...and then went into that spiel I just imitated.

I was still numb with exhaustion. The cadence of his voice made my mind drift. He kept his repeating rifle of words. I had no idea what he was saying. The pressure of the previous days and weeks was seeping out of my body. I had the energy of a soggy noodle. I just sat there grunting occasionally in order to prove to both of us I was still breathing. I might have dozed off if it hadn't been for that approaching storm.

Finally he gazed across his car lot and saw my beaten up Plymouth. He gradually moved his eyes back at me and re-directed his attention to my bedraggled appearance. At that point old T.W. relaxed. I didn't look very threatening. Then he just started talking in that unique style of his...the subject was immaterial.

My watch said it had been almost thirty minutes since I'd sat down beside him. It seemed like three minutes. There was no reason to put off finding out whether this man might be willing to do some business on my terms or not. If he didn't, I had to move on. I'd find another car business the next day in Janesville or Beloit...or even Rockford, Illinois where I'd finally leave the main federal highway between Minneapolis and Chicago and steer south.

While sitting there it again dawned on me that some of those gangsters staying at Chippewa Lodge could be cruising through Madison on the way back to the Windy City depending on the time of a possible raid. The chance of being seen or recognized was still heavy on my mind.

So far I had not volunteered my name...not even a made-up name. Old T.W. didn't seem to mind. Names weren't important to the old guy unless they were a prospect for one of his cars. Then again, his business was based on winning the trust of someone and transacting business in a hurry before the customer had a chance to change his mind or get away. As I rubbed my face to wake up, his conversation changed back to talk of the impending storm. I recall chuckling. If I had been quizzed on anything he'd said since I'd sat down, I would not have passed the test. I think T.W. would have flunked the same test.

It was in the very next instant that my tired but relaxed state of mind was bowled over as if hit by a sudden title wave. Racing down Federal Hwy. 14 right in front of T.W.'s business was a car I recognized. It slowed at a stop sign and then continued on. Sure enough, in it were some of the men who'd been staying at Chippewa Lodge...some for a number of months. I'd seen that car and those men often in Glenwood down at the cafe.

My immediate reaction was to slump down in the chair next to T.W praying they would not take notice of me or my car. I had hoped I'd be safe from ever interacting with any of those hoodlums again. It occurred to me something must have happened that Sunday morning at Chippewa Lodge for them to be that far from Glenwood, Minnesota. Otherwise those men would be still involved in the charity golf tournament back at the Lodge.

When they passed, I couldn't waste any more time. I had to ignore my exhaustion and accept the responsibilities of my new life. I was no longer a patient, conservative manager of a feed & grain mill.

I was surprised how strong my voice sounded as I leaned forward and interrupted my long-winded new acquaintance. He seemed surprised with my sudden robust voice as I said to him, "T.W., for the next five to ten minutes I am going to outline an offer I'm going to make to buy one of your cars. It will be a cash transaction, so you might find my proposition interesting. But, do understand there will be more conditions than just the trade-in value on my dusty old Plymouth sitting out there at the end of your lot. As I explain the entire deal, I want you to stop me at any point you feel any discomfort. I'll just get up and quietly leave...and you'll never see me again."

Old T.W.'s eyebrows rose about an inch. My whole character had changed from less than a half minute before. It made him examine me even closer. But as he did, he only nodded and stayed silent. He knew when to shut up. He'd experienced too many opportunities for a sale lost with too much chatter. Still when he wasn't in control, he figured he was going to come out on the short end of any possible transaction. For that reason he sighed and leaned back in his chair. I remember him looking off in the distance at the approaching lightning and rain clouds and finally saying as if he was surrendering, "Well, son, what do you have in mind?"

What I outlined to him was something that a man in his business could only imagine in his dreams. Even then it was too outlandish. I told him the business I wanted to conduct with him could potentially be repeated often in the future if he could abide by what I was about to propose.

I looked directly into his eyes and spoke confidently. "T.W., after I tell you my proposal, you'll need to analyze the entire deal very quickly...and then be able to give me an answer within five minutes. If it's "Yes", I'll want to close our deal now. If it's "No", I'll be on my way and you'll have a hundred dollar bill in your pocket to forget you ever met me."

T.W. perked up. The $100 offer had touched a nerve.

I continued, "First, I want you to accept $500 cash from me for taking that old Plymouth coupe over there on the side of your car lot off my hands. I never want to see the vehicle again. In its present condition and color, I never want to have anyone else see that vehicle again either. And, I never want anyone to know I ever owned that automobile. That is the first part of our transaction. Is that clear?"

TW leaned forward and nodded hesitantly. I had definitely piqued his interest.

"Secondly, I want to buy that new Ford A 400 Convertible Sedan sitting right in front of us. I will buy it from you for retail plus 10 percent. The extra 10 percent is payment for you to never divulge the name of the purchaser of that automobile. In fact, I do not want to be named on any paper work to the state of Wisconsin or to Ford Motor Company. To help you further, I will be paying you today...and in cash. You won't have to wait around for some two-bit loan to be authorized."

T.W.'s jaw was open so wide I could see his back teeth. He stared at me intently while leaning more forward in his chair. The gears of his brain were smoking trying to evaluate what he'd have to do to make this deal work. I had created some challenges in the potential transaction… no doubt about it. He eyed me carefully as I was about to make my final point to our potential deal.

"Thirdly, I want you to know that I am neither a murderer nor a crook. But, I can almost guarantee that some unsavory hoodlums would like to find me. I'm definitely a hunted man. That's why I don't want any record of our doing business. And, for your own safety, I'm never going to tell you my name. In time you might learn my name, but it is not important for now. Our confidential business relationship will be the only significant factor between us. Privacy is the key to our relationship. If the confidentiality is ever tainted, I will have to end our relationship. And, it will not be to your financial advantage to have our affiliation end."

I finished by saying, "Finally, I have seen one automobile dash by your business already with some fellows who might be looking for me. So, I am interested in finding out if you want to deal right now! If you do, I would appreciate if you would open your garage door so I can hide my very recognizable Plymouth coupe from further view. I would also ask that you drive that new Ford A 400 Sedan into the same garage so I could transfer my luggage and other belongings."

Just then a huge thunderclap with accompanying lightning just west of his car lot exploded as if God was waiting impatiently for T.W.'s response as well. The old guy looked about as stunned as a human could feel.

I was done with my demands. Now I had to wait for his reply. "T.W., can you help me? You've got four minutes left to make a decision."

I had taken control. As planned, I was not going to spare any money from helping myself survive those crucial first couple days of my escape plan.

T.W. looked like he was either pondering the meaning of life or he had an intestinal gas build up second to none. He got up from his easy chair and strolled over to his new Ford A 400 Convertible Sedan as if deciding if he wanted to part with one of his star athletes. He told me later he was actually relieving some gas pain in his stomach.

He gazed back at me for a few seconds, spat on the ground and then exploded in laughter only slightly less loud than a simultaneous thunderclap overhead. Pointing at my Plymouth he directed me to drive it over to his garage as a few droplets of rain began to fall. In the next minute I drove my old beater into his garage and he followed me with that new Ford. As he closed the garage door, the rain came down in buckets. We were both glad he didn't need the full five minutes to make up his mind.

I recall him getting out of his Ford, scratching his belly as he strolled over to me and stuck out his hand. We both said nothing. The deal was consummated with the silent handshake. It cemented a relationship that lasted as long as T.W. lasted. At the time neither one of us could realize the extent that our new friendship would bear on each other's futures. In 1931, I was just interested in buying absolute secrecy along with a new car and ridding myself of my old coupe. He would not learn my true name for many years, but that didn't matter. He always called me 'Son' anyway.

Over the next decade right through World War II, I did my car buying exclusively through old T.W. He was able to find what I wanted even through the difficult war years and the sparse times immediately thereafter. I can always hear that same voice when I opened up a telephone conversation with him. I'd try to always call him on Sunday either at his home or at his car lot. I'd say, "T.W., you want to make a sale on a Sunday afternoon and make 10 percent over retail?"

I'd hear him chortle in that unique wheezing manner and then in that boisterous twang he'd respond, "I say son, how you doin'? You still being chased by those God damned hoodlums. Son, we'll keep things quieter than a rat walking by a cat convention. You just tell old T.W. what you need and when and where you want the vehicle ...and, it'll be there."

And, it always was. Yes, we did a lot of business over the years."

Lawton noticed a slight tear in Henry's eyes and the older man stopped for a moment to blow his nose. It was obvious that Henry's story covering so many years would at times refer to people who had sadly passed on. Lawton stayed quiet as did Lill and Ashley until Henry composed himself again.

Then a smirk crept back on his face as he continued.

"I slept in the back room of old T.W.'s business that Sunday night during the storm. He offered me a room at a local hotel, but I told him I just wanted to sleep on his office couch for a few hours. It would feel safer. I wanted to wake and take off in the pre-dawn hours.

The $1700 T.W. received for my new Ford was actually more than 20% over the retail price of $1400 he had priced the car. He tried to give me back the extra money I'd paid him, but I refused it saying, "Let the extra cover some future long distance collect calls next time I need a car."

While he appreciated the potential car sale opportunities, he asked how he would know the call was from me.

I responded simply, "You'll know me. I'll just say I prefer buying my automobiles on a fine Sunday afternoon from the best damned car salesman in Wisconsin."

He doubled over in laughter.

I also paid him that $500 extra to destroy my old Plymouth. He assured me by 8:00 the next morning, before some of his mechanics even made it into his shop, my vehicle would be in pieces. He said he'd have a friend show up at 6:00 AM to break down the car...then sell the parts to different auto shops for salvage. He was going to make some extra money off my old clunker. Old T.W. was my kind of businessman.

After the storm subsided, he went home with a bounce to his step and my promise to lock the door whenever I left early the next morning. He had $2200 in his cash box that he didn't have when he got up Sunday morning. As for me, I'd just pulled off a major step in ensuring my well-being. After transferring the hidden cash from my old Plymouth to the new Ford sedan, I bedded down on his office couch that Sunday evening content that I was about as safe as I could ever hope to be given my circumstances...at least for that night."

Chapter 10

"It was 4:00 when I awoke that June Monday morning and drove south toward Janesville and Beloit. Once I got into Illinois daylight was breaking. Traveling south out of Rockford on State Hwy. 51, I became less concerned about anyone from D'Annelli's gang in my rear view mirror. Their route would have them turning east toward Chicago. My direction was across the entire length of Illinois toward Paducah, Kentucky by nightfall. At that point I planned on disappearing into the vast American countryside ending my sojourn at my new home on a coastal island off South Carolina. I planned on being so isolated in the weeks ahead, it would be virtually impossible to find me.

I had lunch at a little café out in the middle of Illinois near a town called 'Normal'. It did occur to me then how my life was so distant from the meaning of that word. My new Ford A 400 Convertible Sedan gave me a fresh sense of self-assurance. I'd never driven an automobile with that much horsepower. I felt as if I was flying as I sped down the straight highway toward Decatur, Illinois. I was passing old cars and tractors like they were standing still. I had no timetable to reach my destination. It just felt good to be free from the burdens I'd been carrying for so long.

Driving thru that long state of Illinois felt like I was driving around the world. The state would never end. The flat terrain made it next to impossible to stay awake despite my solid eight hours of sleep I'd had in T.W. Thompson's office sofa the previous night. I must have stopped ten times for water, fuel for the car, and various things to eat just to remain alert. Every time I did take a break, all I saw were the same corn stalks, bare farmland or periodic groves of trees over the same flat land. Minnesota had not the most interesting geography on earth, but it looked like a national park compared to the tedious, flat farmland of Illinois.

Admittedly, I continued to stare at my rear view mirror out of habit. It would take me that day before I accepted D'Annelli's boys would not have a clue as to where I was on the planet. My next concern, though, was the preposterous amount of money I had transferred to my new Ford A 400 Convertible Sedan from my old Plymouth the previous night. With that additional $50,000 I hadn't been able to return to the mill basement, I now had a satchel in the back seat holding that money along with $200,000 hidden in every dark place in that automobile. The old Plymouth had camouflaged the likelihood that I had but five dollars in my pocket. That new more sporting car stuck out like an advertisement that the driver had some wealth.

Still I was thrilled to have that old Plymouth gone from anyone's sight. If that old sedan had broken down, I was very susceptible to being robbed. By that night, though, I would mollify my concern about the cash I was carrying. My destination was just across the Ohio River...a river town called Paducah, Kentucky. I had a friend there.

I recall being so excited at the Illinois-Kentucky border as I crossed the new spectacularly colored blue bridge over the Ohio River to reach that historic city. The only knowledge I had of Paducah was its background of serious flooding every spring...as if the Ohio River overflow couldn't get to the Mississippi River soon enough. But, it represented a milestone...another important step away from my former life. There were so many emotions rolling through my head. The river was so wide. It seemed forever before I traversed that bridge. I guess when you're fleeing for your life, each minute has its own importance.

Once I drove into Paducah, as slow-moving as that old town was, the sight could not mellow my elation. I believe I truly allowed my lungs to completely fill with air since leaving Minnesota. My entire chest seemed to untighten.

It didn't take long for me to experience some disappointment with Paducah. Truthfully, I thought I'd driven into another country... and a very poor one at that. I observed both races, but predominantly black. Whatever the color, folks looked so downtrodden. That Monday had been just another hard day in the fields or loading boats. There was a palpable sense of exhaustion and hopelessness. I'd seen similar bleakness on faces back in rural Minnesota. It was a bit discouraging. It would be written about in future years about those traumatic times in American business, social, and economic history. The Depression had seemingly decimated whatever hopes still remained in rural America's populace. It didn't matter which state.

The sun was low in the westerly sky as I drove slowly through the town. With the heat and humidity, my shirt stuck to the back of the driver's seat as if glued. Stopping by a dilapidated gasoline station, there were four Negro men smoking and chatting in front of the station's garage. The men just stared at me and my new A 400 Ford Sedan. That was the first hint I should be very cautious in my travels. My new car would get unneeded attention and could place me in some difficult situations…and not just in Paducah, Kentucky.

My saving grace at that gasoline station was that all four men were much older and didn't look motivated or physically fit enough to assault me. One of those gentlemen finally got up and trudged over to the pump. He nodded, but didn't say a word to me as he filled my tank. I had an urge to go to the bathroom, however, with the amount of money hidden in that car, I felt it more prudent to wet my pants rather than leave my car unattended.

I walked over to the small garage office and took a Coca Cola from an ice chest. I looked back at the man filling my tank and raised the soda so he could see I intended to pay for it. He gave me an ever so slight nod and then looked away. He didn't seem real excited that I was spending money at his gasoline station.

I was parched and downed half the bottle with my head back and my eyes closed. The three remaining men by the garage mumbled something and their shoulders shook as if they'd never heard anything funnier. I had a feeling it was at my expense. I could not make out what they were saying, but it was obviously something not very complimentary. Of course with their accents, I could have been sitting next to them and I wouldn't have understood them.

I took another long swig of pop finally dousing the dryness in my throat. I'd progressed two days into my plan that was months into the making. I'd always felt once I got to Paducah my life had a chance to continue more on my terms. In that southern town lived a very good friend of mine…someone I'd spent time with during my service overseas in the 'Big War'. I had the directions to his place from downtown Paducah. All I had to do was recognize downtown Paducah.

Despite the shabby looking buildings, the closed store fronts, and the dusty streets, I guessed I was there.

As the attendant finished, I noticed a public telephone. It was close to the time I'd set for calling back to Minnesota. I could only hope the connection would be clear enough to allow a conversation.

Connecting the telephone lines between that location in Paducah and Rich Brey's room at the Lake Mille Lacs resort took some time, but finally I heard the operator speaking to his voice. He seemed relieved and anxious to hear from me. He yelled into the speaker, "Henry, are you all right?"

Rich's voice sounded muffled and a million miles away. Still, it was a relief to hear a familiar voice.

Yelling back, I shouted, "Rich, fill me in. What's been happening back in Glenwood?"

As Brey started talking, those Negro fellows were eyeing my car and me. I thought I was going to have to make yet another escape.

Then a patrol car drove up with his eyes glued on me and my new car...and those fellas sitting hungrily at the front of the filling station sat back in their chairs. The cop then just stopped and stared at me like I was nuts. Apparently I was in the wrong part of town. If he'd known the amount of money I'd crammed under the seats and in the side panels of the vehicle, he might have considered joining forces with those fellows drooling over my car.

Brey was quite upbeat. The hollow sound to his voice on the line couldn't hide his glee. "Henry, the news is all good so far. As it turns out that Miss MacPherson had collected enough evidence and she called in the state patrol and the Bureau of Investigation on Sunday. And, as the cops were rolling into town, D'Annelli got caught up in the damnedest sting you could ever hope to see. He was caught red-handed with stolen goods and counterfeit money in that storage area at the mill. I'm not certain who planned out that scam, but it worked like a charm. It probably was Miss MacPherson, but I don't know how she could have pulled it off by herself. Anyway, Clarence and I have already told the authorities that you had offered that storage space to D'Annelli a year and a half ago just to hold cash from the Calcutta. We told them you had no interest or concern what else D'Annelli might have in the mill basement...that you had given him the free storage area in appreciation for the good he'd brought to the community."

Rich was talking fast. I was having trouble picking up everything he said with the static on the line. I then heard him say something about "the Lodge tumbled like a house of cards…and the authorities……. arrested……known criminals hiding out in the cabins…and verified the year round gambling operation at the Lodge."

When Rich added that D'Annelli was currently sitting in the Pope County jailhouse and being questioned by state authorities, I felt like dancing.

I asked him, "Rich, what about your resignations. Did our plan work out for you and Clarence?

I caught his chuckle as the line got clearer. "Henry, you wouldn't believe how smoothly the resignations went earlier this afternoon. The authorities might question us some more, but both Clarence and I did exactly what the three of us discussed. We feigned embarrassment when we got back from Lake Osakis Sunday night. Then this noon we promptly and humbly resigned our positions.

Some townsfolk were crying when they heard about our shame filled response to having a community of gangsters living under our noses out at the Lodge. The whole thing was crazy. So many people in Glenwood admitted they had at least some idea what was going on. They knew damned well Clarence and I only kept quiet with no arrests all these years because it was in the community's best interest. Anyway, Henry, that had to be the best acting job Clarence and I ever did. The town is still shocked over our high morals and our apparent humiliation. People were still begging Clarence and me as we drove out of town to reconsider and tear up our resignation letters.

I should also tell you the great thing that the MacPherson lady told the authorities in our favor. She said in her findings that you, Clarence and I had no connection with the gangsters at the Lodge. She understood we were in a tough spot. The group at the Lodge needed goods and services. What were the local businesses supposed to do, ignore their needs out at that lake resort? She knew we stayed quiet for the good of the community.

Even when she saw the two of us before we left town today, she tried to talk us into keeping our jobs. She of course had no idea we have other plans. She appeared really saddened that by doing her job, she had ended the good times for the town. Glenwood is going to be just another community struggling to survive from now on. The town is going to miss Loni D'Annelli and his crowd...even if they were hoodlums."

Then Rich added one more piece of information confirming again the generous side of Loni D'Annelli. He said, "Henry, our resignations even had an impact on D'Annelli. He saw us momentarily while he was let out of his jail cell to use the john. As angry as he was about what was happening to his businesses, he mumbled to Clarence and me that he was going to say nothing about the minor security work we'd done for him outside the Lodge. The three of us knew his monthly security guard payment to Clarence and me was made to keep us from nosing around in his affairs. We'd kept our side of the bargain for the benefit of the town. He also knew we couldn't have been involved in his arrest and the police raid or why would we have resigned our jobs?"

Inquiring about the reaction to my own exodus from Glenwood, Brey again had to yell into the receiver. "Henry, we made certain your letter of resignation was found at your home before we left town a few hours ago. At first, people were concerned about your well-being. Everyone now believes your safe and simply on your two-week vacation. They figure you'll likely stop back in town before you begin your new job wherever that may be....and that you'll be shocked to hear about what happened to D'Annelli. Miss MacPherson came through for you as well. She explained to the state police and the agents of the Bureau of Investigation that all evidence pointed out that you dealt with D'Annelli on behalf of the town and you had no illegal involvement. As a result, the authorities have little interest in talking with you considering they have plenty of evidence against D'Annelli.

But, I do have to warn you. As we expected, D'Annelli ordered a couple of his boys who'd had no charges filed against them to find you. When your resignation note was found, he hit the roof and repeatedly told those same guys to find you if they had to spin the globe.

So, Henry, wherever you are now, keep moving. Don't worry... in your next telephone call, we'll keep you posted with whatever we hear. Clarence and I guess some of Loni's boys will eventually look us up and ask if we know anything about where you went. It'll be easy for the two of us to play dumb. I think you'll be plenty safe where you're going."

It was a relief hearing all the news. Hiding out had become a reality.

The telephone line then deteriorated and I was only picking up some of what Rich was saying. He was repeating something we'd discussed before. He was shouting, "Henry…if you can still hear me in all this damn static, we'll wait for you to inform Charlie Davis about Clarence and me. And, don't be concerned about Davis learning your identity. He won't find out from us. But, you can bet he'll be surprised when he learns it'll be the two of us who will be taking over the reins of the two resorts."

The line then got so bad I could only yell a farewell. I hung up feeling greatly relieved but knowing the odyssey had just begun. It was in my imminent plans to have my two friends and business associates meet Charlie Davis. I had already informed him that I'd been training two men to eventually take over the management of the two resorts. Again, over my nervousness that Charlie might walk away still prevailed. If he heard the two humbled Glenwood law officers were my choices, his and my relationship might be affected. I had to wait. He was just too valuable to me."

Following that telephone call back to Minnesota, I sat down on a bench at that Paducah gasoline station drinking another coke with those four Negro fellows now eying me like I was a victim just waiting to be robbed…and the cop looking at me in the same way. When I finally got back in my 1931 Ford A 400 Convertible Sedan, the cop drove over to me with a stern look on his face. In the deepest country accent, he drawled, "Mister…you got a death wish? If I wasn't here, you'd apt to be sitting on your ass on the pavement watching that fancy dan car of yours peel on down the roadway with some other fellers driving it. I'd suggest you follow me out of here and get on to where you're going."

I took him up on his offer. If he'd known the cash hidden in my vehicle, he might have driven me to a doctor to check my sanity. I followed the cop until I saw my turn on a county road in the direction where my friend's house was located. I'd sent a letter in the recent weeks indicating I would be stopping by his town sometime in the weeks ahead and would be looking forward to seeing him.

Heading down that road every house looked dismal. I wondered if there was a better part of town. My mind flew back in time as I visualized my friend's smiling face. His name was Ezeriah Hamilton. He was "Ez" to me and I was just "Henry" to him. We had become friends soon after I arrived with my unit in Paris right at the end of the

'Big War'. He was a cook for my division and a person with darker skin. I was in the supply part of the military. We saw each other at lot, laughed a lot, and together began exploring the back streets of Paris when we had leave. There was not much stigma walking the streets of Paris with him and me being of different color. We ended up traveling together around France, Switzerland, and northern Italy before returning to the states.

Ez seemed to know how to find the ladies, the good food, and some of the historical sites that interested both of us. It was a very exciting time in my life and I owed him a lot. He dragged me along wherever he went. I never thought I added much to our travels. He was the one who could speak French and he knew the history. I didn't need help with the ladies, but I would not have met as many without him.

We discussed often how difficult our travel would be if we were back in the states. With prejudice so deeply rooted in our country, and some people still fighting the Civil War, it would have been challenging for us to have the kind of adventure we were having in our travels in Europe.

When we returned to our respective homes from France, we continued meeting in various cities twice sometimes three times a year until we got too busy with our jobs. Then it was only once a year. How often did we just shake our heads when roving around the U.S. during the 1920's? So many people had a problem with a friendship like ours. While we mostly ignored the disapproving looks, there were times I had to say Ez was my steward so no further problems developed. While on those trips we often talked about working somewhere together, but the times made it difficult and our home locations were inconvenient.

Over the years Ez and I typically met in Chicago, St. Louis, and even twice in Washington D.C. With his businesses he couldn't be gone from Kentucky for very long. No matter how hard life got, I always saw his sincere smile and an incomparable positive spirit whenever we got together. He was a real entrepreneur in his business dealings. Based on the cars he told me he owned, I sensed he was doing whatever it took to make ends meet...and better.

In the last couple years as I knew it would be inevitable I'd be leaving Minnesota, I invested a fair amount of brain power trying to develop a business we could partner. That was another motivation for using D'Annelli's money...to create a partnership.

Our last dinner together was in October 1930 in Chicago. By then I had been making some very good money off the 'borrowed' money from D'Annelli's fortune. Ez commented on my change. He said I seemed more aggressive…even careless.

I remember him saying, "Henry, my friend, you seem to be flying much higher these days. Something's happened in your life? Have you met a woman?"

We both laughed. I was about as confirmed a bachelor as you'd ever meet. I said to him, "No, Ez, I've just gotten into some other businesses in a big way. I'm going to be making some changes in my job and my location."

He looked at me curiously not because he thought I was irrational, but because he could tell I was serious.

I continued, "The changes are fairly dramatic even to the point that I'll be leaving Minnesota. And, I have to tell you I'm going to need some help. I've got to turn to a friend like you to assist me if you can find the time and are willing."

He gave me that uniquely patient grin of his and joked, "So what's taken you so long to get your act together?"

We then sat in this old dive on the south side of Chicago while I told him what was happening in my life. I also related to him some of the further risks I was about to take. I didn't get into all the dealings I was doing with Loni D'Annelli's money, but he got the general picture of what I owned and why I eventually had to leave Glenwood for good.

I then outlined a business we could share if he was interested. I said, "Ez, I have very few people I can really trust besides you. I need someone to help me out in buying and developing properties in the southeast, particularly the South Carolina and Florida coasts. When I leave Minnesota, that's the area I intend to be based."

He looked at me in a very doubtful but appreciative way. He really couldn't believe what he was hearing. It took another few weeks by phone, but we were able to solidify our partnership allowing him to keep running his own businesses out of Paducah…at least until he saw our collaboration in South Carolina as wise and solvent. I had already closed on my Kiawah Island land purchase in South Carolina. In my mind it had become more a place I could hide out rather than to live. Everything I read about the island…which wasn't much…indicated the place was as wild as the Everglades.

Initially Ez and I agreed he would check out some hotel properties in and around Charleston before I got there. Being such an obvious Yankee the local people wouldn't give me much consideration. I'd be looked upon as a damned carpetbagger. With Ez, he at least knew the ways of the South and would have as good of a chance or better working around the ignorance and prejudice of that area.

I wired money to him in February, 1931, for his travels to Charleston. He wasn't excited about staying in a city still ensconced in pre-Civil War haughtiness and post-war abject poverty. The shambles from the stock market crash of 1929 only added to the misery. Recovery seemed a distant dream, yet I thought there might be opportunity. I'd traveled through the city twice during the middle 1920's. Despite the determined class society left over from the eighteenth century, I still saw a charm to the city. The history, the beaches off Sullivan's Island, Isle of Palm and Folly Beach as well as the more agreeable weather showed a tremendous upside with tourism, especially if the economy could make a turn for the better.

After his first trip to the city, he called and confirmed that there were some interesting investment opportunities in the city. But, I could tell it was difficult for him. Despite his educated manner and sharp looks, he still had to listen to the habitual condescending comments flowing from the mouths of too many ignorant white business brokers or real estate attorneys. I even had $20,000 set up in a corporate account at the Bank of Charleston in the name of Triple H Development, Inc. and still Ez, as a principal, was not given much consideration."

There was a sudden break in the flow of Henry's story. Lawton looked up and saw that the older man had turned sad. There was a flash outside the hotel restaurant. A spring rainstorm was building. Lawton had been so absorbed in Henry's account of Charleston in 1931 that he hadn't even noticed the light downpour. An ensuing distant rumble of thunder brought him back completely to the present day.

He then noticed Lill was dabbing at her eyes. Pulling the facts together, it was not difficult to realize Lill Hamilton had been the wife of Ez Hamilton. Something had happened to the man.

Ashley gave Lill his handkerchief and Henry stroked her hand. It was a very beautiful but heart-wrenching scene among the three of them. They had lived through a lot together in the last quarter of a century. The friendship they shared could only have been gained from the respect and affection they had for one another.

Lill nodded her head for Henry to carry on. He took a long swig of his tea and continued. His voice had softened noticeably.

"......It was in late April that Ez and I were discussing by phone whether to bid on a hotel property near Market Street. He kept telling me how beautiful springtime was in Charleston and some other business ideas we could generate once I eventually arrived in the city. He said the very next day he planned on taking a side trip to Kiawah Island to peruse the land I'd purchased before he returned to Paducah.

Then I didn't hear from him for one...then two...weeks. I was concerned enough that I phoned him at his house. Lill answered the phone. I'd talked to her many times but had never met her personally. Ez always spoke so highly of her; I felt I knew her.

By her tearful voice on the telephone, it didn't take much to understand something was wrong. That was when she came forward about an illness Ez had contracted right after he and I had met in Chicago the previous October. She said he'd lost a lot of weight since then. He wouldn't let his condition keep him from that trip to Charleston.

Then she said the day after he'd returned from a second trip to Charleston he'd passed on. He'd been doing some maintenance on one of his automobiles in the garage. She said she went out to see if he wanted some lunch and found him slumped over the wheel of his new 1930 Marquette 34 Sports Roadster. The horrible illness had sapped his strength and put too much pressure on his generous heart. He was but forty years old and was taken way too early. Ez was my best friend in life. I'm not a crier, but I sobbed freely that night.

So, it was with a heavy heart that I looked for Ez's address that Monday evening. Lill knew I would be passing through town, but wasn't certain of the date. It didn't matter. I knew she was as kind and generous as her late husband.

My memory of that drive to the Hamilton household was how darkness fell so quickly in that overcast sky. I drove eastward along the Ohio River on the outskirts of Paducah toward Ledbetter, Kentucky. Following along that the historic river I imagined what it must have been like a hundred years before with the Ohio River being the primary method of transportation from the populated eastern U.S.

to the Mississippi River. In many ways it seemed that time had not moved. I met very few cars. There were many people walking along the side of the road, apparently going home from their day job. They looked very poor and forlorn. In 1931 I was witnessing that scene so often wherever I traveled.

At a road sign, I took a left hand turn and ventured up a slight bluff to a sizeable cabin overlooking the river. There was a light in the window. When I stopped by the house, a very attractive female appeared at the door of the cabin and stepped out on the porch. Her left arm remained inside the door frame. I took for granted she had some type of gun or rifle ready to use if I turned out to be unfriendly.

Upon seeing me, even though she'd never met me, her left arm dropped to her side. She came down her wooden front steps and approached me without hesitation throwing her arms around my shoulders. Somehow I must have answered her vision of what Henry Hanson looked like...and her trust in me was implicit.

Her first words were, "Henry, why don't you drive your vehicle over to the barn and park it inside where it will be safe for the night. Then, come on in. I'll get some food on the table. We've got a lot of catching up to do."

There were tears in both our eyes. I felt like I was home even though I had never set foot in that state in my life. Following her directions I parked my new car inside that barn. It was not the only impressive automobile. There were several other vehicles in mint condition. Ez's 1925 Julian Sports Coupe had to be worth a pretty penny. Next to it was his 1930 Marquette 34 Sports Roadster he'd driven the last time we'd met in Chicago. Parking my Ford A 400 Convertible Sedan beside Ez's two cars had to have made that barn one of the more valuable storage areas in the Paducah area.

I walked to the cabin and shyly tapped on the door. Lill had a bright, but sad smile, some warm food and a cup of coffee. It had been a long day of travel across Illinois and I hardly cared what was being served. Our conversation started seconds later and really hasn't stopped all these years we've known each other. That night we had laughs and tears. She seemed to enjoy my rendition of her husband's and my time together during and after the war.

She described Ez's various enterprises. His chief business was in transportation. He owned two boats that transported various goods down the Ohio to the Mississippi River and then north to St. Louis or south to New Orleans. She lamented how he was gone too often, but had a gift for making money.

Not surprisingly she explained how he was a key person of their race in their community. He was respected for his calm common sense as much as his business acumen. The downside was that too many people on both sides of the race issue depended upon him to handle some tough social and political situations in the community. Nevertheless, Ez never could appease both sides at once. He was described by the low class white folks in the area as "uppity"…and by the black folks as never doing enough.

Lill also shared with me how his friendship with me always made him smile. He would look forward to meeting with 'Henry' wherever and whenever that was possible. I found the only thing she really didn't know much about was the business partnership Ez and I had formulated. I guess it was so early in developing that there hadn't been much to discuss.

I remember being bone tired and telling her I'd tell her a more recent story about Ez and me the next morning. She nodded her head. "Henry, I have an idea you'll be telling me in the morning about Triple H Development, Inc. Is that right?"

I chuckled. "Yes, it's a partnership we finally conceived in during the past year."

I recall her smiling and saying, "Those checks from Triple H Development, Inc. came every two weeks and now they still arrive even after his passing. I'll look forward to our breakfast in the morning."

I went to her guest room and collapsed in the bed.

* * *

Tuesday morning I awoke refreshed as much as a man on the run could be. Lill was gone but left a note saying she'd be back shortly. Upon returning, she explained how she'd been forced to resume Ez's transportation business while trying to maintain her own businesses. Being down by the river barges was not the type of work a classy looking lady was normally involved, but she couldn't let it simply dissolve. Lill had to deal with the drags of society who strolled around looking for loading work along the docks of the Ohio River. She was also looking for a buyer for both of Ez's rigs.

Her businesses included a seamstress shop and woman's clothing shop. She admitted to me an even more profitable third business…Miss Lill's Evening House. It was one of the most respected 'houses' in that sector along the Ohio River. Her employees when not working at the bordello could put in some lower paying work at the seamstress or clothing shops. From Lill's standpoint she at least offered employment for these ladies and regular medical care when needed.

Lill said she had some relatives down the road who watched the house when she was gone during the day. She felt relatively safe in the evenings thanks to a shotgun by the front door, a rifle by her bedside, and two pistols in drawers in the kitchen and living room.

She was obviously being stretched way too far. I was sitting with a very determined and responsible business person. It didn't take much intelligence for me to inquire if she'd consider working with me down in Charleston whenever the time was right.

I told her, "Lill, I'll drop you a note where to contact me after I get to South Carolina. I need only a couple days to arrange living quarters for you. But, until you arrive, Ez's checks will keep on arriving in your mailbox."

I think she was stunned with the proposal and had enough belief in me to know the offer was real. I left Wednesday morning thinking my next destination would easily be gained that evening. My next stopover was Chattanooga, Tennessee, less than three hundred miles from Paducah. I didn't relish the idea of driving through the hilly, backwoods country of Kentucky and Tennessee with so much money hidden in my new car. After seeing Paducah, I had decided to hold my hidden quarter of a million dollars in my vehicle until got to Lookout Mountain. There I had no doubt where to store my exorbitant amount of cash.

My goal that Wednesday was just to keep my sports coupe moving without tire repairs, running out of gas, or getting in a wreck. Upon leaving Paducah, I found out my objective was more challenging than I figured. I was crossing over some very rough terrain. With the lack of state funds, it was as if the two states hadn't been able to improve the roadways since the pioneer days. At times I thought I was driving on a plowed field.

As it turned out, there were thunderstorms, tornado threats, and a huge rut in the road that cost me one tire. I made it only to Clarksville, Tennessee that day. With the tire fixed I had the choice of staying the night in Nashville down the road, driving in the night all the way to Chattanooga through the backwoods, or staying in Clarksville. Seeing the jailhouse only a couple blocks away, I decided to make a deal with the county sheriff. I asked him to impound the car for the night while I slept in a county jail cell. I lied and told him the sedan was to be delivered to Georgia Governor Lamartine G. Hardman in Atlanta and preferably in one piece. He agreed if I'd stayed in downtown Clarksville and parked my Ford A 400 Convertible Sedan on the street, I'd likely not see it the next morning.

I paid twenty dollars to the constable to impound the automobile and enjoy that night's accommodations in the Clarksville jailhouse. It was a slow night for him given the incessant rain. He and I played gin until we both couldn't see straight. Contributing to our fogginess was whatever we were drinking that night. It left an oily taste in my mouth. That next morning I had a headache that could have killed a rhino.

That stay in Clarksville made it possible for me to continue crossing Tennessee with my life, my money and my car still intact. I made a lot of stops that day for gasoline, so I wouldn't be caught in hillbilly country with a fancy new car looking to fill my tank. Also my appetite had returned. That entire trip from Madison, Wisconsin to Chattanooga I was starved as a mother lioness. I had lunch every time I stopped for gasoline.

That two day trip from Paducah to Chattanooga still leaves me with vivid memories. I drove through communities in Kentucky and Tennessee that would have been abjectly poor without the Depression. The squalor at times left me both shocked and feeling hopeless. If I used all the money I was carrying in my vehicle I wouldn't have known where to begin making even a dent in the living standards of what I was witnessing mile after mile.

My mood was rather dour as I reached the outskirts of Chattanooga and seeing Lookout Mountain that Thursday evening. I was looking forward to seeing someone who'd always been special in my life. It had been three years since I'd last been in Chattanooga on one of my many trips out east while living in Glenwood.

Sally Middleton-Carter was my youngest aunt...and as you'll hear shortly, she was a corker. She'd lived in Chattanooga for a long time, but right after my last visit, some things changed in her life and she moved atop Lookout Mountain into what she described in a letter as a 'nice home on the bluff'. Just the thought of seeing her energized me. She was always full of ideas and advice whether a person appreciated her contributions or not.

People said Aunt Sally had lived in the Chattanooga area since shortly after God finished shaping Lookout Mountain. She really wasn't that old. If she'd been around when God was completing the geography of that unique mountain, she would have made some suggestions for improvement before 'He' signed off the completion. People in Chattanooga thought of her as the last great confederate living in the area, even though she'd not seen the light of day until 1876, six years after Robert E. Lee had died. Somehow, people thought she was a young lass when he was still alive. She certainly admired the man and often used reference to him when there was something she though needed to change. She'd use phrases like, "Bobby Lee wouldn't approve of that idea"....or "The General would never have allowed it".

Sally's father was a partner in the Broad Gauge Investor Group who invested in the Lookout Inn built up the mountainside in conjunction with the first inclined railway. The "Incline" descended down to the main city with a tram on the move every hour. Without the "Incline" the trip up the mountain would take three to four hours back before the horseless carriage. When that rail line opened and the construction of the popular hotel on the precipice of the mountain was completed, Chattanooga suddenly had something to feel really proud other than just another battlefield area of the War of Northern Aggression.

Sally's mother had northern ties but that information was kept very confidential from the sensitive ears of the local Chattanooga citizens. If Sally had any knowledge of relatives up North, she ignored the insulting thought. Her mother died shortly after Sally's fifth birthday. With three older brothers she became the princess of the family. She got her own way with her father, with her brothers, and with almost any other person she came in contact. Later, her brothers all moved from Chattanooga to take on various other types of occupations. With the demonstrative Sally, they probably did not want to be considered second fiddle to their little sister. Headstrong would be a mild and grossly inadequate description of the young Miss Sally.

Completed in 1890 just above the historic Craven House that had been so badly damaged during the fabled "Battle above the Clouds in 1863 during the North-South conflict, the Lookout Inn became a favorite social place for Miss Sally with the convenience of the Incline transporting her. For a short time she became quite the popular single lady in Chattanooga society until she married into a fledgling but big idea Chattanooga business family. The Carter name was very well known. Her husband, Gerhard, was a relatively conservative local banker, real estate investor, and insurance man compared to his older brother, Garnet.

After the marriage of Gerhard and Sally, the Lookout Inn sadly burned to the ground in 1908, but the couple remained living on the mountain as a statement of support for the growing community on that precipice.

Sally contributed much of her time on local committees aiming to restore old historic buildings and parks. She was active in gaining funds to build the impressive commemorative military park where the Battle of Chickamauga had taken place in 1863 just south of the city. The fact that there were an equal number of former northern soldiers involved in the undertaking made Sally a bit prickly, but she was able to lay her concern aside for the good of the national battlefield memorial project.

Meanwhile her husband and his entrepreneurial older brother worked on other endeavors. The older brother, Garnet and his wife, Frieda, became prominent outside of Chattanooga. They initiated 'Rock City Gardens', a unique tourist interest on a rocky slope overlooking the city. It was being completed about the time I stopped there in 1931. It was known for beautiful gardens and extraordinary walkways through rock formations and breathtaking views towards parts of bordering states. Garnet's real money, though, came from something called Tom Thumb miniature golf. During the time I was investing cash from D'Annelli secret funds back in Glenwood in 1930-31, my Aunt Sally's brother-in-law had introduced miniature golf all over the country.

Her husband Gerhard enjoyed a piece of that business but primarily forged his wealth through his banking and real estate businesses. When he died accidentally in a fall from Park Point atop

Lookout Mountain in 1929, local folks wondered if it had truly been inadvertent. His death occurred shortly after the Crash of the same year.

Gerhard was still able to leave Aunt Sally in reasonably good financial standing, thanks to an exorbitant insurance policy and some timely investments with some inside traders in New York. It was at least one case where her dislike for people from the north was abandoned when finances came into play.

Aunt Sally was not my only relative, but she was my closest one despite the miles between us. I was the only one in my family who communicated with her...and I'd done so since I was a kid. She more recently had the idea from my letters that I was about to embark on a life away from Minnesota. I believe when I shared with her about my purchase of a piece of land near Charleston, she thought I'd finally seen the error of my ways and was coming to my true homeland in the South. I had to let her know that I was not moving to Charleston to resurrect the secession issue. I was simply trying to establish my business in South Carolina because I found the area having great potential and preferable weather.

My hope was that she might even have some contacts in Charleston who might help my efforts. It wasn't as if I was begging for some working capital. I believed my quarter of a million dollars might give me some kind of credibility. She would not disappoint. I would learn from Aunt Sally one of her first cousins lived in the historic district of Charleston and that he was 'connected' in the city's society. She emphasized it was that cousin's son who would be my best first contact. I did eventually meet this character...a very questionable chap I might add...by the name of Ashley Cooper Carter."

Ashley raised his glass with a smile and only nodded apparently not wanting to interrupt the pace of Henry's storytelling.

Henry continued.

"To be named after two local rivers, it would be assumed he was a native Charlestonian going back to the Huguenots. Actually he was only a second generation Charleston man which he kept confidential. Before I met him in 1931, he had opportunely dropped off the 'Carter' part of his namesake and gone just with his two 'river' names. Whether known as Carter or Cooper, though, he's become one of the true aristocrats of this historic city…and thankfully without the attitude."

Ashley interrupted once again showing some comical disdain for Henry's rare compliment. He countered, "Now Henry, that's not entirely true. I try to maintain some conceit just to remain in good standing with my local haughty friends from multiple generations of Charlestonians."

Ignoring his good friend's aside, Henry stayed focused.

"My arrival in Chattanooga that Thursday evening didn't end my travels that day. I had to find the roadway on the east side of Lookout Mountain in order to ascend to the broad, flat mountaintop. At night the city was beautiful, but the steep twisting road had my heart in my mouth. It was a harrowing climb with few street lights. I felt as if slipping the clutch just one time would find me arriving in downtown Chattanooga backwards in less than two minutes.

Once up on the crest of the mountain, the view through the tree branches was spectacular. I drove to the northeast edge of the mountain top where my aunt said she now lived. All I saw was a grandiloquent iron gate with a large metal golf club attached diagonally across the metal entry. I should have been sharp enough to pick up on that hint but I was too tired to put any meaning to the metal emblem.

Not knowing where to go, I parked across from the entrance to the estate and next door to a small hotel. I figured they had to know where my aunt's house was located.

For a Thursday night, the atmosphere inside the hotel was lively. Built on the edge of Lookout Mountain it seemed a slight jolt could cause the entire building to end up at the base of the mountain. Nonetheless, people were dancing and singing; others were drunk and disorderly. Still others were actually trying to eat dinner. Everyone seemed to be doing their best to disregard the mess the country was in at that time.

I asked the night manager if he'd heard of Sally Carter. He just looked at me and grinned. "If you're Henry, she's out having dinner on the patio. Your aunt said you'd be coming in one of these nights and told us to be on the 'lookout' for you." He laughed at his own pun and walked away.

Strolling out to the balcony, there was a lady facing away from the doorway and sitting with five other people. She was entertaining them with some kind of story...or plotting the next secession. I needed to look no more; I'd spotted my aunt.

That evening she was wearing a stylish, high neck dress with a shawl. Mid-summer evenings on that mountaintop were generally cooler than down in the city. As I maneuvered around to face her, her eyes were bright with excitement as she blurted out the final line to her tale. The entire table erupted in laughter. This woman was not just comfortable in her environment, she was the environment.

I started laughing and I hadn't even heard her anecdote. She looked up and peered for only a moment before jumping up to hurry toward me. It was always a pleasure to feel appreciated and that was the feeling I always got from her. Aunt Sally, who no one in my family up north was able to communicate with but me, was hugging the one Yankee she could love.

For the next hour Aunt Sally introduced me to every living human being including the hotel staff. She told everyone I was a World War I war hero and owned a big business up north. My aunt's hyperbole was boundless. Rather than denying most of her exaggerations, I just let them pass. I figured most people wouldn't remember the accolades anyway. Besides, I was used to her embellishments. Her letters were always teeming with overstatement and histrionics. That night she was at her creative best in describing her most favorite nephew.

Another hour later and I had forgotten how tired I was. She had the hotel kitchen bring out whatever I wanted to eat and drink. As I dined, she told of my exploits during the war. I even had the impression by the end of dinner that all would have been lost in the Big War had it not been for my single-handed efforts.

Then over some late night drinks with twenty people sitting around our table, her eyes got wide as she described how I'd weathered the dismal, icy plains of the Midwestern winters as well as the cold, miserable people who lived in that area before I'd finally made my escape. She made it sound as if I'd left Custer's regiment in the nick of time before he marched onward to the Little Bighorn.

I can't remember all the lies and exaggerations she told about me that night, but as I said, it didn't seem to matter. Most of the patrons including my aunt were fairly well plastered. The only real point made that evening was that my aunt was very proud of me.

With that as my entrée to some prominent folks in Chattanooga society that Thursday evening, I only wished Aunt Sally lived in Charleston. She had more energy than any three people together. We left the hotel restaurant shortly before midnight after bidding good-byes to everyone at the hotel… including the staff. With my car parked close by, I asked her where her home was as we ambled slowly along. She pointed across the street toward the ostentatious iron gates. I should have guessed.

As we drove through the gates and forward to her huge Georgia style brick house, I was pleased for the second time I'd gotten rid of my old Plymouth. My new Ford Sedan was more appropriate parked in front of her mansion.

Inside her stately home, she rang a bell and someone from the kitchen came out to greet us. Introducing the maid, she asked Elma to show me to my room. Aunt Sally actually admitted to being slightly tired. Her honesty relieved me since I'd been failing for the past hour. She then kissed me good night and said, "Henry, I'll be peppier in the morning. I know we have a few things to discuss."

When she headed down that long, lonely hallway to her room, the house seemed too big and too lonely. She was better in a room full of people. At least there was Elma. She was a few years younger in age and obviously represented more sanity in the household.

The matronly woman showed me to the guest room on the second floor. It was complete with roofed bed, my own bathroom, and a liquor cabinet. I was tired enough that I didn't partake of the liquor cabinet. I believe I was asleep before my head touched the pillow. I would awake the next morning still in my travel clothes and lying on top of the bed cover."

Lawton looked up as Henry became quiet. He noticed all three hosts had become more melancholy as Henry talked of Sally Carter. Doing some quick arithmetic, Lawton calculated that the older woman would be in her middle 80's in the current year. It was quite obvious by some sniffles she had passed on.

To reduce some of the sadness around the table, Lawton quietly asked if his folks or Charlie Davis had even met Sally Carter. Henry smiled and nodded. Ashley responded more enthusiastically. "You better believe she met your folks and she knew Charlie even better. The two of them liked scotch and playing cribbage. They all saw her plenty when she was on the corporate board of directors. She always said she never had any interest in talking with Yankees until she met Charlie. He frequently sent her bottles of wine when he traveled and his tales about Minnesota and its people had her constantly laughing. Eventually she had to admit there were some Yankees who were good people. She was especially fond of your mother, Matt. She considered Lindy Lawton the daughter she never had."

Ashley then got up to pour more iced tea while adding another spirit from a flask in his pocket. Without any prodding, Henry returned to his place in his story.

"When I woke up that Friday morning, I just lay in bed not believing all that had taken place in just a week. I was feeling both lucky and...well, mostly lucky. Now, here I was in a mansion on top of Lookout Mountain in Tennessee away from any mob threats. The smell of breakfast permeated the gigantic manor. Quickly cleaning up, I walked down the spiral staircase with portraits of Robert E Lee, Jefferson Davis, and General Pierre G.T. Beauregard neatly arranged along the wall. I wandered through the library with the elegant picture above the fireplace of the Lookout Inn taken at the 1900 Centennial celebration. The opposite wall had a picture of the Battle of Chickamauga, a battle where the South gained a major victory in 1863. Unfortunately as Aunt Sally often repeated, that the old bastard Confederate General Braxton Bragg, never followed up the victory so nothing was really gained by the South other than extending the war. Eventually Chattanooga fell and as so often happens, too many lives had been wasted for nothing. Such was war and poor leadership. 'Bastard' was always her word for the indecisive and largely incompetent Confederate leader during that conflict. I noticed that Bragg's picture was not framed on any wall in her mansion.

The French doors were opened to the outside patio from the library. The fresh cool morning air saturated the room with the most aromatic smell. Working out in the patio and garden were two people with long sleeved blouses and wearing dirty blue jeans. One person looked white but was so dirty and grungy from the garden work that I was not certain. The other person was dark-skinned and equally mud-pasted. The possible white person removed her hat. I was not surprised. It was my eccentric aunt.

Upon seeing me, she chortled, "Henry, my dear, breakfast will be ready in fifteen minutes in the patio. Elma and I have to clean up."

While the two ladies handled that chore, I sauntered around the property. She'd obviously come into more money, but it didn't change her approach to her daily life. She wasn't impressed by her elevated standing; neither did she expect other people to be.

She always wore her feelings and attitudes right on her shoulders in the letters she sent me. I didn't understand half the things she said during my youth, but I certainly enjoyed her fiery comments about politics. She always referred to Presidents McKinley, Roosevelt and Taft as a waste of time. She had wanted them to invest more in helping bring the South back to life. She thought Woodrow Wilson should have remained a teacher but of course liked him better than the next two Republicans, Warren G. Harding and Calvin Coolidge. In her letters she thought Harding had been elected for his looks...and she wondered if Coolidge had a heartbeat.

Her political frustrations always seemed centered around garnering more Federal aid to help refurbish her city. When she came into more money, she gave up on the government and had taken on the task herself. For over twenty years she'd been working on programs to upgrade Chattanooga. She had become a well-known and respected lady in her city.

From the side patio the view looking down at the city from atop the piedmont of Lookout Mountain was breathtaking even through the early morning mist. The homes at that level atop the flat mountain were mostly above the cloud cover.

It took my aunt only ten minutes and then she burst through the double doors to the patio. Her sparkling vigor and even the brightness of her dress made the morning even livelier. And, that was her style... not bawdy, but certainly ostentatious.

That morning over breakfast we talked and talked...mostly her doing the speaking. Then, as if needing time to rest her vocal cords, she stopped abruptly. It was my turn to talk. She said, "Henry, it's about time you tell me what's causing all these changes in your life. If memory serves me, you've worked in that town out in the Midwest for over ten years. There must be quite a story for you to leave your job with the national economy lower than the standards of General Grant. For you to curtly leave your home state, buy land on an island off one of our dear southern states, and telling me in your last letter you plan on setting up your business interests in a city like Charleston, South Carolina...well, it tells me this is more than just a life change. You don't look ill. Your brain seems to be functioning. For you to leave your beloved state... what is it, Dakota or some other kind of Indian name...well, there has to be some pretty serious consequences if you had remained."

While I chuckled over her dismissive reference to Minnesota, I always had to give her credit for her astute observations. I tried to gloss over my being caught in the middle between the townsfolk and some gangsters at a local lake resort. Certainly I didn't intend to mention how I 'borrowed' funds from the head mobster without him knowing about it.

It didn't work. She had an incredible way of probing in places I didn't want her to ask. When I told her I'd invested some money and had been quite successful doing so, she wanted to know where I got the seed money. When I alluded to taking out loans from some unaudited funds of a gangster that were stored in the very basement of the place that I managed, she started chuckling. When I told her I unfailingly paid back the principle I'd borrowed, she shook her head and laughed uncontrollably. And when I told her my final attempt at paying back the last of the principle I still owed only the previous Saturday night... and the interruptions that kept me from doing so...she hooted until tears came from her eyes.

Responding to her question about Charleston was easier. I said to her, "Choosing Charleston was almost too logical. Where I come from in the Midwest, that city is considered part of the wasteland of the post-Civil War era. No one goes to Charleston from Minnesota; no one even thinks about that city. So, not only do I believe I'll never be found in Charleston, I already carry an assumed name complete with false I.D. Furthermore, I've incorporated my company just over a year ago. Right now it's composed of two Minnesota lake resorts, some land investments, and a reasonable cash base. In the last few months I've had a partner explore certain hotel properties in the Charleston area. I have the money to move forward on a purchase if I choose to do so."

She perked up when I mentioned my resorts in Minnesota. Having been in the hotel business herself from the time she could walk through a lobby with her father, Aunt Sally obviously approved of my new business ventures. "Hotel blood must run deep" was all she said.

When I finally stopped she was already rubbing her chin and thinking ahead. She exclaimed, "Henry, you'll need help breaking into the Charleston society. It could take a couple generations unless we can embellish your alias. Your northern blood will not be an asset. I have a relative in Charleston. We'll work through him to change your background and enhance your image."

The gears in her head were spinning. She was surprisingly calm as she related her thoughts to me. "First of all, my dear nephew, listen carefully. You are not 100% Northerner.... thank the good Lord. You are my closest kin and my most favorite one to boot. I will walk on hot coals for you, but I shan't think that will be necessary. You must understand that you are Sally Middleton Carter's nephew. Except for your horrible accent, you have at least some rebel blood in you. The last two years of your life have proven that fact. When you leave this house for even one minute.....or, for the rest of your life, you will have a room and address here in this mansion. As of this moment you are from Lookout Mountain, Tennessee. In time your voice will partially take on the beautiful southern tone with our own colloquialisms and people will hear you as one of them. If there is ever any doubt in any southerner's mind, you just say you have Middleton-Carter blood and you lived at Lookout Mountain. That's going to take you far with that "nose in the air" mentality of the upper crust of Charleston."

What she'd just presented was very generous, yet, she had only begun. She added, "Henry, I have two names in the Charleston area you'll need to contact right away. A distant cousin, the Reverend John Middleton of the First Presbyterian Church on James's Island between Charleston and Kiawah Island should be one key contact. He's older than me by one year and a bit too religious. But, that's his life, so I have to respect his choice. I'll call him before you arrive in Charleston. He'll be expecting you."

Then she quickly added, "Let me also suggest something to help your introduction with him. His church is struggling. I think you and your business mind can assist him. I believe he thinks he owns the bells, pews, organ, and even that old church building. That damn church is the most important thing in the man's life. Unfortunately he's as conservative as a northern republican. I tell him he thinks more of his church than he does of his family. He gets all riled until he realizes I'm razzing him.

I'll let him know you've got some ideas that might help his church. You'll have to think on your trip down to James Island what those ideas might be. Anyway, he'll appear tense when you first meet him because that old fart is not good with change. But, if you can deliver some kind of assistance to him, you'll automatically become one of his relatives however distant that blood flow might be. Above everything, he's absolutely trustworthy. You can depend on him to say and live by his word. You'll like him once you get to know him.

The other fellow is my husband's nephew, Ashley Cooper Carter. He's very well known in Charleston. He should be if they named two rivers in Charleston after him as he claims. 'Ashley Cooper', as his friends call him, is a city contractor. He's really a politician but he won't admit to it. Ashley has his head so far up some of the top Charleston leader's behinds, I'm afraid we'll never see him with gray hair. But, while Ashley is a sycophant, he also happens to be just cynical enough to be rather normal. The bottom line is that he knows how to get things done in Charleston. He's one of my favorite people. He'll be a very good man to have on your side."

Then she gave me another questioning look. Her eyes narrowed and she asked, "Henry, you mentioned something about a cash base. Where are you keeping all this money and are you certain you can't be traced through your accounts with whatever bank you are using?"

I had to grin over her assumption I was using a bank. I didn't want to admit I had little confidence in the shaky U.S. banking system, especially since her husband had been a rather wealthy banker. Embarrassed, I cleared my throat and told her, 'You won't believe this... but I left Minnesota with $250,000 stuffed in suitcases and in various places in my car. Some of it is even inside the lining of the upholstery in the car.

Seeing her eyes bulge, I couldn't help but laugh. It really was ridiculous the chances I was taking.

Her explosion of convulsive laughter even had me chortling. She finally blurted out, "It's obvious, Henry Hanson, it's the making of money that's the challenge and the motivation for you. Once you've made it, you seem to lose interest in it unless you re-invest the money. I think there're a lot of people who'd definitely like to partner with you! You'd do the money "makin" and they'd do the money "savin".

Aunt Sally just shook her head and suddenly got up from the table. She bellowed, "Henry, I'll get some suitcases and you get that money out of the hiding places in your car. Let's go downtown and walk into my family bank. It's time you open an account. You'll get all the personal attention and advantages of a new bank client. Just as important, with this money and your new Lookout Mountain address, it will further authenticate my fine city as your home until you get established in Charleston.

That day I deposited $230,000 in the Southern Bank of Chattanooga. The remaining $20,000 I chose to take along with me. I needed immediate investment capital if I had to make some financial decisions requiring prompt payment.

I stayed at Lookout Mountain for almost a week in order to regain my strength and become somewhat of an expert on the city of Chattanooga. If I was going to claim I was from Tennessee, I had to know as much as I could about the city…and likewise about the state. It helped that Aunt Sally knew everything that had ever happened in the city from the time of its first log cabin…and almost everybody born since that time.

The following Friday morning, June 19, I bid farewell to my spirited aunt. Descending Lookout Mountain to continue my journey to Charleston, I felt connected to Chattanooga. I had a Tennessee bank account, an address on Lookout Mountain, a bed to sleep in if I ever needed it in Chattanooga and a relative who would stand by me if there ever was a question about my background. What more did a man newly adopted by the state of Tennessee need?

Chapter 11

On a thin cement highway I raced toward Atlanta on Federal Hwy. 41 with the hope of ending up in Augusta, Georgia that Friday evening. It didn't get by me that I was following the initial route of General William Sherman across northern Georgia just sixty-seven years before. His passage left a good part of the state even more devastated than it already had been by the ravages of war. Aunt Sally had mentioned her extreme dislike for the man almost daily.

The red hue of the Georgia soil made it look infertile or at least lying in waste as if Sherman's men had only recently trampled over the ground once again. As I drove along, Negro farm hands were everywhere continuing my impression that their lot in life had not improved much since the bondage of slavery.

My trip around Atlanta and then to Augusta was relatively uneventful considering my previous stays in Paducah, Clarksville, and Chattanooga. I stayed Friday evening outside Augusta, Georgia at a rooming house down the road from what I found to be a very interesting project. Construction was taking place in an area formerly called The Fruitland Nurseries. A much esteemed golf course was in the process of being built on the Nursery land by a group led by the famous golfer, Bobby Jones. I'd definitely heard about this Georgia sportsman. A few years before he'd won one leg of the Grand Slam of golf in Minnesota at the Interlaken Country Club. Apparently retired as a golfer, Bobby Jones and his investors were naming the club Augusta National and establishing it as a national membership club.

I rode over to the construction site before sunset driving along a rugged driveway lined with a long row of already matured magnolias. They had been planted before the Civil War and gave the entrance a stately look even before the club opened. The property with the rolling hills and tall pines looked like a nice choice for a golf course.

I recall thinking that in the tough economic times the nationally renowned reputation of Bobby Jones was enough to keep the new golf course on solid enough financial ground. I guess my mild concerns at that time never materialized...especially considering this year in 1960, just days ago, the exciting young golfer, Arnold Palmer, won Bobby Jones' annual Master's Tournament for the second time at that now venerable golf course.

The trip across South Carolina on Saturday was similar to the trip from Paducah to Chattanooga. The hilly geography eventually gave way to flatter topography, but the roads were thin and rundown. I felt nervous every time I met an oncoming car given the skinny width of the road. The grass at the exact side of the roadway was so long in places that you took your life in your hands if you drove too fast or met another car. Anything could pop out of the tall grass.....cows, pigs, opossum, snakes, dogs......or people. There was no relief until I got into the low country nearer Charleston.

Aunt Sally had given me directions to take a short cut to James Island rather than drive straight into the city. The short cut across the upper Ashley River proved unreliable. The ferry was under repair.

Unperturbed, I did drive into the city and took the Hwy. 17 bridge toward James Island where I was to look up Sally's distant relative, the Reverend John Middleton. It was Saturday late afternoon when I stopped at a one-pump gas station with an old Negro fellow alone and rocking back in forth to the tune he was humming. I figured he could give me directions to the James Island First Presbyterian Church.

He seemed to only guess that I required some fuel. Between my apparent accent and his toothless drawl we had little chance of meaningful communication. Somehow he did understand the word 'Presbyterian' after I'd said it six times. He pointed down the road. I paid him and took off, but not before I heard him mumble something about that 'white boy cain't talk too good'.

I was kind of disgusted when I drove off. After all, it was modern day 1931 and all Americans supposedly spoke the same language. I began to wonder if South Carolina had actually seceded and spoke a type of colloquial English. Except for the secession part, I would find the second part of my thought quite accurate...until I got used to it.

Not two minutes later, I saw a church with a steeple so rundown it was a wonder it hadn't sunk into the main structure. There was a dilapidated old Model A Ford parked in front of the church's entrance. I drove into the parking area hoping to meet Reverend John Middleton.

Well, it turned out to be much more than just meeting the man. My relationship with that church began immediately upon walking through the front door. Middleton had been waiting in his church office since the afternoon after hearing from Aunt Sally about my imminent arrival. While he tried to be calm, I could immediately tell he was comparing my coming to James Island as divine providence.

Middleton was a kindly, bear of man who seemed to be naturally unruffled. Looking at his sparse surroundings, I couldn't imagine what kept him so positive. I surmised his congregation was small with revenue from weekly offerings equally meager. His smile was engaging and he offered me some fish and some kind of rice looking concoction he called grits that he'd brought from home. He figured I'd be hungry when I arrived.

I don't remember much about the meal other than I scarfed it down. I liked the fish but those grits never held my interest from that day on.

We sat down that night in the sanctuary, just getting to know one another. I talked about Aunt Sally and my sojourn to Charleston, but nothing about my life back in Minnesota. He covered his work in the church and his dream of building a congregation that could support a strong belief in community and helping others. The man had as big a heart as he did a body.

Finally I asked him what Aunt Sally had told him about my coming to Charleston. I wanted to deal with her exaggerations before any meaningful conversation could ensue.

He laughed and said, "Henry, we both know Sally can be both officious and loud, but her efforts are always for the good. She's a great lady. I can tell you she said you had some personal needs that mostly you would handle, but that in exchange for putting you up and keeping you fed, you might have some ideas to help me grow this church. Like most churches we're surviving on prayer and very thin contributions. Sally did say you had an affiliation with a church out in the Midwest and you might have some thoughts how to help out. But, let me be clear. Whether you do or you don't, just understand you've got a roof over your head and food in your mouth as long as you're here in Charleston. I'll make certain of that."

It warmed my heart to hear such generosity from a man who didn't have that much to be generous with beyond his goodness. I wasn't thinking about Reverend Middleton or his church when I drove up, but suddenly I was offering some marketing ideas as if it was a business. The first thing I suggested was to complete the needed repairs. The church itself looked like a structure about ready to collapse.

I could tell he had his doubts about my suggestions until I laid a thousand dollars out in front of him and proposed we get busy the next day. I did tell him that the only prerequisite for my financial and planning support would be his promise to keep my real name and background confidential.

With eyes on the money and a curious look in his eye, Middleton admitted he knew something about my past life from Sally. He even had an idea of his own to help me out.

He looked at me and winked. "I've been thinking about hiring an assistant pastor at the church. Reaching for the thousand dollars he added, "…….and you seem like a kind and I might say generous man, which makes you a viable candidate. And, for your protection we should create a new persona until you feel comfortable having any of us refer to you as Henry.

It was from that small discussion where the name 'Reverend Hank' was created. I was the new assistant pastor of the James Island First Presbyterian Church. Reverend John Middleton had struck a deal with 'Reverend Hank'.

In the next few days, he would learn further advantages of hiring me as his assistant pastor. Reverend Hank not only had experience at financing church building projects, but I brought along the financing to boot. In exchange there was a private room in the loft of the church where I could reside until I got a place of my own, a church basement closet where I could store my belongings, and the peace of mind that would let me sleep soundly during the nights. I still had hopes of establishing some kind of living arrangement on my Kiawah Island property, but I had to find it first. When I mentioned the land purchase to Middleton, it was the only time he looked at me as if my deck was missing a few cards.

He said to me, "Reverend Hank, you have more faith than I've given you credit for if you decide to live out there."

His inference was obvious. I decided to delay any venture out to Kiawah and first concentrate my efforts on revitalizing his church building. I still had that extra $50,000 from Loni D'Annelli's secret funds. I had determined if I ever used that money it would be for someone's need or for the benefit of a group. I couldn't think of a better way of putting some of that money to work than to help out Reverend Middleton.

True to Aunt Sally's words, when I showed him my list of suggested improvements for his church to make it more inviting...and safer...he was hesitant. He didn't want the $1000 I'd promised him to be squandered away with fanciful ideas.

To ease his mind, I said to him, 'Tell you what, you take that $1000 and earmark that cash for whatever you feel you need in the church. As your assistant, let me handle the improvements of the grounds and building...including the financing.

Within a week, some construction projects around the church property were already under way. Unemployed parishioners had paid work. Not only was the steeple repaired, but an addition to the church was built to hold meetings and classes. Every now and then Reverend Middleton would stumble by the construction project in progress and murmur to me, "Reverend Hank, you apparently found some very reliable financing."

Through all the excitement of the church improvements, I tried to remain out of the limelight as much as possible. I acted as construction foreman but telling everyone it was under the aegis of Reverend Middleton. While people certainly wondered where Pastor Middleton was getting the financial support to expand and upgrade the church, when asked, Middleton and I only said that 'it was high time to invest in the future of the church and the community'. Those words certainly sounded comforting and altruistic, but they were mostly empty. However, he and I did prove that making that church more appealing visually besides spiritually would stimulate an increase in membership.

It was a belief that required a lot of faith. Candidly, prayer didn't have a lot to do with paying off the construction debt. It was purely and simply profits from a gangster's gambling business that helped establish the James Island First Presbyterian Church as the new up and coming modern church of 1931.

It wouldn't take long until word spread about the wonderful improvements…and the work being done by many faithful and willing members of the church…and they were being paid for their efforts!

As far as I could tell, the coincidence of my being hired as an assistant pastor and the sudden improvement in the church was never considered by the local folks. As I hoped, credit was given to Reverend Middleton despite his personal discomfort in taking that praise. We had quite a few discussions about the acclaim. I explained to him he had to now take advantage of that recognition not for his sake but for the sake of so many desperate people who wanted to believe in something when life was so difficult.

In a short time as the church building rounded into shape and the grounds around the church became garden-like. Then he did what he did best as a minister. He preached. He energized his choir. He organized programs for kids. He set up programs of parishioners helping other parishioners in need. He had a new enthusiasm at the pulpit. As for that $1000 I'd given him, he invested that money in weekly Sunday noon teas and luncheons for parishioners and prospective members after the services. His success with that idea contributed to me using the same idea at the East Bay Street Hotel.

One other addition I brought to the church that summer of 1931 was a telephone line. It wasn't done altruistically. Selfishly I needed a private line to talk with my contacts back in Minnesota. Reverend Middleton thought I was setting up a direct line to God. I told him he could believe what he chose, but he was thirty years late entering the twentieth century.

Once that phone line was in, I reconnected to my three primary contacts up north. We had prescribed times we'd talk every other day. The incessant static was frustrating, but given the times I had no complaints.

By Saturday, the fourth of July, I'd been keeping a low profile out at St. James Island for the two weeks since arriving. Building projects at the church were progressing. My temporary quarters in the church loft were comfortable, and I was ready to check out my property out at Kiawah Island. I didn't think I'd ever live out there for any extended period of time. I only wanted a place for escape if that ever was required.

I chose that weekend to check out my property. As I made my way on a dirt road toward a ferry that would take me across to the island, I was beginning to have my doubts. I already felt I was in another country just living for a short time on James Island. I wanted safety not isolation. The further I drove the more the latter became more apparent.

I wasn't even certain if I could find the property even if I somehow got to the island. Reverend Middleton did advise me to talk with a young fisherman-farmer who also operated that ferry. His name was Thomas Rutledge Brown. He said Thomas knew the area and would take me to my land for a dollar...roundtrip. I didn't like the sound of that.

What bothered me more was Middleton's warning about some animals who were more accustomed to living on that island. He strongly suggested Thomas should be my guide so the journey would not be my last. That admonition sounded even worse.

I asked the Reverend about Thomas' name. "Isn't Rutledge a rather well-known and respected name in South Carolina? Is he part of that family?

"Thomas and I joke about that all the time," Middleton laughed. "He says any number of times people are anxious to meet him until they see his color. Then they seem to lose the interest. His great-grandparents and grandparents were slaves of the historic Rutledge family. The name stuck when they became free. Truth is that Thomas is a highly regarded man in these parts. The venerable Rutledge kinfolk should consider themselves fortunate to have a man like Thomas in their family."

Following Middleton's directions, I drove out to an inlet on Sunday afternoon, July 5. Tom's house was at the end of a long dirt driveway with a huge lagoon on the left side of the roadway. Across some marsh next to that lagoon was another body of land. According to a map given me by a worker, that was Kiawah Island. I drove slowly up the driveway and tried to drive around a huge branch. As I turned, the branch moved swiftly into the tall grass on the side of the road. The snake had to be seven feet long and as thick as my forearm.

I drove onward to the Brown home and there was a sudden movement as quick as lightning slapping at the water. It was another animal of some kind. I thought it a large lizard until I saw it floating on the water. My eyes didn't want to see it, but my brain knew what it was. I was in alligator country. It had become quite clear I needed to become friends with Thomas Rutledge Brown, not only to see my property, but to survive the day. It never occurred to me I would be risking my life when I bought the parcel of land along the coast.

Thomas came out of his airy dwelling with a quizzical look on his face. He'd sized me up as alligator bait in about five seconds. Again I had difficulty when he spoke. His dialect was almost indecipherable, but he somehow understood me…and he knew I was coming. I had no idea how Middleton could have gotten word to Thomas. There were no telephone lines or electric lines. Nighttime had to be darker than Thomas' skin color.

A pleasant looking woman with two small children came out of the house and we introduced ourselves. For some reason she was much easier to understand than her husband. Dell Rutledge Brown wore a summer dress and her two kids wore normal kid's clothing. They had shoes. They did not look impoverished. They all were simply dressed consistent with the hot, humid day.

After shaking my hand and knowing my purpose from Reverend Middleton for stopping by, he disappeared around the corner. When I asked Dell about a ferry, she looked at me with her eyes dancing and said, "Reverend Hank, I think you want to leave your car here at our house. There are some paths over at Kiawah, but I wouldn't call them roads."

Then I heard a roar of an engine. It sounded like the freight trains that howled through Glenwood at odd hours during the day or night. Suddenly Thomas thundered up to his dock in a huge motorized boat. He de-accelerated only moments before taking out his entire dock. Dell shook her head in that "kids will be kids look" and motioned for her offspring and me to move to the dock and get in the boat. She and her kids wanted to go along for the ride…and probably see the look on my face when I discovered where my property was located.

I had barely stepped into the boat and we were off. The motorboat sped on the smooth water as a sled on ice. Thomas started talking. Between the din of the motor and his unique accent, I could just as well have been deaf.

As we rounded the corner of the island we looked out onto the Atlantic Ocean. He slowed the boat down as we rode parallel to the most extensive, lonely beach I'd ever seen. It went on forever. He stopped the boat and pointed to the edge of the island we had just come around and then about a half mile down the coast. He looked at me and said, "That's your land".

I looked at Thomas and then at his wife and then back at the beach. If I wanted remote, I had to be happy. There were no roads to it. If I thought a dwelling could be built and I could survive on the island, I guessed it was possible in about twenty years. For the time being I had to hope my room at the church on James Island would provide me the safety and isolation I might need if D'Annelli's boys ever heard I was living in the Charleston area.

Seeing my consternation, Dell tried to soothe me. She said, "Reverend Hank, this is a very desolate island. There is a group of people living on it, but they stay to themselves. The land mass has wild horses roaming all over the island. The entire island has been owned by a family named Vanderhorst for at least five generations. Way back they actually had a reasonably successful cotton plantation before the Civil War. After the surrender, the fifth generation Mr. Vanderhorst just kind of gave up. He didn't have the slave labor required to keep the cotton fields productive."

She shook her head. "You should be aware that the sale of this land might not even be valid. A lot of city folks get taken for a ride. Reverend Hank, you'll need to talk to the firm that sold you the property. Unless they represent the Vanderhorst family, your title is as phony as that politician Franklin Roosevelt's claim that he can walk."

Thomas turned the boat around and headed back to his home on the channel off the Atlantic. I realized whether I owned the land or not, it was of little value. If the deed was fraudulent, so I lost $2000. I'd gained or lost more than that in a week in some of my commodity trading the last couple years. However, the question of the title would give me reason to get to know some folks in Charleston who dealt in appraisals and property values.

I bid Thomas and Dell Rutledge Brown and their kids a friendly good-by giving him an envelope with payment for his time and effort. He thanked me but refused it. He said he had better luck trading than using money. I believe he was just trying to be generous. I promised myself I'd help him out if he ever needed it.

Heading back down their driveway to the main road, I passed by that same lagoon. There was the alligator sunning himself on the side of the water. He looked large enough to eat me... and my car. I also saw the same long snake. His head was up and swaying with the breeze as I drove by.

I left the Brown's property with a sense of relief. I found out Kiawah was unlivable. It was the wildest place I'd ever visited in all my travels including the nude bar a couple avenues from the Eiffel Tower in Paris. That was a different type of wild. This part of South Carolina along the remote coastline was totally out of my element.

When I returned to my small room in the loft at the church that evening, I felt like I was back in civilization compared to where I'd been that afternoon. When I arrived there was a note on my door from Reverend Middleton saying I should urgently call a number. There was no name, but I recognized the number. It was from Rich Brey back in Minnesota.

With that church phone giving me access, I promptly called. It rang only twice after the operator put through the call. Brey had been waiting at the Lake Mille Lacs resort office phone. When the operator was off the line, he didn't waste a breath.

"Henry," he yelled, "I just got word that Loni D'Annelli has been gunned down on a Chicago street yesterday. It's in all the newspapers, especially since it's been only a month since his whole operation at Chippewa Lodge fell apart. This might just put a whole new picture on your life. I hate to be blunt but with him gone, you might not have to be looking over your shoulder."

I kind of mumbled my appreciation for his call. Honestly my emotions were mixed. The mob had actually marked D'Annelli. There must have been other troubles I was not aware. Admittedly I was numb hearing about his death. I'd known the man for five years. He was a crook...and one of the best businessmen I'd ever met. While I couldn't call Loni D'Annelli a friend, there was a part of me that respected him.

As Brey gave me more details about the shooting, I had no belief I was out of the woods just yet. I'd known some of D'Annelli's boys. They had a deep loyalty to him. I had a feeling some of them, especially his two main associates, Whitey Malooley and Billy McCoy, would continue coming after me simply for the sake of revenge. To them I was the whistle blower that caused the police raid. And, when I left town so secretly, why would they not think I did so with a fair amount of D'Annelli's money from the mill basement?

My drifting thoughts were interrupted by Brey's voice echoing in the long distance phone line. "Henry...Henry...are you still on the line? What do you think?

My voice was placid. "Rich, I can't let down my guard. Rumors will be flying. The perception that I left in a hurry is difficult to refute. I'll be vulnerable for some time until things calm down."

Brey tried to quell my concern saying D'Annelli's fortune had been confiscated by the authorities. There would be no public record of how much money was in that mill basement. His point was that how could I be pinned down for walking away with even one dollar of his treasure chest if there was no accurate accounting in the first place?

I had to disagree. "Rich, you know how their minds work. They deal in thievery and deceit. How could they not believe I stole some of D'Annelli's fortune? I believe any number of D'Annelli's people will seek me out just to satisfy their sinister minds. If they'd been in my place, they'd have taken as much of D'Annelli's money as they could fit in their suitcases and pockets."

After hanging up I remember not sleeping well that night. The loft in the church was too quiet and my mixed thoughts were too loud."

There was a pause. Lawton looked at Granville. It was becoming apparent his interest in continuing his story had waned. Ashley picked up the cue as well. He changed the subject to some events coming up in Charleston in the coming week. Shortly thereafter the session ended although the hour was only 10:00.

Minutes later Lawton was in his eighth floor suite while the other three ventured down to the lobby. Henry and Lill would leisurely drive back to Mt. Pleasant; Ashley still had some where to go yet that evening.

Standing out on his deck overlooking the harbor and feeling the breeze, Lawton was not ready to settle down. No bars would be opened that Sunday night, but he felt like a stroll out on the Battery.

Slipping down the back staircase and out a back entrance onto East Bay Street, he watched as Henry and Lill took off for Mt. Pleasant from the hotel parking lot. They had just sped up at the Broad Street intersection when Lawton saw movement in the open second floor window of the dilapidated office building across the street. The building was supposedly vacant.

What he saw next was totally unexpected. In the darkness there was a faint figure of a man and he was pointing something out the opened window. From Lawton's angle it looked as if something was being aimed at Henry's car as it passed below the darkened office window.

In that instant a loud guttural noise exploded and it was not the discharge of some kind of firearm protruding from the window. The piercing blare was his own voice yelling, "Hey....hey there...what are you doing!"

It wasn't a question meant to be answered, just a noise to rankle the man in the dormer window. The barrel of the rifle hastily retracted back into the dormer. Lawton's shout had done the trick. Henry's Cadillac continued undisturbed along East Bay Street.

His roar created a sudden fury within him propelling Lawton to cross the street toward the darkened office building. All he could think was how so completely preposterous the action was that he'd just seen. Why would someone be firing a weapon at Henry Granville? What would be gained? No money would result...only pain for those close to Henry. If that was the case, the man aiming the rifle would have to be deranged.

Lawton was not about to cower back to the safety of the hotel. He wanted to get a glimpse of the unstable character for possible identification later to the police.

Stopping at the corner of the building, he listened for any hint of a man running or breathing heavily. After two weeks in Charleston, he knew his way around the historical area. He was not intimidated by the streets or the alleyways between the row homes.

Hearing nothing he ran up Broad Street hoping the potential shooter might be escaping by car. With his heart thumping against his chest wall, he slowed to catch his breath. Then he stopped again listening carefully. Sure enough...there was an unmistakable sound of a car engine starting up. It was close...maybe two blocks away. It could be a resident...then again maybe not.

Running towards St. Michael's Episcopal Church along Broad Street, he could hear the car's engine coming his way. He arrived breathlessly at Meeting Street just as a dull-colored Ford Falcon slowed at the intersection. Lawton couldn't be certain if the car was being driven by the unbalanced fellow in the office dormer window.

In the next couple seconds his questions were answered. First, the driver of the car turned his head just long enough for Lawton to see the man's eyes bug out. It was a startled expression followed by immediate anger. While Lawton caught only a glimpse of the man's face, the Panama hat he wore gave him away.

Then the car took off before the light turned green...a definite giveaway that the driver was trying to escape detection.

Lawton then did something impulsive. As the driver made one more look at him, Lawton held his arm straight out as if pointing a gun... an imitation of what he'd seen someone do the previous Sunday night as Granville's car had passed. The young man had every belief he was dealing with the same man.

That action caused the driver to accelerate his vehicle even faster. Lawton was unable to see the license plate, but he would never forget the dirty tan color of the Ford Falcon. He walked out into the intersection and continued to just stand there with his arm extended toward the speeding automobile. He didn't bring his arm down until the car had disappeared from sight. He knew the driver would still see him in the semi-lit intersection in his rear view mirror.

Lawton felt a wave of satisfaction...and then a chill of fear. While he walked slowly back toward the hotel, he wondered if he'd really thwarted some troublemaker against Henry...or had he just transferred this man's focus from Henry over to him.

* * *

When Darrel O'Donnell heard the startling shout from across the street at the hotel, he'd pulled his rifle immediately from the window. Escape and not being seen were his only thoughts. His heart raced as he slipped his binoculars and the rifle back under the loose floor board of the vacant office. Then in the familiar darkness he snuck down the hall to a back staircase and exited onto a thin walkway between two buildings three feet apart. With his car parked two blocks away, he stopped a couple times to listen for footsteps. Hearing none he finally arrived at his car with sweat pouring from his balding head.

Starting his engine in the quiet night was like an explosion. Cringing he propelled forward very slowly toward Meeting Street. He began to breathe easier as he approached the intersection of Broad and Meeting streets. He'd had a close call. Someone had seen his rifle pointing out the vacant office window, but the darkness had certainly made it difficult for anyone to recognize him.

O'Donnell swore a blue streak thinking how stupid he'd been. He wasn't even going to do anything rash. His intent was not to kill. He was only going to shoot out the back window of Henry Granville's vehicle. He wanted to scare the man he so hated and push his blackmail scheme to a faster completion. His plan was to then to call Granville the very next day and make a final demand for the hush money. The idea had seemed to easy...so potentially effective. Now after failing to even get a shot off...and worse yet, being seen pointing a rifle out that office window, O'Donnell had just received a devastating blow to his confidence.

As he was thinking once again how he might not have the know-how and grit to pull off a successful extortion attempt, he then received yet another major jolt. Slowing for a stoplight on Meeting Street, he spotted a person just standing by one of the pillars of St. Michael's Episcopal Church. The fellow just stared at O'Donnell's car. For just an instance both their eyes met and the chill sliding down O'Donnell's back made his sweat feel icy. There was that young man...that kid... he'd been following. This individual had already upset O'Donnell's timetable for completing his blackmail scheme. Now this damned kid had somehow sniffed out his trail.

Then suddenly the person moved a step forward and pointed his arm and a finger right at O'Donnell...as if aiming a weapon. It was the very same action O'Donnell had done the previous weekend in a fit of frustration as Henry Hanson Granville's Cadillac passed by him on the street. Tensing up, O'Donnell hit his accelerator before the light turned green. His thoughts shouted, 'That bastard is mocking me... and he's onto me!'

That truth hit him like a hammer. The hair stood up on the back of his neck. His car could now even be identified.

O'Donnell was seething. He didn't know what to do. If his license plate number could be detected, the local police would be looking for his Ford Falcon the very next morning. He'd been in Charleston for a couple months intimidating Hanson and finally making his blackmail demands...and what happens... suddenly his entire extortion plan was in ruins.

He drove around Charleston for the next hour wishing he had more natural skills as a crook. He couldn't figure out why Henry Hanson Granville hadn't reacted like a normal blackmail victim and just paid the money. What was going wrong?

O'Donnell's fear that night built to the point that he couldn't sleep. He left the city before the sun rose the next morning. He didn't stop until he reached Savannah, Georgia. All through that two-hour drive he wailed at himself for being such a loser. Not only had he failed to frighten Granville, he'd been seen. Even his surveillance spot in the vacant office building across the street from the hotel had now been compromised. The final insult was that the damned kid could identify O'Donnell's old tan Ford.

With his blackmail plans up in smoke, the next threatening call to Granville he'd scheduled for Monday morning was no longer going to happen. He had to now find out what the young man's next action might be. Surely he'd contact the police. Surely he'd say something to Henry Granville. That night in Charleston had been a huge setback.

And then that old spark of hope rekindled itself. O'Donnell took great satisfaction that during those times in his life where things seemed at their worst, another thought would ignite to inspire him to keep going. He'd had plenty of stumbling blocks in his life to be familiar with the feeling. That Monday morning he rationalized that it would be in his favor if the young man informed Granville about the previous night's incident. It would supply the same fear and anxiety if O'Donnell had gone through with shooting out the back window of Granville's Cadillac. The intimidation would be accomplished.

With that kind of flawed reasoning, he forgot about his own car being recognizable or the rifle barrel being seen. The dim-witted man had justified to himself how his extortion plan might still be salvageable.

Stopping by a cheap motel on the outskirts of Savannah, the lights were out in the motel office and a sign said 'No Vacancy' even though there were only two cars in the parking lot. The proprietor had obviously wanted an uninterrupted sleep.

The intrepid blackmailer napped in his old Ford in the parking lot of that flee-bag motel with his sweaty clothes stuck to his skin until the owner began cleaning the two rooms he'd rented out the night before. O'Donnell had always visualized his one major crime attempt might be done in a classier mode. Renting a room at 9:00 that Monday morning and with nothing better to do, he sprawled across the stained bedspread in his smelly room. It had been a hell of an Easter Sunday. He expected to return to Charleston later in the week to begin a renewed surveillance on the East Bay Street Hotel. He could observe if those people around the wealthy hotel owner were behaving more protectively. Also, if there were more police in the vicinity of the hotel that would indicate the young man had visited with the local law enforcement.

Now, the game had changed. He had a new competitor to take into account. In O'Donnell's continually twisted mind he figured he had a new target if he wanted to get Granville's attention. That young man...that kid...was someone special to the owner of Triple H Development, Inc.

If O'Donnell could eliminate this new player, he could kill two birds with one stone. There'd be no one any longer who could identify him... and his blackmail scheme would be back on track.

Chapter 12

It would not be until the next Friday night, April 22 that the four were scheduled for another dinner. Lawton was primed to inform Henry each day that week there was a lunatic out there who could be dangerous. But, each day with no sighting of that weird, overweight man with the Panama hat or a Ford Falcon parked near the hotel, Lawton's reasons for bringing up the macabre subject seemed unwarranted.

That week Lawton had followed his own routine of walking through the historic district pausing often to stop and tie his shoe just to sense if anyone was following him. Not once did he have that feeling.

Tuesday morning he'd even crossed the street from the hotel and investigated the vacant office building. Opening the door to the office where he'd sworn he'd seen a rifle barrel pointing out the second story window, all he found was a huge empty space. Except for some loose creaking floor boards he discovered nothing of proof that a would-be murderer was using the room. He did take note, however, that from the dormer window a complete view of the entire hotel complex was available including the bay window area of the restaurant where the interview dinners with Henry, Lill and Ashley had taken place. It gave him a chill realizing some maniac with a weapon would have a clear shot at anyone at that location as well as the entry of the East Bay Street Hotel.

By Thursday with nothing unseemly happening, the incident took on less importance. Lawton didn't want to create angst where none existed. Instead, he let the previous Sunday night's incident diminish in his mind. He began to question whether he'd seen the entire spectacle accurately.

The week did turn out to be more eventful in other ways. Lawton continued to either go to the beach or play golf each afternoon.

Since the previous Friday night card game, he, Jefferson Brown and Lou White would meet for lunch either in the staff lounge or at some other local cafes on Broad Street.

Jefferson was the closest to his age and the two of them had similar senses of humor. Lou White was a generation older, yet seemed to enjoy his younger friends. The man was difficult not to like. He was always active, very resourceful, and had a smile for everyone. One forgot he had but one arm as he handled all the chores as head of maintenance for the hotel with a skill that surpassed any disability.

When Lou and Jefferson learned that Lawton was playing nine holes of golf alone on many weekday afternoons, the three of them made plans for that Friday afternoon to play together. The obvious first concern was Lou having but one arm. Jefferson saw Lawton's surprise at Lou looking forward to playing golf. Before they teed off that afternoon he whispered to Lawton how the only worry he should really have with Lou White was whether Lawton would still have some money in his wallet at the end of the round of golf.

Lawton saw it for himself that afternoon. It was obvious Lou had been a fairly good player in his younger days with two arms.

There was also a second concern. It was not discussed, but it was predictable. Lawton had seen too many examples of segregation in the city. He didn't want Jefferson being embarrassed if there was any rude treatment directed his way by the golfers or the staff at the city owned golf club.

It turned out on that beautiful April afternoon in 1960 that an incident would occur, but the result was nothing like Lawton...or Jefferson Brown...would ever have expected.

In the short few weeks he'd been in Charleston, Lawton had learned much about the inception of the city. He'd marveled that the original community in the late 1600's had been founded upon a determined foundation of religious freedom. All types of religions and people were tolerated as the city grew to be at one time the fourth largest in colonial America. There were other matters that militated against that laudable groundwork as the decades passed. Social class and skin color dictated life more and more...and Charleston was certainly no exception. Even amongst the white population, there was social level and prejudice. The planters were at the highest level. White workers on the plantations were at the lowest levels, just above slaves. Other groups...shippers, merchandisers, and government officials...were at levels in between.

In the almost hundred years since the 'state's rights' conflict between the northern and southern states, the emotions of the 1860's still could be felt. At least Lawton sensed it. Religious preference was still tolerated but social stratum was still very important. And skin color was the easiest way to keep at least one group of people segregated.

That very week Lawton had read up on prominent figures locally so he might know their politics or beliefs if they happened to attend one of the popular Sunday buffets at the East Bay Street Hotel. He'd met one attendee, Federal District Judge J.W. Waring at the previous Easter Sunday buffet. Introduced by Ashley, Lawton found the Judge amusing with a surprising knowledge of the Midwest. That was uncommon. Most locals looked at him blankly when he mentioned Minnesota. While Judge Waring was delightful in conversation, Lawton would learn he was not a very popular magistrate. He was known for making more and more judgments favoring civil rights. That had elevated Lawton's respect for the man.

Mayor Bill Morrison, another acquaintance of Ashley Cooper, had attended the get-together that previous Sunday as well. Ashley later explained to Lawton that Morrison was in the difficult position of trying to allow more desegregation despite the concept being very unpopular amongst the dominant 'voting' constituency...that is, the white population. As Ashley said despondently, "The integration process will be glacial in this city. It may take a couple generations for real respectful and noticeable change to take place."

The golf course incident that happened that Friday was a very personal example of Ashley's point. There was a new golf course manager standing out on the porch of the clubhouse looking at the links as if it was his personal plantation. He saw Lou, Lawton....and Jefferson...taking their golf clubs out of the trunk of one of the hotel's vehicles and his eyes narrowed. It had begun to sprinkle so there were not as many players out on the course. Still the manager looked annoyed and motioned for Lou, the oldest of the threesome to join him for a private conversation.

Lawton would not forget the look in Lou's eyes as he calmly asked Matt to carry his bag over to the first tee box. Jefferson began to hesitate going forward. He had the most disgusted, yet understanding look in his eye. He expected to see what he'd seen too often in his life.

As Lawton carried his golf bag and Lou's bag toward the first tee, Jefferson stopped him whispering, "Might as well wait a moment, Matt. We might not be playing. Let's just see what happens. I think we're getting into a situation."

Lawton wasn't certain what that meant until he saw the arrogant look on the golf course manager's face as he began talking with Lou. Being just out of earshot, Lawton watched as Lou's face reddened. His eyes widened as he looked at Jefferson's similar reaction. Neither of them had ever seen Lou's face that shade of red.

It was less than twenty seconds later when Lou had his nose about one inch from the golf course manager's face. He was not shouting, but Jefferson and Lawton both stood in silent shock seeing a vein protruding from Lou's neck as he spoke. When Lou raised his one good arm to point a finger at the manager, the man seemed to wither. The conversation didn't last long. In fact it was not a conversation at all. It was more a demonstrative monologue...and quite effective.

When Lou was finished he didn't even go into the clubhouse to pay the green fees. He just calmly walked back toward Jefferson and Lawton now standing on the first tee box. His normal facial color had returned as if the altercation had never happened. He smiled at his two young friends and said casually, "Gentlemen, we'll be playing for no charge today. The clubhouse manager insisted on it."

Then, he stared more intently at Jefferson and Lawton and asked, "So, what's our game and who's hitting first?"

Lawton had never experienced seeing a man go from absolute rage to such a calm demeanor. It told him something about Lou...that this wasn't the first time this man with the salt and pepper hair had handled something unpleasant. From that day on, Lawton hoped if he was in a squabble of any sort, he hoped Lou White would be on his team.

They never asked Lou what he'd said to the man nor did the subject ever come up again. But in all the times they played again at the Charleston Municipal Golf Course, there was no green fee collected and the three of them played without any interruption...and that was before the golf course by municipal law became desegregated.

After that round of golf, Lou had to take care of some maintenance problem at the hotel. Jefferson and Lawton went to a bar for a beer where both of them could be served. It was a local dive with primarily a black clientele. Once Jefferson introduced Lawton to a few of his friends, Lawton felt more comfortable. It was still a place he might not come again without Jefferson at his side.

Jefferson and he re-lived the scene of Lou dealing with the racist golf course manager. Lawton learned from Jefferson that Henry had donated a fair amount of money to the city to keep the golf course solvent. That point was undoubtedly made clear by Lou…along with a demonstrative statement that the manager's attitude better change or he'd no longer have his job.

They got talking about the number of years Lou had been employed at the hotel. Jefferson only knew that Lou had just started working at the hotel upon recovering from his injury apparently caused by German bullet to his shoulder at the Battle of the Bulge. Jefferson was one of the closer people to Lou but still didn't know Lou's full background…only that Henry and Lou might have known each other prior to World War II. However, that was a subject Lou or Henry would limit any further discussion.

Lawton then shared something personal with his new friend. "You know, I can't imagine working anywhere for that length of time. I've worked for a publishing company in Minneapolis for a couple years and I'm ready to leave. In fact, I'd be gone except I was asked to take on this assignment down here in Charleston. I'm not supposed to talk about the task, so I won't. But, once I complete this job, I guess I'll be going back to Minnesota to find a new opportunity."

Jefferson gave him an understanding smile. "I tell you, Matt, it's different for me. I guess I could go other places. I have a college degree thanks to some help from Henry. But, it's never dull at the hotel. I keep gaining further responsibilities. It's like Henry makes certain I keep experiencing new things in the management and marketing of the hotel business. He's even insisted I travel occasionally up to Washington D.C. and New York City on business with him. Last year he, Lill and I were overseas for two weeks. I've been to France, Holland and Great Britain to take note how certain international hotels are run. Henry also admitted to me he thought it a good idea for me to experience areas where the color of my skin didn't quite have the stigma that it unfortunately has in my own country."

After two beers they left the small bar. Lawton had an appointment for another round of talks with Henry, Lill, and Ashley that evening. A message in his hotel box changed his plans. Lill's note was an apology for the last minute alteration. Suggesting instead Saturday or Sunday evening, she said there would be no problem if Lawton already had those nights planned out.

Again Lawton had to smile sardonically. His hosts were thoughtful to a fault. Not only would he cancel anything to be able to continue the Henry Granville interviews but his evenings were always predictably clear. In fact, the prospect for much social activity with a more interesting young lady than an uninspiring bar waitress looked hopelessly bleak.

He placed a return note back in Lill's hotel mail box saying that a 6:30 Saturday night dinner would be fine...and that he'd see Henry and her about 6:45.

*   *   *

That week verified further why his assignment would likely continue at a snail's pace. Henry's daily schedule kept him in his office unless he escaped to go sailing...an activity that might happen on a whim. Otherwise, the hotel magnate was typically having lunch with clients, local businessmen or attending some function in the city.

By the end of the week, Lawton had put aside the image of that strange fellow he'd seen the previous Sunday night. He was still alert to the possibility of being followed, but it was no longer a preoccupation. Saturday morning a call from one of Henry's sailboat crew found him in the downstairs staff cafeteria having coffee. It was an invitation for a run down the coast to some place called Kiawah Island...a mostly uninhabited island with wild horses running along the beach.

Lawton was at the pier within the hour. He barely got back in time to shower before the scheduled interview session that evening. He made it down to the hotel restaurant at 6:40, ten minutes late, confident Henry and Lill wouldn't be there yet. He was right. Within five minutes Ashley loped in having just left an afternoon get-together at one of the recently restored ante-bellum homes on Meeting Street. The two of them only had time to exchange some brief overviews of their day including Lawton telling of the great way Lou had handled a golf course incident the day before. Then a wave of conversation flowed through the hotel lobby indicating Henry and Lill had arrived.

Upon arriving the man looked tired and was apologetic. "Matt, I so sorry I've not been around the hotel for us to chat. However, from what I've heard you're keeping yourself occupied learning about the city. Lou tells me you've donated a few dollars to his cause on the golf course."

Lawton snickered. "Lou golfs well for a man with one arm. His strength, though, is negotiating how many strokes I have to give him. At least I was able to lighten Jefferson's wallet by a few dollars to make up for my losses to Lou."

Henry seemed delighted that Lawton was gaining some friends on the staff. "Well, that's just fine. And, that was good of you to jump in and help out with the preparation for last Sunday's buffet. That was very nice...very nice indeed."

Lawton nodded blankly. Henry behaved like it was a sacrifice. To Lawton it was just assisting some newly made friends. It had not been a big deal. It wasn't as if he didn't have some spare time. He'd also helped Lou a couple times. They'd put in some new light fixtures in the restaurant Friday morning. Lou could have done it alone but the work went faster with two men and three arms.

Henry seemed more pleased with Lawton's other activities than the writing project. The older man looked at Lill and asked, "So tell me, is our young writer being treated properly here at our flagship hotel?

Lill looked at Lawton and hoped her nod was accurate. "Yes, Henry, I'd say Matt's doing just fine. He's doing everything we hoped he would do since he arrived.

Lawton gave a vacuous grin while wondering why she'd added that part about 'doing everything we hoped he would'. At times he felt he was staying at the East Bay Street Hotel for more than just the writing assignment. He couldn't put his finger on it.

Ashley then spoke of the dinner Lawton and he had the previous Wednesday night as well as the upcoming invitations he hoped Lawton would attend as well. "Matt, Tuesday night we'll have dinner with a friend of mine, a Mr. Gedney Howe. Mr. Howe just completed ten years of service as the City Solicitor. I think you'll enjoy meeting him, especially after that slight altercation you told me about at the municipal golf course with you, Lou, and Jefferson. Mr. Howe is a local attorney and political leader here in this city. He's a World War II hero and has been a real champion of racial equality. You'll also meet him tomorrow at the Sunday buffet. He's one of the regulars who will always stop by for a cold libation even if liquor is supposedly not being served."

Ashley then patted his breast pocket where he kept his omnipresent flask and winked at Lawton.

Ashley also mentioned a Thursday engagement at another anti-bellum home near White Point Garden. It was to be a night to enjoy the company of visitors with special backgrounds in the arts.

Lawton, thinking about this sudden change to his normal uneventful social schedule, just nodded his head, smiled, and wrote down the invitations. With Ashley, he did not ever want to miss an invitation from this highly social man who seemed to know everyone in town...including visitors.

Why Ashley had mentioned the incident with Lou at the municipal golf course, Lawton didn't know. Ashley had then given Henry a silent shake of the head indicating that there had been no major confrontation. Though Henry seemed to accept Ashley's nonverbal sign, Lawton could tell Henry was troubled.

To get Henry's mind on the interview, Lill took charge and motioned for the waiter to begin serving. "So Henry dear, are we going to get started or do you want to first have dinner?"

Henry smiled respecting her ability to get the purpose of their meeting back on track. He responded, "Let's have some ice teas and talk for a while. We can eat a bit later if that's all right."

A furrow showed on his brow as if recalling the discomfort he'd felt back then. Hesitantly he murmured, "Matt, it's time I introduce you to two other men who will be discussed repeatedly from this point forward. These two individuals definitely were not friends of mine. I've mentioned their names in passing in one of our previous sessions. They were Loni D'Annelli's most trusted associates. Their names were Whitey Malooley and Billy McCoy. They would figure prominently in my life for a long time even after I left Minnesota.

Some of what I'm about to tell you comes through Clarence Petracek and Rich Brey who had some interaction with these two gangsters after I'd arrived in the Charleston area. I also will include the story from the perspective of these two fellows, Malooley and McCoy. I got their viewpoint as a result of knowing someone who knew these two gangsters and what their life had been like following the death of Loni D'Annelli. What made their story especially interesting was how they were trying to find me while being pursued by several hitmen assigned to kill them. To the mob, they were as guilty as their boss in that counterfeit problem D'Annelli had with his mob colleagues. It would become a problem that cost him his life."

Lawton showed puzzlement while Henry tried to ignore his young writer's understandable confusion. Noticing the slight tension in the air, Ashley rolled his eyes exclaiming, "Henry, for the love of God, just tell the young man about Malooley and McCoy. And Matt, don't be concerned how Henry happens to know what happened to them. It'll all get straightened out as Henry divulges more information."

Lawton shrugged in agreement and Henry grinned at his friend. Ashley had cleared enough of the air of doubt for Henry to continue. Blowing some thin cigar smoke toward the fan above their table, the older man finally launched into the next refrain. Lawton's pen could barely keep up.

"I was acquainted with these two men, Malooley and McCoy, for years before I departed from Glenwood. As Loni D'Annelli's right hand men, I knew them well enough to greet them in town although with no real enthusiasm. Often times I didn't know D'Annelli was at the Lodge until I saw either one of the two men at the local café. Both men gave themselves away as front men. They had slicked hair, sharkskin suits, and a tough outer core. They also were ostensibly union stewards in the D'Annelli led union. I would come to know better.

One of their main jobs in Glenwood was to be Loni's eyes and ears. They knew the mayor, town council members, church ministers and most of the local business owners by first name. If anything was said or done that might cast aspersions on their boss or if any negative gossip was bandied about in town about the activities or the guests out at the Lodge, Malooley and McCoy would report the hearsay to their boss. From there, D'Annelli would remedy the problem, often times with my help. He knew my interest was the town and I just wanted things to run as smoothly as possible.

These two men were able to keep themselves clean for the most part from the law. They had not been arrested that often, but by no means were these guys former choir boys. At the time of the Chippewa Lodge raid, D'Annelli was arrested, but Malooley and McCoy were questioned and released when no known criminal record was found.

Until being extradited to the Hennepin County jail in Minneapolis two days after the raid, D'Annelli was held in the Pope County jail in Glenwood. While there, Malooley and McCoy were able to visit and take orders from their boss. That was where he got the lowdown about the U.S. Attorney's office in Minneapolis being responsible for his eventual arrest. He couldn't believe a young undercover woman investigator from that office working as a free-lance magazine writer had been the cause of his undoing...and all by herself! He would never accept that notion despite her determined statement to the press that she worked alone up until calling in the state patrol.

D'Annelli was more obsessed with what brought her to Glenwood in the first place. It had to be someone who had a pretty fair idea what was going on at the resort.

He read and reread the newspaper accounts of her story....that she'd been in town for two full weeks before she began to realize there might be more than a gambling ring in the Lake Minnewaska area. In fact, she knew that fact after the first day of arriving in Glenwood. What she didn't tell the press was that it took the remaining time before the raid to find the evidence needed to prove who was in charge. She was careful in her story to the reporters to make it sound as if her discovery at Chippewa Lodge was accidental...and that she started to recognize many of the guests and golfers at the resort from wanted posters back at her office. With so many known racketeers, wanted criminals, jail escapees and various other lowlifes, she was quoted in the newspapers as saying, 'I just figured where there was smoke there was probable fire'. She'd said this prompted her to focus her investigation on Chippewa Lodge.

D'Annelli wasn't buying her simplistic story. How in just a few days was she able to discover his stored business profits in the mill basement when no one else but Henry Hanson knew that secret hiding place. To him, there was a limit how lucky she could get in such a short time. It was inconceivable that she worked single-handedly.

Those thoughts haunted him as he sat there in the Pope County jail. He could think of only one man who could have clandestinely led her to the Lodge, then later to the mill basement, and then finally worked with her to schedule the raid conveniently after I'd left town. Those factors sealed my guilt in his mind.

Though I had planned for and was ready to defend myself from being found, I wouldn't realize how badly his reputation within the mob community would be tarnished when word got out about the counterfeit money found in that mill basement. There wasn't all that much…maybe $80,000 to $100,000 of fake bills…but it was enough to promote the perception he used the fake money when paying off winning wagers amongst his own kind. That daunting noose hanging over his head would have him constantly in a defensive mode with not just the authorities, but more significantly with the Chicago syndicate as well. Both these concerns would seriously impede his search for me.

When I learned from Brey that primarily his two trusted lieutenants, Mr. Malooley and Mr. McCoy, were assigned to move heaven and earth to locate me, I was frankly quite relieved. I knew D'Annelli and those two bloodhounds had a formidable task ahead of them. I'd covered my tracks and left no scent. They had no idea where to begin in their efforts to find me.

When D'Annelli finally got bailed out of the Hennepin County jail in Minneapolis, it was Wednesday, June 10. He went back to Chicago to control the damage caused by the counterfeit money. With Malooley and McCoy staying in Minnesota to track me down, it was up to D'Annelli alone to defend himself with his mob brothers.

Unfortunately time was not on his side. He was constantly dealing with his exorbitant legal problems. The warrants for operating an illegal gambling operation, grand larceny, harboring known criminals, holding stolen goods, and running booze were big time crimes. His lawyers had always figured ways to help him beat the rap on the dirty things he was doing in Chicago. Up in Minnesota he'd actually been caught red-handed.

The bottom line was that all these charges would not amount to spit in a stained urn if he could not convince his associates in crime he had not conned them. That perception of using counterfeit funds was sticking to him like tar and feathers. Each passing day…every wasted hour that he couldn't verify his innocence to his compatriots… put him deeper in trouble within the mob.

When Malooley and McCoy returned to Glenwood less than a week after the Sunday police raid, they would hardly recognize the community. They were used to seeing a vibrant community with people bustling about town. The aftermath of the raid as well as the ten-day festival being over, Glenwood seemed more like a ghost town. Chippewa Lodge had been closed down since the owner and manager Darrell O'Donnell had been arrested. There was still garbage and residue from the festival in City Park. The locals seemed to have given up knowing their heydays were over. Without the 'guests' at the Lodge needing the supplies and services from the town, Glenwood would now become just another downtrodden, struggling town trying to survive the tough economic times.

Clarence Petracek and Rich Brey had already resigned their respective law enforcement positions and were no longer living in town. Locals knew the two men had purposely looked the other way for the community's benefit. They felt as badly for Clarence and Rich no longer at their posts as the Lodge being abruptly closed.

With townspeople's nerves frayed, Malooley and McCoy found little help. They were aware of my letter of resignation and that I'd supposedly taken a job out-of-state. Legitimately no one had any idea where that job was.

Whitey and Billy stayed in Minnesota for another three weeks eventually finding some people who would talk about me. They learned of my penchant for spending many weekends in Minneapolis. They came in contact with three friends of mine at the Grain Exchange Building who'd given me advantages with their inside information relating to commodities. That information did raise a flag. I had to have some money if I traveled to the Twin Cities that often and had some close association with three commodity brokers.

Malooley and McCoy also bribed one of the workers at the branch office of the U.S. Attorney's office to find out if Lindy MacPherson had admitted to having others help in her investigation in Glenwood. While some of her officemates were jealous of the young lady's rise, there was no indication that her actions were anything but a singular act.

Even the newspaper reporters they chatted with weren't helpful. Most were still mesmerized by the huge story and behaved as if they didn't really want to hear she'd had accomplices. To them she was a Minnesota Supreme Court Justice's daughter who was making good on her own. Her popularity was undeniable and would carry on for years.

The final lead they kept pursuing was the whereabouts of Clarence Petracek and Rich Brey. They found the resignations of Sheriff Petracek and Police Chief Brey to be odd. The two men had simply declared their shock and humiliation over what had been going on out at the resort…and their story was accepted by the authorities after Lindy MacPherson had verified their innocence from her investigation. Their statements specified that the county and city required better law enforcement than they had given, prompting them to resign and leave Glenwood that very day. Word was that they couldn't get out of Glenwood fast enough and showed little angst or concern about their futures.

It was reported in the newspapers they relinquished their jobs 'because of their personal embarrassment over the entire Chippewa Lodge scandal. To Malooley and McCoy, it made no sense during the hard times of the Depression for anyone to surrender any job so willingly. Embarrassment was not a good reason.

I should add that Clarence and Rich's supposed humiliation was one of the finest performances since Will Rogers last performed at the old Lyric Theatre in downtown St. Paul back in 1921. Their resignations had been planned out and their words well-practiced amongst the three of us. Frankly they delivered their lines so well even the townspeople felt compassion for the two peace officers. The mayor and town council members felt even worse. They had a better perspective on what was going on at Chippewa Lodge and knew the two law officers had looked sideways for the town's benefit for many years. Mayor Charlie B. Good made a special effort to persuade Clarence and Rich to remain. But, by then, my two friends were more than ready to leave town and get on with their new jobs at the two lake resorts.

When Malooley and McCoy finally heard the two men were holed up at a lake cabin twenty miles from Glenwood at Lake Osakis, the two gangsters sought out the two former law officers. It was a week and a half before they found Petracek and Brey, since the two former officers were seldom at the lake cabin. Malooley and McCoy thought they were traveling around Minnesota trying to find work. When they did intercept Clarence and Rich, they expected to find two men highly distraught and wondering about their next meal. Instead they found them having lunch at a Lake Osakis coffee shop. The two former cops seemed neither distressed nor anxious…behaviors inconsistent with their supposed dire predicament.

Clarence, Rich and I had discussed this eventual meeting and were ready. Rich was at his theatrical best when he responded to their first question about my possible whereabouts. He deadpanned, "I think he moved on."

Malooley and McCoy looked at each other and rolled their eyes. Keeping his patience, Malooley probed further. "We know he was friends with you fellows. Did you hear where he moved to or where he's living now? We just wanted to ask him a few questions."

That brought out laughter from Clarence and Rich. Rich got to the point and responded, "You guys don't actually think that tall thin turkey had anything to do with causing D'Annelli's arrest, do you?"

Whitey and Billy didn't know what to say. Of course they did…or why were they sitting at some lakeside dive in the middle of Minnesota?

Clarence added, "Boys, I think you're barking down the wrong path. You've known Henry for a couple years. He wouldn't pull any shenanigans against the likes of Loni D'Annelli. He's too smart for that."

Rich added more deceptions. "If you gentlemen have been reduced to believing that a church deacon and festival chairman could mastermind a plot to overthrow Loni D'Annelli's smug little operation at Chippewa Lodge, then you guys must be desperate to find someone to blame."

In his best delusive display of ignorance, Clarence mumbled, "Besides, I thought the young lady from the U.S. Attorney's office was given the full credit for her undercover investigation and planning the raid. Don't you boys read the newspapers?"

The two gangsters just shook their heads. They were getting nowhere. What had just been said was so easy to accept. They knew Henry Hanson as being straight as a preacher, a no-nonsense and detailed finance man, and in no way looking for trouble.

Clarence looked them straight in the eye and provided another lie. "Rich and I weren't surprised to hear Henry had left town for good. Hell, he'd been hinting as such for the past year. It made sense that he fulfilled his duties as the festival chairman before he departed. Furthermore it was typical of him to just leave without saying good-by to anyone…even to Rich and me who often had coffee with him. He always said he was horrible at saying farewell. That's why he wrote that letter of resignation knowing it would eventually be found at his house."

Rich chimed in again. "And now he'll probably never go back to Glenwood even to visit because of the personal shame he felt over the town being duped by Loni D'Annelli for so many years."

Malooley and McCoy had no further reason to detain them. The strange mixture of two gangsters and two former law officers having coffee in a small café by Lake Osakis ended in pleasant but quick handshakes.

As the two Chicago hucksters shuffled out to their 1930 Packard, Clarence and Rich headed for their old Ford truck filled with hunting and fishing gear. They looked all the part of two men with no place to go but to the next fishing hole.

When the Packard was out of sight, my two business associates doubled over with laughter. They had pulled off the stunt. There would be no more reason for the two gangsters to ever shadow their door again. As planned, they would now get more involved in their jobs with Triple H Development, Inc. The expected discussion with D'Annelli's boys had been completed.

By the end of June they would be spending even less time at the Lake Osakis cabin. Three weeks later their cabin would basically lay empty as Petracek and Brey were staying at the respective lake resort properties of which they were now in charge. Friends and neighbors in Glenwood had no idea of their two former law officers' new lives.

* * *

Back in Chicago during the remainder of June, D'Annelli continued his earnest attempts of assuring his brethren in the mob of never having used the counterfeit money in his possession for his gambling operation payoffs. He was having a difficult time regaining the trust among the mob elite.

Malooley and McCoy returned often to Glenwood during those weeks before July 1 in the hopes of hearing something about me. If anything the townspeople said even less with each passing day. It was as if the entire community was in a state of mourning having lost two of their most prominent leaders...Loni D'Annelli and me. Even the reporters flowing into town to find more dirt about the town left disappointed.

On Thursday, July 2, D'Annelli's two most trusted comrades finally called their boss claiming they'd hit a stone wall as far as finding any leads as to where I went. They confirmed there was no proof of any connection between Henry Hanson and the U. S. Attorney's office investigation. They also had become convinced my leaving came as no surprise to anyone in Glenwood. I'd done the same thing in previous years at the end of past festivals. And, while my resignation was unique to the previous departures, many locals weren't surprised. They'd said I'd grown beyond Glenwood and I probably needed to pursue new horizons. Malooley and McCoy concluded they'd found nothing supporting D'Annelli's hypothesis that I was the brains behind his downfall.

D'Annelli finally relented and ordered Malooley and McCoy back to Chicago. He needed help with his ongoing efforts to restore his reputation within the mob community. Besides, the three of them figured over time they would eventually find me. Then they'd put to rest their questions for me once and for all. Retaliation had no time barriers.

That afternoon before departing Minnesota for the Windy City, Malooley and McCoy played golf in St. Cloud. They were in no hurry. They enjoyed Minnesota in the summer. On Friday July 3, they arrived in Madison, Wisconsin and played another round of golf.

The next day, Saturday, July 4th, they were not to meet with their boss until later in the day. It was a national holiday and D'Annelli wanted to wait for the traffic to ease from the Independence Day parade in Chicago. They were not looking forward to meeting him. In the previous weeks when talking to him from Minnesota, he had become more and more irritable...even more irrational and frantic. His world was crumbling around him and he couldn't find an antidote to repair the damage.

They decided to stop in Elgin, Illinois and play what they considered their last round of golf for quite a while considering the warpath the boss was on. He faced going to court that Monday, July 6th to answer even more federal charges against him. Since his devastating loss at Chippewa Lodge, not only was his mob reputation taking a hit, but his entire business operation in Chicago needed to be rejuvenated and re-charged.

Malooley and McCoy had just doubled their nine-hole wager and were teeing off on the tenth hole at the Elgin, Illinois golf course when Loni D'Annelli was gunned down in the Chicago loop. Since returning to Chicago three-and-a-half weeks before, he had devoted his time to self-preservation and restoring his name. That afternoon he spent an hour lying in a pool of his own blood on a Dearborn street corner with sixteen bullet holes in his body until the coroner's office finally had the corpse taken to the Cook County morgue. His efforts to clear his name with his mob group had been futile. His arrest in Glenwood, Minnesota with so much evidence against him was injurious to his entire being... his reputation, his businesses, his ability to slip by prosecution, and his standing within the Chicago syndicate. It just took Loni until July 4th to actually die from those injuries.

He officially had been bested not only by a young female U.S. Attorney investigator and that unknown group of fellows who quietly helped her out that weekend...but as well by a conservative looking and frail feed & grain mill manager. It could be argued that the bullet holes in D'Annelli and his accompanying death were accomplished figuratively one month before by all six of those people.

Malooley and McCoy would finally hear about D'Annelli's murder while eating at the Elgin golf club restaurant after their round of golf. They would overhear some golfers talking at the adjoining table about the gangland slaying of their boss. The two of them had been part of the mob community long enough to know their close association with D'Annelli would likely mark them as targets as well. Less than two hours from the loop, they wisely decided Chicago should no longer be their destination if they valued their lives.

There can be epiphanies even in a gangster's life. In that very hour of hearing that their boss was gone, their perspective changed. They no longer had to deal with the anger of Loni D'Annelli. They faced a new and unpredictable future. Where they would go and what they would do became the sudden questions. That very afternoon they also became men of limited resources as they no longer were on D'Annelli's payroll. It was demeaning to think they'd have to return to their former lives of petty crime to support themselves until they could re-establish themselves in another city.

Over yet another beer, they had to decide where they would best be safe...even that very night. Their Chicago connections were over. As their fast-talk babble continued, they kept revisiting the topic of Minnesota. Not only did they like the summers in the state, but over the last five years they'd become familiar with the area. It seemed like a logical place for them to hide out for as long as was necessary. If they were to become hunted prey in the weeks and months ahead, they had a better chance of survival in a state where they knew so many back roads.

They wasted little more time in Elgin. Two hours after stepping off the golf course...and an hour after hearing of the death of their boss, they were on the road back to Minnesota. With a much different future without D'Annelli, they reassessed everything. Their own survival was at stake. In those hours of travel my name kept working its way into their conversation. They also admitted to each other how curious it was that townsfolk in Glenwood, especially the two former law officers, Clarence Petracek and Rich Brey, seemed to hold no concern or interest where I'd gone. The two former cops also had repeatedly scoffed about my being part of any plot against D'Annelli...almost to the point of their words being contrived.

Furthermore, Lindy MacPherson's adamant statements to the press and to the authorities about my having no part in her investigation had so summarily been accepted. And, no news clips ever divulged how she discovered the private chamber under the mill office where D'Annelli stored his illegal profits.

By the time they reached the Minnesota border, they'd smelled not just one rat, but a bunch of rodents. They'd conjured up so many exaggerations about my guilt; I became a bigger conman than D'Annelli himself. McCoy made the presumption I'd escaped with a pile of Loni's dough...enough to pay off Clarence Petracek and Rich Brey for their silence and certainly enough to disappear anywhere and set up a new life with a new identity. His accusation of course couldn't be proved unless they found me, but the allegation provided their primary motivation from then on. In their minds there was now a pot of gold at the end of the rainbow."

Henry suddenly let out a yawn. He'd been talking for a long time and now expressed some interest in dining. He showed some relief completing that portion of his story.

Emphatically he uttered, "Matt, you now have your notes up to date with Loni D'Annelli's death in 1931, as well as some new information about two desperate characters very interested in tracking me down. However, they had an added stress. They had their own lives to protect with various gangsters being paid to eliminate them. They had to stay under cover until they felt their own safety was no longer as much of an issue. With them staying low, I wouldn't even be conscious of their efforts to find me for a long time."

With the interview abruptly ended, food was served. There had not been near the time investment of previous interview sessions. Lawton wondered why but didn't ask his hosts. The interviews were on Henry's timetable. As Lill, Ashley, and Henry turned the conversation into talk of the hotel and of the upcoming travels, it was yet another indication there would be plenty of intervals between interview sessions.

After just two weeks in Charleston, Lawton found himself not minding the delays.

*   *   *

With the Saturday evening interview having come to a close followed by a more upbeat dinner conversation among the four of them, Lawton accompanied Henry and Lill down to the lobby. The night was still young for him. He was inclined to getting some exercise and taking in a few bars before calling it a night. Waving good-by to his hosts until the next day's Sunday brunch, Lawton was ever mindful of the crazy man who could be lurking nearby.

As the Cadillac departed the hotel property, Lawton focused on the second story vacant office building window. There was no indication of either a barrel of a rifle or even a silhouette of a human being hiding in that darkened space. He was relieved.

Re-entering the hotel, Lawton was still contemplating whether he wanted to walk down the street to have a purposeless conversation with another bar maid or just go back to his suite and read. Then one of the desk clerks motioned for him. She had a note in her hand. Lou and Jefferson were at a bar on King Street. The note said to drop by if the interview session didn't go too late...or even if it did. His evening promptly became more active.

Hoofing it along Broad Street to King Street, he was conscious there might be a set of eyes watching him. Yet the streets were too busy that Saturday night for him to really care. When he arrived at the bar, there was not only Lou and Jefferson, but the poker players from the previous week. He had a good feeling that some friendships had been established.

He compared his new friends to the ones back in Minnesota. The difference was noticeable. Back in his home state those fellows were friends from his youthful uncaring college days. Many of them were still struggling to find themselves in the working world...and maybe delaying the process for as long as possible. In Charleston, the four men he'd gotten to know were all over thirty...in Lou's case, well over fifty...and all were more established in their careers. Lawton found that difference more energizing.

That Saturday night ended after midnight with the Lou, Jefferson, and Lawton walking back to the hotel. It was supposed to be a relaxed walk, but it turned out not to be. There would be yet another slanderous assault aimed at Jefferson. Two young locals near the intersection of King and Broad Streets felt compelled to target Jefferson with some racial slurs. It was embarrassing to Jefferson...and to Lou and Lawton as well. Experience made Jefferson walk stoically ahead trying to ignore the ignoramuses. Lou tried to calm the situation by telling us to disregard the two idiots.

Whether it was a few too many beers or the confidence of having Lou White behind him, Lawton wasn't willing to listen to further contempt aimed at his friend, Jefferson. He began crossing the street telling the two dead heads to get lost...exactly what the two troublemakers were hoping. Staying right at Lawton's side with the intent of protecting the young Minnesotan from his own stupidity was Lou White. While Jefferson didn't want to get his two friends involved in any race related brouhaha, the situation had turned hot. He hurried to catch up.

Halfway across the street with Lawton in his own foolish ignorance telling the two nitwits what he thought of them, the two young locals began to smile. Lawton was being supported by a man without a left arm who appeared to be more than twice their age. Also, the focus of their mockery, Jefferson Brown, was a slender guy and not very intimidating.

The two ruffians sensed they had a definite edge against three fellows who looked vulnerable. They then began taunting the one-armed Lou calling him a cripple. Lou shook his head showing a slight disgust. With a small grin he said to Jefferson and Lawton, "Gentlemen, please step aside for just a moment. Let me handle this one. I'll let you know if I need any help."

Something about the way Lou said it caused Lawton and Jefferson to follow the request. Lou walked up to the two young men with their insipid smirks and quietly said to them, "You boys need to leave this street corner and not bother any more good citizens. If you don't leave, you'll probably get hurt."

They sneered at the words of the one-armed man. Then one of the young men pulled out a knife and menacingly asked Lou, "So, who do you think is going to get hurt?"

Jefferson and Lawton froze for a moment not knowing what they should do. Lou never hesitated. The young man with the knife never knew what hit him. Lou's right foot kicked the youth's wrist causing him to lose the knife. A power blow from Lou's formidable right fist left the young man with a nose that was almost flattened against his face and exploded with blood. When the other youth rushed Lou, the powerful and surprisingly skilled older man stopped the assailant in his tracks. In an instant, Lou had grabbed the young man's testicles.

The fellow's eye balls went from evil slits to looking as if they were about to explode from their sockets. While the one youth lay writhing on the pavement with what most assuredly was a broken nose, Lou squeezed what was most dear to the second young man. Lou's tone of voice did not change as he softly said to the incapacitated youth, "I guess you have an apology to make to my friends. But, you're too dumb to apologize, aren't you?"

The youth moaned out an affirmation.

Lou continued, "You two are so worthless that I'm embarrassed to be seen with you. You shouldn't even be allowed to be out this late away from your mothers, should you?"

The youth moaned another 'yes'.

In a very patient tone with a vice grip still on the boy's crotch, Lou explained to the two miserable thugs, "Boys, I never want to see you again until you grow up. During that time I suggest you read a book about the golden rule and manners. Does that sound fair?"

Another wail was heard from the youth with the now excruciating pain in his groin. Lou released his grip and the former smart-mouthed kid just slipped to the pavement like a melting snowman.

The other youth sat on the walkway not saying anything and just holding his bleeding nose. Lou hailed a cab and gave the cabbie five dollars to deliver the two unfortunate youths to the local infirmary.

Lou told the cabbie, "I believe these two boys were fighting and one of them might have trouble breathing through his nose for a while. The other guy will recover. He just had his ignorance bruised."

The cabbie didn't exactly know what Lou was talking about, but he hungrily took the five dollars and sped the two contemptuous youths down the street and apparently to the local hospital. Lou picked up the knife and threw it in the garbage at the corner of the street.

The entire incident ended as quickly as it had begun. Jefferson and Lawton just stood there with their jaws hanging open. The very idea of Lou needing some help with the two youths never entered their minds.

As they stared with even greater appreciation and respect for their friend, they hardly knew what to say. Lou looked at them, grinned as if nothing really important had happened, and said, "Young guys like those two imbeciles give this city a bad image."

Then he began walking down the street with Jefferson and Lawton hurrying to catch up while looking at each other with eyes like saucers. Seconds later, Lou began talking about the Sunday buffet the next morning. His mind had already moved on to something more pleasant.

*   *   *

Sunday, April 24, turned out to be as bright and invigorating spring day in Charleston. Jefferson, Lou, and Lawton had placed extra tables and chairs out in the hotel patio overlooking Charleston Bay before they'd ended the previous night. As a result the morning buffet event was prepared an hour before locals and hotel guests began entering around 11:00.

Lawton showed up fifteen minutes early wearing a white sportcoat and nicely pressed black dress pants. Both items had been hanging in his open closet when he arrived back at his suite the preceding night. There was a note from Lill saying it was a small present from Henry and her.

Back in Minnesota he might not have considered wearing such a bright looking sportcoat. In Charleston he found the gift not only appropriate but quite pleasing. He was able to thank both his hosts as they arrived surprisingly early at 11:15 that morning.

Henry's comment was something a Minnesotan might say as he admired the white sportcoat. "Matt, your tan helps. You don't look so washed out after a long winter in the Midwest."

As Lawton gave Lill a hug for the present, Jefferson, hearing Henry's remark, leaned into Lawton's ear a minute later saying, "You still look washed out to me."

As had become custom, there was a huge turnout for the brunch. Important civic leaders, many friends from the First Presbyterian Church of James Island, owners of many small businesses in the historic district and various guests of the hotel were all enjoying the noon time event. For the next two hours people would be coming and going.

There was only one mild interruption when a law enforcement friend of Granville's, asked one of the staff if Henry could spare a moment. Lawton noticed Sheriff Will Rockingham was not in a festive mood as he edged toward the hotel mogul. Lawton strolled over to find out what might be agitating the law officer.

Lawton picked up the conversation with Rockingham murmuring, "Henry, you know we've got to keep this racial thing from blowing up in our faces in this city! We can't have one of your people beating up on one of our young citizens just because the young man might have said something impolite."

Henry nodded and responded quietly. "I'll look into it, Will. Thanks for not making this a bigger deal than it probably really is."

It was obvious to Lawton what the subject was…Lou's handling of the previous night's confrontation. When he heard the Sheriff's description of the two young hoodlums as 'young citizens', he reacted immediately. Sticking his hand out to introduce himself, Lawton started talking before the law officer could say another word.

Though miffed, Lawton was able to maintain some tact. "Sheriff, I'm glad you stopped over. It saves me time having to go over to your office and press charges."

Rockingham was surprised. "What do you mean?"

"Well, a friend's life and my life were saved last night by this hotel's head of maintenance and security. Thank God Lou White with his cool head was there to stop two young hoodlums who were not only yelling unkind things at my friend Jefferson Brown and me, but one of those 'young citizens', as you called him, threatened us with a knife. Lou was with us and disarmed the youth. His action prevented the situation from getting out of hand."

The Sheriff smiled sardonically at Lawton and replied, "Disarmed him, son? Those poor youths showed up at the hospital, one with a nose flattened against his skull and another youth whose testicles are so sore, he fears for the next time he has to relieve himself. The youths said they had no weapons and they were provoked. We saw no knife at the scene."

Lawton kept his voice calm. "Those two young men concocted a good story for you, Sheriff. Unfortunately, Jefferson and I saw the whole thing. If it hadn't been for Lou, I wouldn't be standing here. I believe if your people looked in the garbage container at the street corner where the incident took place, you'll find the knife. I think your two young citizens may have had a lapse in memory."

The Sheriff nodded showing he now had a new perspective on the incident. In a lowered voice he asked, "Son, when we find that knife, I'd like you to stop by my office at your convenience and sign a complaint.

Lawton nodded. Rockingham then made a quick exit as if he was sorry he'd interrupted an otherwise enjoyable Sunday event.

As he left the hotel, Henry showed a more serious concern. He put his arm around Lawton's shoulder and whispered, "Matt, seriously, how dangerous was the situation?"

Lawton had nothing to hide. "Henry, I can tell you Jefferson and I undoubtedly would have been in some trouble if Lou hadn't been with us."

Henry normally didn't show much alarm, but he was distressed. Looking Lawton straight in the eye, his voice quavered ever so slightly. "Matt, if you're with Lou from now on, he can't be allowed to be put in those situations. I have no question he can handle himself, even with just one arm. But, it's dangerous for Lou. He needs to keep his record spotless."

Lawton was waiting for a further explanation, but it was not forthcoming. A local city council member came up to greet Henry and the host changed his mood in the next second, smiling and shaking the man's hand. However, as the local man dribbled on about some city problem, Henry gave Lawton one last look of unease.

Lawton simply nodded his understanding. It was a subject that would likely be discussed later in their upcoming interview sessions. Like Henry, Lou obviously had a story as well.

*   *   *

There was something else that happened on that Sunday for Matt Lawton that would have some longer term significances. Having met the renowned Judge J.W. Waring at a previous brunch, Lawton was looking forward to conversing with the Judge and his vibrant wife once again. The couple reminded him of his own parents given their penchant for jest and affection for each other. Lawton was so focused on the Warings that he didn't notice the young lady walking slightly behind them. She was making conversation with someone she apparently hadn't seen in a while. The young woman turned out to be their daughter about to graduate from the University of North Carolina. The introduction of the Waring daughter to Lawton turned out to be a short and not memorable as she turned away again when yet another attendee at the luncheon tapped her on the shoulder.

Lawton drifted away from the three Warings not wanting to disturb their family outing, but he found himself repeatedly staring at the daughter in the remaining half hour of the Sunday event. She was taller with strawberry blonde hair that fell casually down her back. Lawton liked her confident air and her refreshing smile. While her manner was relaxed, it was her penetrating green eyes that kept him ogling.

He realized he hadn't met a girl outside of the hotel who was willing or able to carry on a conversation since arriving in Charleston. The idea of taking a female out for dinner hadn't even entered his mind, especially since the few girls he'd met started looking at their watches when he mentioned either Minnesota or the Midwest. He had a feeling some of them didn't know if Minnesota was a state or a foreign country.

As the Warings appeared to be moving toward the exit, Lawton just for a moment thought he saw Laura Waring glance at him. It was fleeting, but in his mind the possible gesture was enough for him to stroll over to Ashley Cooper. If anyone knew something about the Waring daughter, he'd put his money on Ashley.

Ashley was in the middle of a story with two ladies from the 'Daughters of the Confederacy'. He seemed to be looking for a way to escape.

Lawton gave him a needful glance and the conversation ended with Ashley apologizing to the two elderly ladies. He said business was summoning him.

Sauntering away unhurriedly but obviously relieved, he whispered, "Matt, thank God for the reprieve. Those ladies were about to hit me up to be a guest speaker at their upcoming gala. I've been to one of those events. Purgatory has more enjoyable evenings. So, why the desperate look? Is it the Judge's daughter?"

Lawton wrinkled his face. "For God's sake, Ashley, is it that obvious? Just please understand, I'd just like to hear something about her. Then I'd like to talk with her a few minutes before you bring up whether matrimony is a possibility. It's the sequence of steps I'm more comfortable in following. Consider me old-fashioned."

Without letting Lawton off the hook, Ashley smirked, "Naturally…protocol would prevent such haste. Anyway, it's about time you demonstrate some level of libido. You weren't brought down to this lovely city to lose all interest in the opposite sex. Let me tell you about Laura. As you can see, she's beautiful and you can bet your knickers she's got some guys pursuing her…especially now that she's about to graduate from college. In talking with her mother, Laura is enthused about her summer work here in Charleston before going onto law school this autumn. I'd say the two of you are perfect for each other. You both plan on being here only for the summer. Doesn't that about sum it up?"

Lawton mumbled at his older friend, "Christ Almighty, Ashley, you are a romantic. I'll just forget that I even asked you about her. She just made me realize there might be some sharp gals in this city after all."

As Ashley snickered, Lawton walked away and ventured toward the punch bowl. Feeling like an eighth grader at a church social, he decided to roost there hoping the Waring daughter might get thirsty before she exited the get-together. Giving attention to his previous month's lack of female social interaction, he thought, 'God….get me out of circulation for a month and I utterly lose whatever touch I had meeting the opposite sex!'

His intuition actually paid off. While her parents were interrupted once again by some local citizen, the young lady excused herself and began striding in his direction. His heart leaped for just a moment until he realized she was simply moving over to talk with another local acquaintance she hadn't seen for a while. Deflating as that was she also never made eye contact with Lawton. If she did make it to the punch bowl, thirst would be the only reason she'd move in his direction.

Lawton was experienced enough to steel himself. Still it was a bit dispiriting. The room was filled with predominantly middle-aged and older people. The fact that he was one of the few males at the Sunday brunch even close to her age left Lawton thinking he was more a pariah than a prince.

As she continued talking, suddenly Ashley Cooper appeared and pulled her from her frivolous conversation. Her reaction was instantaneous. Breaking into a huge smile and giving Ashley a hug, she responded exuberantly, "Uncle Ashley, how are you? I haven't seen you since last fall."

He took her arm and began strolling in Lawton's direction by the punch bowl…but taking his time. Lawton couldn't hear a word they were saying, but he did see Ashley looking at him over her shoulder. Ashley was having fun leaving Lawton twisting in the breeze.

With Lawton giving a show of annoyance, the older man finally led the young lady toward the punch bowl. Ashley then made amends by immediately making what would be the second introduction of

Laura to Lawton. She barely remembered meeting him just a half hour before.

This second introduction turned out to have a better result. Ashley described Lawton as a future Pulitzer Prize winner in Literature as well as a very close family friend of the entire management group at the hotel. The false aggrandizement of his importance was comical, but it got the young lady's attention. When Ashley was called upon to perform, he did very well.

Ashley repeated more formally that Laura was about to graduate from the University of North Carolina...and had plans to attend law school in Washington D.C. that fall. Ashley's eyes brightened in fun as he explained how Lawton was on a special writing assignment for Henry Granville and would unfortunately be returning to Minneapolis, Minnesota when the task was completed...maybe in a year or two!

With the mention of Minnesota, Lawton expected Laura Waring to begin looking for her parents in order to make a quick exit. Instead, she surprised him by asking if he believed any schools out East could beat the University of Minnesota in football.....or, if any schools in the Big Ten could beat the University of North Carolina in basketball. He found himself momentarily speechless. That kind of sports question normally didn't come out of a young lady's mouth.

Recovering quickly, he kidded, "Yeh, maybe some of your top schools could score a few touchdowns against the Big Ten's last place teams."

It was meant as a joke, but she appeared slightly peeved. She countervailed, "Do all the schools in the Big Ten schools play basketball...or is it just an intramural sport? The two of them then commenced debating the sports questions as Ashley gradually drifted away.

Fifteen minutes later they were interrupted by Judge Waring. "Laura, you can stay if you'd like, I just have to catch a flight later on this afternoon for New York...and I have to pack."

Laura was about to make the unnecessary introduction, when the Judge fixed his eyes on Lawton and asked, "Matt...I didn't ask you last weekend, but are you Jamie and Lindy Lawton's boy?

Lawton could only nod in astonishment.

The Judge continued, "I know your folks. Henry has introduced them and that shameful card shark, Charlie Davis, to my wife and me.

Delightful people...Charlie and I have played some gin...and drank some as well. I didn't know your father when he was your age, but you certainly are built like him...although you do have your mother's eyes."

Lawton could only nod his head in thanks while wondering how many people in Charleston knew his folks and Charlie Davis. All those trips to Atlanta or Florida when he was growing up...obviously they'd spent a lot of time in Charleston.

Laura broke in, "Well, I've got to be getting along as well. Nice meeting you, Matt."

She shook his hand showing no revelation that anything earth-changing had transpired between them. She grabbed the arm of her father and was out the front entrance of the hotel before Lawton had gathered his wits.

He suddenly realized how dim-witted he'd been. He mumbled, "I didn't even ask for her phone number. What a moron."

Ashley sauntered over and nonchalantly inquired when Laura and Lawton were going out next. Sheepishly, Lawton responded half in jest, "Hey, we'd only gotten to the point of disparaging each other's college sports programs. Don't rush me."

Ashley just shook his head. Walking away he muttered something about youth being wasted on certain people.

*   *   *

Meeting Laura Waring made that Sunday brunch quite unforgettable for Lawton. He resolved never to miss one of those occasions if she was going to attend. Still, he had to face facts. A female of her caliber would probably have every guy in the city knocking on her door. He was nothing more than a foreigner from Minnesota. There was no reason to believe the two of them had anything in common? He sensed his chances with her for coffee or miraculously having her submit to a dinner date with him were about as fleeting as another South Carolina succession.

With nothing better to do, he again helped out Jefferson Brown and his staff with the clean-up after the Sunday brunch. Given the East Bay Street Hotel had become his Charleston home, it was second nature to jump in and assist where he could. His automatic willingness to help out was not lost on the staff members.

As the third week began since he arrived in Charleston, another meeting with Henry, Lill, and Ashley had not been scheduled. He wondered if his hosts would detect some lack of initiative. He could only imagine his boss, Bud Brey, being disgusted that he was taking the writing assignment so lightly.

That Monday morning he left a note in Lill Hamilton's mailbox inquiring whether the following Friday or Saturday evening might be convenient for another interview session. He didn't get a return message until Tuesday afternoon. He was hardly bothered by the delay.

That morning Lawton had donned some work clothes in the hotel basement and helped Lou clean the fountain in the hotel patio. Jefferson Brown came out to kibitz with them and suggest some golf later that day. Casually he mentioned to Lou and Lawton they could play until sunset, but then they might want to be back at the hotel for the staff party following a fund raiser that evening. There would be plenty of leftover food and desserts. The suggestion was made as if Lawton was one of them. Lawton felt complimented.

There were about thirty-five people in the basement staff conference room later that night across from Lou's maintenance and security office. Jefferson and Lawton were the last ones to leave the staff party. About midnight both walked around making a final check on the clean-up.

Lawton found himself enjoying the hotel business. He'd never had that feeling while working at University Publishing in Minneapolis. He wasn't certain why that was the case, but it left him not looking forward to the day when his writing project was completed.

With the hotel clean-up having passed the test, Jefferson and Lawton were lounging on the hotel patio. They caught Ashley Cooper returning from some other social engagement. Seeing the two young men laughing and chatting, he joined them just long enough to ask Lawton a completely unrelated and peculiar question. With a glint in his eye, he said, "Matt, do you have any interest in anti-bellum homes being restored in Charleston?"

Lawton gave him a cockeyed look as if he knew he was being set up. He smiled patiently and countered, "Well, Ashley, I'd have to admit I wasn't sitting here just now with that singular thought. What did you have in mind?"

As Ashley ambled away toward the hotel elevators, he impishly retorted, "I might suggest you take a stroll down East Battery after your coffee tomorrow morning and stop by the house on the corner of Tradd Street and East Battery Street. You might see something quite interesting."

Then he entered the elevator, turned and winked as the elevator door closed.

Lawton looked at Jefferson and said wryly, "That man doesn't know how to be subtle. I met a girl at the Sunday tea. Her name is Laura Waring. She's Judge Waring's daughter. The only thing I know about her is that she'd involved in a summer project with some ante-bellum home restorations and she's about to graduate from the University of North Carolina. Ashley thinks she's an answer to my dreams. I'll be surprised if she remembers that we met. She must have enough beaus chasing her skirt to keep her busy whenever she's back in this city."

Jefferson gave a noncommittal shrug. "You never know, Matt. I can't imagine it, but maybe she's got a thing about Minnesota. She's worth checking out. Besides, it's not as if your social life has been buzzing since coming to Charleston."

Lawton could only laugh.

Chapter 13

Matt Lawton woke with a start Wednesday morning. He was amazed how his chief purpose for being in Charleston had hardly entered his mind since Saturday evening. He hadn't even looked at his interview notes. He'd been living the hotel business daily, touring the city or its beaches each afternoon, playing some later afternoon golf, and attending some evening engagements with Ashley Cooper.

He'd had a few beers at the previous night's staff party, but those drinks hadn't clouded his memory. He remembered Ashley's suggestion the previous night to take a stroll down to Tradd Street.

Taking the elevator down to the basement level for his morning coffee in the staff dining area, he sat down next to Lou who was reading a newspaper.

Lawton asked him, "Hey, Lou, what do you know about restorations in this city?"

Lou patiently put his sports page aside and a story about the previous day's Chicago Cub victory and looked at his young friend. "Well Matt, there must be a hell of a reason for that question, but I'll give you some background. There's quite an effort in this city to save or restore old Charleston architecture. In recent years, there's a guy named Frances Edmunds who has been raising capital for an organization called the Historic Charleston Foundation. They buy old homes, restore them, and then sell them to people who by contract would agree to protect the home's historical integrity. He's got some important people behind him, but the question will always be if there's enough money. Henry is on the board of Edmund's new foundation. No doubt Henry is donating a lot of money. So far, they've started buying a few homes, but their plan is to make more dramatic numbers of purchases in the future. The idea has some merit. Historic buildings could become a wonderful tax shelter for some folks who have money that needs to be protected as well as a source of funding for the Foundation."

It was more information than Lawton required. He got to the heart of the matter. "Is there one of these projects going on down by Tradd Street?"

Lou thought a moment. "Yes, there is."

Lawton needed no more information. Saying "thanks' he got up from the table leaving Lou shrugging his shoulders as to the implication of what just got said.

Walking out of the hotel and down East Battery, Lawton's destination was but two blocks to Tradd Street. Looking ahead he saw some scaffolding encircling an old mansion. The whole place gave the impression it could fall in a heap with a good gust off Charleston Harbor. Only the strong chimney and brick wall on one side of the house showed some sturdiness. There were two workers laying bricks. Another person was on top of the chimney leaning into it. By the shape of the person's posterior, he could tell the rear end did not belong to a male workman.

Deciding not to be timid, he figured to ride the glorified introduction Ashley Cooper had given him the previous Sunday. He shouted up to the top of the three story house, "Laura, is that you?"

Indeed it was. She pulled her head from the chimney opening and shielded her eyes from the bright sunlight. He could tell she was struggling as to who he was. He hoped it was only the blinding sun that made any recognition difficult.

She called back, "I'll come down… just a minute!"

She could have just waved and stuck her head back in the chimney, but Lawton appreciated the more favorable response. When she finally descended, she maintained her pleasant look and seemed to remember him. Unfortunately she asked, "How did you know it was me bent over into the chimney.

Fumbling, Lawton was able to recover. "Ashley Cooper told me you'd be working this summer with Frances Edmunds on some restorations following your graduation. He mentioned you were working a couple days this week before you went back to finish up your finals at school. I thought I'd come down and see what you do?"

She looked him over not fully convinced of his interest. She queried, "Why does a northerner from Minnesota have any interest in the restoration of ante-bellum homes in Charleston?"

It was a direct but fair question. Wearing some blue jeans and one of her father's sports shirts, she seemed more approachable.

His eyes glinted. "Hey…I've been living here for almost a month. I would think you'd like the fact I've become quite fond of your city."

She was only partially impressed with his response. "So, where do you live?" she asked pointedly.

"I have a guest suite up on the top floor of the East Bay Street Hotel through the end of the summer or until I complete a writing assignment I have with Henry Granville."

She looked down East Battery Street toward the hotel and nodded approvingly. His smile reflected someone who seemed quite genuine, quite a change from some fellows she'd been meeting.

Then she tested whether his interest in restoration was legitimate. "You want to climb up the ladder? I'll show you some of the neat things found within the walls of this old house. It's like an archeological dig besides being a restoration project."

At the top floor of the house, she talked fondly of the Foundation. "Yes, it's my second summer doing this type of work. Even though I'll be graduating from UNC next week, I wanted to do one more summer in Charleston before I get serious about my life this fall. So far, I've been accepted at Georgetown University for law school. I'm not certain if that's what I want to do, but at least that's one path I have. In the meantime I'll have fun doing this project over the next few months."

Lawton's reaction was abrupt. "You seem more excited about this kind of work than going to law school."

She nodded. "I'm afraid you're right. My folks think I'm a bit of a tomboy and prefer to see me dressed up like I was at the hotel brunch. I don't mind getting dressed up, but I certainly feel I'm doing important work here. The work is a bit dirty, but I feel more fulfilled."

He was on that third level with her for twenty minutes before he realized he'd better let her get back to her work. Looking at his watch he had an inspiration. Without thinking, Lawton just blurted out, "Laura, why don't you join me for lunch at the hotel? You have to eat and it would be convenient and cooler for you. You don't have to feel conspicuous in your work clothes. We'll eat in the basement staff eating area where everyone else is in their work clothing as well."

She reeled back slightly not expecting the invitation. She then looked at the dirt on her clothing and her head began to shake.

Not letting her respond, Lawton tried to minimize her doubts. "Tell you what…let me make a suggestion. If it's convenient at 12:00 and you want to cool off, I'll have a sandwich, ice tea, and a salad waiting for you. We can continue our conversation. You look just fine… in fact, you look more than fine just the way you are. Enter the hotel on the side entrance and take the staircase down. I'll be there waiting for you….that is, if you decide you want some company for lunch."

Not waiting for her reply he stepped onto the ladder and descended quickly before she thought of a reason to decline. As he walked along the battery enjoying the view of the harbor, he didn't notice a heavy set older man in a tan suit watching him from behind some bushes along the Battery. The man could have been standing in the middle of the street wearing his customary Panama hat and holding a rifle at his side and Lawton likely would not have noticed the man. Lawton had just asked a very attractive girl out to lunch and she hadn't said no. There was nothing else entering his mind as he continued along the Battery.

*   *   *

Having just arrived back in town from Savannah that Wednesday morning, April 27, Darrell O'Donnell had built up the courage to carry on his blackmail attempt against Henry Hanson Granville. He now had another addition to his manic hatred…that young man now staying at the East Bay Street Hotel. The kid had become a menace. Ever since arriving in Charleston, this visitor had been nothing but trouble and bad luck. The pest had seen O'Donnell pointing a rifle out the vacant second floor office window ten days before and then stared at O'Donnell at the corner of Meeting and Broad Streets as he drove from the scene that Sunday night.

That small incident had caused O'Donnell to flee Charleston. He'd been secluded in a cheap little motel across from a pulp plant in Savannah, Georgia ever since fearing the authorities might be looking for him. Only in the last day or two had O'Donnell's nose adapted to the foul smell of the paper plant across the road.

For a week-and-a-half O'Donnell wandered aimlessly around the historical area of Savannah feeling like a tramp, smelling like a longshoreman on a hot day, and wondering if he was at all cut out to be a criminal. He'd thought blackmail would be a much cleaner type of crime, especially considering he held so many strong cards against the former Henry Hanson.

He kept wondering if his planning was flawed. He was no closer to collecting any of Granville's money. Was he just going through a streak of misfortune? Was he too cautious and unskilled? Or, was it just a combination of ineptitude and gutlessness?

Those days in Savannah he had to decide once and for all if he was going to boldly continue his blackmail quest or submit to his own fears of being caught and jailed. The bottom line came down to a choice between taking a waiter job in one of the riverside restaurants in Savannah...something more consistent with his abilities...or would he prefer living in Europe with a flow of extorted money from Triple 'H' Development, Inc.?

Finally he realized he was in the clear. He'd not fired a shot at the hotel mogul's car that Easter Sunday night. There had been no reason for that kid to contact the police. He had to make contact with Henry Granville. It had been three weeks since his last contact. He'd not kept the pressure on his intended victim as he should have. He was way overdue to continue his threats if his demands for payment weren't met.

O'Donnell finally accepted his own challenge and returned to Charleston on that Wednesday. He'd checked into a roach infested motel in North Charleston determined to remain in the city until he'd contacted Granville. Still worried that his car could be identified, he'd taken the public bus downtown. Seeing his dusty Ford Falcon in the motel parking lot was disappointing. It matched the kind of clientele staying at that particular flophouse. He didn't want to admit he might be in that same classification. He was hoping he'd begin seeing a bit more glamour connected to his criminal efforts.

He accomplished one thing that Wednesday morning despite striking out once again with Henry Granville being unavailable by phone. He found out Matt Lawton's name by asking the front desk clerk. Following the young man numerous times earlier that month including to the local municipal golf course, he simply inquired, "I played golf with a young guy recently who's been staying at your hotel the last couple weeks. I know because he drives one of your hotel vehicles. I wanted to invite him out for another round of golf, but I don't have his complete name. Would you know who this person might be?

The desk clear chuckled and was most accommodating saying, "Oh yes...you mean Matt...Matt Lawton...our Minnesota guest. He's out right now. Would you like to leave a message?"

O'Donnell was amazed how the life of crime could at times be so easy. That one response had given him the information he sought and he promptly hung up the line. The name Lawton was oddly familiar. He couldn't place the name. That the young man was from Minnesota and was apparently close to Granville...all that meant something. If O'Donnell needed to get Granville's attention for the payoff, young Lawton was an obvious target.

It was the middle of the morning when O'Donnell arrived at the vacated office building across the street from the East Bay Street Hotel. His small perch in the second floor dormer had been a lucky find. He had the entire hotel complex right before his eyes from the window.

He checked if his second-hand rifle and binoculars were still under the loose floorboard. His adrenalin rushed as he felt the barrel of the weapon. He wondered if he really had the stomach to aim at someone and pull the trigger. He didn't want Henry Granville dead; he just wanted the man to cooperate and pay the silence money. At least this visitor...this Matt Lawton...might conceivably spur the hotel owner if Granville was made to understand Lawton might face injury...or worse. O'Donnell realized he might have to use the weapon on Lawton anyway. The young man was the only person who had seen him.

At that moment O'Donnell glanced out the discolored office window and saw the very object of his evil thoughts. There he was... leaving the hotel and walking in the direction of White Point Garden. For a brief moment O'Donnell considered taking aim from the window and just end the threat that Lawton represented.

The portly man luckily hadn't lost all his faculties as yet. Having followed the visitor when he first arrived in Charleston, O'Donnell knew Lawton was often predictable in his actions...morning walks over to Market Street, ventures to the golf course, and evening stops at some bars down the street from the hotel. In the would-be blackmailer's twisted mind he figured it might be wise to tail the young man again. He might be able to size up possible locations where taking out Lawton could be done more privately if that decision had to be made.

Five minutes later O'Donnell was walking on the battery a block behind Lawton. Moving along carefully so as not to be spotted, O'Donnell watched Lawton enter a construction site and begin conversing with one of the laborers. The worker turned out to be a female...full of dirt and grime on her trousers.

In the next instance, he saw them climbing up a ladder to the top of an antebellum home being restored where he observed them laughing and talking three stories above the street. It made no sense to the chubby man. Lawton was staying in the plushest hotel in the city and he was now hustling a female construction worker.

As he stood there staring in disdain, O'Donnell suddenly realized Lawton was intently looking down in his direction from the construction site. Turning away quickly O'Donnell hustled away from the battery walkway pulling his hat lower over his eyes. As he did so, he realized he was wearing the same Panama hat when Lawton had last seen him. Once again O'Donnell figured he'd blundered.

Without transportation, he jumped in the first taxi he came upon. As luck would have it, the taxi driver was gone. O'Donnell looked back and saw the young man marching in his direction. O'Donnell's heart was on overdrive as he sat there motionless in the taxi. He didn't know what his next move should be...maybe denial...maybe playing dumb. The latter would be easier.

Just as Lawton approached the car, O'Donnell scrunched down in the seat and waited for the altercation. But, nothing happened. The young man sauntered by the vehicle with a smile on his face and showing no concern or anxiety that he'd been followed. He'd not seen O'Donnell down on the street after all. The only thing on Lawton's mind seemed to be that he'd had a fruitful conversation with his lady construction worker friend.

Seconds later the cabbie returned somewhat surprised he had a fare waiting in his back seat. O'Donnell gave the address of his temporary living quarters in North Charleston The driver mumbled something incoherent, nodded his head, and finished off the last bit of liquid from a bottle he had in the front seat.

Rolling his eyes O'Donnell again thought how his renewed blackmail effort was not getting off to a good start. He was now reduced to spying on a lovesick kid. He slouched in the back seat of the cab realizing how ridiculous his entire life had become since quitting his waiter job in New York. What made it even more ludicrous was his feeling that Henry Granville had reduced O'Donnell from an adversary to more of a nuisance. Why would Granville take the blackmailer's demands at all seriously given O'Donnell's erratic efforts?

Then in the warmth of the beautiful spring day, O'Donnell pondered his one dependable alternative. He could chuck the entire blackmail idea and work in one of those riverside restaurants in Savannah. At least he wouldn't have to put up with the constant reminders that he was not cut out to be a blackmailer...or at least an effective one.

Arriving at his stop near his ramshackled motel in North Charleston, Darrell O'Donnell's run of bad luck would continue. After paying the cabbie, he opened the door and absentmindedly took a step in front of an oncoming car. He was hit with a glancing blow and felt himself airborne before landing awkwardly on the pavement.

Immediately the taxi driver and the person driving the car were at his side. Both men looked alarmed, although the driver seemed more perturbed than sorry since he'd had little chance to avoid the mishap. He was only going thirty miles an hour when the man with the low-brimmed Panama hat stepped right out in front of him.

The driver kept repeating, "What's with this guy? Did he have a death wish? Is he all right?"

The groggy but conscious O'Donnell finally sat up and was helped to the curb. He was in shock along with a lot of pain. His left arm seemed strangely askew. If his arm wasn't broken then his shoulder was certainly separated. The driver, relieved that the man was breathing, ran down the street to a gas station to call an ambulance while the taxi driver tended to the badly shaken O'Donnell.

Fifteen minutes later the writhing and ashen-faced victim was taken to the Charleston Municipal Hospital. Before the ambulance left the scene, the recently arrived patrolman tried to ask him a few questions. All O'Donnell could do was babble incoherently about that 'damned Hanson' and that 'damned kid'. Neither the cop nor the other two men could make any sense out of his dribble.

As the ambulance pulled away, the taxi driver verified the driver's story that O'Donnell had mindlessly stepped right out in front of the approaching car traveling no faster than the speed limit. The cop took the driver's name and license number and the cabbie's name and told them he'd be in touch later...if at all. The entire episode took about thirty minutes from the time O'Donnell was hit by the green Oldsmobile to his arrival at the clinic.

As the driver and taxi driver left, the cop called in his report to headquarters. As he pulled away from the scene, his right tire mashed a dirtied Panama hat. The flattened fedora would remain at that curb until a street cleaner picked up what was left of it two days later while performing his normal duty. The worker would lament how the hat had been very stylish at one time. On that hot, humid afternoon, the worker wished he'd owned such a hat just for protection from the sun. With no chance of saving it, the Panama styled hat saw its last daylight before being unceremoniously thrown into the worker's dumpster.

As for Darrel O'Donnell, his arm had been broken in two places and his shoulder had been dislocated. After having it jerked back into place, he spent that night at the hospital. Without checking out the following morning, he dressed slowly and snuck out the back hospital maintenance door. After taxiing back to his motel, he slept the remainder of the day thankful that no hospital bill would find him.

The next morning he retreated yet again back to Savannah, Georgia, this time to heal. In less than two days he'd gone from re-vitalizing his extortion efforts to withdrawing once again from Charleston with his tail between his legs. He hadn't even made contact with Henry Granville. He wondered if his hated enemy would even remember him when next they spoke.

The two-hour drive to Savannah took O'Donnell three hours because of his pain and discomfort. He felt a bit better just opening the door to his small motel room with the single bed, the black and white TV, and the Gideon Bible on a small bureau. As he lay down to rest, there was a knock at the door. He was ready to give up. The cops had found him.

Opening the door it was not someone with a badge but instead the motel's proprietor. He'd seen his injured guest hobble into his room and was now standing outside with ice in a discolored plastic bucket and holding some worn but clean towels. It was the kindest deed anyone had done for O'Donnell...he hated to admit it...in years. With the ice on his shoulder and the chance to sleep, the stench from the paper mill across the road was hardly noticeable.

With his injury coming at the end of April, O'Donnell decided to temporarily give up on his mission against Henry Hanson Granville. Giving up completely, though, was not a consideration. He felt a deep obligation to himself to make every effort to profit from the background information he had against the former Henry Hanson. He figured in a month or two, he'd be on the mend enough to carry on his blackmail scheme.

O'Donnell spent the next few weeks convalescing at his cut-rate motel. While regaining some of his strength and mobility, he played checkers with Figgie Jones, the motel owner, walked down to a local café for his meals, and watched a lot of mindless quiz programs and soap operas on his black and white TV. He found himself actually enjoying his quiet, problemless life. The atmosphere at the small motel was friendly despite the wretched smell from the paper mill and the discolored pond across the highway. Whether the other guests at the motel felt sorry for him with his injuries, he looked forward to chatting at the end of the day in his favorite rusty lawn chair.

If it wasn't for his dwindling money supply, he would have thought he was on vacation. It was two different worlds for him between Charleston and Savannah. His preference was unmistakable. There was something about Charleston. Every time he was in that city something went wrong.

By the middle of May he was more mobile. He wore a long sleeve shirt to camouflage his forearm cast. He interviewed and got a job at the Pirate's Cove restaurant in downtown Savannah. The restaurant wasn't river side, but it was one of the busier eating establishments in the city. O'Donnell's arm and shoulder still hurt like hell for his few first evening shifts but the pain gradually subsided as he once again was making some money.

* * *

It was that same Wednesday when the slightly soiled Laura Waring sheepishly slipped through the side door of the hotel for the first time on Lawton's invitation and hesitantly went downstairs to the staff cafeteria for lunch. Lawton in preparation for the possibility of her arrival had asked Jefferson Brown for something special that could be prepared for her lunch. His friend eyed him not believing food prepared in the staff cafeteria would be a first date. Nonetheless, he gave Lawton a tolerant and reassuring nod thinking Minnesotans had an interesting way of picking up women.

When the young lady cautiously entered the eating area, Jefferson met her with a smile and a glass of ice tea. Conversing with Lou White, Lawton had missed her entrance. Jefferson politely escorted her to the table where the two men were seated and formally introduced the guest. "Excuse me, Mr. Lawton, the lady wants to sit by someone who won't bother her while she enjoys a special lunch we've prepared for her. I thought you'd be the perfect candidate."

Lawton gave his friend a wry grin. "Thank you, Mr. Brown. Now please leave."

The young lady got a kick out of the two friends bantering, but still looked a little uncomfortable. Lawton eased her immediately. "Hey Laura, I'm glad you could make it. I asked the kitchen to do something better than a sandwich and a salad. You've got a seafood pasta dish about to be served. Also I hope you like Charleston ice tea. It's a perfect drink for a classy female construction worker."

He then introduced her to Lou and Jefferson. Her distrust slowly evaporated with the attention being given her by the three males. When the food arrived, Lawton's two friends were courteous enough to take their leave.

Wiping away some of the cement dust on her forehead, the couple continued their chat from earlier that morning as if they'd known each other for years. The rest of the staff at that luncheon room kept their distance realizing they were possibly seeing something quite wonderful happening between two people.

Their lunch went for an hour. It gave Lawton the self-assurance to suggest they continue their conversation over dinner Friday night.

While her response was positive, it came with reservations. She explained, "Matt, dinner would be great; however, I've got to get back to Chapel Hill tonight to complete one final test. I'll be back next Tuesday for a couple days of work. Then I graduate on Mother's Day weekend, May 8. I might be available next Wednesday or Thursday. How about if I call you if I can make one of those evenings?"

He sighed thinking he'd just gotten a brush-off. Nonetheless he promptly agreed. What else could he do?

Having dinner with Ashley Cooper the next evening at a small Market Street restaurant, his older friend asked with a twinkle in his eye, "Matt, have you ventured down to any restoration projects recently?"

Lawton rolled his eyes knowing Ashley already knew the answer. He responded vaguely, "I might have. Why do you ask?"

Cooper danced around with his response. "Well, it's important that people in your generation show some interest in the Charleston Historic Foundation. Who knows who you might meet?

Lawton chuckled, "O.K., Ashley, you can stop with your hopeless innocence. You probably already know that I asked her out to dinner and got shot down...or, at least I think I got shot down. Can you imagine her twisted priorities? She claimed to prefer completing her college career and then graduate rather than going out to dinner with me."

As Ashley took pleasure in Lawton's quip, the younger man added, "The fire isn't completely out. She did say she might have time next Wednesday or Thursday when she's back in town. I think it'll be a cold day in Hell if she even remembers her suggestion about dinner. But, just on the chance it might only be chilly in Hell, Ashley, give me some restaurant recommendations where she might be impressed with both the food and me for choosing it."

Ashley snickered over Lawton's directness. Leaning toward him he gave Lawton some hope. "I think she'll go out with you. All her other beaus are up in North Carolina. She'll be in a festive mood finishing school; she'll want to celebrate her upcoming graduation. No doubt she'll go out for dinner...even with you."

Lawton gave him a droll grin but stayed quiet for more advice from Ashley. "You might get a reservation at the Wharf just down the street. I know it's one of her family's favorite restaurants. I also suggest after that dinner, the two of you take the horse drawn carriage around the historic district. That would be a pleasant way to finish your first date."

Lawton picked up the check that night despite Ashley's objection. The very next morning he took advantage of Ashley's inside information on the Waring family and made the reservation for the next Wednesday at the Wharf just on the possibility she'd be willing to go out.

*   *   *

A lot happened on that Wednesday, April 27. Laura and Matt Lawton had their casual lunch at the hotel staff luncheon room. Darrell O'Donnell met with his accident and limped back to Savannah after yet another failed attempt to jump start his blackmail scheme. It was also the afternoon when Lou White walked into Henry's office to discuss if anything more had developed regarding the extortion attempt against Henry. It had been almost a month since Henry had fielded his last threatening phone call from the blackmailer. And then...as if the fellow fell off the edge of the world, the extortionist hadn't been heard from since.

In amazement, Lou remarked, "I tell you, Henry, we've had to deal with a few odd people over the years determined to prove you were Henry Hanson or disprove you are Henry Granville. Whether some of that Chicago mob or various nosy reporters and business magazine writers, we've been able to prevent any disasters. But, this situation is different. This imbecile is in a real position of strength...and apparently doesn't know it. He's got enough background goods on you to create a lot of trouble. But, just like that, the damned idiot just disappeared. It doesn't make any sense. He's got us down for the eight-count and now it appears he's thrown in the towel. Damndest thing I've ever seen. It's as if he died."

Henry nodded, "I can't imagine what happened to cause this guy to get cold feet. It's like waiting for the executioner and he decides to take a vacation. I've been expecting his call every day. But, each day goes by and no contact...and I wonder what this blackmailer's next step could be. There's a chance he's lost his courage. He's certainly the most patient con I've ever met. He first started bothering me two months ago. Apparently he believes his threatening phone calls and notes are essential in order to wear me down. Like you say, he's got a strong position. He knows people, places, and things from back during the D'Annelli era in Glenwood. Besides having the goods on me...and possibly you, Petracek and Brey are vulnerable as well as Charlie and the Lawtons back in Minnesota. He holds a lot of people's reputations in the palm of his hand."

Lou nodded. All he could do was assure Henry there were plenty of other cards to play before they had to begin sending money monthly to a Swiss bank account.

It was a short meeting. As Lou was departing, he warned once again, "Henry, let's not get complacent. Like always, we just have to be ready. This joker could suddenly pop up out of nowhere and renew his threats. When he does, we'll find this guy."

Henry nodded as Lou closed the office door. He continued staring at the door even after the man had left. Lou White had been a trusted friend for so many years and had handled many difficult circumstances since he began working for Triple H Development fifteen years before. Henry felt responsible for so many people and Lou had always made problems vanish...at times without Henry knowing the actual method.

The telephone rang and Henry stared momentarily at the mechanism on his desk. Could this be the call? He hesitantly picked up the receiver and immediately heard the voice of his secretary, Irene. Her tone sounded normal. "Henry, the mayor is on the line. He says he needs some help from our hotel. Do you want to call him back later?

Henry chuckled, "No, Irene, put him through. I think I know what he wants."

Seconds later, Henry was joking with the mayor. The serious conversation with Lou had dissipated...like an Atlantic hurricane barreling toward the southeast coast and suddenly changing course to the north and out to sea.

Still, while danger had been reduced, it was nonetheless still a hurricane.

Chapter 14

No one was more surprised than Lawton when he got a message delivered to his room Monday night May 2 from Laura Waring. She had returned from her final test at her university and dinner was on for Wednesday night. He tried to play it cool and not ring her back right away. He lasted ten minutes before he called her to confirm the time. Following Ashley's recommendation, Lawton proposed the Wharf Restaurant as if it was his own idea. When he hung up the phone, he congratulated himself on revitalizing his rusty dating skills thanks to some essential assistance from an old Waring family friend, Ashley Cooper.

When Wednesday finally rolled around, Laura Waring met him in the lobby of the hotel. They strolled the few blocks to the restaurant with Laura talking about the cap and gown ceremony the coming Saturday at her school in Chapel Hill. As she chatted Lawton occasionally glanced behind to see if someone was following. Even while dining, he periodically took his eyes away from Waring to casually peruse the dining and bar area for someone who resembled the rotund man with the distinctive low-brimmed hat. It had been two-and-a-half weeks since they'd eyed each other at the corner of Broad and Meeting Streets. As was the case since that night, Lawton had never felt threatened.

Concentrating on his date, he could see she was enjoying herself. It occurred to him that she was just on a high with college graduation coming up within days. Whatever the reason for her happiness, he had a feeling before the night was done he'd suggest another dinner date. Upon asking for the check, the waiter whispered in his ear that the bill had been covered...and that a carriage was waiting in front of the restaurant for an evening tour of historic Charleston. Lawton smirked. It was just like Ashley not to leave things to chance.

The carriage ride took them to the harbor landing where a boat was waiting to cruise them out onto Charleston Harbor. Laura was as impressed as Lawton was. She commented, "If this is a first date, I don't see you or anyone being able to top this night on a second date."

Just the mention there might be a second date was encouraging. When the cruise was completed, another carriage deposited the two of them at the front door of the hotel. Accompanying Laura to her car, he suggested they go out again the next week after she returned from her graduation ceremony.

Her response was refreshingly definite. "Yes, of course I'd like to go out again. I'm curious how you could improve upon this evening."

Then she sighed, "Unfortunately I'll not be returning until Tuesday. I should be back at work at the restoration project next Wednesday. I've also got some engagements next week, so I'll have to check my schedule when I get home. However, I'm certain we can find an open evening."

Lawton said no more. He understood he was likely in a troop of pursuers. He didn't like his odds being from so far away, but at least he was in the game. As she took off in her car, he just shrugged and reminded himself that Rome wasn't built in a day!

*　　*　　*

The next day Lawton would learn about Henry and Lill's business trip planned for the Italian and French coasts leaving the following week. They'd be gone for most of May. Lawton was impressed with their confidence that the hotel would be managed very professionally while they were gone. There was no one person in charge, but every department head was expected to work efficiently with the rest of the staff. The procedure had apparently worked quite effectively in the past when the two of them traveled.

It had been four weeks that Lawton had been on his assignment. Whether another interview session would be scheduled before they left hadn't been discussed. His concern now became more of guilt. His main purpose for being in Charleston...the writing project... would again be put on hold, but this time for an extended period of time. He'd even caught up with his notes from previous interviews and had actually started a partial draft of Henry's background story so far. He literally had nothing more to do on the manuscript until there was another interview session.

As much as he enjoyed the fine accommodations and meeting new people, Lawton sensed he should suggest to Henry that he fly back to Minneapolis for a few weeks until his host was ready to resume the interviews. It would be irresponsible not to make that recommendation to Granville.

That Friday noon while having lunch with Jefferson and Lou in the staff cafeteria, a note was delivered to Lawton. Jefferson quipped, "I'll bet it's a note from your recent date. She's now desperately going to throw herself at you and we'll never see you again."

Lou gave Lawton a shrug as if he was agreeing with Jefferson and then returned to a newspaper article he was examining about a man hit by a car in in North Charleston a few days before. The accident didn't raise his eyebrows as much as the report did. It said the visitor refused to give his name and address, was patched up at the hospital, and then left without handling the payment. The article said police were still looking for the injured man.

Lawton's note turned out to be from Lill Hamilton. It was a suggestion of Charleston ice tea and dessert…a bit later than normal… on the coming Saturday night, May 7, on the top floor terrace patio of the hotel around 8:00.

Lawton appreciated his two hosts still giving thought to his true purpose for being in Charleston. He figured that night would be the time to suggest him going back to the Twin Cities until they returned. That alternative was certainly not his preference. In fact, he was ready to propose he be allowed to work a hotel shift in any capacity…even maintenance or as a part-time bellboy…anything that might keep him busy in Charleston while they were gone.

That Saturday Lawton had golfed into the early evening with Lou and Jefferson. The three had dined at a harbor restaurant in Mt. Pleasant. A bit light-headed, Lawton arrived back at the hotel thirty minutes before the scheduled evening interview session. He gambled Henry and Lill would be later than normal and took a longer shower to burn away his fuzzy head.

At 8:10 he walked down the hall to the silence of the outside eighth floor patio where they were to meet. It was a winning gamble. Even Ashley Cooper hadn't arrived as yet. Lawton felt refreshed. Relaxing and enjoying the view for the thousandth time of Charleston Harbor, he questioned whether he should even bring up the subject of returning to Minneapolis. Henry might agree with the idea.

It was 8:20 when Ashley arrived dressed as if his evening would continue after the interview session was completed. He immediately inquired about Lawton's date with Laura Waring.

Lawton was still thanking Ashley for his part in making the Wednesday dinner memorable when Lill and Henry entered the patio. There were the normal warm greetings before Henry showed a spark that he wanted to jump right into his story. While the kitchen staff brought up some choice desserts and the predictable Charleston ice tea, Ashley still chided his friend. "So, Henry, I hope tonight's addition might last long enough to make it worth my while having left a lively party over on Meeting Street. I figured tonight might be a most important segment... the time when I get introduced."

Smiling, Henry was quite prepared where next to take his story. Placing a thin cigar into a holder, he mused, "I'm sorry it'll be a while before our next interview, Matt, but I wanted to give you some more background before Lill and I take off this coming week. I believe you have a good foundation from our last session about those two conmen, Whitey Malooley and Billy McCoy. You are now aware of their renewed quest to track me down after Loni D'Annelli was gunned down in Chicago on July 4, 1931. Let's start there tonight, shall we?

There were nods around the table. Henry began speaking before he'd finished lighting his thin cigar.

"Well, by the time of D'Annelli's unfortunate shooting death, I was firmly entrenched in my church bungalow at the First Presbyterian Church on James Island here in South Carolina. In fact I had more and more people calling me 'Reverend Hank' because of my supervising the construction work at the church.

I would be unaware of the more determined efforts by those two D'Annelli boys to find me until much later that month. Revenge against me for being the catalyst in D'Annelli's death would eventually become secondary. While investing more of their time staying low and hiding out from the hired guns from Chicago, they had plenty of time to fill their perception that I had escaped with a significant amount of their former boss' money."

Granville then sneered while looking at Ashley. Both men shook their heads nonverbally reliving a time they both shared so many years before.

"Anyway, Matt, getting the news from Rich Brey about Loni D'Annelli's murder, I decided to make my way into Charleston leaving the construction crew on the Reverend Middleton's church to continue their work unsupervised. I was ready to move on with my life and go meet the other key contact recommended by Sally Carter. In Ashley Cooper Carter, she guaranteed this man had wide connections in Charleston going back to his father's efforts to rejuvenate the city after the conflict during the 1860's. Ashley's father was given credit for arranging to have the first President of the U.S. visit Charleston since the Civil War. William Howard Taft was president in 1910 when he made the stop. In many ways Charleston was still despised for its rebel activity in leading South Carolina to secede and where the first shot was fired in that conflict. Taft's visit helped Charlestonians once again feel they were part of the U.S...and not just a bastard relative.

Ashley could have ridden his father's fame, but he built a reputation of his own. His efforts in supporting renovation projects and cultural programs within the city were highly noted. His real claim to fame, however, was his uncanny ability to get things done behind the scenes with local government officials.

I recall the Thursday morning only days after hearing of Loni D'Annelli's death when I walked into Ashley's office on Broad Street. There were five people waiting to see him.

I introduced myself to his receptionist by saying, "Mr. Carter knows I'm coming. He'll want to see me right away."

Everyone in the office looked at me like I was in the wrong office or on the wrong planet. No one referred to him with a surname of 'Carter'. It also could have been my accent.

His secretary hardly blinked upon hearing my name. She accompanied me to an adjoining conference room and whispered, "Mr. Granville, Ashley has been expecting you. By the way, he prefers 'Ashley

Cooper' and then just 'Ashley' after the introductions. He'll see you in just a minute."

It was indeed barely a minute after the secretary went into Ashley's office that his voice could be heard. He bounced out of his office and greeted every person in his waiting room by name. A couple people he set up appointments with later so they wouldn't have to wait. The others he asked that they stop by the next day as his calendar wasn't as full. I thought it was one of the more respectful ways of handling people who'd just stopped by hoping to see him with no appointment.

When he burst into that conference room he behaved like we were old friends. As he closed the door, he vigorously shook my hand saying, "Henry, if you're the favorite nephew of Sally Middleton Carter, you're automatically a favorite of mine. If the South were to rise again, we'd ask old Jeff Davis to step aside and let Sally take over the reins. When she comes to Charleston from that mountaintop in Tennessee, there are parties up and down Meeting Street and along East Battery until she leaves the city. She called and said you were coming down to get some business established in our fair city. I love to hear it! We need some more Northern money invested in this poor downtrodden city. Henry, you just tell me what you need done. I'll see what I can do to smooth some roads for you."

It was an amazing start to a business relationship and friendship that has lasted to this day. I'd hardly said 'how do you do' to this man I'd never seen before and he was offering to open the city up to me within thirty seconds. I was grateful if not a bit wary.

I started out by asking Ashley about my small parcel of land I'd purchased and had recently visited at Kiawah Island.

I recall him chuckling, "So how many acres did you buy?"

"I purchased ten acres along the ocean unseen....for $2000." I was a bit embarrassed to admit that factor, but it was true.

Ashley could have been very condescending and called me a damn fool, but he didn't. His face tightened as he spat, "That cheap-ass real estate firm in town gives Charlestonians a bad image. They advertise land in a couple national travel magazines on that God awful inaccessible island for $200 an acre. They hope to get some desperate Northerners or foreigners to plop down a couple thousand dollars for a parcel of land. Then they bait and switch the property to another location in Charleston after the person can't even travel to his land much less find it without renting a boat and fighting off the alligators. Most people don't know they can get their money back by just making a few threats of suit. The real estate firm guarantees your money back or they'd land in jail. The trouble is their very poor at answering the telephone or answering their mail. They only respond to individual investors who seek them out personally."

Ashley lit up a cigar and continued, "I know the Vanderhorsts. The land on Kiawah is part of their estate. That family is just looking to get any money they can for any acreage on that out-of-the-way island. Henry, I'll contact them and have a check from the bank by Monday if I can have your bill of sale."

I handed it over to him from my briefcase without a second thought. He'd just made another problem go away. I was getting my $2000 back. Life looked good.

Ashley then began asking me question after question. They were unending. He was literally pushing for ways to find where he could be of help. He offered me a drink of tea or water...or some bourbon... and I nodded for the water. His drink was neither the tea nor the water. He sat down at his eight-seated conference table and proved he'd been talking with Aunt Sally.

He queried, "Sally tells me you've got your own land development company in Minnesota. What are your plans here?"

I liked the way that sounded...your own land development company. I wasn't embarrassed at all to explain my dream. "Yes, I'm looking to add some resort or hotel property here in Charleston and eventually further south into Florida. My idea is to attract business people from up north to travel down to this wonderful historic city. I want to publicize my properties in Washington D.C., Philadelphia, New York, and possibly Boston. People up in those parts get sick of the cold weather once the Christmas and New Year's holiday seasons end. I want to promote business meeting accommodations for companies, associations and governmental agencies so people can feel warm again much sooner than waiting for April. Right now Charleston's historic charm is only an overnight train ride from New York...even less time from Washington D.C. As air travel gets more acceptable, there will be even more interest in this city.

Charleston is still thought of as the cradle of the Confederate cause, even though it's been sixty-six years since the war ended. This city needs to overcome that impression. It needs better marketing for the cultural, historic, and social aspects that go back before the Civil War as well as the music and art appreciation that are developing as we speak in this fine city. If there are parties and events when Aunt Sally travels to Charleston there is no reason this city shouldn't have events and special occasions when regular tourists discover the allure of this place."

I recall he gazed at me and finally sighed, "We must have dropped off the same branch, Henry, though I don't know how. You have just given a northern version of the same thing I've been pleading my fellow Charlestonians to believe in. Unfortunately, I'm a Charlestonian native, so I don't have a lot of credibility beyond the borders of this historic city. It brings joy to my heart that at least one northerner knows there is such tremendous tourism potential. This city was around when New York was called New Amsterdam; Washington DC was a bunch of tall pines; and the New England states so proud of its religious tolerance in the original colonies had no idea religious freedom was already being practiced here since the end of the seventeenth century."

We both sounded like two candidates bidding to head the Charleston Chamber of Commerce. It was a terrific first meeting…a great way to initiate a very purposeful and productive relationship."

Ashley raised his glass as he acknowledged Henry's words. Ashley was rarely emotional or speechless. At that moment, he was.

Henry then talked on.

"Those two developments…my anonymity as Reverend Hank, Assistant Pastor of the First Presbyterian Church on James Island… and meeting Ashley…were the two major factors that spurred my actions in Charleston. In the remaining months of 1931, I would be introduced to a number of local leaders through Ashley. As for my temporary home at the church, even when I moved out, I continued serving as Pastor Middleton's financial officer for many years.

After the summer of 1931, the good pastor's congregation grew at a gratifying rate. Folks from Charleston were even crossing the Ashley River to attend services at the First Presbyterian Church on James Island. It was the talk of the Charleston area. It was a good story. Pastor Middleton and his church members were given credit for taking a risk and contracting needed upgrades on the church. The gamble was that the increase in attendance and therefore contributions would handle the payback for the renovations. Of course what people didn't know including the parishioners was that the church improvements were already paid. Much of that borrowed $50,000 I hadn't repaid to D'Annelli's fund ended up in the church coffers. D'Annelli had given much to the churches in Glenwood during his five years there. It made sense to me that he continue his generosity post mortem by helping another church.

Over in Charleston some even grander things began to happen regarding my business interests. I was not 'Reverend Hank' in the city. I was Henry Granville from Chattanooga, Tennessee moving down to Charleston. Verification only had to done by calling the queen of Chattanooga, Sally Carter.

With Ashley's help I gradually became more visible in the closed society of Charleston. Ashley took me to all the local clubs, associations, and business groups. He always introduced me as a relative of both himself and Sally Carter.

By that fall Ashley and I had been checking out any worthwhile opportunity for purchasing land or even a run-down hotel property. We found that potentially restoring an old hotel was very well received by the local business community, especially the banks. Rather than simply destroying the old structure, our idea to renovate showed respect for the city.

Our chance came when Ashley called me about an old hotel near the wharf that was about to close its doors. It had a phenomenal location off East Bay Street and Broad Street. With the hard times, the old hotel needed a facelift along with an image improvement. A great deal of cash was required of which I happened to have at the Carter bank in Chattanooga. The actual price of the dilapidated hotel was a steal. I didn't even have to use much of my cash. Instead, just to build some local business relationships, I established some financing from my new contacts at the Bank of Charleston. They verified my former residence with Sally Carter and the bank accounts I had in one of Tennessee's more prominent banks. With Aunt Sally as my reference, everything was authorized. The purchase went through without a hitch.

That little business venture proved again how friends in right places can make a real difference. Of course, my bank account didn't hurt my prospects either.

With Ashley's contacts, I had acceptable bids from two local contractors. The renovations on my new hotel began within a week after I had purchased the hotel that October. From the very day the refurbishing effort began, the hotel was renamed the 'East Bay Street Hotel'. Three months before I had been in Glenwood, Minnesota concerned for my very life; now I was heading up a major hotel reconstruction project under my alias, Henry Glanville, owner of Triple H Development, Inc. Life was moving pretty fast for a former feed and grain mill manager.

While the hotel was being restored, I traveled every other week to Washington D.C., New York, or Philadelphia. I made contacts with business, government, and association business leaders to promote the objectives of my new hotel. I only had artist renditions of the new hotel and the offer of a free two-night stay when the hotel officially opened. That marketing ploy impressed a lot of northern business people; it showed that the hotel was on a firm financial base.

With that amount of travel, I still had to monitor the restoration project. I repeatedly called Lill back in Paducah, Kentucky to please join my development company. I needed someone I could trust who wouldn't be bothered about my past life. I thought she could be very helpful overseeing the construction project.

She still had the burden of running those three very diverse Paducah based businesses including her deceased husband's river cargo business. It was too much for any one person to handle. She finally turned over those businesses to her relatives. Smartly she didn't divest herself of those businesses completely. After all, it was a hell of a gamble coming down to work for a northerner in a notoriously self-absorbed aristocratic, socially biased southern city. She figured the transition into the social community of Charleston would be challenging even if she were white. I kept telling her not to worry. Whether she believed me or not, she finally gave in and joined me in January, 1932 about four months before the scheduled launch of the new hotel.

We have now been partners in business and life for over twenty-eight years. It's something we don't talk much about to others because of the race issue in this country. We've never married because we knew that concept would be too difficult for too many people to accept...and we had a growing business we needed to keep profitable. We've long agreed to allow our ignorant, unforgiving society to prevail on this one point.

What's so sad is that if a highly competent female hotel manager happened to wed a reasonably wealthy owner of a development company... and they were of the same race...the event would likely hit all the social pages and magazines. However, you put color into the equation and people go crazy. To this day, Lill and I keep our relationship to ourselves. And, that's just the way it is.

As for her arrival in Charleston, I still recall it vividly. It was the day after New Year's Day in 1932. I met her at the train station. I had the top down on my vehicle enjoying the warmer sixty degree weather. I remember carrying her luggage out to my Ford A 400 Convertible Sedan. People in the terminal area, black or white, could not understand why this tall lanky white fellow was carrying the luggage of this colored woman and talking so animatedly with her. I hardly noticed the looks. Lill was more observant, but patiently smiled as I talked.

In the car I told her she had the guest room at my temporary Mt. Pleasant home directly across the Cooper River from the city...and that she should be in no hurry to find a place of her own. I wanted her to be comfortable and not feel lonely. There was nothing strange to me or her about the invitation. She'd opened up her home to me in Paducah the previous June. Why wouldn't I do the same for her?

As we drove toward the construction site, I enthusiastically told Lill about the business trips to New York and Washington D.C. and the results I had so far achieved. I had invited hundreds of senior executives and Association Directors from the North down to Charleston to look over and seriously consider my new hotel as the meeting center for their spring and fall national meetings. By January 1932, the hotel was already semi-booked for May.

When she saw the structure in its half completed condition, she looked at me like I was irrational. The dirt circular driveway was full of concrete machines and building supplies. It was a Saturday and many of the men were working half speed. She looked at me and asked, "Henry, where are your guests going to stay in May...at the local military base or tents set up out on the beach?"

With that she got out of the car and marched up to the foreman of the crew asking if he planned to come to work the next day. He gave her a curious look and a snicker and replied, "Why no ma'am, tomorrow's the Sabbath."

She said to him that there'd be no more Sabbaths for him and his crew until Easter when he could make amends with God at the celebration of the resurrection. Then she shouted at the slow moving crew, "Gentlemen, you're training days are over. It's now time to get to work."

It was another hour before she stopped giving directions to the workers and told them what she expected from their work each day. She and I didn't take a tour of the unfinished inside of the hotel for another hour after that. When we did she saw another crew working on the drywall and flooring at a snail's pace on the sixth floor. Her voice could be heard outside when she yelled for the foreman of the crew. I'd never seen a group of men snap to attention for a woman until that day.

And, that was the way it was every day she was at the construction site. The workers knew I was the owner and financier of the project, but somehow they realized this lady walking with me was the new boss in town. She had no time to be concerned about how white or black people reacted to her. I believe within forty-eight hours she knew all the construction workers by name. They saw how I depended on her judgment. If they had a problem with her color, they either got over it or they were asked to leave. Within a few days she was accepted by everyone connected to the reconstruction project.

Taking the freight elevator to the eighth floor, I remember how radiant her face was as she panned over the entire bay with Ft. Sumter looking so distant and lonely on the Atlantic Ocean side of the Harbor. I pointed out where I lived on the opposite side of the Cooper River as well as some landmarks like the new bridge over the river and the St. Phillips and St. Michaels church steeples. She was mesmerized.

While her face was stern with the crew, her look with me was always tender and kind. I recall her simply saying softly but determinedly, "It'll be close, Henry, but I think we can get this place ready before your first guests arrive in May."

She then told me she'd be busy the next few hours and to pick her up at the end of the work day. I didn't know if she truly believed the hotel would be presentable by the end of April, but I always liked that quality in Lill….that everything was possible.

Towards supper time that Saturday evening, I drove up to the dirt circular driveway and there was a filthy looking lady with a dusty skirt still giving directions to one of the crew chiefs. She finally walked over to me with that same sweet smile and said, "Now let's go home so I can get unpacked. Work starts early for the crew and me tomorrow morning."

We toiled together every waking hour including those Sundays. Her ideas and opinions on everything from finding the right construction people and getting them working on a schedule to adding touches of class to the design of the hotel interior and exterior were essential in making this investment the special place I hoped it would be.

In the weeks ahead as the completion date actually looked possible, it never dawned on me she had never been certain of her role in my business other than recognizing what needed to be done each day. Her work ethic forced me to drag her away from the construction site each evening.

I recall in early April how she was showing me the near completion of the administrative offices on the second floor. She said, "Whoever works in this office will not want to go home with this magnificent view of the harbor."

Grinning I replied, "That's the idea! I hope you will make this office more personal when you get the chance to acquire some more local prints and watercolors from various art shops down the street."

The surprise on her face was priceless. Lill couldn't believe what she'd heard.

She said, "Henry, what kind of job did you bring me to Charleston to handle after the construction is done?"

I was somewhat taken aback that she didn't know. Without blinking an eye, I responded, "Lill, I told you I wanted to use your business and management skills. You built that bawdy house in Paducah into a profitable and acceptable business. You and Ez started a couple other businesses together as well. You personally had the respect of white and colored people back in your area. That ability and experience doesn't just grow on trees. I'm damned lucky to have you with me. And, as you well know, building a business doesn't stop with the completion of the structure. I need you to acquire the staff for this hotel and train them. I've got other properties I'll be buying. My travels won't be reduced. When we open the doors in May, I'll be General Manager in name only. It'll be your place to run."

Once she got over the shock of her new responsibilities, she took control of every facet of managing a hotel. Ashley Cooper, who at the time was continually putting me in contact with the right people in Charleston was immediately impressed with Lill's class and competency. I watched him literally laugh as she'd jump from one construction crew to the next keeping them focused on their work.

When word spread that 'Reverend Hank' had bought an old hotel near the Battery in Charleston and was refurbishing the property, the congregation at the First Presbyterian Church on James Island supported my project in every way they could including seeking jobs. That was how Thomas Rutledge Brown from Kiawah Island and his wife joined our staff. They've worked with us over these many years. And, now his son, Jefferson, as you know, is one of our staff managers.

From the moment of our hotel grand opening that spring in 1932, the East Bay Street Hotel was the talk of the Charleston area. The hotel could not rely very much on local revenue, but what we got we appreciated. Again thanks to my friend Ashley, we received more 'frosting' in our restaurant revenue than we expected. Ashley seemed to be a member of every important business and social group in town. He really paved the way for our hotel showing a profit that first year.

But, it was Lill who was the primary person who made this hotel what it has become. She's been the de facto general manager from the start. It was difficult for some local upper crust Charlestonians to accept her role given her heritage. Over time the bigotry generally dissipated against Lill just because of the kind of person she is. I've been very lucky having her in my life."

Lill smiled at him as he reached over and patted her hand. Any doubt or wonder Lawton had at the beginning of the assignment regarding the relationship of Lill and Henry had long disappeared. It was just very pleasing to observe.

Henry leaned back and lit another thin cigar before continuing.

"As that summer of 1931 proceeded, Whitey Malooley and Billy McCoy had no leads as to my whereabouts. Their primary aim to protect themselves from the Chicago syndicate was however more successful. They still made cautious stops in Glenwood in hopes of hearing any rumors about my whereabouts. Mostly they stayed hidden at a small lakeside motel near Alexandria fishing and playing golf while keeping an eye over their shoulders.

They did learn that the two former officers had been much closer friends of mine than they realized. To the two gangsters it wasn't logical that the friendship ended just because of a police raid at a local resort. They eventually tailed Petracek and Brey and found that the two law officers were no longer hanging out at their lake cabin but were spending a bulk of their time at two lake resort properties. In fact it looked very much like they had found work.

Financial needs did start to cause problems for the two hoods. They had agreed that if no leads came to roost by autumn about me, they would have to revert back to their former days robbing gasoline stations or small town banks. It was a huge come down from their more lucrative life of crime in Chicago. For the time being they maintained their focus because I still represented too big of a payday if I was ever found.

There was one incident, though, that did provide them a new lead. It was pure happenstance. On Sunday, August 2, they registered under assumed names to play in a one-day public golf tournament at the Little Falls Golf Club. It was the same town in central Minnesota where Charles Lindbergh was born...of which they could care less.

The two of them had warmed up and were ready to tee off with a local kid and a druggist from Cambridge, Minnesota in their foursome. Suddenly a biplane was sited flying low over the ninth fairway. Then, unbelievably, the small flying machine actually landed on the fairway and drove over to the maintenance shed where it parked. The pilot carrying his golf clubs and a young woman with long hair blowing in the breeze then began making their way toward the clubhouse. People were laughing. Some had seen this spectacle before. The pilot was known for showing up at different Minnesota golf courses in his biplane. He'd created quite a reputation.

For Malooley and McCoy, the pilot was a sight for sore eyes... at first. They recognized the man as none other than the guy the two of them...plus their boss...had played with at the four-man team competition only eight weeks before at Chippewa Lodge. The pilot's sterling play had won them a lot of money that weekend. In fact, that money was what they'd been living on that very summer.

Malooley and McCoy were about to quietly greet him, thinking he was one of their kind, when they stopped in their tracks. Strolling with their former teammate in the same flying garb as the pilot was someone they'd also seen at the Chippewa Lodge tournament. More significantly they'd observed her picture more than once from various newspapers. She was big news that summer as the undercover journalist in Glenwood who was given full credit for foiling the gambling ring at Lake Minnewaska. She was the one who brought in the troopers and the Bureau of Investigation agents who eventually made all the arrests. Though she hadn't pulled the trigger, her undercover action had led to the arrest and eventual death of Loni D'Annelli.

In more recent weeks they'd read in the *Minneapolis Star* she was the likely replacement for her boss who was retiring at the branch office of the U.S. Attorney's office. The articles also disclosed her father was a judge on the Minnesota Supreme Court. To them, everything about her was objectionable.

Seeing her striding toward the clubhouse laughing and holding hands with the pilot suddenly made that golf tournament feel a bit too crowded. Malooley told the tournament director that his partner had become ill and they were going to have to withdraw. He was actually telling the truth for once. McCoy suggested just shooting her, but Malooley outlined the consequences. He surmised that with her prominence in the Minnesota criminal law community, the two of them would be caught within twenty-four hours by a statewide dragnet and be hung the next day.

Retreating to the gravel parking lot, Malooley and McCoy threw their clubs in the back seat of their 1929 Plymouth Model Q Roadster and prepared to leave the golf club. That was when another odd thing happened. A voice from the automobile parked next to them interrupted their retreat. There was a big guy with an old fisherman's cap covering his forehead and eyes. He was resting in the driver's seat of his premium model 1922 Wills St. Claire A-68 Roadster. Without moving or opening his eyes, the man said, "You gents have one nice looking roadster. I'll bet it's got an engine to match."

Malooley looked over where the voice had spoken and received his second shock of that morning. There was yet another person he recognized. In fact it was difficult not to remember the large man. He was wearing the same loud, repulsive chartreuse golf shirt he'd worn at the Chippewa Lodge charity tournament. He was the friend of the pilot who'd just landed at the golf course. For a moment Malooley wondered if that was the only golf shirt the fellow owned.

With his eyes wide he motioned for McCoy to get in the car. Pulling his own hat lower over his eyes, Malooley dully responded, "Yeh, it's a good car. Looks like you got a vintage one yourself. Have a good day."

Then Malooley accelerated the engine, backed his Roadster up, and sped away in a cloud of gravel dust. McCoy got a glimpse of the shirt and sank deeper into the passenger seat.

As for the man taking a nap in his Wills St. Claire Roadster, he'd just rearranged his hat and was about to talk with the two gents when they peeled away as if they were late for that morning's church services some place in town. He didn't even see the Illinois license plate as the vehicle disappeared in the dust it created.

It was not two minutes later Jamie Lawton and Lindy MacPherson who'd just flown in, snuck up on the relaxed man in the ugly shirt and started beating on the fender to wake their friend up. Charlie Davis had been snoozing in his car for the past hour waiting for the two of them to fly into Little Falls for the golf event.

Charlie had been looking forward to that weekend for a couple of reasons. He needed some recreation considering he'd been so busy recently with his largest client, Triple H Development, Inc. It wasn't easy being general counsel for an owner of a company who insisted on anonymity.

Later that day he was also going to handle another matter. He was to meet the two men his client had trained and hired to take over the entire management of the two lake resort properties. Charlie knew of their existence, but hadn't yet heard their names or background. He was looking forward to decreasing his time allotment invested in my development company. After all, he did have a law practice with other clients he was trying to maintain.

As for me, I was concerned about his reaction when he met my two former law enforcement friends, Clarence Petracek and Rich Brey. I thought he'd be apoplectic considering the reasons for their recent resignations from their jobs in Glenwood. At the very least, he'd wonder if I'd injured my head. At the worst, he might not want to be associated any longer with my corporation.

I considered this transition to be my biggest hurdle. I didn't want to lose Charlie Davis. I had to depend on our two-year relationship and the generous retainer I was paying him to overcome his shock and anguish.

As for Malooley and McCoy, they were out of Little Falls as fast as their roadster would take them, that is, until Malooley suddenly slowed the car having second thoughts. He said to his partner, "Billy, do you realize we're driving away from the best leads we've had since hitting a dead end with the two Glenwood cops. We've talked about that woman investigator probably having some assistance in bringing Loni down. We've always thought that help came from Henry Hanson. But, we just saw something quite interesting. She's now close to the pilot who played golf with us that weekend. No doubt they were meeting their friend sitting in that vintage car today.

McCoy wasn't following his partner's thoughts completely, but didn't object when Malooley turned back toward the Little Falls golf club. Malooley wanted to find out those two fellows' names and follow them. If they were in cahoots with Henry Hanson, Malooley had a gut feeling all three probably knew where I was located.

And, that was what they did. By the afternoon while keeping a low profile in the gallery at the Little Falls golf tournament, they learned the names of Charlie Davis and Jamie Lawton and found out where the two men lived. Given the closeness of the lady investigator with the man named Jamie Lawton, they focused more on Charlie Davis. They didn't want to be anywhere near the lady.

As luck would have it, I had chosen that same Sunday evening for Charlie to meet Clarence Petracek and Rich Brey at the Lake Mille Lacs resort. As I said, I expected problems. I had called Charlie repeatedly leading up to that Sunday meeting emphasizing to him how I trusted the two gentlemen completely and how they would free up his time to take on other legal business.

After the golf tournament at Little Falls, he fueled his roadster for the short trip over to Brainerd. From the moment he left that golf course Malooley and McCoy trailed him.

The dinner meeting was set for 7:00 PM. When Charlie checked in at the Lake Mille Lacs resort he was given the best room in the complex. There was some wine on his desk in the suite. I halfway hoped he would down the entire bottle before meeting Petracek and Brey.

That evening Charlie sauntered down to the restaurant wearing a sport coat over his chartreuse golf shirt. He rarely dignified any meeting with a sport coat. When the maître die brought Charlie to the table where the two managers were waiting, Clarence and Rich reported to me later how Charlie's golf related tan turned rather gray. The astonishment was unquestionable. He had heard through Lindy MacPherson about Petracek and Brey's infamous resignations. He'd paid little heed to that bit of news until that moment.

What I could not have known was he suddenly had other anxieties beyond the needs of Triple H Development, Inc. His apprehension centered on what they might know and if there could potentially be a breach in the secrecy he, Jamie, and Lindy were trying to maintain. Hesitantly he sat down wondering if those two fellows were aware that he and Jamie had been in Glenwood on that bizarre June weekend only eight weeks before.

As it turned out Petracek and Brey had never seen Jamie or Charlie that weekend. They'd been out of town fishing upon request by the town council.

Sitting at that table, Charlie and my two new managers were on a completely different thought wave. They were concerned more with Charlie's response to them as ill-fated law officers.

Immediately Rich gave Charlie a letter…a letter of introduction from me. It was signed by my code name, 'Granville' just to reemphasize my need for confidentiality. Charlie stayed quiet and read the letter. It covered the situation my two friends had been in as County Sheriff and City Police Chief. I told him of their dilemma. While they could have shut down Chippewa Lodge at any time, they were more caught up in the benefits the town was receiving from providing the goods and services to Chippewa Lodge. Conscious of keeping my own identity secret, I lied and said a long term friend of mine had vouged their blind and uncommon loyalty to their town that otherwise would have fallen into the abyss of the national Depression.

The note did ease Charlie's concern about the business matters, but his primary fear prevailed. Much of that evening Charlie danced around the subject of the raid at the Lake Minnewaska resort in order to discover what other facts they might know, especially about Lindy MacPherson. To his relief they seemed to know very little other than what they'd read in the newspapers. They told me later how they remained absolutely silent about her simply saying they had totally been taken in by her claim to be a freelance writer for a travel magazine. They didn't want to explain themselves any deeper than was necessary.

Once Charlie's nervousness had dissipated, the three men got along famously based on the hangover all three had the next day. No one was more pleased than me. When I heard from all three gentlemen the next day, Charlie was satisfied the two lake resorts were in good hands. Clarence and Rich liked that Charlie didn't challenge them as to who Henry Granville really was.

What the three of us would learn much later was that as a result of that dinner Sunday night, Charlie Davis had confirmed in his own mind that Henry Granville was indeed me. At that point it no longer mattered to him that I felt it necessary to keep my actual persona confidential. By then we'd worked effectively together for almost two years and had developed a strong sense of trust. He simply respected I had my reasons for my secrecy. He was confident I'd divulge my true identity to him when I was comfortable in doing so.

Unfortunately, Malooley and McCoy had followed Charlie Davis to the Lake Mille Lacs resort that Sunday evening. They had no idea where he was going until they witnessed him checking in and then meeting Petracek and Brey in the resort restaurant. That one episode... that connection with Charlie, Jamie Lawton and Lindy MacPherson... and then he with the two former Glenwood law officers convinced them some kind of conspiracy had brought D'Annelli down. They also figured the five people would have a link to me.

They would follow Charlie for a couple days with the assurance that he was the break they were seeking. That deduction proved fruitless. They had an inclination to strong arm Charlie Davis into talking, but they still had to be conscious of their own precarious situation with the Chicago syndicate. Malooley and McCoy decided to remain patient so as to keep from being detected. They had a strong feeling if they kept their eyes periodically on Davis, Petracek, or Brey something would open the door to my location.

The last half of 1931 would turn out to be a very frustrating time for the two hoodlums. With money being short, they did in fact end up robbing some general stores in Annandale and Paynesville as well as a few gasoline stations in Moose Lake, Perham, and Walker. They found the latter type of crime particularly demeaning and too visible…and the return had not been that profitable. Central Minnesota was nothing like the robbery opportunities in Chicago.

Eventually with their funds pathetically low, they had to concentrate on their own survival. They did try one more major hit in late 1931. They targeted the community bank in Elk River, Minnesota. They were literally ready to rush the bank at the end of the workday with their guns pulled when the shades were suddenly lowered and a sign was placed in the front door window saying, 'Closed until further notice'. Some workers began exiting the bank with their heads hung low. There was no doubt, the bank had defaulted. Malooley and McCoy would have been laughed right out of the bank had they tried to rob it.

They found an inexpensive cabin near Brainerd for the winter for the purpose of remaining close to one of the three men who might lead them to me. Clarence Petracek at the Mille Lac's Lake Resort was only two miles down the road. They both knew a change had to be made in the way they were conducting their lives. Theft was not going to be a reliable way of keeping food on the table. At some point they'd be caught. They'd be imprisoned. The mob would get wind of their location. Being wasted on the inside by another prisoner being paid by the mob was not their choice how they wanted to leave this world.

In January, 1932, Malooley found a job as a mechanic and McCoy did odd jobs having to do with snow removal. Living in that small cabin in the Brainerd area and periodically checking on Davis, Petracek, and Brey would be their life for the next year and a half. While not picking up any hints as to my locality, at least the mob was having no luck finding them either. In fact, with each passing month, the two gangsters were hoping the vendetta against them would start dying from lack of interest."

Henry then sat back and seemed disinterested in going on with his story. It obviously wasn't a part of his life he enjoyed remembering. It was also a sign that the evening interview was over much sooner than expected.

Lawton placed his new notes neatly in his leather briefcase. Sighing, he then felt it was time to discuss with Henry the subject of traveling back to Minnesota until his hosts returned from overseas in late May. Even then there likely would be no interview sessions until sometime in June. It was disappointing, but he felt it necessary to bring up the problem. He couldn't see wasting the hotel's money being in Charleston and doing nothing.

And, just like that, Lill promptly put an end to his unease. As Henry helped her with her shawl, she put her hand on Lawton's arm and brought him closer to her. She seemed very determined to make a request. Her words were like a pint of straight plasma being shot into his body. "Matt, while we're gone, I need to have you cover for me on a number of my duties. You know enough about our hotel that I'd like you to sit in on some marketing sessions with Ron Taylor. We're looking at producing some better promotional materials. With your experience at University Publishing, you might have some helpful thoughts. I told Ron you'd be attending the sessions and he'd welcome your contributions. Also, I know Jefferson would appreciate your assistance in the upcoming Sunday teas for set-up as well as being one of the hotel greeters. In addition, when that D.C. association group is in town for their meeting this coming week, just take over and help them with any questions or requests they might have. Finally, Lou is meeting with some designers to do some more landscaping on the harbor side of the hotel. I know he'd like your involvement. Other than that, I'd consider it a favor if you'd check all the maids and valet schedules each day so we're covered adequately.

Just like that Lawton felt busy again. Nothing she asked seemed overwhelming. In fact he was surprised how familiar he was with all aspects of what she'd requested. He assured Lill he'd take care of those duties.

A smile also crept across his face as he thought about Judge Waring's daughter. He would still be in town to see her. Though he was likely only one in a crowd of beaus, he liked being in the game. For all he knew, he might just be a fling until she got engaged to one of her University of North Carolina classmates, but he was willing to take that gamble.

Lill and Henry left while Ashley stayed on the outside balcony finishing his drink with Lawton. The two of them watched the automobile carrying Henry and Lill ride along East Bay Street to Hwy. #17. It disappeared amongst some low lying buildings and then reappeared crossing the far off Cooper River Bridge before finally disappearing on the other side into Mt. Pleasant.

Ashley poured Lawton a small drink from his flask. Raising their glasses, he toasted the work Matt was doing on Henry's behalf.

Lawton reacted sheepishly. "Ashley, you know as well as I this is a fantastic short term job. He's giving me more than enough time to complete the project. I have to admit I'm not looking forward to going back to Minneapolis to my other job."

Ashley smiled. "Well, I can tell you this much. Everyone here at the hotel has really enjoyed your time as a resident of the property. It's obvious you've taken a real interest in the hotel as well. The staff tells me you've jumped in whenever help is needed no matter how menial the task. Jefferson especially welcomes your assistance in setting up the meeting rooms and cleaning up after many of the hotel functions. Matt, I'll say this, many people... myself included... hope Henry will never finish his story so you'll never complete the manuscript. That way you'll be compelled to stay in Charleston. Of course, that has to be something you want."

Lawton was flattered. Nothing else was said. The two of them finished their drinks and then retired to their separate suites at the hotel. Lawton was tired and fell asleep reading a book on Charleston's history. He never heard Ashley leave his own room down the hall for another engagement that evening.

* * *

As Lill and Henry rode the elevator down to the lobby, their voices were murmurs. He whispered, "So, what was Matt's reaction? Did he seem interested in helping you out while we're gone?

She gazed at his eyes and responded with a huge smile, "Henry, you are the most conniving man I hope to ever meet. I think I know what you're up to...and I think you're dreaming. Matt's a Minnesota boy. I don't think he'll want to live down here in the South. Besides, he's got his real job back in Minneapolis. Why would he leave the opportunities he has back there?"

Henry leaned toward her as the bell rung as the elevator reached the ground level and gave her a buss on the cheek. "Because, my dear Miss Hamilton, opportunities can grow in different places. I think my past proves that. I'll need some more time, but I believe our young friend will recognize opportunity if I have time to present the right one to him…and he feels he could do the job. He's getting involved in our business; let's give him time. Stalling on completing these interview sessions will not be difficult. I certainly have some traveling ahead of me when we get back from Europe. It might be good to have him accompany me on a couple of those business trips.

Lill smiled knowing the sly nature of the man she'd been with for almost thirty years. He'd persuaded her in a similar fashion many years before to come to Charleston. In time it had turned out to be more than just a business relationship. She knew when he was determined Henry Hanson Granville had a strong record of winning.

Chapter 15

While Henry and Lill were traveling overseas, Matt Lawton covered those assigned chores for Lill Hamilton with ease. The hotel staff worked like a fine Swiss watch. Jefferson Brown handled his duties with his catering staff faultlessly. Lawton continued helping in set up and clean up after various functions. As requested he attended the marketing meetings chiming in when asked his opinion by another friend, Ron Taylor, the marketing manager.

Working with Lou on the new landscaping plans was more fulfilling. Though a generation apart they communicated as if they'd known each other for years. Agreement was reached in two meetings with the landscape architect. They both monitored the work through the month.

During May, Lawton got a taste of all facets of the hotel business, often times without realizing he was working. In down times he retreated to his suite and worked on the manuscript...and still escaped to the beach to jump the waves.

And then there was his intrigue with Laura Waring. While he was only able to take her out twice in the evenings during the two weeks after their first date, it was the lunch times that provided the chance for them to get to know one another even better. When she was unavailable for lunch it was because she was traveling to New York and Boston to check out some law schools where she had also submitted applications. When she was back in Charleston, she was often busy with family engagements as she called them in the evenings.

She had a standing invitation at noon each weekday. Often times he'd walk down to Tradd Street just to take interest in her work. That effort seemed to please her.

The last weekend in May Lill and Henry were set to return to Charleston. On that Saturday afternoon Laura Waring joined Lawton, Jefferson Brown, and Lou White for some golf at the local municipal golf course. She and Lou walked away with the money. The relationship of Waring and Lawton was moving ahead without either of them really acknowledging that fact. Both considered their time in Charleston to be limited. They'd be going their separate ways that coming fall. It was part of what made their connection so easy. There was no pressure that their relationship could blossom into anything but a friendship given their eventual plans requiring them to live so far from each other.

On Sunday morning, May 29, Lawton got a call in his suite from Lill Hamilton. He'd been in a deep sleep. The previous night had been late with poker at Jefferson Brown's apartment. When golf had ended that afternoon, Laura had joined the group but complained she hadn't played cards in years. Despite the assertion she showed remarkable card sense. The guys weren't easy. She returned some of the money she'd made on the golf course. After walking on the battery overlooking the moonlit bay Lawton didn't get her home until after 1:30 AM.

Lill's voice was surprising fresh for all her overseas travel and getting back to Charleston only the previous evening. Her tone was too strong and echoed inside his head. "Matt...good morning...and thank you again for covering for me. We can talk tomorrow morning when I'm in the office. Lou tells me your nose was in everything...in a good way."

Lawton groggily responded trying to find something invigorating to say. All he could muster was, "Yes, I was happy to help out. I don't think I got in the way too often."

She chuckled. "Far from it, my dear, Ron Taylor appreciated your input. Lou was pleased with the results of the landscaping plan."

Lill was entirely too lively for that hour. Lawton wondered why she was calling. Normally she just left notes in his mail box.

She finally got to the point. "Matt, given Henry's travels the next few weeks, he suggested the four of us meet this afternoon on the sailboat for an interview session. It promises to be a great afternoon with little threat of rain. Would your schedule allow it?

Lawton grinned into the phone. Lill was so considerate. Of course he was available. There would have to be an invitation from President Eisenhower for golf at Augusta National for him not to be ready on a moment's notice. She seemed to forget the main purpose of his being brought to Charleston.

With a stronger voice he responded, "Lill, sailing would be just fine. What time should we meet?

That afternoon Henry and Lill picked up Ashley and Lawton at the front of the hotel fifteen minutes later than Lill's estimated time of 1:00. The vivid sky and crisp blue and green glimmer of the water made for a beautiful day. The crew of three men volunteered on what otherwise would be their day off in exchange for some fishing time off the front of the thirty-foot vessel.

It was not until 2:30 that Lill and Henry finished sharing highlights of their trip to the French and Italian Mediterranean coasts. Finally the four of them settled down allowing Henry to continue his story. It had been almost a month since the last interview and Henry predictably asked Lawton where his notes ended. That got Ashley started. "Henry, I'm glad you weren't in charge of writing the Declaration of Independence. This country would still be a colony."

Lawton however was prepared. He brought the other three up to day talking about the two henchmen of the departed Loni D'Annelli looking for leads to find Henry in the remaining months of 1931. Also, he reminded the group that Charlie Davis, Clarence Petracek, and Rich Brey had finally been introduced.

With that update the older man nodded and brought out some notes of his own. Before beginning he showed some empathy for his scribe. "Matt, you will continue having some questions how I know what I'm about to tell you. I'm not ready to reveal any names, but have faith. You'll learn their names soon enough. For now, don't be overly concerned. Is that all right?"

Lawton showed some momentary confusion, but then nodded in agreement. Henry then got started.

"1932 was a real bellwether year for Triple H Development, Inc. The refurbishing of the East Bay Street Hotel was completed. Lill Hamilton was here in Charleston taking over the management of the hotel. Her efforts freed me to continue my business travels to New York and Washington D.C. to attract future business clientele.

By the beginning of 1933 I had enjoyed almost a year and a half of anonymity as Henry Granville in Charleston, South Carolina.

I'd had not one threat from anyone connected with the mob. In fact I tended to believe I had completely voided those years in Glenwood. I hardly thought of myself anymore as Henry Hanson.

I had also put some more thought into where I wanted to live in the area. I found if one lived south of Broad Street, you were part of the perceived aristocracy of the city. Living further north of Market Street outside the historic district was not a safe part of the city. The further west from the city and the smell of the ocean breeze would be lost. That was why I was drawn eastward across the Cooper River.

With the new Cooper River toll bridge making Mt. Pleasant more accessible, I'd rented a small beach home until the house I'd purchased was completed. The house was built on a peninsula. On one side of the house faced the bay with a good view of historic Fort Sumter. The adjacent side of the house gave me a vista of the city of Charleston with the steeples of St. Michaels and St Phillips rising above the tree line. I could of course also see my eight-story hotel as well.

This community gave me the freedom to keep my circle of business friends guessing as to my political preferences. No one quite knew where I stood on various issues. It helped in breaking down people's inclination to pigeonhole me while deciding whether to support my new hotel or not. It was all part of the society game a local businessman has to play from time to time.

Business groups from key northern cities had arrived and held meetings at the hotel. The city itself helped the hotel's image. Walking along the Battery or through the many historic streets could open anyone's mind to how interesting this beautiful old city really was. The various smells of the vegetation and flowers were always intoxicating as long as the street cleaners did their job.

While my many business trips were paying off with new business coming to Charleston, there were still some local stick-in-the-muds who didn't appreciate me soiling the city by marketing to so many northerners. It proves again that you can't please everyone.

As time went on, my cover remained solid. Whether being called 'Reverend Hank' by my James Island friends or 'Henry Granville' by all others, I felt safe. If someone wanted to check my background, I had my bank accounts in Chattanooga, Tennessee and the dependable reference of Aunt Sally Carter.

It was still up to me and those closest to me to maintain a very private stance about my past. I was never open to any reporters seeking interviews. However, even then it was difficult to keep curious journalists from gleaning information from my hotel staff. Luckily everyone connected with the hotel and Triple H Development, Inc. took my lead and generally complied with my wish not to discuss anything about my background. I wanted nothing to do with the limelight, only to be the secluded owner of a privately held and growing hotel and resort conglomerate.

Even with all that understanding and support, I knew it was still possible for my cover to be blown. It was in 1933 that it happened...and it was as you might guess, a fluke. A freelance journalist who had been covering the theatrical, artistic, and literary explosion of Charleston since the early1920's was in town and staying at our hotel. He became intrigued upon hearing the assistant manager was a colored lady from Kentucky. He wanted to do an article on her rise to such an exalted position. Lill and I discussed it and we decided the publicity would be all right...as long as my name was not discussed very much in the article. The interview with Lill went very well and the journalist told her the story might appear in a few southeast newspapers. We expected some promotional value from the article. We got more than we bargained for.

Meanwhile, back in Minnesota, Clarence and Rich had been doing outstanding jobs at running the lake shore properties. I authorized a 10 percent ownership for each of them in the property they managed. Whether the partial ownership factor was an influence or they just got better at managing and promoting the resort properties, both gentlemen were keeping those two lake resorts profitable.

By 1933, Charlie Davis had now been my corporate attorney for almost four years and we still had not met personally. I began to think it peculiar he wasn't more insistent that we either meet or I disclose to him who I actually was. The retainer I paid him was money well spent. He'd been essential in helping me make decisions in buying some other Minneapolis lake front property as well as properties in the Alexandria area. I knew I'd be making inroads into Florida seaside properties very soon along with his help. The depressive economic conditions were providing some astonishing land and property opportunities.

It was the late spring of 1933 when I decided to make a return journey back to Minnesota. It was just a year since opening the East Bay

Street Hotel. I was feeling more confident about my business holdings and management group. Besides meeting me, Charlie also wanted me to see some possible land acquisitions in the Twin Cities. I was of the mind that my secrecy with Charlie Davis primarily to protect him had become unnecessary. I also looked forward to seeing my old friends and now business associates, Clarence and Rich. Maybe deep inside I also wanted to verify I was no longer a hunted man by anyone connected to the former D'Annelli crime group.

Lill was very much against my returning to Minnesota. I recall Ashley also chimed in with his apprehensions, but for different reasons... something about me perishing in the cold. I had to remind him it would be the summer that I would be making my visit. He looked at me as if that factor made no difference.

Nonetheless, despite their misgivings I made my plans to return to Minnesota in late June and early July...a beautiful time to be in the state."

Henry was then interrupted by Lill. She appeared still irritated by his decision even after so many, many years. Lawton didn't quite understand her animus as she exclaimed, "Henry...that was probably the worst decision you ever made in your life. I was against it then and I still shake my head wondering how and why you made that trip."

Ashley didn't say much, but nodded his head in agreement. Lawton looked at Henry to respond, but he ignored their reactions. The subject had likely been discussed too often over the years.

Henry wrinkled his face and continued.

"Anyway....the fellows in Minnesota welcomed my plans to return in that summer of 1933. They certainly hadn't heard of any rumors or dangers that might befall any of us. But, they were still careful. Charlie Davis offered to pick me up in St. Paul at the train station and drive me up to the White Bear Lake resort to meet with Rich and Clarence. I would arrive on Friday, June 30 allowing us to enjoy a weekend at the resort.

While I was looking forward to the trip up north, I still felt the anxiety of being recognized. Beginning two months before I was to make the journey, I allowed my hair to grow even longer and added a fuller beard and moustache. I also planned on making my travel wardrobe strictly South Carolinian in style...that is, very light and loose fitting. I wanted to be unrecognizable even to my own parents had they still been living.

I left Charleston on June 26 to do some promotional business in Washington D.C. From there I planned brief stops in Pittsburgh, Cleveland, and Chicago before arriving in St. Paul on Friday evening. Inviting top management for corporations, government agencies, and even unions down for free stays at the hotel for meeting considerations had become a very effective marketing ploy. I was also considering buying another hotel or resort property in Charleston just to handle the overflow potential tourist and business group revenue. The contacts in Pittsburgh and Cleveland went well enough, but at the last minute I decided not to make any stops in Chicago. Despite the large size of that city, I still feared running into someone who might have been part of D'Annelli's clan. Suddenly being gone for two years seemed like yesterday.

It was while I remained on the train at the Chicago stop and was paging through the *Chicago Tribune* that I became aware of something that appeared innocent, but would eventually blow my cover to the wrong people. That freelance writer who had interviewed Lill a month earlier had done some investigative work on his own about me. He obviously meant no harm. He just wanted to showcase Henry Granville for being the person who'd given Lill Hamilton her opportunity at the East Bay Street Hotel.

His article turned out to be quite popular ending up in major newspapers around the country. While it emphasized the rare career rise by Miss Hamilton, the article referenced her boss as a former Chattanooga businessman who also owned some lake resort properties in Minnesota. The reference to Minnesota was so unnecessary that it momentarily jolted me. The information would cause questions to anyone reading the article. Why would a Chattanooga businessman own some lake resorts in Minnesota of all places?

Then the reporter also brought up my generosity to a First Presbyterian Church in the Charleston area....and that I had an affectionate name amongst that congregation as 'Reverend Hank' for the donations of time and financial support I'd provided them. While the article was a phenomenal advertising piece for the hotel, the reporter had dropped a mind boggling number of hints to anyone who might be looking for the long departed Henry Hanson. I could only hope anyone in the mob who'd been part of the D'Annelli disaster two years before would not read the article."

Henry then paused as the sailboat floated by Ft. Sumter and continued out toward the open Atlantic Ocean. The four of them were drawn toward Ft. Moultrie on their left. Ashley talked briefly about the history of the eighteenth century fort. It gave Henry a chance to moisten his throat and collect his thoughts. Lawton normally appreciated Ashley's historical contributions, but not this time. He wanted the pregnant pause to end.

Henry finally leaned back in his deck chair and stared directly at Lawton.

"Well, Matt, before I tell you about my arrival in Minnesota, I believe it's best to bring you back to what was going on with Whitey Malooley and Billy McCoy. They had virtually disappeared in that winter of 1931-32 since they were hot targets of the Chicago mob. Into the summer of 1933 they were still living full time in that rented cabin near Brainerd and just down the road from my resort along Lake Mille Lacs. At times they'd tried to resurrect their search for me, but all attempts had been unproductive. They began to wonder if I was even still alive.

Malooley was busy with his mechanic's job leaving him little time to concentrate on searching for me. McCoy found a job with the county in the spring and summer doing landscape maintenance. Both were frustrated that Brey and Petracek gave no tipoffs as to where I might be. They had no interest in Charlie Davis. His rare stays at the Mille Lacs resort were usually only for a dinner and overnight before checking out.

They had made one decision after another long winter in Minnesota. If by the end of the 1933 summer they hadn't uncovered anything more about my whereabouts, they'd concede and move to the west coast. It was a big decision for them. They'd be giving up on finding what they thought was a treasure chest of D'Annelli's funds that I'd swindled when I'd disappeared.

It was Sunday, July 2, when McCoy was sitting on a stolen easy chair on the porch of their rented cabin thinking of the better times in Chicago. He was perusing the five day old Minneapolis Sunday newspaper he'd swiped from the Lake Mille Lac resort foyer. An article in the 'People in the News' section caught his eye. It was about a colored woman who had become the assistant general manager of a large successful hotel in Charleston, South Carolina. Billy scoffed at the article wondering how a woman, especially a colored woman, could be competent enough to run a business. He figured the owner of the hotel, a 'Henry Granville' had to be nuts.

The article went on to mention that Granville, a very private man, also owned a couple lake resorts somewhere in Minnesota along with the new hotel in Charleston. When Billy saw the words "resort", "Minnesota", "two years" and "South Carolina", even his slow mind was joggled. He yelled over to Malooley who was sitting on the small decrepit porch with an old fishing pole in his hand hoping to catch that night's dinner.

It was the last couple of sentences in the article that caused them both to stare at each other. The reporter added that the reclusive owner of the Charleston hotel was known affectionately as "Reverend Hank" and had lived for a couple of months at a local First Presbyterian Church in the Charleston area as he was getting himself settled.

Malooley and McCoy began to scream for joy. They remembered I was the guy who handled all money matters for the First Presbyterian Church in Glenwood. They had lived two years in hiding and working dead end jobs, but they'd finally got a major break in locating the man who could be their future financial life line. They could practically taste the opportunity to bring their lives back to the glory days when they were respected members of the Chicago syndicate.

Most of all, the article confirmed in their minds that Henry Hanson under the alias of Henry Granville had pilfered money from the D'Annelli's stored business profits. How else could a feed and grain manager have money enough to finance the sizable hotel in Charleston as well as purchasing two Minnesota lake properties?

I was the answer to all their problems...including their current money woes. This was most of all now a textbook blackmail opportunity. It was overdue that they force their way into Clarence Petracek's office down the road to verify that Henry Granville in the news article was me.

At the front desk, though, they learned that Clarence was gone for the weekend at the sister lake resort property in White Bear Lake.

Twenty minutes later they were traveling down State Hwy. 10 toward the Twin Cities ready to confront both resort managers. They were now certain they'd been duped for the last two years by Petracek and Brey… and they were mad.

*   *   *

I had arrived two days prior on Friday evening on June 30 at the train station in St. Paul. Charlie's and my face-to-face meeting was anticlimactic. We'd built up such a strong relationship by phone and letters. While he'd figured who I was, upon seeing me he had his doubts. When I exited the train that evening his eyes got bigger the closer we got to one another. I did look like I walked out of a picture of a South Carolina plantation owner with my light baggy suit, longish hair, cigarette holder, and white plantation hat. It was a dramatic alteration from my former self.

He recovered quickly and even gave me a bear hug, something foreign to male behavior at that time. The great thing about Charlie was that he paid little attention to supposedly acceptable behaviors. He practically picked me off the ground with his hug. I don't recall much about the drive up Hwy. 61 to the White Bear Lake resort other than we never stopped talking.

At the resort, Petracek and Brey were at my suite having already imbibed some of the booze they'd brought to my room. It was a great time reliving old times. We kept joshing each other about our new looks. I was so impressed how they had changed physically from their days as dispirited law officers in Glenwood.

As we were departing to our rooms later that night Charlie mentioned he'd invited a few friends over to the resort Saturday evening for dinner and then for some golf on Sunday. He added, "Henry, if that makes you uncomfortable, I can cancel the get-together. Frankly, I don't believe you have to be concerned. No one should know you as Henry Hanson, especially with your southern gentleman appearance. To everyone, you'll just be a client of mine from down south."

When those friends began checking into the resort Saturday afternoon, the group turned out to be fifteen in number. They looked somewhat familiar to the group I'd first seen with Charlie almost four years before at the Alexandria speakeasy. However, there was one

321

young gentleman who arrived late. I recognized him immediately. For golf attire, he still favored knickers…the same style I'd seen him two years before with Lindy MacPherson on that last night at the mill in Glenwood.

That Saturday afternoon, July 1 became the first time I'd ever spoken to your father, Matt. He'd just come from a golf match at his club and he and Charlie were like two kids as he told his friend about the results of his round of golf. Charlie was just as excited about Jamie's victory that day.

Over that weekend at the White Bear Lake resort, I would meet a wonderful collection of people. The only time I became concerned about being recognized was Saturday evening when two other people arrived separately for the dinner. I knew them immediately and couldn't believe they couldn't identify me in a glance. Luckily, my disguise passed the test.

There was a young man probably twenty years old who age wise didn't seem to fit with the older group of men in their thirties. He was Adam Bailey from Glenwood then a second year student at the University of Minnesota. I'd watched him grow up and his father, John had been one of my best friends in Glenwood. That was one of the difficulties with my disappearance. It cost me that friendship.

The kid now was a strapping lad almost as tall as Charlie, but very thin like his father. He had the same mannerisms as his father, but was more spontaneous and laughed easily. His father, John, had gone through a horrific situation in middle 1920's. It sapped his zest for life, but hadn't kept him from being one of the more generous men I'd ever known. Like most farmers at that time, he had little money. What he gave was his time when folks needed him.

Adam was the biggest surprise to me at that dinner. I knew he'd caddied for D'Annelli out at the Lodge golf course whenever the man was staying at the Lodge. He also got paid handsomely for doing odd jobs for some of those gangster fellows at the resort. He'd been like a nephew to D'Annelli much to John Bailey's distress.

I recall John being troubled that Adam was spending too much of his time with those guests out at the Lodge. What I saw that Saturday night was that John needn't have been concerned. His son was turning out just fine.

The other person who arrived later for the dinner was a female…
and a very attractive lady she was. Lindy MacPherson hardly looked a
day older than the last time I'd seen her in Glenwood. Judging by the
affectionate greeting she got from Jamie…and the ring on her finger…
it took no great effort to guess she had become Lindy Lawton. I would
find out that night the two of them had been married for almost a year.

When I first saw her that night I ducked down in my booth and
concentrated on talking with Petracek and Brey. Only two years before
I'd had coffee with John Bailey and her down at the Glenwood Café.
She hadn't trusted me then given my relationship with Loni D'Annelli.
Somehow after all the arrests at the Lodge, she'd avowed my innocence
in anything dealing with illegalities at Chippewa Lodge. It let me be
free of the federal authorities hunting me down. I only had D'Annelli's
people to worry about.

I looked at Charlie a couple times that evening questioning if
my camouflage was passing the test. He didn't appear nervous. Little
did I know at the time my identity was totally safe even if Lindy, Jamie,
or young Adam had recognized me. They'd always considered me part
of their conspiracy without me knowing it given the help I'd supplied
them in pinning D'Annelli. They just never had any idea where I
had secretly relocated…and Charlie Davis certainly wasn't going to say
anything as my attorney.

Matt, you have to understand up to that very night at the White
Bear Lake resort, the only people I thought might have helped Lindy
MacPherson bring down Loni D'Annelli was Charlie Davis and your
father. They helped her locate D'Annelli's money at the mill. For two
years I thought they'd simply split town either that night or before the
raid on Sunday. What I saw and heard that night left me awestruck.

It all started when I bid the group a good night and went back
to my suite. I'd purposely stayed clear of talking with Adam, Jamie or
Lindy, even though I would have liked to share past times with them.

It was an hour later and I still wasn't sleepy. I guess the excitement
of being back in my home state kept me awake. I decided to visit the
bar once again to have a nightcap before retiring. The bar was open
facing the huge lake and the humid but cool evening breeze. Wood was
being burned in the patio fireplace to bring warmth and ward off the
mosquitoes. At that late hour there were only a couple small groups of

guests sitting and enjoying the view of the picturesque lake from the patio.

I was about to step outside when I saw a side view of Charlie, Jamie, and young Adam leaning very closely to Lindy as she sat at a table. They were talking very intensely and didn't notice me. I'll not ever forget that image...like a close knit family huddled together talking very seriously one minute and laughing uproarishly the next.

I don't think I realized until that very moment that Charlie and Jamie likely had more to do with helping bring down D'Annelli than just helping Lindy find the crucial evidence at the mill. And, with Adam Bailey sitting so closely to the other three, I had a fairly good idea the young man had joined forces with them as well. And, if Adam Bailey was involved, so likely was his father, John.

The coincidence was unmistakable. They'd all met by accident that weekend and something had caused them to have a close tie. Bringing down Loni D'Annelli and his unlawful businesses had to be the common denominator.

I had this overpowering urge to go over and introduce who I really was, but I still had some uncertainty. Except for Charlie, Rich, and Clarence, I felt I could trust no one else to keep my identity a secret. I was about to retreat back to my suite when I heard the voice of Adam saying, "So...my Dad wanted to know if everything is all right. As Charlie knows, he's still travelling but was curious if anyone has been snooping around about any of us?"

Hearing that question I stopped. I don't normally listen in on other people's conversations, but I couldn't help it. I positioned myself to the side of the fireplace and let my nosiness prevail. From that spot I could hear what they were saying with surprising clarity.

Lindy's response was soft but it carried adequately enough. "You can tell John not to be worried. After two years any of D'Annelli's boys would never admit having worked for him if they cared about their health. Still, the five of us need to be ever cautious. We've done well not to slip up so far. But, there are still those two fellows who were really close to D'Annelli and played in Loni's foursome at that charity tournament with Jamie. Malooley and McCoy have been missing since the day D'Annelli was gunned down in Chicago. We might assume they were taken out as well, only the rumors on the street are that they are still hiding out...some say even back here in Minnesota. It wouldn't be a bad decision. They gained a lot of familiarity in the central Minnesota lake region from their D'Annelli days. If they are still in this state, the only logical reason has to be that they're still trying to locate Henry Hanson. They have to believe Henry disappeared two years ago with a lot of D'Annelli's money.

That assertion got a rise out of Charlie…and certainly one out of me as I sat obscured by the corner of the stone fireplace. I was in shocked silence. Up to that point, I had considered Malooley and McCoy totally out of the picture.

I could tell the discomfort of Charlie as he then tried to re-direct the discussion away from the subject of me. He said with tongue in cheek, "Wherever Henry is right now, I'm sure he's safe. He's been not heard from in the two years since he disappeared. We can't be concerned about him right now. Our awareness has always got to be that those two hoods saw Jamie, Lindy, and I together at that charity golf tournament. If they ever surface, they could be trouble for us."

Then Jamie added something that made me gulp. He said, "I've always wondered how those two D'Annelli guys didn't sense Lindy got some help that weekend. The only other person who knew the location of D'Annelli's vast sums of money was Henry Hanson. It would be logical to think Henry tipped off Lindy. Then with me in their foursome and Charlie and Lindy following our group, why would they not think Chas and I helped her out. I agree with Charlie. If Malooley and McCoy ever confront us, it would be a logical question they will ask."

Charlie reacted from another angle. "I think they do know who you, Lindy, and I are, but have to be wary about approaching us. By now they know all three of us are lawyers, that Lindy's now in charge of the regional U.S. Attorney's office, and maybe even that Jamie and Lindy are now hooked up. If they make trouble for any one of us, it could make trouble for them. I believe the mob still has them on their hot list."

There was another moment of silence. I thought for a moment I'd been detected until Adam wisecracked, "Yeh…I guess they hooked up given Lindy's condition!"

Apparently she'd earlier announced to the group that Jamie and she were expecting their first child."

Henry paused as Lill and Ashley looked humorously at Matt for his reaction. He was still finishing his notes and looked up not realizing what just got said. Then he broke up laughing saying, "I guess that was the first of many times I've been to the White Bear Lake resort. You'll have to forgive me for not recalling the experience. As an embryo I was a bit limited with sight and sound."

Enjoying the comical break, the iced tea was replenished, including the addition Ashley chose to top his drink. Then the four sat back and waited for Henry to continue.

"Anyway.......with the sudden laughter out on that courtyard, I slithered away from the patio and back to my cabin. By pure chance, it had been verified the four of them hunched together in private conversation plus my Glenwood friend, John Bailey, had all been part of an impulsive plot to bring down the D'Annelli operation the very night I'd vanished from Glenwood.

I sat in my room that night feeling very vulnerable...and even more responsible for other people's lives. A bead of sweat rolled down my back as I thought of places I'd been where I could easily have been recognized. Having an alias or being disguised as a Southern gentleman had worked up so far. I began to question how long the concealment of my background could last. I was scheduled to leave from the St. Paul train station on Monday morning, but I had a sudden urge to leave Sunday.

By the following morning I'd calmed down. Charlie and I toured some lake front properties for sale in the Twin Cities. I went fishing with Clarence and Rich Sunday afternoon before we met with Charlie for dinner that evening. With no disturbances that day, I was ready to depart Monday morning right on schedule."

Whether it was a sudden gust of wind off the Isle of Palm coast or Henry being caught up in the emotion of that time, he abruptly stopped with his story. He seemed preoccupied as he excused himself to go talk with the three crewmen. Lawton heard him inquiring about the cloudbank moving toward the coast. Lill seemed unconcerned as she was resting, obviously still recuperating from the long overseas return flight from two days before. Ashley appeared to be recovering as well, but only from his endeavors the previous night on the town.

As the sailboat turned back toward Charleston Bay, Henry sat back down at the deck table. "Judging by the possible weather problem, we're returning to the marina. I'll keep our session going until we reach shore. He then talked on as if there'd been no interruption.

"So...that very July weekend in 1933 when I was back in Minnesota, Malooley and McCoy still hiding out in Brainerd had read the article about Lill Hamilton and her probable connection to me. They were on their way to White Bear Lake north of St. Paul to put the squeeze on either Petracek or Brey as to where I now lived.

Arriving Sunday night...the same night I was having that dinner with Charlie, Rich, and Clarence at the resort restaurant...they pulled up right in front of the resort's restaurant window. Immediately they saw Petracek and Brey and the man they'd come to know as the lawyer from Alexandria...and friend of the woman who was now head of the local U.S. Attorney's office. They were not about to confront the two former law enforcement officers with Charlie Davis sitting there.

From their angle what they didn't realize was a fourth member to the dinner group was just out of eyesight. I was blocked by some greenery inside the restaurant.

When I rose to go use the facilities, the two gangsters sat forward and took immediate notice from the front seat of their vehicle. To them I was a peculiar sight...almost foreign looking. Moving their car for a better view when I returned, they became focused on my every move. As I sat down at the table, they noticed I sat with a very straight posture. My longish graying hair hanging below my back collar was completely contrary to that day's hair styles for men. And, the graying beard was even a deeper color than my hair which still had some dark waves in it. I also wore a very light-colored suit, something no one usually wore in Minnesota. It was as if I'd just flown in from Havana. Beyond my physical appearance, it was my energy that belied my supposed age. My gestures and laughter depicted a much younger man.

Malooley and McCoy mumbled to each other how the man had to be a guest at the resort the way the other three men paid such close attention to what I was saying. The banter at that table continued for another half hour with Malooley and McCoy rolling their eyes waiting for the party to break up. All they wanted to do was to catch Brey or Petracek alone and force out the real truth about Henry Hanson.

Amazing as it was, Malooley and McCoy had no inclination it was me sitting in that booth with the other three men. Their image of me back in Glenwood prevented that thought.

Sensing the dinner and drinking was going to continue into the night, Malooley abruptly changed their plan. He said to McCoy, "Hey, we don't need to create a scene. Those three fellows with their guest won't likely be up early tomorrow morning with the amount of alcohol and food they're putting away. We have the name of the Charleston, South Carolina hotel from the article. Tomorrow morning we'll just call and try to talk with that Henry Granville fellow who owns the hotel. We may be able to verify he's the actual Henry Hanson without having to talk with these former Glenwood law officers."

At daybreak on Monday, Malooley was putting through the long distance call to the East Bay Street Hotel. In an attempt to break thru any resistance or unawareness from the hotel operator, he remembered something else from the article...close friends of Henry Granville called him "Reverend Hank" since the first time he'd arrived in Charleston.

When the operator answered, Malooley smartly asked, "Is my good friend, Reverend Hank in this morning? I'd like to speak to him.

The friendly voice on the line responded, "I'm sorry sir, he's out of town this week. Is there a message?"

"Well, ma'am, it's real important that I talk to him. I'm an old friend. Is there a number where I can reach him?"

Trying to be helpful, the operator said very sweetly, "Would you like to talk with Miss Hamilton? She's in charge while he's out of town."

Malooley stayed patient. "Young lady, I don't want to bother anyone. Would you simply have a number where he could be reached or where Reverend Hank is traveling that I could call him?"

It was then that Malooley heard what he never expected. The operator, thinking she had her hand over the receiver, called over to the desk clerk and inquired, "Bernie...is Henry still in Minnesota!"

When she came back on the line, Malooley had already hung up and had both fists in the air. McCoy thought Malooley's revolver had gone off accidentally.

Upon hearing the operator say "Henry" and "Minnesota", his mind went right back to the man in the light-colored suit sitting at the restaurant table the previous night. Malooley was inventing new expletives to his partner as they ran out to their vehicle and retraced their tracks back to the White Bear Lake resort less than a mile away. They couldn't believe I'd been the fourth member of that dinner party with Petracek, Brey, and Davis.

Once at the lake resort there'd be no asking questions. They'd break into my cabin and let me start begging for my life in exchange for the D'Annelli money I'd taken.

McCoy was almost giddy as he walked into the White Bear Lake resort office to find out my cabin number. That was when the bad news was shared with McCoy. The desk clerk confided, "I'm sorry sir, but Mr. Davis and Mr. Granville have already finished breakfast and checked out. Mr. Granville has an early train to catch in downtown St. Paul.

Barely under his breath, McCoy wheezed the word, "SHIT!" Like a shot, he was out the door of the resort and back in the awaiting car. Within seconds, their roadster was traveling at breakneck speed south on Hwy. 61 toward the St. Paul train station.

As for me, my Monday morning had started early. Charlie and I had breakfast before he was to drive me to the train station. He seemed preoccupied and in a rush. When we were driving he was forever looking in the rear view mirror. When we got to the station, he had me wait in his vehicle while he checked on the train departure. I thought it strange until I saw him walking with a man who was wearing a suit similar to the one I had worn the previous night. Besides the white suit, the man was bearded and wore his gray hair in a longish style. I swore it was a wig…and a cheap one at that. However, there was no mistake that he was made up to look exactly like me! I knew something was wrong.

Charlie then left the man standing by the station ticket master and returned to the car. Squeezing into the smallish driver's seat, he didn't waste any time telling me what was going on. In a muffled tone he said, "Henry, last night while the four of us were dining, I noticed two guys sitting out in front of the restaurant in their car. They sat there for the longest time watching us before they finally took off. Not only did I think their behavior strange, but I swear to God I'd seen them before.

He then looked at me intently and wheezed, "I think I recognized one of the as Whitey Malooley, one of D'Annelli's henchman. I think the other guy was McCoy. I have some familiarity with them since they were in Jamie's foursome during that charity golf tournament two years ago. I was sure enough about their identities that I phoned Lindy last night and told her of my concerns. We came up with an idea and it's already in place this morning. She's got one of her people dressed like you and the cops ready to pounce on anyone who might approach that man on the train platform in your disguise."

Still not believing what was going on, I shrugged now more intrigued with what Charlie and Lindy had concocted than concern for my safety. I sensed I was in good hands.

As we lay low in the front seat of his car, Henry whispered, "That fellow there camouflaged as you will start walking around the train station platform making himself very obvious to anyone who might be seeking you out."

I remember being in a constant state of astonishment. I hadn't expected to be in any danger...not in just three days on my first trip back to Minnesota after two years.

Noticing my anxiety, he tried to ease my thoughts. "Henry, your double has plenty of support. That photographer supposedly taking some pictures of the train station wields a weapon in that camera case. Those two guys sweeping up the ticket area also have revolvers under the work clothing. If there is a move to attack your double, you'll see at least three or four undercover guys respond before you take your next breath."

It was still twenty-five minutes before 9:10 Zephyr was scheduled to leave. Spellbound, I watched as my double sat down on a bench with three other people. He appeared relaxed as he read the *St. Paul Pioneer Press* while fifty other people milled around the station. From the vantage point in Charlie's vehicle, we had a good view of the entire station platform.

And then it happened. It was so subtle. Suddenly two men sat down in unison right across from my double with their eyes beaded on him. They were scruffy looking and unfortunately their backs were to Charlie and me. Charlie bumped my arm and pointed to them whispering, "Tell me if either of those guys look familiar to you."

With my bad angle, I could only shrug my shoulders. Then, as if my 'double' heard my frustration, he got up and walked over to the train station window. The two disheveled men got up from their bench and wandered closer to him. It seemed they were having some difficulty making certain the man was me. Then they turned around in unison facing the parking lot where Charlie and I were located.

A wave of fear hit me like a flash. Both men I had seen innumerable times back in Glenwood. There in front of my eyes were the two primary associates of the former Loni D'Annelli, Whitey Malooley and Billy McCoy. They somehow had found me…and within only forty-eight hours of my being back in Minnesota. I was stunned.

They looked a little worse for wear but they were recognizable. They'd spent more time at Chippewa Lodge than Loni D'Annelli had. One of them I'd been on a relative friendly basis with when I saw him in downtown Glenwood…at least well enough to say 'hello'. The other shorter fellow had been more callous and always ornery. There'd been no reason to acknowledge his presence back then.

Seeing my shock and ashen face, Charlie needed no more of an answer. His thumbs up signal to the undercover guy selling newspapers provided the verification to move forward.

Transfixed at the sight of these two hoodlums, I was mortified they felt I was that important to track down. I couldn't imagine them feeling I was the answer to how wrong their lives had been over the previous two years.

Then I noticed Billy McCoy began to get fidgety. Abruptly he became wary as if something wasn't quite right. As he panned his eyes, he made the briefest of glances toward Charlie's roadster…a vehicle he'd seen many times. Momentarily seeing us in the front seat, his eyes grew slightly bigger. Immediately something was said out of the corner of his mouth and both men split as if a bomb was about to detonate. Walking in opposite directions, they intermingled and were lost in the mix of other travelers on the platform. The undercover agent selling newspapers looked one way and then the other with his hands out showing a sudden frustration as to which way either one of them had gone.

McCoy and Malooley were good…in fact, very good! They had detected something was wrong and didn't wait around to confirm it. McCoy and Malooley had gotten away. My stomach flipped realizing a vendetta was still being held against me. I wouldn't have known I was still being sought by them if I hadn't come back to Minnesota. The thought exploded inside my skull that it would be just a matter of time before they'd find me. What then? Already my mind began to process my options.

Charlie and I sat in his roadster not believing what we'd just seen. He was swearing under his breath that the sting had failed. Nonetheless, I sincerely thanked him for the effort.

He answered me with his typical humor, but now in a more sardonic and disappointed tone, "Anything for a client."

Charlie and I sat in that roadster for the next twenty minutes and then twenty more after the 9:10 had left the station. Then the railway platform area was empty with only the ticket agent counting the money he'd taken in. Charlie seemed particularly perplexed why those two D'Annelli associates were so determined to find me.

That was when I came completely clean and told him why they were so motivated. Malooley and McCoy had to believe I'd run off with a significant amount of their former boss' money stored in the basement of the mill when I skipped town.

I then decided to share the complete story with him about how I'd gained the capital to fund Triple H Development, Inc. I felt it was best that he know. More than Petracek and Brey could comprehend, Charlie would have more the understanding and perspective how my experience and knowledge along with the insider trading advantage had made my risk taking certainly dangerous but potentially quite profitable.

I recall him looking at me in wonderment as if he didn't know me after all. I'd never seen a more dismayed human being. His response showed no humor as he said to me, "Henry...anyway you look at it, you've been damned lucky. I can't believe the chances you took. Many would say what you did with D'Annelli's money took more guts than brains….and that's not to diminish the latter."

I could only agree with him actually feeling slightly embarrassed. "Sometimes even I can't believe what I did. I guess I'd come to that point in my life when I felt my life was going nowhere unless I was willing to take some risks. Many people would say they were wild risks; to me, they were all calculated. If the investing had not worked out, I would have quit using D'Annelli's money. I did nothing I didn't feel capable of accomplishing. My mindset was just reckless enough to take advantage of the opportunity."

Then I paused before asking him, "So, as my attorney, I have to ask you whether I've broken any laws?"

Charlie was back to his joking self. He chuckled, "Oh, you mean like attempted suicide."

Then he smiled. "If I think about it long enough, I know I could articulate a few errors in your ways. There's no doubt you held back evidence for a number of years regarding the illegal activities at Chippewa Lodge. Then again, practically the entire town could be accused of that charge. However, in your case, anything construed as unlawful would be thrown out in court because of your efforts with the U.S. Attorney's office to end D'Annelli's unlawful run at Chippewa Lodge. As for your other unbelievable feat… borrowing someone else's illegally made money…and then paying it back…well, I believe that story should stay between the two of us……..forever! No one got hurt. Let's call it privileged information and move on."

We shook hands on it.

Then our minds returned to the present situation. Charlie made some immediate assertions. "Henry, if these gangsters wanted you dead, I guess they had a few opportunities last night and this morning. They desperately want whatever amount of money they perceived you pocketed two years ago from their boss. Furthermore, my guess is that they somehow found out your location in South Carolina."

That was when I surmised they'd read the newspaper article about Lill Hamilton and digested the added information about me in the same commentary. I showed Charlie a copy of the article.

Perusing the points about me, he only shook his head. "Henry, if they can escape the law in the Twin Cities, they'll be heading your way. An advantage we have is that selfishly they'll keep what they know about you between the two of them. They don't want any competition pursuing you. They want all the money you supposedly took for themselves."

Seeing the faint look crossing my eyes, he tried to mollify me. "Don't worry, Henry. We'll get you through this."

That's when he started up his roadster and we headed off. He had a shine in his eyes indicating that he was way ahead of me in our next steps. As we twisted through traffic he was already talking through some ideas. "O.K…. we have to get you out of here and it's not going to be by train. I'm going to suggest you drive. Your trip will let things settle down a bit and get us prepared for your return to Charleston. With luck maybe those two characters can be picked up by the law before you arrive back home."

I hadn't considered driving back by automobile, but the more I thought about it, the better I liked the idea. I'd be escaping from my home state of Minnesota for the second time in two years. I wouldn't be seen by anyone I knew. There could be a stop in Chattanooga. Sally Carter had been ill over the last few months and hadn't made any trips to Charleston. It would give me a chance to see how she was doing.

Then my own mind sparked. I also had a friend in Madison, Wisconsin, who would sell me a car on whatever conditions I required. He'd come through for me two years before. I told Charlie about old T.W. Thompson. All I had to do was somehow get to the Wisconsin capital city.

Hardly a minute went by when he reacted with a huge grin on his face. "That shouldn't be a problem. I know someone who owes me a favor. That was always the case with Charlie Davis. He always had a friend who could help him.

As the two of us continued west toward Minneapolis, we unwittingly passed two bent over figures hiding in the back booth of the St. Paul Hotel coffee shop. Whitey Malooley and Billy McCoy were sitting off in a dark corner away from any windows. They had escaped the authorities and were then discussing the best way to get themselves out of the Twin Cities without being recognized. They knew where to look for me; it was all a matter of time before they'd make it to Charleston. That city did provide some challenges. They had no idea where that city was located. Living in Chicago for most of their lives, the two of them were not world travelers. Their idea of North was Chicago; South was Florida; West was California; East was New York. The rest of the country didn't matter to them!

Finishing their coffee, they found a downtown St. Paul car dealer and pawned off their late model Plymouth Roadster. It was in bad condition after a couple winters in Minnesota, but they walked away with enough money to buy train tickets to South Carolina…and a little extra. They weren't worried. They figured once they arrived in my new home city, any cash woes would be solved. In their minds, I represented the only real money and future they had.

They took the evening 8:40 train out of St. Paul. It would take until Wednesday evening, a day later before their arrival in Charleston. They had no idea where they were when they did arrive. Their only vision was soon seeing me beg for my life and my reputation as they declared the amount of money they'd need to preserve both."

With that Henry again stood up. Lawton could tell the man was losing interest in going further that evening. In two months he'd gotten to know the older man's habits. Ashley took the cue of Henry's sudden silence and told some old war stories about Ft. Johnson where the first shots in the Civil War were aimed at Ft. Sumter. Moving back into the harbor area, the sailboat crew wasted no more time with the approaching cloud cover and docked back at the Ashley River marina.

In their short ride back to the hotel, Henry informed Lawton of his upcoming schedule. "Matt, I have more business to conduct and I'll be quite indisposed in the next couple weeks...even gone next weekend. I'm afraid it's going to be the second weekend in June before we can have another interview session."

Lawton didn't find the statement surprising considering that afternoon's interview session had been the first one in three weeks. More assertively, he asked Henry, "Shall we set up a time right now for the next interview or wait?

Henry gave Lill and Ashley a pensive look and then turned slyly toward his young scribe. "Let's wait. Lill will again accompany me. Frankly it would be quite helpful and much appreciated if you could stay close to the hotel and cover for Lill once again like you did the previous weeks."

Lawton reacted matter-of-factly, but secretly he was delighted. In the two months since arriving in Charleston he'd come to know more about the hotel business than he could in estimating the completion date of the manuscript on Henry's life. He responded dutifully, "Certainly, Henry, I'll naturally help in any way I can."

Turning to Lill, Lawton offered, "Lill, just leave a list of meetings or responsibilities you want covered. I'll work that in along with collating my notes from today's session and continue drafting the manuscript."

He thought Henry would be pleased, but the nod and smile were forced. The older man responded quickly, "No rush, Matt. Make the hotel and covering for Lill your priority while we're gone. I don't believe your publisher in Minneapolis will complain. You can report to him that I'm very satisfied with the progress we're making on my memoirs."

Lawton only nodded not understanding how Henry could be pleased. The manuscript was going at a snail's pace.

That Sunday evening there was a function at the hotel for the Charleston Historical Society. Lill had mentioned she and Henry would not be attending. Instead she inquired, "Matt, Ashley will be there this evening, but depending on your schedule it would be helpful if you could stop down and greet many of the guests on behalf of the hotel along with him. I'm sorry for making such a last minute request."

Lawton nodded again. Getting cleaned up and putting on a tie and white dinner jacket would certainly not be a strain. Besides, he'd gotten to know a few people in Charleston thanks to Ashley. Local events like the historical society affair would be enjoyable. He thought Laura Waring might be present that evening as well. She'd been rather general about her plans that Sunday. He figured that meant she had another engagement Sunday afternoon and evening with one of her other pursuers.

That night it was a typically beautiful evening in the hotel patio area. The man gaining a reputation as a restoration expert, Francis Edmunds and his wife were talking with the mayor. Judge Waring and his wife arrived without their daughter. Lawton greeted them graciously...and disappointedly. Ashley was his usual social self and waved to them while entertaining two ladies in the society. Moments later Ashley came over and escorted Mrs. Waring to the punch bowl leaving the judge and Lawton standing alone.

Judge Waring then leaned toward Lawton and murmured quite seriously, "So, Matthew, I've been meaning to ask you something. I heard about the run-in you and Jefferson Brown had on Broad Street with some young roughnecks. I was pleased to hear your other friend Lou White was able to persuade the two local young men to direct their mischief elsewhere."

They were interrupted momentarily by a passing friend of the Judge before he leaned back and continued, "With what I was told, those two young men came out on the short end of the deal...one with a broken nose and the other…shall we say walked around rather uncomfortably for a couple days."

Lawton was surprised the Judge had even heard of that particular incident. Noting Lawton's furrowed brow, he laughed, "Matt, I do have some communication links with my daughter…not strong mind you… but effective enough to even hear some things about the two of you. She seems to like having lunch with you…and apparently she feels quite safe when going out with you and your friends."

There was nothing for Lawton to say in response except nodding in appreciation and hoping the Judge's daughter hadn't gone into too much more detail. What he really wanted to know from the Judge was how friendly his daughter was with various other suitors. It was of course not a prudent question to ask the father.

As the Judge slid away to greet some other friends, he winked at Lawton and added, "I think she'll be strolling in pretty soon…in case you're wondering."

The evening perked up from that moment forward until Laura arrived…unfortunately with another escort. Lawton pestered Ashley as to who the other fellow might be and Ashley made up four names of possible local beaus just to make Lawton's discomfort more unbearable. The young man turned out not to be a date but the son of Francis Edmunds and his wife. While she spent the early part of her evening talking with that son along with Francis Edmunds and his wife, as the party began wrapping up, she floated over towards Lawton and Ashley now performing the social duties of saying farewell to the many cocktail party guests.

Lawton couldn't help but throw one wisecrack at her asking if the son of Francis Edmunds had finished grammar school and would she have to drive him home before his bedtime. Laura was ready for the comment and countered, "Yes, I said I'd pick him up at the airport for the Edmunds. He's a bit young, but in a couple years he should be quite eligible. Maybe I should wait around for him."

The two of them continued kibitzing about their social lives until the last guest left. Then they left and walked along the battery until the start of the staff clean-up party that Sunday night. The party actually ended before midnight. Laura would not get home until well after 2:00.

When Lawton groggily stopped by Lill's office Monday morning, she was already gone. She had made a list of twenty meetings and other responsibilities she wanted Lawton to handle in her absence. Many were things he'd already been involved. Ron Taylor, now a weekly card playing friend, had some marketing meetings scheduled. Lawton continued to help Jefferson Brown's hospitality staff set up meeting and evening events. He also made out the daily maid schedule and followed up making certain the work was done promptly and completely. He was busy enough that the manuscript job was left on his desk in his suite and not attended to but twice during the entire time his hosts were gone.

Lou, Jefferson, and Lawton continued to have their morning coffee in the staff cafeteria, but that started even earlier than normal. They all took their functions even more seriously during Henry and Lill's absence. As for Laura Waring, she understood lunch would be waiting for her each weekday noon. Lawton told her if she didn't show up...work clothes and all...the lunch would be left to mold and smell on the table. He said it might cause enough of an odor in the hotel that guests might check out early causing the hotel to lose money and in time would require the closing down of the entire complex...all attributed to her missing lunch with him.

She was amused...but she never missed a lunch. The entire staff got to know her during those weeks in June. He could sense she felt she was among friends every time she set foot in the East Bay Street Hotel.

By mid-June when Henry and Lill finally returned from their extended business trip in the Northeast, Matt Lawton had been living in Charleston for two and a half months and enjoying his new life. He continued to check in with his boss, Bud Brey, back in Minneapolis, but the discussions with him seemed less important. He wondered if Mr. Brey, as the younger brother of Rich Brey, still the manager at Henry's White Bear Lake resort, was at all tuned into the background and affiliation that his older brother had with a man named Henry Hanson. For certain, Lawton never brought up the subject with his boss.

Bud Brey kept voicing satisfaction that Lawton should stay in Charleston as long as the writing project required. The statement was made repeatedly enough that Lawton felt no guilt about spending the rest of the summer in South Carolina. The timing was as good as it could be. Laura Waring would not be leaving for law school at Georgetown

University until the beginning of September. He couldn't see his writing assignment being completed until after she left for Washington D.C.

After hanging up the phone from those calls with Bud Brey, Lawton would always marvel how the assignment in Charleston had come at the right time. His whole world had opened up. He sensed he was capable of accomplishing far more than his tasks at University Publishing. He knew he'd be resigning as soon as he found a new job in Minneapolis.

The return of Henry and Lill on Friday, June 10, was reminiscent of their May trip. Lawton was actually sitting at Lill's desk checking over some fall marketing plans sent up to the office from Ron Taylor when the two travelers walked into the hotel. Lawton got up from the desk ready to give up the reins immediately to Lill. She looked tired and asked him to sit back down until she got her energy back that weekend. Nonetheless, they ended up talking for the next hour. He brought her up to date with every detail of the previous twelve days.

Before she left the office for the day, she suggested an interview session on the roof patio of the hotel on Sunday evening. The meeting was set for 7:00.

Chapter 16

It was that same Friday, June 10 when Henry and Lill were returning from their elongated business trip that Darrell O'Donnell arose early despite having the late waiter shift at the Pilgrim's Cove in Savannah the night before. He'd arranged to have the day off. Still recuperating from his broken arm and internal injuries acquired during his previous Charleston trip six weeks before, he had grown impatient and decided to make another effort against Henry Hanson Granville.

He'd rationalized his previous blackmail attempts as failing due to inexperience and misfortune. He also had directed his wrath at the young man named Lawton. This time he was going to ignore the kid and concentrate on Granville. Once in Charleston he'd make his first call...he was embarrassed to admit...in two months. He'd be the laughing stock of all blackmailers everywhere if they knew of his bad luck and delays in reaching his intended victim.

On that June trip to Charleston, he planned on dealing with Granville from a Charleston pay phone so the call couldn't be traced. O'Donnell expected to read to the hotel magnate the article he intended to send around to various newspapers all over the east. The piece would describe Henry Granville as having been mixed up with the mob back in Minnesota. All matters of Granville escaping to South Carolina with a racketeer's money after being a stool pigeon to the authorities would be explained. The clincher would be when he'd accuse Granville in the article of financing the East Bay Street Hotel as well as other properties in the southeast with mob money.

His written words were likely not all true, but that was not important to the blackmailer. It was the damaging perception that was his real objective. He relished being able to say to his hated foe how the first monthly money installment would be the only way of preventing the article from being shared with the public.

Darrell O'Donnell took off from his motel room next to a bug infested marsh and across the road from the putrid smells of the Savanah paper mill for the two-hour drive to Charleston. He was in anticipation of a huge pay day. The trip was relatively smooth other than he ran over a skunk and a slow moving turkey buzzard got caught in his grill. Half way to his destination, there was a knocking sound in the engine of his 1955 Ford Falcon.

Arriving in the city mid-morning he was first inclined to update his surveillance on the hotel. He drove by the East Bay Street Hotel three times before stopping a block down the street from the circular entrance. The beautiful, southern-styled hotel sickened him as he thought how Henry Hanson had gotten all the advantages over the years and O'Donnell had to get by being a waiter. It angered him enough that he immediately sought a phone booth down the street at one of the restaurants on East Bay Street. There was no reason to delay his phone call to Granville any longer.

When the hotel operator answered, he learned quickly his luck had not changed. After asking for 'Mr. Granville', the reply from the hotel operator was quick and rote, "I'm sorry, sir, Mr. Granville is out. He'll be returning to the hotel later today. Can I take a message and have him return your call?"

O'Donnell snapped back. "No Missee. I'll call him later."

Slamming the phone back onto the hook, the black cloud of misfortune was nipping at his heels. Mentally he'd been ready to take on the hotel owner and now he wasn't certain if he'd even get a chance to talk to the man he so hated. 1960 had started out so well; now the new decade seemed so unkind and ominous to O'Donnell.

The would-be extortionist decided he had no choice but to wait. He'd watch the front entrance to the East Bay Street Hotel for Granville's arrival. Besides, it was better that he continue letting his mending broken arm and various bodily aches and pains rest. The moment he saw his nemesis enter the East Bay Street Hotel, O'Donnell would hurry to a pay phone.

For the rest of the morning he was parked along the battery watching the semi-circle entrance to the East Bay Street Hotel. About noon his heart jumped as he recognized the young man who'd seen him six weeks before now walking along the sidewalk directly at him. O'Donnell scrunched down and pulled his new tan-colored fedora over his eyes swearing again about his bad luck.

The young man strolled right by his car without so much as a glance. A half block down the street he stopped as a young lady met him. They then turned together and began walking back toward O'Donnell's car. The older man felt his heart skipping a few beats. He started his car and gunned it out of his parking spot to get as far away from the couple as possible. With his luck that damned kid would recognize the car.

Just past the hotel, the aspiring criminal experienced another bad break. He'd been so involved in observing the hotel, he hadn't noticed the change in weather. The slight cloud cover had become threatening. As he drove down the street, he observed the young couple in his rear view mirror running across the street to the hotel entrance just as the cloud burst let loose.

The wind was violent very suddenly. Debris and leaves were flying all over. Without warning, a palm tree plopped down right in back of his car. Then a piece of roofing sailed right at his windshield. He ducked hoping his rusty Ford Falcon would be spared. Seconds later the object shattered the right side of his windshield and left two major cracks in his driver's view. The shock caused him to barrel into a palm tree on the other side of the street.

O'Donnell looked in his bent rear view mirror and saw blood on his face. He looked closer and was relieved to see only a few particles of glass from the windshield had actually hit him. Yet, with the blood flowing down his face, he looked like he'd lost a fight.

Getting out of his car he inspected the sunbaked, rusty exterior of the car and determined it was still drivable despite half his windshield in pieces on the floor of his vehicle. The words coming out of Darrell O'Donnell's mouth were not for the faint of heart. Throwing the piece of roofing off his car, he just started shaking his head and lifting his arms as if talking to demons from another world.

Being near the hotel, one of the first people to arrive at the accident scene was the older man O'Donnell had seen hundreds of times while doing surveillance on the hotel from the vacant office building across the street. It was the Negro valet and O'Donnell was in no mood to be helped...and certainly not by one of Granville's employees.

He wiped the blood from his eyes and face and got back in his damaged automobile. As he backed away from the palm tree, his head was moving back and forth in exasperation. Angrily shifting the car into drive the car puttered away as the wind and rain began to dissipate. Bystanders saw a distraught driver muttering incoherently to himself.

O'Donnell suddenly had a great desire to get out of a city he was now comparing to Gomorrah. There would be other days to harangue Henry Granville. Right then he just wanted to make it back to Savannah alive without having his car towed. His face was no longer bleeding profusely, but it was streaked with blood. The rain and wind had stopped, but there were still rain clouds in the sky.

With half his windshield gone, he proceeded through downtown Charleston until he got to S. Hwy. 17. Along the way people pointed at his damaged car as if it were a bizarre float in a parade. They looked carefully to see who the lunatic was who was driving the dented Ford Falcon with only half a windshield. When he stopped at a stoplight he felt the eyes of the city looking at him. There were cars in better condition than his in repair shops. He just looked straight ahead expressionless.

By the time O'Donnell turned left onto S. Hwy. 17 and headed toward Savannah another rain cloud had opened up with more pouring rain. His wipers still worked with the passenger side windshield wiper passing over open air. The rain was coming into his car as if someone was holding a fast spewing hose. Nonetheless, he drove on…his head now nodding in submission instead of shaking back and forth.

Finally he was forced to stop at a gasoline station and have his right front tire repaired. Naturally the rain stopped the moment he drove into the station. When he asked the mechanic to repair the tire, the man looked at the remains of O'Donnell's car, scratched his chin and said, "Why?"

As O'Donnell sat on a bench waiting for his tire to get fixed, he was so numb he no longer felt the constant ache in his arm and shoulder from his accident two months before. He kept whispering to himself repeatedly about the adversity he had to face every time he entered the God forsaken city of Charleston. There was no denying every time he ventured into its city limits, it was as if he was a marked man. He was certain someone was carrying out a conspiracy against him.

O'Donnell had to stop three times on his way back to Savannah to open his driver's side door and let the water out of the interior of his car from the incessant rain. Thirty miles from Savannah, the skies cleared and then the bugs started hitting what was left of his windshield. Those not hitting the windshield came into the car and seemed to relish the bloodstains on his face. He couldn't swear out loud or he'd get a mouthful of gnats and mosquitoes.

When he finally returned to his motel that afternoon after the three-hour trip, his radiator was smoking and he could sing 'Mr. Sandman' to the beat of the knocking noise in his engine. He bandaged himself up in his motel room and just sat and stared at the blank TV. He had neither the energy nor desire to turn it on.

O'Donnell had lost count of the number of times he'd tried to go after Henry Granville. The previous two trips had been such wretched failures he'd barely made it back to Savannah alive. There was no question now in his mind Charleston was someplace evil and a place he should seriously consider never re-visiting.

When he finally calmed down, he knew there would be a next time, but he expected the next attempt would be well into the future. Not only did he have to repair his car windshield and the hood, but he doubted the Ford Falcon could even make another round trip to the hated city. The engine was ready to scrap; the body of the automobile looked more like a left-over from a county fair demolition derby.

The final insult was his realization that he'd likely have to take the bus to and from his place of employment in the downtown historical area of Savannah…at least until he could afford another car. He wondered if other hoodlums and extortionists had to go through the kind of hazing process he'd been experiencing before carrying out a successful crime. If so, the life of crime he was trying to initiate was hardly worth it.

The next day Darrell O'Donnell found himself looking forward to going back to work at the Pilgrim's Cove restaurant. At least life was more pleasant at the eating establishment. People respected the job he was doing and treated him well enough. As far as his living conditions, the motel proprietor had become a friend of sorts. The man didn't talk much but the two of them played a lot of cards and watched soap operas together on O'Donnell's days off. He was far more in a comfort zone in Savannah as a waiter and living at a motel than in Charleston as a novice blackmailer.

O'Donnell went to bed early that Friday night. He was going to play canasta with some of the regulars staying at the motel that night, but he didn't want to have to explain his newly acquired injuries on his face. Before he lay down he inspected his injuries wondering if any of the wounds would leave a scar. He hoped not. He wanted nothing to remind himself of his inglorious visits to a city he'd come to hate.

Back at work on Saturday at the downtown Savannah restaurant, many patrons expressed concern about his bandaged facial injuries. He mentioned he'd been in another unfortunate car mishap. When his shift ended later that Saturday night, he found his pocket full of more tips than he'd ever earned previously. It made him feel as if Savannah was a much luckier place to live. He sensed he wouldn't make another play on Henry Granville until the end of the year…maybe well into the spring of 1961. Maybe by then he'd have a more workable plan to subdue the wealthy hotel owner, get the payout he'd been dreaming about for so long, and be fully recovered from his wounds.

* * *

That Sunday evening, June 12, Matt Lawton and Ashley Cooper were relaxing on the hotel roof deck waiting for Henry and Lill to arrive. That evening's interview session was expected to be short given that Henry and Lill were still recovering from their recent heavy travel schedule. The two men so different in age talked as if they were related. One topic of conversation covered the abrupt and surprisingly strong Friday storm. It had uprooted some palm trees and caused uncountable damage to tree limbs and branches. The resulting clean-up made traffic run quite slow over the weekend.

Lawton shared with Ashley the tale of the wounded motorist who had been hurt in an accident just down the street from the hotel. Lawton was trying not to laugh as he told the story. "Thomas said a piece of roofing fell on a car during the height of the storm. From his valet desk he saw the whole thing and rushed down the block to see if he could help. Not only did the car incur some serious damage, but the driver lost control of his car and hit a palm tree. He ended up with multiple light cuts on his face and a more noticeable gash on his forehead. He was bleeding profusely but didn't seem to care. His car lost half a windshield and looked as if it should have been hauled away. Thomas offered the guy some help but this fellow waved him off, pushed the huge roofing piece off his car, backed up hitting a fire hydrant, and drove away mumbling something about 'bad luck.... always bad luck'.

They had a quiet laugh between themselves while silently hoping that kind of misfortune would never cast its shadow on them. Ashley changed the subject to something more pleasant. "So Matt, have you seen the Waring girl recently?"

Lawton's wry grin indicated an answer was hardly needed. He and Laura had been out on the hotel sailboat until dusk the previous day and then had a late dinner right there at the hotel.

Ashley then jibed, "Yes...I've heard that a lady construction worker comes over to the hotel each noontime for lunch. I guess she likes the lunch menu."

The wisecracks were just beginning when Lill and Henry stepped off the elevator. As they took in the view from the roof patio, Lawton could see they never got tired of the panorama. The four of them stood and chatted for a few minutes while some servers arrived with ice tea and a tray offering some small sandwiches and desserts.

Lawton marveled at how different and relaxed the banter was at the start of their interview sessions. The discussion covered more about the hotel staff, the hotel events, and about Henry and Lill's business travels...almost as if the interview session was secondary.

Finally Henry looked at his watch. They sat down with his simple words, "Matt, where did we leave off at our previous interview session?"

Lawton opened his notebook appearing more disorganized than normal. After quickly paging through his notes and faking confidence, he stated, "Henry, it was Monday morning July 3, 1933. You'd just left the St. Paul train station after you were almost accosted by Malooley and McCoy. Charlie Davis and you were discussing the best and safest way for you to get back to Charleston, South Carolina after that weekend in Minnesota."

Henry sighed, nodded his head, and began organizing his thoughts. He then snickered, "Yes...that's a good place to start, Matt... that return trip to Charleston from Minnesota. I was looking into buying another car from T.W. Thompson over in Madison, Wisconsin and then make my way southeastward from there. But, first I had to find some way of traveling to Madison. That was where your father entered the picture once again. He was instrumental in helping me with my second exodus from Minnesota. I might add that he was still flying that dilapidated old biplane...the same one he landed outside Glenwood two years before."

Lawton nodded, "Yes, my mother has mentioned many times how she and my Uncle Charlie finally set fire to that plane just to keep my father from flying it any longer. He was so mad he threatened to have both of them arrested for arson and destruction of personal property. Charlie countered declaring how my mother and he should be given a medal for saving my father's life."

Lawton then locked his eyes on Henry and asked, "You didn't actually fly in that old contraption, did you?"

Henry grinned. "We're getting a bit ahead of ourselves. Let me take you back to the phone call to old T.W. later that Monday and then how your father helped me out."

Quite different from previous interview sessions, Henry showed a boyish glee as he continued his story.

"My call to T.W. Thompson in Madison, Wisconsin started feebly but improved when I finally got a chance to get a word in edgewise. T.W. answered his phone with a telephone sales pitch before I even said "hello". He went into a harangue about the Ford Motor Company being the best danged car manufacturer in the U.S. and anyone would be nuts to consider another type of automobile.

When he eventually took a breath, I yelled into the phone, "T.W., you old goat, you remember doing business on a pleasant Sunday afternoon a couple summers ago? You remember an old Plymouth you sold for parts?"

There was a silence on the other end of the phone. Then I heard a completely different voice gasp, "By Jesus, son, I say is that you? Is that the same fella who drove out of here in one of my convertible sedans after sleeping in my garage over night?"

He didn't give me a chance to respond. Not believing what he was hearing, he gurgled, "Is this the same fellow who pays 10 percent above retail as long as there's no record of sale?"

In an equally hushed tone, I jokingly replied, "That's right. Have you got a problem with the way we do business?"

T.W. almost choked in pure jubilation. He chortled, "Son, you just tell old T.W. how many you want, and by God Almighty, I'll work out the details. The governor of this state himself will never find the paperwork for the vehicle you are about to purchase. Tell me, son, do you want me to chop up a trade-in like last time?"

He remembered me very well. "No, my friend, I'll be down in Madison by late Tuesday or early Wednesday to pick up my new car. We'll work out the details."

T.W., like a good salesman, wouldn't let me off the line without further commitment to the sale. He inquired, "I say, son, how you gettin' down to old T.W.'s place? If you need me to pick you up anywhere… including Hell….I'll be outside the gates waiting for you with the engine running. I've got a couple of new 1933 models that'll make you cry they're designed so perfect. You'll have your pick of the litter when you get here."

The man was a consummate salesman. I ended the phone call saying, "Don't be concerned. I'll get myself to Madison…and this time I won't sneak up behind you and scare the hell out of you."

All I heard was a roar of laughter as I hung up the phone.

I imagined T.W. grabbing a beer and happily going outside at his business to sit on his easy chair enjoying the rest of that July day whether he sold another car or not.

After that phone call, Charlie and I drove toward the tallest building in downtown Minneapolis, the new Foshay Tower, where Jamie had his office. I didn't know it was Jamie we were going to see until we got to the twenty-first floor and entered the busy but comfortable offices of Lawton, Nelson, and Gustafson. We were directed into the conference room.

Like I said, I'd seen your father, Matt, only a few times including the prior weekend at the White Bear Lake resort. I really hadn't talked with him, your mother, or Adam Bailey at that dinner. I just didn't want to be recognized.

While waiting for your father, Charlie informed me that Jamie owed him a favor and would transport me to Madison. He didn't tell me how I was going to get to my destination…only that Jamie had some business in Lacrosse, Wisconsin on Wednesday. Madison was a bit out of the way, but that didn't matter to Charlie.

He added, "Henry, you'll be able to leave early Wednesday morning since Jamie's meeting is not until that afternoon. I'm certain you'll enjoy the flight as long as it doesn't storm."

With that Charlie got up in a rush and left the conference room to look for Jamie. When the word 'flight' finally registered in my slow mind, I was like a shot out of a gun as I trailed him down the hall.

I found them bowled over in laughter in Jamie's office with Charlie crowing, "Henry, I bet Jamie it would take you less than six seconds to come bouncing out of that conference room when you heard you'd be flying to Madison. Well, I just made a dollar, thank you very much."

My mouth was wide open in shock. Charlie's additional comment didn't help me. "And Henry, except for flying in the worst contraption known to mankind, you'll be flying with an equally unskilled pilot."

The introduction was not needed now that Jamie and Lindy had found out who I was when Charlie summoned their help to hopefully round up Malooley and McCoy that morning. Though the morning attempt had failed, it did give me the time in the next day and a half to get to know your folks. And, I'll say this….from what I witnessed and experienced, Matt, you were lucky to be born! How your father lived long enough to marry your mother and have you and your siblings is a testament to good fortune. His propensity for flying that biplane back in the 1930's was a lesson in risk-taking that belies logic. Of course, you could mention my comments to him today and he wouldn't have any idea what the problem was. To him, that dilapidated biplane was as dependable as Charlie's old 1922 roadster.

I recall Jamie trying to relax me about flying down to Madison. He countered Charlie's joking comments by saying. "Henry, I've actually flown for years. It's no inconvenience to drop you off in Madison. From there it's only an hour flying time over to Lacrosse if I don't have to buck too big of a wind."

I was oversensitive to anything he said. I didn't like the way he described me being 'dropped off'. I hoped I didn't have to parachute. At that moment I wanted him to make no effort. I would have preferred hitch-hiking.

Charlie kept commenting on the poor condition of the biplane, which didn't help my comfort level. I was certain he was mostly joking. I would find out soon enough he was not.

Before I met your father, Matt, my impression of him was unfavorable. I considered flying a biplane as reckless. However, in the coming days, I would learn that not only was he a skilled pilot, but a very capable attorney as well. And, knowing he was part of the conspiracy against D'Annelli two years before, he had my respect as well.

Later that Monday I made contact with Lill back in Charleston. I informed her of my change of plans saying that I had run into a couple old friends and had to extend my trip in Minnesota…and that I'd bought a car.

She saw through my half-truths. Even if I had seen some former friends, she knew I would not have acknowledged them for fear of compromising my alias and the secret life I was leading in Charleston. Finally forcing the real truth out of me, she was incensed and highly concerned about my safety.

She insisted I leave my home state immediately or she'd call the FBI and have me arrested as an undercover Klansman doing recruiting in Minneapolis. I understood her point. I'd likely be safer in jail."

Henry then took a huge drink of his untouched Charlestonian ice tea and looked over at Lill once again. "Matt, if there was ever any doubt you can now see how important Lill has been to me in my life. When I talked with her again from the Lawton home that Tuesday afternoon back in July, 1933, she was still concerned for my welfare. She hadn't gotten over my insistence that I made the return trip to Minnesota. When I'd left Charleston she pretended to be mad and said that if the mob got me, she wouldn't attend my funeral.

I laughed at her remark then, but a week later the laughter was gone. Anyway, that pending flight with Jamie made me ready to deal with the Devil if I was allowed to survive that portion of my voyage back to South Carolina."

He put his tea down and jumped back into his story.

"In those two July days with my two lawyer friends, they entertained me as if they'd planned it for weeks. We had a dinner engagement at the Minneapolis Club that Monday evening. I was invited to stay at the Lawton lake home. Charlie needed no invitation. He always stayed there when he was in the Twin Cities.

Tuesday being the Fourth of July was a day off from their work so they showed me a couple investment opportunities before we went out again that night. I recall sometime Tuesday evening I had been told our flight would initiate at Flying Cloud Air Field southwest of Minneapolis…providing we were still standing. I did inquire whether either man ever took time to sleep. They looked at each other, shrugged, and told me they were unfamiliar with the word!

Without going into detail, I saw very little of Jamie's lake home either evening. I remember my mind being in a constant buzz from either the activity or the food and drink. Those two attorneys were a few years younger but their metabolism worked entirely different than mine.

A particular pleasure both nights was that Lindy accompanied us on both evening adventures. She drove. Within five minutes she was asking about what I'd heard if anything about the folks in Glenwood. She'd come to like a lot of the people in that community, but had not been back since the police raid at Chippewa Lodge.

Funny how there was no surprise when she first saw me that Monday night. She just seemed content I was all right after two years of wondering what had become of me. She also carried a lot of admiration for the circumstances between Charlie and me. She realized he and I had obviously been working together and he'd never mentioned it to her or Jamie.

By Tuesday night I was feeling quite old given the schedule Charlie and Jamie were keeping. Lindy, bless her heart, leaned over to me at dinner on Tuesday night and bolstered my confidence by admitting, "Don't feel badly, Henry, both Charlie and Jamie will be so tired by Wednesday morning, they'll barely be able to see. They usually get a good night's sleep on Wednesday and Thursday nights in order to build up their reserves for the coming weekend. They normally don't drink like this either, but you seem to be bringing out some youthful exuberance in both of them."

Her words were a nice tonic. With my premature grey hair I was afraid I'd crossed over some unseen barrier that no longer allowed me late nights and carousing.

Seeing Jamie crash into his bed that Tuesday evening did invite the question whether he'd be able to answer the bell the next morning.

That night, hitch-hiking again occurred to me as a viable and preferred option to flying with him to Madison, Wisconsin.

I had called T.W. Thompson earlier Tuesday letting him know I'd be flying into Madison late the next morning. I told him we'd fly low over his business so he'd know we were arriving and then touch ground at Madison airfield just down the road.

T.W. asked me twice just because he thought his hearing was damaged. He bellowed into the telephone, "I say son, am I hearing you right? You're going to 'fly' for the love of God?! You're flying to Madison from Minneapolis?!! Tell me again!! No, don't tell me again!! For Christ's sakes, for an extra $50 I'll drive to Minnesota and pick you up. Son, I don't like those flying contraptions. I deal in ground transportation!!"

Interrupting old T.W, which is the only way to get a word in edgewise, I shouted in the receiver, "I'll be fine. I'll see you tomorrow morning!"

Then I hung up before I heeded his warnings too seriously. T.W. certainly could not be accused of being a trendsetter when it came to other forms of travel.

Wednesday morning arrived too early. Jamie looked like he'd died; I didn't feel much better. The previous two nights had definitely taken their toll. His look did not instill confidence. Charlie was among the living, but it didn't matter. He wasn't flying that day. He had only to drive back to Alexandria.

I took the steering wheel of Jamie's 1930 Bentley 6-Speed Tourer to the Flying Cloud Air Field with Jamie giving me directions while moaning about the bumpy roads exacerbating his headache. I stayed on State Hwy. 5 per directions from Charlie and ignored Jamie's shortcut to the airfield altogether. He was still barely awake.

As we got closer to the airfield, Jamie began regaining consciousness. He now only looked wounded, not comatose. With a cup of coffee from the airfield office, he started to make a miraculous recovery. For a cadaver only one hour earlier, his resurgence was inspiring.

An older man named 'Sam' wheeled the biplane out and Lawton looked at the machine like it was his only child. The look of affection in that man's eyes for that contraption was almost unnatural. I on the other hand did not share his fondness for this rattletrap of a flying machine. I'd flown but not in a biplane or one in that kind of condition.

I might not have been an experienced flyer, but that didn't mean I couldn't recognize garbage. The biplane would have been considered old when it went on spying runs over Germany back in 1917. In modern day 1933 it looked at best like a museum piece that needed restoration.

Jamie grabbed my bags and threw them in the fuselage behind his seat. I was to sit in front of him in the two-seater plane. He then gave me a plastic oversized coat mumbling something about 'possible rain'. I gazed at the slightly overcast skies realizing my last day on earth might be caused by the weather and not engine failure.

He jumped enthusiastically into the cockpit and motioned for me to get in that open seat in front of him. I would have charged the German lines naked without a gun in the Big War before I wanted to get in that death trap. Somehow Lawton's bravado was contagious and I climbed into my cramped seat. I didn't leave that morning's breakfast on the ground, but it was close.

Lawton revved up the engine and we started down a dirt road toward what looked like too short of a runway. At the end of the airfield the land fell over a cliff toward the Minnesota River flowing peacefully in the valley below. I'd fished in that river; I'd never considered my life would end in it.

Jamie motioned for me to put on my goggles and cap. Then he waved to Sam apparently indicating everything was all right. I couldn't see anything that was right. That morning I learned how a man felt when he was about to be hanged.

We began moving forward at a speed that was tolerable but with a noise that was not. All of a sudden he increased the speed by double, the noise level tripled, and my heart rate quadrupled. I was about to dive out of the fuselage and end my life on my terms when suddenly there were no more bumps. We began gliding smoothly into the air. We were not far off the ground.... until Mother Earth gave way to the valley below. My breath disappeared for an instance. We seemed very high, very quickly.

Jamie steered the biplane into a southern breeze and then turned gradually eastward. The Foshay Tower in downtown Minneapolis was off in the distance to our left. The Minnesota River was directly below and the long line of the Mississippi River was straight ahead far off in the distance. I also could see a large bank of clouds much further to the south. I tried to ignore it, but I knew that cloud cover would likely be something we'd reckon with during our flight to Madison.

Competing with a possible thunderstorm added to my angst. I turned around to my gifted pilot and pointed to the cloud system to the south. He looked to his right and then back at me. He smiled and shrugged as if to say, "You see one storm you've seen them all". Somehow I did not like the thought of seeing even one storm while five thousand feet in the air.

The noise of the engine was deafening, but the feeling of flying was exhilarating as every minute in the air felt like I was cheating death. Amidst the deafening roar, I examined this flying casket as if it might be the last thing I ever inspected. What kept it together was a mystery. There was actually some stretched canvas covering one part of a wing. I looked down at the floorboard and saw ground between a couple cracks in the base. I could only shake my head and look further skyward for some assurance from a higher power.

When we got to the Mississippi River we followed its southward course over Hastings and then past Red Wing. These were familiar towns from my youth. Now seeing them from this heightened perspective was something I could never have dreamed back in those years.

Everything was quite scenic, but it was getting rougher with the increasing cloudiness. Jamie kept bringing the plane to a lower altitude. As long as we could see the ground apparently my intrepid pilot was going to mush on. When raindrops started pelting into the windshield, I lowered myself into my small cockpit seat to stay as warm and dry as possible. My pilot continued his setting with the Mississippi River directly below. We were no higher than a thousand feet above the water and so far there was no lightning or thunder in the distance.

At our next landmark, Winona, we flew at the same height as the top of the bluffs on the Minnesota side of the river. People on the ground actually waved at us. I could see their faces. I looked back at my pilot wondering if he was going to touch his wheels to somebody's roof. He just nodded at me as if trying to inspire my faith. Our flight continued at that elevation with occasional breaks in the clouds and with intermittent droplets of rain. Each time I saw blue sky I actually had hopes of living through this experience.

Then Jamie turned our heading more to the east. For the next hour we flew over the Wisconsin farmland thru recurrent clouds and only a smattering of rain. But, all along the flight pattern there were some distressingly black clouds further south and west. We were staying ahead of the easterly moving weather system but definitely not increasing our lead.

Jamie tried to fly around the puffy clouds in front of us, but sometimes we flew through them. The biplane bounced around as if a toy. The plane would creak and groan…just like my heart.

Finally, as we turned south, we could see Madison and the impressive state capitol building off in the distance. Unfortunately that thicker weather system was moving west to greet us. There was a good chance it would beat us to the Madison airfield.

Then a lightning flash streaked across the distant weather front. Jamie had told me the night before how he'd had to land his plane in the damndest places over his many years as a pilot. I was certain this would be another one of those times.

Motioning my trusted pilot to go lower so I could spot Hwy. 14 and where the airfield was located, we were now close enough to the ground to see the road signs. And, there it was…a highway sign indicating we were right over Hwy. 14 and the airfield was just ahead. I actually had a feeling of jubilation. I could not believe how courageous and flexible a person had to be when flying a small biplane.

Jamie followed Hwy. 14 as the wind grew fiercer. There was no time to spare as another bolt of lightning lit up the sky off to the west. I looked back at him and he was unbothered. He just smiled with his eyes lit up behind those goggles. He gave me another quick wave. He seemed to be enjoying himself.

Making a ninety-degree turn into the westerly headwind, the sky was lighting up like a Thomas Edison display at the World's Fair. I could feel my hair follicles turning snow white in fear. The next moment with both my eyes wincing, the biplane's wheels touched down on the grassy airfield. The rain began to pelt harder. Another lightning bolt hit the ground not a hundred yards away. As if he had done this numerous times, Jamie calmly drove the plane right up to an old shed and through an open door. As he cut the engine, there was a moment of silence and then the heavens burst. A deafening roar of rainwater cascaded on the metal roof of the shed. Accompanying thunder echoed within the tin shack.

We had landed with not a second to spare. T.W.'s car business was only a mile from the airstrip. I figured he would not have even considered any possibility of our arrival.

I was so rattled...and so excited about being alive...I felt like dancing once my feet touched the ground. I turned back to see my pilot's reaction to our death defying landing and he was coolly removing his goggles and rain jacket as if it was just another day in the skies.

I yelled amidst the clatter of the heavy rain on the roof, "Lawton, that was a pretty close call, wasn't it?'

He looked at me as if puzzled and replied, "What do you mean?" He had no idea of my concern.

He then smiled and finally nodded, "Oh...you mean the rain. Nah, I've flown enough that if it gets dangerous I'm the first to get out of the sky and land the plane wherever I can safely. I don't like to take any chances. I knew where the airfield was and where the storm was, so I wasn't that worried. Now I just want the storm to blow through so I can fly over to Lacrosse for my afternoon meeting."

I thought, 'For the love of Christ, he doesn't like to take any chances! I didn't know how we could have played it any closer! I hated to think what he considered truly perilous!

I'll always remember how my impression of that young lawyer/pilot changed that day. Since I'd started to get to know the man the previous two days and nights, I thought he was quite casual, often not serious, and very spontaneous. He was quite an enjoyable chap in conversation with a lot of subjects he liked to discuss. But, what I saw during that breathtaking flight was a man quite impervious to pressure. In fact, he seemed to enjoy the stressful circumstances. I decided right there under that tin roofed airfield shed that he could be on my team any time he chose.

As we were drying off in this metal barn the thunderclaps echoed within the shed, another noise began to close in on us. It was the sound of a powerful automobile engine racing across the airfield in the pouring rain to our little airfield shelter. It drove right into the small shack at full speed before screeching to a halt. It was a brand new 1933 Cadillac Fleetwood Cabriolet. I was barely out of the cockpit and enjoying the feeling of firm ground when out popped old T.W. from that fancy Cabriolet. He was looking like he hadn't missed any meals since I'd last seen him, but his energy was unabated. He would prove immediately his outgoing sales approach was still unrivaled.

He rushed up to me and shook my hand vigorously. The cadence to his speech was like a repeating rifle. He roared, "By God, son, congratulations on starting your next life cause you just gave up your first one. Holy Christ! I say son, I was closing the doors to my car garages with lightning and thunder not one mile to the west when I see you gents flying right over my business and heading for the airfield. If you were one minute later you would have been fried in the sky. I say son, you boys have got whiskers where hair don't grow!"

Then the man howled at his own joke causing even Jamie to break up laughing. I could see your father's look of disbelief. T.W. was exactly as I'd described.

The excitable T.W. continued, "Shitfire, son, I feel like I'm about to sell a car to an angel. And, I'm telling you, my boy, if that's true, my Edna will be so happy. By Judas, tellin' her this tale should get me out of going to her damned church for the next six months. Glory be! That would be a prayer answered. Those goddamned Dutch Reformed people have to be the most boring humans God ever created."

Then he looked skyward momentarily and more gently saying, "No offense."

Not a second later, he was right back to his normal volume. "Hellfire, I don't even wait around to eat their damned church lunch after the service...even though Edna always brings my favorite meat and rice casserole! She usually makes sure there's some left so I can eat some later!"

Again he exploded with his one of a kind humor literally drowning out the rumble of thunder. T.W. was so wound up from seeing me and no doubt relieved that he still had a sale. Motioning for Jamie and me to get in the car, he shouted, "My friends, I'm taking you boys to lunch."

He paused and then added, "But don't be too appreciative. The lunch tab will be added onto the price of the car."

Again he burst forth. His laugh was infectious. I would say one thing for my friend, T.W. Thompson, he sung the blues about the tough times of business, but he truly enjoyed making a sale.

It was an hour later after finishing lunch at a diner across the road from the airfield that T.W. had already switched his focus toward

Jamie in order to sell him a vehicle as well. As T.W. could only say it, "Son, I want to save your life and sell you a car. I won't even charge you for hauling that thing you call an 'air-o-plane' out to the dump."

It took some doing, but Jamie was able to somehow delay the possible sale.

When the storm had blown through, Jamie was anxious to get back to the airfield and continue his flight over to Lacrosse for his mid-afternoon meeting. Dropping him off at the tin-roofed shed, he gassed up his biplane and made his routine inspections to see if his contraption, as T.W. accurately called it, was still air worthy. Both T.W. and I agreed the flying machine hadn't been airworthy for years. To Jamie, everything seemed fine. We all shook hands. Another friendship had been sparked.

He got in his biplane, revved up the engine, and exited the metal shed with the sun now poking its head through the skies. Increasing his speed across the soaked field, the biplane bounced a few times through puddles before becoming airborne. He gave a bravado wave and disappeared into the clearing skies.

My adventures in the air were over. I was to live to see another day. Now it was necessary to get on the road and head back toward Charleston. T.W. and I drove over to his business. He had a brand new Marquette 34 Sports Roadster that had just arrived. I looked at the Cadillac Fleetwood Cabriolet he driven over to the airfield and then back at the Roadster. The flying experience must have put me in a more adventuresome mood. I chose the Marquette 34 Sports Roadster.

T.W. got his 10 percent above the retail price with a cash sale, no paperwork, and the entire transaction to remain confidential. T.W. was delighted. He didn't even add on the price of lunch.

When I was ready to leave, he was quite somber as he wished me farewell. He said, "Son, it's always a pleasure doin' business with you. I don't know your name and I won't ask it until you choose to tell me. But, I want you to know that if there is a God in Heaven, I want him to be with you until you can feel safe again."

It had to be the most sincere thing T.W. had ever uttered.

I repeated that 'doing business on a Sunday afternoon' would be my calling card and I'd be talking to him in the future. We shook hands. I got in my new Marquette 34 Sports Roadster, drove out onto Hwy. 14, and began my long haul down to South Carolina. I was off for a second time by automobile across the central U.S. plains towards the low country.

This time I was not stopping in Paducah, Kentucky. I was heading directly toward Lookout Mountain, Tennessee to see my favorite relative, Sally Carter. She had visited me in Charleston twice... once just before and the a few months after the hotel opened in 1932. Yet, in the first half of 1933, we'd only talked by telephone. I figured the South Carolina low country might be too hot for her Lookout Mountain blood.

The new Marquette was a powerful machine. The journey would be a two-day ride to the other end of Tennessee from Wisconsin including that mind-numbing drive the length of Illinois followed by the sobering jaunt through the poor hill country of Kentucky and Tennessee."

Henry unexpectedly stopped talking and yawned against the warm breeze off Charleston harbor blowing over the top floor patio. Lawton could sense that night's interview session could be coming to a close. The conversation changed to that of hotel business...something Lawton was now very readily involved. Henry talked of acquiring a couple more hotels...one in the Boston area and another in the Naples area of Florida. That discussion continued for another half hour before Henry helped Lill to her feet. Both his hosts seemed more animated about the business prospects than Henry's background story.

Nonetheless Henry alerted Matt that he'd be more determined to continue when next they met. "I'll then pick up the story with my return trip to Charleston via Chattanooga and the sudden challenges faced as Whitey Malooley and Billy McCoy came after me."

As for Lill her mind was already on the coming week. "Matt, if I don't see you right away tomorrow morning, would you add to your calendar to attend the luncheon for this fall's art show on Tuesday. There are some other functions on Thursday and Friday at the hotel that I'd also appreciate your help. Jefferson will be busy with some association meetings and your help in setting up the other meeting rooms would relieve him. Also the Historic Charleston Foundation responsible for buying and refurbishing historic properties is having a gala event next Saturday evening. I'll have a tuxedo delivered to your suite. If you'd like, you can escort a date. I trust your choice might be someone more attractive than Ashley, Jefferson, or Lou.

She was of course alluding to the three people who'd become Lawton's closest friends since arriving. Glancing lightheartedly at Lawton, she clarified, "And, if your date happens to be Miss Waring, please ask if she'd like to join you in greeting invitees. Ashley will be there a little late. He's the emcee at a Daughter's of the Confederacy gala at the Exchange Building."

When the meeting finally broke up, it was not yet 10:00. Lawton hustled from the hotel to meet Laura Waring. For him the evening was just beginning even if was a Sunday night.

A street cab had him in front of a King Street restaurant just minutes after Laura had arrived. She was waiting at the bar talking to the bartender, a local friend of hers. She looked stunning. He'd been getting used to her grimy, dusty look at lunch when she'd pop over to the hotel staff eating area during the week.

It had occurred to Lawton how in recent days there'd been no interruption mentioned about other engagements. She'd been available for playing cards with his friends the night before. That night she was even willing to go out for a late dinner on a Sunday night. Though nothing could come of the relationship with their future plans not coordinating, he still enjoyed winning her time from the other admirers pursuing her.

He shook the bartender's hand and ordered a local drink requesting it not be served with the umbrella. Wasting no time, Lawton set forth on securing her for the upcoming Saturday night Historic Foundation Dinner at the hotel. He also asked her if she'd like to attend a staff party after another function Thursday night. Almost in the same breath he finished by suggesting dinner on Tuesday night. To his great satisfaction she met his invitations with enthusiasm.

Voicing her excitement, she said, "Francis Edmunds wanted me to attend the Historical Society function anyway. Going with you will make it more fun. Let's plan on it."

Then she added, "Dorothy Legge, who had pioneered the rehabilitation of Rainbow Row back when Henry and Uncle Ashley first purchased the East Bay Street Hotel will be at the event as well. Apparently, Henry donated a nice sum to help Ms. Legge's project."

Those events were the beginning of a frequent number of evenings out with Laura including many social and cultural event invitations...some on behalf of the hotel and others just for fun.

Henry, Ashley, and Lill were often in attendance as well and noticed the blooming relationship despite Lawton and Waring saying the summer fling was great but unfortunately temporary. While Lill and Ashley thought it somewhat sad to see a romance being limited with the arrival of September, Henry only saw the positive.

*   *   *

Times became so busy that through the remaining days of June, Lill, Ashley, Henry, and Lawton could not find a convenient time for another interview to continue Henry's life story. Lawton was up to date with his editing, but was procrastinating doing any more drafts of the manuscript. Without any complaints even from his boss back in Minnesota, he saw no reason to hurry along the writing project. Besides, he was very aware of trying to gauge the completion of the manuscript to coincide with Laura Waring leaving for law school in the fall.

His time during the day had also become quite different than his first weeks in Charleston. Lill kept asking him to cover for her on hotel business matters, especially anything related to business development and marketing. Those kinds of meetings were becoming part of his daily routine and something he looked forward to attending. The inference from Lill and Henry was that his presence at those meetings gave him a better perspective of Henry's business life.

It was the last of June when word came that Ronald Taylor was being moved to Naples to head up the marketing effort for the new hotel acquisition of Triple H Development, Inc. It left Lill with more responsibilities than she had time to handle. Lill left a note in Lawton's mailbox asking him to help her out including a meeting with their outside advertising agency from Atlanta on Tuesday, July 5.

It was not a strange request since in her absences he'd been involved in many advertising and marketing plans with Taylor. Lawton knew what questions to ask and what results were expected.

Although the writing project had slowed, he continually contacted his boss, Mr. Brey, back in Minneapolis. While his purpose was to inform Brey on the progress of Henry Granville's memoirs, each phone conversation surprised Lawton. The impatient Brey generally seemed satisfied even with very little headway. He kept emphasizing how the manuscript could be a huge best seller in the business marketplace right away. Lawton would reiterate that the toughest part of the job was simply corralling the very busy hotel owner just to sit down and talk.

While those phone calls satisfied Lawton that he was doing his job for University Publishing, he was also discomfited. Information being discussed in the interviews at times seemed quite sensitive even years after the fact.

After going to the Charleston Historical Society and the Historic Charleston Foundation functions with Laura, they began to be recognized as a couple highly interested in the earlier times of Charleston. They were being invited to dinners, even in private homes, as many as three times a week. At least two other nights she would have invitations from Lawton to hotel functions or some weekly hotel staff post-function party. At times, she seemed as much a part of the hotel as the staff. When there were no social invitations, they spent a few evenings with the Judge and Mrs. Waring playing bridge.

To Lawton after three months in Charleston, he couldn't believe how life had steered him. He knew the summer of 1960 would always be special. Like a typical Minnesotan, he wished the summer would slow down.

Chapter 17

It was Friday, July 8, when a note appeared in his hotel mailbox from Lill Hamilton. She was suggesting another interview session either Saturday or Sunday afternoon...if that was convenient. He smiled at her thoughtfulness...as if his schedule really mattered. He would have normally agreed to Saturday, but times had changed. He was in no rush. He hoped his return note wouldn't appear too inattentive as he counter proposed the next Wednesday or Friday....if Sunday, July 10 was too soon!

Seeing him later that day, she made a more convenient and even surprising idea. She said, "How about an evening cruise on Sunday, the seventeenth...and if you'd like to invite Miss Waring, she is most welcome. Henry and Ashley know her family very well. We know she can be trusted if she were to hear parts of Henry's story."

Lill also made another request asking Lawton to help out with some potential business clients from Washington D.C. on Friday, July 15. She explained they were interested in bringing their group of two hundred fifty to the hotel for a four-day national business meeting. As she phrased it, "Matt, with your publishing background in Minneapolis, you could help the hotel a great deal in potentially landing this potential client. This D.C. organization is in the legal publishing business."

At the time Lawton had only shrugged and put no particular importance on the assignment. After three months of seeing how the hotel operated, he had no qualms about responding to questions on how the hotel could serve the group. He would look back to that July sales encounter and always wonder how blind he was to what was happening in his life. His focus was always on completing the manuscript. He was doing all the other things asked of him because he had the time and he

363

enjoyed the people connected with the East Bay Street Hotel. He'd also built up quite a volume of local historical knowledge.

Later that week Lill also asked him to lead a tour of the four person decision-making group around Charleston. Even he was surprised how conversant he'd become. The group seemed particularly interested in the reincarnation of some of the historic anti-bellum homes as well as the artistic and cultural offerings of the city. One man kept asking him how many years Lawton had lived in Charleston.

He was going to tell them he was simply pinch-hitting for the hotel's general manager but he realized that was unimportant. Instead he responded, "Certainly long enough to take pleasure in the beauty and background of this city. There is so much to enjoy in Charleston no matter the time of year."

He sensed they liked his reply.

After showing them around the hotel and taking them on a Charleston harbor cruise, they dined Thursday evening at one of his favorite restaurants that he and Laura Waring enjoyed on King Street.

Lill and he were supposed to meet the publishing executives at breakfast on Friday to make a proposal to the group, but she left another note in his box saying she was called away. She asked that he manage the meeting since he already knew the room pricing and the food and beverage costs as well as the organization's needs. She simply ended her note saying, "Good luck, Matt. I think you can handle the transaction."

The breakfast went smoothly. As the D.C. group was about to leave for the airport, Lawton asked what he considered the obvious final question. "So....is there anything the East Bay Street Hotel lacks that would keep you from giving us not only favorable consideration, but actual commitment? We'd really like to be your meeting choice."

The Vice President of the legal publisher smiled. "I wish we could get our sales representatives to voice such a comfortable and to the point question when trying to gain a client."

There was laughter, but Lawton wasn't certain he'd done the right thing. He hadn't meant to appear so driven to get the business. He'd just gotten caught up in his own enthusiasm for the hotel and the city and how they blended with the requirements of the Washington D.C. organization.

The man in charge said he would likely have an answer by the beginning of the next week. Lawton was disappointed he didn't get a better response but he'd done his best. All in all, he enjoyed the sense of action and the act of careful persuasion.

By the afternoon his mind had switched over to seeing Laura at her break over at the construction site around 3:00. It was 2:45 and he was about to wander down the street to see her. It was Lill who interrupted his exit asking him to step into her office.

Inside were Henry, Lou, and Jefferson. They were smiling. Lill said "Congratulations!" We got a call from the publishing representatives you were with this noon. They wanted to commit to their main group meeting this fall and to several marketing seminars with their clients over the next eighteen months. All told we expect this commitment to be close to $210,000 in revenue. We don't usually get an answer from groups that quickly. They were really impressed with your presentation and how personable you were with them. They said if you weren't happy with your present job, they'd like you to consider their company. Matt, we just want to thank you for the job you did. Frankly Henry and I had every confidence you'd represent the hotel and the city very well. So, from all of us, thank you."

There were some glasses already on her desk and some champagne was poured. Henry chuckled, "Matt, this isn't the normal way we celebrate, but we thought this was pretty special."

Lou and Jefferson then shook his hand and kidded him about being a salesman at heart. He wasn't certain they meant it as a compliment, but he decided to take it that way.

Lill then added, "You've got a reward coming. How about thinking of anything we could do for you and give Henry and me a chance to make it happen."

Lawton's response was spontaneous. I know exactly what I'd like. I'll leave a note in your mailbox."

Their impromptu meeting ended and Lawton walked down to the foyer with a sense of satisfaction he hadn't felt since his college days. He'd accomplished something that even he could appreciate. Before leaving the hotel to see Laura, he wrote that note to Lill. The reward he wanted was new tables and chairs for the staff cafeteria. It just seemed like the right thing to do. The staff members had been nothing but kind and thoughtful to him since he'd first arrived at the hotel. He strolled down the Battery towards Laura's project feeling good and sensing the East Bay Street Hotel was becoming part of him.

Two evenings later Lill and Henry picked up three passengers at the front of the hotel for the ride over to the marina on the Ashley River. The hotel sailboat would be waiting for them. Seated next to Lawton and Ashley was the newly invited extra passenger, Miss Laura Waring.

Before the sun went down on the warm, humid evening, the five of them with a two-man crew sailed leisurely up and down the Cooper and Ashley Rivers. Shrimp and she-crab soup…and of course the Charleston ice tea…had been added to the supplies.

Laura had been prepped by Lawton to just sit back and enjoy the sights…and, if she wanted to listen to Henry's story, she was welcomed to do so but every word had to be held in the strictest confidence.

She chose to sit closely to the conversation. Lawton's admonition had made her particularly curious.

It had again been a couple weeks since the last interview session. Lawton had to consult his notes to remind everyone around the table on the boat's deck where Henry had stopped. As he turned his notebook to his final notations, Laura noticed the animated conversation up to that point had changed to a more nervous anticipation of what was about to be told.

As Ashley poured something from a pocket flask into his iced tea and Lill rested back on a pillowed chair with her eyes softly taking in the view, Henry was patiently placing a thin cigar into his holder. Lawton was in his own zone flipping through pages nervously trying to locate the previous ending point.

Finally Lawton said confidently, "You're leaving Madison"… that was all it took for Henry to nod and begin.

"While I was on the road from Madison, Wisconsin back to Charleston in that new 1933 Marquette Sport Roadster, those two gangsters, Whitey Malooley and Billy McCoy, took separate trains to Cincinnati, Ohio so they wouldn't be seen together. There they met up and bought tickets to Charleston after McCoy lifted a man's wallet at the train station.

They really had no idea where Charleston was located…other than it was somewhere near Florida. They didn't bother to look at a map. They just depended on the train tracks and the engineer to get them to their destination. They also had no awareness of the typical mid-summer weather conditions in the low country of South Carolina.

There was humidity in Minnesota in July, but that was no comparison to Charleston in July. They were also used to the evenings cooling down in the central Minnesota lake region.

Both men were miserable the moment they stepped off the train in Charleston. It was just past supper time Thursday evening, July 6, 1933. The two rough, unshaven characters were greeted by a wave of heat that felt like the aftermath of a gun battle they'd experienced inside a garage on LaSalle Street back in their younger days in Chicago. Malooley didn't think the climate was as bad as his partner did, but both were drenched in sweat as they strolled along the Charleston train platform wondering where to find a room for the night.

McCoy commented to Malooley about all the 'coloreds' in Charleston. He kept asking what country they were in...and what language was being spoken. Neither one could understand the accent of the locals.

They got their luggage and walked the 'wrong' way up Meeting Street to find a rooming house. They figured that part of town was like the rest of the southern city. It had recently rained so steam was rising off the tarred streets. McCoy kept commenting that if they weren't already in Hell, the gates had to be just down the street. Everywhere they looked they saw old row houses, abject poverty, and people walking in slow motion because of the heat. The smell of garbage was overpowering. Even Malooley began to wonder if McCoy's instincts about Charleston having the Devil as the mayor might be more truth than fiction. Their hope was that they wouldn't be spending too many nights in this God-forsaken hell-hole of a city anyway.

They finally checked into the best of the dilapidated rooming houses hoping to sit in front of a fan until the evening might cool down...which of course it did not. The man behind the desk talked incessantly about a fish he'd caught five years before while getting them a key. They were not required to even register as long as they paid cash in advance. McCoy kept repeating to Malooley about whether they should have a passport or not. The only saving grace to either of them was that the clerk behind the desk was the only white man they'd seen since exiting the train. They thought that commonality might earn them better accommodations.

The room was on the third floor. There was no elevator which surprised neither man. The stairs were stained of things Malooley and

McCoy had certainly seen before, but generally had not seen baked into the wood. Their slow climb emphasized with each step how low their life had descended since Loni D'Annelli had been killed.

Gritting his teeth and covering his nose, Malooley said, "Billy, I say we find a better place to sleep or we may die from some disease just breathing the air in this scrapheap."

Before leaving the rooming house to find something to eat, both used the bathroom down the hall. It would be the last time either would set foot in that little room.

Back downstairs they asked the weird clerk where the East Bay Street Hotel was located. The man stopped jabbering, looked at them for two seconds, and then broke out in a coughing seizure of derisive laughter that appeared life threatening. The best he could do was point down Meeting Street and choke out, "That way."

That was progress. It was the first communication Malooley or McCoy had understood from anyone since they arrived in the city. They had hoped sign language would not have to be the primary form of communication.

Then the scruffy clerk mumbled something sarcastic about a limousine arriving to pick them up and then convulsed into another paroxysm of laughter so loud and full of choked coughing there was a question if the man had a death wish.

Thoroughly disgusted, they left the semi-conscious comedian and ambled down Meeting Street toward the center of the city to find the hotel. McCoy complained all the way of his aching joints and his constant thirst. The sweat dripping off his right ear lobe actually flowed.

They asked a colored guy directions and it was again futile. Figuring they had no chance understanding any Negro dialect, they finally found a drunken, ruddy white guy sitting at the curb drinking his dinner. They asked if he'd ever heard of the East Bay Street Hotel. His speech pattern was completely incomprehensible as well. The man did point and uttered the word 'Broad' which was a minor victory. McCoy thought the drunk was indicating where they could find some ladies of the street. Malooley was ready to sign up for a tour just to get understandable information.

After walking by an old market place and structures that looked as if they hadn't been cared for since the preceding century, there were finally signs of more habitable buildings and houses including some restaurants. McCoy commented how they'd passed through Hell and made it out the back exit. A few blocks later McCoy leaned against a post holding up the overhang of a hotel called the Mills House. It was the best conditioned hotel they'd seen so far. It appeared they'd returned to civilization.

Getting directions and continuing their sojourn to the East Bay Street Hotel via Broad Street, every piece of clothing was stuck to their bodies when they finally stood across the street from the large complex. The hotel was an anomaly in an area of predominantly aged buildings. The fountain spewing water was surrounded by a paved, circular driveway. Beyond the fountain was the hotel entry into an impressive atrium.

They were speechless as they shuffled through the front entry while the valets stared at them with questionable looks. There were ceiling fans everywhere in the lobby. Malooley's eyes were riveted to the unbelievable cleanliness and classiness of the hotel. McCoy noticed nothing. He was just looking for relief from the God awful humidity.

They could not believe Henry Hanson owned this hotel under the name Henry Granville. Two and a half years before, I was a lowly feed & grain mill manager. The only thought they shared was where else could I have pocketed the money to make this kind of investment than from D'Annelli's fortune. Actual retribution for Loni's death had long been forgotten. They only wanted money! And, as far as they were concerned, any remaining D'Annelli money was their money…and my hotel represented at least a portion of that sum.

They were staggered by what I had accomplished since leaving Minnesota… especially since they had done little more than dodge possible mob reprisals against them and waste time trying to locate me. They were blinded by how much I now could be worth. Not expecting to see me at the hotel that Thursday evening, they sat down in some elaborate chairs in the lobby just to cool down. They would finally reluctantly leave the hotel a half hour later to sojourn back to their dubious accommodations. They already looked forward to staying for no charge in the East Bay Street Hotel once they intercepted me. It would all be part of the deal they would make with me for their silence and my life.

While this was going on with those two hoodlums, Lill Hamilton was on a rampage. The sparse details I shared with her about the St. Paul train incident and why I was driving back to Charleston caused her to call Charlie Davis on Wednesday. She demanded to know the facts and he was most forthcoming considering there were now more lives at stake than just mine. He revealed how the two former D'Annelli boys had somehow sniffed out my location and my alias. Both understood the two thugs were likely in transit to Charleston. Lill had to be on the lookout.

She then alerted Thomas Rutledge Brown at his valet station and the desk clerk staff to be wary of two sinister looking men asking about me. For not having met them her description was quite accurate. She said they'd speak with a northern accent and likely be wearing clothes not suited to the hot, humid climate of the southeast.

It was just a day later...on that Thursday evening that Thomas called Lill at home from his valet desk. He'd speculated he'd just seen the two hoods casing the hotel. Describing them, he said to her, "Lill, there were these two men in the hotel lobby who looked like two carpetbaggers with intentions of nothing good. They're sweating like field hands and scoffed at me when I asked them if I could be of any help. One of them slurred, 'Not now, but we'll be back.' I tell you, Lill, it's been a long time since I've seen such miserable looking creatures."

At that very minute Lill began plotting against them. In fact she was relieved I wouldn't be back in Charleston until Saturday. She calculated correctly that Malooley and McCoy would be back before then and she wanted to be ready to deal with them in her own way.

Oblivious to having been spotted, the two gangsters dragged themselves back to their decrepit rooming house stopping by two cafes on the way to get a cold drink. To McCoy's constant chagrin and with Prohibition still being the law of the land, he was unable to get anything but water or sweet tea. McCoy's repeated complaint was that his thirst was never satisfied with the southern tea. And when Malooley suggested water, he only got a look of disgust from his partner.

During their trudge back to the rooming house, Malooley got more serious. "Billy, let's face facts. We lucked out running into Hanson back in Minnesota. He's changed his whole life thanks to having the money and the friends to help him out. Grabbing him and demanding money is not going to be as easy as we figured."

McCoy rolled his eyes. "Well, we can't wait too long. I'm not going to last much longer in this inferno. I've always felt when I finally go to Hell, I'd be seeing more of my kind of people. But, with this constant, overpowering heat and humidity, I've got second thoughts. I may have to take on religion and get forgiven for my sins."

Malooley chuckled appreciating his friend's humor. McCoy always depended on Malooley to make the plan and as of that Thursday evening Malooley had no idea how to proceed other than returning to East Bay Street Hotel until they found me. So far they had done nothing illegal and if asked could claim only to be looking for their old friend 'Henry'. No one could be arrested for that purpose.

After seeing the grandeur of my hotel, their choice of accommodations that night became particular hard to stomach. Between the overbearing heat and the paper thin walls, neither man remembered sleeping.

They grabbed their belongings early the next morning and left the rooming house. Having seen some more respectable hotels the night before; they were not going to lower their standards anymore...not with a king's ransom just waiting for them to acquire.

Their exit from that neighborhood was further humiliating when they faced an attempted robbery. A gunman approached them as they walked toward Market and King Streets. McCoy just rolled his eyes and kept walking when the gunman demanded money. It was beneath McCoy to even acknowledge the desperate half-drunk slob. As for Malooley, he just shook his head, kicked the gun out of the robber's hand, and sent the poor excuse for a mugger flying with a forearm to the man's sternum. He then picked up the weapon, emptied the chamber of bullets, and threw the weapon at the burglar telling him to get lost. Malooley and McCoy hardly broke stride during the incident.

By the time they strode the six blocks to the Francis Marion Hotel on King Street, they didn't look or feel much better than the drunkards on the rooming house staircase they'd stepped over that morning. A ten dollar tip to the desk clerk got them some respect and a room despite the early morning hour.

Once cleaned up, their outlook improved. That day they planned to meet the person second in command at the hotel if their 'good friend Henry' was not yet back in town. By that Friday morning, Lill already knew they were on my trail. She was ready for them if and when they returned. Unfortunately for them, they had no idea they were going to be dealing with our beloved Miss Lill Hamilton.

371

It was already a steamy morning on July 7 so Malooley and McCoy took a taxi to the East Bay Street Hotel. Clean shaven and dressed more acceptably, they looked nothing like they had the previous night. They strode right by Thomas Rutledge Brown at the valet desk and he didn't recognize them.

It was at the front desk, however, that they were spotted by one of the desk clerks. The taller of the two men had a definite northern accent when he asked to see Henry Granville. Both men showed irritation when told I was out of town.

The desk clerk, as coached, then volunteered, "Sir, would our Assistant General Manager be able to help you?"

Malooley looked at McCoy and winked. 'Yes, that would be fine.'

The desk clerk called upstairs and one minute later Malooley and McCoy were making their way up the curved foyer stairway to the second floor offices. Following orders, the clerk then called a personal friend of both Lill and mine, Police Chief Brooks Calhoun.

At the top of the staircase, the two men were met by a very attractive and professional looking colored woman. She greeted them politely and led them down the hall.

Malooley and McCoy smiled at each other as they entered a very stylish professional looking office. They sat down figuring to wait for the assistant manager.

Then instead of leaving the office, the lady went around the desk and sat down. Very composed, she said, "Now then, gentleman, how can I help you? I'm Lill Hamilton, the Assistant General Manager."

Lill often jokes how those two fellows could have been blown over had the office ceiling fan been on. They didn't know what to say. Not only was she a woman manager, but she was a colored lady besides! It wasn't possible she was in the position she was in.

Malooley having more the brains of the two eventually recovered enough to follow his pre-planned illusory introduction. "Ma'am," he said, "we are looking for a long lost acquaintance…er…a friend you might say…from back in our days in Minnesota. His name is Henry… ah….Granville. We hoped to arrange dinner with him and …ah… talk about old times."

McCoy with his empty grin nodded in agreement. He always liked the way his friend could regain control of a situation.

Lill went along with the ruse hoping to find out what the two scalawags really wanted. She coyly asked, "As the clerk downstairs informed you, Henry is not expected in for a couple days. Is there a chance we could offer you a room here at the hotel until he returns hopefully by this Sunday? I'll be talking with him sometime today and will tell him that you gentlemen are awaiting his return. I'm sure he'll be excited to seeing you. Who shall I say is calling on him?"

Malooley was completely caught off guard by her professional manner and the kind offer. He gave Lill a fictitious name for himself and hesitated a bit on coming up with a false name for Billy. Lill had to hold back laughing at the antics of these two clowns.

Malooley pressed on hoping to find out my location. While he tried to show patience with Lill, McCoy began to show one of his strengths. He began smelling a rat. Something was askew. Without asking, he got up as if to pour himself a glass of water on Lill's office credenza by the window. Looking out he immediately saw the arrival of three police cars in front of the hotel.

After the kidnapping attempt in St. Paul, the law had somehow caught up with them once again. Whitey and he had fallen into some kind of trap. His only focus at that point was escape.

Malooley was still trying to get Lill to talk about me when McCoy abruptly interrupted. "Well, thanks for the offer of the room, ma'am, but we've got other accommodations and we've got some other business in town anyway. We'll just check back when Henry returns on Sunday."

Malooley was puzzled. His friend rarely interrupted. His antenna went up as he realized even the young woman could not be comporting herself normally. Malooley wasn't used to someone being so cordial and patient with them. In a flicker he knew something was up.

He got up while still talking to Lill and walked toward the water pitcher on the credenza. Seeing yet a fourth cop car arriving at the circular driveway of the hotel, his throat suddenly got drier.

Lill no longer could keep them in the office. Tripping out the door as they said their farewells, they were back in their comfort zone as they raced toward the back fire exits. Escaping from the cops was not new to them.

Taking the fire escape out to the back hotel patio, they spotted a work crew trimming the bushes and shrubs with their boss examining an apparent set of new nursery plans. Malooley showed his guile. Without hesitation he went over to the man and began complimenting the work being done by the crew. "I'll tell you," he said, "as the new head of maintenance here at the hotel, we're really pleased with your work."

The surprised supervisor beamed and began shaking Malooley's hand. McCoy stood there like a lawn ornament having confidence that his partner was likely doing the an effective maneuver in order to evade the police.

At that moment four policemen came scurrying across the patio. Malooley now holding his sport coat over his arm pretended to be concerned. He said, "Officers, please be careful where you walk. Our crew is cutting down some limbs. We don't want you hurt."

One of the officers looked at Malooley who seemed to be in charge while McCoy sat in a lawn chair trying not to wet his pants. While eying McCoy, the officer asked, "Did any of you guys see some strange men sneaking around the facilities?"

The crew supervisor's eyes got big, but Malooley stayed in charge. Picking up a rake as if trying to keep anyone from tripping over it, Malooley used it as a prop as he approached the officer. Showing concern, he lowered his voice to a whisper. "No officer, we haven't seen anyone back here not affiliated with the hotel. Do you know what they look like?"

The officer squinted into the sun looking frustrated. "Nah… we're just looking for two fellows who might be on the run."

Malooley patted the officer on the shoulder as he pointed at McCoy "Well, if we see anyone, I'll send William, our finance officer sitting over there on the chair into the hotel to find you gentlemen."

Then not losing any cadence to his ad lib, Malooley exclaimed, Now, make certain you and your men go in and get something cold to drink. I hate to see you out here in this heat in those hot uniforms."

The officer gave Malooley an appreciative nod and then motioned his men to continue the search.

McCoy sat in his chair admiring his friend. Whitey was a maestro at getting out of jams…using words and lies to mollify the situation. If that didn't work, Malooley didn't hesitate changing to stronger action. McCoy was ready if the officer hadn't bought into Malooley's deception. His hand was on the small revolver in his suit coat pocket on his lap.

When the cops were gone, Malooley again thanked the supervisor for his good work and motioned McCoy to start walking toward the harbor's beach. It was a signal for them to split up and meet later.

Malooley then waved at nobody toward the inside the hotel. He shook the supervisor's hand and said, "I'm being summoned. Thanks again for your fine efforts."

Malooley then walked across the garden area completely the opposite way of the hotel until the supervisor watched him disappear amongst some buildings. While he couldn't help but feel good about all the accolades he and his crew were receiving, his smile weakened as he wished he would have gotten the new hotel maintenance man's name. He seemed like such a nice man.

A half hour later McCoy entered the room at the Francis Marion Hotel. He was soaked from hiking the indirect, side street route back to the hotel. There was Malooley propped up on the bed drinking some ice water and reading the local paper. He looked at his friend and asked, "Billy, what took you so long. I thought you didn't like the heat?"

It was the first time McCoy smiled since he'd arrived in Charleston. He said, "Which heat are you referring to?

They both laughed over their narrow escape from the cops. There were times McCoy truly enjoyed being Whitey Malooley's partner. That morning was one of those times.

When Lill heard the two hoodlums had slipped away from the police, she was mortified. As instructed, the desk clerk had called Police Chief Calhoun. He'd sent over four squad cars but didn't divulge to his officers the backgrounds of the two men in Lill's office...only that they were wanted for questioning. Lill knew he could be trusted not to reveal that two mobsters were pursuing Henry Granville. That would have been a major news story in the local papers and opened up curiosity to readers about me. It was the last thing Lill wanted to have happen... bad publicity for the hotel chain and dangerous for me considering my actual background.

Now she was sorry she'd ever brought the police into the matter. She'd thought a quick arrest and holding the two hoodlums until I returned would provide me a fairer environment. Having them behind bars seemed a fairer way for me to carry on a conversation with them.

Unfortunately, they had not only escaped, but they now knew they were being sought.

Police Chief Calhoun was equally upset the two men had gotten away. Added to his concern was Lill Hamilton's follow up comments. She said she'd been too hasty. The two men were only former adversaries and had only wished to make amends with me. She asked the police chief to call off any search for them and assured him if she felt threatened, she would call him personally.

Calhoun hung up the phone and complied with her wishes. However, he sensed something wasn't right. She'd described them as hoodlums the day before. Now she was changing her story. That very morning after Lill's phone call, he assigned a couple round the clock non-uniformed policemen to keep their eye on the hotel and put Lill under protective custody until I returned.

While all of this was going on without my knowing, Lill decided it was necessary to fill in Thomas Brown and Ashley on the backgrounds of the two racketeers. She also called a fellow board member, Sally Carter from Lookout Mountain and shared the same information. Both ladies had become good friends since Sally joined my new board of directors for Triple H Development, Inc.

Surmising the two thugs would unlikely leave the city until they had their chance to see me personally, Ashley and Thomas Brown put the word out to their contacts on the streets to be on the lookout for two fellows from the north who looked rather seedy."

Lawton taking feverish shorthand suddenly interrupted Henry. He was confused and asked, "Where were you when all this was going on?"

His eyes showed sadness as he readied his reply. Lill and Ashley showed the same emotion. Unconsciously Laura scooted over closer to Henry becoming even more intrigued by his story. She sat motionless and attentive while Henry responded.

"I was on at least my second life as I left Madison, Wisconsin on that Wednesday afternoon July 5. Within a half hour of Jamie taking off in his mud splattered biplane toward Lacrosse, I had purchased that new Marquette 34 Sports Roadster from my friend, T.W. Thompson and was speeding down the highway toward Janesville. I wasn't out of danger, but it certainly felt good being out in the open country where almost no one could find me. During that road trip I recall knowing Malooley and McCoy obviously knew that I now lived in Charleston. I knew I had to be better prepared when I arrived home.

Traveling across the hot, dry flatland of Illinois, I marveled how much my life had changed in the two years since I had last driven on the same highway. On the contrary, it was discouraging how little had changed in the raw countryside of the Midwest. If anything the farm land looked worse.

With the inauguration of Franklin Roosevelt earlier that year, change was expected. Transformation of course couldn't happen overnight. I sensed the country had a better leader to help folks through the tough times. When I finally drove into Tennessee, it was refreshing to read in the area newspapers about the jobs connected with the new TVA program. I wished every state had a TVA to create more jobs.

Mostly I felt humbled as I drove along. At any time in the last few years even before I'd left Minnesota I could have been one of the many poor souls pondering what the next sunrise would bring. There have been many nights over the years I wake up sweating thinking how reckless I'd been in using Loni D'Annelli's funds. In retrospect I'd do the same thing again. My motivation was to alter my life and risks were part of the package. As I gazed at all those blank faced Americans walking along the roadways in the states as I passed through, I remember concluding that none of those people would have had the impudence to do what I'd done...even if they'd had my investment knowledge and experience. I'd been reckless but I had a lot of things going in my favor as well.

As I traveled south in my Marquette roadster, I was mostly oblivious to the many things then happening back in South Carolina. I called Lill on Friday, but she never referred to the two hoods who'd visited her that morning.

That afternoon Charlie got a call from Lill. It was then he learned Malooley and McCoy were already in Charleston. With the lives of his four co-conspirators from two years before along with the dangerous situation for me, he was already making plans to travel to Charleston.

On that same Friday afternoon I arrived in Chattanooga. I hadn't called Sally but she was aware from Lill that I'd be passing through. I could only assume she was home as I drove up the scenic, serpentine roadway that ascended Lookout Mountain. Driving right up to the front gate of the Carter mansion, there was a cloud cover bringing rain to the top of that bluff. Parking across the street by the restaurant where I'd first seen Sally two years before, I went in to give her a call so I could gain entry to her estate.

Approaching the matre deis to ask for use of their phone, he seemed to vaguely remember me. I noticed a distantly sad look in his eyes as he said, "If you're looking for Miss Sally, she's in the patio having a drink with a few lady friends."

The melancholy in the man's eyes, though, was displaced with a brighter light as he brought me to her table overlooking the city below. There she was sitting in the middle of a table of five ladies conducting some laughable story to the delights of her audience. However, I noticed a difference in her appearance. Although her eyes and mouth were smiling, she was noticeably thinner.

Then I gulped hard as I saw she was sitting in a wheelchair. She was obviously in ill health, yet ignoring whatever affliction she had. She'd never mentioned her condition to me. When she saw me, she raised her arms in greeting with her usual excitement. She did not stand but had me lean down to kiss me. My throat was so tight I couldn't say anything.

After introductions and several more minutes, her lady friends gradually departed leaving her and me together. I acted mad. "Sally, tell me what is wrong and I will go to the end of the world to help you. Nothing is more important to me right now!"

She said patiently, "My dear nephew, I am being well taken care of by a number of doctors. You just sit down and relax. Lill called and told me you'd be arriving. Now just have something to eat and we'll talk."

It was 6:30 PM when I wheeled Aunt Sally out of the restaurant and down the street to her beautiful mansion. My own challenges seemed rather mundane compared to my aunt's health. She'd told me her illness was diagnosed as a respiratory ailment…possibly Tuberculosis. She had apparently contacted the disease somewhere during her many travels. The mountain air of Lookout Mountain was supposed to be a helpful antidote as the doctors worked to beat whatever ailment she had.

As I pushed her wheelchair up the driveway to her oversized mansion, she finally admitted that Lill and she had been talking. Sally knew of the St. Paul train station incident; she also disclosed to me that Malooley and McCoy were already in Charleston looking for me...and the police were on the prowl for them.

As Sally could only say it, "Lill told me I should do anything short of breaking your legs to keep you here in Chattanooga until those two savages are found."

Then knowing me as she did, she added, "Well, we both know I'm not going to injure your legs, so more on point, what's your plan when you get back to Charleston tomorrow evening?"

We had always been straight-forward with one another. I replied, "Sally, if they wanted to murder me, they would have had plenty of chances while I was in St. Paul. I just never expected I'd encounter them. They obviously think I disappeared from Minnesota with a lot of their former boss' money. They want the money back...as if it's partially theirs."

Then pausing for a moment, an idea flashed in my mind and I shared it with Sally. "You ask my plan. In fact, what I am going to do when I arrive in Charleston is to park very visibly in the semi-circle of the East Bay Street Hotel and continue making myself highly noticeable. I want these two fellows to approach me. They'll do me no bodily harm, not until they figure how much money I might be worth.

I also believe by coming out into the open last Monday at the train station, these two conmen have created problems for themselves. They've been targets of the Chicago mob and now word about their having been seen will cause more interest within the syndicate. There's a chance I can use the renewed danger they now face as a possible bargaining chip."

I recall Sally not liking my impulsive notion. She retorted, "Henry, you're leaving yourself too vulnerable. They could kidnap you. You've become successful. They could hold you for ransom and threaten to make you fish bait unless your company pays them off. You can bet they'll be asking for a lot more than what you are willing to give to them as a peace offering."

Her point was well made, but I was head strong. I left Saturday morning, July 8, determined to get to the bottom of this mess with Malooley and McCoy. I'd known them for four years...not well...but enough that I figured we could have a rational discussion.

My Marquette Sports Roadster sailed over the back roads of Georgia and South Carolina that Saturday. Again, nothing had changed in the last two years on those roadways. From the piedmont to the low country of my new home state, the farmland looked desolate. More people were walking along the side of the highway seeming not to know where their next meal was coming. On most of the roads there was no shoulder, just high grass to the edge of the pavement. At times it was as if I was driving thru a tunnel with no top. Some walkers would step into the tall grass and disappear while I drove by. Others would just stand at the edge of the roadway eerily staring at me with those blank eyes. The car I was driving represented another world to them.

When I arrived in the city early Saturday evening, I felt like I'd been gone for months. I felt no lingering tiredness, only relief. I was anticipating seeing Malooley and McCoy and having the chance to bring our conflict to a close.

Pulling up in front of the East Bay Street Hotel, Thomas Brown seeing my car from his valet desk initially didn't recognize me because of the new vehicle. When he finally saw me, he looked oddly apprehensive. He said without thinking, "Henry...what are you doing back so soon?"

His unease tipped me off that he was aware of my problems. Without hesitation I tossed him the keys and gave him a quick handshake. As I entered the hotel foyer, his fretful expression never changed.

There was an event that evening and the staff was scurrying around greeting the arrivals and pointing them to the patio where the function was taking place. Any delusion that my daily presence was required to keep the East Bay Street Hotel running properly was disproven once again.

I recall seeing Ashley out on the patio already enjoying his personal concoction of the ice tea that was being served. When he saw me he gave me a wistful wave...not the usual enthusiasm. He then headed toward me but was cut off by some invitees. The event was a political fund raiser for Mayor Tom Stoney. For those types of gatherings Ashley Cooper was definitely in his element. Even those locals who were entrenched in prejudice and generally boycotted the East Bay Street Hotel because of Lill's color or my lack of Charleston gentility could still rationalize attending this function if Ashley was present.

The veteran mayor, a regular at the hotel's Sunday noontime buffets, greeted me. "Henry, it seems I'm at your hotel enough that I should get a permanent room."

Before I could respond, he was sidetracked by another constituent. He winked at me with the assurance that we'd talk later as he was pulled away. Given my circumstances I recall hoping I'd get the chance to converse with him later.

Lill finally saw me from the other side of the fountain. She excused herself and hurried over to greet me. She was her normal glowing self but her clenched teeth belied her smiling face. She was not entirely happy to see me that evening.

She whispered, "Henry, my dear, do you have a death wish? If you could have given us a few days like Sally asked, we'd have found those two bastards and you wouldn't have had to be deal with them."

I smiled at her. "It's something I've got to handle."

She rolled her eyes at my apparent bluster. Wanting to talk more, we were unable as invitees kept flowing onto the hotel patio and garden area. We got preoccupied shaking hands and greeting people.

Evening events, especially on Saturday, were such pleasing affairs. As good as the Sunday buffet was at bringing people together, there were often times those Saturday nights were as popular with people milling about in the garden patio area of the hotel enjoying a cool drink and the picturesque harbor. It was all Lill's planning. In the past how she'd initiated the same kind of social get-togethers...always in the evenings...during the summers at her Paducah bawdy house. Then, it was to show off the girls. With our hotel, she jokingly said her purpose was to just show off our own "bawdy house".

That same Saturday evening there were other things happening that Lill, Ashley, Thomas and I were not aware. There were two shady looking characters not standing together but taking in the entire affair from opposite sides of the garden area. Both had observed my entrance with great interest.

The surprise to both Malooley and McCoy was how relaxed I was upon entering the patio event as I shook people's hands and entered into familiar conversation. My new persona frankly repelled McCoy. He couldn't imagine a bigger fraud given his belief that everything I owned was financed by their former boss.

Malooley's take was somewhat different. Both wanted to collect money from me for their silence, but he was continually fascinated by the reaction of people toward me and the fabulous hotel I'd built. So, while McCoy simply hated me, Malooley held some respect.

As the evening continued, they realized approaching me was ill-advised. They were satisfied that they had me in their sights. It was just a question of when they would separate me from the pack of people who were surrounding me.

*   *   *

Earlier that night before I had arrived at the hotel, Thomas Rutledge Brown, at his post as the Hotel Bell Captain, thought he'd again spotted the two men he'd seen Thursday evening. They weren't standing together, but each man displayed an uncommon nervousness compared to all other invitees at the event.

What also tipped him off was how one of the two men looked so miserable. As Thomas later told Lill, that short man from the North stuck out like a union soldier drinking some punch at a Daughter's of the Confederacy monthly meeting. No one in Charleston displayed the level of misery for the heat and humidity the way that man did.

By the time Thomas was able to find Lill and report their presence, both men were nowhere to be seen. They had apparently exited upon seeing my arrival.

Disappointed, Thomas returned to his valet post only to see the two men standing across the street under a street lamp lighting their cigarettes. A half-filled horse drawn tourist carriage was clomping by and they boarded it. It wasn't meant to be public transportation, but the bedraggled way the two men looked must have cued the carriage driver to show pity.

Immediately Thomas motioned for one of his trustworthy bell boys, Benjamin, to follow the carriage. A bit perplexed, the bell boy asked, "Who am I following? How will I recognize them?"

Thomas responded unsmiling, "Don't worry...you'll know them. They're the worst looking white folk you'll ever see. One of them is sweating so badly, he'll look like he just stepped out of the shower. There's a really tall fellow with him. Just follow those two until you find out where they're staying."

Benjamin shrugged and went off in pursuit of the tourist carriage. Five minutes later he was strolling thirty yards behind the slow moving carriage. When the sightseers were finally dropped off on Market Street, the bell boy had no problem identifying Malooley and McCoy. The two over-heated out-of-towners dragged themselves down the street as if they were heading for their execution.

Eight blocks later with Benjamin a safe distance behind them, Malooley and McCoy finally arrived at a broken-down rooming house in one of the worst sections of the city. Seeing enough, Benjamin retreated back down the street ready to fight for his own life given the characters on the street. He luckily found a taxi that actually stopped for him likely because he was the cleanest looking human being in the area. The rooming house address was conveyed to Lill once he reported back to Thomas.

As for Malooley and McCoy, the shorter man was half-dead by the time he'd ascended the stairs to his dilapidated room. They'd only stayed at the Francis Marion Hotel Friday night. They simply felt too noticeable at the larger hotel. They'd learned during their life of crime that staying at one place too long could only make it easier for any pursuers to find them.

Returning to the less visible end of town north on Meeting Street where they'd stayed the first night, they chose what they hoped would be a slightly better boarding house. This one had no drunks lying in the staircase. Also, the room had a bathroom in the room instead of one down the hall accommodating all rooms on that floor. It was better only from those two standpoints.

Malooley opened the window for ventilation, but there was none. Their view was the wooden wall of the neighboring building not three feet away. The result was no breeze filtering through the room. McCoy complained about the possibility of moss growing on their skin. The temperature in the room was beyond tolerable. The two men just lay there and wallowed in their misery. Their hope was that their stay in Charleston would end very soon.

As for Lill, when Benjamin returned with information as to where the two men were staying, she smiled. Now she was more in control again. Knowing that I wanted to meet with the two hucksters, she was equally determined not to let that happen."

There was a moment of silence as Lawton caught Henry glancing admiringly at Lill. She only smiled back. It was obvious she'd been looking out for Henry from the day she'd arrived in Charleston thirty years before.

Henry then suggested a short break. Laura, only having been introduced to Granville's story unconsciously shook her head not wanting him to stop.

Ashley reached over and patted her on the shoulder saying, "Laura, honey, it's only taken this man almost three months to get this far in his story. You might say there've been a lot of breaks!"

The delay was only temporary. After walking to the bow of the boat to talk to the two crew members, he returned to the table with the other four interested parties ready to listen.

"Matt, there will be two final people you'll need to add to your notes who became players that weekend of July 8-9, 1933 in Charleston. They had played golf in that same Chippewa Lodge charity golf tournaments your father played in back in 1931. Their names were Vinnie Spagatini and Bert Bertinelli...both hard core members of the Chicago syndicate. These two fellows frankly made Whitey Malooley and Billy McCoy look like schoolboys. As hardened criminals who'd both done time behind bars, they had long since lost count of their arrests.

I was not their main target. They had a mob contract on Whitey Malooley and Billy McCoy since Loni D'Annelli's take down two years before. They certainly had other business to conduct, so their entire focus had not been on the two D'Annelli associates. After a few futile months of trying to find Malooley and McCoy during the remaining summer of 1931, the contract became just a standing assignment to be carried out if the location of the two D'Annelli men was ever unearthed. That didn't mean the vendetta against Malooley and McCoy would be forgotten... just delayed. Mob memories are long.

Even then, it took a stroke of luck for Spagatini and Bertinelli to become aware of the whereabouts of Malooley and McCoy. After two years the targets had blundered. They had carelessly allowed themselves to be seen at the St. Paul train station on that previous Monday morning. Up to then there'd been no leads, not even a whisper, as to where they were. Even the connections Spagatini and Bertinelli had within various police forces, including some Twin Cities cops, had brought no light to the location of Malooley and McCoy.

And then Spagatini got a call out of the blue from a guy named Merlie Swenson, a twenty-year cop on the St. Paul police force. He'd been on the take for many years with one of D'Annelli's former friends, a guy named Willie LaCurso, one of the syndicate's bigwigs in the Twin Cities. Swenson was also on friendly terms with Spagatini.

When that train station incident happened, Officer Swenson knew there was a price on the heads of Malooley and McCoy. Swenson found out from a friend in the new FBI that there'd been an unsuccessful sting against Malooley and McCoy that Monday morning. He further learned that there was some big-wig businessman originally from Minnesota who now lived in South Carolina....specifically Charleston. Swenson put two and two together and figured if Malooley and McCoy had gambled their identities attempting to intercept this man now living in the south, then it would be logical they wouldn't give up. They'd be traveling down to Charleston as soon as they could flee the Twin Cities' authorities.

Swenson called the Chicago hitman Spagatini right away with his findings. The cop added that apparently this fellow on Malooley's and McCoy's hot list was a character right out of the history books. He said I was a bearded, longish gray-haired southern gentleman...almost like a nineteenth century politician.

With that information Spagatini and Bertinelli caught a late Friday afternoon flight on July 7 to Atlanta...and then a train to Charleston on Saturday. They had no idea who I was, nor at the time did they care. I was just the bait that would bring Malooley and McCoy out of hiding. They were looking forward to completing the standing contract and the quick pay off once they disposed of the two bodies.

What made their sojourn to this southern city all the more satisfying was that they expected the trip to be fast. Their hope was that in a smaller city the size of Charleston, they'd find and finish off both of D'Annelli's boys and be back in Chicago sipping martinis on the Gold Coast by Sunday night. Eliminating Malooley and McCoy would be a big feather in their caps...to say nothing of receiving the nice cash reward.

Since I was just an unaware pawn, they figured if they had any trouble rousting their targets, they would find me and force me to bring Malooley and McCoy out into the open. Swenson's distinctive description of me gave them that further advantage of finding me... whoever I was.

Their train arrived in Charleston early Saturday afternoon. They rented a car and asked the attendant for a hotel recommendation. The response was that the East Bay Street Hotel would be a good selection."

Chapter 18

Matt Lawton could sense from the story Henry was telling that the July weekend in 1933 in Charleston was as critical in the older man's life as the June weekend had been two years before when he'd finally left Glenwood. Once those names, Vinnie Spagatini and Bert Bertinelli, were mentioned as Henry told his story, his audience of four sat even more attentive.

As for Laura Waring, she was spellbound. Even the Spagatini and Bertinelli names sounded evil. She couldn't believe this refined hotelier and friend of her parents could have had such a perilous past life.

Lawton watched as Henry's eyes scanned the harbor apparently deciding how thorough he wanted to be. Abruptly he blinked. His eyes were very intense as he unsmilingly retraced that period of his life.

"The next day on Sunday July 9 Lill and I planned on going sailing that afternoon since we'd been away from each other so long. She habitually got up early on Sundays and traveled alone across the river to the farmer's market. She'd typically make a short stop at the hotel and then return home with some food items before 9:00 AM.

That morning the telephone rang early and she answered the phone before the second ring. Upon hanging up she informed me there had to be a change in her normal Sunday habits. She wanted to stop by the hotel and asked if I would meet her there. We'd have a light breakfast, go to James Island for church, attend the Sunday brunch at the hotel and then sail in the afternoon.

That followed well with my plans. I wanted Malooley and McCoy to have every chance to see that I was back in the city.

After Lill left, I got in my roadster and crossed the toll bridge taking a left on King Street. It was my typical route to the hotel. King Street was normally hustling and bustling with open air shops and busy foot traffic. However, this was Sunday. Things were much quieter with people sleeping or getting ready to attend their church services. The entire city seemed to be moving at half speed. As I took another left on Broad Street toward the hotel, there were several people and families walking toward St. Michael's Episcopalian Church. People were dressed in his or her Sunday best. The poor economy did not keep people from getting cleaned up for church.

As I slowed to allow another family to cross in front of me, I was leaning back taking in the sweet smells of the Charleston shrubbery and flowers when, like a flash, a vehicle stopped and parked right beside me on the street. Two men jumped out and then into my vehicle before I could even react. I felt the steel of a gun pressed against the back of my neck. One man was in the front seat; the other with the gun had dove into the back seat. I assumed these two 'gentlemen' were my determined pursuers, but I'd hoped our meeting would be less prickly.

It was the guy in the back seat with the gun at my neck who spoke first. His voice sounded so loathsome. He spat out, "Henry Hanson, you've gotten a bit sloppy with your disguise. We heard someone from Minnesota now lived down here…and looked just like some God damned southern senator from the last century. We've been here less than a day and we found you. It was too easy. We just checked into a hotel and asked a couple waiters if they knew some local businessman who matches that very description…you know, with longish hair and a beard.

One of the waiters joked with another waiter that 'Henry' has that look, but they didn't reveal your name. We stopped at a few other watering holes last evening and asking about a businessman named 'Henry' and lo and behold they said there was a Henry Granville over at the very hotel where we are staying who matched your description. When we returned to our hotel Saturday evening, there you were at some hotel function. We saw you enter the event…and stared at you with great interest. You looked too familiar despite your new looks. It didn't take long. We finally had you pegged. There was our old friend, Henry Hanson, from back in the good old Chippewa Lodge days, the man Loni D'Annelli trusted beyond all others.

Seeing you with disguise and a new name, things began to make more sense. No wonder Malooley and McCoy are after you. It kinda looks like you not only pulled the string on D'Annelli, but you must have gotten away with some of his money."

Then both men broke up laughing as if they'd stumbled upon a pot of gold. As for me, nothing was making sense. I was sitting there stiffly feeling that pistol against my neck afraid to look any direction but forward. I had no idea who was in my automobile with me.

I finally was able to turn my head slightly to see the man next to me. That was when things became less murky. Then I swiveled my head to the back seat to the man laughing gleefully.

Sure enough…it had been only two years and both men were easily recognizable. They'd been part of Loni D'Annelli's golf gang at Chippewa Lodge for five years. I'd seen them more than I cared to remember. Both were Chicago gangsters who'd stayed in the Glenwood area every summer during the tournament week. The man holding a gun to the nape of my neck was Vinnie Spagatini. The man enjoying the ride in the front passenger seat was Bert Bertinelli. With them finding me, I now had an entire different array of problems.

Spagatini took charge and ordered me to drive on past the hotel taking East Battery Street toward White Point Garden where the two rivers met. My mind was buzzing trying to figure a way out of this new predicament. With his gun still pointing at the back of my head, I stopped my roadster by the beautiful antebellum home at 2 South Meeting Street. At that point I was focused only on how to make it out of this ordeal alive.

The two men ordered me out of the car. We strolled over to a park bench near one of the numerous obsolete cannons pointing out toward the harbor. I remember thinking the only weapons that worked in that entire park area were the guns in both gangsters' pockets and they were pointed directly at me.

What immediately became clear was that both men's primary focus was still on Malooley and McCoy. Sitting on that park bench while Bertinelli stood watch, Spagatini wasted no time. He said, "Hanson, we want those two D'Annelli guys. We got our sources and heard they'd be coming down here to look for you. We decided we might just intercept them. Our guess is that they're in this city right now. And, as you can see, you ain't hard to find. We followed you this morning once that lady left your house."

Then he took a less threatening tact. "Hanson, the folks we work with have long memories. They don't like what D'Annelli did regarding the counterfeit money…especially to people who were supposedly his friends. They got D'Annelli, but they also want the hides of those two bums who worked so closely with him. It looks like if you cooperate with us and you help us get Malooley and McCoy, you might get out of this thing alive. How does that sound to you…Mr. Henry Hanson?"

It was my turn to talk, but I was slow to respond. I was not convinced Spagatini and Bertinelli would stop with just the deaths of Loni's men. They'd soon put two and two together and figure if I owned the hotel, I'd gained it through pilfering D'Annelli's money. My worries would not be over. The two grease balls looking me over on that park bench would be coming back at me before their targets had stopped bleeding. I sensed I had one advantage. They appeared uninformed about my stature with the hotel. They seemed to think I only worked there.

Nonetheless, the deep hole I was in had suddenly gotten deeper. I had two sets of crooks after me. I'd had sticky situations in the past, but I couldn't recall a predicament as bad as the one I was in. I frankly didn't understand why I was not panicking.

Funny things what people learn in life. I'd picked up from Loni D'Annelli that wandering from the truth…especially for self-preservation…was fair as long as I could make it believable. I'd deceived people before….D'Annelli….some of his hoods…. some of the folks in Glenwood….even Charlie Davis. It was puzzling how I ever earned the nickname 'Honest Henry Hanson'!

I still wonder what inspired me sitting in that park with those two gangsters. I guess I felt like I had nothing to lose.

Calmly looking at both men, I sat back and put on a performance that I have not matched to this day. The deceptive words just flowed.

I started out speaking softly. "Gentlemen, I think you should know something before I try and help you. You're going to expect me to say I had nothing to do with D'Annelli…so I can save my neck. Well, you both know I worked very closely with the man for five years. I ran his golf tournament Calcutta. I knew some funny business was going on at that resort, but I never said a word to anyone. In fact, I was the one who offered the secret basement under my mill office to store his business profits. I did it for the good of the town. I didn't want to see D'Annelli and his guests leave the area.

As for the loot he stored at the mill basement, I didn't really care. I was more concerned with my town surviving and my church men's club getting its share of the profits from that Calcutta. Anyway, who was I but a lowly mill manager...was I really going to take a dime of his money. You have to give me some credit for having some intelligence. I did and still do value my life.

Both Spagatini and Bertinelli nodded their heads in agreement wondering where I was going with my apparent candor. Up to that point I'd laid the foundation of what I was about to say with truths. Seeing their curiosity, I then let the lies just come pouring out of my mouth.

I told them what I'd seen while working nights at the Glenwood Feed & Grain Mill. Malooley and McCoy were the only D'Annelli men trusted to have access to that mill basement...and they took advantage of their position. I told Spagatini and Bertinelli how I'd seen the two cons taking small shoeboxes of money, especially when D'Annelli was back in Chicago. I didn't say anything to Loni because I feared reprisal from those two fellows. I reminded Spagatini and Bertinelli that I was a deacon at the church. I didn't go around looking for trouble.

I then added, "That night before the raid at the Lake Minnewaska resort, I witnessed Malooley and McCoy lifting more money out of that mill basement. Then the next morning the authorities caught D'Annelli in the mill basement with the remainder of his illegal business profits. If you remember, Malooley and McCoy weren't arrested for anything. I've always felt they were the ones who got cozy with the cops and ended D'Annelli's operation. When I heard the raid was happening, I simply left town rather than face a bunch of questions by the law about my apparent involvement with D'Annelli. I didn't put it past Malooley or McCoy to make me look guilty. So, when I left town, I just stayed away...and eventually just ended up here in Charleston."

I remember hoping my face hadn't turned red with the tall tales I was telling Spagatini and Bertinelli. I recall they just stared at me trying to figure out if what I'd just said made sense.

Bertinelli still looked doubtful. He said, "Hanson, so you're telling us you left Glenwood with not a dime of D'Annelli's money?"

My mind was whirring as I desperately tried to make up a logical lie to any question they might pose. I said to him, "No.... that's not entirely true. As I said, Loni and I had developed a business relationship. He did stake me some money in the amount of $20,000 for us to invest in the commodity markets. I'm not proud to say, but I had some inside information in the commodity trade. After all, I was in the feed and grain business. Anyway, he and I split the profits. I never was able to get that principle back to him because of his arrest and ensuing death. I just left the money invested."

Then I made up a partial truth. "When I arrived in Charleston, I had a contact at the First Presbyterian Church across the river on James Island. I told the preacher I'd give the church that money to invest in exchange for my anonymity. Well, that was a life saver. That church made me an assistant preacher. Hell, with that $20,000 I gave that church, they would have made me 'Pope' if it wasn't a Protestant church."

When both Spagatini and Bertinelli chuckled over that lie, I knew I had them. I just had to remember each lie.

Bertinelli then shot back another question. "So, how did you come to buy that big hotel down the street?"

I was prepared to respond...of course with another lie. "Gentlemen, I don't own the hotel. The Presbyterian Church over on James Island helped finance the Hotel. They won't admit it, but they own a piece of the property and make a substantial profit off their share. The bank owns the rest of the complex. My only job is to manage the hotel. It's the same kind of work I did managing the mill back in Glenwood, Minnesota. However, this job obviously has a bit more class."

The two mobsters just stood there nodding having totally been taken in by my fabrications. The words were falling out of my mouth so smoothly, it occurred to me I may have missed my true calling. I could well have been a cheating, deceitful crook like those two clowns with me that day in the park.

Spagatini kept some pressure on me. "So how did Malooley and McCoy find you in Minnesota?"

I was back on firm ground with my response. "I don't really know. Last week was the first time I'd been back to Minnesota since leaving Glenwood two years ago. I have no idea how they spotted me.

I hope to find out. I've worked hard to maintain my cover. Anyway, it doesn't matter. They found me and now they want to silence me. They have a good idea I have the proof they were the turncoats who worked with the authorities to bring down their boss."

I watched as Spagatini and Bertinelli kept eying each other. Certainly what I'd just admitted, though profoundly false, was not impossible to believe. With their primary mission to kill Malooley and McCoy, my story only gave them more reason to carry out their contract.

Spagatini finally threw the one question at me that tested my resolve and theatrics. "Hanson, beyond that $20,000 you say you couldn't get back to D'Annelli and then gave it to some damned church, did you steal any other amounts of D'Annelli's money?"

It was a test I had to pass with absolute assuredness.

I responded quickly and deceitfully. "I'll say it again. How could I? I managed money for the church and for the mill with a spotless record. Where would I get the idea to say nothing of the guts to steal his money? How long would I expect to remain alive if I got caught…a couple of hours….maybe a day? It would have been totally illogical for me to pinch any of the money D'Annelli stored in the mill basement."

When their heads nodded once again, I was overwhelmed with my ability to mislead. I sat there stunned how the tale I'd just spun had been so effective.

I sensed the discussion was coming to a close. Now Spagatini and Bertinelli would still be expecting me to help them bring Malooley and McCoy out into the open. The two of them chatted privately ten yards away by the gazebo in the middle of White Point Garden. Their eyes kept glancing nervously back at me as if to see any hint that I was distressed. I maintained a relaxed pose. As long as they couldn't see my hands shaking and arms dripping with sweat, my ruse appeared to be working.

Spagatini returned while Bertinelli continued panning around the park looking for any possible threats or interruptions. He examined me closely and then said, "Hanson, we think Malooley and McCoy are in this town right now. If we get them before they get you, you'll come out of this jam in pretty good shape…and we'll make our money on our contract. If everything is as you say it is, we might be out of this town by tonight."

The dry gulp in my throat was almost audible. Not only was I facing the consequences of my lies, but I no more believed these two hoods would leave me alone than I would a sleeping fox feigning interest in a chicken coop ten feet away. I would be seeing these fellows later after they disposed of Malooley and McCoy.

My mind was on overdrive again. Seeing the cold eyes of these two hardened killers, I actually felt a wave of sympathy for the two D'Annelli lugs. I didn't think the two D'Annelli men had any chance against the likes of Spagatini and Bertinelli. Those two criminals wouldn't blink an eye if assigned to kill anyone. Malooley and McCoy might have a slightly better chance of surviving than most people, but I wasn't about to bet a dime on their chances, especially with the element of surprise in their pursuer's favor.

Finally Vinnie Spagatini scratched his chin and growled, "Hanson, I think you know more than you're telling us, but we've got other things on our minds. We're staying at your hotel, so we'll be close. It's obviously in your best interest to let us know if you hear from Malooley and McCoy. That'll be the last time you'll have to deal with them….."

I almost finished the last sentence for Spagatini as I thought…. '….but not us.'

Remaining quiet I just nodded my head as if in full agreement. As far as I was concerned, at that moment Malooley and McCoy were already dead.

The two Chicago professionals then peered around and abruptly strolled away saying nothing. I was left pondering my future on that park bench. How the tables had turned. I only had a day or possibly two before Spagatini and Bertinelli would have completed their contract and likely would find out I was the true owner of the East Bay Street Hotel.

Stumbling across the street to my parked Marquette Roadster, I sensed a black cloud surrounding me…much like the feeling I had before leaving Glenwood two years before. For the first time Sally Carter's idea of me disappearing once again became a more interesting option."

At that moment some lightning appeared west of Charleston. It was not yet close, but the two-man crew wasted no time heading toward the marina. Lawton carefully folded his notes, wrapped them in a plastic container and tucked them into his leather binder. That interview session with Henry had ended. Lill, Ashley, and Lawton were used to sudden stops to his narrative. Laura was the most disappointed. She held her tongue in the hope she'd be invited back to the next rendition.

As the five of them relaxed while sailing toward shore, the conversation ventured toward some of the more current challenges of the day. Laura was asked about the hotter local issues her father was handling. Everyone on that boat knew Judge Waring was making some unpopular but important rulings on various social issues. He'd been more and more in the news in the past year with his decisions increasingly in the favor of civil rights. The consequences had been stressful. A cross had been burned in front of the Waring stately home along the Ashley River. Laura admitted she'd not realized how serious the problems had been for her father until she'd returned home from school.

As the sailboat sailed closer to shore on the Ashley River, she acknowledged another startling fact. "I guess I don't see him remaining in Charleston as a Federal District Judge much longer. Even his marriage to my stepmother is being made to look scandalous. Her northern background has always been a sore spot with many locals. With each of his decisions favoring equal rights, my father and Elizabeth have increasingly become alienated from the local citizenry."

The consternation on the faces of Henry, Lill, and Ashley was evident. Lawton now realized why Judge and Elizabeth seemed so remote and only ventured out to limited engagements including the East Bay Street Hotel Sunday brunch...and why Lawton and Laura often played cards back at the Waring home. Lawton felt badly he hadn't understood the full story about the pressure the Judge and his wife were facing. It was just another example how his fondness for the city had overridden the evil ignorance displayed by too many Charlestonians.

After hearing what Laura had disclosed, Lawton would come to learn in the days ahead that some actions had been taken by Henry and Ashley. Both were on the phone the next day talking with some contacts each had in Washington D.C. as well as in the city itself. By Wednesday there was surveillance on the Waring house by U.S. Marshals and bodyguards were covertly watching over the Judge and Elizabeth.

Upon leaving the boat at the harbor that Sunday evening, Henry also said something Lawton wasn't ready to hear. As the five of them drove back to the hotel, he commented, "You know, I'm almost sorry to say but I believe I can finish this background overview in the next one or two interview sessions. What do you say we plan the next interview session for Friday, July 29? And, Laura, you're certainly invited wherever we have the meeting."

The smile on both Laura's face as well as the appreciative grin by Lawton was noted by Lill, Ashley, and most certainly by Henry. It hadn't gotten by him that his scribe and the Judge's daughter had struck up a closer relationship than just casual, periodic dating.

The remaining days of July continued with Laura being a regular for lunch at the hotel. In addition, Lawton and she continued attending city or hotel social functions, caroused at some local watering holes or played cards with the Judge and Elizabeth in the evenings. Regrettably, the problems of Laura's father seemed to percolate as if the constant July temperatures wouldn't allow prejudicial wrath to cool. The U.S. Marshals were protecting the Waring house much more effectively than the local police had been doing. However, the daily stress of performing his judicial duties so farsightedly, yet with so much slander directed at him, his life had become intolerable.

While playing cards, Laura and Lawton would learn of the Judge's plans to retire before the end of the year and move to New York. As a result of that surprising announcement, Laura seemed to be grappling with her own future. As for Lawton, he didn't want his writing project to end. Neither would admit their struggles also had to do with their budding relationship.

More and more her comments centered on whether law was her preferred career path. She admitted to being affected by the horrible grind her father was experiencing only because he was performing his judgeship duties as fairly as he knew how.

She angrily commented more than once, "I see his reputation being maligned. His hard work and determined efforts to be fair and unbiased just seem so unrequited. I want a career where my work can't be torn apart by prejudice and ignorance.

During their discussions she even broached the subject of delaying law school so she could continue her restoration work with Francis

Edmunds. She lamented, "No doubt my father will be disappointed, but he'll understand I'm not ruling out law school altogether."

Occasionally, Lawton wanted to flatter himself into believing she might also be curious about how strong was their relationship? Yet, he remained humble. It wasn't difficult to recognize her mind was on choosing between the fulfillments of restoring antebellum homes versus the sense of obligation for attending law school. As for himself, he had to admit his meeting Laura Waring was having an impact on his future thoughts. With plenty of female friends back in Minnesota, he'd always figured marriage would be later anyway...just considering his own folks. His father didn't marry until he was thirty-two years old. For Lawton, that always seemed soon enough. Now something was breaking down that assumption.

*   *   *

For that last Friday of July Lawton took it upon himself to invite everyone including Laura to his eighth floor residence at the Hotel for drinks followed by dinner on the large hotel patio outside his suite. With that breathtaking view it was a private and relaxing place to talk. His suggestion of 7:00 for drinks was met by affirmative replies from all invitees.

Ashley arrived early like he always did. Lawton arranged to have his friend's favorite beverage on ice waiting for him...and it wasn't ice tea. Ashley and he always caught up on the happenings of the city even if it had only been a day since they'd seen each other. That night Ashley seemed bent on discussing Laura Waring.

The younger man, as he often did when he preferred not to discuss a subject, acted ignorant. Conveniently, Laura arrived before the friendly interrogation became too pronounced. The conversation then turned to more topical items...like the current renovation she was working on.

Henry and Lill arrived at their normal time.........about fifteen minutes late. Off in the distance beyond Sullivan's Island the sky was being lit up like a Christmas tree. The thunderstorm was forecast to miss downtown Charleston. Henry and Lill were especially interested in discussing some other restoration projects with Laura while Ashley renewed his nosy attack on Lawton about the young lady in their midst.

Lawton finally asked the waiter to have dinner served just to end Ashley's banter. For the next hour, the five of them enjoyed each other's company. When after dinner drinks were served, Ashley sardonically asked when Henry was going to give his patented line, "So, where are we at in the story, Matt?"

Lawton was prepared and so much more confident in taking charge of the interview sessions. With his voice strong, he brought the group up to date. "Henry, when we left off after the boat cruise a week ago Sunday, you had just been visited by those two lugs from Chicago named Vinnie Spagatini and Bert Bertinelli. Luckily they were more interested in directing their attention towards eliminating Whitey Malooley and Billy McCoy…or, I guess you'd probably not be telling your story right now."

There was laughter except for Laura. Her eyes opened a bit wider than normal.

Lawton continued, "You said the blatant lies you told them were persuasive enough that the two mobsters allowed you to go free…with the understanding you'd assist in bringing Malooley and McCoy out into the open."

Henry nodded satisfied that Lawton's notes were accurate enough.

Then Lawton grinned, "I must say, for a man whose namesake back in Glenwood had been "Honest Henry Hanson", I find your first instinct to deceive these two Chicago hitmen to be highly inconsistent."

Henry knew he was being kidded, but replied very candidly, "Matt, you had to be there. My stomach was grinding. I felt the noose around my neck. When that's the case most people including me will say whatever you need to say to survive."

Lawton stopped smiling. Henry's point was made.

Unruffled, Lawton offered a starting place. "Henry, could you bring us up to date on how Spagatini and Bertinelli finally crossed paths with Malooley and McCoy?"

"Oh yes," Henry said as he placed a thin cigar in his holder. "First, however, I'd like to fill you in on two more chaps who we know quite well. Matt, your father and Charlie Davis would enter the story that July weekend in 1933 as well. You'll see again how your father and Charlie Davis operated together back then…..and, I must say, how they still seem to cooperate with each other today. In all my years I have never met two more compatible friends. They would do anything for one another and giving each other a hard time every step of the way... at least until they had to take serious action. I've been very fortunate to count them as friends.

As he lit his cigar, Laura sat close to Henry as if not wanting to miss a word.

"I give Charlie the credit for this part of the story. He's told this tale many times over drinks and each time it's more entertaining. I'll try to reduce some of Charlie's hyperbole though I risk making it less amusing.

Anyway, he was having dinner with Jamie and Lindy and a few of their mutual friends at the Minneapolis Club that Friday after Jamie had flown me to Madison, Wisconsin two days before. He'd shared with your mother and father, Matt, that I was likely still on the road back to Charleston, but figured I was safer in doing so. Knowing I'd be stopping at Lookout Mountain, Tennessee to see Sally Carter that evening, he half hoped I'd remain there until Malooley and McCoy might be rounded up.

Charlie had already planned on traveling to Charleston once the two gangsters were in jail. Because he knew a bit of their history with Loni D'Annelli, he expected to be the primary negotiator in getting the two hucksters off my back. However, that very night he had to move up his travel plans. He received a call at the Minneapolis Club from Sally that she couldn't persuade me to remain a couple extra days in Chattanooga.

Jamie noticed Charlie's discomfort immediately and matter-of-factly asked, "So, there's a new problem with Henry. What time are we leaving in the morning and where are we going?"

My entry into their lives the previous week automatically made me part of their secret accord with the two Baileys. They had to do everything in their power to save me just as they would each other. With the actions by Malooley and McCoy at the St. Paul train station, Charlie again made the assumption the two hoods' primary aim was blackmail and not murder. That gave them time to discuss some defensive strategy.

Before they left the dinner club that Friday evening, Jamie had called and checked into the fastest method by air that he and Charlie could make it down to Charleston. They went home immediately to get some sleep before the early flight out of Wold Chamberlain Field very early the next morning.

Lindy was also able to help in her role as head of the U.S. Attorney's branch office in Minneapolis. She called her U.S. Attorney contact in Charleston and asked him and his office to be on the lookout for Malooley and McCoy. She told them if the two gangsters were found to hold them on any charge...even if it was a late payment on a traffic ticket...until Charlie and Jamie could see them personally.

Saturday morning, July 8, Charlie and Jamie got on a plane that would eventually get them to Atlanta later that day. Jamie hadn't told Charlie, but he knew they'd have to ad lib a bit in order to gain a flight from Atlanta into South Carolina. Northwest Airlines was making daily flights from Minneapolis to Chicago in 1933. Also, American Airlines was flying between Chicago and Atlanta. Although he didn't like flying, Charlie was a bit more contained given it would be a supposedly safer passenger flight. His only previous flights were on Jamie's biplane which would cause most people to swear off flying. It took him only two flights in your father's biplane before he ended his interest in that form of travel. Kissing the ground after the second flight, Charlie had proclaimed, "God wants me to see several more years on this earth. He'd be disappointed if I chanced seeing Him too soon."

Unfortunately those commercial flights were not well coordinated and Jamie had to find some alternative. Jamie explained to Charlie on the way out to Wold Chamberlein Air Field that the two of them were going to fly a couple of mail routes. The plane they were to use was called a Ford Tin Goose Tri-Motor. Charlie liked the part about the "Tri-Motor" but he didn't like the "Tin Goose" description. At least the cockpit was enclosed and it had a single wing.

Jamie was very positive about the freight plane. He told Charlie he could sleep in the back of the plane. Charlie interpreted that to mean he could throw up in the back of the plane.

The flight plan took them to Chicago, then to Cincinnati and then onto Atlanta. Jamie didn't mention their next challenge. He hoped he could be a substitute pilot for another mail route plane to Charleston, but that possibility was not a sure thing...especially on a Saturday.

Everything went smoothly until Atlanta. Then it took a bit of inspired hijinks to keep them from being marooned at that air field. There were only two air mail carriers available Saturday evening and they were not earmarked for Charleston. Moreover, the airport supervisor saw no reason for mail delivery on a Saturday evening. It took Charlie walking down the road to a bar, borrowing the telephone, calling that same airport supervisor and claiming to be the Postmaster General needing one of his planes in Charleston, South Carolina right away. He and Jamie had their plane.

That last leg of the two-hour flight from Atlanta to Charleston was harrowing for Charlie. He liked seeing places where the plane could be set down in case of engine problems. The terrain underneath them in that part of South Carolina was mostly swamp, marsh, or forest.

It was almost dark when Jamie was able to get a visual on Charleston and eventually find the airfield. His flight map showed a landing strip cut out of the trees and marsh miles from the city. He was lucky to spot the small airfield. If there had been inclement weather, he was certain he'd have had to land on a highway which didn't bother him in any way. Charlie's heart would likely have given out.

After the precarious but successful landing, finding a ride into Charleston proved a further trial. Taxis sat out at the airfield only when scheduled passenger flights were arriving. A mail plane landing at sunset didn't earn that type of respect.

Finally the airfield manager offered them a ride into town… for $5.00…as soon as he closed out his chores for the day. It wasn't the example of southern hospitality they were looking for, but they finally made it into the city well past 10:00 Saturday night. They were exhausted and checked in at the East Bay Street Hotel hoping to have a message from Lindy's U.S. Attorney contact in Charleston indicating Malooley and McCoy had been picked up. Unfortunately there were no messages.

They then went to their rooms to sleep. It had been a fatiguing day and they figured they'd have plenty to do the next day. The only people Charlie knew at the hotel were Lill and Ashley. He'd talked to them countless times in the last year on the phone. They'd never divulged that Henry Granville was Henry Hanson. Living up to his word, Charlie never asked about Henry Granville's background either. The three of them, although never having met, got along famously.

As they took the elevator to their rooms Saturday night, they of course had no idea earlier that evening Malooley and McCoy had made a brief appearance at a hotel function. They were also operating in complete ignorance that Vinnie Spagatini and Bert Bertinelli were also in the city...in fact, staying in the same hotel.

Long after Malooley and McCoy had left the hotel function that night, Spagatini and Bertinelli were returning from their night on the town as Lill and I were leaving the hotel. I was tired and not very attentive. I certainly wasn't looking for anyone else besides my two pursuers. I certainly wasn't aware of Spagatini and Bertinelli suddenly stopping and staring at me in the lobby.

When they saw me getting into my roadster with Lill at the front of the hotel, they almost tripped over one another. Not only did they find the replica of the man the St. Paul cop had described but they recognized who I really was as well. Despite my disguise they'd seen me enough at Chippewa Lodge or in Glenwood each summer. It came to them right away why their targets, Malooley and McCoy, had gambled their secrecy and were in pursuit of Henry Hanson.

By Sunday morning they had already found where I lived in Mt. Pleasant and were about to pay me a visit at my home when they saw Lill take off and me doing the same a few minutes later. They followed my roadster into town looking for the right moment to pounce on me. That's when the incident by St. Michael's Episcopalian Church happened and they forced me to drive over to White Point Garden for our personal discussion.

After that Sunday morning encounter with them, my mind was in overdrive. I knew I was in a heap of trouble. Leaving town was not an option like it had been when I vacated Glenwood. I now had too much invested in my new life. The only thing I could think of was to handle one set of gangsters at a time. Helping Spagatini and Bertinelli find Malooley and McCoy seemed like the best course of action. My schedule would give Malooley and McCoy plenty of opportunity to spot me; I just didn't like the fact that I would be the bait leading to their deaths. After all, they weren't out to kill me or they would have done so back in Minnesota.

My mind was in a jumble as I drove those few blocks to meet Lill at the hotel. The weekly Sunday brunch at the hotel patio would begin at 11:00. The last place I wanted those four gangsters to tangle with each other was at the hotel.

I still wasn't ready to tell Lill anything. She was in her office getting ready to attend the church service over on James Island. I begged off saying I had some paper work and wanted to be at the hotel for the start of that day's brunch event. She didn't object which surprised me saying she'd see me later at the brunch. What I didn't know, of course, was that she had her own plan in progress to deal with Malooley and McCoy...a plan she didn't want me involved or to get in harm's way.

Accompanying her down to the hotel front entrance, Thomas Brown greeted us and had her car waiting. Looking across the street, I located Vinnie Spagatini and Bert Bertinelli sitting in their rental car. It was obvious I was going nowhere without the two of them following me.

Lill took off for James Island as Thomas and I stood there. He seemed preoccupied as if wanting to get something off his mind.

He finally murmured, "Henry, did you or Lill ever figure out what those two greasy looking characters prancing around the hotel event here last night wanted. They made me uncomfortable even looking at them. When they called on Miss Lill a couple days ago, I thought the police had picked them up. But, there they were last night, still nosing around. I had Benjamin follow them just to see where they were staying. He got the address over on Wolfee Street. He said the place their staying matches their looks."

That was the first time I had any hint Malooley and McCoy were actually in Charleston and had been for a day or two. My plans that morning changed in that instance. Having the address from Thomas, I unexpectedly had another card to play. Given the deceiving mode I was in, an idea sprung forth.

Wasting no more time contemplating, I went back into the hotel to appease Spagatini and Bertinelli sitting across the street. Without breaking stride, I exited a rear door and hailed a cab. It was an impulse and for what I wanted to do, no one could follow me.

The cabbie looked at me curiously when I told him the address off North Meeting Street. It was definitely not one of the neighborhoods any reasonably well-dressed and intelligent man would want to venture.

He dropped me off a block from the rooming house address Thomas had given me. All the way over, the taxi driver kept asking if I had the right street address. He made the crack, "If I had a Wolfee Street property in this area named after my family, I wouldn't admit it."

He was right. Without a doubt that street was located in one of the more decrepit parts of the city. There were people sleeping on the curb or looking comatose as they leaned against a door trying to recover from their previous night's binge.

I walked purposely to the dirty rooming house address and carefully opened the door. The guy behind the desk was asleep. I looked at the roster of guests and saw John Smith and Tom Johnson in Room #410. I thought, 'God, no imagination…some very appropriate Midwestern names as if these aliases were supposed to hide their identities!'

Ascending the creaky stairs, I was forced to vault over one of the boarders who'd apparently chosen to sleep on the staircase rather than his smelly suite. Wasting no time I simply walked into Room #410.

The space had little ventilation and took on the smell of sweat and booze that permeated the entire four-story complex. It was not my idea of a great evening in historic Charleston.

The two guests hiding out in this horrible cubicle, Whitey Malooley and Billy McCoy, began scrambling around the room as if they had woken up in Hell and were about to be offered a better room further from the main fire. Malooley was looking for his pants to find his revolver; McCoy was crawling across the floor fumbling for his own clothing. Running around the dark, dingy room like chickens in a henhouse, they had to wonder why the intruder had not knifed or shot them yet.

It was at that point I turned on the bedroom lamp and sat down. They stopped in mid-flight as their eyes focused on their guest. They couldn't have been more astonished if I'd been the second coming. Now it was up to me to carry out the impulse I'd had. With the confidence from that morning's deceit with Spagatini and Bertinelli, I launched into an en core that even amazed me. My only guide was that I was dealing with criminals. There were no rules except believability.

Breaking the silence, I spoke. "Gentlemen," I said with false courage, "I'm here to save your lives if you're interested. If you're not concerned, I'm walking out of here unharmed…or you'll have the entire Charleston municipal and county law enforcement group on your collective asses before you can breathe a decent cubic inch of outside air. I'll give you ten seconds to tell me you want my help. One….Two…"

It was Malooley who showed the brains. He responded surprisingly under control. "Hanson, you're in a tough spot to be so self-assured. You've got the floor...for now."

I kept my bland cadence and continued. "You apparently have been searching for me for a long time. I believe after two years, it's time we come to some kind of understanding."

McCoy slowly sat down not saying a word. Malooley kept his eyes leering at me.

I went on. "I know you're after something...probably the D'Annelli money you think I have...but we can cover that misinformation later. You two fellows might just be interested in something that happened to me this very morning. I was impolitely asked to join two other gentlemen from Chicago. We strolled through that park near the harbor. I must say they were not very friendly and they seemed determined to meet up with the two of you. You might know them...Vinnie Spagatini and Bert Bertinelli."

Malooley and McCoy sat on their beds in stone cold silence.

"Anyway, by the degree of their spite toward the two of you, I was very pleased I was not their primary target. Unfortunately I found out you boys have the star billing! They made the trip down to this beautiful city just to meet up with the two of you."

McCoy looked at his partner and spat, "Spagatini and Bertinelli...those were the guys who lost the most after Loni's arrest. How did they find us? It had to be that damned St. Paul train station. They found out who we were pursuing and where he's now located."

McCoy looked back at me with animosity in his eyes, "Where are they, Hanson? We'll take care of them before lunch. Then we'll sit down and have our little discussion."

Undaunted, I kept their attention. "You may want to think twice about that plan. Because of your St. Paul train station disaster, you've got more than just Spagatini and Bertinelli looking for you. The local cops have your description as well. You guys would be better off if you dressed in drag for the duration of your stay in this city. With your dark clothes, you both stick out like statutes in a park. You haven't even tried to blend in to the local style of dress. Are you trying to get caught? Has two years in hiding affected your brains?"

McCoy didn't like the way I was talking to him. He barked, "Hanson, you have a lot of guts breaking into this room. We could shoot you right now...as a burglar."

I ignored McCoy and turned toward the brighter Whitey Malooley who was also the calmer of the two. "Whitey, you guys are looking for something from me. You've apparently had a chance to kill me, but haven't done so. That tells me you need me alive for whatever you want. I'm at a loss. What do you want to know? Or, do you think I have something that doesn't belong to me?"

Malooley actually seemed fascinated the way I was confronting the two of them. He was very upfront with his response. "Hanson, since Loni was killed in Chicago, we've been on the run. We've been looking around every corner knowing that any number of guys from Chicago could be looking to eliminate us like they did Loni. We think you walked away with a lot of the money stored in that mill. Frankly, after observing the two lake resorts you probably own in Minnesota and your impressive hotel here in Charleston, how could we not think that way? How else could you have afforded these properties?

I was equally impressed with Malooley's sound...and true... summation. I looked at both their faces and sensed that William Jennings Bryan couldn't dissuade their thinking in a thousand years, that is, if honesty was the rule. Since it wasn't, in the next five minutes I would tell them untruths that would have all of our heads reeling.

I began with the truth...and then wavered as needed. "Whitey, you're absolutely right. I was aware of the counterfeit money and the other assets Loni had stored in the feed & grain mill basement. But, my question to you boys is how much money did you find missing? I'm certain you knew every coin that was down that basement storage area at the mill. Isn't that correct?"

I was relieved to see them flinch nervously. I was certain no one except me had ever accurately audited how much money was actually stored in that mill basement. Their looks of confusion confirmed my thought.

Then my lies flowed like syrup. "It may surprise you to learn that I never touched a dime. Obviously I certainly thought about it. But, with D'Annelli I was overmatched. I would never take on a man who could douse my lights with a snap of his fingers."

McCoy started to chew on his lip realizing what I was saying was difficult to refute. Malooley just looked like he didn't want to believe me.

I relaxed a bit and continued. "Actually I was too close to Loni's business interests. When I became aware of some law enforcement people nosing around the town that weekend of the golf tournament at Chippewa Lodge, I decided to leave town. I had planned a trip anyway. I had a built-in excuse. In previous years I'd taken a long two- week break after the annual Glenwood festival and charity golf tournament.

Impatiently, McCoy interrupted, "Let's get to the point. How did you come to own those lake resorts in Minnesota and this big hotel in Charleston?"

I was ready with my response. It had worked so well earlier in the day with Spagatini and Bertinelli. I repeated, "Gentlemen, I don't own the properties you speak of. A lawyer up in Minnesota has a group of his friends that collectively own those resorts and the East Bay Street Hotel. In fact, some in the group of investors knew the former County Sheriff Petracek and Police Chief Brey. After these two men resigned their positions in Glenwood, they were asked to eventually manage the two resorts for the consortium. That group eventually got in touch with me and asked me to redesign and build the hotel here in Charleston. I'm just in charge of group sales, so I travel to find business or association managers looking for meeting sites. I have to travel a lot, but it sure beats managing a feed & grain mill, don't you think?"

I could tell the two men were dazed. Malooley showed his doubt. "So...why the Henry Granville alias?"

My answer was quick. "I didn't want to be found. People like you might think I had something to do with Loni's arrest. Why would I want him arrested? Think of the good he did for the town. Why would I want that to end? That was why I worked with him for so many years.... for the benefit of the town."

The two sleepy gangsters were staggered. It was difficult to find fault with my cascade of lies. Every question they asked I had an expedient response with just enough truth. I sensed they were forgetting why they despised me.

More confident, I continued the sham. "Gentlemen, my question is simple. Why do you think a small town mill manager would have the guts to take one cent of a racketeer's money? That doesn't mean

I didn't dream what I could do with even a small amount of that money, but I valued my life more than that money."

Judging by how their heads were hanging, I sensed I had them baffled so I took that chance to change the conversation over to their own fates once again. "I think you fellows have more to be concerned about than me anyway. You were easy to find…too easy. Your mob cronies have marked you for death. Getting back in the mobs good graces isn't likely. How has it felt having your future built around the big target emblazoned on your chest?"

The two of them were silent. Their saturated minds were spinning with the realization I had little to offer them. With such limited options, I almost felt sorry for them.

It was then I showed some sympathy…all part of my impulsive scam. "Boys, I believe we have the makings of a deal. I might be able to help you and we can part company having no reason to see each other again. Face it…you don't have much of a chance of getting out of this city if the two contract killers smell your trail. And, if I'm not in my office in another fifteen minutes, the cops are going to come barreling down on you.

So…I ask you again. I have a proposition to help you…but it has to be done on my terms. You knew me as trustworthy during those years back in Glenwood. Loni wouldn't have dealt with me if I didn't shoot straight. It was tragic what happened to him, but he's now gone. I don't believe you fellows deserve his same fate. I can get you out of this city alive, but it would be wise if you found another area other than here or in Minnesota to continue your line of work."

Malooley and McCoy briefly looked back and forth at each other. When Malooley turned toward me and simply nodded, I believe that was one of the most breathtaking moments of my life. This was the second set of career hoodlums I'd deceived that Sunday morning and it was not yet 11:00.

Now my mind was clicking on all cylinders. I had to think of a way to get these two mugs out of town without them being seen by their pursuers. Then I could concentrate on the two Chicago mobsters who seemed at that moment much more dangerous to me besides the two hoodlums in that flophouse."

Henry then smiled awkwardly, leaned back and just gazed off into the blackened night. He seemed in another world as he contemplated those past times. Ashley for once didn't make a jab at his friend. He also seemed to be lost in those days. Lawton had the feeling both men knew they'd been very lucky back then.

Henry then turned his attention toward Lawton and chuckled. "Matt, a lot was going on that weekend in 1933. By later Sunday morning I was up to my tonsils in lies and deceit. Furthermore, I still didn't know that your father and Charlie were in town. I didn't know that Lill and Ashley had already been colluding about how to deal with Malooley and McCoy. All my close friends were trying to do the right thing in protecting me. And, I was trying to keep those same people from risking their necks for me.

While the others around the table leaned forward hoping there wouldn't be any further delay, Henry finally carried on.

"Matt, meanwhile another incident was happening to your father and Charlie after checking into their rooms at the hotel that Saturday night. All they wanted was a good night's sleep. Unfortunately, a couple undercover officers who were staked out across the street from the hotel under orders from Police Chief Calhoun saw the two of them enter the hotel after 10:00 Saturday night. The rumpled Charlie Davis and even Jamie looked somewhat bedraggled after their day long flights to Charleston. Their disheveled appearance spurred the two cops' attention.

One of the officers went into the hotel as both men registered for a room. All he had to do was hear one sentence from the loud and brash Mr. Davis and he knew he had two Yankees who might just match the culprits their chief of police had described. The call into headquarters happened before Charlie and Jamie got on the elevator. They had become primary suspects.

The result was your father and Charlie didn't sleep much that night. Their rooms were raided just after midnight by orders of the police chief. The knocks at their respective suites brought them out of a very short deep sleep. The police showed them a warrant for their arrest and handcuffed them. Nothing Charlie or Jamie could say was going to make a difference that night. The officers were determined to take them in.

Charlie nonetheless got his wind and began making loud protests about his rights being violated. Jamie told him to calm down. Complaining wasn't going to make any difference.

Charlie acquiesced. Jamie was right. They figured once at the police station they could make their one phone call to Ashley Cooper before they got lost in the Charleston judicial system.

Charlie kept his sense of humor as they were being led away. He pointed at Jamie and said to the cops, "This man here is the one you're looking for. He's completely at fault for whatever crime was committed. My mother warned me not to hang around with people like him. I demand a separate cell, especially if we're to be incarcerated for more than an hour."

Jamie just snickered too tired to come to his own defense. Even the cops started laughing at Charlie's antics. They already were sensing they were bringing in the wrong suspects.

Fifteen minutes later Charlie and Jamie were booked at the jail for attempted murder and kidnapping. Charlie Davis was laughing so hard his sides hurt. Jamie just grabbed a blanket, politely asked not to be shot at dawn, and then requested a quiet jail cell so he could get some sleep.

Charlie still demanded his one phone call. He asked for Ashley Cooper's number and the cops again broke up in laughter. Ashley was well known by law enforcement in the city, not for any wrongdoings but for his support to their police fund.

One of the officers told Charlie that Ashley wouldn't be home for another couple hours if it was a typical Saturday night. At that time it was 1:00 in the morning.

While Charlie and Jamie were sitting in the Charleston Municipal Jail, Spagatini and Bertinelli were enjoying the remaining hours of Saturday night with their respective dates. Bertinelli could not remember whether the woman lying next to him was to be paid or had he somehow hinted to her that he was marriage material. When she finally demanded full payment and wanted to leave, he was relieved.

As for Spagatini in the adjoining room, he had already bid his date a pleasant farewell following a quick tryst after midnight and becoming fifty dollars lighter in his wallet. He was sleeping soundly as Charlie Davis and Jamie Lawton were being fingerprinted and shown to their joint cell to be overnight guests at the local precinct house.

It was 6:00 Sunday morning when Ashley was finally located and ushered to the jailhouse to vouch for the two Yankees who claimed they knew him. Ashley was still wearing his white suit from the party the previous evening. He'd been tracked down as he was getting into his car out in front of the mansion at 2 South Meeting Street. With that light colored suit, his longish hair style, and his wavering walk, the passing squad car couldn't miss him. The patrolman asked if he minded coming down to the station to identify two kidnapping suspects.

Ashley was semi-conscious and was actually thankful he didn't have to drive his car. Pulling away from the large mansion on Meeting Street, he tried to recall the name of the former debutante he'd only met the previous evening. He had no recollection how they'd ended up at the large house since the party was at another location. He finally gave up. It was all just a fading memory."

The others stared at Ashley as Henry described that night. He showed no guilt only meekly saying, "How was I to know the punch was spiked? Whoever that woman was, she got me drunk. Shame on her!"

Lill only shook her head knowing the habits of her good friend. Laura didn't know whether to believe Ashley or not. Lawton only grimaced having a fairly good idea Henry told that part of the story quite accurately. After four months he knew Ashley's late night habits and they likely were the same back in the 1930's.

Henry enjoying the momentary embarrassment on his friend's face then continued.

"When Ashley arrived at the police station in his mussed white suit, it was 6:20 Sunday morning. He had everyone in the station chortling with his attempt at looking innocent. Police Chief Calhoun was even there to meet him, Ashley sobered up very quickly when the officer asked him, "Do you know a guy named Charlie Davis?"

Ashley broke up in laughter. As fellow members of my corporate board of directors, they had actually met only once on a business trip to Washington D.C. six months before. Charlie had never attended a board meeting in Charleston but would always be on the telephone with Ashley and me soon after the meeting ended.

Anyway, it took but that one evening at a grand gala at the historic Willard Hotel near the White House for those two characters to become fast friends.

Ashley's foggy mind did not keep him from having more fun that morning at the jailhouse. Upon seeing Charlie and Jamie playing cards in a cell he proclaimed Charlie not some crook from Chicago but most certainly a miscreant from Minnesota. Seeing Jamie he expressed only sorrow that Charlie's friend had been caught in the web of depravity conducted by the likes of his cellmate.

Jamie piped up and readily agreed. He'd not ever met Ashley but he liked the direction of the humor aimed at Charlie. Even the cops were enjoying the early morning banter.

Charlie just sat there nodding patiently. His only response to Ashley was, "And nice to see you again, Mr. Cooper. When you're done cracking jokes, I'd like to get back to the hotel, shower, and get some uninterrupted sleep before I have to look at your ugly mug again."

Ten minutes later Charlie and Jamie…and Ashley…were being driven back to the hotel in a taxi. Ashley was given the details of the attempted assault on me back in St. Paul the previous Monday. In turn he shared that Lill Hamilton had been visited by Malooley and McCoy at the hotel and that I had only returned to Charleston the night before.

Arriving at the hotel, Ashley then added a final note. "When I arrived at the police station this morning, Chief Calhoun wanted to talk for a moment and took me aside. He mentioned he'd heard from Lill Hamilton about two other gentlemen from Chicago who'd checked into the hotel on Saturday. It might be coincidence but the two men didn't match any descriptions about slovenly dressed northerners. However, their slick personalities and loud, accented voices did bring their attention to the night registration clerks. They called Lill and she in turn called Chief Calhoun to have them checked out."

Ashley then began fumbling for his pockets. "In fact, I've got their names right here on a scrap of paper. The chief told me to tell Lill when I see her this morning that the two Chicago men are legitimate Chicago businessmen who offer no threat.

As Ashley located his note, Jamie and Charlie began eyeing one another …as if something wasn't quite right.

Finding the paper, Ashley had a hard time pronouncing the names. He hesitantly said, "Those two gents' names are...ah... 'Spag...a...tini and Ber...ti...nelli.

Charlie no longer was paying attention to Ashley. Both he and Jamie knew Vinnie Spagatini and Bert Bertinelli very well from that fateful golf tournament at Chippewa Lodge two years before.

Jamie lamented, "Looks like the mob is still after Malooley and McCoy. The word got out that Loni's boys are heading for Charleston. We've got some additional players in the game and yet another threat to Henry."

All three were operating on practically no sleep and were no longer thinking straight. At that hour they figured nothing could be done. They agreed to catch a couple hours of sleep and meet at the hotel restaurant later that morning at the Sunday buffet. Ashley said he'd call Lill and set up a time for the four of them to discuss what next steps had to be taken. Their focus was on keeping me completely out of the picture and deal with Malooley and McCoy on their own. Now that those two hoods were being sought out by Spagatini and Bertinelli, it offered an entirely new set of circumstances."

The lightning still could be seen off in the distance up the coast toward Georgetown, South Carolina. The air was somewhat cooler and less humid. Henry stood up to stretch and rest. Lill got up and joined him while Lawton, Laura, and Ashley remained seated.

Ashley mumbled softly so Henry and Lill couldn't hear him. "Well, Matt, it must be astonishing to think that throughout your life this place, your folks and Charlie Davis have been an integral part of the lives of Henry, Lill, and me...and you never had an inkling this was the case."

He said it for Laura to understand. Somewhat surprised, Laura looked at Lawton for confirmation.

Lawton's nod was slow. "Yeh, that's quite true. Every interview it emphasizes why Henry's life has had to be so private. I've even contemplated whether it's wise for him to document his story...whether for legal reasons or not."

Ashley responded more seriously than normal, "I guess we're getting to the part in Henry's story where you'll understand that the situation back then doesn't only pertain to Henry. His story is mine. It's Lill's. It's Charlie's. It's your father's and mother's. It's Clarence Petracek's. It's Rich Brey's. I believe you'll understand why Henry has taken so long in relating his entire background to you. He wanted you to get a feeling of what has become of his life as well as so many other people's lives who have stood by him over the years. He wants you to truly appreciate the past and the sense of responsibility he feels towards others. If you haven't already realized why your mother and father never mentioned this part of their life to you or to anyone else in your family or to other close friends, it'll become even clearer very soon."

Henry and Lill then returned to their chairs and sat down. Laura was caught up in the tale and little patience for anymore delay. She blurted out, "Henry, so go back to that rooming house and tell us what happened with those horrible two men!"

The group all laughed. Henry, while humored by her interest, stressed an admonition before he continued. He whispered to her, "Laura, we've let you in on this little matter because you've become very special to all of us...or certainly maybe even more to one of us. You've got to remember to keep everything said in these interviews absolutely private."

Her eyes widened not realizing there'd be any doubt. And, when Henry mentioned how special she was to all of them around the table...and maybe more to one in particular, it was as if she woke up to another reality.

As Henry sat back ready to continue, her eyes looked skittishly at Lawton as he prepared to take more notes. The older man needed no reminder as to where to start.

Chapter 19

"I remember sitting in that sweaty flophouse on Wolfee Street after filling Malooley and McCoy with all those lies and deceptions and wondering if I could remember all the fabrications I'd just voiced. The three of us sat nervously looking at one another. I still wasn't exactly certain how they were going to respond. They'd been my pursuers for two years; now practically overnight things had changed making them not the hunters but the hunted. They realized their lives were at stake that morning. Their personal dealings with me had become suddenly quite secondary.

While I sat there listening to their desperate discussion as to what next to do, they kept returning to the same response...kill Spagatini and Bertinelli before they did the same thing to the two of them. I didn't want them to arrive at that conclusion and urgently interrupted them. "Gentlemen, you'd better rethink that strategy. If you kill those two fellows you'll have the entire gangster community hunting you down like dogs!"

McCoy was having trouble with my pretense of support for them. His hatred was so deep, yet what I was saying made too much sense. Malooley, the cooler head...and the more reasonable one...spoke to me hesitantly...even showing some regard. "O.K. Henry, we're willing to listen, but the deal has to include getting us out of Charleston safely. We'll decide later if and when we deal with Spagatini and Bertinelli. We'll need some cash...and your word that no trail will be left behind."

Malooley's request was a major victory for me. For the first time in two years I had a chance to put permanent distance between me and D'Annelli's former henchmen. All the way back to Charleston I'd thought the only way to rid myself of these lowlifes would be to reduce myself to their level. Now I had done so. Still I had doubts about the two of them living up to any agreement.

Irritably I muttered, "I'm not certain a deal can be made. If you think I'm actually going to believe this little thirty minute meeting in this hell hole of a room is suddenly going to make you guys disappear forever….well, I'm just not that gullible. I'm willing to help you guys out of this city and even give you a little seed money to temporarily assist you with food, clothing, and board. But, I need more guarantees that I'll never lay eyes on you two again."

McCoy of course reacted negatively to my tone. He vehemently shouted at me, "Hanson, I have my own way of making certain you won't have to be concerned about us."

He then looked at his partner and sneered, "Whitey, why don't we just shoot him now, take whatever money is in his wallet, and blow town. I think he's bluffing about the cops outside. By wasting him now, we'd probably be money ahead and get a head start on those other two jokers."

Malooley disagreed. "Billy, unfortunately Hanson is right. We made ourselves public. The cops or Spagatini and Bertinelli will find us unless we have some plan to get out of this city. We need to change our identities and set ourselves up in a different location."

Malooley was now in sync with my thinking, but I had to keep the pressure on McCoy. Hastily I said, "You'll have to trust me. My coming to this room alone should give you some reason to believe me."

McCoy started heating up again, but Malooley gave his partner a stern look before saying to me, "Keep talking."

I was devising my strategy almost as fast as I was relaying it to the two of them. I told them, "You'll need to check out of this rat hole immediately and be ready to be picked up in a 1933 Marquette Sports Roadster down the corner at Wolfee and North Meeting Street in about thirty minutes. I may or may not be driving the car, but just dive into the back seat when it slows and stay low. You'll be driven to a place over on James Island where I will arrange other transportation for you to leave this area permanently. I'll also get you some travel money.

While you're escaping, I will deal with Spagatini and Bertinelli. If things go right, they might also be in a big hurry by tonight to escape the eyes of the local law enforcement people. I plan on telling them the cops have been hounding the city for three days and not found any indication the two of you are even in Charleston. I know the police chief. I'll make him understand the actual descriptions of the two of you more closely match Spagatini and Bertinelli. Once out of the city, you two will have the chance to go anywhere else in this country, change your names, and start a different life if you choose.

The deceit flowed off my tongue so naturally. "Just remember, contacting me ever again will be like committing suicide. You can bet I'll find a way of defending myself. You have to remember I knew a bunch of D'Annelli's friends during those five years in Glenwood. I'll not hesitate contacting Spagatini or Bertinelli. Consider me no longer a target, but a trigger."

By their hunched shoulders, I could see their confusion and now their desperation. My final threat of contacting some gangsters in Chicago if they ever shadowed me again, that was the last thing I would have done. But, they believed that I would and that was what counted.

It was time to leave that wretched rooming house. I no longer feared Malooley and McCoy. I had manipulated a workable plan to rid myself of those two pursuers. Walking toward the door, they hardly looked at me. Before closing the rotted wooden door, I looked back and repeated, "A half hour from now on the corner of Wolfee and North Meeting Street."

Malooley actually showed an appreciative nod. McCoy was irascible as ever shouting, "We'll be there, Hanson, and that car better be there too."

I then left, but to this day I believe if Whitey Malooley hadn't been in that room, I doubt things would have worked out as they did.

Proceeding out the door I was not fully certain I wasn't going to get shot in the back if not by Malooley and McCoy, then by some other guest at the broken-down rooming house. I was lucky it was still morning and the scalawags in the dingy lobby and out on the street were still recovering from their previous night. Not until I hailed a cab on Meeting Street and was out of shooting range did I believe there was a chance of living through that part of the ordeal.

The taxi returned me to the hotel where I slipped through the supplier's door and up to my office without being seen. I was still of the mind that I had to work this entire matter out myself. The less people involved, the fewer people would get hurt. That was my thinking...and it was so flawed.

With my schedule tight having to get Malooley and McCoy out of town, I then had to figure a way of furtively leaving the hotel once again without being seen by Spagatini and Bertinelli still keeping an eye on the front entrance of the hotel. Nothing was simple that morning. Every step seemed to get me into a deeper quagmire.

Life was ticking on like normal when I entered the hotel lobby. The weekly brunch event had already started and Lill was waiting for me in her office having just returned from the James Island church services...or at least that was where she claimed to have been.

Trying to be nonchalant she said, "Henry, your clothes smell like booze and cigar smoke. If I didn't see you fall asleep last night back at the house, I would swear you'd been on a binge."

I didn't have time to enjoy any conversation. I spoke rapidly in tones she rarely heard from me. It was too difficult to hide my desperation and fear. As serenely as I could I said to her, "Lill, you're going to need to trust me and let me deal with a problem that's developed. I'll need your help right now...and please, no questions."

She was silent as I motioned her over to the second floor window of her office. Pointing to the two sharply dressed gentlemen now out of their rental car and sitting leisurely on a bench across the street from the entry into the hotel's circular driveway, I whispered, "Lill, those two gentlemen down there are named Vinnie Spagatini and Bert Bertinelli. They are checked into this very hotel and are following me in hopes of finding two other fellows they want. We all go way back. I can't explain the relationships just now."

Then lying, I told her, "I'm in no danger, I just need these people off my back so I can help the two other fellows get out of town. Again, there's no time for questions. I just need your assistance now. I have to be someplace in less than fifteen minutes."

What I've always liked about Lill is how she can recognize immediacy and not ask questions. She was heading out the door toward the lobby before I could say another word. Before the office door closed, she called back, "Henry, give me three minutes. Then take off from the back parking lot. I'll take care of the two gentlemen. Just call me as soon as you can so I know you're safe."

The office door closed and she was gone. I looked at my watch and began walking down the back stairs to the back parking lot. I wasn't certain what she was going to do, but I had long since learned not to doubt her. At the back of the main floor I stood out of sight. Not a minute later there was a loud clatter of celebration throughout the lobby as people from the brunch on the patio even came inside the hotel to see what the merriment was all about.

Spagatini and Bertinelli, showing great discomfort, were being ushered into the lobby with all employees applauding them. Even the two plainclothes policemen assigned to the hotel by Chief Calhoun had gotten caught up in the festivity. They'd not paid any notice to the two nattily dressed men sitting on the bench. Their appearance didn't match anything like the description given to them regarding the slovenly dressed Malooley and McCoy.

It was Lill who stood before the hastily created ensemble and greeted everyone. Her voice was strong and warm. "Ladies and gentlemen, we wanted to acknowledge Mr. Spagatini and Mr. Bertinelli as our first guests from Chicago at the East Bay Street Hotel. We've been looking for them so we could offer our hospitality and thanks for considering our humble hotel and great city for their next function."

Champagne was then offered. Leave it to Lill to create such a ruse. She'd literally walked across the street and rounded them up. Spagatini and Bertinelli were sheepishly accepting the praise and adulation having no idea what Lill was doing. Happily they accepted the free booze. Even the two cops were quite satisfied to get out of the sun and have a cool glass of champagne even though they were on duty...and Prohibition was still the order of the day.

I slipped out the side door and into my Marquette Sports Roadster. I was driving down Broad Street to Meeting Street before Spagatini finished his first glass of the contrived congratulatory drink. It would be twenty minutes before they realized I wasn't attending the Sunday brunch or even at the hotel.

It was just after noon that Sunday when I reached the corner of Woolfe Street and North Meeting. Churchgoers were strolling slowly in the growing heat back home. It was a poor part of town, but the local churches were usually filled. My new Marquette Roadster stuck out noticeably.

My intentions were not to spend a lot of time in that part of town. I wanted to find my two gangster 'friends' and be off. I had decided to take them to the First Presbyterian Church on James Island where I would find a couple parishioners who would like to make a

quick fifty dollars to drive Malooley and McCoy to either Columbia
or Savannah. I knew some very ominous looking church members who
could keep the two former D'Annelli associates in line.

As I drove thru the intersection, Malooley and McCoy were
exiting the door of an old General Store. Heading directly to my
automobile, they got in the back seat and remained low as I'd directed.
Accelerating my vehicle toward Hwy. 17, I suddenly felt the metal of
a pistol against my neck. It was the second time that day I'd felt that
sensation and both instances were unpleasant.

It was McCoy's cold voice that gave me the bad news. "There's
been a change in plans, Hanson. We thought it might be nice if you
supplied us with this nice car and the money in your pocket. We don't
trust that you can keep Spagatini and Bertinelli off our backs, so we
may have to just cancel you out of the picture."

That was when I started to sweat. I had no answer to their
sudden preference. I was given instructions to take Hwy. 17 towards
Savannah. They had called my bluff. They had no intention of leaving
me with what they perceived as the good life when their entire future
looked pretty grim. They had figured they were in a no-win situation.
It made them drunk with carefree power. I sensed their only concern
was where they were going to dump my body after they shot me.

Passing over the Ashley River toward James Island, I turned off
the main highway and headed toward Folly Beach. Both men put their
guns to my head and wanted to know where I was going.

I shouted at them, "Being dumped in a river is not my idea of a
nice way to spend a Sunday afternoon. You guys said you wanted some
money and I don't have anything on me. I'm going to go where I store
some of my money and maybe where we can come up with a better deal
for all three of us."

They didn't say a word and let me drive on. The sudden detour
gave me some time to collect my thoughts. Both gangsters seemed
satisfied with my interest in buying my freedom and my life. Experience
told them I was behaving more normally. However at that bleak point
in my life I had no illusions that money was going to spare my life.

Thinking of my familiarity with the newly renovated First
Presbyterian Church on James Island, I grasped another idea. Again I
yelled. "There's a church ahead. I'm a deacon and I lived at the church
when I first arrived in this area. I have some money hidden away there."

Lies...lies...lies...but it was the only thing I could think of to extend my life. They both shook their heads and laughed derisively remembering my days connected with a church in Glenwood, Minnesota.

I now had fibbed so many times my own head was spinning. With my knowledge of every back room and staircase in that church, I at least had a whimsical chance to survive. I also was depending on the church grounds being empty since the services had been over since 11:00. I knew many of the church goers were at the hotel brunch or had gone home.

Parking my car I showed no delay and got out of the car heading for the church entrance. Both men not knowing what was going on but not questioning my movements tried to stay with my rapid pace. The only thing going through my mind was to come up with something quickly or I may as well stay right in the church for my forthcoming funeral.

I practically jogged into the church and into the main vestibule without slowing my pace. Luckily no one was in the church. Malooley and McCoy were looking around as if mesmerized by the unfamiliar surroundings. I headed directly to the podium at the altar and up the four steps toward the church organ. I glanced behind and they had only made it half way down the church aisle. There was now enough space for me to make my move. I quickly ducked through a small back door behind the organ to the minister's private office. Slamming the door, I heard McCoy shouting, "Where'd he go? Where's the God damn door?

It was that moment I fled down a small hallway to an exit leading to the parking lot where I'd just left my roadster. Through the door and not breaking a step as I ran toward my vehicle, my heart went to my mouth as I heard a shot ring out and something whistle past my left ear. Then I heard the sound of another shot but strangely from another direction...as if the bullet had reverberated back toward the man who had shot at me.

Immediately there was a cry of pain and I realized it wasn't me. Looking back, one of my assailants, Whitey Malooley, was writhing in agony on the hot gravel of the parking lot after taking a shot to the left shoulder. I didn't slow down my run until I got to the safety of my Marquette Roadster. I turned quickly just to see where McCoy was located. And there he was...running out the same door I had just exited.

He was leveling his weapon and taking straight aim at me. Standing in front of my car, it looked like I had no chance to dive to the pavement before he squeezed off at least one shot. I took one more glance at Malooley squirming in pain on the gravel parking lot wondering if I'd look like that in the next second.

Closing my eyes to wait for the leaden bullet from McCoy's gun to enter my body, something strange happened instead. Before McCoy steadied his aim, another shot rang out and something hit his hands like an exploding bomb. His gun disintegrated in his hands and blood began running from his right hand. He fell back like he had just been kicked by a mule. I stood there in shock. There was Malooley in obvious agony by the front door of the church....and McCoy was sitting on the gravel clasping his mangled hand as he tried to stop the bleeding. Both men were in shock.

I looked around and could see nothing but an old 1923 Chevrolet Utility Coup across the road. It had not been there when we entered the church. The driver's side door was opened as if a shield. There was a man ducked down behind it.

The passenger side door then opened and both men made themselves visible. It was Charlie Davis and Jamie Lawton, both with firearms in their hands. They ran across the road checking to see first if I was all right. I kind of nodded blankly. Both of them then ran onto the injured men they'd just shot to further disarm them and tend to their wounds.

Malooley was hurt the worst with that slug in his left shoulder. McCoy was more angry than hurt. His right hand was definitely damaged.

Charlie tore off Malooley's shirt and applied pressure on the man's shoulder to stop the bleeding. Jamie simply frisked McCoy to make certain he didn't have another weapon on him. He then yelled for me to go into the church and call the police and an ambulance.

In a trance, I followed his instructions."

Henry stopped his story for a moment as he and the rest of the small group were staring at Matt Lawton to see his reaction. He had stopped taking notes and was just sitting in total astonishment. He could not believe what he'd just heard. His vision of his father was that of a very competent, polished corporate lawyer with a silvery tone to his blondish hair. His father's primary weapons were his brain, his voice, his legal mind, and his golf clubs. Visualizing his father and his lighthearted Uncle Charlie taking aim and firing at two human beings was totally out of their character...at least from Lawton's perspective.

He'd never given it much thought about his father, Charlie, his mother, or for that matter more recently Henry, Lill and Ashley as ever being his age and having the energy and spunk they all showed at that time in their lives. Now they were a generation older. It was overwhelming and humbling. Lawton wondered if he had the intestinal fortitude to have reacted as they had.

It was Ashley who got the young man out of his stupor. "Matt, are you still with us or are you going to be the cause of another postponement of this saga?"

Laura answered for him. She leaned over to Lawton and affectionately rubbed his face and scratched his head of hair to bring him back to the present time.

Still a bit dazed and reflective Lawton folded his notebook to a new page and nodded at Henry. "Go ahead."

Everyone's eyes returned to the older, creased face of Henry. He closed his eyes momentarily obviously reliving those moments at the church parking lot on James Island.

"The police and an ambulance arrived at the First Presbyterian Church on James Island within ten minutes. Thanks to Charlie, Malooley despite losing a lot of blood looked like he was going to make it. McCoy just stared at his right hand with Jamie holding a gun on him.

As those two gangsters were being led away by the police to the hospital, I couldn't help saying to them, "Boys, you could have been on the train for freedom right now. You should have known that I could be trusted! Life is full of choices...and today you chose poorly."

They probably didn't appreciate my parting comments.

The police asked me to stop over to the station to press charges. For a moment I wondered for what? They hadn't done anything to me yet. It took Charlie and Jamie to put my mind back in perspective. They said practically in unison, "Yes...charge those two bastards with kidnapping...and attempted murder. The magnitude of what had just happened finally became quite real. Those two charges alone could put the two men behind bars for a long time.

Though I nodded, I still had second thoughts as to how the situation should be handled. Given my growing stature in the city, the story would definitely reach the newspapers. Even national newspapers including those in Chicago could well carry the story. All I could see was jeopardizing people's lives when all I really wanted was to protect them...especially the two gentlemen who'd just saved my life.

When the police and ambulance pulled away, I looked over at my Marquette Roadster. Charlie and Jamie were talking as if they were just awaiting their tee time. I could not believe they had traveled to Charleston. I couldn't have felt more indebted.

Though I was shaken, they weren't rattled in the least. I tried some fake swagger commenting, "Nice of you fellows to come visiting. I hope you'll consider staying at the new East Bay Street Hotel while you're in town."

Then I hugged them both. I felt a pent up relief that had taken me two years to release.

When I'd calmed down, my first question was directed at their shooting prowess. I asked, "You boys looked as comfortable with a weapon as you do a golf club. Where'd you learn to shoot like that?"

Charlie broke in with a wry grin. "Jamie and I both thought we were going to be in criminal law, especially the way our first year of law school went. We weren't exactly at the top of the class...especially given some of the non-legal areas of interest we pursued. Turned out we met a few guys while going to school who became friends on the Minneapolis police force. They taught us how to shoot. They surmised with our probable incompetence as lawyers, this skill might be necessary."

I asked them how they knew where I was going and they just shrugged. Jamie responded, "It was Lill. We met her this morning and she asked that we not let you out of our sight. She even had an old rental car delivered to the hotel for us. We were only a block behind you when those two fellows jumped into your car. We had no idea they were Malooley and McCoy until you stopped at the church. Charlie and I agreed you should consider a better caliber of friend."

I could only shake my head. All the while I figured my life was about to come to an end driving out to James Island, the two of them were on my tail. We then sat down on the running board of my roadster and I filled them in on what I'd been facing that morning...including the impromptu meeting with Vinnie Spagatini and Bert Bertinelli.

Surprisingly they only nodded hearing Spagatini and Bertinelli had traveled to Charleston to carry out a hit on Malooley and McCoy. They got a good laugh as I informed them of all the lies I'd told the two hitmen. Even with them beside me, I didn't believe my future looked that bright. Once Spagatini and Bertinelli heard that Malooley and McCoy were in custody, they'd turn on me.

Despite my gloom, Jamie and Charlie just sat there on that running board sharing a drink from Charlie's pocket flask. They hadn't said a word, but they were both obviously deep in thought.

It took Charlie to apply the final insult to Malooley and McCoy. The rented 1923 Chevrolet Coupe was left on the side of the road across from the church. There was a bullet hole in the windshield and one of the tires had blown out. He would report the vehicle as stolen by the two injured gangsters...just to stick another charge on them.

On the way back to the hotel in my roadster they behaved as if the church parking lot incident was past history They kept asking me about the lies I'd told Spagatini and Bertinelli...and then exploding in laughter and patting me on the back for my originality. Both had the most mischievous smiles on their faces as we crossed the Ashley River Bridge...as if they were proud of me.

I wasn't as festive. I was certain Spagatini and Bertinelli had figured out that I'd deceived them. I expected them to be awaiting my return to the hotel anxious to wring as much money out of me as possible in some kind of quickly concocted blackmail scheme."

We drove along Calhoun Street toward the hotel as Charlie and Jamie kept mumbling to each other...sometimes quiet and other times snickering. They seemed hardly daunted by my situation. I could sense they were formulating some kind of plan.

Approaching King Street, Jamie told me to pull over by a small rundown café and park under a beautiful overhanging magnolia tree. Heading toward the coffee shop, Charlie mumbled, "Henry, it'll be just a moment. I've got a telephone call to make."

While Charlie was in the phone booth, Jamie just sat there relaxed, blowing his cigarette smoke out the window, and asking me random questions about the two Chicago gangsters who accosted me that morning. He just nodded...sometimes smiling...as I responded. He was the picture of a man totally unperturbed...completely the opposite of how I felt.

Charlie returned smiling. "Henry," he said, "We're going to make things a bit hectic for your two mob friends you saw this morning. I doubt the inconveniences they will be facing will cause them to leave the city, but we need them otherwise engaged so we have time to set up a larger plan to deal with them. In the meantime Jamie and I think we have a few more moves to make with Malooley and McCoy. They're in custody right now, but they aren't out of our lives."

Getting back in the car, he calmly continued. "I called Ashley to set up an emergency meeting of the Triple H Development, Inc. board of directors in about fifteen minutes at the hotel. Spagatini and Bertinelli will be on ice by then. Shortly they'll be coming into some very bad luck and will be hauled into the Charleston police station. They'll be asked to tell their whereabouts at the time of a murder in North Charleston that has absolutely nothing to do with them. Also, they'll be queried about soliciting prostitutes at the hotel last night, which is the only offense that has some truth according to some hotel staff witnesses.

Jamie then explained how Charlie and he acquired the firearms. "Your local police force mistook us for a couple gangsters. Charlie and I were detained the entire night. We finally got a hold of Ashley to help us out only early this morning.

Then he looked humorously at Charlie and said, "While Ashley and I were talking with the cops and signing exit papers at the station, my sticky fingered friend accidentally walked off with two law enforcement pistols…and some ammunition. We figured the trouble you were in, the pistols might come in handy."

Shrugging as if it was all in a day's work, Charlie then added something else the two hitmen would have to face with the cops. "When we get back to the hotel, we'll sneak these 'borrowed' revolvers into the hotel rooms of Spagatini and Bertinelli. When the cops search their rooms and find these weapons, those two slugs will have even more things to discuss when they're brought to the station. We need to keep those two occupied for as long as possible. The next hour of that Sunday afternoon worked like clockwork. Charlie, Jamie and I arrived back at the hotel and shimmied up the back stair case to the board room where Thomas Brown, Lill and Ashley were waiting for us. Spagatini and Bertinelli were still enjoying the royal treatment down on the hotel patio with the free food and drink as the Sunday buffet had long ended

Passing the 'borrowed' police revolvers over to Thomas Brown, he immediately wiped the weapons free of fingerprints. With the hotel house keys he snuck up to the two hitmens' rooms slipping those pistols into each man's suitcase.

As hoped, Charleston police arrived while Spagatini and Bertinelli were bleary-eyed with champagne and resting out on the hotel patio. They were told of the pending charges against them and were ordered to go down to headquarters to be questioned. They were also told they answered the description of two suspects driving away in a 1923 Chevrolet Utility found at a shooting scene earlier that day on James Island. The two Chicago men reacted humorously figuring they were being set up. They hardly showed concern knowing it was just a matter of time when the charges would be dropped and they'd be freed. Then they planned on getting their revenge against me.

Even when a warrant to search their hotel rooms was shown to them, they hardly cared. The brazen grins left their faces when the officers found the two missing guns...missing from the police station... with some slugs gone from the chambers. They now wondered how far this game was going.

While at the police station, Spagatini and Bertinelli heard more about the shooting out at a James Island church. The two hitmen learned that two 'gangster types' were being treated at the hospital before being brought to the station to be arraigned.

It didn't take much for Spagatini and Bertinelli to understand their targets had come out of hiding once again to take care of Henry Hanson. To the two hitmen they were pleased. Their targets would now be easier to find. Once the various trumped up charges were dropped, all they had to do was locate the hospital where Malooley and McCoy were being treated.

When they also heard my name having some connection to the shootings, they were astonished to say the least. First, they'd thought I'd been at the hotel the entire morning. They were keeping me under surveillance while I supposedly was going to roust Malooley and McCoy for them to complete their contract. Spagatini and Bertinelli were stunned that I had bolted from the hotel without them seeing me...then, got into an apparent gun battle with my two pursuers...and bested them!

They suddenly realized the Henry Hanson they thought they knew was no longer an easygoing former mill manager from Glenwood, Minnesota. The Henry Hanson they'd intercepted that morning had become a more conniving, secretive, and deceitful individual who could now apparently handle a weapon. While sitting at that city jailhouse on those bogus up charges, they also realized a lot of people could well be helping me.

They were street wise enough to also understand the story I'd told them that Sunday morning was a fabrication. The focus of their journey to Charleston, South Carolina changed in that instant. The Malooley and McCoy contract could be put on hold. Laid up in a local hospital under police guard, those two second-rate hoods could be dealt with later.

The two Chicago hitmen had little more to say to the cops. Expecting to be released yet that afternoon, they did have a legitimate setback. Police Chief Calhoun found background information indicating Vinnie Spagatini and Bert Bertinelli had some Chicago mob affiliation. They were held over that Sunday night until any pending charges up north were reconciled.

At dawn on Monday, all charges against Spagatini and Bertinelli were dropped. Breakfast was coffee and a hard roll of which both men ignored. By 8:30 the cell door was opened and the two men walked outside to a waiting cab. They were back in their hotel rooms ten minutes later.

The news of their release was called over to my office immediately by Chief Calhoun. By then my board had met and we'd formulated our own strategy to deal with both sets of thieves. With Malooley and McCoy recovering at the local hospital, it was clear we should deal with Spagatini and Bertinelli right away that morning.

As the two men cleaned up in their respective hotel suites, a messenger, Thomas Brown, politely knocked on each man's door. He presented both men an immediate invitation for a special breakfast in the hotel restaurant. He explained, "Gentlemen, our entire staff here at the East Bay Street Hotel feel so badly about the misunderstanding that took place with the local police. Not only will we not charge you for your rooms, but Mr. Henry Granville would like you to be his guest down in the restaurant as soon as it could be arranged."

The two conmen were in no mood to waste any more time. They agreed to see me in fifteen minutes. After the previous day, they were on alert I might be trying more hijinks. However, breakfast seemed innocent enough. The sooner they confronted me, the sooner their own demands could be discussed.

At a corner table in the restaurant, they were greeted not by me but instead by a taller man looking very relaxed in a sportcoat and open-collared shirt. That was as formal as Charlie Davis ever dressed. Both looked at him like they'd seen him before, but they couldn't place him.

Charlie got right to the point. He motioned for the two gangsters to sit. Without stating his name or acknowledging that he'd ever seen either man, he curtly said, "Gentlemen, I'm the General Counsel of the hotel and we are aware that you have some business interests you want to discuss with Mr. Henry Granville...or Henry Hanson as you know him. He works for this hotel and I'm here on his behalf. Apparently you have some false impressions that Henry is guilty of something... like taking money from a Mr. Loni D'Annelli back in Minnesota. Apparently you also believe he owns this hotel. Well, we could go through a litany of denials, but Henry believes you won't change your minds. With that in mind, we've decided to cut the games and find out what you want from this man.

Spagatini and Bertinelli were delighted with the positioning they were being given. In their game, if accused, the first thing to do was deny everything. They looked at Charlie Davis as if he was incompetent. He was apparently ignorant of the normal procedure. They now saw themselves in the driver's seat with a windfall of money about to be bestowed on them. They weren't certain whether I owned the hotel or not, but that was no longer important now that they were ostensibly dealing with the primary legal representative of the hotel.

Bertinelli and Spagatini glanced at each other with a glint in their eye...like their ship had finally come into port. They had the feeling they could ask for anything and probably get it from such a non-combative attorney.

They began looking around the hotel as if they already owned it. They were wondering whether they should drive my Marquette 34 Sports Roadster back to Chicago or take 1st class rail instead. Spagatini even showed his impudence by sarcastically asking, "So, where is your client? Is Henry planning another disappearing act?"

Ignoring the question, Charlie remained cold. "Gentlemen, you've proven your experience by seeing through our ploy of trying to intimidate you last night…though it was intended for your own good. We were hoping you'd be on a train back to Chicago by now. Disappointingly, that didn't happen. We were told that you slept very comfortably at the police station last evening. You must be very adept at getting away with murder."

Spagatini was the first to realize that Charlie's attitude was continuing to be strangely superior…almost arrogant. Based on what he was admitting, they were expecting the attorney to show more desperation and fear.

Spagatini suddenly flashed his short fuse. He leaned toward Charlie and hissed, "Listen you dime store lawyer, we don't feel like listening to you anymore. We have some demands for your client or he's going to have a very uncomfortable future. We have a few friends back in Chicago who feel badly about what happened to Loni D'Annelli two years ago. It's a situation where our associates don't like that Loni not only was taken down but was swindled by a small town feed and grain mill manager. He's done real well for himself.… with Loni's money. We think he owns this place…and probably other things as well. Your Mr. Henry Granville better be willing to share some of the dividends he's gained thanks to the D'Annelli money. Are you getting our drift?"

Charlie was purposefully provoking the two swindlers hoping to understand everything. He didn't hold back his disdain for the two hitmen. "I believe I'm feeling some kind of breeze…but it smells.…just like those spent shells that were used to gun down Loni D'Annelli in Chicago those same two years ago. I guess there was a limit how badly you two felt about D'Annelli's plight."

The steam began billowing out of Spagatini's ears. "Look, lawyer, we dealt with D'Annelli the way he deserved. Now we can see that Hanson was really deep into D'Annelli's operation and took advantage of his position. How else could he have bought this hotel?

Charlie showed no respect for the words from the two hucksters… and he'd just got more information than he expected. Spagatini, in his wrath, had just admitted being one of the shooters who brought down D'Annelli.

Now Charlie showed impatience as if he didn't want to be sitting with the two hoodlums any longer. While looking at his watch, he spat out, "Let's shorten this meeting. What do you want from Henry Hanson?"

It was Bertinelli who was more in control than Spagatini. He summed up what they would expect in order to keep their mouths shut about Hanson's involvement in the D'Annelli episode as well as the riches supposedly rifled from the Mill basement. "More specifically, he said, "We want a 50-50 split with everything Hanson owns. It's as simple as that."

Charlie, in a grandiloquent gesture, laid his napkin on the table and stood up saying, "Gentlemen, I'll get back to you Wednesday morning. I'll need to consult with my client. He's currently indisposed. You'll have our answer then."

Charlie then walked out of the restaurant with not even a glance back at the two hoods.

Spagatini and Bertinelli sat at the table looking at each other. They did not understand Charlie Davis' behavior. He didn't react to their demands. He simply said he'd get back to them. The result of the brief discussion was puzzling. They'd thought the cards were stacked in their favor, but they never felt in control.

They finished their breakfast uneasily but hopeful. The cops would no longer be bothering them. Waiting two days wouldn't be impossible. It might even give them time to take care of Malooley and McCoy before they were released from the hospital and brought to the Charleston jailhouse. Whether their targets were going to be arraigned in South Carolina or extradited to Illinois or Minnesota, Spagatini and Bertinelli wanted to end the lives of the two former D'Annelli associates before they left the city."

Henry paused to take another deep drag of his slender cigar. It was getting late. Lill picked up on his fatigue and suggested the meeting end for the evening. Her voice was soft. She and Ashley understandably knew much of the rest of the story and felt no rush for Henry to complete his tale that night.

She gently suggested, "Henry, it's late. Let's schedule another get-together. Matt's got plenty of notes to keep him busy in the days ahead."

Laura and Lawton didn't want him to stop, but their wishes didn't matter. Then again it was only the end of July. Lawton didn't want his purpose for being in Charleston to end too soon.

Chapter 20

The last days of July, 1960, ended a smoldering hot, humid month that only continued into August. Matt Lawton had been putting some time into completing his notes, but found little motivation for bringing the first draft of the manuscript up to date. He welcomed other assignments relating to the East Bay Street Hotel and hadn't suggested a time for what would likely be the last interview session.

When Henry made the offer for Lawton to accompany him on a business trip to Washington D.C. and New York City, he accepted enthusiastically without a trace of guilt for snubbing his main purpose for being in Charleston. Even his boss' attitude was slack. Each telephone call back to Mr. Brey in Minneapolis had his boss repeating, "Yes, my boy, you're doing just fine."

The business trip turned out to be as much pleasure as business. Along with Henry, Matt Lawton met ten association clients in D.C. over a four-day period. Their travels then took them to New York City where they saw only three clients. The remainder of the two days Henry and Lawton visiting the typical tourist spots...the Empire State Building, the Statute of Liberty, the United Nations Building, the home of Theodore Roosevelt out on Long Island and some prominent museums. Lawton noted Henry's enthusiasm even though the older man had visited these places a number of times in the past. Rarely did the manuscript ever come up in their conversation the entire trip.

Returning on Wednesday, August 10, they decided to make the upcoming Friday night the likely final interview session. That timing seemed acceptable to Lawton. Laura would be leaving for law school the first week of September and Lawton could arrange his first draft to be completed around that time.

Lill set up a dinner reservation at the main restaurant with that fabulous picture window view of Charleston Bay. The 7:30 reservation again included Laura Waring who had become a welcomed addition to the group.

Ashley arrived early and shared a flask of brandy in his coat pocket with Lawton before their other three invitees arrived. They conversed about the unfortunate Waring situation. Judge Waring had announced his resignation as a federal judge as soon as his Charleston house sold. In a newspaper article the Judge showed class in saying how much he and his wife would miss Charleston.

There was disgust on Ashley's face that Lawton had rarely seen. They both knew a highly qualified judge was being virtually driven out of his own city as a result of the man performing his duties so competently.

With the Judge moving, Laura Waring would no longer have Charleston to call her home. It left Lawton noticeably silent.

At that moment a radiant Miss Waring walked into the restaurant to sweeten up the regrettable conversation about her father and step-mother. Her look was so dramatically different from the blue-jeaned, dusty contractor Lawton had lunch with earlier that day. She was now the refreshed and attractive young lady he had become accustomed to seeing most evenings. The two of them had been spending most of their free time together which seemed to be more obvious to her parents, Henry, Lill, and Ashley than it did to the young couple. They still saw their lives as inevitably separated once September arrived. There was no real alternative in their minds.

Henry and Lill arrived only ten minutes late. Dinner was served immediately. Initially, all the talk was about anything but Henry's past. There was more discussion about the upcoming restoration projects Francis Edmunds would be bidding on. The topic of the East Bay Street Hotel and possible improvements in the facilities entered the conversation as well. Henry also intimated some other properties in Florida he was interested in buying.

With dinner completed, Henry seemed ready to proceed. After dinner drinks were served and to the delight of his dinner mates he picked up exactly where he'd left off from the previous interview session two weeks before.

Taking out his omnipresent thin cigar holder, he said, "Matt, I believe we were right at the point in our last conversation where Spagatini and Bertinelli were feeling very confident about the probability of blackmailing me into submission. Let's pick the story up from that point, shall we?"

Only the clanking of some dishes in the kitchen on the opposite side of the restaurant could be heard as Granville began.

"Charlie Davis took the elevator immediately up to the eighth floor after that awkward Monday morning meeting with Spagatini and Bertinelli in the hotel restaurant. He was heading back to the board room where all the Triple H Development, Inc. board members had congregated…including someone who'd just arrived. Sally Middleton Carter had been in close communication with Lill on Saturday and Sunday and had flown into Charleston the previous night on her private plane from Chattanooga, Tennessee.

As Charlie walked into the boardroom, there was Lill Hamilton talking with Ashley and Jamie Lawton. On the other side of the table he saw me talking with Sally and Thomas Brown. She looked surprisingly spry since I'd stopped by her home on Lookout Mountain only three days before. Seeing her in a wheel chair, we all expected her energy to be low. Instead, she had fire in her eyes and was anxious to hear the report from Charlie.

Everyone, including Sally, was up to date with the developments of the past two days. Before Charlie started, I had one piece of business to conduct as part of our official board meeting. That morning Jamie Lawton joined the board of directors as well.

The roundtable of handshakes was barely completed when Sally cackled, "It was bound to happen sooner or later, Henry. You've been traveling and promoting. Lill and you have made the East Bay Street Hotel a highly regarded and visible property in the southeast. You are and will become more and more noticeable no matter how much you try to hide behind your longer hair, your stylish beard and the southern plantation design of your clothing. We've got to set up a better defense in dealing with these damned carpetbaggers. We recognize the concern for the corporation as well as your life."

435

Then she turned to Charlie who'd she talked in the past but was only meeting him for the first time that morning. "So, Mr. Davis, how did the breakfast meeting go this morning with those two bastards?"

Everyone at the conference table broke up at my aunt's feistiness.

Charlie raised his cup of coffee to her and began. "We all pretty much have it right. Spagatini and Bertinelli know of Henry's connection to the hotel, but not his place in the organization. So, those two chums have no idea of his actual worth.

They were shooting from the hip and demanded half of whatever he owns apparently hoping he might have a piece of the East Bay Street Hotel. That ultimatum didn't surprise me nor did their threat about delay in paying them. They wanted me to pass along that without imbursement they'll have the mob in Chicago so tuned in on who and where the former Henry Hanson is located, he'll have regular guests from their brotherhood visiting Charleston and staying at this hotel. This could become another haven for gangsters much like Chippewa Lodge was back in Minnesota. There's no question we need to deal with Spagatini and Bertinelli very seriously."

There was silence around the table and I finally spoke. "Folks, one obvious solution should be considered. I could disappear for a while. I know this corporation is in good hands. The name of Henry Granville doesn't have to be the owner of Triple H Development, Inc. I could put it into a trust under all your names. It would verify to Spagatini and Bertinelli, or anyone else looking into my background, that I was always only an employee.

I tried to remain strong, but the entire group in that board room saw my shoulders sag slightly. I couldn't help it…and I know it pained them to see me in another bind.

Then they all started talking at once. There was Lill taking her loyal and loving approach saying, "Henry, you are going nowhere. Two years ago you were not really known beyond Glenwood, Minnesota. Now, you have become a well-respected citizen of Charleston and an equally well-known businessman in cities like New York and Washington DC. Having you evaporate into another time zone is not an option."

I tried to make my proposal more agreeable by adding, "I could sell all of my holdings and start over again. I've done it once. I could do it again under a new name."

Every head in the room shook back and forth. Charlie spoke for the group. "Henry…no….we can do better than that. This is just the first major test on protecting your future from your past….and it's not just you, others need protection as well."

Then he pointed to Jamie and himself as examples. "So, let's stop this talk about anyone disappearing."

Then in the momentary silence, Ashley clicked his glass of iced tea as he poured something alcoholic into the brew. Everyone turned towards him as he cleared his throat. "My friends, I have had the chance since late last night and this morning to rummage through an alternative plan with one Miss Sally Middleton Carter. We've done a bit more than just get caught up in family matters since she arrived. If we might, Sally and I would like to float an idea amongst our present board group that has a favorable chance of freeing our dear Henry from this quagmire.

While Ashley liked the stage, Aunt Sally couldn't wait. Characteristically she interrupted, "What if we find a way for them to take care of each other?"

The rest of us looked at each other like we'd missed something.

She looked irritated that no one was catching on. Impatiently she bellowed at me, "Are brains wasted on your generation? My dear friends…we have two lowlifes sitting in a hospital just waiting to be attacked by Spagatini and Bertinelli. They know their situation and they have to be feeling desperate. Ashley and I are suggesting we arrange the possibility of Malooley and McCoy saving their own skins by eliminating their pursuers? I believe they'd be highly motivated to listen to any alternative to the one they have right now at the hospital."

There were still many quizzical looks.

She continued, "We have to remember where these villains come from…the background they have…and that their word is no better than little turds floating in a contaminated pond."

Sally was not one to clean up her metaphors.

"The two hitmen have lived a life of crime and by now feel they're immune to justice. Well, Ashley and I believe we should deal with them in the same unsavory and hard way that they intend on dealing with not only Malooley and McCoy, but eventually with Henry."

Ashley then added, "The beauty of this idea is that we don't have to be involved in any of their violence. We're proposing to let those that live by the sword...to let nature take its course. Malooley and McCoy are due to get out of Charleston Municipal Hospital on Wednesday morning and then be arraigned at the county courthouse that afternoon. Those two already know their days are numbered, especially if they are extradited back up north to face charges lodged against them in Minnesota. That's where the mob will finish them off whether in jail or out on bail.

The only way Malooley and McCoy will live is to escape while here in Charleston. And, even better, if they get a chance to face the two hitmen on more favorable ground...let's just say the ensuing battle could be quite...deadly."

Charlie and Jamie stayed quiet as they pondered the merits of the idea. Lill and I didn't like a possible wild shooting to take place somewhere in our city, especially at the hotel.

Showing respect, Jamie inquired, "If I'm hearing this correctly, you're suggesting we spring the two gangsters who've been after Henry for two years and allow them to concentrate on two other targets who are staying at this hotel. I take it that little trick might need a little assist from us as well."

Both Ashley and Sally nodded in agreement.

Then Jamie scratched his chin while looking at Charlie. "You know, it's not a bad thought. It'll take some time to set up...and a little luck."

Then he paused before saying, "Yeh...I like it. I'm only sorry I didn't think of it."

Charlie for once was silent and just nodded. My mild-mannered friend, Ashley, was surprising me with his aggressive posture.

He wasn't done yet either. Ashley added, "If we can spring them and they take care of the Spagatini and Bertinelli matter, we should also offer help for them to complete their escape. We'll have to make it clear the consequences if they ever cast a shadow over Henry again. We'll need to make it clear their identities and location will be slipped to the Chicago mob any way possible.

The board room was quiet once more. People's minds were trying to consider the holes in the plan presented by Sally and Ashley.

Lill left no doubt her feelings. "I guess Malooley and McCoy are in no physical condition to just run once we helped them escape. With Malooley having taken a slug in the shoulder and McCoy's right hand damaged, they'll need more than a little assistance against those two hitmen. However, their survival instincts and some advantages we might give them should help them complete their task."

Again there was a silence in the room. Sally broke the stillness with her loud, impatient voice. "Are you boys going to keep staring at your shoes or are we going to move forward?"

Charlie chuckled, "It seems like a crazy thing to vote on in a board meeting. We're voting whether to help two villains escape incarceration and arm them so they can be freed to hunt down two mobsters sent to kill them. What happened to those normal issues we used to vote on regarding acquisition and business management? Do we have any other new business that's not quite so lethal?"

Jamie just leaned back and looked around the table before saying, "Let's roll." Lill had a stunned look on her face as she nodded affirmatively. I recall she mumbled, "Sally... Ashley...who are you two? I never want to be on your bad side."

There was some chuckling, but it ended quickly. Seconds later the whole group was talking about the strategy in springing Malooley and McCoy at the hospital. There was agreement that facility would be the only logical place for a successful escape.

Meanwhile Charlie and Jamie were whispering intently to each other. I had a feeling they were already talking about an alternative if the escape plan didn't work.

The situation over at the city hospital with Malooley and McCoy looked bleak. Malooley was lucky to have survived the serious wound in his upper arm. The bullet had entered his arm by the shoulder but fortunately it had struck no bone. Still he'd lost a lot of blood and the pain was requiring a lot of pain killers. The side effects of the medication made him woozy. He of course knew better than to tell the doctors he was feeling better. He was in no hurry to be checked out of the hospital and transported to the Charleston jail. As foggy as his mind was, his primary attention when conscious was whether there was any way to escape from the hospital.

To make it easier for the local cops to guard them, McCoy was right next door in an adjoining hospital room. Malooley could hear his partner complaining about his damaged hand. From check-in Sunday through Monday, neither was able to converse with one another. By Monday night both could communicate by having the windows by their adjoining wall opened. Talking softly, both agreed to continue to show they were suffering from their wounds. The more time in the hospital, the better chance they might see a way to escape. More pills were dispensed to both men. The used the medication sparingly in order to keep their minds clearer.

McCoy carried out his complaining with sincerity. His right hand was wrapped so tightly in a lower arm and hand cast that he couldn't tell if his fingers of his right hand worked or not. He was crying the blues that he wouldn't be able to hold a golf club properly.

At times Malooley had to chuckle. Here they were under felony arrest about to be extradited to Minnesota or Illinois, both were injured with twenty-four hour guards at their respective hospital doors, two Chicago hitmen were likely bearing down on them...and Billy was worried about his injury preventing him from playing golf. Malooley would have laughed harder but the movement pained his shoulder.

That Monday afternoon doctors concurred that Malooley's wound was not as bad as it first appeared. Though still heavily bandaged, both gangsters were informed they would be moved from the hospital to the city jail on Wednesday. From that prognosis, Tuesday would have to be the day they had to find a way to bolt from the hospital.

When Tuesday morning arrived, the medical staff removed the old bandages and applied a longer term wrapping around his shoulder for when he departed the hospital. The pain still kept him lightheaded, but he fought the need for medication. McCoy also had a new dressing placed on his right hand. While the bandages weren't as tight, he was able to move his fingers but it was painful. While he was somewhat relieved, both he and Malooley couldn't see any opening for escape.

It was under these circumstances in the early evening of Tuesday night, an older lady in a wheel chair from a local church rolled confidently up to the police guards insisting on visiting the two injured criminals as she had other patients earlier that day. She had a fruit basket for the patients and wanted to read them a bible verse.

The police normally would have rejected her entry into the gangsters' rooms, but that night figuring the old lady just wanted to display an act of kindness, they allowed her to speak to each man. As the guard stood out the open door, the lady rolled in and showed no fear of either hoodlum.

First, staring Malooley straight in the eye while handing him the small basket of fruit, she rasped quietly, "Our church would appreciate it if you would fill out the suggestion card in the basket. We want to know if our fruit baskets are being appreciated. She looked sternly enough at him while pointing to the small envelope that Malooley actually sat up straighter. Something was going on.

Then she repeated the same action in the adjoining room to McCoy. In his case he was rolling his eyes barely showing patience with her interruption. When she shoved his hand onto the envelope in his fruit basket with her eyes burning into his, even the dull-witted McCoy took notice.

When she finally rolled her chair down the hall requesting one of the two guards to help her, Malooley and McCoy had opened their small envelopes. Both notes said the same thing:

Spagatini and Bertinelli will be checking out of the East Bay Street Hotel on Wednesday. You'll not leave Charleston alive. If interested in defending yourselves, be ready at 11:00 tonight.

That was it. Both men didn't know if this was a set up by Spagatini and Bertinelli or legitimate help from some unknown person. But, they were not about to ignore an opportunity to escape.

The notes gave them some hope. Whitey's shoulder didn't hurt quite as much. Billy's fingers hurt like hell, but his carping lost volume.

As the evening progressed, both Malooley and McCoy had no urge to sleep. They watched the second hand move as if stuck in molasses. About 11:00 they both jumped when they heard some shuffling in the hallway outside their rooms. They knew the noise could be Spagatini or Bertinelli making their way down the hall to finish them off....or... it could be whoever was offering them the chance for freedom. They strained to hear as some discussion was taking place outside in the corridor. It sounded like a change of guards.

Then suddenly, a guard stuck his head in Malooley's room while another officer opened McCoy's door. The two hoodlums didn't know what to think when they saw in the semi-darkness both officers with masks over their faces.

The guards hissed the same thing at both injured men. "Get dressed. We've got to move fast."

Malooley and McCoy needed no other urging. A minute later both gangsters staggered out of their hospital rooms wondering if what was happening was good or bad. While the officers were holding guns on them, their hopes were definitely raised. It was apparent the masked guards desired to hide their true identities. If the guards had been Spagatini and Bertinelli, the two of them would already be dead.

The four of them stole down the hall through the exit door and then down a flight of stairs to the first floor where the two guards stopped. Malooley and McCoy had no idea what was happening but they put their faith in what they could only believe were two dirty cops being paid by someone to help them. Why anyone would help baffled them completely.

One of the guards checked out the back parking lot while the taller more intimidating guard kept his gun trained on the two injured men. Hurrying back, the other guard nodded his head indicating the coast was clear. No sound was made except the heavy breathing of the four men.

Heading down one more level to the hospital basement, Malooley kept asking, "Who are you? Why are you doing this? Where are we going?"

One of the guards finally whispered loudly, "Shut up! You'll know soon enough!"

The other masked guard then pointed toward the basement exit door and murmured, "Through that door at the top of the stairs is a Plymouth coupe. That'll eventually be your vehicle to drive your way out of this city…if you follow our directions and don't ask too many questions. But, you have a couple choices before we go further."

Malooley was straining to hear every word. "What do you mean…choices?"

The larger masked guard spoke matter-of-factly, "You can get in that car now and leave town. I can tell you you'll be chased down by the cops….or you'll eventually be found and murdered by Spagatini and Bertinelli."

In the dark of the basement it was McCoy who practically shouted, "Well for Christ sakes, thanks for the great choices! Why did

The Disappearance of Henry Hanson

you bring us this far if our chances for escape are hopeless? It sounds like you're just sending us away to be shot."

Still in the dark of the basement, the other guard snarled, "O.K., you've got another choice. Think about this. We're going to give you the chance to do something about the two men after you...Spagatini and Bertinelli...before you leave town. They are both staying at the East Bay Street Hotel in adjoining rooms #408 and #410. We'll help you get to the hotel and we have a master key for the fourth floor suites. They are occupied down in the hotel restaurant right now with some free drinks offered by one of the waiters. But, they'll be returning to their rooms shortly. We suggest you be in their adjoining rooms when they arrive. They'll be some weapons provided for you in room #410 under the bed. Once they do return, you'll have the advantage for a short time. Once they see the shape you two are in, they will be looking for a way to overpower you. Obviously, you'll lose if there's any kind of ruckus."

Malooley and McCoy looked dazed. What the guard was saying made sense. Something didn't smell right why the two of them were being offered a chance to escape, but neither man was about to question the true motives. The chance to neutralize the two hitmen would be a key if they were going make it through the rest of the night alive.

The taller guard continued to talk very fast. "If you want to go after your pursuers, go out and get in the back of the Plymouth. We'll drive you over to the hotel, and drop you off at the back entrance. It'll be up to the two of you to get Spagatini and Bertinelli out of the hotel and into the Plymouth. It would be a bad idea to waste them at the hotel. The gun shots and noise would only create noise and commotion. Again, you'll have the cops on your tail. A better idea is to take Spagatini and Bertinelli out of the hotel and out of town in that Plymouth. Once you're miles from Charleston, you can decide yourselves what to do with them."

There was a momentary chill that passed through that corner of the hospital basement. All four of them knew what the guard had just insinuated.

The other guard became impatient. "It's time to go. We'll give you five seconds to make up your minds....then, we're out of here... five....four....three.

Desperately Malooley and McCoy simultaneously cried out, "All right!!!

Without so much as another blink of an eye, the four of them moved out the basement door and up the stairs to the parking lot into the sticky, humid late night heat. The two injured gangsters crawled into the back seat of the Plymouth clarifying their willingness to go to the hotel. Both made minor groaning noises from their injuries but made no other comment. Their elation and relief suppressed any pain they felt.

Seconds later the guards were in the front seat heading for the hotel. As the car sped down the street, the guard in the passenger seat turned back toward the gangsters and added more detail to the escape plan. "Now listen carefully. Like we said, this vehicle is your transportation out of town. The element of surprise will be very important when Spagatini and Bertinelli return to their rooms. Don't delay. Get them down to the car right away and head out of town via northbound Hwy. 17 over the Cooper River Bridge. We can delay the cops learning of your escape only for a short time. That route will be the quickest in leaving the city. Just remember, any bloodshed at the hotel or in the city and the police will be on you like flies. If you stray from this plan in any way, you'll likely find yourselves back in jail no matter what happens to Spagatini and Bertinelli."

Then the guard driving the vehicle bellowed, "One final thing and let's be clear. You stalk Henry Hanson anymore at any time in the future and you'll be found and dealt with faster than those gunshots that hit you yesterday. Whatever you think regarding his worth or his guilt back in Minnesota better not matter to you anymore…that is, if you value freedom and good health."

Malooley like always was the one who had listened the closest. From the back seat his stunned voice could barely be heard. "Who are you guys and why are you doing this for us. There's no assurance we'll be able to complete our side of the bargain and force Spagatini and Bertinelli out of the hotel. Besides that, how do you know to trust us that we'll not come back after Henry Hanson?

The answer from the front seat by the guard in the passenger seat was surprisingly cordial. "Gentlemen, you're being given another chance at life tonight. We're doing this because you've done nothing to harm Henry yet. If you decide to come back after him in the next couple days or the next couple years, you should be aware simply by what we're able to do with you fellows this evening. We'll always be prepared never to let people like you bring harm to him in any way. We'll do whatever has to be done. If you don't want to believe us, we can drop you off at the county jail."

Malooley responded in an equally sedate voice. "We'll go along with your plan."

The guard in the passenger seat mumbled, "Good decision."

As the Plymouth pulled into the back of the hotel, the parking lot was quiet, just like a typical late Tuesday night. The guard who was driving stopped the vehicle by the dumpster, got out and promptly walked over to the maintenance door of the hotel. He was making certain it was not locked. He waved to the other guard in the front seat.

As the two wounded gangsters readied themselves to take on the next part of the plan, the masked guard still in the car leaned back toward them. In a hushed whisper he said, "We'll leave the keys under the driver's seat."

He hesitated slightly before making a final warning. He seemed more desperate as he spat out his final admonition. Grabbing Malooley's good arm he said, "And… one last warning and listen carefully…if there is a police chase…get out of the car! Don't hesitate. Let Spagatini and Bertinelli drive on. If you've maintained control of the situation, those two killers will feel lucky to get away from you. Their tires will be kicking up dust just to get away from those guns you'll have pointed at their heads. Remember…the cops may be your friends tonight, but only if you get out of this car before any shots are fired. There's no reason for four men to die tonight."

Then in a less fretful tone, the strangely helpful guard mumbled, "If you find yourself on foot, make your way back to this hotel. You'll be safer. Once here, you'll have the pass keys to get into the hotel through the back maintenance door as well as into those same suites on the fourth floor. If things work out, Spagatini and Bertinelli shouldn't need those rooms after tonight. Someone will be in contact with you tomorrow morning. One way or another, we'll get you out of this city."

Malooley and McCoy glanced at each other and shrugged. The plan being given to them gave them a better than average shot at defending themselves against Spagatini and Bertinelli. Beyond that, the rest of the plan left a lot of questions…of which there was no time to ask.

Slipping warily out of the backseat of the Plymouth, they shuffled slowly in the black night groaning ever so slightly from their injuries. Waving for them to hurry, the taller guard helped them through the maintenance door. He then handed McCoy the fourth floor pass key and whispered, "Go to Room #410; #408 connects it and the adjoining door is opened."

With his upper arm and shoulder heavily bandaged under his shirt, Malooley grabbed the guards arm and put his eyes very close to the masked guard's face. He said to the guard very earnestly, "We'll take care of this. You tell Henry not to worry about us anymore…and to have a good life."

The taller guard blanched under his face cover not expecting to hear such a genuine farewell from a gangster who was supposed to be heartless. He then watched the heavily bandaged gangster split up the back stairs behind his partner.

Meanwhile the other guard was busy performing another part of the plan that would be not known by Malooley and McCoy…and not even by his fellow guardsman. He ran over to another car, opened the trunk, and pulled out a two-foot by two-foot box. He brought it carefully over to the Plymouth and placed it in the trunk.

When his taller compatriot returned, that deed had been completed. They both stripped off their masks and their police guard uniforms. The key was placed under the driver's side seat of the Plymouth. Charlie Davis and Ashley Cooper took a deep breath and shook each other's hands relieved that the bizarre escape plot was so far moving along as planned.

Hurrying around to the side of the hotel, Davis looked up and waved to a man now seeing them from the eighth floor deck. With the return wave the two of them whisked along the sidewalk in the shadows of the semi-moonlit night and slid through an auxiliary entrance into the hotel. Now, they all had to wait and see if the two injured gangsters would actually follow the directions given them. There was also the obvious chance they would simply take out Spagatini and Bertinelli as those two men returned to their hotel rooms. It wouldn't be the worst finale, but I had been adamant not to allow any bloodshed in the hotel if at all possible. I was still concerned as always about adverse publicity that might rain on the East Bay Street Hotel…and in turn draw attention to me and the very people who were protecting me.

With that possibility of Malooley and McCoy shooting the two hitmen and then driving away in the Plymouth, Jamie was ready on the eighth floor terrace deck with a revolver overlooking the back parking lot. His eyes were now concentrating on the dimly lit Plymouth Coupe. If any shots were fired anywhere in the hotel, Jamie would shoot the tires out of the old Plymouth rendering it unusable. Malooley and McCoy would be immediately picked up by the police and shortly thereafter would face murder charges of the two hitmen. At the very least they would be incarcerated for life given the other charges against them as well. So, all of us in that boardroom would be safe either way. The only question at that hour of the night was whether Malooley and McCoy would be smart enough to carry through with our plan for their eventual freedom.

With Jamie outside on the deck Thomas, Lill, Sally, and I were waiting nervously inside the suite by the telephone ready to react if anything went wrong. There had not been much else for us to do but count the minutes.

Meanwhile Malooley and McCoy had made it up to the fourth floor but were interrupted by some bad luck. The head maid had just finished checking #401 and was exiting the room. She looked at them cautiously. Malooley stayed calm and greeted her with his good arm. Smiling he said, "Good evening, ma'am. We forgot something in my suite."

She looked at both men doubtfully and checked her list. "Yes... er... Mr....."

He interrupted her immediately. "Spagatini...Room #410."

Instantly she was satisfied. "Well, Mr. Spagatini, have a good evening."

Both men smiled at her as she strolled towards the elevator. She looked back as Malooley masquerading as Spagatini opened #410 with the master key given him by one of the masked guards. They waved back at her as they entered the room.

Closing the door they hurriedly checked under the bed for the two pistols as the guards had instructed. McCoy was astonished when he actually found the two loaded weapons. They'd obviously been planted when the two Chicago hitmen were out. Neither Malooley nor McCoy had ever experienced such support from people they didn't know.

Malooley opened the adjoining interior door to #408 and searched the other room. Their luck continued. A couple fifths of scotch whiskey were found in a suitcase in Bertinelli's room. Both took a long swig to settle them down. The last half hour had been fast moving and a bit perplexing.

It was another half hour later well after midnight when Malooley and McCoy heard footsteps and gruff voices coming down the hall. They were relieved not to hear any lady's voices. That was yet another potential problem they fortunately were able to dodge.

While Malooley stood in the adjoining room doorway with the planted pistol, McCoy huddled behind the entry door. When Spagatini opened his suite, he was discussing the two men having a 'night cap'. Those were the last relaxed words either man would say again that night.

When the light turned on in Spagatini's room, they had no chance to reach for their weapons. McCoy slammed the door shut...and Malooley moved to the middle of the suite with his weapon in his good right hand and arm trained on both hitmen. With their arms raised, McCoy quickly frisked them and removed two revolvers in their coat pockets and a derringer in a leg holster on Bertinelli.

The stunned look on the two hitmen's faces was gratifying to both Malooley and McCoy. The complete shock had left the two Chicago men momentarily speechless even though their minds were in overdrive trying to figure how to handle this new predicament.

Seeing the obvious injuries to their intruders, the two hitmen were ready to take any advantage without hesitation. Spagatini began speaking rapidly in obvious discomfort. "Whitey, Billy-boy, it's good to see you guys. It's been a long time. We didn't know you were in town or we would have invited you out for dinner."

McCoy scoffed at the poor attempt at deception sharply telling Spagatini to shut up. Bertinelli stayed quiet observing every detail happening each moment.

Malooley's voice was odious. "We know you boys are down here to kill us. The only thing that keeps us from pulling the triggers is the untidiness we'd create. One wrong move, though, and the room gets real bloody. Understand?"

Spagatini and Bertinelli nodded glumly.

Malooley continued, "We're going to take you gentlemen out of this hotel and go for a little ride. We need to find some quieter place away from this city where we can discuss all of our futures."

That was good news to the hitmen. Considering the injuries to their foes, both could see better chances to reverse the present circumstances.

No time was wasted. Guns were pointed at the hitmen's skulls as they left the suite and headed for the exit stairwell. Down the back staircase, the Plymouth coupe was waiting. Spagatini was ordered into the driver's seat with his partner directed to the back seat behind him. Malooley and McCoy took the other two seats so they could hold a gun on the man sitting next to them.

Spagatini was ordered to drive along East Battery. Feeling the gun pressed against his neck, he followed the command. Bertinelli seemed ready to pounce on McCoy in the back seat until McCoy put the barrel of his weapon right on the nose of the gangster. He barked, "Bertinelli, it would be a shame if you were killed in the backseat of this car with a bullet between your eyes. It'd be a hell of a way to die."

Bertinelli sat back swearing under his breath.

It was but a few blocks from the East Bay Street Hotel when the quiet night suddenly changed. Distant police sirens could be heard. Malooley's and McCoy's escape from the hospital had been discovered. It appeared the masked guards had only been able to hold off the police for too short of a time. Malooley pressed his gun harder into the side of Spagatini's neck and ordered him to drive faster toward the new Cooper River Bridge.

Minutes later the Plymouth approached the entrance to the toll bridge. Spagatini slowed only slightly as the sleepy toll operator had some coins thrown at him from the opened driver's side window. The dazed operator gave a half-hearted wave wondering what the rush was all about.

The sirens were getting louder. Malooley and McCoy glanced back and saw the flashing lights of some police cars off King Street already turning onto Hwy. 17 and coming in their direction. The two men eyed each other realizing their escape attempt might be coming to a close. Bertinelli and Spagatini waited to hear Malooley's and McCoy's next directives.

At that moment the warning from that shorter police guard in the car flashed through Malooley's brain… something about 'no reason for four men to die that night'…and then 'to get out of the car if pursued by the cops'.

That caution kept echoing in his mind until he heard himself holler, "Stop the car!" The shout was guttural...almost panicked. The car lurched to a stop.

McCoy looked at his partner oddly as Malooley bounded out of the car. With their pistols still aimed at the two hitmen, McCoy followed suit but not as willingly.

He yelled, "Whitey, what are you doing?"

Malooley ignored his partner and shouted at Spagatini, "You'd better take this chance to get away from us because you can bet we weren't going to make this a pleasant night for either of you! So, hit the accelerator and high tail it out of here! If you can outrace the cops, you might live. Now scoot...or we'll start shooting at you."

Spagatini and Bertinelli took a look at each other and momentarily tried to consider other options. A couple cop cars were less than a mile away and gaining on them. With the siren volume, there seemed to be other police vehicles joining the chase. While they wanted to simply stop the car and let the cops arrest them, they didn't have that choice. Malooley and McCoy were standing there ready to blaze away at them if Spagatini didn't hit the accelerator immediately.

Spagatini floored the gas pedal. Across the bridge they could slow down and let the police catch them. Then they had to hope the cops wouldn't shoot first and ask questions later.

Malooley and McCoy as quickly as they were physically able, jumped around a hedge alongside the roadway entering the bridge. They watched through the branches of the bushes as the Plymouth coupe sped away and began climbing the steep incline of the Cooper River Bridge. Not thirty seconds later, four patrol cars sped through the tollgate within a couple feet of where the two gangsters were hiding. Shots began bursting forth from the patrol cars toward the fleeing Plymouth coupe as it reached the apex of the bridge.

Malooley and McCoy just sat in that bush staring in awe at the spectacle. From the light of the moon and the headlights of the cop cars, they could see the back window of the coupe suddenly get blown out. They gulped knowing that either Spagatini or Bertinelli could easily have been shot in the rampage of bullets...to say nothing about themselves if they were still in the vehicle.

Then they watched as the automobile began weaving uncontrollably at the top of the long, high bridge. It appeared the driver may have been hit. Another shot blew out the back rear tire of the Plymouth causing the car to veer to the right and instantly flip once on the pavement.

But, it didn't stop there. The speed of the car caused a second unbelievable flip that resulted in the damaged Plymouth smashing against the side of the bridge...and then impossibly it vaulted over the mesh railing.

The night got suddenly and deathly quiet. No more shots were being flung at the car. No longer was there the sound of screeching brakes or engine acceleration. Even the squawking sea gulls were silent. There was only the appalling vision of the damaged Plymouth flying through the air as if in slow motion as it made a half summersault in its descent to the broad river below. Malooley and McCoy sat there motionless realizing that shocking picture would remain in their minds as long as they lived.

The Plymouth finally landed upside down on the rippling water of the Cooper River smashing its roof into the driver and passenger seats. As if that wasn't enough, the rear of the vehicle literally exploded as the car made contact with the water....as if there were unused cannon balls being stored in the back of the Plymouth. Any life form existing before the vehicle hit the river was now obliterated by the sickening explosion.

The remains of the car and anything in it were reflected by the moon for only a couple seconds before the pieces slowly sunk into the water. Amidst bubbles barely visible, the residue of metal frame and whatever remained of Spagatini and Bertinelli slowly sank to the bottom of the deepest point in the river. Whether killed by law enforcement bullets, by the explosion from the rear of the vehicle, by the contact with the Cooper River, or by drowning, Spagatini and Bertinelli were now part of the bridge's lore. They had met their fate in a way that many would say was deserved.

Malooley and McCoy remained almost attached to the hedge to shield themselves from being seen by more patrol cars passing right by them on the other side of the thicket. Still in shock over what they'd witnessed, McCoy began to make mumbling complaints about possible poison oak or ivy in those bushes...or getting bit by a snake. His dissatisfaction seemed so unimportant compared to the disaster before their eyes. Malooley, on the other hand, was elated to be alive. It did not get past him that there was some reason why he wasn't in pieces in the river floating among the fish and the charred portions of what remained of that Plymouth coupe.

Another cop car whizzed by the thick hedge giving Malooley time to appreciate that the police would have every reason to believe the speeding escape vehicle had to be driven by the two escapees...he and McCoy.

The vision wasn't entirely clear, but something told Malooley that while no one could predict the Plymouth was destined to tumble into the water, it certainly was set up to be bushwhacked by the chasing cops. After all, he and McCoy were dangerous escapees. The law had every right and reason to shoot to kill. The only problem was that the wrong culprits were in the fleeing car...as apparently had been planned.

As McCoy kept itching from the bushes, Malooley watched in the distance as the cops peered over the damaged railing down to the water far below. They had to assume it was the watery grave of Whitey Malooley and Billy McCoy.

As Malooley considered the next move to make, he remembered yet another directive the masked guard had given him and McCoy. They should make it back to the East Bay Street Hotel and hide out in the suites of the two now dead hitmen. That now seemed like the only choice they had. The guard had said they'd be contacted the next morning where a secondary plan would be put into place to get them undetected out of town. Malooley had no reason to doubt that guard's word.

Malooley motioned for his partner to stay low as they crawled down the embankment to the river's edge. It was dark. They wouldn't be seen by the cops high up on the bridge. Stumbling along the shore line, they felt no pain from their injuries. They were dirty, sweaty, and somewhat in shock, but contrary to the two hitmen, Malooley and McCoy were still breathing.

A half mile from the bridge and seeing the hotel only blocks away, both men were groaning as the pain of their injuries returned. Their adrenalin was dissipating. Nonetheless, they stayed quiet as the waves along the shoreline of the harbor slapped against their feet and pant legs in the darkness.

Slowly creeping along, those words of warning from the guard kept echoing in Malooley's head. It was as if he was living another life.

By all rights he and McCoy should have been blown to bits with their body parts sinking slowly but steadily to the river's bottom. His thought wave would have been overwhelming if his journey back to the hotel hadn't required so much of his concentration.

McCoy initially thought his partner unwise for wanting to return to the hotel. As they wheezed along the sandy shore of the river to the East Bay Street Hotel, McCoy was no longer arguing the choice. He just wanted to rest. Malooley kept reminding him they could hold out in Spagatini's hotel room and live on room service until the next move in their escape could be initiated.

Twenty minutes later the two of them were hiding in heavy grass between the river and the parking lot of the hotel. Though it was very late, they cautiously panned the entire area making certain no one was watching or whimsically out for a late night stroll on such a beautiful night.

Sneaking along the edge of the hotel parking lot, they made it to the maintenance door with shoes sloshing and their clothes attached to their skin from perspiration. They didn't need the pass key after all... the door had been left unlock. Moving swiftly up the staircase to the fourth floor, they could only hope their good fortune would hold out until they made it to Spagatini's suite.

Malooley with the master key opened #410 and they stumbled into the suite sprawling on the bed and sofa. Neither said it but they both knew they'd just experienced the most unbelievable night of their lives. Seconds later they were like crazed kids muffling their laughter and recognizing they had a story that never could be told considering they both had died less than an hour before...that is, according to yet to be written police reports.

Each one knew they could never acknowledge their own names again. They were no longer alive in the eyes of every patrolman witnessing that old Plymouth diving into the depths of the Cooper River. Within twenty-four hours the accident and their deaths would be reported in the press and likely be conveyed to all national newspapers. Even to the crime families in Chicago who wanted them dead, the news would bring a satisfying end to the D'Annelli episode. The cops in Charleston, South Carolina had taken care of that wish.

And what a story! It wasn't as if their names were so well-known. It was more the way they died. Major newspapers in every state in the union would relish having the story on their front page describing the horrific scene at the Cooper River Bridge. Readers from California to Maine and Montana to Alabama would shudder thinking how utterly horrifying it would have been plunging off that high bridge into the murky watery grave below.

The two gangsters went from giddiness for being alive to exhaustive sleep. They would wake periodically because of the pain of their injuries, but neither would complain. Each would lay there in that room sometimes chortling loudly and other times in reflective silence.

Around 4:00 AM they again had awakened. They decided to clean up expecting the next part of an escape plan to start at any time. Trying on some of the clothing in the suitcases of the two former hitmen, Malooley and McCoy drank liberally from one of the bottles of whiskey found in Bertinelli's suitcase. They eventually drained the bottle helping them to drift off into another exhausted sleep...Malooley on the bed covers and McCoy sprawled on the sofa.

It was only an hour later when Malooley jolted awake. There was absolute silence in the pitch black room. For a moment he wondered if he was dead until he felt a shooting pain in his shoulder again.

His mind was racing. He thought of the old lady in the wheelchair who had visited him at the hospital who was part of the escape plan. He recalled the masked police guards so strangely protective and conscientious in their part of the plan. He thought about the person who'd planted the pistols for them under the bed in Spagatini's room. He thought about the maid who'd been on their floor when they first arrived. Was it possible she was part of the team helping them escape?

He kept rolling the details of the night over in his mind. Henry Hanson had an impressive list of friends...and it was equally extraordinary the lengths those friends went to protect him. As diligent as those police guards had been with McCoy and him, they left no doubt why they were involved in the escape. They wanted Spagatini and Bertinelli dead as much as Malooley and his McCoy did.

What he couldn't get over was how straight-forward the people were in providing the means to escape. That firm caution for he and McCoy to get out of the car immediately if chased by the police saved their lives. There had been no explanation why...just an emphasis to do it. That caution reverberated within his skull time and time again as the image of the car flying off the bridge and the trunk portion of the old Plymouth exploding on impact with the Cooper River. When he imagined pieces of metal and flesh sinking to the harbor bottom, he had to shake his head to end the ugly thought.

Malooley suddenly got a dull pain in his stomach. He turned away from the window and called out to McCoy sleeping on the couch. "Billy….Billy….wake up!

McCoy bolted awake automatically reaching for the revolver beside him. The pain shot through his mangled fingers as the end of his forearm-to-hand cast rammed into a chair beside the bed. Still half-asleep, he yelled, "What….for Christ sakes….what!"

Showing no concern for his partner's agony, he gasped, "Billy, you remember there was an explosion in the rear of the car before it hit the water?"

McCoy rubbing his head moaned, "There must have been a full tank of gasoline."

Ignoring the response, Malooley muttered through clenched teeth, "I think there were some explosives in that trunk. Those guards who helped us last night…I swear to God they knew there was some kind of dynamite in the rear of that automobile. We got warned to get out of that car in a police chase. They knew the Plymouth would be riddled with bullets during any kind of police pursuit. Let's face it, one bullet could set off a blast and all four of us would have perished whether the car went sailing over the bridge railing or not.

But, that guard…the shorter one…he seemed determined not to let us die. You remember in the car…he even grabbed my arm and made me heed his warning. That guard saved our lives…for whatever reason."

His partner grabbed the last bottle of whiskey and took a long swig. Malooley walked over and took an even larger swallow. The two of them had sidestepped the law with a lot of help…and then snubbed death as it stared them in the face.

They polished off that last bottle without saying another word to each other. Eventually, they fell back asleep…their drunkenness dulling their minds so they could do so."

Henry then sat in silence letting that vivid part of his past sink in. Lawton sat in awe looking at Henry, Lill, and Ashley trying to put himself in their shoes twenty-seven years before. He thought of his father…Charlie Davis…and Sally Carter. What would he have done or said if he'd been part of that 'board of directors' who'd come up with that deathly scheme and then determinedly made it work? Would he have had their temerity, their resolve...or their coldness?

There was silence around the restaurant table as Lawton lay down his notebook and took a long swallow of his ice tea. Henry was even shaking his head over what he'd just shared. Laura was transfixed and just stared at Henry. Lill and Ashley were lost in their own thoughts thinking back to that time.

Easing the tension, Lawton slowed his own voice while summarizing. "So....the police killed Spagatini and Bertinelli thinking they were Malooley and McCoy escaping in the missing car. And... while they were shooting to disable the car...and maybe to incapacitate the driver and passenger as well...they had no idea there were some explosives in the trunk of the car. Is that right?"

Henry nodded.

Lawton continued, "The cops were obviously told to not let the escapees make it out of Charleston alive. Once they saw the Plymouth speeding up that bridge, they would supply a rain of bullets that would by all estimations hit those explosives in the trunk destroying the vehicle and everyone in it. As far as the cops were concerned, they had no reason to think there was anyone but Malooley and McCoy in that car.

In addition, I gather all seven of you back at the hotel in that eighth floor suite were witnesses to the horror that occurred that night. But, you couldn't have been sure if there were two or four men in that automobile. You were too far from the bridge to see Malooley and McCoy exit the car before it sped to its eventual doom."

Henry nodded his head slowly as Lawton caught his breath. Then he continued, "Henry, you had to think your plan had succeeded either way. You suddenly didn't have anyone connected to the Chicago syndicate hovering over Henry Hanson Granville anymore."

Pausing again, he finally added, "Am I arriving at the right conclusion?"

Henry didn't respond right away. He was just shaking his head remembering that night so long ago.

Lawton was not going to let the story end there. Prodding the older man to continue, he queried, "So what went on with the six of you as that night continued? I can't believe you calmly went home or back to your respective guest rooms and simply had a good night's sleep. And, for that matter, what really became of Malooley and McCoy?

Anticipating the question, Henry sat back. When he finally spoke his voice was almost inaudible. "No, Matt, your conclusion is not entirely accurate. We assumed Malooley and McCoy had perished with the two hitmen. I personally wouldn't know they had survived until years later.

However, there was one person who did know, but not until later that night."

Everyone at the table leaned forward. Henry looked at Lawton and motioned for him to close his notebook. He said, "Matt, this part of the story should never be recorded, but I will tell you what actually happened that night…and even the next morning."

As Lawton put down his pen, the older man talked on very softly.

"Once we saw these four men in that Plymouth pulling away from the hotel, it was Sally Carter who immediately called the police. She knew the police chief and had set up a signal when the escape car was leaving the hotel. The person she spoke to only had to hear her voice. Her words were succinct. "You can start the chase. They're heading for the Bridge." Then she hung up the phone.

It was barely a minute went by when we heard a flood of sirens. I recall talking with the others how fast the police were responding and how a possible gun battle was likely. Malooley and McCoy had the guns. They certainly weren't going down without a fight. Going back to jail was certifiable suicide. The mob would get them at some point.

We wondered if Malooley and McCoy would eliminate Spagatini and Bertinelli before leaving the city and then if caught by the police claim those two hitmen pulled them out of the hospital and were taking them out in the country to shoot them. A lot of things were a possibility that night. We were mostly wondering if they were going to follow our directions or not. If not, we had the cops on their trail as soon as possible with the police chief's order to blast away at the car. One way or another we wanted Spagatini and Bertinelli eliminated that night. For certain, however, none of us ever visualized the car being hit by a hail of bullets causing it to lose control and catapult over the bridge rail. That was a form of death far beyond our consideration.

457

From our perch atop the hotel we could see the Plymouth coupe race down East Bay Street. Simultaneously, we saw flashing red lights from police vehicles racing in the same direction from King Street. For a moment it looked like the cops might beat the Plymouth to the toll bridge.

When the Plymouth approached the entry to the bridge it slowed momentarily at the toll booth and then disappeared as some trees and high shrubbery blocked our vision. Then the car came into view once again speedily charging up onto the long bridge. We assumed the four men were in the car.

Then our hearts were in our throats as we saw the flashing lights of a couple police cars rapidly gaining on the escaping vehicle. As many as four police vehicles were pursuing as the Plymouth drew near the apex of the bridge. We became transfixed as we could hear distinct shots being fired.

The Plymouth suddenly began to waver. Then as if there was another force at work, the car pulled toward the edge of the bridge flipping one time...then again. Our gasps were audible as we watched in silent horror as the vehicle jumped upside down over the bridge railing on that second flip and suddenly became airborne. As it plunged there was a silence among all of us ...all like a bad dream...until it reached its watery grave below.

We thought the tragedy would be completed when the car hit the water, but as if an exclamation mark to the entire episode, the old Plymouth exploded in a fiery ball simultaneously to hitting the water.

Someone in the suite wheezed out loud, "My God." I still don't know who said it. It may have been me. The seven of us just stood on that terrace patio stunned. If there was any chance that anyone lived through the long plunge, the explosion ended any such miracle.

It was the most unique feeling any of us had ever felt. There was some unspoken remorse in the room how death had come to those four human beings in such a horrible way. Yet, there was also a silent understanding that those gangsters had died quite consistent with the violent lifestyle they followed.

It was my dear Aunt Sally who broke the silence with her bluntness. Rolling her wheelchair over to the liquor cabinet, she poured herself a stiff drink before declaring, "Some individuals have been eradicated from this world who invested their time into making money dishonestly and causing misery to so many people. If they didn't die that way, they would have died violently another way. They were the dirt of society."

She then downed her drink as if not wanting to participate in anyone second-guessing whether the right decision had made. She proclaimed, "I'm going to my room and read myself to sleep. Good night, everyone."

Ashley offered to wheel her down to the elevator, but she waved him off saying curtly, "I can make it up and down an elevator." It seemed like she wanted to be alone with her own thoughts.

The rest of us also partook of the liquor cabinet before retreating to our respective rooms for the remainder of the night. Lill and I even grabbed a spare room at the hotel.

The story of the escaped detainees at the hospital meeting their death at the Cooper River Bridge would be the talk of the community the next day. The seven of us would have to be at our best to feign surprise when hearing the horrible news that Whitey Malooley and Billy McCoy had come out second best when fleeing the hospital and then the police. The strange detail missing in all the reports was that Spagatini and Bertinelli were in that car and no one knew it but the seven of us. It was a secret that had to be kept.

Weeks later after parts of the bodies were found, it would be reported that a partial identification had been found showing a man named Vinnie Spagatini was tragically killed in the Cooper River Bridge accident as well. He'd been reported as missing along with his friend, Bert Bertinelli. Nothing was ever found proving the friend was a fourth person to die in that horrible scene, but the fact that he seemed to have disappeared into thin air made investigators eventually reason that this fourth man had likely been in that automobile catapulting off the bridge as well.

Newspaper reports would eventually investigate and find that Spagatini and Bertinelli might have been even bigger crime suspects than the two escapes from the hospital. To the authorities it looked like the two guests at the hotel had actually assisted Malooley and McCoy in their departure from the hospital…at least that was how the final report would read.

As far as the crime syndicate in Chicago was concerned, there was satisfaction that D'Annelli's two most trusted associates were now dead for their part in dealing counterfeit money within the mob family. However, there was confusion why Vinnie Spagatini and Bert Bertinelli would have helped Malooley and McCoy escape from hospital. They were in Charleston to kill D'Annelli's former right hand men!

Mob members would often talk about the decision by Vinnie and Bert. Why didn't they simply sneak into the medical center and shoot both of D'Annelli's boys as they lay injured in their hospital beds. It would have been the most expedient manner of caring out the murders, especially with the morgue just down the block from the hospital.

The most important result of that entire night was the reasons for Malooley and McCoy even being in Charleston, South Carolina. That question died with their supposed deaths. The Chicago syndicate had no idea Malooley and McCoy were in that southern city to track down the man thought to be the cause of Loni D'Annelli's house of cards caving in two years before.

My alias as Henry Granville was secured once again as were the backgrounds of the people who were so close to me. I was of the mind that all serious remaining threats from the D'Annelli era had disappeared into the Cooper River on that July night in 1933.

I've faced other questions since then about my background from reporters and business magazine writers, but those have generally been easy to fend off. I've also had other small level gangsters from back at that time somehow track me down and accuse me of being Henry Hanson. Those attempts at blackmail have always been dealt with effectively thanks to those same colleagues who helped me that night."

Lawton was impatient. "Henry......so Malooley and McCoy were still alive, but you say you didn't know it. What happened?

"It was not until some years later just before the outbreak of World War II that I learned of the actual outcome of Malooley and McCoy. It was after my Aunt Sally's funeral in 1940. A close friend of hers in Charleston had been sworn to secrecy until after she had passed. He was my friend too. Police Chief Brooks Calhoun, a week following her burial, called ahead and asked to see me on a business matter.

Accepting my offer of ice tea, we sat down. He said he finally had the permission to talk to me about something additional that happened back during that unforgettable July night in 1933.

He was a strong, burly man, but he was surprisingly emotional as he began disclosing a deal he and my aunt had made with Malooley and McCoy as part of the escape plan...a pact that spared the two gangsters' lives. He said it was an agreement that went beyond the escape plan the board members had concocted that Tuesday night.

I felt a numbness growing in my body as he talked on. "Henry," he said, "Your Aunt Sally and I went back a long ways even before you even thought of coming to Charleston. She used to come to this city a lot before she got married. You might say we got to know each other. I'll just leave it at that. Anyway we were always good friends. We thought the same way and we always said what was on our minds to one another. Well, from that kind of relationship she never had any qualms about calling me...including that time in 1933 when your life hung in the balance.

She told me of your long term problems you had with not two but four gangsters from the Chicago area who were now in Charleston. I hadn't heard of the first two fellows who were apparently tracking you, but when I heard the names Vinnie Spagatini and Bert Bertinelli, that got my response. Those birds were notorious. I think every police chief in every major city in the country likely knew of those two hoods by reputation. Those two underworld freaks had dodged so many murder accusations and numerous other unlawful charges. I'll just say it was understood in the law enforcement community that at some point those two fellows had to go down.

When she told me those two villains were in my city's own backyard, her needs and my needs coordinated quite nicely. It was my opportunity to do something about Spagatini and Bertinelli.

Anyway she and I met sometime that Monday the day before the horrible incident on the Cooper River Bridge. I was crestfallen seeing her wheelchair bound, but she told me not to be concerned. I might add that was the last thing said about her condition. All I saw was a sharp-eyed, quick-witted lady as feisty as ever.

She told me about your board's plan to spring the two injured convicts from the hospital in order that they take out Spagatini and

461

Bertinelli...with the further guarantee they'd never shadow Henry again.

Naturally those two thugs agreed to the terms. Who wouldn't?

Well, I wanted Spagatini and Bertinelli wiped out as much as you and your board did. However, I had my doubt the two injured gangsters could pull off such an assignment given their injuries. That was when Sally and I devised an additional element to the plan to better insure the results we all wanted. We didn't think you or anyone else on your board had to know. We just went along and did it.

It was our scheme to put some explosives in the trunk of the car. Ashley Cooper helped us out not totally realizing what he was doing. Sally said it was important he transfer a box from another car she described in that hotel parking lot to the Plymouth. She said it was clothing for Malooley and McCoy if they completed their break. He had no clue the box held any dynamite. He'd probably not have touched it if he had known.

He was also the one Sally gave strict instructions to warn Malooley and McCoy to get out of that vehicle if any shots started flying. Ashley of course didn't know the depth of our scheme or the amount of explosives that were in that box. He was just trying to keep them from being killed from the rain of bullets from the cops that would be fired at that car with Spagatini and Bertinelli in it.

As for Sally and me, those explosives were placed in the Plymouth trunk as a further guarantee that the murderous and unlawful days of Spagatini and Bertinelli were going to end. We just had to hope Malooley and McCoy would get out of that car with that forewarning from Ashley. That part of our extra plan was purely up to them.

I have to admit when I saw that car catapult off the bridge, I thought four gangsters had plummeted to their deaths. I actually felt badly for Malooley and McCoy since they were carrying out their part of the bargain as best they could. They were so close to beginning a new life if their former one had not ended so tragically."

Then he paused taking a drink of that ice tea and lit a cigarette. It was as if he was nervous about how I would take the next part his tale.

Though my office door was closed, his voice was only a whisper as he said, "Henry, I'm here to tell you today seven years later that there were only two major crime syndicate people, Spagatini and Bertinelli, who flew off the Cooper River Bridge to their watery grave that night.

Malooley and McCoy made a second escape that night…from that old Plymouth…just a minute before my boys started shooting at the fleeing car as it ascended the bridge. I wouldn't learn of Malooley and McCoy miraculous exit of that car for another couple hours.

I was still congratulating my officers for a job well done when Sally Carter called my office. She'd been sitting out on her hotel suite deck overlooking the parking lot just in case Malooley and McCoy had made good their escape from that vehicle. If they followed the advice given them to make their way back to the hotel and stay in Spagatini's room the rest of the night, then Sally would activate the next part of hers and my plans for them. To their credit they followed the directions by the masked Ashley Carter to the last letter. Frankly they had little choice. They were in no condition to go anywhere else that night.

When she saw the two stagger across the unlit parking lot about an hour after the car explosion that was when she called me. We decided to meet those two chaps the very next morning in their suite.

When your board was assembling the next morning, Sally had been up in #410 discussing the final details of the continuing escape plan with Malooley, McCoy and me. Sally then left our little powwow and went to your board meeting where of course she said nothing about the two injured gangsters recovering four floors below.

Fifteen minutes later I was seen leaving the hotel with two of my deputies. It was simply assumed by the hotel staff that my deputies and I were making a routine investigation. No one really noticed the two deputies. The police uniforms covered up the shoulder wound of one. The other deputy concealed his severely injured hand with a checkered cloth from a fruit basket. The three of us got in my squad car and I drove straight out of town on the Savannah highway to a few miles past the old highway to Kiawah Island. An old Chevrolet Coupe was parked a half mile off that road under a large magnolia tree near a weed infested pond."

Once there I insisted on getting the uniforms back from Malooley and McCoy. I didn't like seeing them in a uniform I respected. Clothing in the Chevy Coupe was provided and I waited around while the two injured men struggled with the change of clothes."

Then Calhoun grinned before continuing with the seven-year old story. He crowed, "Henry, there was a moment as they were changing where I scared the holy hell of both those fellas. I pulled out

463

my revolver, fired it, and killed a water moccasin slithering towards one of them. When they saw that gun, their eyes were like saucers. They obviously felt the escape plan had just been nullified. Well, I tell you what, I wasn't about to take either of them back to Charleston to be treated for a snake bite.

The shot made them hurry even more. They were as anxious to leave the area as I was to see them go. When they finally got the other clothes on, I reached into my breast pocket and pulled out two envelopes containing $1000 for each of them and two separate I.D. cards from a couple deceased men formerly living in Georgia. Then I threw McCoy the keys to the Chevy Coupe.

I truly think that was the moment they realized they'd not only completed their escape, but they had a chance to wipe the slate clean and follow a new path in life…that is, if they were truly willing.

With no other fanfare, I grabbed the deputy uniforms and bid them farewell saying, "I'd stay out of Georgia. Those names might get you in trouble. Good luck on making better choices in life from this day forward."

Then without further delay, I got into my police vehicle, backed over the dead snake, and promptly drove back toward Hwy. 17 and then onto Charleston. I saw the two injured gangsters in my rear view mirror get in their newly acquired used Chevrolet Coupe and drive off the opposite way. I never looked back again."

Henry pulled out his handkerchief and blew his nose. He seemed content to make his visit with Chief Calhoun the finish to his story. But, he wasn't quite done. As he leaned back in his chair and lit up a slender cigar, he added one more morsel.

"I remember greeting Sally as she rolled her wheelchair into the conference room that next morning for our 9:00 board meeting

I brought her some coffee and informed her about the latest word on the previous night's incident. I told her, "Sally, the morning scuttlebutt is that all four gangsters were in that car when they went over the bridge. With the bullets, the explosion and the contact with the water, they had no chance of survival. Their remains may never be found."

I recall she only nodded as if satisfied that would be the result reported in the newspapers. She moved her wheelchair over to the conference table and asserted in her own inimitable way, "Henry, they live and die in a different world. They got what they deserved. Now, let's start the meeting. I want to hear about those possible acquisitions in Florida!"

We all laughed at her business-like demeanor and the energy she brought to the boardroom. I called the meeting to order with no knowledge of how Sally and Chief Calhoun had collaborated. All I felt was relief. It was the most unburdened I'd felt in years."

Then he added, "And, I guess Sally and the Police Chief made their points very clear to those two guys. I never heard from Whitey Malooley and Billy McCoy ever again. Their names died with that horrendous car crash, but their bodies and minds with new identifications lived on."

Henry's story had been told. An unnatural cool breeze drifted through a corner window in the restaurant as each member of the dinner party reached for something to drink to remedy their dry throats... each one lost in their own thoughts. Ashley made some odd comment about the uncomfortable draft being the forbearer of possible inclement weather and Lill wondered whether one of the hotel events scheduled the next day might have to be moved inside. The talk then declined to empty prattle about the recent 1960 political conventions in Chicago and Los Angeles. Henry just sat seeming obliged to just rest his voice.

It was now up to Lawton to complete his notes, draft and edit the copy, and complete the entire manuscript before his assignment was officially completed. From there it would be up to Henry what he wanted to do with the journal of his life.

Yet, after four months of living so close to Henry Hanson Granville's current life and hearing the man's background through so many interviews, Lawton found himself now especially dubious whether the text should ever be seen in public. If the manuscript was supposed to tell the actual truth of various misunderstandings or temper the hyperbole in Henry's past life, Lawton realized he may have to take some of the actual happenings out of the text. The purpose was not to create a piece that was damaging to Henry and various other people connected to the corporation including Lawton's own father and mother, Charlie Davis…and even Clarence Petracek and Rich Brey. The mob might no longer be interested in retaliation, but why chance the possibility…or having reputations besmirched over some past deeds done so many years before.

The interview session ended shortly thereafter and everyone seemed shell-shocked except Henry. He not only showed relief but some actual energy now that the ordeal of telling his story was apparently over.

He stood up and thanked his contemplative dinner guests for sitting through the series of interviews. And then, with a vigor in complete contrast to the rest of his dinner guests, began talking about his coming business trip.

While helping Lill with her chair and her shawl, he looked appreciatively at Lawton and said, "Matt, unless you have other plans, I'd like you to accompany me. You haven't seen one other side of the business. Those properties I'm considering buying in Florida…how about flying with me down to Miami Beach and then up to Naples this coming Monday. It would give you another perspective on our business before you finish the manuscript."

Then he repeated a statement Lawton had heard too many times to count, "Besides, there's no timetable on getting your writing assignment done. You can finish the text later."

Just like that Henry had changed the somber mood of the completion of his story to that of enthusiasm for the coming days. As he and Lill walked to the restaurant's exit, his fervor continued, "It should be a wonderful trip. We'll be back on Thursday. How does that sound?"

Lawton couldn't help but laugh at Henry's enthusiasm. He'd come to appreciate that attribute in the older man. "Yes, I'll look forward to joining you. You just tell me the time of the flight. I pack lightly."

Henry's zest sparked the group and everyone left the restaurant feeling almost but not quite as inspired as the older man. Ashley said he had some place to go. Henry and Lill were heading back to Mt. Pleasant. Lawton and Laura went back to the Waring house to see if the Judge and Elizabeth might want to play a few hands of bridge.

It had been an unforgettable night.

*   *   *

Upon returning to Charleston the next Thursday after the Florida trip, Lawton would invest the remainder of August editing his notes on Henry's story and completing the first draft of the manuscript. He could have done the writing task in half the time had he not continued to be asked to take on certain hotel business responsibilities. There were three times each week Lill requested he be with her when they met some potential clients invited down to the hotel to inspect the property for future meetings. It was Ashley and he who took these representatives out for dinner or out for a sail on Charleston Harbor with hopes of winning their business.

In addition, Lawton became part of the marketing team of the hotel. Though he had no specific title, it was just understood his contribution was desired in those meetings.

While he could have made time in the evenings to work on his main purpose for being in Charleston, so often his interview notes remained untouched. More importantly, he had no desire to miss an evening with Laura Waring whether attending a hotel function or just being by themselves.

By the end of August, the relationship between Laura and Lawton had grown stronger. She tried to make her chief challenge the decision whether to attend law school at Georgetown that fall or to continue her beloved restoration projects in Charleston. But, her dilemma had become more than those two considerations.

Lawton believed he had no decision. Once his writing task was done, life would move on. He would be returning to Minneapolis and continue his job at University Publishing, Inc. until he found another career path.

It was during the week before Labor Day weekend that Lawton came to a decision of his own. He recognized he simply didn't want to leave Charleston. Since the spring he'd gained some true friendships that were based more on the hope of the future than the memory of past experiences. He liked working with people who shared a common interest...in this case, making the East Bay Street Hotel the best example of southern hospitality. The jobs he was asked to do in support of the hotel he'd always done willingly and with great satisfaction.

He'd been repeatedly told by Lill that his extra work gave him a better perspective on Henry's business thereby making his writing more real and effective. While her sage words turned out to be true, what was more truthful was that he simply enjoyed his involvement in the business. He'd regained his energy and focus that had deteriorated while working at University Publishing, Inc.

It was that Friday before Labor Day weekend he had decided to jokingly announce to both Henry and Lill he'd lost all his notes and the entire interview process would have to be repeated. He hoped they might grasp what he was insinuating. He then planned on requesting consideration for a job at the hotel wherever a void needed to be filled.

The response was more positive than he ever imagined. Henry's reply was simple and to the point. "Matt, do you really think we'd let you get away. The only way you'd ever be allowed to leave us is if you wanted to return to Minnesota."

Chapter 21

The years passed from that spring and summer of 1960 in Charleston, South Carolina. Henry Hanson Granville's memoirs would remain unfinished and unpublished in a glass-enclosed shelf in Matt Lawton's personal library. He'd never completed drafting the final chapter of Henry's story discussed on that August night with Henry, Ashley, Lill, and the enthusiastic listener, Laura Waring. Only Lawton's final notes from that night were a record of that last interview session.

Lawton thought at times how someday he'd finish editing those final notes and write the story...as a fiction piece. He'd have to change the name, the location and certainly the identities of so many people involved. He could let nothing even hint of the former Henry Hanson being the present day Henry Granville. However, the idea seemed not only arduous, but somehow superfluous and even disrespectful to all those who'd made the real truth happen. What he'd come to appreciate was how his own life had been formed as a result of Henry Hanson Granville's life as well.

And what a life the older man had lived. Lawton always marveled at the risks so many people had taken...people who'd been part of his formative years. Lawton saw again and again how the good fortune of close friendships could have such wonderful lasting effect on various people's lives.

He would also think often of the actual final interview session with Henry...not the one at the restaurant with everyone included, but the one that came only two weeks later when Henry and he were alone in the older man's office. It was while Lawton was trying to complete his first draft of the manuscript during that last week before Labor Day weekend.

Lawton caught Henry at the end of the day when Lill was out of the office. The older man thought his young scribe had stopped by to report on a luncheon he'd had the day before with some prospective clients from Washington D.C. Henry had just learned the association visitors had enjoyed their time with Matt Lawton and wanted to secure dates for their annual meeting at the East Bay Street Hotel for the following fall.

Before Henry could share the good news and congratulate Lawton, the young man launched into a question relating to Henry's background story. The gnawing question came out direct and blunt, completely in line with the close relationship the two of them had developed over the previous months.

Lawton asked, "Henry, you mentioned to me during our interview sessions...a couple times in fact... that you would tell me how you knew the perspective of the story from the viewpoints of Whitey Malooley and Billy McCoy. You never did divulge that information to me...and it's causing me some difficulty in finalizing this writing assignment."

Henry sat back and nodded his head. Lawton could see he was putting the man in a discomforting position. He also sensed Henry was not surprised by the query.

Granville got up, closed the door to his office and chose to sit opposite Lawton on the sofa in his office. He then said, "Matt, make yourself comfortable. Let's make this the truly last interview session and one that I'd prefer you keep between the two of us. What I have to tell you may help you complete the manuscript...or, it may not.

What he had to say would make the color on Lawton's face disappear. "Matt, sometimes friendships are born out of the strangest of circumstances...and I'm about to relate to you one of those instances. It was about thirteen years after that tumultuous evening in July 1933. The potential mob threat on my life and my business had been greatly, but not entirely eliminated. World War II had been over for less than a year but the aftermath was fresh in everyone's minds all around the globe. It was a time I felt very lucky that my group of hotels had remained solvent after I'd let two of my properties in Florida be used for soldiers convalescing from injuries received during the war.

In 1946 the East Bay Street Hotel was thriving again and my five hotel properties in Florida along with my two lake resorts up in Minnesota were either showing profits or moving again in that direction. I had been traveling a lot the previous six months, especially to Washington D.C. and New York City to remind clients that the East Bay Street Hotel and my hotels in Florida wanted to be at the top of their list when thinking about future business or association meetings. It was the last week of March and I recall thinking how even more inviting Charleston was now that the war years were behind us.

Monday morning usually meant I was catching up on a lot of paper work after any extended travel. I was reading the *Washington Post* and the local newspapers when Rose at the front desk called me and told me I had a visitor. She also whispered into the headphone out of the visitor's hearing range, "Henry, he's a war veteran. He has an injury. It would be nice if you could spare some time for him."

I didn't figure I had more than ten minutes, but the tone of her voice intimated that I should use those ten minutes with this man. I took her hint and asked her to send the man up to my office.

Greeting the man at my office door, I hoped I might recognize him, but it was not to be. He was about my height and seemingly younger, but the gray in his full beard and moustache made me guess we were about the same age. While he wasn't wearing a suit, he was clean and casually dressed with a sport coat. His hair style was a bit longer for the postwar style of men's hair, but then again so was mine.

Offering him a chair, I didn't notice his injury immediately. My focus was more on his eyes and manner than his physical condition. Finally when he sat down, I observed his missing left arm. Whether it was his apparent unfortunate war service or just the possible hard times of life he was now experiencing, I found myself wanting to give the man whatever time he sought.

Without giving me his name, he began talking. He confirmed he was a WWII veteran and had fought in the European theatre. He was looking around my office and seemed really pleased to be talking with me.

I stared intensely at him as he was speaking. He started to look familiar but then the beard, the weather beaten skin and the softer look in his eye left me puzzled.

I asked him more about his war experience and he responded but I could tell that wasn't the reason he'd come to see me. Then suddenly, he got more personal in his comments. He said, "Henry, I've had many years to think about my life since an occurrence way before the war...as well as during the many years trying to survive more recently over in Europe. I have to tell you, you've been part of those thoughts. There would be no way you would know this, but you've had a tremendous impact on my life. Believe it or not, I've had a unique opportunity to watch how you've grown and prospered going back to your life in Minnesota."

When he brought up 'Minnesota' I flinched. Not many people knew that part of my background and I'd rarely mentioned my home state in the fifteen years since arriving in Charleston. But, he didn't seem as if he had ulterior motives, so I let him go on.

His voice was very warm when he said, "Henry, from the first time I met you back in Glenwood to the last time I saw you, I've always been impressed with the loyalty and respect your friends showed to you...even the last time our paths crossed in this city. That leads me to my purpose in wanting to see you as I'm passing through Charleston...a city I haven't been in for many, many years."

He seemed to choke for a moment but then recovered. "Henry, I just came to apologize to you and guarantee that I would never want any harm to come your way or to your friends and associates. It's something I've wanted to say to you for years...and I want you to consider me a friend very willing to help you if ever that need should rise."

In all my years up to that day in 1946, I'd never had anyone say something like that to me. Normally people were asking me for help... not that I ever minded. But, having someone...a complete stranger... make the statements he was making left me both touched, yet still bewildered. My only hint was that he had to be someone I'd dealt with back in those trying times of the early 1930's...and maybe even prior to that since he'd mentioned Glenwood, Minnesota.

I tried to visualize some of those characters who owned businesses back in Glenwood or near Lake Minnewaska but I could recall no one of his size...especially no one with such an obvious kind heart. I remembered those Glenwood business owners and many of its citizens as people who were just trying to survive a major economic breakdown around the U.S. Having a kind heart and generous nature weren't attributes of many of those folks.

Then just like that this bearded man held out the hand from his one good arm hoping I'd reciprocate. Of course I did...and with alacrity.

As we shook hands, he introduced himself. "Henry, I'm Whitey Malooley...although I haven't gone by that name for thirteen years. Ever since I was given a new chance at life by that woman in the wheelchair and by the police chief here in Charleston, I changed both my name and my life. And, I know it was not just those two people who saved my life. I have a strong feeling you and a few other folks were part of that escape plan. It makes me even more beholden to you."

Matt, as you can imagine, when he said the name 'Whitey Malooley', I could have been blown over by a slight breeze. What surprised me was my reaction. There was no fear...in fact, quite the contrary. There was something about the man's calm, sincere demeanor that completely belied his former self. We sat there in my office and talked like old friends for the next hour. I postponed two meetings. He was delightful. In fact, our conversation was so pleasant I had a hard time accepting he could have been the same man fifteen years before who was plotting along with his partner against me. I'd rarely thought about the man since 1933. In fact, I'd thought he was dead. It was a conversation I would never have believed possible.

Whitey mentioned he and Billy McCoy had gone separate ways shortly after leaving Charleston on that July day in 1933. He'd learned years later that Billy had been killed in the streets of New York City before the war. As for him, Whitey said he'd done odd jobs in Florida and California for a number of years... and kept his nose clean. He'd enlisted in the military in 1938 with his new identity showing his age to be seven years younger than he actually was. Since the war's end the previous year, he said most of the work he'd found was working more odd jobs driving delivery trucks in places like Philadelphia and Miami. He said he was actually heading towards Florida to take on another job he was considering as a security guard.

What impressed me was the man's complete lack of dissatisfaction. I could sense he was now a man at peace with himself and a determination to live life straight up. And, despite his sincere offer to help me anytime I might need it, I eventually had to ask him, "Whitey, you've obviously turned things around for yourself and you're handling the loss of your arm with courage. But, let me ask you if I can assist you in any way?"

That was the only time he looked bothered. His response was polite but measured. "No, Henry. My purpose in coming to see you was not to ask for any handouts. I simply wanted to apologize to you and thank you."

Sensing his time was coming to a close, he began to rise from his chair. I found myself inventing things to ask just to keep him from leaving. He sat back very pleased of my interest in his altered life.

As we talked on, I tried a different tact to possibly help him. I wanted to be so careful not to upset the man's pride. I told him if he'd be interested I might be able to find him another opportunity that he could at least compare with the job he apparently had in Florida. He seemed appreciative, but repeated again his genuine purpose in seeing me was not to bother me.

I guess I was struck by the guy. I liked him and I liked how unwavering he had to have been to keep his life clean. I also came down with an idea that would help both of us. I'd employed many people in the past, but in just that hour of conversation I realized I knew him better than most people I'd hired in my career.

I finally said to him, "Whitey, I've got something to say to you and I want you to accept it as words from a person you've known for getting on twenty years. We have some things in common and I have great respect for your resolve in your service overseas and even more what you've done with your second chance at life. Making good on any second chance, you have to admit, that's certainly something we share. Otherwise, I'd probably still be storing feed and grain back in Minnesota.

He nodded appreciating our commonality. It made it easier to again offer my assistance in finding him a better job. There was something about him...and something about me...that created a trust. You had to see the man's eyes...and hear his words. There was not a spec of malice in his voice. It was as if we'd been in some kind of fraternity years and years ago.

I don't know when the flash hit me, but I wanted this man in my growing organization. I recall thinking to myself how a man like Whitey with his military background...and even some of his experiences back in the 1930's…..might make him quite appropriate for a position I had been looking to fill in my organization.

To this day I've never felt so good about offering someone a job…and being quite confident that it was the absolute right decision. I had taken risks in my life, but that didn't feel like a huge risk.

That very morning I told him I wanted him to consider something and I'd be personally affronted if he interpreted what I had to say as a hand-out. I told him there was a position in security at my hotel I was eventually going to fill when I found the right person. I told him I needed someone I could trust and if in the next week he'd like to discuss the job further, he had only to call me.

He was definitely moved that I would even consider him. He said he had to check out that job in Florida and then he'd get back to me by the end of the week. He called a few days later and returned to Charleston that next Friday. We talked over a long lunch and those feelings I had about him in our first meeting five days before were further confirmed. I could see myself trusting this man literally with my life.

While I had the job outlined, he suggested I also use him in some maintenance work since he would be working nights at the hotel. It turned out he was as valuable doing repair and maintenance as security. Despite having but one arm, I felt like I was employing two men in one."

As Henry paused, Lawton asked a question proving he wasn't seeing the entire story. He said, "Henry, helping a man like that was not only a risk on your part but highly generous. Tell me, what became of this man…this Whitey Malooley? Where's he now?

Henry gave Lawton a huge grin. "Matt, you know him quite well. One of your best friends in Charleston and certainly one of my dearest friends is working right here at the hotel. Whitey Malooley is 'Lou'. He's been in charge of Security here at the East Bay Street Hotel since I offered him the job back in 1946. You can imagine he and I have guarded each other's secrets as if our very lives depended on it. And, in at least my case, it often has.

Anyway, Matt, I didn't talk much about Lou in my background story because I don't want to create any problems for him. After all, he did have some run-ins with the law when he was Whitey Malooley. We have always got to be very careful not to unveil too much about his past life. Since establishing his new name, he's never run into any problems… and we want to keep it that way. We have a special confidence in one another that we have always maintained. It's the exclusive merit in a truly trustful friendship."

Lawton was once again completely flabbergasted with another of Henry's disclosures.

*　*　*

In the years since that private discussion in 1960 between Henry and Matt Lawton, Whitey Malooley or 'Lou White', as Lawton would always know him, continued as Director of Security and Maintenance at the hotel. It was ten years after Lawton had arrived in Charleston that Lou passed away…a ten-year friendship uncommon considering the generation and a half difference in their ages.

By 1970, as General Manager of the East Bay Street Hotel and CEO of Triple H Development, Inc., Matt Lawton felt honored to give the eulogy at Lou's funeral at the First Presbyterian Church on James Island. Lou was godfather to Matt and Laura's first son and like an uncle to the other two Lawton offspring. No one at that memorial service ever knew of a Whitey Malooley…only Lou White…and that included Lawton's wife, Laura. Lawton never even acknowledged to Lou that Henry had confided Lou's true identity. To Lawton, discussing that fact served no purpose. The individual he'd gotten to know was a completely different man than the one first described to him by Henry from back in those Minnesota days of their lives. As second chances go, Lou took advantage and made a monumental success of his subsequent life.

Whenever Lawton recalled his first months in the city, he'd look over at that unfinished Henry Hanson Granville memoir in the glass enclosed shelf…and just smile. The whole task back in 1960 documenting some of the questionable times in Henry's life…it had also been a ruse the older man had set up to get Lawton to come to Charleston. Henry would later admit how he'd always had the notion if he had a chance to get the young man under his wing, it would be worth the effort. That intuition turned out to be highly perceptive. In the many years that followed, Henry's confidence in Lawton grew as the young man was able to feed off of Henry's vast business acumen.

Lawton's advancement to CEO of the corporation at the youthful age of thirty-five was as natural as the sun rising the next morning.

Henry had the joy of adding to the product Jamie and Lindy Lawton had brought up. He considered his efforts a privilege as well as carrying out a responsibility to his large corporation of finding a capable and talented successor.

It would be four years later Lawton's mentor, Henry Hanson Granville, would follow Lou White in death. Lawton again gave a warm and appreciative tribute, but that one was even more difficult to complete. In his acclaim he voiced how he couldn't imagine where his life would have gone without Henry's interest in him and how fortunate it was that Henry connived to get Lawton to come to Charleston back in the spring of 1960.

Lawton had a tear dripping down his cheek as he looked at Laura and his three kids, at his folks, Jamie and Lindy, at his Uncle Charlie, at Lill Hamilton and Ashley Cooper and then at so many people from the organization and friends from Charleston who were attending the funeral. His voice choked for a moment as he said, "I wouldn't have all of you in my life…and I just can't imagine that not happening. I owe so much to Henry."

With those two men gone from his life, there would often be times Matt Lawton would stare out his second floor office window at Charleston Harbor and marvel how lucky he'd been. He'd officially taken over the helm of the Triple H Development, Inc. chairmanship shortly after Lou had passed on. Those following four years he thankfully was able to share and discuss business matters with the retired Henry Granville. They were warm and gratifying years. Lawton could see the pride and confidence the older man had in him as Lawton seamlessly took charge of the overall responsibilities of running a huge hotel and resort conglomerate.

He so missed that daily contact with Henry and Lou. He still had Lill Hamilton and Ashley Cooper who remained on the board, but they were no longer as active in the business. He loved and respected both of them dearly, but it wasn't the same as when they were so impassioned day to day in the operation of the East Bay Street Hotel.

Lill and Ashley would retire shortly after Henry's death and live on enjoying a pleasant life in Charleston. They were still seen regularly at the hotel for lunch or dinner with a number of their friends. They spent a lot of time and traveled together. They were regulars attending the Sunday brunch still scheduled at the hotel patio during the warm months or the Saturday evening cocktail party during the cooler times of the year.

Also, Lawton was still close to his longtime East Bay Street Hotel friend, Jefferson Brown, who now managed another major property owned by the Triple H Development Company, Inc. on the coast of Florida near Palm Beach. The hotel conglomerate was also employing another Jamie and Lindy Lawton offspring. Matt's brother, Nick. He'd been working under the tutelage of Jefferson since graduating from college.

Needless to say, Lawton never went back to his publishing job in Minneapolis. He resigned his position with Mr. Bud Brey's company, University Publishing, Inc. in September 1960. Mr. Brey was not surprised. Lawton went to work for Henry accepting a job at the East Bay Street Hotel as Director of Sales & Marketing. He continued living in that top floor suite until he got married in the summer of 1961 to Laura Waring.

She never did go to law school at Georgetown University that fall of 1960 or any year thereafter. She found she just had other interests. Whether Lawton's decision to stay in Charleston affected her choice became immaterial. Initially, the primary reason she gave to her father and others for not wanting to study the law was the passion she felt for antebellum historic restorations in Charleston. That interest continued right through her marriage and birth of the Lawton's three children and beyond. It would be logical to say two passions kept her in Charleston.

The Lawton's wedding day, June 3, 1961, was a huge affair. It was just fifteen months after Lawton arrived in Charleston and fourteen months after Laura Waring and Matt had met. There was certainly the predictable local talk questioning why a nice southern girl would choose to marry a guy from the North. The feeling was that she was too good for him. Whether said in jest or seriously, Lawton would always agree with the comment.

The ceremony was across the Ashley River on James Island at the First Presbyterian Church. The church couldn't hold the number of invitees, but there was more room for everyone at the reception in the patio garden area of the East Bay Street Hotel. The hotel had a skeleton crew during the church ceremony with so many staff members filling the pews. At the reception, the crowd challenged the hotel patio and lawn for having enough space. Guests at the hotel were invited along with the Lawton and Waring family members and friends to the party…just as if the reception was one of those Saturday night teas or Sunday morning brunches. Nightly patronage by guests always brought membership to hotel sponsored events.

There was one unfortunate occurrence that did happen that Saturday of the Lawton wedding. It was in Charleston, but had no effect on the special event in the least.

A hefty man wearing a very used and grimy white suit was seriously injured outside the Charleston bus terminal. He'd just ridden up to Charleston from Savannah by bus and had been making a call in an outside phone booth. Another bus just leaving the terminal cut a corner too sharply and smashed into the phone booth.

When they pulled the man from underneath the rear of the bus, he looked as broken as the booth itself. Miraculously, the mangled man was alive but badly injured as the ambulance workers separated the pieces of the booth from the unfortunate caller. In the medical vehicle on the way to the Charleston Municipal Hospital, the man was conscious, but the medical team feared he might have a brain injury. He kept repeating his extreme hatred for the city of Charleston and someone named Henry Hanson.

Darrell O'Donnell was in the hospital for four days before he snuck out of the facility. Looking more like a corpse than a passenger, the bus company almost refused to sell him a ticket to Savannah, Georgia. He had bandages on his head, his left arm was in a cast, and a knee brace caused him much pain.

When he finally told them one of their damned buses almost killed him the previous Saturday, the bus company finally acquiesced. They said they'd deliver him back to Savannah if he'd sign a waiver saying the bus company would pay his hospital medical bill if he'd not pursue them with any other legal action. If O'Donnell had the proper legal help, he would have never signed that waiver. Given his desperation to get out of Charleston, he signed the document with an eagerness that defied his physical condition.

O'Donnell returned to Savannah and his one-room motel that had become his home. It took him a couple months to recover from yet another disastrous journey to Charleston. He was unable to continue his job at the Pilgrim's Cove restaurant in downtown Savannah until that autumn...unfortunately when the tourist season had diminished and the tips on average had decreased.

He would live at that motel for another four years and continue his job at the Pilgrim's Cove in downtown Savannah. He walked with a limp but was able to carry out his job as a waiter. His manner was professional and his physical limitations brought sympathy in the form of higher tips from his customers.

His personal quest to blackmail Henry Granville ended with that final bus accident except for one more attempt by telephone. He still had those tales he'd written about the real Henry Hanson who'd been living as Henry Granville for over thirty years. He was certain those stories would be a damaging to the reputation of his hated enemy and all those hotels the man owned. Once those stories became articles in newspapers and news magazines all across the country, the former Henry Hanson and his organization would be ruined. The thought always brought a smile to O'Donnell's face. He just wanted Henry Hanson Granville to feel the extreme pain for what he'd done to O'Donnell and his lake resort at Lake Minnewaska back in 1931.

O'Donnell finally built up enough courage to threaten Granville one last time. Physically he couldn't make it up to Charleston. With his limp and accompanying back pain, it was problematic enough just taking the bus to and from the restaurant where he worked.

It was his day off on Friday on a nice spring day in 1965 when he forced himself to call the East Bay Street Hotel from his motel room across the road from the Savannah paper mill. He wondered if he could make his voice fierce enough to intimidate the hotel mogule into paying him some money to remain silent and to destroy those incriminating letters he had ready to send to various newspapers.

As the operator connected his call to the hotel, O'Donnell wondered why he didn't have his old feistiness that had propelled him to make so many threatening telephone calls back in the winter and spring months of 1960. It was as if his heart was no longer in the challenge. Maybe it was because he didn't look forward to the same strong defensive game Granville and his protectors would certainly wage. He knew the hotel owner would deny everything O'Donnell was going to say. His arch enemy would also no doubt bellow harsh things on the phone to O'Donnell...something the now more docile man didn't want to hear. Worst of all, he expected Granville might agree to pay some blackmail money just to end the phone conversation and then do everything to combat O'Donnell with no intention of paying the hush money.

O'Donnell knew he wasn't a natural criminal. He just wished Granville would acquiesce just once and pay him something so the whole blackmail scheme could be put to rest.

When the call went through from O'Donnell's motel room to the East Bay Street Hotel, he asked the hotel operator to connect him to Henry Hanson's office. She of course had no idea to whom he was referring.

She inquired, "Sir, are you certain you have the right hotel? We have neither a staff member nor a guest by that name.

It had been so long since O'Donnell had thought of Hanson's alias, the name 'Granville' had not readily re-surfaced in his mind. It had been four years since his previous attempt had ended when he'd been run over by a bus in a Charleston phone booth. Besides that, he realized he was suddenly going blank about the sum of money he had planned on demanding for his silence.

There was no fight left in Darrell O'Donnell. He rationalized his immediate embarrassment was not loss of memory, but more loss of focus. The one-minute call was like the final insult. After all the injuries and close calls he had being identified in Charleston, his resolve had perished. If he couldn't remember Hanson's alias, how could he expect to conduct this nefarious business of blackmail with the man he so hated. He blanched thinking how embarrassing it would have been if Hanson had gotten on the phone and asked for a price for his silence. O'Donnell would have sat there blubbering over how much to ask.

Darrell O'Donnell would simply hang up on the hotel operator. He couldn't face any more humiliation. His career as an extortionist was over. The only things that had really happened during his short stint as a blackmailer was that he'd almost been caught and identified... and he'd incurred enough injuries every time he'd visited Charleston, South Carolina to make that city a place he never wanted to visit again.

That afternoon after a nap, as he did so often on his days off, he limped slowly out to the metal rusty chair on the grass in front of the motel where he could rest his leg. There he could watch the traffic drive by, consider what the billowing smoke from the paper mill across the street was doing to the air he was breathing, and sip some of his cheap wine out of a paper cup. Now that his blackmail days were over, he wondered what would occupy his mind.

He would be found later that afternoon slumped over apparently having fallen asleep from too much drink. Unfortunately, he wouldn't be going to work the next day or any days thereafter. Darrell O'Donnell would be the last man from those D'Annelli days back in the 1930's who wanted a piece of Henry Hanson. Now he was gone.

As for Henry Hanson Granville, during the latter years of his life, he would at times think about that last serious blackmail attempt from a man who knew too much about his past. It happened during those first months of 1960. Lou White, Jamie Lawton, Charlie Davis, and he had labored many hours strategizing how to defend against that extortionist. They considered this man as the most formidable threat they'd encountered since that time back July, 1933 with the four gangsters.

And then Matt Lawton arrived in the spring of 1960, and strangely the blackmailer was never heard from again. There was no reason to believe the two factors had anything in common; however, the coincidence was often brought up in conversations with Jamie Lawton and Charlie Davis when attending one of the many board meetings for Triple H Development, Inc.

As time progressed Henry would joke about that oddity as just more validation how he'd chosen right when he brought Matt down to Charleston...as if the younger Lawton had brought a lucky charm to ward off further extortion attempts. As much levity as his statement caused, Jamie, Charlie...and Lou White would often times only nod with much relief.

As for the younger Lawton, especially during that first year in Charleston, he would occasionally wonder what happened to that peculiar, portly, and sinister-looking man with the light-colored suit and Panama hat. Matt had definitely seen someone in the shadows across the street from the hotel. He'd sensed too many times that he'd been followed in his first weeks in the city. And, there was no question he'd observed a frightening silhouette of a man in the vacant office window across the street from the hotel aiming a rifle at a vehicle Henry was driving.

Then the man had vanished as if he'd never existed. Like bad dreams, those uncomfortable images would arise less and less in Matt Lawton's mind. Over time, those distressing visions would gradually die away until they would disappear altogether...rarely if ever to be thought of again.

* * * *